THE TRYST.

VOLL

CW00521227

THE SERPENT IN SPRING

BARBARA LENNOX

ISBN 979-8-3858-5487-5 (paperback)
ISBN 979-8-3864-7815-5 (hardback)

1st edition April 2023
10..9..8..7..6..5..4..3..2..1

DEDICATION

To my late parents, who gave me that greatest of gifts,
a love of reading.

BONUS MATERIAL

Link to longer synopses of *The Wolf in Winter* and *The Swan in Summer*

Link to a scalable map of The World of *The Serpent in Spring*

Link to a Spotify playlist for *The Serpent in Spring*

Link to trailers for *The Trystan Trilogy*

CHARACTERS, SETTINGS AND TRIBES

CHARACTERS

(Principal characters in bold)
*characters who appeared in *The Wolf in Winter* and *The Swan in Summer*

From The Lands between the Walls:

Lothian:

*__Corwynal__ – half-Caledonian son of the King of Lothian
*__Trystan__ – Heir to Lothian, Corwynal's half-brother
*__Rifallyn__ – King of Lothian
*__Blaize__ – half-brother to Rifallyn, Corwynal's uncle, also half-Caledonian
*__Ealhith__ – Corwynal's Angle slave
*__Aelfric__ – Angle from Bernicia, son of Herewulf of Gyrwum
*Caradawc – Ealhith's son
Taliesin – Ealhith's son
*Madawg – Leader of Lothian's warband
*Janthe – Corwynal's mare
*Rhydian – Trystan's stallion

Galloway:

*Marc – King of Galloway
*Gwenllian – Marc's late sister, Trystan's mother
*Garwyn – Bishop of Caer Lual and Galloway
Hereydd – Abbot of Rosnat
*Andrydd – Lord of the Galloway Fleet and Lord of Loch Ryan
*Dynas – Steward of Galloway
Gwrast the Ragged – Marc's late father
Caswallon – stonemason
Pwyll – a guard
Gryn – a guard

Gododdin:

*Lot – King of Gododdin, Overlord of Lothian and Manau, Duke of
    the Britons
Gawain – Lot's son
Gaheris – Lot's son

Manau:

*Arthyr – Consort of Gwenhwyvar, and War-leader of the Britons
*Gwenhwyvar – Queen of Western Manau
*Bedwyr – Arthyr's companion
Culhwch – one of Arthyr's men
Cynog – one of Arthyr's men

Strathclyde:

*Dumnagual – King of Strathclyde

Selgovia:

*Essylt – Queen of Selgovia
*Kaerherdin – Her half-brother

From Dalriada:

*Brangianne – sister to Feargus, King of Dalriada
*Yseult – ~Feargus' daughter
*Ferdiad – Fili of Dalriada
*Oonagh – villager in Carnadail
*Ninian – apprentice healer at St Martin's
*Feargus – King of Dalriada
*Ciaran – Abbot of St Martin's Monastery
*The Morholt – late Champion of Dalriada
*Eoghan – former Steward of Dalriada
*Loarn – Feargus' foster brother
Domangart – Loarn's son
*Ethlin – Feargus' late wife
*Aedh – late husband to Brangianne and former Lord of Carnadail
Osric – Oonagh's son

From Caledonia:

Atholl:

Seirian – Royal Lady of Atholl
Kirah – her daughter
*Domech – Archdruid of Atholl
Ciniod – King-regent of Atholl
*Broichan – his son
Maelcon – former Archdruid of Atholl, Kirah's father
Urguist – former Archdruid of Atholl, Seirian's grandfather
Gaelen – former Royal Lady of Atholl
Belig – a druid
Fothla – former Royal Lady of Atholl
Marag – former Royal Lady of Atholl
Bruide – former King of Atholl, Seirian's uncle

Other Caledonian lands:

Drest Gurthinmoch – High King of Caledonia, and King of Badenoch and Mar
*Arddu – God of the forests and empty places
Nechtan Morbet – former High King of Caledonia
Tarain of Fortru – contender as Consort to Seirian
Wroid of the Creonn nation – contender as Consort to Seirian
Elpin – King of Circind
Deort – King of Fortru
Forcus – King of Ross
Gede – King of Buchan
Ase – God of Death
Taranis – God of Thunder
Vitiris – God of War
Ludus – God of the Sun
Latis – Goddess of the Waters

On The Island of Eagles (Former Caledonian training camp):

Conn of the Dal n'Araide tribe – boy on The Island
Lutrin of the Creonn nation – boy on The Island
Sinnan of the Ui Niall tribe – boy on The Island
Uuran – tutor on The Island, a Brehon (judge)
Galan – tutor on The Island, a Fili (poet and historian)
Deort – tutor on The Island, an Armourer

Others:

***Azarion** – The Dragon, leader of the Dragon-riders
Scathach – Attecott swordsmith
Marius – unit leader of Dragon-riders
*Maredydd – trader from Rheged

SETTINGS

In the Lands between the Walls:

The Mote – Principal stronghold of Galloway (The Mote of Mark, near Rockcliffe)

The Rhinns – Southwest coast of Galloway (area around Stranraer)

Loch Ryan – Harbour of Galloway's war-fleet (Stranraer)

Rascarrel Bay – Bay in Galloway west of The Mote (Rascarrel Bay)

Carraig Ealasaid – island claimed by Galloway (Ailsa Craig)

Rosnat – Seminary in Galloway (Whithorn in Galloway)

Alcluid – principal stronghold of Strathclyde (Dumbarton Rock on the Clyde)

Iuddeu – principal stronghold of Western Manau (Stirling)

Dun Eidyn – principal stronghold of Eastern Manau (Edinburgh)

Dunpeldyr – principal stronghold of Lothian (Traprain Law hillfort)

Trimontium – settlement on the border of Lothian (Melrose)

Meldon – principal stronghold of Selgovia (Black Meldon hillfort in the Scottish Borders)

Llyn Llumonwy – The Beacon Loch (Loch Lomond) site of a battle in *The Wolf in Winter,* also known as Loch Laoimin

Drumquhassle – fort near Llyn Llumonwy (near Drymen in Stirlingshire)

Malling – fort (near Lake of Menteith in Stirlingshire)

In Eriu (Ireland):

Dalriada:

Dunadd – principal stronghold of Dalriada (Dunadd hillfort in Argyll)

St Martins' Monastery – Monastery near Dunadd (Kilmartin, in Argyll)

Carnadail – settlement in Ceann Tire (Carradail on Kintyre)

Dun Treoin – private residence of Abbot Ciaran (hillfort of Duntroon, near Dunadd)

Crionan – port near Dunadd (Crinan in Argyll)

Other lands in Eriu:

Ulaid – area occupied by various Scots tribes (Ulster)

Dun Lethglaise – principal stronghold of The Dal Fiatach tribe (Downpatrick in Ulster)

Old Dalriada – original lands occupied by the Dal Riata tribe (northern part of Ulster)

In Caledonia:

Atholl – Caledonian Kingdom (roughly Perthshire)

Dun Caled – Principal stronghold of Atholl (hillfort near Dunkeld)

The Nemeton – Centre of druid worship in Atholl (near Kenmore on Loch Tay)

The Crannog – Seirian's residence on Loch Tay (near Ardeonaig on Loch Tay)

The Sacred Mountain – Mountain in Atholl (Schiehallion)

Circind – Caledonian Kingdom (roughly Angus)

Badenoch – Caledonian Kingdom (roughly Badenoch and Strathspey)

Mar – Caledonian Kingdom (roughly Moray)

Buchan – Caledonian Kingdom (roughly NE Aberdeenshire)

Fortru – Caledonian Kingdom (formerly around Stirling, but now part of northern Aberdeenshire)

Ross – Caledonian Kingdom (roughly Easter Ross)

Island of Eagles – former location of the Caledonian warrior and druid training camp (Glen Brittle on Skye)

Dun Tarvos – Principal stronghold of Mar (Burghead in Moray)

Orc Islands – Caledonian Kingdom (Orkney Isles)

The Island of Eagles – former location of the Caledonian warrior and druid training camp (Glen Brittle on Skye)

Dun Sgiath – ruined fort on The Island of Eagles (near Tokavaig on Skye)

The Long Island – land of the Attecotts (Outer Hebrides)

Other locations:

Raineach – lands occupied by the Dragon-riders (Rannoch Moor)

Rheged – Briton Kingdom (Cumbria)

Caer Lual – stronghold in Rheged (Carlisle)

Gwynedd – area with a number of Briton Kingdoms (North Wales)

Bernicia – Angle Kingdom (Northumberland)

TRIBES AND NATIONS

The Britons:

The Kingdoms of Gododdin, Lothian and Manau (Votadinae tribe)
The Kingdom of Galloway (Novantae tribe)
The Kingdom of Strathclyde (Dumnonae tribe)
The Kingdom of Selgovia (Selgovae tribe)
The Kingdom of Rheged (Carvetii tribe and others)

The Scots:

The Kingdom of Dalriada (The Dal Riata tribe, originally from the north of Ireland, Ulaid (Ulster) but who've expanded north into Western Argyll)
Dal n'Araide (tribe occupying lands to the south of the Old Dalriada)
Dal Fiatach (tribe occupying lands to the south of the Dal n'Araide)
Ui Niall (tribe occupying lands to the west of Old Dalriada)

The Caledonians (a generic term for all 'Pictish' tribes):

The Kingdom of Atholl (Caledonian tribe)
The Kingdom of Circind (Veniconn tribe)
The Kingdom of Buchan (Taexel tribe)
The Kingdoms of Badenoch and Mar (Vacomag tribe)
The Kingdom of Ross (Decaen tribe)
The Kingdom of Fortru (Verturon tribe)
The Ram tribes (The Kingdoms of The Creonn, The Carnonacs and The Caerenn)
The Bird tribes (The Kingdoms of the Smertan, Lugaids and Cornavs)
The Kingdom of the Orc Islands (The Orc tribe)
The people of the Long Island (Attecott tribe)

The Anglo-Saxons (Germanic tribes from the continent):

The Angles – Originally from Denmark, now occupying Northumbria
The Saex – Originally from Saxony, occupying lands to the south of Northumbria

MAPS

MAP 1   THE FOUR PEOPLES OF *THE SERPENT IN SPRING*

MAP 2   THE LANDS BETWEEN THE WALLS

MAP 3   CALEDONIA – TRIBES AND LANDS

MAP 4   ATHOLL IN CALEDONIA

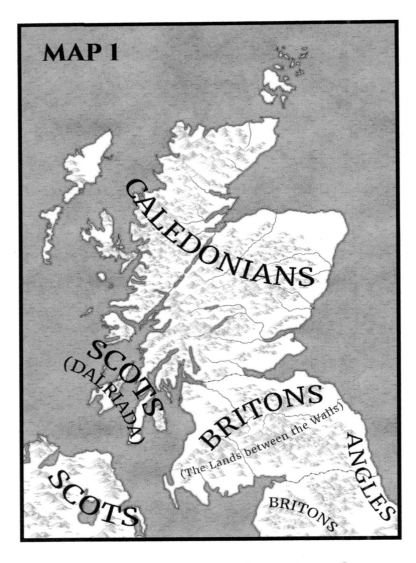

MAP 1

CALEDONIANS

SCOTS
(DALRIADA)

BRITONS
(The Lands between the Walls)

ANGLES

SCOTS

BRITONS

THE FOUR PEOPLES OF *THE SERPENT IN SPRING*

THE LANDS BETWEEN THE WALLS

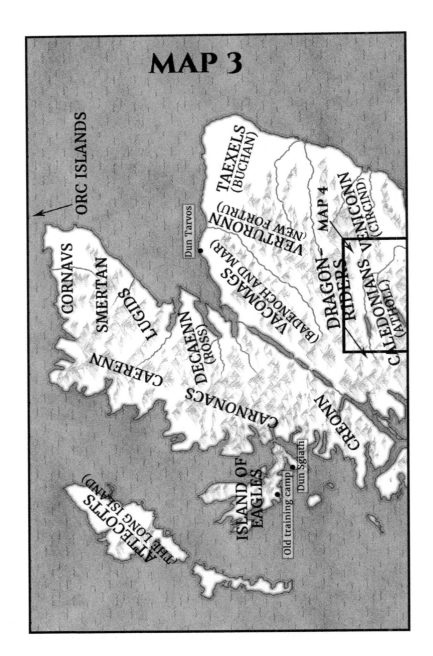

MAP 3

CALEDONIA – TRIBES AND LANDS

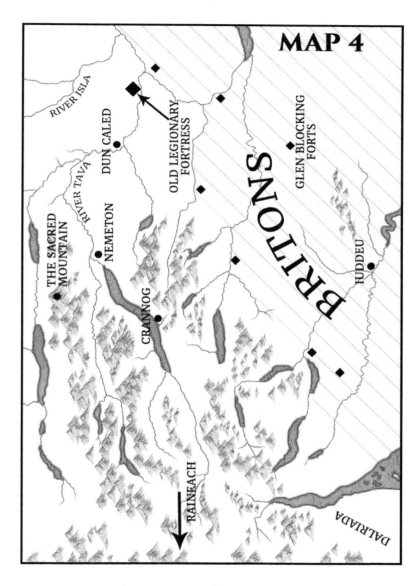

MAP 4

RIVER ISLA

DUN CALED

OLD LEGIONARY
FORTRESS

GLEN BLOCKING
FORTS

RIVER TAVA

NEMETON

THE SACRED
MOUNTAIN

BRITONS

IUDDEU

CRANNOG

RAINEACH

DALRIADA

ATHOLL IN CALEDONIA

THE STORY SO FAR

In *The Wolf in Winter*, **Corwynal**, son of the King of Lothian, is forced to abandon his dreams of being a famous warrior to become the guardian and tutor of his half-brother, **Trystan**.

Seventeen years later, Trystan has turned into a charismatic and skilful young warrior, desperate to prove himself a hero, but Corwynal has recurring nightmares of Trystan's death in a fight with a man wearing the sign of the Black Ship, so when war between the Britons and Caledonians is declared, he goes to war with Trystan to protect him.

They journey to the secret Kingdom of Selgovia to persuade them to join the war, but Trystan ruins Corwynal's negotiations by seducing and marrying **Essylt**, daughter of the king, to get the promised warband for himself. Corwynal is furious at Trystan's callous behaviour, but their disagreements are put aside when they learn that the Scots, led by **King Feargus** of Dalriada, have allied themselves with the Caledonians. Corwynal and Trystan almost succeed in persuading Feargus to abandon the fight, but treachery by Trystan's uncle, **King Marc** of Galloway, ruins everything, and Trystan, Corwynal and the Selgovian warband are forced to fight the Scots against overwhelming odds. Nevertheless, they win the battle, and Feargus, who wears the sign of the Black Ship, flees, so Corwynal believes he's averted the death he'd dreamed.

After the battle, Corwynal, believing him too young, refuses to support Trystan as War-leader, and **Arthyr of Gwynedd**, is chosen. Hurt by Corwynal's lack of support, Trystan goes to Galloway and accepts a challenge from **The Morholt**, Champion of Dalriada. As the Dalriad ship leaves for the island where the challenge is to take place, Corwynal sees the sign of the Black Ship on its sail and realises the death he's dreamed hasn't been averted after all. After a desperate journey, aided by the captured Angle warrior, **Aelfric**, Corwynal reaches the island, and is forced to watch the fight unfold as it had in his dream. In the end, however, Trystan kills The Morholt, though he's badly wounded himself.

In *The Swan in Summer*, **Brangianne** sister to **Feargus**, King of Dalriada, aunt to Princess **Yseult** and a healer, flees to the remote settlement of Carnadail to avoid an unwelcome marriage. Meanwhile, **Trystan** is dying and **Corwynal** decides to take him to Dalriada to be healed, but they're shipwrecked at Carnadail. Fearing discovery by their enemies, Corwynal and Trystan keep their identities secret. Brangianne mistrusts the Britons, so she too keeps her identity secret, even when she and Corwynal fall in love.

Ferdiad, The Morholt's lover, arrives in Carnadail, bringing Yseult with him as part of a plan to break Corwynal and Trystan's hearts. When Brangianne and Yseult discover Corwynal and Trystan's true identities, the Britons only just escape with their lives. Only the threat of war enables Brangianne to begin to forget Corwynal. The Creonn, old enemies of Dalriada, supported by mercenary cavalry, the Dragon-riders, led by **The Dragon,** are poised to invade Dalriada. Determined to help, Brangianne joins the army.

Ferdiad, dissatisfied with his revenge, persuades Corwynal and Trystan to help Dalriada. Trystan is forced to fight The Dragon when Brangianne and Yseult are captured. Trystan wins but is poisoned in the fight. Corwynal struggles to save him, but Ferdiad drives a wedge between them and persuades Trystan to claim Yseult on behalf of his uncle **Marc**, King of Galloway. Trystan, not knowing Yseult is the girl he met in Carnadail and fell in love with, agrees, and Yseult, not understanding he's offering marriage with his uncle, accepts.

Brangianne's own chances of happiness are dashed when she learns that Corwynal has married his former slave, **Ealhith** in a fruitless attempt to forget her. They separate after a bitter argument, neither expecting to see the other ever again, only to learn that Trystan has agreed to escort Yseult and Brangianne to Galloway.

Corwynal confronts the architect of all this heartache – Ferdiad, forces him to fight and hurts him so badly his ability to make music is lost. Ferdiad threatens to destroy him one day but Corwynal is more concerned with Trystan's future than Ferdiad's threats. Corwynal, together with Trystan, sails to Galloway to witness Yseult's marriage to Marc, but is determined to prevent Trystan from ruining his life over a woman he can't have.

THE TRYSTAN TRILOGY

ENDING AND BEGINNING

Dunpeldyr in Lothian,

Spring 491 AD

Tomorrow, the man who changed my life will burn his father, and Lothian will have another king. He'll be a man worth serving, a man worth following – and I should know, for, in another time, another kingdom, I followed the same man.

So maybe that's why I'm here, lurking in the shadows of Dunpeldyr, fort of the stockades, on the night before a burning. Perhaps I've come to offer him my loyalty once more, for good or ill. But I doubt he'd accept anything from the man who broke his heart and tried to destroy everything he cared about.

Much lies between us, both in the past and in the present, and forgiveness doesn't come easily to either of us. We've been enemies more often than we've been allies, and neither of us have forgotten why they called me Ferdiad the Serpent when I was Fili of Dalriada. I have a new name now, of course, and new allegiances that surprise me still but, perhaps, like myself, he doubts my transformation.

Names are strange things: the names we're given, the names we take, the names we win, the names we try to live down. I'm familiar with all of these and can slip off any name as a snake casts off its skin. I can become anyone – even the hero of my own story.

And so this tale is not only that of the man who paces the starlit rampart high above me, but of myself, the dark twin who tried and failed to destroy him. It's the story of Ferdiad the Serpent, of his fall, and of his rise, of his becoming everything he'd long dreamed of but never truly believed in, then becoming something else entirely. It's a tale that, like all tales, could begin anywhere. But the journey of that becoming starts, perhaps, in a Dun on the edge of a fretful sea, in Dalriada, a few weeks after Lughnasadh, four years ago.

THE SERPENT IN SPRING
PART I

DUN TREOIN IN DALRIADA,

AND THE MOTE OF MARC IN GALLOWAY,

AUTUMN AND WINTER 487 AD

PROLOGUE

Dun Treoin in Dalriada

Samhain 461 AD and summer 487 AD

REMEMBERING

*T*hey came for them at Samhain. All over the west and north they came for the eight-year-old boys on the night they called The Night of Endings. But for the boys themselves it was a beginning – the start of their lives as the men they were supposed to become.

Ferdiad had always known what he was destined to be, for didn't he bear the name of the greatest warrior of Eriu, but for one? His path lay as clear before him as the path of a rising moon spilling over open water.

Those who, like him, were tall and strong, would also become warriors. Others with a different sort of strength would be smiths. Those with pure clear voices would be poets, the argumentative ones judges, the dreamers priests. In truth, Ferdiad could have been any of these things, and, as they travelled north in the care of the quiet-eyed kindly men who'd be their teachers, he moved easily from group to group, welcomed for his keen wits, his silver looks, his golden voice, his gift of tongues, knowing that these other boys would become comrades, friends, rivals perhaps, and that he'd outshine them all.

And so, on the Night of Endings when they took him away, he

was one of the few who didn't weep as he stepped out into his moonlit future. Not then, nor on any other night down the long years. Never. His mother wept, as all mothers did, and his father's eyes were moist with pride, as were the eyes of all fathers. But Ferdiad didn't look back as the Dal Fiatach ship sailed out of Dun Lethglaise and headed for The Island of Eagles and the training schools, its grey sails straining in the wind. Other ships joined them as they travelled north - from Old Dalriada, from the Dal n'Araide lands, from the holdings of the Ui Niall, lands of enemies and allies alike.

And when they dropped the anchor stone in the bay beneath the mountains, they saw the sleek black ships of the Caledonians that had brought the eight-years-olds from the lands of the Creonn and Carnonacs and from further east beyond the great forest where the Taexels, Vacomags and Veniconn dwell – boys from Atholl and Circind, Buchan and Mar. No-one came from the islands of the Attecotts, of course. The little dark people of the outer islands were ever slaves. And only one boy ever came from the lands of the Britons.

In the end, however, Ferdiad didn't become a warrior, despite passing all the warrior tests and beating all the others. His voice was too pure, its gold deepening to honey, his memory prodigious, and his gift for languages too valuable to be wasted on a mere warrior. So he chose instead to become a poet. When he was nine, he made his first harp from holly wood strung with horsehair. It fitted into the curve of his left shoulder like a fifth limb, and, before long, he was drawing forth not only the old tales and songs but new ones he began to make, sad songs for a people given to easy tears. But he never wept. Never.

This was a long time ago now, but he remembers it as if it was yesterday – the huts huddled at the roots of the black mountains, the waterfall plunging in its mist-filled gorge, the pool beneath an archway of rock where the boys dived into bright blue water, the sound of drums from the warrior school as they stamped out the rhythm of lunge and thrust, and the chanting from dormitories hazed with woodsmoke as boys recited the laws. He remembers all the other boys, his friends and rivals – wiry little Conn of the Dal n'Araide, big Lutrin of the Creonn nation, red-haired Sinnan of the Uí Niall, and he remembers his teachers too – Uaran the Brehon, Deort the armourer, Galan the Fili. He remembers everything, as if it was yesterday. Everything. From the moment he was chosen on that Night of Endings, the journey to Dun Lethglaise, the grey sails of the ship—

'The Dal Fiatach never shipped out of Dun Lethglaise, and nor, in those days, were their sails grey.'

To Ferdiad, enmeshed in his past, the voice seems to come from the future. But he's wrong. The voice is from the present, and it rushes over him like a wave tumbling on a grey and stony shore. The fingers of his right hand brush against fur and wool, and he smells tincture of poppy and hot wine, sweat and peat smoke, cattle dung and freshly-cut rushes. He can smell seaweed too and hear the thump and hiss of waves, the patter of rain and the dull moan of the wind. He tastes wine on his lips, something bitter beneath his tongue, and bile at the back of his throat. He knows that if he opens his eyes there will be firelight, and the old Abbott will be looking down at him with those dark eyes that see a great deal too much, and Ferdiad's afraid he'll see kindness there, or pity, so he keeps his eyes shut and tries to slide back into the past.

'Grey, white . . . It doesn't matter.' His voice, once so golden, is an abomination in his own ears. 'And if it wasn't Dun Lethglaise, it must have been somewhere else. It was a long time ago.'

'But you remember everything, don't you Ferdiad? So tell me; your mother, the one who wept when you went away – what colour was her hair?'

In his memory, his mother is turning away, back into darkness, as the ship slips into the night.

'Dark,' he guesses. 'She had dark hair.'

'And your father?'

But he too, the man who stood so proudly as his talented son stepped into a golden future, is also turning away, and Ferdiad can't see what he looks like.

'Fair,' he says. 'Fair, like me. Why does it matter?'

The Abbott's hand comes down on his right hand and grips it hard. He can't feel anything with his left hand.

'It matters because none of it's true,' the Abbot says with his kind – too kind – voice. 'You're not of the Dal Fiatach, are you? You're not from Eriu at all, and Ferdiad isn't your name. You took that name from a story. My dear, dear boy, it's all just a story.'

Ferdiad opens his eyes, sees the old man looking down at him with tears in his eyes, and he squeezes his own shut once more and tries to dive back into the past where everything he remembers – as if it was yesterday – is right and true and straightforward, where a boy lived the life he was meant to live, and never had reason to weep. Not once. Not ever. But the present hooks him like a fish and won't let him go.

'Who am I then, old man? If everything I've told you is a story, what's the truth?'

'I don't know, my dear. Only you know. So tell me, if you can – what happened to you on The Island?'

But he can't – or won't. A memory such as his should have been a gift, but instead it's a curse. He remembers everything. *Everything!* The boy who never wept weeps now as a man, coiling himself up like a wounded animal as he keens for his past as a woman keens over a corpse. The old man puts his hand on his shoulder and Ferdiad tries to push it away with his left hand but pain flares along the bones of his arm and he – who's never forgotten anything – remembers the one thing he's been trying to forget, the reason he's here with the old man, the reason for the wine and poppy and the bitterness and bile in his mouth.

He remembers he no longer has a left hand.

A ROYAL MARRIAGE

'I can't bear this!' Trystan whispered.

'You must.'

'It's too soon!'

Corwynal and Trystan were standing near the front of Marc's chapel, and Corwynal glanced around in alarm, but no-one in the crowd that pressed in behind them appeared to be listening. Nevertheless, he replied in the Gael tongue that few in Galloway would understand.

'It has to happen sooner or later. Best get it over with.' He moved towards Trystan until their shoulders touched. *I'll see you through this*, he'd promised him, but he was finding the whole situation hard to bear himself. Sunlight flooded through the high windows of the chapel, and, though the doors stood open, the wind that had blown them so swiftly and uncomfortably from Dalriada to the Mote had died away and the place was stifling. Corwynal was wearing a black tunic embroidered with silver, a bad choice for a hot day. It smelled sweetly of the herbs in which it had been stored, but the scent couldn't mask the smell of sweat trickling down his ribs, nor the stench of the crowd jammed into the chapel to see the King of Galloway marry his foreign Princess.

Trystan was right, however. It was too soon. They'd only arrived in Galloway that morning, and he'd expected a few days at least to pass before the marriage took place, but Marc had always been impatient. News of the alliance had reached him long before the ship bearing the bride to seal it, and everything had been ready for the marriage. The Mote was as packed as it must have been only a few days before for the Lughnasadh fair. All those who weren't important enough to gain a place in the chapel itself had crowded into the courtyard and, when that was full, had spilled through the gates and down into the port. Everyone was dressed for a festival, woman and children waving bunches of flowers and men blowing trumpets or banging on anything they could find to make a noise.

Corwynal felt a headache coming on. The floor was still heaving from the motion of the ship, and his sea-sickness had returned. His clothes itched abominably, he was desperately thirsty, and his tongue tasted of bile.

'Here she comes!'

Everyone except Trystan craned their necks towards the door. Even Marc, standing stiffly at the altar beside Bishop Garwyn, turned his head. He'd asked Corwynal to stand with him, but he'd pleaded illness. Trystan needed him more than Marc.

'Not long now,' he said bracingly, for even in the heat of the place Trystan looked cold and clammy, and he was bone white. He didn't reply and threw Corwynal a glance of sheer desperation.

'I can't watch this!' His voice cracked with panic, and he might have turned and fled if Corwynal hadn't gripped his arm.

'Do you want everyone to know?' he hissed. 'Do you want *Her* to know?' It was the threat he'd used on the ship, the only one that might work. 'You'll watch it because you must, and you'll bear the feast too because you must. But then we'll leave, tonight if you like, and never come back.'

Then Trystan would recover from this madness – if that's what it was. But was it? The question had tormented Corwynal all the way to Galloway. Was all this just an effect of the poison that had nearly destroyed Trystan in Dalriada? Was Trystan's love real? Was any love? Or was love itself a form of madness? Corwynal's head hurt just thinking about it. Nevertheless, madness or not, he was determined Trystan would survive with his honour intact, if not his heart. He'd escape, as Corwynal had failed to escape all those years before.

'Here she is!'

Behind them, the crowd parted, and Corwynal was aware of a veiled figure pacing slowly towards the altar, but he was more interested in the woman walking behind her. Like him, Brangianne was dressed in black. A gold cross studded with pearls hung on her breast, and she appeared older and sterner than he knew her to be. *Have I done this to her?* He shuddered with guilt and caught her eye. She held his gaze for a heartbeat before allowing it slide away with no change in her expression. Unable to bear the coldness in her eyes, he turned his attention to the woman everyone but him was looking at.

Abruptly, the chapel vanished, taking the crowd with it. The shouting and banging faded away to a dull thudding, and he was no longer standing in the stifling heat of a summer afternoon but in torchlight on a cold evening in spring with the mist rolling off the sea and wreathing the rock of Dunpeldyr in a grey fog that smelled of salt and weed and the cold waters of the firth. She was wearing the same dress – *the same dress!* The fine linen was dyed the colour of new elm leaves, and the neckline and cuffs were embroidered with the ravens of Galloway, their eyes seed pearls, their wings slivers of jet. She was wearing a veil of linen and a narrow filet of gold set with a pale jewel. Corwynal knew that beneath the veil was a waterfall of auburn hair and eyes that were the same green as her dress, but that wasn't who he saw. The woman he was seeing had hair like spun gold, eyes the blue of a speedwell and a body that, beneath the dress, was deeply familiar. Nor was it Marc standing at the altar but a much darker man – his own father. And Corwynal couldn't stand it.

But that had been twenty years before, and the woman he was imagining was dead to the world. He took a deep breath to steady himself as the veiled woman passed by, close enough to touch, and breathed in a scent he'd forgotten. On the shoulder of the dress was a faint line of stitching where a tear had been mended. He'd forgotten that too.

I can't bear for him to touch you! he'd told Gwenllian when it was far too late to do anything about it. They were alone for a brief moment, and he'd pulled her towards him, but she'd jerked herself out of his grasp, tearing the dress in the process. *Not here! Not yet! Stop it, Corwynal!* '

'Corwynal? Corwynal!'

He blinked. Eyes as blue as a speedwell, hair like spun gold . . . 'What's wrong?'

The floor heaved beneath him and he grasped Trystan to stop himself from falling. The crowd crushed against him and the walls closed in. The old fear of enclosed places took him by the throat.

'Get me out of here,' he croaked as his gorge rose. 'Get me out!'

'I hate this dress,' Yseult muttered, plucking at the green linen.

The wedding feast was well under way by then, the hall of the Mote full to bursting, the heat intolerable, and Brangianne regretted her own choice of dress which, being made of a thick wool, was more suitable for winter. But it was the only one she had in black, and she'd wanted to make a statement to one man in particular. *Look what you've driven me to . . .*

She eyed Yseult critically. She'd expected hysterics, but Yseult was surprisingly calm. She hadn't said much since they'd arrived that morning, but hadn't objected to any of the arrangements, not even to wearing the hated dress. It suited her, for it matched the colour of her eyes, and was a gift from the King, an honour, apparently, for it had belonged to his sister, the woman Corwynal had loved twenty years before and perhaps still did.

He'd left the chapel before the marriage had been solemnised, Trystan supporting him, and hadn't been the only one to have been taken ill in the stifling heat of the chapel. *Not that I care!* she reminded herself fiercely. Nevertheless, she couldn't stop herself from glancing along the table to where he sat on the far side of the King between Trystan and the Bishop of Caerlual. He was still pale, and she'd heard the King ask if he'd recovered. He'd nodded and smiled wanly, and the King had smiled back at him. She'd always thought Corwynal to be a man with no friends, but the affection between him and the King of Galloway seemed real, despite Corwynal having secretly loved his sister, a thought that made her look away and turn back to Yseult.

'It's old,' Yseult complained. 'Look—' She plucked at the shoulder. 'It's been mended.'

'Stop fussing about your dress,' Brangianne said briskly. 'And smile. Remember who you are.'

'Were,' Yseult corrected her. Nevertheless, there was a noticeable lift of her chin, and when the King – her husband – turned to her with some question, she answered him politely enough, and Brangianne, whose other companion, some Galloway sheep-lord, was deep in conversation with his neighbour, was free to allow her attention to wander.

So this is Galloway, she thought with an unsettling sense of unreality, for everything had happened so quickly. Their ship had arrived not long after dawn at the principal stronghold of Galloway, a place called The Mote. It seemed a strange name to one whose Briton was still far from fluent, despite her studies of the language while incarcerated in St Martin's, and Kaerherdin's tuition during the journey. The royal residence was built on a rock overlooking an estuary which the ebbing tide revealed to be a network of mudflats and sandbanks. A river ran close to the Mote, its channel so thronged with Galloway's famous trading fleet that she'd wondered if there would be room for their ship at the wharves. But a place had been reserved for them. Indeed, everything was in readiness, and even at that early hour men and women, with children on their shoulders, had crowded the dockside, shouting greetings in the tongue she'd yet to master.

The hall in which they now sat was a vast place of carved timbers soaring into high rafters, lit by day by openings in the roof, and at night by lamps of beaten bronze. A line of firepits ran the length of the hall but, the day being hot and sultry, remained unlit. The walls were newly painted and gilded and hung with huge elaborately-woven hangings in which Galloway's symbol of the raven featured prominently. Only slightly smaller than the hall was the royal residence which stood at the far end of the walled enclosure on the rock's summit. It had its own small meeting chamber, spacious quarters for Yseult and her household and, on the other side of the meeting chamber, for the King. A door led from the central chamber to a courtyard which looked out over the estuary and reminded her of Dunadd's royal terrace.

The Chapel in which the marriage had taken place was a stone-built, whitewashed building separated from the royal residence by the kitchens that provided the seemingly-endless platters of meat and bread, and jugs of ale and mead and wine. Even now, when everyone had surely eaten their fill, baskets of pastries stuffed with honeyed fruit and scented with spices were circulating, but Brangianne, feeling sick, waved them away.

Is he here? She scanned the hall, searching for the leader of the raiders who'd come to Carnadail and destroyed her life all those years ago. *Maybe he's dead.* Was that what she wanted? She was no longer sure. Ciaran would want her to forgive the man, but she didn't know if she could, or what she'd say to him if she met him. The raven bracelet he'd tossed her years ago was concealed by the long sleeves of her dress, an ambiguity that matched the state of her mind. *I don't want him to be here. I don't want to face him.* Nevertheless, she scanned each of the sweating faces in the hall, from the high tables at the head of the hall where the King and nobility of Galloway were seated, to the benches near the door where the lesser people sat and where she could see Oonagh, Aelfric and Kaerherdin. But she didn't know if she'd recognise the raiders' leader. Like her, he would have changed, grown older. All she could recall about him with any certainty was the look in the man's eyes. Even so, she caught and held the eye of each of the men in the place. But none seemed to recognise her, and none was familiar.

He isn't here, she decided with a flood of relief and was able to turn her attention back to the wedding feast. There was cheering in the hall and Yseult grasped her hand, for Trystan had left his place beside the King and strolled out into the centre of the hall, a harp in his hand. He looked flushed, which was hardly surprising given the heat in the hall, but there was a wildness in his eyes Brangianne didn't like the look of. His tunic was undone, his shirt open at the neck, his gait not entirely steady. *He's drunk*, she realised in alarm, for she'd never seen him more than mellow with drink. *Be careful, Trys.* She couldn't stop herself from glancing at Corwynal in whom she saw the same anxiety. She'd known Trystan loved Yseult ever since that awful night in Dunadd, a love Yseult returned, though neither knew the other's feelings – and it had to stay that way, for such a love was doomed. *Please be careful!*

To begin with, however, he was. He took his place on the bard's chair and plucked a few chords from the harp to catch the attention of everyone in the hall. The crowd grew quiet as Trystan's voice began to fill the vast spaces of the hall like a golden mist, all the richer for the wine he'd drunk. But the song, however expertly delivered, was nothing special, something in praise of women in general. at least to begin with. Gradually, however, it changed as odd harmonies crept in, a minor key that was discordant and soulful, and a completely different song emerged. Yseult's hand gripped Brangianne's even more tightly, for it was one she and Trystan had sung together at Carnadail, a sad song of separation and longing, a song that silenced the crowd entirely. *Don't give yourself away, Trys! Not in front of Yseult!* She would have jumped up and made some excuse to stop him if the King himself hadn't intervened.

'A bit gloomy, Trys!' he boomed. 'Why don't you give us something more cheerful?'

Trystan broke off half-way through a verse. He'd been in

Carnadail, Brangianne realised, but now he was back in Galloway, back in control.

'My apologies, Uncle,' he said, getting to his feet. 'I was mourning Dalriada's loss when I should have been celebrating Galloway's gain.' He tilted his head towards Yseult, a narrow smile on his lips.

'I can't do this,' Yseult whispered as Trystan bent to his harp once more and sang a jolly song Brangianne couldn't follow but which must be amusing, judging by the laughter that began to rock the hall. 'Not while *He's* here.'

She was quite white, her grip on Brangianne's hand so tight she felt as if her bones were being crushed.

'Talk to the King,' Yseult pleaded. 'Tell him it's too soon, that I'm tired . . . sick. Tell him I have my moon-blood. Tell him anything. I can't . . . I just *can't!* Not tonight, not while *He's* here . . .'

She was close to breaking, close to jumping up and running away, but there was nowhere to run to. Yseult's unnatural calm had been because she'd been asleep. She'd sleepwalked into this marriage, all the way from Dalriada, but now she'd woken up, not out of a nightmare but into one.

Brangianne glanced doubtfully at the King, who was chuckling at Trystan's song. He was older than she'd expected, but not ill-favoured, a man who might once have been handsome had he not let himself run to fat, though he was tall enough to carry off the extra weight. He still had all his teeth, and his hair, a raddled golden grey, was thick and well-groomed. It could have been worse. Of his temperament, however, she knew nothing as yet, for she'd exchanged no more than a few words with him, a polite greeting in which it was clear he assumed she'd return to Dalriada as soon as the marriage celebration was over. Not unnaturally, he'd been more interested in the woman who was now his wife, and of whom he had . . . certain expectations.

But he appeared to be good-natured, affectionate to Trystan and Corwynal, and popular with his people. Someone who'd ruled

Galloway for as long as he had must be intelligent enough to make allowances for the fears of a young bride and might be persuaded to give her time to grow used to the idea of marriage, to grow used to him. In a few days, tomorrow perhaps, Trystan would be gone – Corwynal with him – and, once they'd left Galloway, Yseult might be ready to fulfil the duties of a queen and a wife.

'Very well,' she said, not relishing the conversation. 'I'll talk to the King. I'll talk to your husband.'

'Look at it,' Ciaran insisted as he unwound the bandages from Ferdiad's arm.

They were sitting on a bench outside the wall of the Dun that perched on a small promontory on the north side of Crionan's loch. It was fair for once, the storms of early August having given way to gentler weather as the days shrank into autumn. The wind had dropped to little more than a breeze, heavy with the scent of kelp, and the sea, which for days had lashed the stony shore below the Dun, was suspiciously benevolent, gentling the land and murmuring to itself beneath a sky tumbled with clouds.

Ferdiad had been at Dun Treoin, Ciaran's private guesthouse, for half a moon by then, and Ciaran had told him his wound had begun to heal. But that meant nothing. Was his missing hand growing back? No. Then he'd never be healed. There were some wounds to a body, or a life, from which one never recovered.

And you know who to blame... Arddu's voice oozed from the bones and sinews of his missing hand, and the fever-beat of what was left of his blood.

'Not now,' he muttered tiredly. He was in no condition to argue with a God.

'Yes, now,' Ciaran said. 'Look at it.'

Reluctantly, knowing that at some time or other he'd have to, Ferdiad forced himself to look. He'd imagined it of course, red inflamed flesh and stinking weeping scars, but none of his imaginings had prepared him for the sight of his arm and the way it ended in . . . nothing. He jerked his head away, but Ciaran reached out, grasped his jaw in surprisingly strong fingers and forced him to look, and look, and look . . .

'You'll get used to it in time,' he said, and Ferdiad glared at him with such ferocity the old man let his hand drop, if not the subject.

'You must,' Ciaran insisted. 'And you need to decide what you're going to do now.'

'What can I do? I can't play the harp anymore.'

'You still have your voice. You still have your mind. You're still Dalriada's Fili.'

He shook his head. He wasn't that man anymore.

'What do you want, my dear?' Ciaran asked him in his gentlest voice, the one Ferdiad had come to loathe.

'I want my life back,' he replied without thinking. 'The life stolen from me by Corwynal of Lothian.'

You want revenge, Arddu reminded him, and Ferdiad's missing hand curled into a fist.

'I want his death,' he said.

Not death. Is death enough to pay for your hand, for Trystan, for The Morholt? For what happened on The Island . . . ?

Ciaran clicked his tongue in disapproval. 'My dear boy—'

'I'm not your boy!' Ferdiad snapped and jumped to his feet.

'All men are my children,' the Abbott reproved him so gently Ferdiad wanted to weep. The man he'd become was shamefully tearful, and only anger could keep those tears at bay.

'Why am I even here?' He waved his good hand at Dun Treoin. 'Why not St Martins?'

He'd seen no-one but Ciaran since the Abbott had brought him to the Dun, not when he was in his right mind. In the wound fever, or when dosed with poppy, he'd seen others, some of them long dead, but only Ciaran had been real.

'St Martin's is too public. I believed you needed privacy.'

A wounded animal brought to a lair in which to die, Ferdiad thought with an odd mixture of gratitude and shame. Then he understood.

'Everyone thinks I'm dead, don't they?'

Ciaran shrugged. 'Your absence has been noted, but you were always one for coming and going. Only one person asked if you were alive or dead—'

Him!

'—and I told him the truth,' Ciaran continued. 'That few men recover from such an injury. He assumes you're dead. He seemed . . . troubled.'

Ferdiad smiled. It made his face feel strange. *One day – dead or alive – I'll take everything from you, and everyone you hold dear. One day I'll destroy you.* The last words he'd ever said to Corwynal of Lothian. 'Good. I want him troubled. Now tell me why you let him believe that.'

'Because death is a threshold. A door opening. A choice. A chance. An ending. You tell me you want revenge, but that's not what you truly want.'

Ferdiad regarded the old man sourly. His hands were clasped together, his body relaxed, his eyes calm. How could anyone be so . . . *calm?* It was altogether infuriating.

'You don't know what I want or don't want. You know nothing about me!' He folded his arms and glared down at the Abbot, but he just tilted his head to one side and smiled that secret smile of his.

'But I do. You talked, my dear. In the fever. You talked a great deal.'

Ferdiad's legs almost gave way as the shock ran through him. Had he told him *everything?* Then the fury was back and he reached out, grabbed Ciaran by the throat and half-lifted him from the bench. *If I squeeze the breath from your body, it will all die with you.* His fingers tightened, but his anger shrivelled when he realised he couldn't. Not with only one hand.

'Sit down, Ferdiad,' the old man said, still infuriatingly calm, when Ferdiad let him go. 'Your secrets are safe with me. Come . . .' He patted the bench beside him and Ferdiad, feeling hollow and thin, as if the wind was blowing through him, slumped down onto the bench, leant back against the warm stones of the wall and closed his eyes.

'You killed them, didn't you,' Ciaran said. 'The boys you claimed were your friends – Conn and Lutrin and Sinnan.'

'They were never my friends,' he said dully. 'And yes, I killed them. Years later. I killed the druid Uuran first though. I offered his heart to Arddu. It was still beating.'

For the first time, the Abbot's calm seemed to desert him. He frowned and his eyes were troubled when he turned to Ferdiad and laid a hand on his arm.

'Don't listen to Arddu! He'll use you and destroy you.'

For answer, Ferdiad lifted his arm, the one with the missing hand. 'There's little left to destroy.'

'Enough!' Ciaran snapped, no longer the calm and gentle healer, but Abbott of St Martins and Bishop of Dalriada, a man who ruled as a king rules. Kindness was gone. So too was compassion.

Good! Ferdiad braced himself.

'How dare you indulge in such self-pity! You have your life. You have your sanity. Both were in question. You should be *grateful* to Corwynal—'

'Grateful?! After what he's done to me? The Morholt—'

'Died in single combat – which *you* arranged.'

'He tricked him. And he took Trystan from me.'

'Trystan was never yours, and never would have been.'

Ferdiad flinched at that particular truth. 'I loved him,' he protested.

'Did you? Wasn't it rather that he reminded you of who you might have been? You didn't love Trystan, but rather a vision of yourself.'

Ferdiad's heart stopped at that, and he had to reach for the anger to get it going again.

'What I might have been was taken from me – by Corwynal of Lothian! If I talked so much, you know what happened on The Island.'

'I know what you believe happened.'

'There's a difference?'

'The difference I see is this; you searched for and killed the druid and those boys, but not Corwynal. Why not? You've had plenty of opportunities to kill him in the past two years, so why isn't he dead?'

'Because I wanted to make him suffer.'

'You certainly did that,' Ciaran said dryly. 'So why isn't it over? Why did you fail to kill him with The Dragon's blade when you had the chance? What was it he did to you that was different?'

Ferdiad turned away to conceal the flood of relief that swept through him. So he hadn't revealed everything in the fever.

The Abbot laid his hand on his arm once more and squeezed it for emphasis. Ciaran the healer was back. 'Give up this idea of revenge. There are other pathways for you now, difficult ones perhaps, but they'll take you to a place where you can be at peace.'

'I don't want peace! I want revenge. I'm going to strip away everything that matters to him – his honour, his secrets, his future, his past, everything he loves and values.'

In his mind, in his nerves and bones, Ferdiad heard Arddu repeating his words, his voice rich and amused as he turned them over as one might turn over gems in a chest, or bones in a grave. He heard the echo of his own oath. *One day I'll destroy everything you hold dear. And then I'll destroy you.*

'And only then will you kill him?' Ciaran asked, frowning.

Ferdiad shrugged. 'If I'm feeling merciful, which is unlikely.'

'Don't listen to Arddu,' Ciaran said once more, as if he could hear the God's voice for himself. 'All he wants from you is your soul.'

'And what do *you* want from me, Father.'

He'd called the old man 'Father', intending it to sound sarcastic, but somehow it didn't come out that way. Ciaran's eyes brightened, a dazzle of sunlight on deep implacable waters, and he smiled a smile that was both promise and threat in one.

'The same thing, my child. The very same thing.'

'Madam . . . ?'

King Marc clearly expected his bride to be waiting for him in his bedchamber and was rather put out to find her aunt in the anteroom. Yseult, at that precise moment, was waiting anxiously in the bedchamber for Brangianne to persuade her husband to forego his conjugal rights, at least for the moment. It wasn't a conversation Brangianne was in any way prepared for.

'The queen is tired from her journey,' she began. 'It's been a long day for her, Sire.'

'A long day for us all.'

'Indeed, Sire. But it's all been so . . . sudden. We arrived only this morning and Yseult hasn't had the chance to get to know you. Might it not be better to wait before . . . ?' She made a helpless gesture, her grasp of the Briton tongue faltering, but the King understood her meaning and his brows snapped together.

'You expect me to forego my rights?' She could smell wine on his breath, and strong male sweat. 'You expect my servants, in the morning, to discover not only no queen in my bed but no maiden blood staining the sheets?'

Heat flooded into her face and she raised her hands to her cheeks to conceal her embarrassment. 'Please, Sire—'

'What's this?' He stepped forward, grasped her wrist and dragged her sleeve back, revealing the raven bracelet. 'Where did you get this? Who gave it to you?'

She stared at him. She hadn't expected this. After finding no-one in the hall she recognised, or who recognised her, she'd thought it was over, that her long-planned revenge had died the death it deserved. And she'd been glad of it, so she'd decided to throw the bracelet away and try to forget what had happened.

But The King recognised the bracelet, so he must have given it to the man who'd led the raiding party. If she truly wanted to know who the man had been, all she had to do was ask. But her tongue had stuck to the roof of her mouth and her lips refused to open, for there was something in the King's voice that wasn't right. Something more than surprise. The King recognised it because . . . because . . . The world lurched and spiralled around her, and her gorge rose. *Because . . . because . . .*

'You gave it to me.' Her voice came out as a reedy whisper. She wanted him to deny it, to offer some other explanation. He was a King. He was Yseult's *husband!* The leader of the raiders has been young, clean shaven, and this man was bearded, his face fuller, his skin slack, his features sunk into flesh. All that was left of the man she was trying not to remember were the eyes. And now, in a flicker of torchlight that reminded her of a farm burning, she saw they were the same – not in their colour, which she'd forgotten, but in their expression of grief. They belonged to the man she'd hated for twenty years.

He let go of her wrist and stumbled back, his face crumpling. Then he fell to his knees as if he'd been hamstrung, dropped his face into his hands and wept great tearing sobs.

King Marc? Yseult's husband? Her mind was caught in the eddy of some vicious current, and her thoughts kept circling and circling and going nowhere. But out of that whirlpool two images emerged from her dream of revenge: the first the man kneeling at her feet in remorse, the second the rusty knife in her hand. She gripped the hilt, ready to drive it into his stomach, but her fingers closed on nothing.

The King struggled to his feet, cuffed his face dry with a sleeve, took a long shuddering breath, then strode to the door that led to the main chamber, jerked it open and yelled for a servant. 'Find Trystan and Corwynal! Bring them here!' Then he slammed the door shut once more.

'It has nothing to do with them!' she protested, prey to a foreboding she couldn't identify.

'They have to know,' he said bleakly. 'And you have to know the reason.'

Nothing made sense anymore. Time had stopped, and maybe that was for the best. But time rarely stopped for long. There were voices outside and the door opened.

'Uncle . . . ? Sire . . . ?' Trystan came into the room, closely followed by Corwynal, whose eyes flew to hers, his brow snapping together when he took in Marc's tear-ravaged face.

'What's happening?'

Marc curtly dismissed the servants before turning back to them.

'The Lady Brangianne and I have met before,' he said, leaning back against the door. Trystan stared at him, puzzled, but Corwynal stiffened, his eyes widening.

'It was you?' he whispered.

'Who?' Trystan asked. 'What?'

I should never have come to Galloway! Brangianne thought. *I should never have begun this! I should deny everything.*

But if she did, Aedh's death would mean nothing. And so the words had to be said.

'Twenty years ago, my husband was murdered by Galloway raiders at the Beltein truce,' she told Trystan tonelessly.

'I know, but . . . ' She watched Trystan's expression change as understanding dawned. Then he turned on his uncle. 'It was *you?*'

'Not directly, but, yes, I was to blame.'

'Why?'

If she'd known what was about to happen, she would have stopped it. She would have said it was a long time ago, that revenge accomplished nothing, that he'd ruined her life but she'd managed to build another, that there was no rusty knife in her hand nor ever would be. Maybe that was all true, but she still wanted to know why. She needed there to be a reason for the night that had changed her life. And so she said nothing.

'I'd just learned that your mother – my sister – had died giving birth to you,' the King told Trystan. 'And I was mad with grief because . . . because I was responsible. I wasn't in my right mind. I did things I'm ashamed of, but none of them was worse than the sin I'd already committed. I've done penance for it, and the priests tell me God has forgiven me, but God doesn't matter. It's you I wronged – all of you.' His gaze swept the room and caught sight of the white-faced girl who was standing in the doorway to the bedchamber, a shawl about her shoulders. 'Come in, child. You should learn what sort of man you've married.'

'Listen, Marc . . .' Corwynal moved towards him, a hint of panic in his voice as if, like Brangianne, he knew something appalling was about to happen and was trying to stop it. But Marc flung up his hand.

'Don't touch me! Not until you've heard what I have to say.' He took a deep breath. 'I killed your mother, Trys. I went mad when she died – because *I'd* killed her.'

'But . . . but she died in childbirth, didn't she? You just said so.' Trystan turned to Corwynal in puzzlement, but Corwynal just stood there, horror dawning in his eyes, and Brangianne, swept out of the circling eddy and into the vicious current, knew what that horror had to be.

'That's how I killed her.' Marc dropped his eyes. 'We were more than brother and sister, you see . . .' The river rushed on and Brangianne saw, black and jagged, the rocks on which they were all about to break. 'I'm your father, Trystan.' The King raised his head to look at him.

'No!' Trystan turned to Corwynal. 'It's not true. It can't be.' But Corwynal, bone-white, said nothing. 'Why don't you deny it?!' Trystan's voice was shaking with desperation.

He can't, Brangianne thought. *He can't speak. He can't think. He's clinging on to this moment because, if he lets go, the river will sweep him not onto those rocks but over the edge of a great fall.*

'It's not true,' she said, but no one listened, and Trystan's face turned ashen as he waited for his father? – no, his brother – no, not that either – to speak, and when no answer came, he flinched away as if he'd been struck.

Outside, away from this room, away from this unfolding horror, the sky rumbled as the thunderstorm the day's heat had set off rolled over the Mote.

'It is true,' Marc insisted. 'You belong to Galloway, Trystan, not Lothian. It's Corwynal who should be heir to Lothian, not you.' He turned to Corwynal. 'So I wronged you too.'

And still Corwynal said nothing.

'You're despicable!' Trystan snapped at the King, his face flooding with anger, and there was something in his eyes, a madness that had nothing to do with the wine he'd drunk. 'You don't deserve to rule Galloway! And you don't deserve *her!*'

Everyone looked up. Yseult was still standing in the doorway, half-hidden by the hanging, looking young and frightened and confused.

'You're right,' Marc agreed gloomily. 'But I can't send her back. Not now. I can't risk war with Dalriada. She's Galloway's Queen if not yet my wife, but Galloway needs a maiden's blood to seal the bargain, and you're my son, Trys, whether you like it or not. So that task must fall to you.'

It was a moment before Trystan realised what he meant, a longer moment before everyone else did so.

'No!' Brangianne protested.

'Don't be a fool!' Corwynal echoed her plea.

'I'm not a fool,' the King replied. 'I'm a sinner, and this is my punishment. So take her, boy. She's young and so are you. You deserve one another.'

If Yseult had protested, she might have broken the spell, but she just stared at Trystan and he stared back as if they were the only people in the room.

'I won't let this happen!' Corwynal eyed the knife at Marc's waist, the only weapon in the room, but even as he moved towards him Marc whipped out the knife and grabbed Brangianne by the shoulders. Then he pulled her against his chest and laid the knife against her throat.

It wasn't the first time a man had laid a knife at her throat to threaten another man. She hadn't believed it then, and didn't do so now, but Corwynal wasn't so sure of the man he called a friend.

'You wouldn't!'

'Don't try me,' the King snarled. The knife bit into her skin, and a trickle of blood ran down her neck. 'Go on.' The King jerked his head at Trystan. 'Go on, before I change my mind.' His body, pressed against Brangianne's, was shaking, and she knew that if she could see into his eyes at that moment, she'd see the raider of Carnadail, desperate to assuage grief in violence.

'Don't, Trys,' Corwynal begged, as Trystan took a step towards Yseult. He stopped, but only to whirl around, his eyes flashing.

'Why should I listen to you? What are you to me now?'

Only Yseult could stop this. It would only take a word or a plea, but Yseult loved Trystan and she wanted him, even in these appalling circumstances. So she just lifted her chin. *Take me*, that lifted chin seemed to say. *But don't expect it to be easy.*

'Yseult, don't . . .' Brangianne pleaded, but it was too late. Perhaps it had always been too late. Yseult watched Trystan walk towards her, her eyes narrowed with hatred, but not for him. It was herself she hated. It was shame for her loss of pride, because, even now, believing he despised her, she still wanted him. And so when he took her wrist and pulled her into the bed-chamber she didn't protest. Nor did she say anything when the hanging fell down behind them and did no more than gasp at the sound of her bed-gown tearing.

Outside, lightning cracked, thunder rumbled and rain began to drum on the roof. There was a taste of iron in the air, and the sound of laughter from the sky. But the old Gods' amusement couldn't drown out the sound of Yseult's screams. Not of pain or fear or pleasure but of fury, because she wanted this, but hated herself for it. This was no rape, but only Yseult would know it, and after it was over there was silence. Then they heard cursing and Trystan threw back the hangings, his face flushed with pleasure and anger and shame.

Marc had let Brangianne go long before. The knife had fallen away, and he'd slumped down the wall to rest on his heels, his face in both hands. Brangianne had struggled to a chair, just making it as her legs gave way, but Corwynal remained upright, as stiff and unyielding as a standing stone, rooted to the earth, his expression unbearable. He didn't even move when Trystan brushed past him and slammed his way out of the room, nor when Yseult came to the door of the bedchamber, a shawl covering the ruin of her bed-gown. She was crying now.

'I want my father,' she was saying. 'I want my *father!*'

Marc looked up, got ponderously to his feet, went over to her and patted her shoulder tentatively. 'I want my father,' Yseult repeated and, to Brangianne's surprise, flung herself against the king who'd given her away to another man, buried her face in his shoulder and wept hysterically.

Yseult didn't need her any more, but Corwynal did. Brangianne got to her feet, went over to him and touched him on his rigid shoulder. But he didn't look at her, and when he spoke his voice was as cutting as a blade.

'So, you got your revenge . . .'

'Revenge?'

'Do you know how many lives you've ruined by your spite?'

'My *spite?!*'

'What else? Against him.' He nodded at Marc. 'And against me too. Do you know what you've taken from me tonight? But you do, don't you? You, of all people, knew *exactly* what you were doing. And I'll never forgive you for it. Never, do you hear me? *Never!*'

2

LOVE AND MADNESS

It took Corwynal all night to find Trystan, and, by the time he'd done so, dawn was breaking weakly in the east, throwing a nacreous yellow light over the Mote and the estuary. The mudflats gleamed a dull pewter and curlews cried mournfully along the edges of the swelling river. Trystan was standing with his back to him, looking across the mudflats to the Island of Lepers, connected to the mainland only at the lowest of tides, but he'd heard Corwynal approaching for he spoke without turning.

'I don't know who I am anymore.'

Corwynal put a hand on his shoulder, but Trystan flinched away.

'You're the same person you've always been.'

'Whoever that is.'

'Listen, Trys, we don't need to talk about last night. But we do need to leave – today – and never come back. We'll go to Rheged . . .'

Across the Firth, swimming above a thin layer of mist on the sea, lay the mountains of Rheged, hard-edged against the narrow band of light.

'You're right,' Trystan said. 'And wrong. We *do* need to leave, but we also need to talk about Marc claiming he's my father. I want to know what you believe.'

Trystan turned around, and Corwynal's heart contracted at the expression in his face. He was lost, hopeless, grieving, and

Corwynal knew how he felt. His own belief was a thing of the heart and not the head, a belief Marc's claim, so horribly plausible, had stolen from him, leaving him rootless and doubtful. Between them, his oldest friend and the other half of his soul had robbed him of the one truth that had given his life meaning, that Trystan was his son. But still he clung to that belief.

'Listen, Trys. Marc isn't your father. I'm sure of it. But only your mother could say for certain, and she didn't.' *Except for a name called out in the night, a name that wasn't Marc's.*

Trystan turned away once more to gaze at the calmly tilting sea as it ate away the mudflats, the incoming tide fighting with the river over the bar.

'I wish he'd never said anything, never claimed me.'

So do I. 'What man wouldn't be proud to claim you as his son?'

'Should I be proud of my father? Or he of me? I've no reason for pride. Quite the opposite. Yet, if Marc really is my father, doesn't that give me an excuse? If I'm no more than the result of his . . . transgressions, am I not doomed to repeat them?'

It was the question Corwynal had been asking for the whole of Trystan's life.

'I don't know.' His eyes were gritty with lack of sleep, and he was still wearing the same clothes as the day before. They were hot and itchy, despite the dawn chill. He didn't want to be here, didn't want to have this argument. Behind them, the port was waking up, smoke pluming from hearth-fires, fishing skiffs rowing down the channel against the flooding tide. 'We need to leave.'

'Not yet.' Trystan turned back to face him, and this time his expression was hard and accusing. 'Why didn't you deny it?'

'I was . . . shocked.'

'But not surprised, knowing Marc as you do. You must have suspected, but for all these years you said nothing. For all these years you've lied to me.'

'No, I haven't.' That too was a lie. 'I didn't suspect.'

'You didn't *want* to suspect. But you knew all the same.'

'No—'

'You've always made allowances for him, always forgiven him.'

Not this time. 'Is that why you were so hard on me when I was growing up? Because you didn't want me to be like him?' *Because I didn't want you to be like me.* 'Well, you failed, for here I am, having done something just as bad. That wasn't me last night. That wasn't the person I thought I was. That was Marc's son!'

'I don't believe that.'

'Then give me a better explanation. Make me understand why I . . . I raped the girl I love.'

Trystan's voice broke, and he dropped his face into his hands to grind his fingertips into his temples. 'I wanted her, so, so much. I couldn't bear for Marc to have her, so when he gave her to me, I didn't hesitate, didn't *think.* All I could do was feel, and I convinced myself she wanted me, even though it made no sense. But I was so sure of it that I . . .' He dropped his hands and looked at Corwynal, his mouth twisted with self-disgust. 'I suppose that's what all men think when they . . . do what I did – they justify it. But I can't. I'm so *ashamed!'*

'We all do things we're ashamed of.'

Trystan gave him a long searching look. 'What have you done?'

So many things . . . 'Nothing I want to talk about, because that's how we deal with shame, Trys. We keep it inside us. We tell ourselves we'll make recompense, and yet the years go by and we do nothing until it's too late. But shame scabs over, like an old wound that still aches in cold weather.'

Trystan stared at him, as if trying to penetrate the dark places of Corwynal's past, then laughed. 'When I was a child and did something I was ashamed of, I'd tell you and you'd thrash me. I always felt better for it.' Then his humour faded. 'Thrashing isn't going to fix this.'

'No. But leaving will help.'

'We can't go together.'

Corwynal's old fear roared into life. 'Why not?'

'Because if I'm not Marc's son, there has to be some other explanation for what I did. Perhaps the poison hasn't left me, and last night I was as mad as I was in the earth-house when I tried to kill us both. Maybe it would have been better if I *had* killed myself, because I can't live like this, always being afraid of what I might do and who I might harm.'

Corwynal gripped him by the shoulders and shook him. 'It wasn't the poison. Or, if it was, it was a different sort of poison. *Love* is a poison. Love is madness. It makes fools of us all, makes us do things we'd never dream of doing.' He wasn't sure he believed what he was saying, but Trystan needed to hear it. 'We have to get away from Galloway, Trys. *I* have to get away, from Brangianne, and Marc. I can't forgive either of them, and if I stay I don't know what I'd do.'

Trystan took a deep shuddering breath and tried out a shaky smile that tore at Corwynal's heart. 'Very well. We'll leave, but I have to do something before we go. I need to apologise.'

'You don't need to, not to me.'

'Not you. Her.'

A tremor of foreboding gripped him. Yet he couldn't have said why. The girl hated Trystan, didn't she, and now had more reason to, so how much more damage could an apology do?

'I went to Dunadd to apologise to her,' Trystan said. 'Now I have a lot more to apologise for, but if I can just explain . . .'

In Corwynal's experience, women didn't listen to explanations, but maybe Trystan would feel better about himself if he tried.

'Very well. But after that we leave.'

If only it had been that simple. If only he'd known. But who could comprehend a woman's heart? And maybe, even then, it was already too late.

Oonagh knew Galloway would be trouble as soon as she set foot on dry land.

It was foreign, of course, and Oonagh, despite her own complex origins, didn't care for foreigners. She didn't like the way they smelled, the way they looked, or the way they talked in a language she struggled to get her tongue around.

'I thought you could get your tongue around anything,' Aelfric had remarked with a leer, whereupon Oonagh had punched him hard in the stomach. A man like Aelfric needed to be kept firmly in line.

Not that there was much point, since he'd be heading off with Trystan and that Caledonian when they left Galloway. Indeed, she'd expected him to have left straight after the wedding feast, which was why she'd been generous with her favours that night. But, three days later, the big oaf was still in Galloway, as were the boy and the Caledonian, both of whom looked as if they didn't want to be there at all.

It was a sentiment Oonagh agreed with. Why *had* she come to Galloway? She didn't owe Brangianne or Yseult anything, so why hadn't she gone back to Carnadail? Maybe it was because the world seemed a little larger than Carnadail now, and perhaps that was why she'd come to the land which hitherto had been no more than a smudge on the horizon. Or maybe it was because Brangianne and Yseult needed her help, poor creatures that they were. Not a particle of common sense between the pair of them, especially in matters of the heart.

What made it particularly galling was that Oonagh still didn't know what had happened on the night of the wedding. Aelfric, if he knew, wasn't telling, and both Brangianne and Yseult had kept their silence on the matter. But anyone with eyes in their head could tell it must have been bad. Yseult had kept to her rooms since that night and refused to see anyone. Brangianne looked haggard and distracted. The Caledonian was even grimmer than usual. And now here was Trystan, looking as if he hadn't slept in a month.

'Will she see me today?'

He'd come to the Queen's private chambers every day since the wedding but Yseult had refused to speak to him. It was driving Oonagh mad. Caught up in her own affairs in Carnadail the previous year, she'd failed to see the signs, but, looking back, it was clear the pair had fallen in love. All that fighting had been because they'd refused to admit it to themselves. And now neither was going to admit it to the other. They both needed a good shaking.

'I'll ask,' she said. 'But I reckon you'll get the same answer as yesterday.'

'Tell her I can't leave Galloway until I've spoken to her.'

That's new! At least he knew he ought to leave.

'I can't see him.' Yseult's eyes were wide with panic when Oonagh had conveyed this message. 'I *can't.*'

'You must,' Brangianne said. 'You can't stay in your room any longer. What do you imagine everyone's thinking? You're Galloway's Queen.'

But this just set Yseult crying once more. She'd done a lot of weeping in the last few days. Annoyingly, tears didn't mar her beauty. Brangianne and Oonagh, on the other hand, never looked their best when crying, which was why Oonagh was careful not to let anyone, especially that big Angle, reduce her to tears.

'Come on, Yseult!' Brangianne abandoned the chest she was unpacking and went to sit beside her niece. 'This isn't like you. All you have to do is listen to whatever he has to say – it will be an apology I'm sure – then say something gracious and he'll go. You'll never have to see him again. Isn't that what you want?'

'No . . . Yes . . . I don't know!'

'We won't leave you alone with him,' Brangianne added, glancing at Oonagh for confirmation.

Good! I'll finally get to find out what happened. But Yseult still looked doubtful.

'You have to do this, my love,' Brangianne coaxed. 'Come – dry your eyes and remember you're a Queen, and he's your subject. You can pretend even if you don't feel like it. You were always good at pretending.'

So, in the end, an uncharacteristically nervous Trystan was shown into the Queen's private chamber and was met by a girl pretending to be a Queen. Yseult was dry-eyed and straight-backed, and met his anxious gaze steadily enough and concealed the shaking of her hands by curling them into fists in the folds of her dress.

'Well?' she said coolly. 'As you can see, I'm rather busy.' She gestured at the room, in which chests stood open, dresses and cloaks spilling from them, their colours rivalling those of the hangings on the wall, the scents of dried herbs and fragrant wood filling the air. For three days, Yseult had insisted there was no point unpacking since she wasn't staying in Galloway, but Brangianne had finally persuaded her to do so. 'I'd thought you'd left Galloway already,' Yseult went on. 'For wherever it was you were going. To join your wife perhaps?'

Trystan flinched at that, and a little colour stained the pallor of his cheeks.

'I couldn't leave until I'd explained—'

'An apology will be sufficient, Trys,' Brangianne cut in quickly, but he ignored her.

'—explained why what happened . . . happened.'

'I'm not interested,' Yseult said, turning away.

But I am! Oonagh watched Trystan's face crease with frustration and something close to desperation as Yseult, her back to him, picked one of her dresses from the chest at her feet and shook out the creases as if she'd forgotten his existence.

'I love you,' he blurted out. 'From the first moment I saw you in Carnadail, I loved you.'

'Trys, no!' Brangianne stepped towards him, placed a hand on his shoulder and urged him towards the door. 'Yseult hates you and has even more reason now. Please, just go before—'

It was too late. The dress Yseult had been holding slipped from her fingers to pool about her feet in a drift of blue linen. 'I thought *you* hated *me!*'

'No. I pretended.' He smiled ruefully. 'I'm good at pretending.'

'You've had your say, Trys,' Brangianne went on desperately, still trying to move him towards the door. 'Yseult's flattered but can't return your feelings, so you should leave right now.'

But Trystan was deaf to everyone but Yseult. 'You pretended too?'

'To you. To myself. I ought to have hated you and I tried to. But I didn't succeed.'

'Then . . .the other night, it wasn't . . . I didn't . . . ?'

What?! Oonagh wanted to scream with frustration.

'No. It wasn't. You didn't. I . . .' Yseult dropped her eyes, her cheeks flushing a rosy pink. 'I wanted you,' she whispered.

Brangianne let Trystan go and dropped her face into her hands with a groan, but looked up after a moment. 'Come on, Oonagh. I think we'd better leave these young people alone.'

They were already alone, oblivious to everything except one another. Yseult was staring at Trystan, and he at her, their faces alight with something Oonagh hadn't felt in years, and the memory of it was both sweet and treacherous.

'I don't think that's wise.'

'It's not,' Brangianne agreed, but put an arm around Oonagh's shoulders and marched her out of the bedchamber. 'But it's inevitable.'

'It's madness, that's what it is,' Oonagh insisted, conscious, on the other side of the door, a gasp, a cut-off laugh, a groan, the creak of a bed. 'If the King ever finds out . . .'

'The King already knows.' Then Brangianne finally – *finally* – told Oonagh what had happened that night, an account that shocked a woman who thought herself beyond surprise.

'What will happen now?' she asked, unsure if she wanted to know.

'At worst? Discovery, disgrace, even death.' Brangianne gripped Oonagh's hand. 'Which is why you and I are going to guard them until this burns out. Because it will. It must.'

But Oonagh wasn't so sure. And nor was she so sure about Brangianne's motives.

'Trystan won't leave Galloway now,' she pointed out. 'And if he doesn't, neither will that Caledonian. Is that what you want?'

A faint flush ran up Brangianne's neck and she looked away. 'No . . . yes . . . I don't know.'

And if the Caledonian stayed, then so too would a certain Angle, and it occurred to Oonagh that if anyone had asked her the same question, she might have given exactly the same answer.

'That's her horse, isn't it?'

Corwynal was standing inside the entrance to the Mote's stables when Trystan led in his bad-tempered grey stallion, Rhydian, and a neat little bay mare. Both were wet to the knees from the early morning dew.

'Whose?'

'Yseult's.' Corwynal still thought of the girl as Ethlin. 'The Queen's. Marc's wife.'

Trystan flinched. 'What of it?'

Corwynal hadn't seen much of Trystan since he'd gone to apologise to Yseult almost a moon before. He didn't know what had happened, and the only person who could tell him was avoiding him as assiduously as Trystan himself. But it didn't take much imagination. Even now, despite the smell of horse sweat he could detect Yseult's distinctive perfume, and, beneath that, the unmistakable smell of sex. The Queen, Marc's wife, was the reason Trystan no longer wanted to leave Galloway. And that meant Corwynal's own plan to leave Galloway was in ruins.

'You've been riding?'

Trystan snorted. 'What an amazing piece of deduction!'

It was raining, a fine persistent drizzle, but Trystan's tunic was dry, which meant they hadn't been riding, but had been inside somewhere.

'Don't be facetious. Did you take a groom?'

'I don't need a groom.' Trystan let Rhydian's reins drop and gave him a slap on the rump that sent him into his stall while he led the mare into another. 'Where are those cursed horse-boys?'

'I sent them away.'

'Wonderful!' Trystan hauled the mare's saddle off, picked up a couple of brushes and tossed one to Corwynal. 'If you intend giving me a dressing down, you might as well make yourself useful while you do it.' He began to groom twigs and leaves out of the mare's tail. At least he hadn't walked away. Corwynal eyed Rhydian warily, for the big stallion was inclined to bite. The animal swung his head and bared his teeth when he removed the saddle and bridle but did no more than stamp a hoof as he started to brush him down.

'Say what you have to say and be done with it.' Trystan brushed the mare's flanks in long deep strokes and the animal whickered softly, used to Trystan's touch. Too used to it.

'You have to stop seeing Yseult.'

'I can hardly avoid seeing my uncle's wife.'

'You know what I mean.'

Trystan laid down his brush and turned to face him.

'You hate her, don't you?'

Did he? Corwynal hardly knew the girl. She was lovely, certainly, but he'd never trusted beauty. Yet, lovely as she was, she'd blossomed since the night of the marriage, and Corwynal didn't think it was Marc who'd caused that.

'I liked her better when she hated you.'

'She doesn't hate me. She never did. And I love her. I loved her from the moment I saw her, and it was the same for her. It's not something you can talk me out of and, yes, it's madness, but I don't care if you think it's due to the Dragon's poison. I *love* her and always will. Can you even begin to understand that?'

Corwynal's mouth twisted at the irony of that particular question. He'd loved Trystan's mother in exactly the same way, and that had been madness too – all those stolen assignations, breathless and exciting before deteriorating into frustration and bitterness. He wasn't going to let that happen to Trystan.

'I understand that you love her, but what you feel now won't last.' Again, that twist of irony. He'd grieved for one woman for almost twenty years and now, having ruined one last chance at happiness, expected to grieve for another for the rest of his life. Perhaps love was sent by the gods to send men and women mad.

'You have to leave Galloway before you're found out.'

'We won't be.'

Corwynal's stomach contracted at the certainty in Trystan's voice. Someone was helping them, and he knew who it must be. This was Brangianne's revenge for Corwynal rejecting her when Feargus had forced him to. She'd had her revenge on Marc too, but Corwynal didn't care about Marc. He couldn't forgive him and hadn't been able to speak to him since that night. His own feelings didn't matter, however. Trystan's did, and what they might lead to.

'If you carry on, sooner or later you'll be discovered.'

'Marc doesn't care,' Trystan said with a shrug, but Corwynal wasn't so sure. He'd seen Marc look at Yseult with guilt and remorse to begin with, but there was something else in his eyes now, and it was growing.

'Don't be so sure. And even if Marc doesn't find out, someone else will, someone who wishes you or Yseult ill. Think of her, if not yourself. Think of the disgrace, of your own honour. You have a wife, Trystan. Yseult has a husband. You have to stop.'

'I can't,' Trystan said quietly, but with finality, then turned on his heel and walked away.

Corwynal didn't follow him. He'd recognised the quiet desperation in Trystan's voice, because it had been the same for him. He hadn't been able to stop either. But he'd protected Trystan all his life, and would continue to do so, even if it meant fighting the girl who threatened to ruin Trystan's future as Gwenllian had ruined his. He'd break Trystan's heart rather than let that happen.

'Won't I, boy?' he asked Rhydian, and the big stallion nodded his head and snorted, then rolled his eyes, swung around, baring his teeth, and bit him on the shoulder.

Seirian dropped the bundle of old rushes into the fire and stepped back to avoid the billow of acrid smoke that plumed from the bonfire set on the pebbly beach of Atholl's sacred loch, downwind of the Crannog. Her women were bringing out the rest of the rushes and the old bedding and throwing them onto the fire. Fresh rushes had already been cut, and, once the Crannog had been swept out and the wind allowed to blow it clear of its summer staleness, they'd be spread out on the floor and her possessions could be put back. For the moment, however, everything – the chests and pots, looms and bundles of wool, her precious stocks of herbs and dyes – were all laid out on the shore, the blankets and sleeping furs tied to lines stretched between the alders that grew along the stream were flapping in the breeze.

Please, Latis, Lady of the Waters, don't let it rain until everything's back inside.

The morning had dawned clear and cold, with dew sparkling on the spiders' webs that presaged the turn of summer into autumn, and the sky had been covered in a high layer of cloud. It hadn't looked like rain, and so, tired of the stink of the Crannog after a damp summer, Seirian had decided that today would be the twice-yearly clear-out. For once, it looked as if Latis was going to cooperate, for the loch that lay at Atholl's heart in the sinuous cleft of the mountains was clear and bright beneath the thinning cloud. Even as she looked northeast down the loch, the clouds broke up, and she had to shade her eyes against the low morning sun.

It was then that she saw the boat rounding the bend in the loch and rowing swiftly towards the Crannog. She could make out water surging at the prow as the rowers bent and straightened, and in the stern, sitting upright, gold glittering from his vestments, the last man she wanted to see: Domech, Archdruid of Atholl.

Trust him to come when everything was in chaos! *You might have warned me, Latis!* For answer the Goddess of the waters sent a gust of wind that swirled the smoke about her, set the blankets flapping and drove her women back from the fire. The wind rose steadily and the boat was heading right into its eye; there was still time . . .

'Quickly!' Seirian clapped her hands. 'Get everything back into the Crannog.' She looked around for Kirah but couldn't see her daughter. 'Someone find Kirah and tell her to keep Ninian out of the way.' Her women ran off to do her bidding, and Seirian would have run too, had Atholl's Royal Lady not been required to maintain a certain dignity.

'So, Domech, this is a pleasant surprise,' she said coolly when the Archdruid ducked his head to enter the Crannog. There hadn't been time to replace the rushes but everything else was back inside, piled into the side alcoves and concealed behind the woven hangings. The fire in its stone cradle sent up a tendril of peat-scented smoke that snaked fitfully in the draught from the doors, open to both loch and shore. Her chair stood on one side of the fire, a bench on the other. Empty of the usual women's clutter, and with the floor bare, the place looked austere, and from below their feet light was reflected from water lapping and tilting beneath the Crannog. The light pierced the gaps in the floor that would normally have been covered by rushes, spearing the room in a shifting pattern of woven sunlight. Seirian was rather pleased with the effect, for it was a reminder that the Crannog was the domain of the Goddess of water and wind, and the cold depths of the loch. Domech, priest of stone rooted in the land and the predictable shifts of the stars, looked noticeably unsettled, but Domech was never unsettled for long.

'A surprise, Seirian? But you know what day it is.'

'Of course.' It was the day after the night of the new moon, the night on which the Druid College met. She should have anticipated this visit. 'But you so rarely come to give me the benefit of your deliberations, I didn't expect you today.'

The Crannog brightened as the sun shone through a gap in the thinning cloud, and the light from the door lit up the Archdruid's face, a thing of planes and angles dominated by a long narrow nose that resembled the blade of an axe, and a pair of hooded eyes. His long iron-grey hair was braided and bound with feathers and bones, and more feathers hung from the staff he carried. It was topped by the skull of a marten, and faceted quartz, set in the sockets of the marten's eyes, gleamed with an almost human intelligence.

Seirian shifted uncomfortably on her chair, for her own ceremonial dress was too heavy for the late summer warmth. The dark wool was embroidered at hem and cuffs with the curved lines of water, the under-tunic scattered with embroidered moons in all their phases. She wore a heavy silver lunula about her neck and the chain was cutting into her skin. Sweat was trickling down her back, and not just because of the heat.

'The Druid College is unhappy, Seirian.' Domech clasped his hands behind his back and leant towards her.

It wasn't surprising. There was always tension between the Archdruid and the Royal Lady, between the gods of stone and stars and the Goddess of water and wind.

'With me?' She raised an eyebrow.

'You grow old,' he said bluntly.

'We all grow old, and you're a great deal older than me.'

'Agreed. But it will be many years before my age prevents me from serving Atholl. Your usefulness, however, may soon be at an end. The College therefore requires you to make your choice of Consort and bear Atholl its next King before it's too late.'

'Since when have such matters been the province of your sorry bunch of star-gazers?' she asked sharply.

His flint-coloured eyes narrowed. 'All matters regarding Atholl's place in the Confederacy are the province of the Druid College, and your continued refusal to accept a Consort weakens Atholl. Maelcon might have tolerated your intransigence, but I warn you that I won't.'

She allowed the anger to surge through her. 'How dare you! You may be Maelcon's successor but you're not half the man he was! You forget to whom you speak. I'm Atholl's Royal Lady by birth and training. Do you imagine me to be unaware of my duties? And have I not fulfilled them? I took Maelcon as my lover, as demanded by the Druid College, though he was old enough to be my father. I bore a daughter to be Atholl's next Royal Lady, and I'm training her to fulfil that role as I was trained. As to the Consort, once I've chosen him, I'll bear a King as tradition demands. If I've been— How did you put it? Intransigent? —it's because the right man has not yet presented himself.'

'Many suitable men have presented themselves, but you've rejected them all.'

'They were *not* suitable! I'm Atholl's Royal Lady. It's given to me to know the Consort, not you. It's the one right I have, and I've no intention of giving it up for your political convenience.'

Domech's eyes narrowed once more, but he inclined his head. 'The choice is yours, naturally,' he said mildly. 'All the Druid College requires is that you make it. Because if you don't, you'll be put aside.'

The sweat running down her back turned to ice. 'You can't do that. You don't have the authority.'

'I can get it. There are precedents . . .'

'I see,' she said. He'd persuaded the Druid College that if she didn't agree to his demands, he could approach the High King's druid for the authority, and Seirian knew he'd get it. If she was to be put aside for some other woman, then Kirah, whom she'd raised to be Atholl's next Royal Lady, would have her future taken from her – and she couldn't allow that. 'So, who do you want me to take as Consort?' she asked sweetly. 'Who does the Druid College recommend?'

Domech seemed taken aback by such a rapid capitulation but recovered quickly. 'It will be your choice, of course. The College was quite clear about that. We did, however, consider that, while tradition demands it be a stranger to Atholl, traditions are changing. The Creonn, for example, no longer require it, and nor do the Taexels. So you could choose a man of Atholl. Ciniod, for example . . .'

Ciniod, King-regent until her as-yet-unborn son came of age, Ciniod who was a vain and weak man controlled by Domech. His weakness must have begun to outweigh his usefulness, however, or Domech wouldn't be here.

'No,' she said flatly.

'His son then. Broichan's a better man than his father.'

'He's just a boy.'

'Then perhaps someone from the Druid College . . . ?'

She stared at him, wondering if he meant himself. He'd succeeded Maelcon in everything but her. Did he want her too? Did he see a way to rule Atholl more firmly than through the vacillating Ciniod, by siring Atholl's next King? It was unthinkable, for all sorts of reasons, and she mustn't let him make the offer, for if she rejected him it would mean war between them.

'No, it has to be an outsider. My mother flouted tradition, so I must not. If Atholl's to take its rightful place in the Confederacy, it would be better to avoid the accommodations of the Taexels or Creonn. Very well. You may send word to the other tribes that I'll consider possible contenders at Samhain.' She gave a thin-lipped smile. 'Samhain is for endings, after all.'

'And you'll choose one of them?' he asked suspiciously.

'If one of them is the right one.'

'Seirian—'

'And if none of them is, I promise I'll choose someone else – a stranger to Atholl as tradition demands.' She leant towards him through the coiling tendril of smoke from the fire. 'And you know who that would be.'

The blood drained from his face and his hand tightened on his staff for support. 'You wouldn't!' he whispered.

'Don't threaten me, Domech,' she hissed.

They glared at one another, priest of the gods, priestess of the Goddess, and Domech was the first to back down.

'All I want is for Atholl to be great again,' he said plaintively. 'To be at the heart of the Confederacy, not on its edge. Isn't that what you want too? Atholl is weak because of what happened twenty-five years ago—'

'We will not talk of that!'

'As you wish. But though what happened was neither your fault nor mine, it falls to us to deal with the consequences. Work with me, Seirian, not against me.'

An axe can kill but it can also shape. Was she wrong about Domech? Was his ambition not for himself but for Atholl? Was his passion not for her but for the land they both served?

'We have the same aim,' he urged. 'We shouldn't be enemies.'

He held out his hand through the smoke and, after only a brief hesitation, she took it. His grip was strong and warmer than she'd expected.

'Peace then,' she said.

But the water went on dancing, netting them in its web of light, and the wind sighed through the timbers of the Crannog with the voice of the Goddess. *For the moment*, it said. *Only for the moment*.

WHO IS THE EXILE?

The hand was lying on the ground, broken off at the wrist, the hair a litter of yellow chips among the grass, the face a ruin of plaster. Only one eye remained, a blue the colour of speedwells, and it looked out from the wall accusingly. *What have you done to me?*

Brangianne was more concerned about what might be done to her. She'd been summoned to meet the King, a summons she'd been dreading for weeks. She hadn't spoken to him apart from a few brief public exchanges since what she'd come to think of as 'that night', but she'd been aware of his gaze in the hall and was conscious that, by helping his wife betray him with Trystan, she was deceiving a powerful and dangerous man.

In her defence, she hadn't expected the affair between Trystan and Yseult to have lasted as long as it had. She'd thought it would burn out, given time, but, far from burning out, the affair had grown in intensity and recklessness. Had Marc found out? Was she in danger? The thought kept her awake at night, even though she was Feargus' sister and Galloway couldn't afford to upset Dalriada. But would Marc remember that?

Then there was that other matter – Aedh's death and the promised revenge she didn't know whether she wanted. Marc was no longer the leader of the raiders but Yseult's husband, a man as shattered by the events of twenty years before as her. More shattered perhaps, but not so broken as to overlook her involvement in Trystan and Yseult's affair.

Yet, if he'd summoned her to explain her actions, it was strange that he'd asked her to meet him on the little terrace that lay beyond the royal quarters, a place too peaceful for recriminations. It was a sunny triangle of flagged stones set about with lavender and sage and mats of thyme in which a few late bees browsed lazily in the afternoon sunshine. The only thing that marred the place was the damaged mosaic on the east-facing wall. She guessed who it must represent and wondered why it had been allowed to fall into such ruin.

'It was beautiful once.'

The voice made her jump, and when she turned to face the King, her heart was hammering.

'I smashed it because it wasn't beautiful enough.' He bent to pick up a few of the pieces of mosaic. 'Shouldn't have done it, of course.' He looked up at her, still turning the pieces between his fingers before letting his eyes slide away. He seemed more sad than angry. 'Shouldn't have done a lot of things.' He rose to his feet and tossed the coloured cubes from hand to hand. 'You deserve to know why I did. It's taken me this long to steel myself to explain. I'm not a brave man when it comes to certain things . . .'

Brangianne's heart slowed. This wasn't about Yseult and Trystan after all. It was about her.

'There's no need . . .' she began, though it wasn't true. She still wanted to know more than had been revealed on the night of the wedding, so when he gestured to the bench which stood beside the ruined mosaic she sat down without demur. He leant one shoulder against the wall, still fingering the pieces of mosaic. The bees went on buzzing fitfully and gulls cried raucously as they swooped overhead, riding the southerly breeze. From below the walls, Brangianne heard people shouting and laughing, and the clamour of a port going about its business.

'Did you ever hear of my father?' he asked eventually. 'They called him Gwrast the Ragged, because he was a mean bastard. My family has Roman blood, but it turned him hard and inflexible. He thought a son should be dutiful, a daughter meek, and when we were neither we were beaten. Our mother was dead, and any servants we grew fond of were taken away. We only had each other. One day – I forget the reason now – I was beaten worse than usual, and that night Gwen sneaked into my room to comfort me. She was fourteen and I was sixteen.' He paused, staring into the distance, into the past. 'It didn't feel wrong, not then, nor later, not even when my father died of an apoplexy – thank Chrystos – and I became King in his place.' He'd been clutching the fragments of the mosaic but now he opened his fingers, tilted his palm and let them fall to the ground. 'If I'm honest with myself – a rare event, I assure you – it still doesn't seem wrong. I loved her.' He looked down at Brangianne, meeting her eyes for the first time, and she saw they were the pale blue of a winter's sky. 'I think you're a woman who understands love.'

'I loved my husband,' she snapped. He flinched at that, but his eyes still held hers.

'You don't know what it is to kill the person you love. I didn't want to send Gwenllian to Lothian, but she wanted to be a queen so I gave in. When I heard she'd died in childbirth less than nine months later, I knew the boy must be mine because that old man – Rifallyn of Lothian – couldn't have fathered a child on my lovely girl. So it was I who killed her, and for a time I wanted to kill myself. I suppose, in a way, I did, because after she died the man I'd been died too. I took to drinking and whoring and fighting, consorted with the scum of the taverns and went raiding rather than ruling a Kingdom – the consequences of which you're aware.'

She nodded curtly.

'You were so happy, you see,' he explained. 'It wasn't until I saw the fires on the hill that I realised it was Beltein. Breaking the Beltein truce didn't bother my men, but it bothered me. I was about to call them back to the ship when you appeared – so young, so happy – and I understood that I'd never be happy like that ever again. So I didn't try to stop what happened until it was too late.' She stared at him. Had Aedh been killed simply because they'd been *happy?*

'If it's any consolation at all – and I know it won't be – that was the end of it,' he went on. 'Not because of what happened, since we'd done worse in other places, but because I realised what I was doing wasn't helping. I came back to Galloway and, though I'd never been much of a Christian, I went to the Bishop in Caerlual and confessed everything – and I mean *everything*. You've met Garwin. He's not an easy man to shock, but I succeeded.' He smiled ruefully. 'I was given penances to serve, but I'm a King and the Bishop's a politician, so the penances were largely financial. But it wasn't enough. The Bishop couldn't punish me as I deserved, but God could, and he did. The grief and the guilt didn't go away, and I started to drink again. I made bad decisions, fell out with Strathclyde and Rheged, and worsened our relations with Selgovia. I raided the lands of the Dal Fiatach and the Dal n'Araide, and attacked Dalriada's fleet. But I didn't go whoring again. I . . .' He was struggling to hold her eyes now. 'I couldn't. That was my punishment, you see, for incest with my sister. For being weak.'

Brangianne nodded, for she'd come across cases like this before. He'd become impotent.

'And now?' she asked, unable to suppress a professional interest in his case.

'I don't know,' he said. 'In the last year my – incapacity – vanished. Do you imagine I would have offered for Yseult if I hadn't been . . . able? Now, however? As I say, I don't know. I've done as you asked that . . . that night and left her alone.'

Because he's afraid. She was aware of a growing and unwelcome feeling of empathy.

'What you did that night was unforgiveable.' She could still feel the blade at her throat, still hear the accusation Corwynal had hissed in her face. *Do you know how many lives you've ruined by your spite?*

'I know,' the King replied heavily. 'Yet that's what I need. Forgiveness. God might have forgiven me, but God doesn't matter. You do. I need everyone I've wronged to forgive me. I know it won't be easy, given what I've done, but I won't have peace until I've been forgiven. Which is why I asked you to meet me here.' He waved at the terrace and the ruined mosaic that symbolised so much about him – a man who destroyed what he loved.

'You asked me here so I could forgive you?' she asked, astonished.

'And to offer you recompense.'

Astonishment was swept away by a tide of outrage.

'My husband died three days after your men struck him down. Do you know what it's like to die from a stomach wound? You and your men ruined my life, and you tried to buy me off with a trinket. Did you think I was some sort of whore? I'm the sister of the King of Dalriada. How dare you suggest there's any possible recompense for destroying my life!'

He stepped back from her fury, holding up his hands as if to defend himself.

'You're right. I can't give you back the life taken from you, but I can offer you another life. You're a healer now. I owe you Trystan's life – my son's life. We don't have healers like you in Galloway, but I want that to change. I intend to build a healing centre here at the Mote. Look—' He pulled her to her feet and marched her over to the southern tip of the terrace where the wall was lower. The rock fell away steeply down to the port below and the views were extensive. To the west lay the estuary and an island where a small colony of lepers dwelt. To the south a small fort crowned a promontory, but the King pointed to the fields that lay below the fort. 'It's good land,' he said. 'And there's a spring on the high ground.' She could make out a ribbon of water in a channel of birch and low scrub. The fields themselves were dotted with grazing cattle; it was rich land indeed.

'I'll send for builders from Caerlual and Gwynedd, men who know how to work with stone. You can design it yourself and run it as you choose.'

I'm dreaming, she thought. This was the life she'd always longed for. How ironic that it should be offered by a man she'd every reason to hate.

'I can't accept it,' she said with a tremor of regret. 'I'm returning to Dalriada when Yseult's . . . settled.'

'Why? What waits for you there? Why not stay, get to know me? I'm not as bad as you imagine. I've changed. And I'm not the only man who wants you to stay in Galloway . . .'

In spite of herself she coloured. 'You mean Corwynal?'

He blinked in surprise but recovered quickly. 'Was it you he was eating his heart out over last winter?'

She shrugged. 'His heart appears to have recovered.'

'He's a difficult man. Always was. He was my friend once, my best friend, though we're as different as day and night. I could always trust him to tell me the truth, especially when I didn't want to hear it. And I trusted him with my sister – he was the only one I could. Trusted him to bring up Trystan too. He thought he was his brother, of course, but now I've robbed him of that.'

You've robbed him of a great deal more than you think.

'He doesn't forgive easily, but I need him to forgive me too. Dynas is old and tired, and I want Corwynal as my Steward. So perhaps if you stay . . .'

'I see. You make me an offer you claim is recompense because you think it will make *him* stay?'

'That wasn't the reason. I didn't realise there was anything between you until now. When I said someone else wanted you to stay, I meant that young Selgovian, Trystan's friend.'

Her heart sank like a lead weight. For a moment, she'd believed Corwynal loved her enough to have confessed it to Marc. But he didn't love her at all. *I'll never forgive you. Never!*

'And Trystan and Yseult? Do you need them to forgive you too?'

she asked, then wished she'd held her tongue. To have linked their names like that . . .

'They're in love, aren't they?' he asked abruptly.

The wind dropped. Even the noise from below in the port disappeared. All she could hear was a buzzing in her head that might have been bees. Or it might have been sheer panic, for this painful meeting seemed to be about Trystan and Yseult after all.

'Why . . . why do you say that?' Her voice came out as a croak.

'They're young and beautiful, high spirited and courageous. It stands to reason.' He smiled without humour. 'The irony is that when I was Trystan's age, I was just like him, but Yseult can't see it. All she sees is a tired old man.'

She looked at him properly then. He wasn't old, not really. She knew him to be only a little older than Corwynal, but a life of dissipation and disappointment showed in his face. It was as if the man he was had sunk into his own flesh. Only in the eyes could you see the real Marc of Galloway – a man who was weak and unhappy but tried to be neither, who could have been a good King if he'd surrounded himself with good men, a man who had the capacity for self-deception and had only been willing to listen to the truth from the friend who hated him now. He was dangerous and powerful, sad and desperate, a man she found herself, against her will, beginning to understand. Was this empathy the foundation of forgiveness, or did she still hold that rusty knife in her hand?

'What should I do?' he asked as if he was genuinely seeking her advice.

Send Trystan away. It's what she should have said. It would save the marriage, save the treaty. But he'd said *in love*, not *lovers*. Was that what he believed? That it had only been that one night? That it had gone no further? Or was that what he wanted to believe? Was this conversation a warning or a plea? Was the price for her forgiveness that he'd let them love one another for as long as it lasted? *This is part of your punishment*, she could tell him, and make him believe it. Maybe she wasn't doing this for Trystan and

Yseult because she believed in love, and Corwynal, apparently, didn't, but for darker older reasons. Perhaps she did indeed still hold that rusty knife in her hand, ready to thrust it into the heart of a man who stood with his arms wide open expecting – deserving – the blow. *What should I say?* The bees went on buzzing in her head, and the smell of thyme crushed beneath her feet was so strong it almost choked her. *What do I want?* Too many irreconcilable things. But she had to choose one of them.

'I think when you send for builders for your – our – healing centre, you should find one who can repair a mosaic.'

And so Brangianne, for good or ill, or both, bound herself to Galloway, the land she'd hated, to a king she'd hated too but had to learn to understand and forgive – then betray.

Seirian wasn't sure how long she'd been sitting there, watching the smoke coil from the smoored fire and brooding over everything Domech had said. Time was indeed passing and – though she'd never admit it to him – she had doubts about her assertion that she'd know the right man to be Consort when she met him. But what if he didn't come, or didn't exist? Or, if he did, what if he was deformed or cruel? All the Goddess required of the Consort was that he be strong, but strength could take many forms. Might it not be safer to do as Domech suggested and take one of the men she already knew as Consort? *I'll wait*, she decided, *and see who Domech comes up with by Samhain.* If none of them were suitable, she'd pick someone from Atholl, one of the warband, or one of the younger druids.

'You could choose Ninian.'

Seirian looked up as Kirah emerged from one of the curtained alcoves where she'd been hiding.

'You heard everything? You understood?'

Kirah gave her a scornful look. She was only seven but clever for her age. She'd make a formidable Royal Lady when the time came, and Seirian would do anything – *anything* – to ensure that happened.

'I *like* Ninian,' Kirah announced. 'So do you.'

Too clever by half.

'Where is he?' Seirian asked. 'I left word for you to keep him away from Domech.'

Kirah smiled slyly. Clearly those orders had been ignored. Sometimes Seirian wondered if she'd been too lenient with her daughter, and if a good spanking might improve matters, though it was probably too late for that.

'Where is he?'

'At the end of the pier, fishing.'

'So Domech saw him?'

Kirah grinned. 'He went like this—' She drew herself up, her hands at her side, as stiff as a dead tree – a powerful parody of the Archdruid. 'Why is he afraid of Ninian?'

'He isn't afraid. He just doesn't like priests who serve a God he doesn't recognise.'

Kirah frowned at that, aware that this was less than the truth, and that there had to be a reason why a priest of the Nailed God had been permitted to remain in Atholl. The normally garrulous Ninian hadn't told Kirah the real story, however, so Seirian forestalled her inevitable questions by getting to her feet. 'Shall we see if he's managed to catch our supper?'

She laid aside the lunula, unbound her hair, threw off the stifling over-tunic and strolled to the end of the pier that thrust out onto the loch and where Ninian was sitting, his feet dangling, a fishing-rod in his hands. This was sacrilege, of course, for the pier was for sacrifices and divination, not fishing. It was where Seirian stood on the nights of the full moon to offer up whatever was appropriate to the season to Latis, Goddess of the sacred waters of Atholl. But Latis was older and less cruel than the Druids' gods of stone and stars, and wise enough to tolerate Ninian's presence on her pier. She'd even allowed him to build his bee-hive shaped hut close to the farm settlement, where he prayed to his God and told stories to anyone with the time or patience to listen.

Seirian sat down beside him and dipped her feet into water that, even in autumn, was bitterly cold. But the wind, which had blown up just before Domech had arrived, had died down now, and the evening was still, the loch darkening as the shadows of the mountains slipped across its surface. The smoke from the fires in the settlement drifted over the Crannog, bringing with it a smell of food roasting that made Seirian's stomach growl.

'Have you caught anything?'

He shook his head. 'The son of my God was a fisher of men, but I'm not even a fisher of fish.'

'You don't have a worm on your hook, do you?' Kirah accused him sternly.

'It's too fine a day for a worm to be dying,' he said peaceably. 'Or a fish,' he added, smiling that gentle smile of his, the one that made Seirian's heart turn over.

Why him? He had a pleasant face but wasn't handsome. His body was slight, his hair a jumbled shock of tumbled mouse-brown curls that fell into his eyes. He was younger than he pretended, a boy really, aged by something he refused to speak about, though she knew what that was. Domech had nailed him to a tree and marked him with death, but Ninian had survived, thus earning the right to claim sanctuary in Atholl, sanctuary she'd been pleased to grant, if only to annoy Domech. Now it was for the man himself, for Ninian had a core of strength she admired, and she'd come to love him, this stranger to Atholl who struggled with its tongue and whose accent held the lilt of distant lands. Sometimes he'd tell her of those lands, and of the sea that lay beyond them. Seirian couldn't imagine a sea, but sometimes she'd dream of a loch so vast it had no further shore. In her dreams, she'd step into a boat beached on the edge of waters that heaved and sighed beneath her and set sail into a sun setting into a sword-sharp horizon. Sometimes, in the dream, there was a man with her, but she couldn't see his face. She knew, however, it wasn't Ninian.

You'll know the Consort when you meet him. It was one of the many things her mother had impressed on her before she'd died of the fever that had failed to kill the five-year-old Seirian. Little of what her mother had said had made any sense, but she'd forgotten none of it, and later, with time and experience, she'd come to understand. *You may not like him. He may not like you. But you will know him.* What her mother hadn't warned her was that she might meet a man she could have given her heart to, but who wasn't the right one either. She could still choose Ninian, of course, but it would destroy the peace in him, and she wasn't sure she could do that, even if he was the man she was waiting for.

'What did the Archdruid want?' he asked, oblivious to her heart-searching.

She shrugged. 'The usual.' She'd explained her circumstances to him. It was a mark of his obsession with his God that it had never occurred to him that she might have chosen him. 'The Druid College – by which he means himself – requires me to take a Consort without any further delay.'

'And will you?'

'I said I'd consider possible contenders at Samhain.' She smiled brightly to mask her uneasiness. 'But maybe the right man will turn up before then.'

Samhain was only a little more than a moon away, so there wasn't much time. She stared down into the water beneath the pier and tried to see the future in its shifting depths. Surely if the man she was supposed to take as Consort was one of those who'd come – warriors or leaders of some of the other tribes – she'd be able to see him in her future? But, like the man in her dream, he remained hidden, trapped in his own world, not even moving towards her.

'I see him!'

Beside her, Kirah had turned on her stomach and was staring into the depths of the loch. Her face was bloodless, and Seirian reached for her in alarm and pulled her to her feet. 'The Consort? You see him?'

Kirah's eyes were wide, the pupils black with vision, but she shook her head. 'There's a mountain and fire and—' She caught back a cry. 'I'm falling and there's a man . . . No, he's not a man.' She stared at Seirian. 'He's *you,* and it's me who's falling!' She began to sob uncontrollably, and Seirian pulled her into her arms, not so much to comfort the child but to comfort herself, for Kirah hadn't seen the future. She'd seen the past. She'd seen what had happened twenty-five years before.

'Who is he, mother?' Kirah whispered when her sobs had quietened to gulps. 'Who is The Exile?'

'I'm not well, you know.'

Corwynal sighed. He'd suspected Dynas, Galloway's Steward, had been leading up to this. Anyone could see the man was ill; his face was shrunken, his skin had an odd yellow tinge, and his movements were slow and careful.

'Then see a healer.' He glanced down the hall at the only healer he knew. Brangianne was sitting next to Kaerherdin, laughing at something he'd said. When, Corwynal wondered waspishly, had the Selgovian become so amusing?

'I have.' Dynas followed his gaze. 'She said nothing could be done. I've not got long, Corwynal. Galloway needs a new Steward.'

'Agreed. But it won't be me.'

There had been a time when this was exactly what he'd wanted – a chance to help a reformed Marc run a Galloway that one day would fall to Trystan. Corwynal would have preferred Lothian, naturally, but Lothian was barred to him, and Trystan thought Lothian too small and safe. Galloway, on the other hand, offered more challenges, and he might have been content there with Corwynal as his Steward – had that not become impossible.

Corwynal scowled at Yseult who was sitting beside Marc, talking animatedly and making him laugh, for all the world as if the events of the night of their marriage had never happened. Trystan was watching her coolly from further down the hall, his normally mobile face expressionless, the only man in the hall, apart from Corwynal himself, who didn't appear to be besotted with her. Even the women had begun to copy her dress and hair style, and called her the Flame of Dalriada – and not without cause, for she attracted men like moths and let them flutter about her, scorching themselves with her beauty. To Corwynal, that beauty was more like a blade than a flame, a weapon she used to defend herself, and to wound, but Trystan would hear no criticism of her, especially from Corwynal, and had taken to avoiding him. Galloway had become a place where everyone avoided everyone else.

'Is it settled then?'

A hand fell heavily on his shoulder, and Corwynal cursed himself for not noticing that Marc, the man he'd taken the greatest pains to avoid, had left Yseult's side and come down the hall to join him and Dynas.

Dynas threw Corwynal an apologetic look and slid out of his seat to allow Marc to take his place. Corwynal moved to get up too, but Marc's hand slid from his shoulder to his wrist, pinning his hand to the table so he'd have to make a scene if he wanted to get away.

'If you mean is it settled that I'll become Galloway's next Steward, then the answer's no.'

'Why not?'

Corwynal closed his eyes. *Why not?* How did one even begin to answer that question?

'Because I'll be leaving Galloway when Trystan does,' he said, pulling his hand away.

'Trystan's going nowhere.' Marc turned to the high table where Trystan had joined Yseult and was being persuaded to take up his harp and play for her.

Doesn't he see it? Corwynal glanced at Marc, who was looking at

Yseult with the same besotted expression as every other man in the hall.

He doesn't sleep with her,' Trystan had told him, as if that justified his own relations with her.

What if she has a child? Trystan had stared at Corwynal as if this possibility hadn't occurred to him.

Then it will be mine.

And Marc will know it.

But Trystan just shrugged. *We'll deal with that if it happens . . .*

Corwynal wanted to shake him. Trystan was living in the present when he needed to think about the future. But Trystan refused to think about anything except the girl, which meant Marc was right; Trystan was going nowhere.

'Listen, Corwynal,' Marc said, lowering his voice. 'I know you're shocked and angry about what happened all those years ago, but you need to understand. I was young and so was Gwenllian. What happened couldn't be helped.'

Corwynal flinched at the mention of her name. He'd always known he hadn't been the first to awake the sensuality that had been sleeping, but he'd never imagined her first lover might have been her own brother, his best friend. So he wasn't angry. He was bereft.

'I'll make it right,' Marc said blithely.

'Make it *right?*'

'I'll name Trystan my heir. If Yseult has a son, he'll be Trystan's heir, and if Trys renounces Lothian, Rifallyn will have to name you his successor.'

'Don't be ridiculous!'

He felt sick. Indeed, ever since that night, he hadn't felt well. The hall was too hot, too smoky, and smelt too strongly of grease and wine and dogs. His head ached from the noise and, needing fresh air and darkness, he tried to get up, but Marc laid a hand on his arm to stop him.

'I need you to forgive me, Corwynal,' he said seriously.

Forgive him?

Corwynal wasn't sure he could, even though his illusions had been his own. Had Gwenllian ever said she'd loved him? Or that he'd been the first? She'd cried out his name before she'd died, but what did that mean? Yet he'd built a life on that cry. It had been his choice, his mistake, but he still felt betrayed.

'I loved her,' Marc said fiercely.

I loved her too! He shook Marc's hand off and grasped the cup in front of him to stop himself from yelling it in Marc's face.

'You wouldn't understand,' Marc went on. 'You were always a cold-hearted bastard, though . . .' He nodded down the hall at Brangianne. '. . . maybe not so cold these days? It's her isn't it? If you want me to get rid of that Selgovian, just say the word.'

Did Marc think he could make that right too?

I'll never forgive you! he'd yelled at her. He didn't seem to be a very forgiving person. Looking back now, he knew he'd overreacted. She couldn't have known what would happen when she found out Marc had led the raiders to Carnadail, but by the time he'd gathered the courage to apologise it was too late. She'd taken her revenge by doing the worse thing possible, by actively encouraging and concealing Trystan and Yseult's affair. A woman wronged and rejected was a dangerous creature indeed.

'She's going to stay in Galloway,' Marc added. 'I'm to build her a healing centre, here at the Mote.'

Corwynal's grip on his cup tightened until the metal started to distort. So, Marc had bought her forgiveness. Corwynal hadn't thought she could be bought, but what did he know about women? Yet if Marc imagined he'd stay in Galloway for her sake, he was wrong.

'I'm not going to be your Steward.'

'I'll give you whatever you want – lands of your own, the authority to do anything you like in my name. You're the only one I can trust,' Marc insisted. 'You're my only friend, and I need your advice.'

Send Trystan away before someone makes you face the truth. If he had any advice for Marc, that would be it. But Marc had always had the ability to believe anything he liked, and he evidently believed there was nothing between Trystan and Yseult. Should he tell him the truth? But Marc was unpredictable, so if the affair was going to continue – and, with Brangianne's connivance, that was likely – then it might be better to use Marc's trust in him to conceal it. He had the experience, after all; hadn't he carried on an affair with Gwenllian under her husband's, his own father's, nose – a man not known for self-deception?

But Corwynal couldn't do it. Brangianne might have sold away her principles, but he wasn't going to.

'My advice?' He slammed down his cup and got to his feet. 'Find yourself another friend.'

'I can do it myself!'

Ciaran held up his hands and stepped back, allowing Ferdiad to struggle with the laces of his shirt. With only one hand, even the simplest thing became a battle, but, in the end, he defeated the laces, though the fight left him drained and irritable. Irritable was an improvement on tearful, however, so he must be getting better.

It had been two moons since he'd lost his hand. No, not lost – that implied a degree of carelessness on his part – had it stolen from him. What was left, the stump, had healed, and Ciaran had one of the local smiths make a hook which was attached to a cup of leather and strapped to his arm by a complicated series of belts and buckles. The hook allowed him to do more, but not tie laces.

'Another step forward,' Ciaran remarked when Ferdiad was able, finally, to pull his shirt closed against the increasing chill in the wind. The Abbot's calm optimism was driving Ferdiad slowly insane; had he survived The Dragon's poison only to go mad in a different way? It was past time for him to leave Dun Treoin, but he had no idea where he might go or, worse, why he should go anywhere at all.

You are going to destroy Corwynal of Lothian, Arddu reminded him. He'd come to loathe the God's voice as much as he hated Ciaran's. *Leave me alone, all of you.* But they wouldn't.

'It's about to rain,' Ciaran remarked, shading his eyes to look out to sea. They were sitting on the bench outside the Dun in a little sunshine, Ciaran reading a manuscript in Greek, Ferdiad pointedly doing nothing. The tide was out, the rocky shore an expanse of brown weed glistening in the wan sunlight. But even as Ferdiad's gaze followed Ciaran's, the light turned flat and dull, and the wind whirled about the Dun, ruffling the dry autumn grasses and scattering the yellowing birch-leaves in a shower of gold. There were black clouds out to sea, and the afternoon darkened as they moved towards the land, trailing rain in their skirts.

Ferdiad had come to like rain – the sound of it hissing on the thatch, the rush and gurgle in the drain below the eaves of the roundhouse, the growing roar as the stream filled with rainwater. He liked the way it forced him indoors and stopped him from thinking about the future.

'I have to go back to St Martin's.' Ciaran rolled up his manuscript. 'But you can stay here as long as you like.'

To be left alone was what Ferdiad had longed for, but now the prospect of only having Arddu for company filled him with dismay.

'I'll be leaving too.'

'And going where?'

Ferdiad shrugged. 'Wherever Corwynal of Lothian is.'

Ciaran sighed. 'You're still set on revenge?'

'It's all I have to look forward to.' He'd intended it to be a simple statement of fact, but even in his own ears it sounded suspiciously like self-pity. He wished he'd held his tongue, for it would bring on one of Ciaran's lectures about making the best of things, about how, in ways he didn't or couldn't specify, Ferdiad could change the course of his life. *Too late for that, old man.* He'd learned to let these lectures wash over him, to nod and agree and stop listening. But later, at night when he lay sleepless, feeling his absent fingers curve to fit the strings of a harp, some of Ciaran's words would echo in his mind. *Another path... peace... fulfilment...* Then Arddu would laugh, and the words would vanish like smoke on the wind, leaving him with nothing.

'Very well, I'll help you.'

It took a moment before Ferdiad understood what Ciaran had just said.

'You'd help me get revenge? After everything you've said?'

The old man smiled faintly. 'Everything I've said has made no difference to this desire of yours, has it? I rarely fail in my persuasions, so I must assume you're really set on it, even though it's more likely to result in your death than his, and I didn't save your life for you to waste it.'

'I'm not going to challenge the man to single combat! I'm not a complete fool!'

'But it's what you want isn't it? To confront him as an equal?'

Ferdiad glanced sharply at the old man. How did he know that? Had he revealed even this childish fantasy in his fevered ravings? Conscious of Ciaran's eyes on him he looked down and fiddled with the straps of the hated hook.

'That's not very likely, is it? He's a seasoned Caledonian warrior and I'm a Fili. The only weapon I have is satire, so it would hardly be an even match.'

'Quite. Which is why you need help.'

'What *are* you talking about?'

'About another path. One you might have taken years ago, when you were a boy.'

Ferdiad flinched at that. He'd had such dreams then, but Corwynal of Lothian had stolen them. Just as he'd stolen his hand.

'It's not too late,' Ciaran insisted. 'You can become the warrior you wanted to be when you were a boy. I don't believe it's your destiny, but you need to find that out for yourself.'

Ferdiad stared at him. Was this Ciaran's idea of a joke? If so, it was a particularly cruel one. Nevertheless, he forced himself to laugh, if only to keep those treacherous tears at bay.

'I'm thirty-four years old and I only have one hand. But you think I can become a warrior? Are you *insane?*'

'I'm not saying it will be easy,' Ciaran said evenly.

'*Easy?!* That's a masterly piece of understatement, even for you.'

'There are those who can help you,' the Abbott went on. 'If you genuinely want this, I can arrange it.'

'Why would you?'

'Because you need a challenge. Because if, in the end, you still think revenge is the only thing that can cleanse your soul, then let it be clean. It's time to stop being Ferdiad the Serpent and find yourself another name, something with honour.'

'Honour? No-one has ever linked that word with me.'

'No,' Ciaran agreed. 'And that being the case, what I propose could turn you into a monster. It could drive you into Arddu's arms, and he'll destroy you.' He tilted his head and eyed Ferdiad speculatively. 'It's a risk.'

'Whose? Yours or mine?' *Ferdiad the Monster.* He rather liked the sound of that. But he also liked the idea of a clean revenge, of destroying Corwynal of Lothian as an equal, of burning his soul free of a lifetime of hatred, and feeling whole for the first time in his life. But he wasn't a fool. This would be Ciaran's way of distracting him from his goal, of sending him off on the hunt for something that didn't exist or would end in failure. It was his risk. On the other hand, it was something to do.

'Who'll help me turn myself into this monster?'

For answer Ciaran drew from beneath his robe a narrow leather thong from which hung a small wooden medallion carved on one side with an oak leaf and on the other with a symbol Ferdiad didn't know – a serpent crossed with a broken spear. 'You'll know them by their medallions, and they by yours, so don't lose it, and keep it hidden.' He pressed the medallion into Ferdiad's hand and his fingers, gnarled and bony, tightened on his. 'It won't be easy, my dear. You may fail at the first step on the way, for it will be the hardest.' His eyes were dark and compassionate, his fingers still gripping Ferdiad's own as if to give him courage. And that meant courage would be required, that there was every reason for fear.

'If you want to become the man you should have been, you have to go to the place where your path diverged.'

Ferdiad's heart began to gallop like a panicked horse, and that was when the laughter began, running through bone and blood, sinew and nerve – the laughter of a God who knew everything – the past, the present and the future.

'You must go back to The Island.'

4

THE NIGHT OF ENDINGS

'Where's the King?'

Andrydd, Lord of Loch Ryan and Commander of Marc's war-fleet, smelled of the ship he must have arrived on – tarred rope, damp timbers and wet sail-cloth – and as he strode down the Mote's hall, he didn't appear to be in a very good mood.

'He's gone hunting, my Lord,' Dynas said apologetically.

'Why do you want to know?' Corwynal saw no reason for the old Steward to apologise for anything, especially to Andrydd.

'Since when was it your business?'

Corwynal smiled thinly. 'Since Marc asked me to take over from Dynas.'

Andrydd narrowed his eyes at him and glanced at Dynas who coughed but said nothing. It wasn't entirely a lie, and Andrydd believed it.

'It's the Dal n'Araide,' Andrydd said grudgingly. 'They've raided the Rhinns and I need to know what Marc wants done about it. Do I go after them or not? In the old days—' He scowled at Corwynal, meaning before Marc had been persuaded to give up drinking. '—the man who commanded the fleet didn't have to go running to the Mote to be told what to do. Well, if he's not here, I'd better see the Queen.'

'The Queen?'

'She can speak for him, can't she? Word is he does anything she wants, and Dalriada was never friends with the Dal n'Araide. In the Royal Chambers, is she? Right—'

'Wait!' Corwynal leapt up and followed him out of the hall and across the courtyard. 'You ought to get Marc's sanction.'

'Oh, don't be such an old woman!'

Andrydd jerked open the door to the Council chamber and headed for Yseult's quarters.

Let them not be here! Corwynal didn't know whether to be relieved or not when he saw Oonagh sitting on a stool outside the door that led to Yseult's bedchamber. She was clearly on guard, which meant there was something or someone to be guarded. Indeed, he could hear Yseult laughing beyond the hanging across the door.

'The queen's indisposed.' Oonagh got to her feet, crossed her arms, and planted herself in front of the bedchamber.

'I know where Marc's gone hunting,' Corwynal said desperately. 'I can take you there.'

Andrydd ignored him. 'Indisposed?' Again, there came the sound of Yseult's laughter.

'Indeed, my Lord Andrydd,' Oonagh said loudly and the laughter stopped.

'Where's Trystan?' Andrydd demanded. Oonagh's eyes widened and flew to Corwynal's.

'I've no idea,' he said. 'Probably with Marc.'

'Then who—'

The hanging was pulled aside, and Yseult stood there, her hair tumbling about her shoulders, her face flushed, her lips swollen, completely unconcerned about the picture she presented.

'What brings you to the Mote, My Lord Andrydd?' she asked coolly.

His eyebrows rose at her appearance, and it was some time before he recalled his manners. 'I apologise for disturbing you, my Lady. I understand you're indisposed . . . ?'

'A touch of fever,' she said lightly, intending to brazen this out, but, judging from Andrydd's narrowed eyes, he didn't believe her.

'Can't a man make love to his own wife of an afternoon without some bugger wanting something or other?' Marc complained loudly from the other side of the hanging, and Corwynal shuddered with relief.

'It's Lord Andrydd,' Yseult said helpfully.

'What in the Five Hells does he want?'

'The Dal n'Araide have raided the Rhinns,' Andrydd explained.

'Then take care of it! Can't you people use your initiative?'

'Yes, Sire, but—'

'Then sod off back to Loch Ryan and deal with it. Now send my wife back in. We were in the middle of something . . .'

Yseult blushed rosily and slid back behind the hanging. They all heard Marc's growl of approval and the tinkling of Yseult's laughter.

Andrydd stared at the hanging, turned on his heel and marched out.

'That was close!' Oonagh breathed when the door to the courtyard slammed behind him.

Corwynal frowned at her. If Marc was with Yseult, why had Oonagh looked so guilty before and so relieved now? Then he heard laugher once more, but it wasn't Yseult's. Nor was it Marc's. The hanging was pulled aside and Trystan collapsed against the door frame, convulsed with hysterics.

'I wish I could have seen his face,' he declared once he'd recovered. 'Sod off, Andrydd!' he repeated in Marc's voice, still chuckling. Trystan had always been a good mimic.

'You *idiot!*'

'Oh, God, not another lecture!'

'What do you think will happen when Marc finds out Andrydd's gone after the Dal n'Araide without his authority?'

'Oh, Yseult will tell him he she sanctioned it. Won't you, my love?' She'd come to stand beside him, and he put his arm about her waist and smiled down at her. She smiled back before turning her green gaze on Corwynal. *You hate me, but he's mine now.*

'Come on, Oonagh,' Yseult said. 'Let's leave these men together.' She disengaged herself, took Oonagh's arm and marched her out to the terrace.

'Whatever you have to say, I won't listen to it.' Trystan strolled out to the empty Council chamber, poured himself a cup of wine, leant back against the scarred table and crossed his legs at the ankles. 'But I don't expect that will stop you.'

'It's not me who has to stop. It's you.'

'I can't,' he said, and Corwynal believed it. Trystan couldn't stop this anymore than Corwynal had been able to stop his own affair with Gwenllian.

'How do you imagine this is going to end?' he asked harshly, remembering the chamber at Dunpeldyr and how red it had been with blood. *Not that! Please, not that!*

'At best?' Trystan tilted his head, considering the matter. 'Marc will put Yseult aside, and I'll divorce Essylt. Then we can be together openly. That's what we both want. Do you think I enjoy sneaking about like this?'

'The best isn't likely to happen.'

Trystan shrugged. 'Marc gave Yseult to me that night, so what did he *think* would happen? He must know, yet he's said nothing.'

'You don't know Marc like I do. He doesn't *want* to know, but sooner or later someone's going to tell him, someone like Andrydd who means you or Yseult ill. You need to stop this relationship, Trys, but if you can't you need to take more care. Stop meeting at the Mote.'

'It's too cursed cold to meet anywhere else. Anyway, Oonagh's watching out for us.'

'And Brangianne? Is she helping you?'

'Why shouldn't she?'

'You expect me to help you too?'

'No. But you won't give us away, will you?'

'You assume a great deal, Trys.'

'I'm right though.'

'Think, Trys. *Think!* This can only end badly. Think of Yseult if you can't think of yourself.'

Trystan tossed back the last of the wine and laid the cup down on the table with exaggerated care, his head bent, and when he looked up all his bravado was gone, leaving behind a bleak expression shadowed by something Corwynal had never seen before in Trystan's face, something that shook him to his bones. It was fear.

'She's the other half of my soul,' Trystan said softly. 'Do you know what that means?'

'Yes, Trys,' he said, smiling to conceal his grief and desperation and terror. 'I know what it means.'

'I want to talk to you.'

Brangianne's heart rocked. She'd been aware of Corwynal entering the hall and walking towards her. She was always aware of him. It was as if he held all the dark heat of cooling iron fresh from the forge, a warmth she could sense through her skin. *He'll walk straight past me.* He'd done so often enough since the wedding, so she pretended she hadn't noticed him and kept up her bright – too bright – conversation with Kaerherdin about something or other. But this time he stopped.

'Brangianne doesn't want to talk to you.' There was ice in Kaerherdin's voice. He didn't get up from his place on the bench beside her, but his hands curled into fists as he readied himself to square up to the older man. They were like two stags at the rut, except Corwynal was no longer interested in this particular hind.

'It's all right,' she said quickly and forced herself to look at the man she'd been avoiding for over a moon.

He's old! She was shocked by his appearance. The silver in his hair was more evident now, his face drawn down by deep furrows that ran from nose to mouth, his eyes as dull as wind-dried slate. *Have I done this?* But, with an effort, she forced herself to ignore her troubling feelings of responsibility. 'Say what you have to say.'

'Not here.'

'Why not?' Kaerherdin demanded and Corwynal turned on him, planted his fists on the table and leant towards the younger man.

'Because it's *private!*'he snarled.

'Please . . .' She got to her feet before they came to blows. 'Where then?'

Corwynal glanced down the hall to the raised dais where Marc was laughing at something one of his chieftains was whispering in his ear. Beside him, Yseult was gazing across the hall at Trystan, but he, carefully, wasn't looking back.

'The Council chamber,' Corwynal said curtly. 'It'll be empty.'

He didn't speak as they left the main hall and walked across the wet courtyard to the royal residence. She'd thought he might take her by the arm and drag her there, but he didn't touch her, and somehow that was worse.

'Well?' she asked, shaking the rain from her hair once they'd reached the small hall that lay between Marc's quarters and Yseult's. She crossed her arms and turned to face him. 'You've not spoken to me since—' His lips tightened and she stopped. *Since the night that wasn't to be mentioned.*

'You're helping them, aren't you?'

As ever, his accusation came as swiftly and surely as the thrust of a blade to the belly.

'Who?'

'Trystan and Yseult, of course! You're helping them be together.'

'They love one another.'

'And that's all that matters, is it? For the gods' sake, woman, Yseult's Galloway's Queen, and Trystan has a wife of his own.'

So do you, she thought resentfully.

'Marc's no husband to Yseult, and Trys hasn't seen his wife in . . . how long?'

'That's no excuse. They aren't the children of peasants and free to do what they want. Yseult's the only thing keeping Dalriada and Galloway apart.'

'So the only thing that matters is politics?'

'Politics means the difference between war and peace, and if you haven't learned that from your fox of a brother you're a very foolish woman! Trys and Yseult are too important for this affair to be allowed to continue.'

'So, stop it,' she snapped. *A foolish woman, am I?* 'Take Trystan away from Galloway as you intended.' He frowned and shifted uneasily, stirring up dust from the floor. 'But you can't, can you? And that's the only reason you're talking to me now. Because you can't control your precious Trystan!' The colour flared in his face, and she forced herself to laugh. 'You ignore me for two moons. You told me you wouldn't forgive me for what happened that night, when nothing – *nothing!* – was my fault! You didn't even give me a chance to explain. Yet here you are demanding my help. How *dare* you!'

The blood flooded into her own face, and she swelled with indignation, even as the colour drained from his.

'We will not speak of that night,' he said coldly. 'And I dare because I must. What do you think will happen if they're discovered?'

'What do you think I'm doing, you stupid, *stupid* man! They're going to meet one way or another. If no-one helps them, they'll take greater and greater risks. I'm not encouraging them. I'm *guarding* them.'

'You'd do better keeping them apart. If I can get Trystan away, he'll forget her.'

'As you forgot his mother?'

His eyes widened and he glanced quickly about the chamber – at the table littered with rolls of parchment, an empty flagon, a cup lying on its side, the smell of dust everywhere – a room that hadn't been used in weeks and where servants had no reason to come. The place was empty, and all the doors were closed. Nevertheless, he lowered his voice to a whisper.

'That was different.'

'Yes, because she died. You grieved for twenty years because she died. If you take Trystan away now, it will be as if Yseult died for him, and he'll never forget her because she'll always be in his memory, unchanging.' She saw him flinch as each of these arrows hit its mark. 'Let him stay. Let it burn out. A flame like this can't last.'

'They're in danger as long as this continues,' he insisted.

He was right, of course. She could see the fear in him, and felt it in herself, but was still convinced she was right. She unfolded her arms and softened her voice.

'Then it's up to you and I to keep them safe. Come—' She held out a hand. 'We're on the same side in this, so why are we arguing?'

He looked at her, his gaze unfathomable, and ignored her offered hand.

'Is that what you believe? That love dies in the end?'

She'd argued herself into a corner. Yes or no, she'd lose either way. 'I don't know,' she said, and he nodded wearily. This was as hard for him as it was for her. He wanted to leave Galloway, not just to take Trystan away from Yseult but to get away from her. *I've done this to him. And he'll never forgive me.*

'Kaerherdin's in love with you,' he said abruptly.

She shrugged. 'He believes so.'

'Do you?'

'What? Believe it? Or return his affections?'

He glared at her, unable even to ask, so she knew what she had to say. Why wait for their love to die? Why not put such a wounded thing out of its misery?

'It's none of your business. Not anymore.'

She turned her back on him and faced the disorder of the abandoned Council chamber. Behind her, the door opened and the parchments on the table shifted in the draft from the door. The gold of the flagon and cup swam as the evening sun, striking through a gap in the rainclouds, flooded into the room, brightening everything to a blur of sunlit dust, beautiful and perfidious.

Don't leave me!

It was too late. He already had.

The old training school was in ruins. All that was left were tumbled circles of stones choked with nettles and sour with dying bracken. A deer grazing in the long grass of what had once been the fighting ring started at his approach and went bounding off towards the lower slopes of the hills that reared, black and ominous, into low hanging cloud.

The ship that had brought him to The Island of Eagles had already left, running for shelter before a gusting north-westerly that presaged a storm come nightfall.

'Wonderful!' Ferdiad muttered to himself. A storm on its way and no shelter to be had in a place that held so many of his ghosts.

You have to go back to The Island, Ciaran had told him. He'd refused to begin with, not so much out of fear but a blank refusal to even think about the place. *You have to face up to your past.*

And what better night to do so than Samhain, which was for endings? Although he hadn't come for any sort of ending – which was impossible – but for a beginning. A beginning that looked increasingly unlikely.

'The person I'm sending you to is a warrior and a weapons-master. You'll find him in the old training school,' Ciaran had said when he'd browbeaten Ferdiad into agreeing to go.

'I didn't know they'd started up the training school again.'

'They haven't.'

The break-up of the Caledonian warrior and druid school had been the action of the previous Caledonian High King, Nechtan Morbet. The school had too much power that was out of his control, in his view, an opinion shared by Nechtan's successor, the current

High King, Drest Gurthinmoch. Now each tribe trained its own warriors and druids, the best of them being seconded to the High King's court at Dun Tarvos. Ferdiad had been eleven when word had come that the school was to be disbanded, and he'd rejoiced at the news – until he'd learned what his own fate was to be.

'Then why there?'

Ciaran hadn't answered but didn't need to. Ferdiad knew the reason. The training school on The Island was where his ghosts lived, ghosts he had to face. He'd sensed them as soon as he'd stepped foot on dry land, and now, in the ruins, they were gathering, memories flooding back, the old nightmares rearing their heads. It would be bad once the sun set, even without the storm. The wind had blown up to a gale by then and was whining about the ruins. The ship had vanished into a sea streaked with lines of spume, running for shelter back down the coast, but there was no sign of the weapons-master. To be alone here when night came would be unbearable.

The horizon had disappeared, the distant islands vanishing into the gloom, and the cloud which had obscured the mountains had flowed down into the valley, concealing the jagged black crests and high lonely corries behind a grey pall. But Ferdiad could still feel their menace.

'Curse you, Ciaran! Was it always your plan to abandon me here?'

Of course it was! Arddu's voice came out of the gale, from the stones and clouds, the black rock of the mountains, from the mouth of the valley in which the ruins were stumps of rotting teeth. *He wants you alone, but you will never be alone. I am always with you. Don't trust the weapons-master.*

Good advice – if there had been anyone to trust.

Ferdiad was standing in the ruins of what had once been the druid hall. On the other side of the training ring had stood the dormitory of the warriors, beside the boys' house. Further down, towards the river, had been servants' quarters and storerooms. He could have sheltered from the wind behind the remains of some of the walls, but there was no shelter from the rain which began to fall, a shower of stinging drops that merged into a downpour, and the rising wind tore his cloak from his one-handed grip. He peered through the rain at the pass at the head of the valley and wondered if he should seek shelter in that direction. But he didn't know what lay on the far side. More mountains? Bog? Whatever it was, it would soon be in darkness.

You have to face your past . . .

'Curse you, Ciaran,' he repeated as he searched for the one remaining possibility of shelter. It took some finding, for the nettles and bracken grew thickly, and birch scrub had grown up within the walls, but it was still there, a tunnel in one corner of the servants' hall that led into an old souterrain. In Ferdiad's time it had been used to store butter and cheese in the summer, and he'd hidden there on more than one occasion. It was still roofed with stone and turf and, though it smelled of mould, the floor was dry. It was a tight squeeze for the man the boy had turned into, but he managed to crawl out of the rain and the wind. And into his past.

They came almost at once, ghosts who whispered and laughed.

Come out! they insisted. *We know you're in there. You, whatever you call yourself . . .*

Ferdiad, one of them said. *He calls himself Ferdiad.* Laughter rocked all around him.

Ferdiad, then – come out or we'll come and get you. And you know what'll happen then . . . So come out now, and we won't hurt you . . .

They'd been lying. Nothing had been true in that place. Not even his name, a name he'd stolen from a story. It was the one shining memory from those days, the story he'd clung to, the tale he'd found himself in. A dream of a future, the promise of a past, a story that had kept the whispers at bay, then and now. And so Ferdiad pressed himself to the stone at his back, closed his eyes against the black of the night and told himself the tale.

Cuchullain bethought himself how he could prepare himself for deeds of heroism and war. He had heard of a mighty warrior-woman named Scathach who could teach young heroes feats of arms. So he went to the Land of Shadows and abode with her for a year and a day and learned all the feats she had to teach him. And while Cuchullain dwelt with Scathach, his friend above all friends and his rival in skill and valour was Ferdiad, and they vowed to love and help one another as long as they should live . . .

But no story, no matter how shining, could keep the ghosts at bay, not at Samhain, not even here beneath the earth with his back to the wall. And so everything he refused to remember surged out of the dark and into the present. Or not quite everything; he wasn't ready for everything . . .

He'd sought out the first of the boys in the lands of the Ui Niall, a boy who'd become a man and forgotten the child from The Island. By the time Ferdiad had finished with him he'd remembered everything in painful detail. The second had been easier, as had the third and all the others. Only when he'd killed all the boys who'd tortured him, had he been ready for the druid . . .

He woke to his own shouts. Despite his vigilance, he'd fallen asleep. He mustn't do so again, so he clutched the stump of his left arm to remember why he'd come here.

To defeat Corwynal of Lothian, Arddu reminded him, his voice slipping between the cold stones at his back to whisper in his ear. *You want him to grovel at your feet and beg. You want to strip him of any reason for pride. Once you've driven him to his knees, I will take his soul, and you can have everything that is left. But you must promise me his soul.*

Had he dreamed that? Had he promised? Had that been part of the Samhain nightmares? He must have fallen asleep once more, for when he opened his eyes a grey light was seeping past the nettles and bracken at the end of the passageway. The wind was no longer howling, and he could hear no hiss of rain. Samhain was over, the veils between the worlds thickening, the ghosts trailing their way back to the otherworld. He'd faced his past, some of it at least, and his mind, if not his dignity, appeared to be intact. He'd survived, and if he could survive this, he was ready for what came next, the transformation Ciaran had promised him, the name he'd make for himself. Ferdiad the hero, perhaps.

But the hero was stiff and cold and so ravenously hungry he was imagining the smell of frying bacon. He could even hear the crackle of an open fire.

'Breakfast?' someone asked. A shadow moved across the entranceway, and Ferdiad crawled painfully back into the light to find he'd imagined nothing. A man was sitting on the broken wall poking a couple of thick slabs of bacon that sizzled in a frying pan set on a bright little fire. A medallion hung around his neck, an oak-leaf on one side, a beast Ferdiad didn't recognise on the other, the same beast that patterned his face. All Ferdiad's optimism fell away and Ferdiad the Hero had a hollow sound now.

'Is this a joke?' he asked, his voice as stony as the souterrain he'd just left.

'Neither of us is laughing.' Azarion, the weapons-master on The Island all those years before, watched him crawl out of a hole in the ground, his golden eyes speculative. 'Ciaran tells me you want to become a warrior . . . Do you realise how difficult that's going to be?'

'I realise how difficult it would be for a man of your age to train anyone. So maybe we should both give up now.'

Azarion shrugged. 'It would save us both a great deal of pain, but Ciaran called in a favour, so I suppose the attempt must be made.'

'Here?' Ferdiad looked around at the ruins of the training school, the place his hopes had died and where, twenty-five years later, they died once more.

'Here?' Azarion looked at him as if he was mad. 'Of course not! We're going to Dun Sgiath.'

. . . and Cuchullain passed the Plain of Ill-luck and escaped the beasts of the Perilous Glen and came to the Bridge of Leaps beyond which lay Dun Sgiath, the Fort of the Shield. There he found many

sons of the princes of Eriu who had come to learn feats of war from
Scathach, and among them was his friend Ferdiad . . .

'Dun Sgiath? It still exists?' Hope glimmered as treacherously as
a scrap of gold half-buried in the dirt of a ruined life. *Dun Sgiath . . .*
The Bridge of Leaps . . . The sons of the Princes of Eriu . . .
Cuchullain . . .

'After a fashion.'

'And Scathach?'

'Exists too. After a fashion.'

Brangianne didn't feel well. In part it was due to all the rich food
she'd eaten, but mostly it was the wine she'd drunk. And the dead.

It was the feast of Samhain, the night before the first day of
winter, the night when the veils between the worlds were at their
thinnest, the Night of Endings. In Galloway, an empty place had
been set for the dead beside everyone in the hall, be they King or
servant, and Brangianne's dead sat as uneasily beside her as did the
food and drink in her belly.

You should have avenged me. Aedh's ghost leant towards her,
his eyes unforgiving. In his arms was the child she'd lost, a child
who wailed as mournfully as did the wind around The Mote's
feasting hall, a wind that whined and shuddered and blew leaves
through the doorway, for it had been left open to let the dead crowd
in.

Beside her, Kaerherdin was saying something, but she was
finding it difficult to concentrate, for the hall blurred and
shimmered, and the noise pulsed drunkenly all around her.
Brangianne wasn't the only one to have drunk too much that
evening, for few chose to meet their dead entirely sober. Marc had
been carried away some time before, but the empty place beside
him was still occupied. A girl sat there, blue-eyed, golden haired,
smiling knowingly. But, as Brangianne watched, she broke apart

into cubes of mosaic and disappeared, only to reappear beside the man Brangianne had been avoiding, for she was his dead too. For him, this particular ghost was naked, her skin running with water, and there were strings of river weed in that golden hair, and fingers of willow leaves patterning her skin.

But Corwynal wasn't looking at the girl he'd loved, the girl who'd borne a child he'd believed to be his own son but could do so no longer. He was looking at her. She'd been aware of his gaze all evening, cold and stormy, and sensed that he was terrifyingly sober.

If so, he was the only one in the hall. A few seats away, Yseult had a glazed expression on her face, and her gaze was on everyone but Trystan. Trystan's eyes glittered dangerously, for he wasn't entirely sober either and was reaching the end of his fragile patience.

Suddenly, Brangianne could bear it no longer – the deception, the lies, the compromises, the sacrifice, the . . . unhappiness.

'I don't feel well,' she muttered to Kaerherdin.

'You need some fresh air.' He took the cup from her hand, put an arm around her shoulders, helped her to her feet and steered her to the open door. She glanced back once, unable to help herself. Corwynal was glaring at them, but Kaerherdin just smiled.

Her room was in the Royal Chambers, close to Yseult's, and had the rare luxury of privacy. She shared the room with Oonagh, but Oonagh would be spending the night with Aelfric in some barn or other. The room was small, with only a bed, a pallet, two chests and some clothes hanging from pegs. A thick hanging separated the room from the antechamber and a single guttering oil lamp on a high shelf threw a faint glow about the room. Kaerherdin poured Brangianne a cup of water and found, among the clutter on the chests, a twist of dried mint that he sprinkled into the water.

'You remembered . . .' she murmured, drinking down the minted water.

'I remember everything you've taught me.' He sat beside her on her bed since there was nowhere else to sit.

'You're a good pupil.' Kaerherdin had become her apprentice, as Ninian had once been. 'And a good friend,' she added.

'I think you need a friend in this place.'

Her eyes brimmed and tears trickled down her face as his arms went about her. She found herself sobbing against his shoulder, even though, distantly, a warning bell had begun to swing in the wind.

'A friend who doesn't want to see you like this. He hurt you, didn't he? It hurts me to know he's caused you so much pain.'

She began to cry once more, quietly and desperately, and he laid his cheek against the top of her head. 'Let me take away the pain, Brangianne . . .' He kissed her forehead, her eyes, her lips. Her own lips parted beneath his, despite the ringing of that warning bell, louder, closer. *Don't do this . . .*

But she didn't have the energy to stop it. She tasted wine on his breath, mixing pleasantly with the mint on hers. She smelled rosemary, and the sharper musky scent of his skin, and turned her head away. But he held her against him, his hands on her shoulders kneading away her resistance. 'Let me heal you. Let me care for you. Let me help you forget.'

The lamp, that had been guttering lower and lower, finally went out, leaving them in darkness, and she was no longer sure who she was, or who he was, but his hands were confident enough to dispel her own lack of certainty, and he was leading her somewhere she wanted to go. *But not with him!* The warning bell went on ringing, muffled now, as if falling through the water that had closed over her head. She sank deeper and deeper, away from light and hope and anything that mattered. Except for him. She arched up, crying out a name. *Talorc!* she cried out to the man who wasn't there, to the man she'd lost, to the man who was as dead to her, and she to him, as any Samhain ghost . . .

Brangianne woke to a raging thirst, a sweet ache in the core of her body and the conviction that order had been restored to her world.

She'd drunk too much the previous night, which accounted for the thirst and her inability to remember in detail exactly what had led her and Corwynal to make up their differences. They'd had yet another terrible argument before the Samhain feast had begun. Inevitably, it had been about Trystan and Yseult who'd managed, in Brangianne's absence at the new healing centre, to be together. *Do you know how close they came to being discovered? Yet again? So where were you? Where was the guardian?* Which had infuriated her. *Why is it always down to me? I have a life too, you know. Where were you?* He must have apologised later. Or she had. It didn't matter. He was with her now, breathing quietly beside her. She lay there savouring the moment, wondering if they'd made another child in the night, and moved her fingers to her belly, searching for some other presence there. But even the light pressure of her fingers made her feel sick, and the ache that spread through the whole of her body was no longer so sweet, but rather a piercing throb centred somewhere behind her eyes. She must have drunk a very great deal.

'Brangianne . . .' His voice was gentler than it had been of late, but strangely muted. 'Brangianne?' There it was again, his voice coming from the antechamber beyond the door hanging. *How odd!* She eased herself onto her back, and then, head and stomach protesting, onto her side to look at the man lying beside her, his dark hair spread across the pillow, his long lean back to her. But something was missing. The designs of bull and fish she'd traced so often with her fingertips had gone as if she'd smoothed them away. Still asleep, the man beside her turned on his back and she saw why there were no designs. Her stomach clenched and she only just made it out of the bed and across the room to the basin that stood near the door before retching up all the wine she'd drunk.

'Brangianne?' It was the voice again. *His* voice, and it was coming from the other side of the door hanging. 'Are you all right?'

'Go away . . .'

'No. I need to speak to you.'

'Not now.'

'Yes, now. Are you dressed?'

He intended to come in, she realised. 'No! Give me a moment.' She found her skirt in a pile of clothes on the floor and scrambled into it, pulled her tunic over her head and laced it with trembling fingers, then glanced at Kaerherdin – *Kaerherdin?!* – before slipping into the antechamber and twitching the hanging down behind her. 'What do you want?' she asked curtly. Her fantasy about how they'd made up their differences was just that – a fantasy.

'To apologise.'

She closed her eyes. Why now? Why not last night before . . . ? How could she have been so *stupid?!*

'I've been unreasonable. I've blamed you for things that weren't your fault.'

He looked terrible, his face grey, his eyes half-closed as if even the faint light of the antechamber hurt them, and he was frowning. She wanted to reach out and smooth away that little frown, but she couldn't, not now.

'You're right,' he said. 'We should be working together. Not against one another. I know I've hurt you, and I understand why you need to hurt me in return, but, please, don't do it through them.'

She closed her eyes once more, her stomach roiling, wanting to be sick or weep or both.

'I love you,' he said. His eyes were the steel colour of clouds in a sunset sky. 'I've never stopped loving you.'

'But she doesn't love you.'

Kaerherdin's voice came from behind her, as did his arm, going around her shoulders and pressing her back against his chest. He was naked.

May the earth open to swallow me. May the sea rise to drown me. May the sky fall upon me. It was the ancient oath of all the peoples of the North, and right then Brangianne wished the earth would open and take her away from there. She closed her eyes, willing this to be some nightmare from which she would wake up, but when she opened them once more Corwynal was still there. His eyes had turned from cloud to slate. His face was the colour of granite and just as hard.

'I see.'

'Good,' Kaerherdin said, still with his arm trapping her against his chest.

'Just . . . just go,' she whispered. *I know you need to hurt me . . .* She hadn't wanted to, but she had. She, a healer, appeared to have more power to hurt than to heal. He raked her with a look which told her exactly what he thought of her, then turned and walked stiffly from the room. She knew he'd never speak to her again, that she'd lost him at the very moment he'd reached out to her. Samhain, indeed, was for endings. And now something else had to end . . .

'Kaer—' she began.

'Come back to bed,' he whispered.

'Kaer, I—'

Just then a servant carrying some linen appeared in the antechamber. She jumped at the sight of them – the half-dressed woman, the naked man – smiled faintly and left the room once more. *Everyone will know!* Brangianne felt as if the sky was pressing down on her, and her bones turned so liquid that Kaerherdin had no difficulty in steering her back inside the bedchamber once more.

'He's not the only man to love you,' he said.

'I . . . I know.' She'd suspected it for some time, so why hadn't she been more careful?

He went across the room to pull back the shutter, letting the light spill in – too bright, too . . . detailed.

'Someone will see,' she protested.

'I want *you* to see.' He came over and took her by the shoulders, then lifted her face so she had to look up at him. 'You thought I was him last night, didn't you?'

Maybe she had, but in the too-bright morning light all she saw were the differences – the eyes paler, the nose longer. He was taller and younger than Corwynal by at least ten years, younger than she was. She flushed and looked away. 'Didn't you?' He shook her lightly, forcing her to look back at him. 'I thought we were friends.'

'We were . . . are.'

'Did a friend deserve that?

She shook her head. She'd never felt so ashamed. He was a good man and she'd hurt him too.

'Then look at me now.' He bent his head to kiss her. She turned her face away but he wove his fingers into the tangle of her hair and turned her back towards him. 'Look at *me*,' he insisted. 'Know who's here with you.'

This is my punishment. This was the recompense she must make to a good man who loved her. And so she kept her eyes open as his lips moved to her throat, as his hands – the hands of a healer – stripped away her clothes once more. He'd said something about healing last night, she remembered. Now it was her turn to heal, and so she allowed him to do these things to her and pretended a response she didn't feel until it occurred to her that he was right. A good man hadn't deserved her pretence of the darkness, and neither did he deserve this pretence of the light. So she kept her eyes on his as he moved above her, grey eyes the colour of the high clouds of winter that come before the snow, and let the earth swallow her up, let the sky press down and the sea rise up to drown her.

THE CHOOSING

Tarain of Fortru was young but not too young, handsome but seemed unaware of it, strong but not overtly so; Seirian had never been impressed by the size of a man's muscles. She was, however, captivated by his intelligence and dry sense of humour, both of which had kept her entertained all through the Samhain feast. Domech, watching from the other side of the hall, had smiled at that, which meant Tarain was Domech's preference for Consort, and that, in its turn, meant he was the High King's choice.

There were others, naturally, but none of them were real contenders – a Creonn who hadn't thought it worth his while to wash before attending the feast, a Taexel with the hair of a fox and the face of a stoat, and a thick-necked warrior from Circind who had no conversation to speak of. So it was clear who she'd pick in the ceremony of The Choosing later that evening.

She'd come to Dun Caled for Samhain, travelling by boat down the loch and into the Tava River that flowed through Atholl's heart and past the Royal Stronghold which lay not far from the border with the Britons' lands to the south. It had been some time since the last Choosing, so everyone who was anyone in Atholl, and a few who weren't, had crammed themselves into Dun Caled's feasting hall and spilled into the courtyard that overlooked the river swirling around the foot of the western ramparts.

The Samhain feast had been a sombre one, as befitted the Night of Endings, but it was over now. The doors had been barred and the ghosts banished into the wind howling around the stronghold. The little that remained of the feast was thrown to the dogs, who growled and squabbled until the hall's Steward had them whipped out. The fires in the firepits were allowed to die down, and the place stank of ale and roast meat, smoke and excitement. Everyone was wearing their best clothes and rather too much jewellery, especially the King. For once, however, Ciniod wasn't the centre of attention. She was.

'My Royal Lady, may I present Wroid of the Creonn nation, who's come to offer himself as Consort.' Domech looked down his axe of a nose as the man fell to his feet before Seirian and launched into a short speech in which he extolled his virtues and suitability as Consort. On the far side of the hall, hidden among Seirian's women, since she wasn't supposed to be there, Kirah made a face at her. Seirian struggled not to laugh and, once the speech came to an end, arranged her face into something resembling regret.

'I'm sorry,' she said. 'But the Goddess does not choose you.'

The fox-haired Taexel fared no better, though his speech was longer, while the man from Circind made no speech at all and just looked at her soulfully until everyone laughed. Even Ciniod seemed amused. The King-regent didn't want her to choose anyone, unless it was himself or, better, his son. Broichan sat beside his father, scowling at her; he hadn't forgiven her for turning him down at the last Choosing, but hadn't entirely given up hope. Nevertheless, in Tarain of Fortru, he recognised a serious rival.

'My Royal Lady, may I present Tarain of Fortru, of the Verturon tribe, who's come to offer himself as Consort.' Domech raised his voice until it echoed about the hall. An expectant murmur ran through the crowd, and Seirian's women giggled excitedly. Ciniod was no longer amused, and Broichan's scowl deepened. Ciniod's warband exchanged knowing glances, for Tarain's prowess in battle was common knowledge.

Seirian looked for Kirah but could no longer see her in the crowd. She'd intended telling her she was going to accept Tarain, but when they'd reached Dun Caled, Kirah had disappeared into the stronghold's warren of storerooms and granaries. Would she be pleased? Or jealous? Did Tarain like children? Would he be a good lover? Would he be kind? None of these things mattered, however.

You will know him. You may not like him. He may not like you. But you will know him. I promise you that, Seirian. So you must wait until you're certain.

But she'd been waiting for many years now, and Domech was right; she was getting old and must make a choice. Samhain was for endings, but after every ending comes a beginning.

Tarain knelt before her, smiling faintly. He'd make a good speech, she decided. He'd be modest but would make clear his qualities. She glanced briefly at Domech who stood impassively to one side, his hands folded into the sleeves of his robes, a glitter of satisfaction in his eyes. He wanted her to choose this man, which meant he believed he could control him. Did she want a man Domech could control? Might it be amusing to see if *she* could control him? So she waited with interest for the speech. But he didn't make one. He lifted his eyes to hers and his smiled deepened.

'Will you take me?'

Maybe it was the way he'd looked at her, appealing not to the warriors or druids, but to herself directly, as if he assumed she'd already decided to choose him. Maybe it was that overconfident smile. Or maybe it was because when everyone craned forward to listen for her reply Seirian caught sight of Kirah shaking her head urgently.

You will know him, her mother had told her. Breaths were taken and held as everyone waited for her answer, and Tarain carried on smiling.

'I think you'd make an excellent Consort, Tarain of Fortru.' She pitched her voice so everyone could hear. 'But my opinion doesn't matter. It's the Goddess who decides – and, I'm sorry, but she doesn't choose you.'

It takes thirteen years to become a druid, thirteen years of disciplines as harsh and painful as any the warriors have to undertake. A druid has to strengthen not his muscles but his mind, and his reactions need to be just as quick. He has to read not how a man might move in this moment or the next, but how the world might shift this year, this generation. He has to fight for his tribe, not with sword or spear but with the honed weapon of his intellect and the shield of his knowledge. Above all, he has to master himself. He needs to crush emotion and turn desire, ambition, even love, into a force for change or stability. He needs to be the calm centre in the storm of lesser men's passions. None of that is learned in a mere thirteen years. Even after he's won his staff and had the double disc that symbolises the duality of all things pricked into his shoulder and the sign of the serpent of knowledge marked on his forehead, a druid must go on learning. He must strive for that inner calm that is the source of his power. But it's never easy, and sometimes it's impossible.

'Why did you refuse him?' Domech was shaking with anger, frustration and – yes – fear. After all his work! After everything had seemed so promising! After Tarain himself had assured him the outcome was inevitable. 'Women can't, as a rule, resist me,' he'd said complacently, and indeed many of the women in the hall regarded him hungrily. But was Seirian one of them? Domech wasn't as certain as Tarain.

The High Druid, however, would expect him to come up with better reasons for this failure than overconfidence and uncertainty. For Tarain wasn't the High King's choice, as everyone assumed, but the High Druid's, and Domech was going to have a lot of explaining to do to a man who frankly terrified him. The prospect was far from conducive to that elusive inner calm.

'What was wrong with him?'

The ceremony was over by then, the crowd dispersed, and the contenders had left the hall in various states of resentment or relief. Domech had confronted Seirian in the guest hut that had been made available for her and her women, where she was calmly packing her ceremonial robes into a chest, layering them with sharp-scented herbs that made him sneeze.

'He wasn't the right one.'

'I warned you—'

'And I warned you.' She let the lid of the chest fall with a bang.

But he'd had time to think about that. 'If you were going to take that follower of Chrystos as Consort you would have done it by now.'

She flushed at that and had no reply to make.

'You leave me no option, Seirian. I'll have to consult with the High Druid to determine our course of action.'

'Our? Who is 'we'? You and Atholl, or you and the High Druid? Where does your loyalty lie these days, Domech? Do you even know?'

He walked out at that point, knowing he'd say something he'd regret if he stayed. He strode across the courtyard and climbed the inner rampart that overlooked the river. Leaning his elbows on the stone coping, he clasped his hands and breathed deeply to calm himself, allowing his eyes to follow the river as it curved around the rock of Dun Caled, silver in the light of a Hunter's moon. But the calm he needed escaped him.

Between Seirian and the High Druid, Domech had been forced into a corner, something he should have foreseen. What was wrong with him these days? The future eluded him as effortlessly as that longed-for calm. All he could see in the fires, or the wheel of the night skies, was a shadow sweeping in from the west. But why the west when it was north he'd have to go to face the High Druid in person?

He shuddered at the prospect; he was still smarting from a confrontation three years before when he'd been summoned to discuss a course of action he'd undertaken at the High Druid's request, one that had resulted in failure. Any further failure, he'd been warned, would be regarded with – how had the High Druid put it? – with *disappointment*. Disappointment; such a benign little word, so open to interpretation. It could mean anything from a mild clicking of the tongue to the bloody extravagances of the sort of ritual sacrifice that hadn't been practiced in generations.

And all because he cared about Atholl, because its faded glories pained his soul, because Ciniod was a reed that bent with every wind when what Atholl needed was an oak. And because the old ways were fading, the ancient knowledge drifting away like smoke, the minds of his fellow-druids becoming more rigid, the rituals followed with no consideration of the reasons. Atholl needed to regain its past in order to take its place in the future, but Domech had no idea how that was to be achieved.

'Don't worry. It will be all right,' a little voice said from close beside him.

He looked down to see that Seirian's daughter had clambered up the rough wall and was leaning her elbows on the coping stones. Her hands were clasped and she was staring down at the river in a parody of his own posture.

'What are you talking about?' Shouldn't children be in bed at this time of night? Domech didn't like children, and had always found this one disturbing.

'The man,' she said with the patience a woman might give to a particularly retarded child. 'He's coming. I've seen him in the waters.'

'The Consort?'

She shrugged. 'The man,' she repeated, pointing up-river. 'He'll come that way.'

From the west! Had the child seen the shadow too?

'He's been here before,' she added. 'He knows the way.'

'Who? When?' he asked urgently, despising himself for

depending on the vision of a seven-year-old girl. But she shrugged as if neither of these questions were important.

'Kirah!' One of Seirian's women called for her from the door to the hall, and the child jumped down from the wall.

'I have to go now.' She smiled brightly at Domech. 'But don't worry. It will be all right.'

And with that she was gone, skipping across the moonlit courtyard, skipping into a future as clear to her as a limpid pool, while he was blind and deaf and stumbling, and deeply, deeply afraid.

'Do you love me?'

Aelfric opened one eye. 'I just did. Woden's balls, woman, you're insatiable!'

His other eye flew open when Oonagh punched him in the stomach. 'I didn't mean that, and you know it!'

'Oh, you mean that poetry stuff? Why? You want me to recite you a poem? Or warble you a song?'

Oonagh snorted in derision.

'I thought not.'

'I want to know if you care for me at all.'

'Of course I do,' he said, hoping that would be the end of it.

'So, we have a future, do we?'

'Everyone has a future.' He closed his eyes once more to indicate that this discussion was over. They were lying in the hay barn and, though the hay was soft and smelled sweetly of summer, the wind howling around The Mote was distinctly wintry. He pulled Oonagh closer to him beneath his fur-lined cloak, and trailed his hand along her thigh, but she pushed him away, propped her head on one hand and scowled down at him.

'Together, I mean.'

Aelfric let his hand slip from her thigh and sighed.

'I already have a wife.'

'Whom you haven't seen for over ten years and don't seem to care about. You have sons too, but you aren't interested in them either.'

'They're children. Once they're men, I'll be interested.'

'It'll be too late by then. Boys need a father while they're growing up. How do you think Trystan would have turned out if Corwynal hadn't brought him up like a father from the day he was born?'

'He might have been less of a bloody idiot!'

That silenced her, thanks be to Woden, because it was the truth. The boy had gone mad in Dalriada, but this was a different sort of madness, and it wasn't going to end well. If that was love, Aelfric was glad he'd never suffered from it. And it wasn't only Trystan. Corwynal and Brangianne were a mess too, what with Brangianne taking up with Kaerherdin and the Caledonian and Selgovian being at one another's throats. It must be something in the water, Aelfric had concluded, and made the happy decision to stick exclusively to ale. Even the King was infected by the same madness – all those soulful looks at his own wife on the rare occasions he could focus, for the man had taken to drinking heavily once more. What with one thing and another, Galloway was like a simmering pot of milk ready to boil over, and Aelfric wasn't sure he wanted to be around when it happened.

'Corwynal's not his brother,' Oonagh said abruptly.

'I know.' He wondered how she'd found out. Not that it mattered. Brother or father, the Caledonian was following the boy around like an anxious sheepdog, and Trystan wasn't taking it well. But someone needed to keep an eye on the young idiot. Just the other day, Aelfric had followed him to a charcoal burner's hut within spitting distance of the Mote, where Yseult had been waiting for him. He'd given him an earful later, asked him what he imagined would have happened if someone else had followed him, but Trys just laughed, and there was a look in his eyes Aelfric knew meant trouble. It was as if he *wanted* to be found out – and sooner or later someone was going to do just that, especially now the colder

weather was driving them inside, as it had driven Aelfric and
Oonagh into the hay-barn behind the stables.

'Aelfric . . . ?'

What now? He'd drifted off again, but it didn't look as if he'd get
any peace until Oonagh got whatever she had to say off that
magnificent chest of hers. 'Are you telling me to go back to my wife
and bring my sons up?'

'Of course not. If you'd wanted to, you would have left ages ago.'

'You think I'm staying in Galloway for you? You're not the only
woman in the world.'

She punched him again, which was unfair since he'd actually
been faithful to her – more or less. What more did she want? Stupid
question. Women, in Aelfric's extensive experience, always wanted
more.

'I think I'm the only woman who'd put up with you for the rest
of your life. I think it's time you settled down.'

Settled down. Those words had an ominous sound. Settling down
meant no more fighting, no more drinking, no more women, no
more adventuring. The unnerving thing was that the idea had begun
to have a certain appeal, which meant he was getting old. He'd even
thought about going back to Bernicia and reclaiming everything that
was his. Which might be entertaining, at least to begin with, but
would mean making a decision he wasn't ready to make.

'Settled down with me,' Oonagh went on. 'We might as well be
man and wife, especially now . . .'

She gave him a secret little smile and Aelfric had the uneasy
conviction that the world was about to change.

'. . . because I'm carrying your child, you big oaf.'

'Again.'

'I can't . . .'

Despite the cold November wind blowing straight across the
sound, sweat was trickling down Ferdiad's back. The double-

weighted sword was like an iron club in his greasy fingers, the large wooden disc strapped to his left arm more like a door than a shield. His body ached, his throat was raw, and his lungs were burning, but Azarion ignored his protest.

'Again. Or are you giving up?'

Ferdiad glared at Azarion and thought about how much he hated him, because that was all he had left. Confidence had been stripped away, then hope, even determination, and all he had to keep despair and disillusion at bay was hatred for the man who faced him, shield raised, sword held low, and who, despite his advanced years, effortlessly blocked every move Ferdiad made.

'Again,' Azarion growled.

Ferdiad lifted the hated sword and recalled his hopes of only half a moon before, hopes of becoming the man he should have been, the warrior he'd dreamed of being, a man of honour, skilled enough to defeat even Corwynal of Lothian. But they had been a child's hopes, all too easily crushed beneath the unimaginable weight of the disappointments that, one after the other, had fallen on him like the blows of Azarion's sword.

A skiff, which must have brought Azarion to the old training school, had been waiting for them at the mouth of the bay below the ruined school. It was helmed by the strangest creature Ferdiad had ever seen. To begin with, he hadn't even been sure if it was human or some gnome out of the old tales. Even its sex hadn't been obvious. It was a hunchback with a seamed leather face ingrained with dirt, any hair it had concealed beneath a filthy cap, and it was wrapped in furs. But the arms, bare despite the cold, were thick with muscle and scarred with what looked like burns. The creature glared at Ferdiad from beneath heavy brows, the same speculation in its eyes as in Azarion's, judging him and finding him wanting.

Dun Sgiath was a day's sail away, down the sea loch that lay at the foot of the mountains, past a low island, then curving around black mountains and red, and over a wide sound beyond which lay a long finger of land. Behind that lay the cloud-covered mountains of the mainland, layer on layer, fading into the east.

The journey had been made in near silence, for the hunchback hadn't spoken, at least not to him. The few words it had uttered had been to Azarion and in a language whose cadences were disturbingly familiar. But Ferdiad ignored them both and lost himself in the hiss of the swell that surged beneath the boat's stern. The wind, out of the northwest, was bitterly cold, but it blew them swiftly towards the low-lying peninsula and into a tiny bay dominated by an equally tiny dun perched on an outcrop close to the high tide mark and separated from the shore by a narrow channel of shallow water.

That was when the disappointments began.

A stone bridge crossed from the shore to the dun and Ferdiad, still clinging to the old story, wondered if it was The Bridge of Leaps.

For if a man step upon one end of that bridge the middle straightaway rises up and flings him back, and if he leaps upon it, he may miss his footing and fall into the gulf where the sea-monsters are waiting for him . . .

But this bridge had fallen into the sea, leaving a gap across which a reasonably agile man might step if he chose to. But why should he? Dun Sgiath was as ruined as the training camp below the mountains and equally deserted. There were no sons of the Princes of Eriu waiting for them here, no Cuchullain. Only him, the weapons-master and the hunchback. A long low building crouched near the shore, half buried beneath turf and moss. To one side was a workshop of some kind, a couple of outhouses, an empty pigpen and a ring of boulders knee deep in dried grass. The last glimmer of hope vanished. It had only ever been fool's gold, a talisman against the night. Now even that was gone, and it was this so-called weapons-master who'd stolen it from him.

Ferdiad wanted to howl like some wounded animal, because that was what he was – a wounded animal.

'And Scathach?' he asked, after taking in the ruins of Dun Sgiath. Where was the woman who'd trained Ferdiad and Cuchullain? The woman who was meant to teach him how to defeat the man who, like everyone else, had stolen Ferdiad's precious fool's gold of hope. Not here, apparently. But in that he was wrong.

'Scathach?' Azarion asked in surprise. 'But you've already met her.'

The hunchback had looked up at Ferdiad, eyes gleaming with derision and malice, then turned and stumped off to the workshop and disappeared, slamming the door behind her.

'That's Scathach?' Ferdiad's voice, crushed beneath all that disappointment, came out as a whisper.

'You expected her to be teaching you, like in that old story?' Azarion laughed harshly, the croak of a raven, laughter that rocked through Ferdiad's bones and nerves as Arddu echoed the weapon-master's amusement. 'Scathach's not the only one to have taken a name from a story. But she *is* a weapons-master – or mistress. She's a swordsmith, and more. If she judges you worthy, she'll make you a sword.' Azarion glanced over at the workshop. The door remained resolutely shut. Scathach's opinion of Ferdiad's likelihood, now or ever, of being judged worthy of anything was all too clear.

That had been half a moon before. Now, as the days shortened and the weather worsened, the last shreds of his dreams fragmented and were blown away by the frigid winter winds. Ciaran had sent him on a wild goose chase. Why had he believed the old Abbot's promises? How could a man of his age become a warrior capable of defeating someone who'd been fighting all his life? Had he been mad?

Azarion wanted to be here no more than he did, and, as for Scathach, he'd barely seen the woman, if woman she was. She hadn't even spoken to him, and there was no evidence of her making a sword for anyone. The only sound that came from behind the closed doors of the smithy was a light metallic tapping that went on all night and drove Ferdiad insane. Well, there was an easy way to solve that particular irritation. He'd leave. He'd go and find Corwynal of Lothian then he'd ... He'd what? He wasn't sure, but something would occur to him.

But first, he decided, he was going to wipe Azarion's pitying smile from his face. He hefted the sword, raised the shield and stamped forward, forgetting everything he'd been taught about balance and gravity and angles of attack. He feinted right, then thrust his sword in low, and for the first time in two weeks managed to get past Azarion's shield, only to find his low thrust blocked by the man's blade. It caught Ferdiad's own in a clash of metal that reverberated all along the bones of his aching arm, and he fell back, tripped and fell heavily, and the air whooshed from his lungs. The weapons-master stood over him, his shield flung away, both hands on the hilt of his sword, and Ferdiad knew that if this had been a real fight he'd be about to die. He closed his eyes, defeated.

'Better,' the man said.

Ferdiad's eyes flew open. *Better?* The first word of praise in two sodding weeks!

Azarion held out his hand, grasped Ferdiad's wrist, hauled him to his feet and tossed him a skin of water. 'So, what did you do right?'

Ferdiad took a long swallow of peaty water and poured the rest over his sweating face. 'You tell me.'

'You stopped thinking.'

'Wonderful! The one thing I'm good at and you tell me to stop doing it.'

'You don't need to think to fight. A man fights with his heart, not his mind. I could see you stop thinking, so I didn't know what you'd do. That gave you an advantage. That's how you got past my first line of defence. But even if you succeed, you haven't won. You still have your opponent's mind to fight. *That's* when you start thinking, not before. *That's* when you fight with your mind.'

'And how do I do that?'

Azarion laid aside his sword, sat down on one of the boulders that ringed the training ring, and folded his arms. 'You have to trust your instincts. And you have to trust me.'

Don't trust the weapons-master. Arddu's warning rippled through his veins.

'Why should I trust you? You don't believe I can learn what I need to know.'

'What I believe doesn't matter. It's what you believe that counts.'

'I'm old. I lack a hand.'

'But you have a mind. A good one, according to Ciaran.'

'Which you tell me I mustn't use.'

'By the blessed Chrystos, man, do you never listen? You fight with your body and your heart, but you *win* with your mind. You need to think, but not when you fight. Then you need to stop thinking, because if you do your opponent will read your intentions in your face, your eyes, in the way you move. So you must shield your thoughts or, better, fight without thinking. Know your body and your abilities so well you need no longer think about yourself. Instead, you think about your enemy. You need to get under his skin, imagine his secrets, his dreams and his fears, his past and his future, everything that makes him weak. You need to *become* him.'

'How can you kill a man you become?'

Azarion gave a crack of laughter and threw back his head. 'At last! A genuinely intelligent question! How indeed?' He leant forward, his sword across his knees. 'Tell me why you want to kill Corwynal of Lothian.'

'Destroy,' Ferdiad corrected him. 'I want to destroy him. I want you to teach me as you taught him.'

'You were a boy on The Island? I don't remember you, and I remember all the boys.'

'Evidently not.'

Azarion regarded him narrowly, as if trying to recall someone he'd forgotten.

'I looked different then.'

Azarion shrugged. 'Does Corwynal remember you?'

'I intend to make him.' There was an echo of Arddu's voice in his own, cold and relentless.

'Such hatred! Where does that come from? What did he do to you?'

For answer Ferdiad lifted the stump of his left arm. 'This. And more. He took a boy I loved, a man I loved.'

Azarion tilted his head to one side, golden eyes glittering with curiosity. 'So it's about love, not hate.'

'My reasons are none of your business!' Ferdiad leapt to his feet and reached for his double-weighted sword. For the first time, it felt light. For the first time, he could actually wield it, for it was buoyed up by the flood of his hatred. He lifted it until the point touched Azarion's leather breastplate. 'None!'

But the weapons-master just smiled in what looked like satisfaction. 'It is if the reasons help you fight.'

Then the weight was back and the sword's point dropped. Ferdiad let the blade fall and strode away. Trying not to run, he headed across the machair to the dun and stepped over the gap in the bridge. The tide was out and the only monsters beneath the bridge were the sea-anemones in the rock pools. The place smelled of rotting weed and dying stories. He leant against the remains of the outer wall and scowled north, at the mountains of The Island of Eagles in their cloak of cloud, and the rocky little islands of the sound, black against the water. The sea surged mournfully at the base of the rock on which the Dun stood, and a single gull swept over him, screeching with laughter. The tears were back, hot and shameful, and he dropped his face into his hand and let them trickle through his fingers. Eventually, however, he lifted his head but kept his hand cupped. Piece by piece, he built his dream into that small pool of tears – Cuchullain and Ferdiad, their princely companions, their games and laughter, their feats at arms, the bridge and the dun, and Scathach the woman warrior. When it was all there, glimmering like a summer mirage, he tilted his hand to allow them to fall into the sea and dash themselves to nothing on the rocks below. But at the last moment he clenched his fingers on the dream, pressed his fist to his chest and got to his feet.

Don't trust the weapons-master! Arddu's voice was urgent now, but Ferdiad ignored him. He made his way back across the bridge and over the machair to the huts and training circle. Azarion was still sitting on one of the boulders but said nothing as Ferdiad strapped on the shield and picked up the hated sword.

'Again,' he said, bracing himself for battle.

It grew colder as the year slid steadily towards Midwinter. The south-westerly winds brought rain to the hills of Rheged across the firth, and into the uplands north of Galloway, swelling the river that ran close to the Mote, but the Mote itself, and the whole of the southern coast of Galloway, remained unseasonably dry.

'It won't be long before the walls are finished,' Kaerherdin remarked as he and Brangianne strolled around the building site that was to be the new healing centre. The walls of the main building were almost at full height, and the roof supports were cut and shaped and ready to be erected. If the weather held, the place might be useable before winter began in earnest, bringing its inevitable fluxes and fevers. But Caswallon, the stonemason, a surly pessimist from Gwynedd, was less than encouraging.

'Something will go wrong,' he said dolefully. 'Something always does. And no wonder ...'

He glowered at Kaerherdin, scowled at Brangianne, shook his head at the building site, and stumped off to remonstrate with one of the men shaping the roof supports. He considered he'd been brought to Galloway under false pretences, being more used to building Christian places such as monasteries and churches. He'd yet to be convinced that anyone in Galloway was as God-fearing as himself, and didn't believe Brangianne was a real Christian. She was a woman and a foreigner, and everyone knew foreigners, especially women, were ignorant savages. To prove it she'd taken up with a pagan.

'He means me,' Kaerherdin said. 'Would it help if I became a Christian?'

She looked at him in surprise for she'd thought him true to the forest gods he worshipped. 'Do you want to?'

'I do if you want me to,' he said earnestly.

Brangianne's heart sank. She'd hoped he'd be tired of her by now, but they were still lovers because she couldn't see how to stop without hurting him.

'Why stop?' Oonagh had asked when appealed to for advice. 'He's a good-looking man. He's young. He's not that Caledonian.'

But 'that Caledonian' was the reason, though it made no sense. Kaerherdin was a good man, a good friend, a considerate lover, had a dry sense of humour, and they shared a common interest. Oonagh was right; he was an attractive young man, especially when he smiled, which he did more often these days. She ought to be flattered, and if she was sensible, she'd be in love with him. But she wasn't, nor ever would be while Corwynal of Lothian was in the world, the man who despised her, refused to forgive her, had a wife and son, and who looked as though a sword was being slowly driven into his heart whenever Kaerherdin put a hand possessively on her shoulder – which he did whenever he thought Corwynal was watching.

I've never stopped loving you, he'd said. Nor she him, but she couldn't tell him so, not now. All she could do was what he wanted: guard Yseult and Trystan and thus preserve the truce between Galloway and Dalriada. She'd long since given up any hope of the affair burning out. This flame wouldn't be extinguished until it consumed what it fed on. Yseult had already grown thin and, if anything, more beautiful. Her skin was so translucent it was as if a light inside her was streaming out. But Brangianne knew it was the flame, burning her up. Trystan was in the same fire, smouldering with the effort of pretending not to love her, and it was paring him to the bone. He was like a dry reed, ready to catch light at the first spark.

For the moment, however, they were safe, Trystan having taken himself off to some fort along the coast, Yseult remaining in the Mote, pretending not to mope and overdoing it. She played the part of a young queen in love with her aging king so well that Marc, already besotted with her, believed it. But she hadn't convinced the rest of the court, and Brangianne began to hear mutterings.

'Be careful,' she'd warned her.

'Be careful yourself,' Yseult had retorted, glancing at Kaerherdin.

'So, what do you think?' Kaerherdin asked as they wandered around the foundations of what was to be a walled herb garden. 'About me becoming a Christian?'

'I think you should follow your heart,' she said thoughtlessly, forgetting Yseult's advice.

'I am.' He stopped and took her hands in his. 'If I was a Christian, we could be married by the rites of your church.'

'Married?' She laughed nervously and pulled her hands away.

'Why not?' His face darkened. 'My father was a King. My sister's a Queen. I'm as good as anyone—'

'Of course you are.'

'—as good as *him*,' he concluded fiercely. 'Better. I don't have a wife back in Lothian I've forgotten about. So, what's wrong with me? Is it because my mother was a slave? Is that it?'

'Of course not,' she said quickly, for he was touchy on this subject. 'But I'd no thought of marrying. I'm too used to being my own mistress.'

'What if there's a child?'

There won't be. She had to stop herself from saying it. She'd panicked after the night of Samhain, afraid she might have conceived. If she hadn't already known she didn't love Kaerherdin, her relief, when she discovered she wasn't carrying his child, would have convinced her. Ever since then she'd been dosing herself with a foul-tasting infusion of thistle and smartweed to ensure she didn't fall pregnant.

'Why can't we remain as we are?' She slipped a hand through his arm and led him on into the building site. 'You're my good friend, Kaerherdin. Let's not spoil that with all this talk of marriages and children. In fact— The time had come. She had to tell him this must stop.

'I love you,' he said stubbornly.

She knew what he wanted her to say, but she couldn't lie to him.

'I love you so much I'm the only man in Galloway who's not besotted with your niece,' he went on. 'Except for Trystan,' he continued with a short laugh. 'He never falls in love. I used to admire him for it, but now I pity him. If I'd know what a cold heart he had, I'd never have allowed him to marry my sister. It's too late now, but at least he can be trusted not to dishonour her with another woman.'

He doesn't even suspect! Kaerherdin's obsession with her was blinding him to the truth, and that meant she had to go on keeping him blind, for what might he do if he found out? Kaerherdin was a good friend, but she had the feeling he'd be a very bad enemy.

'It's cold,' she said, shivering in her fur-lined cloak with more than the wind. 'Let's go back to the Mote. Let's go on as we are.'

So she'd go on lying to a good man who loved her, for the sake of a man who was neither good nor kind but who loved her too.

6

HARPSTRING

'I want you to go yourself,' Arthyr told Blaize after they'd discussed the latest rather alarming reports from Blaize's best spy in Galloway. 'It may just be baseless speculation, but even that could be damaging.'

He looks tired, Blaize thought. Arthyr was trying to hold together an increasingly fragile alliance in the face of threats from all directions – Angle pirates on the east coast, Caledonian incursions all along the frontier – and he didn't have enough men to fight them. But Arthyr had dealt with such situations before. What he couldn't control, however, were the speculations in his own camp about Gwenhwyvar and Bedwyr. Those might be baseless too – Blaize didn't know and, uncharacteristically, didn't want to know – but Arthyr was right. Speculation itself was dangerous, so it wasn't surprising he was touchy about Galloway. If Feargus got wind of the rumours, the truce between Dalriada and Galloway would be at risk, and the last thing Arthyr needed was a problem on yet another front.

'Find out,' Arthyr said grimly. 'And stop it.'

Easy for him to talk, Blaize thought resentfully as he rode south through the short winter day into rain that was turning into sleet. Arthyr hadn't managed to stop whatever there was between Gwenhwyvar and Bedwyr. If Trystan was staying in Galloway for the sake of the young Queen, Blaize doubted if that could be stopped either. Trystan could be as stubborn as Corwynal, and only death had ended that particular affair.

With luck, however, it would turn out to be nothing more than talk. Just because all the elements of a story were there – a young Queen, a middle-aged King, a handsome young warrior with a golden voice – that didn't make it true.

But one look at Corwynal's face, when he arrived at the Mote and tracked him down to the hall, told him it was.

'You're drinking,' he observed sternly, noting the vagueness in his nephew's eyes, the half-empty flagon of wine in front of him, and the unsteadiness of his hand as he pushed an empty cup towards Blaize and slopped wine into it.

'Why shouldn't I? If Arthyr sent you, you'll know why.'

Blaize sighed. 'You'd better tell me everything.'

Everything, it turned out, was worse than even Blaize's most pessimistic imaginings. He'd been too caught up with Arthyr's affairs, and though he'd heard about the rather surprising agreement between Galloway and Dalriada, he hadn't questioned it further. Now, as revelation followed revelation, he wished he had.

'Marc? Trystan's father? And you believe it?'

'No . . . yes . . . no.' Corwynal dragged his fingers through his hair. 'I don't know what to believe.'

Neither did Blaize. The political implications alone . . .

They were on the rampart by then, the only place in The Mote where one could have a private conversation. The Mote had always been a place of whispers, the rock of the stronghold so crammed with buildings and servants there was little privacy to be had, and the settlement below was such a jumble of dwellings and inns and places of business that a rumour whispered at one end of the port was reported as fact a few moments later at the other. But on the wall that surrounded the stronghold they were alone, if rather cold, for fog had rolled in from the Firth.

'And Ferdiad's dead?' That too he struggled to believe, for Ciaran hadn't mentioned it in his latest letter detailing the deteriorating situation in Dalriada. In comparison, perhaps, the loss of a Fili was a minor matter, though a world without Ferdiad would be a little less bright, if a great deal safer, especially for Corwynal.

'You don't look well.' Blaize regarded his nephew critically. In the hall he'd looked pale and thin. Now, in the muted light of a cold November afternoon, Blaize was seeing his own reflection, and it wasn't a pretty sight. 'I suppose,' he said carefully, 'you've tried talking to Trystan?'

Corwynal threw him a savage look. 'Of course I have! But he doesn't listen to me.'

'He reminds me of someone I knew twenty years ago,' Blaize observed.

'I always blamed you for not stopping me then,' Corwynal said. 'But I don't blame you now.'

'Good of you,' Blaize said dryly, but Corwynal didn't notice the sarcasm and gripped Blaize by the arm.

'I won't let him ruin his life as I did. Something will happen – good or bad – and we'll need to escape. That's the only reason I'm staying.' He loosened his grip on Blaize's arm and turned to lean his elbows on the wall and look down at the settlement below. 'Gods, I hate this place and everyone in it! Marc, Yseult . . .' He paused, his attention caught by something below the walls. 'Them,' he added sourly, nodding at a dark-haired woman walking towards the Mote's lower gate, talking animatedly to a young man Blaize recognised. Corwynal clearly hadn't told him everything.

'What's she doing here?'

'Encouraging them,' Corwynal said bitterly. 'Marc's men killed her husband, and this is her revenge, even though he's bought her off with that healing centre.' He nodded to a building site beyond the Mote. 'She's going to run it with Kaerherdin. They're . . .' He stopped, his mouth twisting. '. . . together.'

'Kaerherdin? The horse-faced Selgovian?'

'Some people like horses, apparently.'

So that accounted for the drinking. Blaize felt the pain coming off the man like waves of heat from a fire.

'Why does it hurt so much?' Corwynal asked. 'Why can't I accept it? I envy you, never being in love, never having to suffer this.'

Blaize hesitated, wondering if this was the way into the conversation Corwynal always slipped out of. Arthyr's curt instruction wasn't the only reason Blaize was in Galloway.

'Don't bother envying me,' he said, and Corwynal stared at him in astonishment. 'What? Do you find it so difficult to believe I was young once?'

'Young and in love?' Corwynal asked doubtfully, diverted from his own problems. 'Who was she?'

'It's none of your business. The point is that I gave her up. I made a sacrifice for something I believed in – something you can believe in too.'

Corwynal was looking at him suspiciously now. 'You want me to go to Atholl, don't you?'

'Listen, Corwynal,' Blaize said urgently. 'Drest has spent years trying to subdue Ross, but now he's done it he'll be turning his attention south. We need someone in Atholl to tell us what's happening.'

'You have spies, don't you?'

'Traders. They can't get close to the druids. But you can.'

Corwynal laughed. 'Close enough for them to tear me to pieces!'

'They might not do that.'

'*Might* not?'

Blaize supposed Corwynal had a point. 'I'm just saying there's meaning to a life away from here and everything you hate.'

'I can't leave Galloway. Not while Trystan's still here.'

'Then let's see what we can do to persuade him to leave.' He patted Corwynal on the arm. 'He'll listen to me.'

Trystan was in the Queen's private chambers idly plucking a harp while she embroidered the border of a cloak by the light of a lamp. The place smelled of rose-petals and was too warm for comfort. A couple of Yseult's women sat at the other side of the room spinning wool, eyeing Blaize curiously as they did so.

'Arthyr sent me,' he told Trystan. 'He needs you in the North.'

'My uncle needs me in Galloway.'

Neither Yseult nor Trystan looked at one another and, when they spoke, were deliberately cool. If Blaize hadn't known better, he might have assumed Trystan to be bored by having to dance attendance on the spoiled young wife of his uncle, or that Yseult was being grudgingly gracious to her husband's sulky young nephew. He might have thought neither liked the other.

'If Arthyr needs you, perhaps you should go,' Yseult said, laying down her embroidery.

Blaize blinked in surprise. Corwynal had told him Trystan had gone to his fort on the Fleet but had stayed barely a day before returning to the Mote. Was it Yseult who'd sent him there? He looked at her more closely, trying to see beneath the surface of her beauty, but it wasn't easy. Even to Blaize, who mistrusted beauty, she was astonishingly lovely. That hair, that figure, those eyes . . . But, looking deeper, he saw that she was little more than a girl both fascinated and terrified by the fire consuming her and Trystan. How often had they tried to stop it and failed? How often had they agreed to part then flown together once more? He saw a desperate young woman pitted against someone who was half-lover, half-enemy, a man who defeated her in every battle they had, and who did so once more.

'No.' Trystan plucked a discordant run of notes from the strings. 'My uncle wants me to stay.'

'And this uncle wants you to go,' Blaize said with what he hoped was a winning smile but apparently wasn't.

'You're not my uncle,' Trystan muttered.

Gods, did the boy actually believe that nonsense of Marc's?

'Listen, Trys, you're needed in the North. Arthyr needs you. Gaheris has your command now.'

'Good for him.'

'Gaheris is a follower, not a leader. Your men need you. The Caledonians are raiding all along the border. Angles are attacking Gododdin. It will be Lothian next. Don't you care? Come on Trys! There's fighting to be done. It's what you were born for. Who is there to fight in Galloway?'

He thought he had him then, but after a moment Trystan shook his head angrily. 'I'm not Arthyr's dog to come and go when he demands.'

'He doesn't demand. He begs.'

Blaize could see him struggle, but in the end Trystan shook his head once more.

'No. The Dal-n'Araide have been raiding our coasts. I need to be in Galloway.'

'Then perhaps you should go back to your fort, Trystan,' Yseult murmured.

'You want me to leave?'

The women looked up at his tone, but Yseult gave them a cat-like little smile. 'We could do with a rest from your interminable twanging.'

The harp clattered to the floor and Trystan leapt to his feet, gave Yseult and her women a mocking bow, and stalked from the room.

'Oh dear,' she said peaceably, taking up her embroidery once more. 'I do hope I haven't offended him. I'd ask you to go after him, but I suspect he'd prefer to sulk.'

It had gone further than Blaize had imagined. They were no longer lovers bemused by the violence of their passions, no longer at the mercy of the urges of two beautiful young bodies. They were like an old married couple, squabbling over trifles, hurtful and inconsiderate with one another, yet each of them trusting the other so much no argument could ever come between them.

Stop it, Arthyr had said. As well try to stop the wind in its tracks, a river in spate or the passing of time. But still he had to try, so he went to see the other party in this appalling situation.

'I suppose Arthyr sent you,' Marc muttered when Blaize was finally granted an audience.

The King stank of stale wine. Sober, Marc, had proved himself to be a reasonable man, willing to compromise, to plan for the future. Drunk, however, he was as stubborn and unpredictable as he'd been for most of the past twenty years. Corwynal had warned him that Marc was closing his eyes to the situation but that others had begun to talk. Andrydd for example, Andrydd who had ambition and no great love for Trystan.

'Arthyr wants Trys back. We need him and Corwynal in the North.'

'Trys is my heir.'

'But you have a wife now. Surely—'

'That's none of your business! Or Arthyr's. Trys stays here. And I need Corwynal too. I want him as my Steward. Dynas won't last long.'

'Has he agreed?'

'No, but he will. He'll come around.'

Blaize sighed at this fresh evidence of Marc's refusal to face facts. Corwynal would never forgive him.

'I hear the Dal n'Araide are raiding your coasts.'

'What's that to you? Or Arthyr?'

'I'm just interested, Sire.'

Marc humphed at that, poured himself another cup of wine, and leant towards Blaize. 'Bloody Andrydd went after them against my express orders. I had a mind to ask Feargus to deal with them to see how far this truce goes. Now Andrydd's ruined that. Claimed he had my authority. Can you believe that? I've summoned him to the Mote. We'll thrash it out at a Council Meeting . . .'

Which was news that caused Corwynal to turn distinctly grey.

'It's all your fault,' Blaize told him crossly, later in the hall, as he reached for the wine jug and poured himself a large cup. 'You could control Marc if you could just divest yourself of those stupid principles of yours. Well, it's too late now. Andrydd will be on his way.'

Corwynal dropped his face into his hands, groaning. 'It's worse than that. Andrydd almost caught Trys and Yseult together, but Trys tricked him by pretending he was Marc and telling him to go after the Dal n'Araide to get him away from the Mote. What in the Five Hells am I going to do now?'

'Well, for a start, make sure you're at the Council meeting. Then get Trys out of the Mote, preferably out of Galloway. Take him to Rheged.'

'Then what?'

'I don't know – go back to Lothian? You've another son, you know.'

Corwynal stared at him. 'Ealhith had another son?'

'You married her,' Blaize reminded him. 'Word is, he looks like you, though I doubt it. Infants, in my experience, all look the same.'

Corwynal ran a hand through his hair. 'I can't go back to Lothian, not yet. I need to make sure Trys is safe.'

'Then take him to Rheged or, better, Gwynedd. Will you do that?'

Corwynal nodded glumly and stared down at his wine, swirling the dregs in the cup.

'Do you remember that prophecy?' He looked up. 'The one you made when Trys was born? You said he'd be a great warrior, a great singer and a great lover?'

'That old nonsense?'

'Does it still apply if he's not my son?'

Blaize sighed. 'I told you; prophecies never mean what they say. And he *is* your son. I'm sure of it.'

He wasn't sure, but it was what Corwynal wanted to hear, and his expression lightened for a moment, but only for a moment. 'How will this end, Blaize?'

He wanted prophecy, of course, but it didn't take a seer to see into this particular future.

'Badly, my boy. Badly.'

'You told me yourself to go after the Dal n'Araide.'

'No I didn't. Why should I?'

The argument between Marc and Andrydd had gone on for some time without coming to a conclusion. Both were right, for once, and both were aggrieved at the other's intransigence. Andrydd's supporters were at the Council meeting too, but some of Andrydd's enemies had got wind of the possible humiliation of the over-ambitious Lord of the Fleet and had come to the Mote to add their voices to the debate. It wasn't the full Council, however. That wouldn't meet until Midwinter, if the roads were clear. But enough of them were crammed into the stuffy Council chamber to make this meeting rather too public. Corwynal had come with Dynas, causing resentful glances, but Marc had been dropping hints about Corwynal replacing Dynas, so no-one objected out loud. Nevertheless, he'd been careful not to say anything until now.

'You did, actually, Sire,' he said. 'I was there. I heard you order Lord Andrydd to go after the Dal n'Araide.'

Andrydd looked surprised, then suspicious, at Corwynal's support.

'I would have remembered that,' Marc complained.

'I've only just remembered myself.' He smiled ruefully. 'Men of our age – we forget things . . .'

And I'll forget what you said that night. I might even forgive . . . He wouldn't, of course, but he was willing to pretend for Trystan's sake.

Marc nodded slowly, understanding Corwynal's unspoken capitulation.

'Very well. If you say I said it, I must have done, though God knows why. However, now I want the Dal n'Araide left alone. Let Dalriada deal with them. They're Dalriada's enemies.'

'And ours if they raid our coasts,' Andrydd pointed out. 'I see no reason why Dalriada should tell Galloway who we should raid and who we shouldn't. I suppose the Dal Fiatach are to be left alone too?'

'They're allies of Dalriada. It was part of the deal,' Marc said grumpily.

'A deal you made against the advice of your Council.'

'I'm the bloody King! I do what I bloody like! And don't try to tell me this deal you object to so much hasn't been good for business.'

For the traders, certainly. And for the settlements along the coast. But for the warband, for the war-fleet, controlled in large part by Andrydd and his supporters, it hadn't been, and none of the Council spoke up in support of their King.

'You were always on at me to marry,' he reminded them testily.

'But not a foreigner who, charming though she is, shows no sign of giving you an heir.'

'Give the girl a chance! We've only been wed for four moons. Anyway, Trystan's my heir. Always has been and still is.'

'I see.' Andrydd's voice was thick with implication.

'Is that wise Sire?' one of Andrydd's supporters asked. 'In the circumstances?'

'What bloody circumstances?'

'There's been talk, Sire,' another said. 'Unfounded, I'm sure. But it's said Prince Trystan spends overmuch time with your Lady wife.'

'At my request,' Marc growled. 'A young woman needs to be entertained, and Trystan speaks her language.'

'No-one denies that Trystan is entertaining,' Andrydd said smoothly. 'Or that your Lady wife is beautiful. She turns men's heads.' He gave a small self-deprecating laugh. 'I confess myself to be as smitten as Trystan. Small wonder he stays in Galloway.'

'He stays for me,' Marc insisted. 'He's my . . . my heir. And I refuse to listen to this . . . gossip when he's not here to defend himself.'

'But his mouthpiece is here,' Andrydd said turning to Corwynal. 'So, where's Prince Trystan?'

'He went to his fort near the River Fleet.' Corwynal thanked the gods Trystan had been persuaded to leave the Mote. 'He was concerned about the Dal-n'Araide raids.'

'Which took place nowhere near the Fleet,' Andrydd objected. 'But perhaps he chooses not to be too far from the Mote?'

'Enough!' Marc jumped to his feet and slammed both fists down on the table. 'I've had enough of these insinuations!'

'My dear Lord, I'm not insinuating anything! How could I when these rumours are baseless? There's no proof.' Andrydd glanced at Corwynal. *Not yet.* 'I am merely telling you what's being said since no-one else has thought to do so. I didn't approve of your . . . arrangement with Dalriada, but since it exists let's not risk it by allowing this . . . speculation to reach the ears of King Feargus.'

'Your concern is noted,' Marc said stiffly, sitting down once more. 'But I don't see what you expect me to do about it. Ship Yseult back to her father and ask him to send me an uglier woman?'

'Of course not. Dalriada's gain would be Galloway's loss. You can hardly put the Lady Yseult aside without proof of her infidelity.'

Put her aside? Infidelity? Had the talk gone this far?

'There's no question of Queen Yseult being put aside,' Corwynal cut in, stressing the title Andrydd had failed to give her. 'That would be disastrous politically.'

'For whom?' Andrydd asked. 'Maybe I too grow old, and my memory weakens also, but I can remember a time when Dalriada was Galloway's enemy, and it was far from disastrous for Galloway.'

There were some mutters of agreement at that, and not only from Andrydd's supporters.

'Any hint of dishonour to his daughter and Feargus would react . . . disproportionately,' Corwynal pointed out. 'It wouldn't be a matter of raiding. It would be war.'

'So?' Andrydd shrugged. 'We have a War-leader these days, don't we? And I believe Arthyr's mouthpiece – your Caledonian kinsman – is also in the Mote. Does Arthyr direct Galloway's policy now? Must we do nothing to upset Dalriada, no matter what the provocation?'

'There *is* no provocation!' Corwynal objected. He seemed to have lost control, or perhaps Andrydd was too clever for him. Yet there was an opportunity here if he could grasp it. 'Any provocation will be in the form of – how did you put it my Lord Andrydd? – baseless speculation. Then let's avoid it.' He turned to Marc. 'Send Trystan to Arthyr, who has need of him.'

Andrydd smiled in satisfaction and Corwynal knew he'd made a mistake. *He knows. He suspected before, but now he knows. Would I have advised sending Trystan away if the rumours were baseless?*

'An excellent idea,' Andrydd said.

Corwynal held his breath. It could solve the whole thing if Marc was to order Trystan north, so why was Andrydd urging the same action? Because he knew Marc.

'No!' Marc turned on the Lord of the Fleet. 'I know what your game is! You always objected to Trystan being my heir, and now you're trying to come between us. I'm sending him nowhere. In fact, I'm recalling him from his fort. So, sod off back to Loch Ryan. Sod off the lot of you!'

Corwynal's heart sank even before he saw Andrydd's glint of triumph, but the Lord of Loch Ryan just bowed and left the room with the others.

'Not you,' Marc said as Corwynal got up to follow Dynas. His stomach clenched, convinced Marc was going to demand the truth. What should he do? Lie or tell the truth? What would Marc do? He no longer knew.

'I want Trys back here,' Marc snapped.

'But, Sire—'

'I won't be dictated to by rumour mongers. I know what Andrydd's game is. He wants me to put Yseult aside and marry someone of his own choosing. But I won't without proof, and there isn't proof, because it isn't true. None of it's true.'

'Sire, that night . . . Corwynal began, feeling his way, but even this was too far, and Marc's face, already flushed with wine, darkened still further.

'We will not speak of that night! It never happened; do you hear me? It's to be forgotten.'

He's mad, Corwynal thought. The evil spirit that had always gnawed at Marc's soul had chewed its way through his hold on reality. Now he occupied a world he'd created for himself, a world in which Yseult was his loving wife, Trystan his loyal son, Corwynal his oldest friend, a world he'd fight everything and everyone to protect even as it crashed around him. For crash it would. Sooner or later, Trystan and Yseult would be caught, and Marc would be forced to face the truth. Andrydd and his supporters would be watching them, waiting for them to make a mistake. *Good or bad, something will happen,* he'd told Blaize. Now he knew it could only be bad, and that he'd have a fight on his hands to get Trystan out of this with a whole skin if not a whole heart. But he'd been fighting for Trystan all his life and wasn't about to stop now.

Snow was falling, great fat flakes of snow falling out of a grey sky like the down of an eider duck. Everything Ferdiad could see was black and white and grey; the mountains on the far side of the sound had turned from black to ash before vanishing into the blur of falling snow. The dark islands lying offshore had blended with the sea and disappeared, and the water, granite under steel clouds, lapped gently at a stony shore softened to white.

The training circle was black, stamped into mud, but Ferdiad didn't care about the snow or the mud. For the first time since he'd come to Dun Sgiath he thought he might be winning. Yet he didn't want to win, didn't want the fight to end, for he'd found something he hadn't expected to find ever again, something he hadn't been warned about or promised.

Music.

His sword swung low and met Azarion's in a ring of steel on steel, the reverberations continuing as a low hum even after they disengaged. Each blow had its own tone and pitch, and Ferdiad felt as if he was moving in a shifting chord of music that slid up and down the scale like the sweet notes of a reed pipe. There was rhythm too in the stamp of feet on the ground and the beat of shield on shield and, as he fought, he found himself moving in time to the fight's own cadences. He was aware of nothing but the music as each note followed the next. He swung his sword and blocked with his shield, each rasp of sword on sword, each beat and counter-beat, building into a song, the first he'd made in over half a year.

But all songs come to an end and this one ended in the usual slither of steel on leather and a cry of pain. But for once it wasn't his own, and it was echoed by a bark of laughter from a small snow-covered boulder that stood outside the training circle. Scathach, unusually, had come to watch their latest fight.

The music faded back through steel and wood into bone and blood and the world returned – the ache in his shoulders, the dryness of his throat as he dragged air into his lungs, the heaviness of the double-weighted sword as it tugged at his right arm, the straps of the shield chafing the skin of his left. The falling snow was no longer as soft and warm as down but cold and wet.

'I won?' he asked in astonishment, staring at Azarion who was clutching his arm.

Scathach laughed once more then stumped back to the smithy, and Azarion crouched down to gather a wad of snow and press it to the wound in his forearm, a long shallow cut. 'If you don't know you've won what use is winning?' Azarion growled.

'I've not had much experience of winning,' Ferdiad let his sword drop to the ground.

'No experience, more like. But don't imagine you're a warrior now because you've beaten a man twice your age.'

But Ferdiad wasn't going to allow Azarion to spoil his hard-won triumph. 'I heard music,' he said, wondering if he'd imagined it.

'Music?' Azarion bared his teeth in what Ferdiad had come to recognise as a smile, and the beast-markings on his face flexed unnervingly. 'Good.'

'You didn't tell me.'

'You wouldn't have believed me if I had, because you still don't trust me.' Azarion shrugged, as if he didn't care. 'But you've begun to trust yourself. That's what matters.'

Don't trust the weapons-master! Arddu still hissed his warning through his bones, but Ferdiad had begun to listen to Azarion and do what he suggested without question. Was that trust? Whatever it was, he was stronger and faster now, more patient, less impetuous. He'd learned to step outside himself, to focus on his opponent, to trust his body, if not yet his mind.

His dreams were still bad, for something had broken at Samhain. By allowing the ghosts past his defences, he'd weakened the barriers that had kept everything else at bay, and now the memories clamoured to be let out, robbing him of sleep. He'd started to long for the beginning of each short winter day and the training to begin so he could forget everything in the fight and the pain, the defeats and humiliations. As long as he fought, he could stop thinking, stop remembering . . .

'—I said I've something for you.' Azarion was scowling at him. 'When I said stop thinking, I didn't mean stop listening. Come.'

He stalked off towards the smithy where Scathach slept and worked, somewhere Ferdiad had not been permitted to enter. The infuriating tapping still went on, but more often now, if he woke in the night, he'd hear the deep breathing of the bellows and the clang of metal on metal, oddly soothing sounds that would lull him into a dreamless sleep, confident Scathach's hammers were beating away the dark.

Now he saw what the swordsmith had been making, and what else could it be but a sword? Yet no ordinary sword lay on the anvil. It was as beautiful as a well-made harp was beautiful, as a horse could be, or a man. It was pattern welded, rods of metal beaten together over and over until they blended together and left a ripple on the surface of the blade like the patterns ice makes on water. The hilt was plain, the grip of twisted wire, the crosspieces gently flared to catch an opponent's weapon, the weighted pommel set with a faceted green tourmaline that drank the light of the fire and threw it back in splinters of green flame. His eyes softened as he gazed at it, then was aware of another's gaze – Scathach, regarding him sullenly from the shadows at the back of the smithy.

'You made it?' he asked.

'You're surprised?'

'Not surprised. Awed.'

'Then try it.'

The pommel slid into his palm and his fingers closed on the grip. The sword lifted itself into the air as if it was made of air itself.

'It will feel light after the training sword,' Azarion warned him.

Ferdiad swung it once, twice, and it cut through air, through light, through fire, its edge vanishingly sharp.

'A sword fit for a hero.' He lowered it reluctantly and offered it back to Scathach, but the swordsmith shook her head.

'It's yours,' she said before sliding into the shadows and vanishing.

Ferdiad, surprised, turned to Azarion. 'I'm no hero!'

The Dragon was leaning against the door, his arms folded across his chest, regarding Ferdiad with narrowed speculative eyes, as if he'd passed – or failed – some test.

'You're whatever you want to be. Hero or not, it's still yours. It was part of the deal I made with Ciaran – that Scathach should make you a sword if you were up to wielding one. Now you have to give it a name. All good swords deserve a name.'

'Harpstring,' Ferdiad said without hesitation.

'Heartstring?' Azarion asked, mishearing him. 'A good name.'

Harpstring, heartstring. They meant the same thing to the man who'd lost music but found it once more.

'Harpstring,' he said, his voice rough with emotion as he laid it back down on the anvil. 'I haven't earned this. You're right. Beating a man twice my age in a single training bout doesn't make me a warrior. Scathach agrees with me.' He peered into the shadows but she'd gone. 'She doesn't want me to have it.'

'All smiths put part of their soul into weapons like this. It's part of our magic. Giving it up is like giving up a child, sending it out into the world in the hands of a stranger. Only when you have a child of your own will you understand that.'

'That's unlikely.'

'As unlikely as you becoming the warrior you want to be? Perhaps.' Azarion shrugged. 'But not impossible, though you still have a lot to learn, and not only about fighting. About yourself.'

'What does that mean?'

'What did I tell you when you began?'

'That I have to become my enemy.'

'And how can you do that if you don't know who you are?'

It was still snowing outside, but Ferdiad longed to be in the clean killing wind, rather than the smoke-filled smithy with a man who knew too much. But was leaning against the door, blocking his way.

'I know who I am,' he insisted, though he didn't, not anymore.

'You know who you are, not who you were.'

'Only the present matters, and the future.'

'A future you have to shape out of your past. You've been given a gift today.' He glanced at the sword on the anvil. 'Two gifts. You've earned Scathach's respect.'

Ferdiad snorted. 'Respect? She despises me. She hasn't talked to me until today.'

'Quite. She speaks to few people. I'm one of them. And do you know why? Because I speak her language. It's kin to the tongue of the Forest People, but she spoke to you in her language. And, without thinking, you answered. How is it, Ferdiad of Dalriada, that you speak the tongue of the outer islands, of the Attecotts?'

'I don't— I can't—' The dark things were stirring once more, things from his dreams, monsters he kept imprisoned in a cage in his memory. 'I heard you talking, that's all. I'm good with languages. I must have picked up a few words.'

Azarion peered at him in the dim light but, to Ferdiad's relief, let the subject drop.

'You won today. You have a sword. Neither make you a warrior, but you're in a better position to decide how far you want to go.'

'All the way.'

Azarion regarded him in thoughtful silence, then sighed. 'Very well. I'll carry on training you. If you pass my tests, you'll go to train with real fighters. But I warn you; they won't be kind.'

'Dragon-riders?' Ferdiad asked with a thrill of both excitement and apprehension that was sufficient to crush the dark things back into their prison.

'Dragon-riders,' Azarion confirmed. 'Do you still want to go on this journey, no matter where it takes you?'

Ferdiad glanced at the sword lying on the anvil. Its pale green jewel picked up the light of the banked-down fire and threw it back like a morning sun reflecting from sea-ice. *Harpstring*, he murmured to himself. The name was like that of a lover on his tongue, like music in his missing fingers.

'No matter where it takes me.'

7

SILVERHAND

I should have made her come to the Nemeton, Domech thought irritably as the boat punched its way into the icy wind, driving west with each beat of the oars, but drifting back a little on the return stroke, making progress slow. Why did the wind always blow from the west whenever he had to go to the Crannog? Did Seirian really have the power to sway wind and waters? He liked to think power lay in ritual, in the certainties of earth and sky, not the imagination of women or the fickleness of the water that lay so cold, so unsettlingly deep, beneath him. But sometimes – today for example – it was difficult to dismiss the notion, and that wasn't a good frame of mind in which to tell Seirian what he'd come to say.

He wished he'd never threatened to put her aside, but there was something about Seirian that made him do the opposite of what he wanted. Maybe it was nothing more than the eternal battle between priest and priestess, though surely their relations didn't have to be this difficult? If only she'd listened to him, they could have worked together. But working together was out of the question now.

She'd forced him to go to the High Druid, an experience that had been as uncomfortable as he'd feared. The weather had been bad, gales and blizzards on the high ground, flooding along the valleys, and, predictably, the High Druid hadn't been pleased she'd rejected

Tarain. Domech had been certain he'd recommend Seirian be replaced by someone more biddable, which wasn't what Domech wanted. That had just been a threat, words that had got out of hand. But the High Druid didn't suggest it. Instead, he proposed something quite different.

'Think you can handle it, Domech?' he'd asked mildly.

No, he'd wanted to say, but a suggestion from the High Druid, no matter how difficult, wasn't a suggestion at all; it was a command. An Archdruid could also be put aside.

'It will... take time,' he said, his voice barely under control. 'Given the season.'

Given the sheer impossibility of the task. Given that he'd attempted it before and failed – a failure the High Druid hadn't mentioned but which hung between them like a rotting corpse swinging in the wind.

The High Druid smiled serenely. 'Then let's say... by the campaigning season?'

'There's to be a campaign? Against whom?'

'The Britons, of course.'

Of course.

He'd seen it then, the game on the board, the pieces massed, the warriors and druids, the kings and consorts, the tribes and their lands, facing the usurpers from the south, with their forts and watchtowers, their cavalry, their ships. He saw Atholl at the heart of the game where he'd always wanted Atholl to be – but not like this. He wasn't looking forward to telling Seirian.

'So, my Lord Archdruid, have you come to tell me I'm to be put aside?'

She was alone but for the child sitting at her feet. He would have preferred the girl not to be there at all. Those eyes saw a great deal too much.

Seirian's voice was light and her lips curved in a smile, but her hands gripped the arms of her chair. The child looked up at him curiously, without concern. In another seven-year-old he would have dismissed that lack of concern as a lack of understanding, but not this one. This one *knew*.

'I should warn you that Ciniod won't permit it,' Seirian went on.

'*Ciniod* won't permit it? That bag of wind?'

'That bag of wind has an efficient warband and an ambitious son.'

So she'd made a deal. He wasn't surprised. In her place he'd have done the same thing. She must have promised herself to Broichan in return for Ciniod's support, or had hinted at a promise. Seirian was too clever to commit herself, Ciniod too stupid to realise it. But it no longer mattered.

'You're not to be put aside,' he informed her.

'I told you so,' the child said with quiet satisfaction.

'Hush, Kirah.'

'Send her away,' Domech said. 'These are no matters for a child.'

'She'll be Atholl's Royal Lady one day. She must learn.'

'About The Exile?'

Seirian's eyes widened. 'The Exile?' she asked faintly. The child looked up and opened her mouth to ask a question, but her mother forestalled her. 'Go, Kirah. Find Ninian and stay with him.'

'But I want to hear about The Exile!'

'Go! And if I find you listening at doors, I'll strip you naked and thrash you in front of the entire settlement!'

The girl turned white, gave her mother a wounded look, Domech one of pure loathing, then ran out onto the Crannog's walkway. Seirian waited until she heard her footsteps crunch into the gravel on the shore before turning on Domech.

'How dare you! He's not to be spoken of, especially in front of my daughter!'

'He must be spoken of, and she'll have to learn of him eventually. Anyway, she knows, doesn't she?'

'Only the name. I've told her nothing.'

She gestured to the chair on the other side of the fire. It was padded with the combed skin of a sheep, and he sank gratefully into

its soft depths. His bones still ached from all that travelling. She laid
a log on the fire – applewood, judging by the sweet resinous scent –
and regarded him wearily. 'Kirah saw something in the waters.'

'The Exile? Where?'

'Where? I've no idea. She saw the past. That's where he is – in the
past.' She leant forward. 'Isn't he?'

'No.'

The colour drained from her face.

'The High Druid has revoked his banishment.'

'He can't do that. It's Atholl's business, not his!'

'I think you'll find this High Druid can do whatever he likes,' he
said dryly.

'But—'

'You brought this on yourself – on us – Seirian. You refused to
take a consort, despite knowing that Atholl needs a strong leader.'

'If I agreed to take Tarain now—'

Domech shook his head. 'It's too late, and your refusal was
merely a pretext for something I suspect has been long in the
planning. Others reasons would have been found. I've been asked –
no, told - to get him back.'

She gave a short incredulous laugh. 'He won't come. Why should
he? It would mean his death.'

'Not necessarily. The High Druid doesn't want him back to have
him killed, though he must be made an example of.'

'I see,' she said coldly. 'You'll offer him an amnesty. You'll declare
him guilty, but his punishment will be a token one. But you've
forgotten something, you and the High Druid. You forget it was me
he wronged and that means the punishment will be mine to decide.
And it won't be a token one. I'll demand his death.'

Ice ran through his veins at that, for he had indeed forgotten it,
but she laughed shortly.

'It won't come to that, however, because he won't come to Atholl.
You tried to persuade him before and failed. Nothing is different
now, and I doubt you even know where he is.'

'Not yet,' he admitted, wondering how he was going to find out. The snows had come early and the high passes were blocked. The traders he depended on for information wouldn't journey to Atholl before the spring. But he'd sent a message to his best spy. He'd know where The Exile was, and then . . . He'd worry about what to do next when he'd learned what there was to learn. 'All men have their weaknesses,' he said with more confidence than he felt. 'It's simply a matter of finding out what his are.'

She narrowed her eyes at that but said nothing and let her gaze drift to one of the hangings – the wolf of Atholl, as fierce as Atholl itself had been fierce, as strong as Atholl had been strong. It was a sight to make any man of Atholl proud, but Domech felt nothing but disquiet, for he had the distinct feeling he was about to grasp the wolf by the tail.

Ferdiad was no stranger to drink. After The Morholt had died he'd been drunk for a month, and when he'd lost his hand, he would have sought a similar oblivion if Ciaran had allowed him. But he preferred to get drunk on his own. Drink loosened tongues, and a man might reveal matters he'd come to regret, or expose a weakness he'd prefer to keep hidden. He'd used it, of course, to ferret out the secrets of others, but was careful himself. Ferdiad the Snake couldn't afford to allow his tongue to be blunted, his wit to lose its edge, or his power to amuse diminish, and whenever he felt the effects of whatever he was drinking, he'd take himself off to either sober up or finish the job in private. But Azarion's invitation to share a jug of Caledonian firewater wasn't one he intended refusing, because, after the past few weeks, he badly needed a drink.

To his relief, Azarion was alone, sitting beside the fire in the main dwelling place, tending a couple of haunches of hare that were roasting over the hot stones of the fire. Scathach wasn't there, presumably being in the smithy where she spent most of her time.

Ferdiad had avoided her ever since she'd given him the sword, and she hadn't sought him out. He was deeply uncomfortable with her now, knowing she was an Attecott, though it should have occurred to him before. The tribe dwelled on the cloud-wreathed island chain that lay on the western horizon, and they were an ancient people, a stockier and darker version of the willowy Forest People of the Ghost Woods, to whom they were related. Half-animal and wholly despised, the Attecotts were raided with impunity and enslaved by the mainland tribes of the western seaboard. To be Attecott was to be a slave, lower than the lowest bondsman, of less worth than a beast. Yet Scathach had made something of such beauty and skill, the sword he still didn't believe was for him.

'Have I been working you too hard?' Azarion asked when Ferdiad lowered himself with a groan onto the stool on the other side of the fire. Every part of him hurt, for ever since he'd won that bout, Azarion had subjected him to a punishing schedule. Mornings were given over to training, even harder than before, and now he could beat Azarion more often than he lost. Afternoons were for more mundane pursuits, and for the past few weeks he'd been cutting fodder for Scathach's scrawny beasts and dragging driftwood up from the shore to be split into firewood. None of this, for a man with only one hand, had been easy, and the callouses he'd developed from wielding the double-weighted sword, were now overlaid with blisters. Azarion himself had hunted, surprisingly effectively, bringing back not only the hares roasting by the fire, but deer and boar which he'd butchered and hung to dry in the smoky warmth of the smithy. The log-store was full, the barn packed with tree-fodder for the beasts, and, with the approach of Midwinter, the weather had changed, the blizzards and storms of early December having given way to achingly blue skies with snow-dusted mountains on every horizon.

Ferdiad reached for one of the haunches of hare. It wasn't quite cooked, but he was famished, and they ate in silence until the meat was gone, the bones picked clean, the bloody juices soaked up with pieces of bannock. Then Azarion poured some spirit into a couple of beakers and passed one to Ferdiad. He inhaled the fumes, scented with peat and honey and heather, and groaned with pleasure.

'I'm leaving tomorrow,' Azarion announced.

Ferdiad had been raising the beaker to his lips, but now he laid it down. *I* he'd said, not *We.*

'So this is our last night together,' Azarion continued.

I'll carry on training you. Then, if you pass my tests, you'll go to train with real fighters. That had been the promise.

'So, I failed . . . ?' To hide the disappointment in his voice, Ferdiad took a deep swallow of the firewater. It was harsh and burned his throat, but when it reached his stomach it sent out welcome tendrils of warmth that spread through his veins.

'I warned you it was a possibility. But no, you haven't failed – yet. There's still a test to undergo.'

A fight, Ferdiad assumed, like the fight he'd witnessed between a much younger Dragon and the boy from Lothian, and perhaps Azarion was remembering the same fight.

'They named Corwynal 'Wolf' for his tribe – for his two tribes - but I always called him Little Wolf. I trained him in secret, you know, for they'd decided he was to be a druid, though he was determined to become a warrior. I suppose it was the same for you; you wanted to be a warrior but they turned you into a Fili, given that's what you are.'

'Were,' Ferdiad corrected him, wincing at a spasm of remembered pain from his missing hand. 'Most of the boys didn't get a choice. I only completed the first few years of warrior training. That will be why you don't remember me.'

Don't trust the weapons-master. But the God's voice was muted by the fumes of the spirit.

'It's odd then that you chose to name yourself after a warrior.'

'I didn't choose it. It's my name,' he insisted.

Azarion ignored him. 'And odd that you chose that particular name,' he went on. 'Any normal boy would have chosen the hero's name, not that of the hero's friend.'

I wasn't a normal boy. But he wasn't going to tell Azarion that, so tried to change the subject.

'Scathach's a name from the same story. Was that chosen or given?'

'Chosen, when she settled here. Dun Sgiath means Scathach's dun, so it's a good name, but she's had many names. Shall I tell you her story?'

'No, I don't want to know—'

Azarion ignored him once more.

'She was captured by Smertan slavers when she was a child and spent years in the slave camps before being sold to a smith, in exchange for a pig. He considered he'd been cheated and took it out on her. Over the years he broke every bone in her body and she was forced to do such heavy work her back began to curve. But when she was older, she was strong enough to fight back. She killed the smith with his own hammer and fed his body to the pigs, then cut off her slave ring and escaped with his best tools to become a travelling smith. She pretended to be a man for many years. It was a lie she came to live with, a lie that saved her life on more than one occasion. What lie do you live with, Ferdiad? And why are you weeping? It's not for Scathach.' Azarion leant over the fire. 'It's for yourself.'

'No! I was . . . I'm not . . .'

The lie I live with every day. Ferdiad cuffed the tears away and tried to get up, to walk away, but he couldn't move. He stared down into his cup and the fumes writhed through his blood, his nerves, his memory, dissolving the iron bars of the prison that kept the black things away.

'Who are you, Ferdiad the Fili? Shall I tell you?'

Don't trust the weapons-master!

'No, I—'

'You're like Scathach. You're an Attecott.'

Ferdiad laughed, or tried to.

'An Attecott? But look at me!'

'I look at you and see the blood of the Northmen.'

'They're just a myth.'

'They're no myth. In a bad year they come to the islands to raid and rape, burn settlements and destroy lives, before sailing back north. But they don't come from the North. They're from a land to the east, beyond the sunrise. They look like you, Ferdiad. Occasionally a woman survives being raped by a Northman and bears a child, but none are to be found on the islands for they're prized by the slavers. Some even ended up in the training camp beneath the mountains . . .'

Azarion's voice had changed, and Ferdiad became aware that he'd shifted into Scathach's language, the language Ferdiad had never learned. The language he remembered.

'You weren't a boy on The Island, Ferdiad. You were a slave, an Attecott slave.'

If he'd had two hands, both of them would have been over his ears by then, but he didn't, so Azarion's voice carried on beating through flesh and bone until he was sick and dizzy.

'Shall I tell you what I've guessed? That your mother sold you to slavers when you were old enough, and they sold you on to the Druids. You were probably a beautiful child, but being beautiful couldn't wipe out the taint of being an Attecott, so I guess you were beaten, but not badly enough to damage your looks. I guess you were raped when you were old enough, if not before. I guess you would have tried to make yourself invisible, to be less than a beast. I guess you would have been called 'slave' so often you forgot your own name, if you ever had one. And when you heard that story, you chose for yourself the name of Cuchullain's friend, because you needed a friend. You needed a Cuchullain. Did he come, Ferdiad? Was he Corwynal of Lothian, the man you want to destroy? What did he do, or not do?'

The Dragon's voice followed him as Ferdiad stumbled out into the moonless night, trying to get away, but tripping over the snow-covered boulders that ringed the training field, and losing himself in the drifts that settled against the outbuildings. Eventually, he groped his way to the barn and threw himself into the furthest corner, and tried to bury himself in the earth, to be surrounded, to be safe. But there was no safety here, nothing to stand between him and the truth inside him. That he was an Attecott. The last dream, the one he'd constructed with such care, was broken – the dream in which he'd been someone, that he'd been stolen from loving parents, that he'd once had a future. But he'd never had a future. He knew that now. He'd been in the wrong place, given life by the wrong man, birthed by a woman who'd sold him into servitude, a slave with nothing to call his own except a dream. Until even that had been taken from him, leaving him with nothing but a stolen name. *Ferdiad the Hero. Ferdiad the Warrior.* What a joke! He was Ferdiad the Serpent, Ferdiad the Fool. Ferdiad the Slave.

They were out of their prison now, the black things, circling around him, eyes gleaming, their vicious beaks grazing his skin as they swept around him, wings beating, beating. Ravens and crows, all the black things . . .

We won't hurt you, Ferdiad. But they always had. The druid hadn't even pretended to be kind. *Come here, slave. On your knees. I said on your knees!*

'No!' He pulled his arms about his head but it made no difference. The voices were inside his head. 'Arddu . . . ?' But Arddu went on muttering the same old thing. *Don't trust the weapons-master. Don't trust the swordsmith.*

'I don't need this,' he muttered, scrambling to his feet. 'Not now. Not ever. It's too *late!*'

It's never too late, my dear boy. Ciaran's voice joined the others. 'Get away from me! All of you. *Get away!*'

With a curse, he went to the door, threw it back and strode over to the dwelling place, his breath puffing white in the firelight that seeped from beyond the door, his heart thudding alarmingly. He paused, hearing voices, his hand on the door, and considered running away, but jerked the door open and slammed it behind him.

The voices stilled and two pairs of eyes looked up at him. The fire had died back to embers, but he could make out Azarion's bulk in their faint glow, and beside him, Scathach's. Had she been there all the time, in the shadows, in the dark?

'I want the truth.' The irony of this demand didn't escape him. 'Ciaran put you up to this, didn't he? That old man!' He jerked his head at Scathach. 'He made you call yourself Scathach, because he knew my story, didn't he? He knew everything about me. *Everything!*'

'Sit down, man,' Azarion said peaceably, hooking a stool towards the fire.

'A man, am I?'

'You're whatever you want to be.'

'That's not true! I never had a chance.'

'You have one now.'

Flame flared as The Dragon placed a log on the fire. Salt blue flames lit the room in an unearthly glow, and pine-sharp smoke misted the room. 'Ciaran gave me a purpose in life,' he said. 'If you allow him, he'll give you one too.'

'I have my own purpose.'

'One that will destroy you.'

'I've had few choices in my life, but that one I can make for myself.'

'Self-pity, Ferdiad?' Scathach mocked.

'You're wrong, you know,' Azarion said. 'Ciaran didn't know everything, but he guessed, as I and Scathach guessed. No-one knows the truth – except for you.'

'Ciaran sent me here, knowing what would happen, knowing what would be unearthed, knowing I'd be stripped of everything I believed in.'

'He's a healer. Sometimes when a broken bone sets awry it has to be broken once more.'

Ferdiad stared into the fire, watched the flames lick the driftwood and shivered. He held out his hand to the growing warmth and his fingers threw long shadows into the dark. All the fight went out of him, and he sagged down onto the stool, but went on staring into the flames, into the past. It was a long time before he could speak, could say the words.

'It was true, all of it . . .'

Beginning the telling was hard, but once he'd started it was difficult to stop, and it was close to dawn before he finished and his voice trailed away into silence.

'Better?' Scathach asked when it was over.

He shook his head but, oddly, it was.

'Did you really make that sword for me?'

'I didn't make it for Ferdiad the Serpent.'

He'd thought not.

She exchanged a glance with Azarion, then a nod.

'I made you something else.' She heaved herself to her feet to retrieve an object wrapped in sacking. 'I made this for the man who'll wield the sword, the man who accepts the truth of himself.' She pulled away the covering.

Don't trust the swordsmith!'

It was a hand. A left hand. His hand, his fingers, his palm, a hand curled lightly as if touching the strings of a harp, and it was made of silver.

The tears came from nowhere and everywhere, tears of self-pity and regret and loss, tears of joy and hope, and everything between. Tears that trickled between the fingers of his good hand, tears that unmanned him.

'Glad you like it,' Scathach said dryly, once Ferdiad had mastered himself. 'Why don't you try it on?'

It was lighter than he expected, made not of solid metal but hollow beaten steel dipped in silver. The fingers and thumbs hinged to enable him to grasp a cup or the reins of a horse. It was a thing of great craft and great art, a gift beyond any deserving, a gift that humbled him.

'I don't know what to say.'

'Well, there's a first,' Azarion said dryly. 'But no doubt you'll find your tongue soon enough, Ferdiad Silverhand.'

'Ferdiad Silverhand?'

'The man who's going to wield Harpstring. Not Ferdiad the Serpent. Not anymore. Ferdiad Silverhand is the man you should have been and can still be - if you choose. And if you choose, you've a long journey ahead of you, to the lands of my Dragon-riders.'

Despite everything, hope flared once more. 'Isn't there another test?'

'There was, but you just passed it.'

He understood then, at least part of it, understood how he'd been manipulated and tricked, how he'd been defeated and allowed to win, how he'd hoped and lost hope over and over, how he'd been unmanned but found himself on a journey that had been longer than the one he was about to make. He thought of the miles that lay ahead of him, across moorland and seas, rivers and forests, bogs and mountains, all of them in winter. And of a harder journey, one that had begun on The Island, a journey to become a man he didn't know and couldn't imagine, a man who had a future, rather than a past.

'Don't you want a child?'

Yseult was crumbling dried hyssop into a bowl while Brangianne stacked the shelves of her newly-built workshop with all her jars and flasks. In the centre of the room, close to the workbench, stood a brazier in which apple wood was burning brightly. But it couldn't dispel the bitterly cold north-westerly that had brought rain and low cloud to The Mote and was poking its wet draughty fingers into the gap beneath the door and setting the oil lamps flickering and dancing.

She did want a child, but every evening Brangianne swallowed the foul-tasting mixture that would prevent one from taking root. *I'm a fool,* she thought.

'I don't have time for a child.' She gestured about the room and, by implication, the adjoining infirmary, which was almost finished. It wouldn't be long before she'd have patients to deal with, men and women to train, herbs and drugs to prepare, a life to build, a life in which a child had no place. That wasn't the reason, of course. A child would bind her irrevocably to Kaerherdin and, fond of him though she was, she didn't want to be bound.

'Oonagh's going to have a child,' Yseult reminded her.

'Don't we all know it,' Brangianne said dryly, for Oonagh's coming child was her sole topic of conversation these days.

Yseult laid down the bunch of hyssop, turned to face Brangianne, and squared her shoulders.

'And . . . and so am I.'

Disbelief came first. 'You can't be! You've been taking the thistle mixture.' Then realisation. She'd never seen Yseult swallow it. She'd always made some excuse to take it later. 'You haven't been, have you?'

Yseult shook her head.

'You fool!' But anger was quickly swamped by fear. 'Oh, Yseult . . .'

'I love Trystan,' Yseult said staunchly. 'I want his child.'

'He's not your husband.'

'My husband wants an heir.'

'He'll know it's not his.'

'He won't care. He doesn't *care*, Brangianne.'

Yseult was wrong. Marc cared so much he'd closed his eyes to what was happening, but what Yseult had done couldn't be ignored. It would precipitate the crisis Brangianne had been dreading. They'd already been standing on the edge of a cliff where a gust of wind would send them tumbling to the rocks below. Now Yseult had deliberately stepped over the edge.

'Marc will divorce me. Then, when I'm free, Trys will divorce his wife and we can be together, as we were meant to be. We're tired of hiding.'

Brangianne stared at her. Was Yseult as blind to reality as Marc? Did she think things would be that easy?

'Bearing another man's child will be proof of your infidelity,' she said bluntly. 'If Marc has proof, you'll be guilty of treason, as will Trystan. You won't just be put aside, Yseult.'

'My father—'

'Your father's too far away. He'll take revenge, of course – for whatever's done to you. It will mean war, but it will be too late for you and Trystan.'

Yseult's bright certainty wavered, and she looked sick.

'Does Trystan know about the child?' Yseult shook her head. 'Then tell him, but tell him you slept with Marc. Make him doubt it's his. It will hurt him, but you must make yourself do it. Send him away and mean it this time. Then throw yourself on Marc's mercy.'

Yseult stared at her. 'I can't *lie* to Trystan,' she said with an incredulous laugh.

'Yes you can. You *must!*'

'I can't!'

'Then there's only one solution . . .' Brangianne glanced around her shelves. Yes, everything was there: angelica, pennyroyal, black cohosh. It wouldn't be pleasant, and might even be dangerous, but it would have to be done.

'No!' Yseult exclaimed, backing away.

'It's the only way. Listen, Yseult—' But Yseult had reached the door.

'Don't touch me! I won't do it, do you hear me? I *won't!*'

She pulled the door open and was off, running down the hill in the rain, her skirts flying, her hair a russet flag, running back to the Mote as if the devil was after her. To Trystan? No, he'd gone hunting with Marc. To Oonagh then. Oonagh would make her see sense. Brangianne took down the pots of herbs and stacked them together on her workbench. She stared at them for a moment, then, with a swing of her arm, swept them onto the flagged floor where the pots shattered, the dried herbs spilling into the rushes to envelop her in a bitter-smelling cloud.

This was a *child,* Yseult's child, a baby conceived in love. No matter how dangerous its existence was, it deserved to be born, to be held in its mother's arms, to live, to grow up. She went to the door, closed it, and gave herself up to tears. *Don't you want a child?* Of course, she did. She wanted the children that should have been hers, the one who'd sickened and died, the other who'd left her in a gush of blood on the Night of Endings. She wept for those children, then wept for herself, for all the things done and not done, said and not said, for the past that couldn't be changed and the future that was sure to end in more tears, because there was no way out and no-one she could turn to.

Certainly not Kaerherdin. He'd asked her outright if the rumours about Trystan and Yseult were true, but she'd laughed them off and made him believe her. If he discovered what was happening, he'd know she'd been lying to him. No, not if. When. Well, she'd wanted an ending to that particular situation. Who then? Oonagh would help, but her power was limited. Could she approach Marc? No, the King was too unpredictable. Feargus then. She'd write to him, explain what had happened and ask him to send a ship to take Yseult away. But, knowing it would mean war, would he risk it, even for his own daughter? To her horror, she wasn't sure he would. Which only left one person.

She hadn't spoken to Corwynal since Samhain over a month before, but she'd watched him when she could, had seen him, like her, laugh off the rumours, watched him talk with one man and the next, painstakingly building alliances in case the worst happened. He'd know what to do. Yet she couldn't turn to him, much as she wanted to, for every time he saw her, he flinched and looked away.

Her very existence hurt him. Even so, she found herself looking forward to going to the hall every evening just to see him. She'd laugh and talk with Kaerherdin and other acquaintances, but all the time she'd be watching Corwynal from beneath her lashes, wondering what he was thinking, what he was feeling, and, unable to stop herself from caring, worrying over his pallor and the likelihood he was sleeping badly. If she was carrying his child, she'd never consider getting rid of it. She shouldn't have suggested it to Yseult, and ought to go after her to tell her so. Picking up her shawl, she swung it around her shoulders and opened the door.

He was standing there, rain dripping from his hair, mud splashed to his thighs. He was breathing heavily, as if he'd run all the way from the Mote. Taking one look at her tear-ravaged face, he moved towards her.

'My heart, I'm so sorry . . .'

She stepped into his arms and wept against his shoulder, clinging to him as he'd once clung to her. His cheek was against her hair, his hands stroking her back, and everything was all right once more. Except it wasn't.

'How did you know?' she asked, wondering if he'd met Yseult. Yet surely he'd be the last person Yseult would tell.

'The ship just came in,' he said. 'Maredydd came to find me. How did *you* know?' He pushed her away to look at her, frowning. 'You don't, do you. My love, it's Feargus—'

Her heart contracted. The rumours must already have reached him, but he hadn't done nothing. 'Is it war?'

Still Corwynal frowned at her, his eyes the colour of a storm, and she knew, from the swooping in the pit of her stomach, that a storm was coming indeed.

'It's not war, not yet, and not with your brother. I'm sorry, my heart, but Feargus is dead.'

8

THE SACRED MOUNTAIN

A wolf howled from somewhere high on the slopes of the mountains and was answered by another. Or perhaps it was an echo. Whatever it was, Ferdiad's horse tossed its head in alarm, rolled its eyes and looked reproachfully at him.

'I don't want to go any more than you do,' he murmured, eyeing the valley that lay ahead of him, a deep cleft in the mountains that narrowed to a high pass well above the snow line, a valley so deep that even now, close to midday, it lay in shadow as if reluctant to let go of the night and the cold. 'But we'd better get going,' he explained to the horse.

Gods, I'm talking to animals now! I'll be giving the bloody horse a name next.

His mount, a solid hairy creature so short in the leg Ferdiad's feet almost touched the ground, turned its head and looked longingly at the settlement where they'd spent the night. Ferdiad had paid for a night's shelter and food, and stabling for the horse, by telling stories, but they wouldn't give him a guide. They'd pointed to a near-invisible track that ascended the valley and disappeared among the rocks at the head of the glen, beyond which lay Raineach. That was the name in the old tongue, but everyone called it the Wolf Moor, which wasn't an encouraging name, especially this close to Midwinter with the sky clouding in the east and the unmistakable smell of snow in the air.

So, snow, wolves and worse, and nothing to defend himself with but an unlit torch, an ember of charcoal in a fire pot, and a sword he hadn't fully mastered.

Azarion had accompanied him on the short journey across the low-lying peninsula south of Dun Sgiath, but when they'd reached the shores of the sea-loch on the far side, he'd been met with a couple of his Forest People, and had sailed off with them in a little skiff, saying he had some private business to take care of, but had given Ferdiad instructions on how to reach Raineach.

'Regard getting there in one piece as yet another test,' he'd said before abandoning him. 'The medallion will help . . .'

Ferdiad still didn't know the medallion's meaning, and Azarion had refused to enlighten him, but it clearly meant something to others. Not long after Azarion had left, another little fishing boat arrived and, on showing the fisherman the token, he'd been taken south, past bays studded with islands, around a great promontory and down a deep twisting sea-loch to a small settlement at its head. There he'd crossed a narrow pass to yet another loch and a little ferry that had taken him across the narrow stretch of water to the mainland proper.

Now, several days after he'd set out, with a lot of uncomfortable miles behind him, and wolves and snow ahead of him, he'd almost reached the end of the journey Ciaran had intended him to take, the one that would turn him into Ferdiad Silverhand.

Don't trust the old man. Don't trust the weapons-master. Don't trust the swordsmith. Trust no-one. You have no friends. Friends are a weakness, and you can't afford to be weak.

'Come on then,' he said to the horse, kicking it into a trot that slowed to a walk as the way roughened and steepened, then to a trudge. The mountains closed in, steep buttresses soaring like giants who looked down on him, incurious and implacable, their hoary heads lost in the thickening and lowering cloud, He felt very small and very alone, though this was what he'd wanted ever since he'd lost his hand – to be alone. Until now, there had always been

someone there, first Ciaran, then the surly captain of the ship that
had taken him to The Island, then the Samhain ghosts, then
Azarion and Scathach. Even once he'd left The Island there had
been the boatman, then guides who'd taken him from one little
settlement to the next, where he'd repaid their hospitality with tales
and stories. Not song though. He wasn't ready for that. Now, alone
at last, he felt oddly bereft and wished there was someone to share
the journey with, to laugh with and argue over the meaning of life.
Was that what friendship meant?

You don't have a friend, Arddu reminded him.

'Azarion's my friend,' he insisted.

Then why didn't you tell him everything?

Ferdiad ignored that, or tried to.

Why didn't you tell him about the boy?

Once he reached the head of the pass, the gradient eased. It had
been snowing lightly all the way to the head of the valley, but now it
began to snow in earnest. The track, faint enough to begin with,
vanished into a bleak wilderness bare of trees or fields or
settlements, a treacherous place of frozen lochs and tarns
concealed beneath a deepening layer of snow. He'd been told to
head south of east, curve around the mountains, pass between two
lochs, then two hills, until he reached a wood where he'd find a track
leading down to the lower lands. But he could see no mountains, no
loch, no hills and no wood. He couldn't even see the sun to tell him
in which direction east lay, and the wind, which had been blowing
in his face all the way up the valley, now changed direction and
swirled around the mountains, making it impossible to find his way
by the wind either.

'Which way, boy?' he asked the horse, but the animal just tossed
his head nervously as a wolf howled from somewhere on his left.
Another replied from the right, then one from behind him. 'Ahead
it is,' he muttered. Maybe he could outrun them. He kicked the
horse into a canter, hoping to find a track smooth enough to allow
the beast to gallop, but couldn't find one.

Arddu! You're the God of wild places. You have power here! But Arddu was silent. Ferdiad caught the rank stink of predators and saw a dark shape keeping pace with him on the edge of sight, then another, and yet another on his other side. Gradually, they drew ahead of him and more wolves joined the pack. One darted in to nip at his horse's flanks, making the terrified animal squeal and rear. Ferdiad grasped instinctively for the mane with a hand that no longer existed, lost his balance and fell.

Then he saw it, beyond the wolves, a beast crowned with antlers moving towards him. *Arddu! About time . . .* But it wasn't the God, unless there were two of him, for another appeared, then another, then more. Something whined past him and one of the wolves yelped with pain and tumbled over, a black dart in its hind leg. Then another was down, and another. A flame burst into light and the rest of the wolves slunk away from torches carried not by gods, or stags, but by men wearing antlered helmets. He'd been rescued by Dragon-riders.

The Riders' massive horses circled him, tossing armoured and plumed heads, snorting at the smell of wolf, their hot breath clouding the cold air, their flanks and muzzles flecked with foam as if they'd been ridden hard. There were seven of them, their antler-crowned riders faceless and threatening, dragon banners droning in the wind. Gradually they slowed and came to a halt but kept their circle tight, facing towards him and his horse. Then the one with the biggest spread of horns, whom Ferdiad took to be their leader, urged his horse a few steps forwards and peered down at him, eyes glittering behind his helmet.

'My thanks.' Ferdiad held out his hand, but the man ignored it, removed his helmet and tucked it under his arm. Ferdiad wished he'd put it back on again for his face was a hard one, scarred and ruined. The nose had been broken more than once, and the skin was pitted with old pock marks and badly tattooed with abstract patterns of blue and green. His eyes were black and couldn't be called friendly, but Ferdiad thought he ought to make an effort.

'I'm . . .' He hesitated. Who was he? Ferdiad the Serpent? Or Ferdiad Silverhand?

Ferdiad the Fool. Arddu's voice rang through his head. *I told you not to trust the weapons-master!*

The man bent down, gripped the thong about Ferdiad's neck and pulled out his medallion, then grunted in satisfaction.

'You're the one?' he asked in the bastard Latin the Dragon-riders spoke.

Ferdiad smiled. His reputation had preceded him. He spread his arms to reveal the sword and the silver hand. 'I'm the one,' he confirmed.

The leader grinned, revealing a mouth of stained and broken teeth, and turned to his men.

'He's the one,' he said. 'Let's kill him.'

'How did he die?' Brangianne had stopped crying but was still clinging to Corwynal as if she'd never let him go. It was so natural, so right, her reaching out to him for comfort, him giving it.

'A Creonn raid, they said. Feargus was in the North, so it could be true. Loarn took prisoners and killed them all in revenge.'

'Loarn's behind it,' she said fiercely. 'He'll have paid the Creonn to kill him.'

'Probably.'

It had been Maredydd who'd brought the news. The Rheged trader had been in Loch Gair when word of Feargus' death had reached Dunadd, so he'd headed for Galloway to sell this valuable piece of information.

'Loarn's King now.' Maredydd had sent word to Corwynal from his favourite tavern, a seedy little place down by the wharves that stank of fish. 'That Steward – what's his name?– Eoghan? – was behind it. Feargus should have killed him when he had the chance, not sent him off to plot.'

'What will happen now?'

Maredydd shrugged, not much caring. Whatever happened, he'd make a profit out of it. 'I didn't stay to find out. War, maybe, but not yet. Loarn will need to consolidate his position first. But then . . . ?'

'Arthyr must be told,' Corwynal said, wishing Blaize was still in Galloway. But his uncle had left the Mote a few days before. 'Can you get word to him? For a fee, naturally.'

Maredydd shook his head. 'You don't know much about ships, do you? Hear that?' He jerked his head at the door banging in the wind that was filling the place with acrid smoke. 'That's a north-westerly. It got me to the Mote fast enough, but as for going back, it's a headwind. It'll be days before it blows itself out, and, until it does, the Goose is going nowhere. If this news is so valuable it'll have to go overland.' He sucked his teeth. 'And at this time of year . . . ? It'll cost you.'

Corwynal had paid the Rheged trader the extortionate amount he'd demanded and went to find Brangianne to break the news of her brother's death.

'I should never have left Dalriada,' she said. 'If I'd been there with Feargus—'

'You'd have died too. Loarn won't leave any of your family alive, so thank your God you're here in Galloway where you're safe. That's all that matters – that you're safe and . . . and happy.'

'You think I'm happy?'

'But you and Kaerherdin—'

'It was a mistake. I drank too much at Samhain because I was lonely and miserable without you. And afterwards . . . well, he's been a good friend and I didn't want to hurt him. I've been such a fool.'

'So have I. I believed you'd deliberately goaded Marc into confessing something I didn't want to hear.'

'I couldn't stop him. I couldn't stop *anything*.'

She began to cry once more, and he put his arms around her. 'We have to try, my heart. We need to get Trys away from Yseult.

We can do it if we stop fighting one another. We can do it together, Brangianne. We were meant to be together.'

'But in Dunadd, you said—'

'I had to say it. Feargus swore he'd put you in a nunnery if I didn't give you up. I had to make you believe I didn't want you. But I did. I do. I always will.'

She was the other half of his soul. How could he ever have doubted her? Why had he doubted himself? He saw his reflection in the rain-washed forest pool of her eyes, eyes that flickered and closed as he bent his head. Their lips touched, tentatively at first, questioningly, then not. They were together once more, and nothing would keep them apart. Nothing but the world.

The door slammed open and Kaerherdin strode in, the man Corwynal had come to hate, a man who hated him in equal measure.

'I see,' he said, an echo in his voice of Corwynal's that Samhain morning. then brushed past him to strike Brangianne across the face. 'You slut! You liar!'

Corwynal caught him by the throat and slammed him against the wall, but the Selgovian tore his hands away.

'You lied to me about *everything!*' he yelled at Brangianne.

'I'm sorry, Kaer—'

'Sorry? I *believed* you. I heard the rumours, but you told me they weren't true and I *believed* you! You made a fool of me, you and that niece of yours. As for Trystan – I'm going to kill him.'

'You'll have to kill me first,' Corwynal hissed, and Kaerherdin turned his pale gaze on him, his lip curling.

'That won't be a hardship.'

'No!' Brangianne pushed her way between them. 'Don't fight. Please. Not over me.'

'It's not about *you!*' Kaerherdin spat. 'I know you don't love me, but I thought you'd need me when you learned what's happened. But you don't, do you? You never did.'

Corwynal felt his hurt as if it was his own.

'That's not true, Kaer,' Brangianne said. 'I always valued you as a friend, and I'm grateful you came to tell me, but I already know my brother's dead.'

'Feargus is dead?' He stared at her, then at Corwynal, and something cold and vengeful flared in his eyes. 'You don't know, do you?' He smiled thinly. 'You haven't heard.' He looked from one to the other. 'Your precious Trystan. Your oh-so-innocent niece.'

Brangianne was staring at him, not understanding, but Corwynal, with a sickening swoop of fear, knew it had finally happened.

'They caught them together in the King's bedchamber,' Kaerherdin said in bitter triumph. 'And there's nothing either of you can do to save them.'

'Is that where the gods live?' Kirah asked doubtfully. She was looking up at The Sacred Mountain from the edge of the trees, her breath clouding in the bitter chill of the December morning. Behind them, on the other side of the wood, down by the loch, lay the Inn that served the crowds who came to The Mountain for the Midsummer rites. In the winter, however, it was deserted but for those who came to make offerings to the Mountain that lay at Atholl's heart.

From north or south, it was a long ridge of rock standing proud of the lower lands, its western edge falling away in great cliffs. But from the east The Mountain was a narrow jagged peak crowned with snow, as brilliant in the too-bright sunlight as the blade of an axe. And just as welcoming.

I'm a bad mother. Seirian looked down at Kirah who was so muffled against the cold in a woollen tunic and leggings, and fur-lined cloak, hat and boots, that she looked like a small round bear. *I shouldn't have brought her all this way in winter. I could have told her everything at the Crannog.* But she hadn't been able to answer Kirah's question - *who is The Exile, mother?* – because the answer required their presence at the place where everything had happened. Atholl's sacred mountain, the dwelling place of the gods, was as central to the story of The Exile as it was to Atholl itself. Yet, now they'd arrived, it was no easier to begin, so Seirian took refuge in her other role in life. She might be a bad mother, but she was a good teacher, and this was an opportunity to test her daughter's knowledge and understanding.

'What do you know about The Mountain?'

'It's the tomb of the Ancestor, the man the Goddess took as her Consort,' Kirah replied promptly. 'She bore him five daughters and gave one to each of the five tribes to be their Royal Lady. And the eldest was given to Atholl, and her name was Fothla, and her daughter was called Marag . . .'

Seirian smiled as Kirah recited the Lady list, each one the daughter of the one before in unbroken succession all the way back to the Ancestor, which none of the other Kingdoms could claim. '. . . and her daughter was called Seirian and her daughter is Kirah!' she ended triumphantly. 'But why—'

'What else do you know about The Mountain?'

I am the Royal Lady, memory of the tribe, guardian of the past and key to the future.

'The ancestor's tomb is covered with bones and skulls and . . . and more bones,' Kirah replied with relish. 'My father's bones are there. A bird took them.'

'That's not quite right. Your father's body was given to the sky. The birds took his flesh so he became a bird like them. That's why the druids can tell the future from the flight of birds since many of them were druids in another life. But you know all that. Your father's bones were taken to The Mountain at Midsummer to join the bones of the other archdruids and the kings. The remains of all the great men of Atholl lie there under the protection of the gods, as the bones of the Royal Ladies are given into the care of the Goddess in the deepest waters of the loch. Now you're seven, I'll take you with me to The Mountain at Midsummer to make the sun offering and see the Ancestor's tomb for yourself. You'll watch the warrior and druid tests that turn boys into men and, when the sun rises – though it's never truly dark at Midsummer – the men will beat the drums to welcome back the light.' *And drive away the ghosts.* 'Then there will be a great feast.'

'I want to go *now!*' Kirah ran off down the sacred way that led to the track that wound up The Mountain but Seirian caught her long before she'd reached it.

'Don't be silly. You can't go now. It's not permitted.'

'But why—?'

'It's dangerous. The gods aren't like the Goddess. They're jealous and can be angry, so it isn't wise to provoke them. No-one goes there except at Midsummer when the druids have made the correct offerings.'

That wasn't exactly true. Some went at other times of the year, bravely or foolishly. Many years before, Seirian herself had gone alone, and not at Midsummer, nor by the sacred way guarded by the druids. There was another way only she knew about, a secret way that crawled up through the western crags, a way hidden even from the gods. But on the summit, there was no hiding, and they'd known she was there. At Midsummer they were a presence in the blood, a beat that was neither drum nor pulse, a power banked down by ritual. Not so at other times of the year, and only her innocence and the sacred nature of her purpose had protected her. She'd been lucky to escape with her sanity.

'If we can't go now, why are we here?' Kirah asked sulkily.

Why? Why? Why?

'Because you asked a question,' Seirian said. 'You asked who The Exile was, and I brought you here to show you the place where he was banished. That's why we've been talking about what happened to your father's bones, because another of your ancestors lies on The Mountain. Who was that? Can you tell me?'

Kirah looked up at The Mountain, a faint frown furrowing her brows. 'My . . . my great-grandfather?'

'That's right. He was an Archdruid too, one of the wisest of men, a far-seer. I learned the lore from my grandmother but I learned of life from him. I had no father or mother, you see, and I loved him as much as I love you.' She smiled down at her daughter and Kirah nodded seriously. If there was one thing Seirian had taught her, it was the importance of love, of loyalty, of family.

'My grandfather – your great-grandfather – was murdered by The Exile,' she said shortly. 'He tried to kill me too. Look—' She pushed her hair aside to reveal a faint white mark on her temple. 'That was why he was banished and his name buried beneath a stone so that it may not be spoken in Atholl. That's why I haven't told you until today. But now Domech wants to bring him back.' She crouched down and gripped Kirah by her shoulders. 'And I won't let him. *We* won't let him, will we?'

'But why—?'

'Just because. Now, enough of your questions.' She straightened and took Kirah's hand. 'You wanted to know about The Exile and now you do.'

'But—'

'Come on.' She marched back towards the wood, dragging a reluctant Kirah behind her. 'It's cold. Let's go back to the Inn.'

Kirah was blessedly silent as they made their way through the trees. The Mountain was out of sight behind them, but Seirian sensed its looming presence behind her, seamed with memories.

She'd been seven when she'd first gone to The Mountain and, though she'd returned many times since that first Midsummer, the details were still vivid: the noise and colour, the drums and laughter, the shouts as the warriors went through their tests, the ring of steel on steel and the cries, sometimes of pain, sometimes of triumph, the smell of sweat and woodsmoke and the taste of charred bannocks and heather honey ale. She remembered the riddles that were the tests of the druids, the quiet hiss of satisfaction when the right answer was given, the calm intensity of those who passed the tests, druid and warrior, the way they moved with a new pride, for they were of Atholl now, and no longer children, but men. And she remembered the one they tested last, the man – still a boy really – who passed every test with arrogant competence, impatient of the ceremony – until he came to the last test of all, that of the Archdruid.

This was the part she didn't want to remember, but couldn't help herself. He'd faced her grandfather on the edge of the cliffs, and the sun, a little below the horizon, silhouetted him so he appeared to be rimmed with light, like the heroes of old. She was never sure what happened next. Even now, everything was jumbled. A question, a command she didn't understand. The boy's reaction, disgust and denial. A hand thrust out, her grandfather stepping back and stumbling, her own hand gripped then let go. She'd grasped his robes and she was falling too. Air rushed past her, then rocks and heather, until the impact, the pain in her head, the soft thud of her body against something that broke her fall – her grandfather's body. He was still alive. 'I was right,' he said, smiling. Then he died.

Right about what? The question still plagued dreams of falling, dreams in which men called out to her, but, hidden in a cleft in the rocks, she couldn't answer. Later, much later, she'd made her way down to the valley floor, through ramps of heather and scree, the secret way down the western crags. Years after that, when they made her Royal Lady, she took that secret way once more and, guided by ravens, the sons of the sons of the birds that had taken the essence of her grandfather into the sky, she'd found her way back to the cleft and the bones. She'd taken them to the summit to lay on the Ancestor's tomb as was his right, but had no gold to give, no words to speak, nothing to still a restless spirit that would haunt the summit forever, tumbling on the wind and cawing its mournful denunciation. The Exile had done that. How could she permit him to come back to her beloved country? How could she ever forgive him? *Why are we here?* Kirah had asked. *To remember,* Seirian should have said.

'...Mother...Mother...*Mother!*' Kirah was tugging at her hand and pointing at the Inn, now visible beyond the trees. 'Look! Horses!'

So he's come after all. Until now, she hadn't been sure he'd come at all.

'Ah, the panders. We were wondering when you'd turn up.'

Andrydd radiated triumph and satisfaction from his position behind Marc's chair. He had a hand on the King's shoulder, and Marc himself was sitting in his chair, staring moodily into a cup of wine. When Corwynal and Brangianne burst in, he looked up, his face unreadable, then lifted the cup to his lips and drank it down in one go, his fingers shaking and wine dribbling down his chin.

'Panders?' Corwynal asked sharply. Anger swelled inside him, but it wasn't strong enough to swamp the fear. Andrydd wasn't the only member of the Council in the Royal Chamber. Others were there, mostly his supporters, so it wasn't surprising Andrydd was confident about his position.

'That's what I said.' He eyed Corwynal with the satisfaction of a stoat who'd cornered a hare. 'What else can I call the man who encouraged his brother to betray his King, his own uncle. And as for you—' His lip curled as he turned to Brangianne. 'You've been covering up this treachery for months.'

He knows everything! Corwynal thought wildly, his anger fizzling in a backwash of fear that rooted him to the floor of the chamber, immobile and impotent. It was Brangianne who reacted, striding past him to strike the Lord of the Fleet hard across the face.

'How dare you!'

Andrydd's head shot to one side, a livid red mark on one cheek, but though his fists balled and his eyes hardened, he carried on smiling his hateful smile of triumph.

'I dare because it's true.'

'My brother—'

'Your brother's dead,' he cut in.

Maredydd, you swine! The swindling, double-crossing weasel must have sold the information to Andrydd even before he'd made Corwynal pay for it. The fear was paralysing now. If it was known Feargus was dead, there was no safety for anyone from Dalriada, especially Yseult and Brangianne.

'There is no treachery,' Corwynal insisted.

'No treachery?' Andrydd raised an eyebrow, still with that smile of sweet revenge. 'They were found together in the King's bedchamber.' Marc flinched at that. 'Your brother sneaked away from the hunt to return to his . . . paramour. Unfortunately for them both, Marc was taken ill and returned early.'

A return that would have been forced on him by Andrydd. Corwynal wouldn't put it past him to have caused the illness too. How long had the Lord of the Fleet been planning this? Not that it mattered; what had happened would have happened with or without Andrydd's intervention. Now Marc had seen with his own eyes what he'd been trying to deny for months, and a man stripped so comprehensively of his illusions was a dangerous man indeed, especially when he wasn't entirely sober.

'Marc . . .' he appealed, not sure what he could say. He could hardly deny it, not if there were witnesses. All he could do was appeal for leniency, but when Marc looked up at him there was no mercy in his eyes.

'I offered you a position of honour in Galloway – and you turned me down.'

'Sire . . .' Brangianne dropped to her knees before the King. 'If any of this is true, you must understand – and forgive.'

Marc's lips tightened, but he said nothing.

'Forgive?' Andrydd gave a bark of laughter that rang around the chamber, echoed by a squalid little titter from his supporters. 'Do you know the penalty for what's been done? It's death. There can be no forgiveness.'

'That's for the King to say,' Corwynal protested. 'Marc, please, let me talk to you.'

'You *are* talking to me.'

'Alone. Please. For the sake of all that lies between us.'

'All of which you rejected.'

So, it was his fault. His resentment of Marc and his inability to compromise had put Trystan in danger. 'For the sake of your sister then. And your sister's son. You wouldn't put her son to death. Not Gwenllian's son.'

Would he? Could Marc even consider it? What father could bring himself to kill a boy he believed to be his own son? Inexplicably, given the bleakness of the situation, Corwynal felt a lightening of the grief that lay on his heart. If Marc could think of condemning Trystan to death, then he couldn't be his father. How could he ever have believed it? No, Trystan was his, and, like any father, he'd fight to the death to save him. 'Gwenllian meant too much to you for you to do that.' There was a threat in his voice now. Andrydd's eyes sharpened, not understanding what they were talking about, but Marc grasped his meaning. *I'll tell everyone if I have to. I'll tell them of the incest, and I'll be believed* . . . Marc's face turned a pasty grey.

'Go away,' he growled. '*Go away!*' He jabbed a finger at Andrydd and waved a hand at the rest of his Councillors, all of whom were listening avidly. 'I want to talk to Corwynal alone.'

'He's your enemy,' Andrydd insisted. 'He's poured poison into your ears ever since he came to Galloway. Don't trust him. Disarm him at least.'

'Sire—' Corwynal protested, but Marc nodded at Andrydd, who removed Corwynal's sword and dagger, and didn't object when Andrydd and his fellow-Councillors retreated only as far as the door of the Council chamber.

'You too,' Marc told Brangianne.

'No,' she snapped. 'I've a word of my own to say to you.' She glanced at Corwynal and an understanding passed between them.

We can do this together, back-to-back, fighting our enemies. Together, as we were meant to be. We can save them.

'Listen, Marc.' Corwynal crouched next to him and lowered his voice. 'You gave Trystan an order on the night of your wedding. It was insane, and he shouldn't have obeyed you, yet he did. Where was the crime in that? But you couldn't have imagined it would stop there. They're young. They loved one another long before they came to Galloway, though I swear neither Brangianne nor I knew that. I tried to tell you what was happening, but you wouldn't listen. I urged you to send Trystan away, but you refused. So, send him away now. Banish him from Galloway if you want to punish him. *Think*, Marc. If you have him killed, you'll have war with Lothian and, while you might welcome that, you won't welcome Arthyr's support for Lothian's cause. You stand to lose everything you've worked for.'

'They'd all think me weak,' Marc objected, glancing over at his Councillors.

'You *are* weak.' Brangianne sank to her knees beside him. 'All men are weak. You were weak when you committed a sin with your sister. And you were weak when you imagined that cursed you, but you were cursed by nothing but your own guilt. You asked me to forgive you for what you did to me, and I've done so. You asked God to forgive you for incest with your sister, and he has. Now it's time to forgive Trystan and Yseult for what's happened between them. What you did on the night of the wedding was a terrible mistake, but you could have stopped it then. Yseult's young. She needs to be loved as a woman, not as a daughter, or a sister. Yes, I know you see in her the sister you sinned with, and you won't touch her because you can't forgive yourself for that sin. But you *must* forgive yourself. She turned to you that night, despite what you did. That was a gift you threw away. I know you love her, but it's not too late to make her love you in return. So do as Corwynal suggests and send Trystan away. Then make your peace with Yseult. Forget your pride and honour. Listen to your heart, not your Councillors. Be strong, Sire. Be a King.'

Marc stared at her, wanting to believe her, and the colour returned to his face. But the men by the door could see him being swayed by whatever the foreign woman and her Caledonian lover were saying, and Andrydd took a step forward.

'She must be punished,' Marc said after a glance at Andrydd and his cronies.

'Not death,' Brangianne insisted.

'No, not death.'

Brangianne turned to Corwynal who nodded his understanding. *It's the best we can hope for. He cares for her. It won't be too bad.* Both rose to their feet. 'Punish her as you see fit, Sire,' Brangianne said. 'But don't put her aside.'

'And nothing will be said of . . . that other matter?' he asked Corwynal.

'Not by me. I swear it.'

'Very well.' Marc sat up in his chair and raised his voice. 'Trystan will be banished,' he announced.

'Banished?' Andrydd strode forward. 'Is that all?'

'He'll be stripped of his titles and holdings in Galloway,' Marc went on. 'His fort on the Fleet – you can have it if you want.'

'And he's no longer heir?' Andrydd asked, looking for more.

'No. My new heir will be . . .' He paused and Andrydd held his breath. '. . . will be decided later, in consultation with my Council.' He looked at the men in the room. 'At the Midwinter gathering.'

Andrydd nodded slowly. The gathering was still a few days away. There would be opportunities for Andrydd to persuade enough of the Council to support him. 'And the girl? Is she to be banished also? Will you send her back to Dalriada? I believe her foster uncle reigns there now. Perhaps he'd be willing to take her in.'

'Please, Sire,' Brangianne said urgently. 'Don't send her to Loarn!'

'The Queen—' Marc said pointedly, '—won't return to Dalriada, but she will be punished.'

'Punished how? She deserves to die,' Andrydd insisted.

'She isn't going to die. I'll decide her punishment at Midwinter too, after considering the views of my Council and the people of Galloway.'

What does that mean? Corwynal felt a tremor of foreboding, but Andrydd appeared satisfied by Marc's decision.

'And them?' He jerked his head at Corwynal and Brangianne. 'They helped your nephew and your wife betray you.'

Marc swept them with his clouded gaze but said nothing.

'I'll leave Galloway with Trystan,' Corwynal said. 'You can regard it as banishment if you choose. The Lady Brangianne will be coming with me.'

At last they could be together, free of the world and the demands of other people. Just the two of them and wherever the future took them. Together. That was all that mattered.

'Won't that be a little awkward?' Andrydd asked silkily. 'Surely you're going back to Lothian, to your wife and sons.'

'Sons?' Brangianne asked, puzzled, turning to Corwynal. 'Sons?'

He closed his eyes. How had Andrydd found out? Blaize had told him Ealhith had had another child, but, caught up in his concerns for Trystan, he hadn't thought much about it, far less considered telling Brangianne – who hadn't, in any case, been very approachable at the time.

'Didn't you know?' Andrydd asked innocently. 'Didn't he tell you? Corwynal's wife bore him another son at Samhain. Mother and child are both doing well, I believe . . .'

'My heart . . .' Corwynal reached out to her but she backed away, her eyes dark with hurt and betrayal.

'Do you seriously imagine I'd leave Yseult alone in Galloway?' she asked in a clipped tone.

Of course she wouldn't, even if he'd told her, even if he'd explained, even if there had been time. But there was never enough time, and now there was no time at all.

'I'll leave tomorrow with Trystan,' he said, looking at her, willing her to change her mind, but she wouldn't meet his eyes.

'Trystan won't be leaving tomorrow,' Marc said shortly. 'He's to be held under guard until Midwinter, until the Queen's is punished, then he'll be banished. These things must be done in public.'

Corwynal stared at him, appalled, even as Andrydd smiled in triumph. His only hope of getting Trystan away was to stop him from finding out Yseult was to be punished. Now that was no longer possible. Trystan would stay and fight, but he'd lose. So Corwynal was going to have to stop him. With or without Brangianne's help, he would stop him.

9

THE DRAGON-RIDERS

'How does it feel being dead?' asked an amused voice. 'Painful,' Ferdiad muttered. His whole body was a mass of bruises.

The first time he'd been killed had been the worst, because he hadn't been ready for it.

One of the Riders had leapt off his horse. 'Piece of piss.' He'd growled, drawn his sword, crouched in an attack stance, then, grinning, had tucked his left hand behind his back in an ironic pretence that this would make him and Ferdiad equal.

'Come on then, Dalriad.' He'd lunged forwards before he'd finished speaking.

They weren't equal. Very far from it. It wasn't long before Ferdiad was lying on his back in the snow, a foot on his chest, a short but very effective and distinctly sharp blade hovering over his heart. 'You're dead.' The man stepped back and held out a hand to pull Ferdiad to his feet.

'What—?' he began, dizzy with relief.

'Next,' the leader barked, and one of the others dropped to the ground, drew his sword and crouched . . .

He was killed six times. On a couple of occasions, he made the bout last longer than a few moments, but that was the best he could do. The leader shook his head, tugged on the reins of his mount and trotted off. The others mounted up and followed, falling smoothly into line behind him. They'd gone some way before the leader turned in his saddle.

'What are you waiting for? Get on that sorry excuse for a mount. You're late, and we've a long way to go.'

That was the last thing anyone said to him for the rest of the day as he tried to keep up with the bigger horses. It carried on snowing, but the Riders appeared to know where they were going. They picked their way across the frozen expanse of the moor, passing between two lochs, then two hills, vague shapes in the snow. Wolves dogged their steps, howling mournfully, and one of the Riders lifted his head and howled back at them. It set them all laughing, but Ferdiad didn't find it amusing. Why wouldn't they speak to him? *Oh, yes*, he remembered. *I'm dead.*

Some time later, the Riders picked up a track by a wood that led to lower ground. Ferdiad expected the going to get easier after that, but he was wrong. As soon as they reached the track, the Riders kicked their mounts into a canter, the great hooves kicking up divots of half-frozen mud and turf, splattering Ferdiad who was riding at the back. His tired horse couldn't keep up with them, and the Riders vanished into the gathering gloom of the short December day. It had stopped snowing by then, the snow having turned to rain, and a thick fog was seeping out of the trees on his left.

'Wonderful,' Ferdiad muttered, spitting the taste of earth out of his mouth and slowing to a walk. He had no idea where he was or where he was going, but the track, he reckoned, must lead somewhere.

What it led to was a pack of Azarion's little forest hunters who coalesced from the gloom, startling his horse and terrifying him. Had he escaped wolves and Dragon-riders only to fall prey to the little hunters with their poisoned arrows? Their faces were painted with ochre and lime, their hair woven with bones and twigs, and even in the cold they stank of fox, but they looked at him curiously as if he was the savage here. Then, after some muttering in their fluting language, one of them came over, took his mount's reins and led him on down the track. The others crowded about him, laughing at Ferdiad and commenting freely, and apparently critically, on his appearance and uselessness. Finally, they stopped at a small campsite, where they gestured him to wait by a smouldering fire, before disappearing as the Riders had done. By the time someone came, he was tired, hungry, cold and furious.

'Was it you who arranged for that particular piece of humiliation?' he demanded when Azarion sat down beside him and tossed some wood he'd brought into the fire.

Ferdiad regarded The Dragon resentfully but without surprise. So much for 'private business to attend to', whatever that had been. Azarion had still managed to get to this campsite ahead of Ferdiad, which meant he'd come an easier route, but when Ferdiad pointed this out, The Dragon just shrugged.

'I said getting here would be a test.'

'And I failed – yet again.'

'Failed? You got here in one piece. And I didn't expect you to singlehandedly defeat six of my best men.'

'Will I ever?'

'Probably not.'

'Then why am I here?'

Azarion poked at the fire with a stick, stirring the embers into flame. 'Because you want to become someone you're not, because you want to kill Corwynal of Lothian very badly, for reasons you're keeping to yourself – don't think I didn't notice. And because Ciaran asked me to give you a chance. I've done that and, to be honest, you've done better than I expected. I thought you'd give up long ago.'

'I'm not giving up.'

Azarion regarded him steadily, judging him, Ferdiad thought. 'My debt to Ciaran is paid now, so any more I do for you will come at a price. Come – let me show you something.'

He got to his feet and gestured for Ferdiad to follow him through the trees. The clearing wasn't far from the edge of the forest that crowned a small hill overlooking lower-lying land. It had stopped raining by then and the fog had cleared. Ferdiad could make out a river and a loch lying in a valley with more mountains on the far side, glittering with snow in the light of a setting quarter-moon. There were campfires down on the land by the river, a cluster of huts surrounding them, and some way off, more fires under the eaves of a wood.

'You see that?' Azarion gestured to the two camps. 'These are my peoples – Dragon-riders and Forest People, the people of my blood and the people of my heart. I'm commander of one and father of the other, but I have to make them one, to carve a place for them both in a land that's far from generous and is surrounded by enemies. It's only because there's so little life to be won here in these narrow valleys and empty moors that we haven't been overrun. My peoples live their lives in camps or on the move. The Riders sell their skills to the highest bidder. The Hunters take refuge in the ancient woodland. Both have turned themselves into myths. I need to make that one reality. I've tried bringing them together, making them fight as one, but haven't succeeded since I'm the only person who can easily walk in both camps. Or I was, until you arrived.'

'Me?' Ferdiad had only been half-listening. He wasn't interested in Azarion's dreams. He had enough trouble with his own. 'Me?' he repeated.

'You speak Attecott. It's kin to the language of my Forest People, and you tell me you're good with languages. So learn their tongue, and be a bridge between them and the Riders. Help me turn them into a new army made up of units of Riders and Hunters fighting together. Together they could be formidable, but first they need to understand and respect one another.'

It was a big dream, an insane dream, but Ferdiad found himself responding to it, as if some trumpet had sounded, calling him into battle.

This isn't what you came for, Arddu reminded him, speaking for the first time in days, but Ferdiad ignored him.

'And what will you do with this formidable army?'

'Fight wherever and whenever we're needed.'

'For whom?

'For our own survival.'

It was only half an answer, Ferdiad thought.

'And you need me as a translator? Well, it's nice to be not entirely useless, but I'm sorry; this isn't what I came for.'

'You came to learn. This is your chance. One unit, that's all it will take. If it works, I can use it to seed other units. I want you to live with this unit, train with them and fight with them. Six of my Riders defeated you without breaking sweat. Train with them and you'll learn to defeat all six. Only then will you be ready to face the Corwynal who defeated me all those years ago.'

Arddu was silent now, but Ferdiad felt his dark sceptical presence. There would be a catch. There always was. 'What do I have to do?'

'The seven men who met you at the border; they're the unit I have in mind. Marius commands them. He's strict but fair, and his lads are rough, but once you're sharing quarters with them you'll get used to them.'

Sharing quarters . . . ? With the men who'd so comprehensively humiliated him? It would be like The Island all over again. His guts liquified at the thought.

'But they're animals!' he burst out.

'So tame them,' Azarion said implacably. 'You wanted a chance. This is it. Take it or leave it.'

The Inn's yard was packed with horses and dogs, and noisy with whinnying, barking and shouting. While Seirian and Kirah had been away, a hunting party had descended on the Inn, and the yard was awash with dung, mud, and pools of congealing blood from a freshly slaughtered deer. The common room was no less chaotic, being full of men yelling for food and drink, banging on the tables, shouting abuse at one another, and laughing in the way men laugh when they've had a good morning's hunting.

They all fell silent when she entered the room. She still had that power. They laid down their tankards and touched their foreheads in the respect due to the Royal Lady of Atholl. All but one.

'Seirian!'

'Ciniod.' She inclined her head to the King-regent of Atholl. He'd been handsome once, and thought he still was. In truth, he was a big man running to fat, and his thinning hair, once thick and golden, was now a dirty straw colour.

'Why in the Five Hells did you ask me to meet you here?'

She ignored the question and turned her attention to the young man beside him. Broichan was a more attractive and considerably more dangerous version of his father. 'Broichan,' she said coolly. He'd never forgiven her for rejecting him as Consort a few years before, but now his eyes turned to Kirah and sharpened with speculation. If he couldn't have Atholl's current Royal Lady he might be willing to wait for the next one.

Seirian's hand tightened on her daughter's shoulder. 'Kirah, this is Ciniod, King of Atholl, and his son Broichan.'

'That man's not a real King,' Kirah said in a penetrating whisper that caused Ciniod to flush with rage, for he hated being reminded that he was King-regent rather than King.

'Seirian – a word.' He slammed down his tankard. 'No, not here. You there!' He snapped his fingers at the harassed innkeeper. 'Clear one of your rooms and bring hot ale – your best, mind. Broichan – guard the door. You stay here,' he growled at Kirah, but she smiled sweetly at him and slid her hand into Seirian's.

'If you think for one moment I'd leave my daughter with your pack of wolves, you can think again,' Seirian said. 'Anything you want to say to me can be said in front of her.'

He scowled at Kirah. 'She knows?'

'She's Atholl's next Royal Lady. Of course she knows!' she said scornfully and bent down to Kirah. 'Listen and remember, but don't ask questions,' she warned her in a whisper.

The room the innkeeper offered them was cold despite a brightly burning brazier that stood in the centre of the room, but it was clean and free of draughts. A steaming jug of ale stood on a bench, watered ale beside it for Kirah. Ciniod poured himself some ale, swallowed it down and wiped his mouth with the back of his hand. Only then did he pour Seirian a cup. She smiled but left it untouched.

'Curse it women, why couldn't we have met at Dun Caled? Or that Crannog of yours?'

She sighed. Did he seriously imagine a meeting in either of those places would have been free of listening ears? To have brought a hunting party was bad enough.

'Because The Mountain is part of all this. I assume you've heard the rumours? You'll have your spies in the Druid College as I have mine. You'll know what Domech's planning. I guess you've no wish to see that man come back to Atholl to reclaim what was once his.'

'No more than you.'

'Then we need to work together against Domech.'

He shifted from foot to foot – he was afraid of Domech – but nodded.

'If you keep your side of the bargain.'

'To take Broichan as Consort? Of course.' She smiled sweetly. 'Once this . . . situation is . . . resolved.'

'If that man returns, I'll kill him.' Ciniod was a man who understood the power of men and muscle and not much else.

'We must work within the law,' she insisted. 'I don't want him here. I don't believe he'll come because he's not a fool, and he can't imagine that what he did has been forgotten. I for one haven't, but I have powers of my own, powers granted me by the Goddess, and I'll invoke them if I have to. Only if that fails, need we talk of the sort of violence you have in mind. Do I make myself clear?'

Ciniod scowled but nodded his assent. Seirian looked away to hide her disgust. A real king would have defied her. A real king would have flouted any law if he thought it right. Domech was correct; Ciniod was a stain on Atholl's reputation, but bringing The Exile back wasn't the solution. If necessary, she'd use Ciniod and his warband to oppose Domech's plans.

'But it may not come to that,' she said, schooling her face into a smile. 'I don't think Domech will manage to persuade him to return.'

'You don't *think?* I thought it was your job to *know.*'

'My duties are to the past, Ciniod, not the future. If the Goddess grants me a vision of what lies ahead, it's at her will, not my command.'

'You don't know,' he concluded.

'*I* do,' Kirah piped up.

Listen and remember, but don't ask questions. Seirian should have chosen her words more carefully.

Ciniod bent down, with an audible creaking of leather, to crouch in front of Kirah. 'You've seen him? You've seen—'

'His name is not to be spoken,' Kirah cut in sternly in an imitation of Seirian's own words and tone.

'Quite,' Ciniod said quickly. 'But you've seen him?'

'Yes.'

'He's coming here?'

'Not yet.'

'What in the Five Hells does that mean?'

But Kirah just shrugged.

'It means what she says,' Seirian said as Ciniod rose to scowl at her.

'It means nothing.' He pushed past her to return to the common room and the things he understood – men and blades and strong drink – leaving mother and daughter alone in the cold little chamber.

'What *does* it mean?' Seirian asked once he'd gone. She

crouched in front of Kirah to look her in the eye, but Kirah's own eyes were unfocussed and distant.

'Poor Exile,' she said softly.

What did that *mean?* Seirian recalled her own words. *Kirah's Atholl's next Royal Lady. Of course she knows.* And she did. She knew more than Seirian had told her, not just the truth but the whole truth. She was clever for her age, but Seirian no longer considered her too clever. She was clever enough to have put the puzzle together, and perhaps it had proved no more of a challenge than the games she'd long since discarded. Maybe all she'd needed to complete the puzzle was to meet Ciniod for herself and to know that the King was no real king, that there was a gap in the records, that the murder, even of an Archdruid, might warrant banishment but not the stripping away of a name, that her own mother's hatred was fierce and implacable and far too extreme, and that even in the presence of the Sacred Mountain she hadn't been able to bring herself to tell her everything. But Kirah had guessed. Kirah *knew.*

'Why do you say that? Why do you pity the man who murdered my grandfather?'

'Because he was his grandfather too. And his name is—'

'—not to be spoken,' Seirian said, fighting back tears of rage and . . . abandonment.

'But it can be whispered,' Kirah said. 'So tell me.'

With those words, Seirian knew her daughter would be formidable one day, for in that moment she could refuse her nothing.

'Talorc,' she whispered. 'His name was Talorc.'

When Ferdiad had killed the Druid, Uuran, and offered his still beating heart to Arddu, thus binding himself to the God, he'd made himself two promises.

Never again would he be invisible. And he'd always sleep alone.

The first had been easy, for after that night his hair had turned silver, and he'd made the most of it. As for the second, though he occasionally longed to share the warmth of the hall with other people, he usually managed to find somewhere private and had become accustomed to the cold.

Nevertheless, sleeping in a barracks room with seven strangers who'd beaten him so easily and now ignored him, thus rendering him invisible once more, was preferable to finding some shelter in the woods of Raineach on a bitter winter's night. But only just.

Getting to sleep, however, proved impossible. He was too used to silence to ignore the noises seven men made: snoring, turning over, crying out. Breathing. So he lay on his back, stared into the dark, and reminded himself why he was there . . .

'He's to be called wolf,' they said. 'But he won't answer to it.'

Word went around quickly. The boys were quick to judge and rarely kind. A new boy had to fit in or be ostracised. But this boy cared nothing for the opinion of the others. He even seemed to welcome the shoulders turned against him. He was different.

'Half-Briton,' they whispered. 'And they say his mother was a slave . . .'

Ferdiad, invisible but listening, pricked up his ears at that and began to watch the boy who made no friends, and whom the other boys picked on. He fought back, naturally, but was small for his age and could often be seen limping about with blackened eyes and skinned knuckles. Ferdiad, with his own hurts, felt a strange identity with the dark-haired boy with the watchful eyes. Eventually, however, the other boys lost interest and found others to torment. Slaves who couldn't fight back were always more entertaining game. But Ferdiad continued to watch the boy, saw him accept the name of wolf, saw him train with sword and spear, listened to him learn the lore of the druids. It was clear he'd be a warrior, and Ferdiad was only slightly less surprised than the boy himself when he was chosen for the druid college, something that amused Ferdiad's particular tormentors who'd also been chosen for *the college and who'd been assigned to Uuran, the druid everyone feared for his sarcastic tongue and other reasons no-one talked about. The boys became his disciples, Ferdiad slave to a vicious man and to boys who considered themselves men and who, with Uuran's encouragement and example, found new ways to amuse themselves at Ferdiad's expense. Those were bad times, but when they were at their worst, when he wanted to die, he'd think of how the dark-haired boy retreated into himself, and he'd try to do the same thing.*

He never spoke to him, of course. Slaves didn't speak unless spoken to. The boy didn't notice him, but Ferdiad was used to being invisible, and he used his invisibility to watch and listen at doors and windows to the lessons the boy refused to learn, hearing how he answered wrongly or not at all. So he knew that something had changed when the boy began to give the correct answers, to do his work quickly then disappear.

'Where does he go?' his tormentors wanted to know. 'You – slave – follow him. Then tell us . . .'

He never did tell. He followed and watched and lied. 'He wanders about. He throws stones in the loch or the sea. No, it's the truth. No, don't. Please . . .'

He kept on following, and watched the boy become a warrior, watched him fight himself free. He gave him a new name then, Cuchullain from the story. For hope. Hope for what, Ferdiad couldn't have said. He was afraid to give it a name for fear it would be taken from him as everything else had been taken. It came to nothing, of course. How else? He'd never had a chance . . .

'Have you come to say you told me so?'

It was tempting, for Corwynal had indeed warned Trystan this would happen, but he shook his head.

'Then why are you here?'

Trystan had been imprisoned in a stinking warehouse down near the river, a barn of a place stacked with bales of fleece and sacks of grain, barrels of imported wine, and jars of oil. The building had thick walls to keep out both weather and rats, strong beams to hold up the roof, and even stronger uprights to hold up the beams.

'To see how you were being treated.' *To see if I could get you free.*

Trystan held up his hands. They were shackled at the wrist, and his ankles were shackled too. Both wrists and ankles were linked to a heavy chain fastened around one of the uprights. It was long enough to allow Trystan to lie down on the pile of sacks he'd been provided with for a bed. To one side stood a jug of water, the remains of a meal and a bucket to act as a privy. 'As you can see, my accommodation is delightful. As is my companion.' He smiled sweetly at the guard standing at a safe distance, one hand on the pommel of his sword. Trystan must have tested the limits of his chain, and the man was keeping out of range, though he was still close enough to hear anything they said.

'None of your foreign talk,' the man objected, for they'd been speaking in Gael. 'If you can't talk like a Christian, you don't talk at all. Lord Andrydd's orders.'

Andrydd would be behind the chains. He'd have informed Marc that Trystan was imprisoned, but wouldn't have gone into detail, and Marc wouldn't have asked. The guards – there were more outside – would be his too, and the only reason Corwynal had been allowed to see Trystan was to demonstrate that any plan he might have to rescue him was futile. But at least it gave him a chance to tell Trystan what was happening.

'You're to be banished,' he said.

Trystan sagged with relief; he must have expected death, and not without cause.

'There's to be a trial at Midwinter in front of the Council. Marc's sent for Abbot Hereydd from Rosnat since he's a judge.'

'That old prune!'

'That old prune will find you guilty.'

Trystan gave a short bark of laughter. 'I expect he'll be given no choice!' Then he sobered. 'What of . . . of the Queen?'

'She'll be judged also and, if guilty, will be punished.'

'He wouldn't dare!'

'Trys – Feargus is dead.'

Trystan's eyes widened, and he paled with fear, but not for himself.

'Punished, how?'

'I don't know. Penance probably.' *Nothing painful or humiliating*, was what he meant.

'I won't—' Trystan glanced at the guard and caught himself. *I won't let that happen.*

'Trys – accept Marc's judgement,' he urged.

'I'll accept yours,' Trystan said after a moment's thought. 'I'll do whatever you'd do in my circumstances.'

What would I do? Would I leave the woman I loved to face any sort of punishment? Would I leave her to the mercy of a man who was unreliable at best, half-mad at worst? Of course he wouldn't. Yet he had to persuade Trystan to do so.

'If I'm to be banished, we'll go back to Lothian,' Trystan went on. 'You must be keen to see your wife and sons again. If I had a wife and a son, wild horses wouldn't keep me away from them.'

What was Trystan talking about? Why mention Ealhith when he knew they wouldn't be returning to Lothian? Trystan stared hard at him and glanced deliberately at the guard once more. There was a message in what he'd just said. But what? Trystan had no wife, not really, nor a son, and yet he'd emphasised that word ever so slightly. Then, with a shudder of some emotion he couldn't give a name to, Corwynal understood. Yseult must be with child, Trystan's child.

He stared at Trystan, a series of emotions washing through him: disbelief, anger, fear, acceptance and, finally, resolve. And with resolve he found his voice once more.

'You're right,' he agreed. 'It's time I went back to them. We should be together, all of us. I ought to be somewhere I can watch my sons grow up.'

My grandson. My son's son. Once more that nameless emotion swept over him. What was it? Pride? Love? Terror? All three? It didn't matter. The chances of persuading Trystan to tamely allow himself to be banished and forget Yseult had been vanishingly small. Now he no longer wanted to try, because he'd meant what he'd said, but not about himself and Ealhith. It was Trystan, Yseult and the child he'd meant. He'd tried to hate the girl and blame her for everything, but none of this was her fault. He couldn't condemn her, not the mother of his grandchild. She was much part of his family as Brangianne and, one way or the other, he was going to get his family out of Galloway.

'That's enough now,' the guard said, bored with their talk.

'It's not long until Midwinter,' Corwynal said to Trystan as he turned to go. 'Once the trial's over, we'll leave Galloway, all four of us. You, me—' He paused and let two names fall silently between them. *Yseult and Brangianne.* '—Oonagh and Aelfric,' he finished for the guard's benefit.

'You can count me out, you Caledonian bastard!'

A big man was lounging in the doorway of the prison. The guard half-drew his sword. 'Who in the Five Hells are you? Who let you in?'

'I'm the Angle.' Aelfric hiccupped then swayed and grasped the doorframe for support. 'They let me in.' He jerked his head at the door. 'I wanted to see my master.' He peered into the warehouse and smiled at the sight of Trystan, chained to the upright. 'Hah!' he exclaimed. 'How do you like it, pretty boy, being chained like an animal?'

'Out!' The guard pushed Corwynal towards the door, and he fell against Aelfric who staggered once more.

'Careful, master.' He clutched a skin of wine to his chest. 'Don't want to spill none.' Then he weaved his way unsteadily into the prison.

'You! Get out too!' the guard eyed the big Angle nervously, his hand on the hilt of his half-drawn sword.

'Me?' Aelfric asked in an aggrieved tone. Then his brow cleared and he laughed. 'You think I want to free him?' He strolled over to Trystan and tugged at the chain. 'See this,' he said. 'They put a chain like this on me when I was captured. Took two of them to defeat me – them two.' He swept a hand to encompass both Trystan and Corwynal. 'They chained me like an animal. Like him.' He nodded at Trystan. 'Here—' He pressed the skin of wine at the man. 'Hold this. Drink some if you like, but not too much mind. I've a thirst on me, but I've got a word or two to say to pretty boy here first.'

The guard grinned, slid his sword back into its scabbard, and took a swallow of wine. 'Say what you like.'

'What are you doing?' Corwynal demanded of Aelfric, trying to push past the guard.

'Shut the fuck up, you Caledonian bastard!' Aelfric snarled, then turned to the guard. 'Don't trust him. He's a treacherous underhanded shit! You want to keep that boy chained up until Midwinter? Then don't let that man anywhere near him. But you won't, will you. I can trust *you*.'

He draped an arm companionably around the guard's shoulders, retrieved the wine, took a long swallow and handed it back. 'See him—?' He jerked his head at Trystan, who was staring at him with a mixture of confusion and outrage. 'They say he's been fucking the little Dalriad Princess. Got me to stand guard so no-one would find out. I was all set to speak out when some son of a bitch beat me to it. But you can tell your master, Andrydd, that Aelfric the Angle's his man. You tell him now.' He clutched the guard to his chest and breathed wine-sodden fumes over him. 'Promise me you'll tell him.'

The man nodded, still grinning. Aelfric let him go and staggered over to Trystan, grabbed the chain and yanked hard. 'Good,' he said. 'There's no way you're getting out of here, you . . .' He dropped his voice and spat some obscenity in Trystan's face.

'How dare you!' Trystan hissed something back at him, but Aelfric laughed and pulled back his fist to hit him.

'Nah,' he said, lowering the fist. 'Don't want to spoil that pretty face before Midwinter. But as for you—' He whirled, pushed past the guard and caught Corwynal by the tunic. 'I'm going to do something I've wanted to do for years. I'm going to smash your fucking face in.'

His fist came up and caught Corwynal below the jaw. It half-lifted him off his feet, and he fell backwards through the doorway to sprawl in the dirt outside. Andrydd's guards cheered ironically and made no move to help him.

'Again?' Aelfric asked with relish, and before Corwynal could struggle to his feet he was kicked down the side of the building and around the corner into an alley that led to the docks.

'Take that!'

Corwynal shut his eyes and threw up an arm to protect himself, but the blow never landed. He heard the sound of flesh striking flesh and opened his eyes to see Aelfric smashing a fist into the palm of his other hand as he looked down at him with his usual good-natured derision.

'Yell, you stupid bastard!' he hissed, kicking the wall of the warehouse. 'Make it sound like I'm hitting you!'

Finally, Corwynal understood, and he yelled as convincingly as he could while Aelfric carried on kicking the wall and smashing his fist into his palm as they worked their way down the alley. Behind, out of sight, the guards carried on cheering and laughing.

'I bit my tongue,' Corwynal complained when they were out of earshot in the warren of alleys that ran down to the riverbank. His mouth had filled with blood.

'Don't be pathetic,' Aelfric said. 'I barely touched you.' Then he started to laugh. 'Odin's balls, I enjoyed that!'

'I don't see how it helps.'

'Are you joking? I've made a friend of those guards, and that's going to come in useful.'

'You have a plan?' Corwynal asked, hope stirring.

'No,' Aelfric said. 'But Trystan does.'

'I blame everything on women,' the guard complained. His name was Gryn and he'd just thrown a two.

'What, everything?' asked Pywll, his fellow-guard, since he'd won that particular throw.

'He's right,' Aelfric said. By sleight of hand, and painfully against his nature, he'd been losing steadily all afternoon. 'Luck's a woman.'

'Luck's not having a woman,' Gryn maintained. 'Not a wife at any rate. Shrew that she is. Her mother too, curse the bitch. And as for that whore at the Three Bells . . .'

'Gave you pox, didn't she?' Pywll said sympathetically. 'Bitch.'

'They're all bitches,' Aelfric agreed, thinking the Britons might be fools but they weren't complete fools. Women were indeed trouble, Oonagh always on about the child and forcing him to think about the future, Brangianne, taking up with Kaerherdin then dropping him and falling out with Corwynal over Ealhith's new child. Ealhith wasn't much better, losing her heart to the Caledonian in the first place, and, as for Yseult, she was the reason Aelfric was here.

Trystan crouched with his back against the barn's central post, pretending to ignore their talk. The two guards and Aelfric were sitting outside the reach of his chains, huddling about a brazier that did little to banish the chill of the warehouse. It was the day of the trial, Midwinter's day, and it had dawned late, the low sun obscured by a thick freezing fog that shrouded the Mote in a white blanket. The fog might prove useful if they could get away, but that was looking increasingly unlikely.

I have a plan, Trystan had said.

Aelfric had been coming every day since Trystan had been taken prisoner to try to find out what that plan was. The guards welcomed his presence, for they found him amusing, but they didn't entirely trust him. They always searched him for weapons and were careful not to let him get too near Trystan, so he hadn't managed to find out what Trystan had in mind. Nor had he thought of anything clever of his own, and today was his last chance, for it wouldn't be long before they came to take Trystan to the trial. *Cutting it fine, Trys!* But that was always Trystan's style. Nevertheless, he could see the sense of leaving his escape until Midwinter for, if they were to get Yseult free, today was the day to do it. Until now she'd been under close guard in the Royal residence. Today, however, she'd be in the hall for the trial, together with anyone who could buy or bribe themselves a place at what promised to be the most entertaining event in a lifetime – the trial of a queen and her lover. With any luck, sufficient confusion could be created to get them both away.

If only Corwynal doesn't go mad. As the days had gone by and Trystan remained a prisoner Corwynal had lost the little reason he had left, and Aelfric was afraid he'd do something they'd all regret. Only four words had kept him sane. *I have a plan.* Aelfric just needed to get Trystan free so he could put that plan into action. But, whatever it was, it was increasingly unlikely it would work.

There should have only been the one guard in the warehouse, but today there were two. Aelfric ought to have anticipated that. Nevertheless, he could take two of them without breaking sweat, even without weapons – though he wasn't exactly weaponless, he remembered, shifting uncomfortably. The big problem was the chains. It would take time to break them. And there were more guards outside the warehouse, huddling about the fire they'd built but coming in at frequent intervals to warm themselves at the brazier inside. Could he deal with them all? It looked as if he'd have to, unless Trystan had a plan for them too.

It was Aelfric's turn to throw and, while the other men's attention was on the tumbling dice, he looked over at Trystan and raised an eyebrow in enquiry. Trystan shivered and wrapped his arms about his body.

'Hey – a six, you lucky beggar! Looks like your luck's turned.' Aelfric grinned, but not because his luck had turned. He'd finally understood Trystan's plan. A risky one, but what plan of Trystan's wasn't?

'Poor thing.' He nodded at Trystan. 'He's cold. Look how he's shivering. Are you cold, master? Do you want me to bring the fire nearer?'

'I'm freezing,' Trystan complained, speaking for the first time that day. 'When my uncle the King finds out how I've been treated he'll have your heads.'

'Maybe he'll be having your head first,' Pwyll replied

'Or maybe they'll burn you,' Gryn suggested. 'You'd be warm enough then.'

'He's scared,' Aelfric said scathingly as Trystan shivered violently once more. 'Look at him – Galloway's champion, and he's scared.' He picked up a brand from the brazier, strolled over to Trystan and waved it at him. 'This fire close enough for you, master?'

Trystan flinched away but glanced significantly about the warehouse as he did so.

'Come on, Aelfric,' Gryn said. 'Leave him alone and let's get on with the game.'

Aelfric turned and headed back. Trystan's stretched out one leg and Aelfric obligingly tripped over it, dropping the flaming brand into the tinder-dry rushes which immediately caught fire.

'You fool!' Gryn leapt to his feet and began stamping out the fire. Pwyll looked about wildly for something to douse the flames and made for the casks of wine standing near the door, but Aelfric barrelled into him.

'Leave it to me.' He grabbed an amphora of oil and threw it at the fire. It smashed, splashing oil everywhere, and the fire spread.

'You moron!' Pwyll yelled, as he and Gryn scuttled towards the door to avoid the wall of flame that sprang up between them and Aelfric. 'You out there! Fire! Fire!'

The others came rushing in but the draught from the door sent the fire roaring upwards as Aelfric threw amphora after amphora into the fire, driving them back.

'Enough, you idiot!' Trystan gasped, coughing. 'You'll fry us both. Now I hope to God you've brought something to get these chains off.'

For answer Aelfric pulled out the chisel which he'd fastened across his back and the lump of granite that had been pressing uncomfortably against his bladder.

'Quickly, man!'

The fire was smouldering in the bales of wool, sending up a greasy choking smoke that made them both cough as they worked on the bolts holding the shackles closed. They were made of more brittle metal than the chains, but it still took several blows before the first one shattered. The fire was raging all about them by the time Trystan was free.

But it had taken too long, for they could hear shouting outside. A crowd had gathered, and the only way out was through that door – without weapons, into a crowd of armed men. But if they didn't want to burn, they had to try. 'Come on,' he urged Trystan. 'Come *on!* What the fuck are you doing?'

Trystan, ignoring the flames licking about him, was banging at the bolt that fastened the ring holding the chains to the upright. 'Help me!' He tossed Aelfric the stone and held the chisel over the bolt. Aelfric smashed the stone down again and again until the bolt shattered and the chains were free. He hauled off his shirt, tore it into four, tossed two pieces to Trystan then wrapped the others about his hands and picked up one of the fire-hot lengths of chain.

'Ready?' he asked, as Trystan did likewise.

Trystan's face was black, his hair singed, but his teeth shone white in the fire and smoke of the warehouse. 'Ready,' he said, grinning. Then they leapt through the flames . . .

'That was almost as much fun as Trimontium!' Trystan declared when, a few moments later, hidden by the fog, they'd found shelter beneath the pilings of one of the wharves. Behind them, there was shouting and a whoosh of fire as the warehouse went up. Smoke billowed through the fog that glowed amber in the light of the fire. Getting out had been easy, swords and shields no match for the heavy chains, Andrydd's guards no match for the two blackened devils who erupted from a fire that should have killed them both. But it had been close, and Aelfric's heart was still hammering, his chest still dragging in lungsful of cold clean air that didn't taste of smoke.

'So, what's the plan?' Trystan asked.

'I thought *you* had a plan!'

Trystan shrugged and looked down at his hands, badly blistered from the fire. He wouldn't be holding a sword in a hurry. Not that he had one. Not that either of them had any sort of weapon, for they'd abandoned the heavy chains at the warehouse once they'd done their job. And now the hunt was up. Orders were being shouted, men fanning through the settlement.

'You said you had a plan,' Aelfric reminded him.

'I said that to stop Corwynal doing something stupid and getting himself killed.'

'So, now what?'

'Now I get Yseult free. I assume Corwynal has some way of getting us away from here once I have?'

Aelfric nodded. 'Oonagh's waiting with horses at that ruined hut in the marshes up the river. They're bound to come after us, but we'll head north then double back for Rascarrel bay. The Goose should be standing off in the bay, if Maredydd's managed to find his way in this fog. He'll wait till high tide. If we don't appear by then he'll leave. If we make it, we head for Rheged, all six of us.'

'Only six? So, Kaerherdin's turned against me. Pity, but I suppose it was to be expected.' He got to his feet. 'We split up now. You get to Corwynal and Brangianne, and tell them I'll meet them at the hut. Make sure they go, no matter what happens.'

'I'll try.' Aelfric scratched his beard doubtfully. Corwynal would never leave Trystan if he was in danger. 'What are you going to do?'

Trystan grinned. 'You don't want to know.'

Aelfric eyed him suspiciously, then decided he really didn't want to know. 'You'll need weapons,' he told him.

'I have all the weapons I need.' Trystan clapped Aelfric on the shoulder and vanished into the fog.

THE TRIAL

They made her swear on a chicken bone. It lay within a jewelled casket on a bed of blue-dyed wool, and was Rosnat's most holy relic, the finger bone of Saint Martin. Brangianne didn't think this the time or place to point out their mistake, and anyway, human or chicken, man or saint, she'd every intention of telling the truth.

'I swear, on this holy relic—' she declared, '—that my niece, Queen Yseult, daughter of King Feargus of Dalriada, has had relations with no man but the one to whom she gave her maidenhead on the night of her marriage.'

Take that! She glared at Marc, who was sitting at the head of the hall on a raised platform. He shifted uncomfortably and wouldn't meet her eyes, knowing she could tell some unpalatable truths about that night. To his left sat Yseult's accuser, Andrydd, Lord of the Fleet, and on his right her judge, Abbot Hereydd of Rosnat, a man who neither liked nor trusted women.

'The late King Feargus,' Andrydd corrected her, his gaze shifting about the room, assessing enemies and allies. The rest of Marc's Council sat on the long sides of the hall. Servants and townspeople, Kaerherdin among them, had crowded in behind them, but the centre of the hall had been cleared to allow everyone to see the accused. That was a mistake on the part of her accuser, Brangianne thought, for, sitting in the simple wooden chair, with the torchlight augmenting the wan Midwinter light that filtered through the fog at the upper windows, Yseult looked both innocent and queenly, a woman wronged, a woman grieving for her father. Brangianne hadn't been allowed to speak to Yseult since the day she'd been taken, but Oonagh had managed to get word to her about Feargus.

'So you swear your niece has never had relations with any man but her husband?' Hereydd didn't approve of women healers and resented Marc's gift of land for a healing centre, being of the opinion that healing should be reserved for the righteous.

'I've sworn the truth on the holy finger bone of St Martin,' she said tartly.

He glowered at her, then motioned one of his hovering acolytes to take the casket with the chicken bone to Yseult.

The hall fell silent. Would she confess? Would she dare lie in the presence of the relic of Rosnat's revered saint? But Yseult followed Brangianne's lead and told the truth.

'I swear I've had no relations with any man but the one who became my true husband on the day I was wed.'

Once more Brangianne glanced at Marc, wondering if he'd dare tell the truth about what had happened that night, but he remained silent, a brooding presence between Yseult's accuser and her judge.

'That's a lie,' Andrydd maintained loudly. 'I saw you with Trystan with my own eyes.'

'I've not asked you to speak, my Lord.' Hereydd was a stickler for protocol and, having reproved the Lord of the Fleet, turned once more to Yseult. 'How do you answer this charge?'

'I don't know what Lord Andrydd saw or imagined he saw,' she replied coolly.

'You were discovered with Prince Trystan in the King's own bedchamber,' Hereydd informed her.

'And why shouldn't I be there? I'd noticed a tear in my husband's tunic and intended to repair it. I went into his bedchamber to find the tunic, being unaware that in Galloway needlework was a crime.'

A ripple of amusement ran through the hall. The mood of the crowd, ever fickle, had shifted when Yseult had been brought in, and now it shifted still further. *Perhaps she can talk her way out of this.*

'You aren't accused of needlework.' Hereydd glared at those in the hall who'd laughed. 'You're accused of adultery with the King's nephew, who was found with you in your husband's bedchamber while the King was out hunting.'

'Prince Trystan had come to tell me the sad news of . . . of my father's death.' She bowed her head and a single sparkling tear trickled down one cheek and splashed onto her clasped hands. A little sigh ran through the crowd.

'That's a lie,' Andrydd objected. 'He couldn't have known of it then.'

'Why not?' Hereydd asked.

'Because the news came to me first, and I didn't speak of it.'

'Not even to the King?'

Marc roused himself from his brooding introspection and looked coldly at Andrydd.

'I . . .' Andrydd began, discomfited.

'I knew,' Corwynal interrupted.

He was sitting on the other side of the hall with Dynas. Like herself, he hadn't been accused of anything, but both knew that if Trystan and Yseult were found guilty, they too would be under suspicion. So they'd been watched and hadn't been able to speak freely since the day they'd appealed to Marc, and Brangianne regretted the coolness that had fallen between them that day. *He has another child!* It still hurt. He hadn't told her, and that hurt more, but her own hurts mattered little right then. *Just get us all out of here*, she prayed, not to God but to Corwynal, in whom she had rather more faith.

'I also learned of the death of King Feargus the day Lord Andrydd was told of it,' he went on. 'From the same man, a Rheged trader by the name of Maredydd. And I have to confess that my first thought wasn't that I should inform the King, but that I should tell Feargus' sister and daughter. I went to find the Lady Brangianne myself and sent Trystan's man-servant, Aelfric, in search of him so he could break the news to the Queen.'

'Lies!' Andrydd shouted. 'They were *embracing!*'

'I was upset,' Yseult said. 'As anyone would be to learn of the death of their father. He was a great King and I loved him. Prince Trystan, understanding that, comforted me in my grief.'

It wasn't true. Trystan hadn't known, but it sounded plausible, and Hereydd threw Andrydd a sour look before turning to question Corwynal once more. But he was listening to a small boy who'd wormed his way through the crowd to whisper something in his ear. His expression didn't change, but Brangianne could see him go very still. Something, clearly, had happened, for just then the main door of the hall opened and one of Andrydd's men, blackened with filth of some kind, hurried over to him and muttered something that made his master turn pale.

'Prince Trystan has escaped and—' Andrydd began, but the noise in the hall drowned him out. There was even some cheering. 'But that just proves it!' he shouted over the din. 'He's guilty. Why else would he escape? And that means she's guilty too!' He pointed a trembling finger at Yseult.

She didn't look guilty. She looked radiant.

It's over! Brangianne looked at Corwynal, expecting to see relief in his face, but he was scanning the hall, judging and measuring, making and revising plans. He threw her a warning glance, but she didn't know what he was warning her about.

'Find Trystan!' Marc rose to his feet. 'He mustn't be allowed to escape.'

'Silence in the hall!' Hereydd roared. For a small man he had a powerful voice, honed, no doubt, by years of shouting at novices. 'This trial is not yet over! Lord Andrydd is right; this escape is an admission of guilt. As for you—' He turned and pointed a finger at Yseult. 'This calls into question your sworn evidence, evidence you swore on a sacred relic! So now, one final question, Lady. Do you, or do you not, in defiance of your marriage vows, love Prince Trystan?'

It went very quiet as everyone in the hall leant forward, holding its collective breath, to hear what Yseult had to say. Would she deny everything to save her own life? Or defy the court that was ready to judge her?

Tell them you don't love Trystan, and you'll walk away from this,' Brangianne wanted to tell her. *Say no, and Marc won't punish you. Lie, Yseult and keep on lying.*

But Trystan was free, and Yseult was her father's daughter. She was no longer willing to lie. She rose from her chair to stand tall and proud and disdainful of Marc's court and everyone in it.

'Trystan's the brother I never had, the friend I had to leave behind, son of one King and nephew of another. He's a warrior and a poet, a swordsman and a singer. Who wouldn't love such a man?'

'So you confess?'

'I confess nothing! I've committed no crime, not in the eyes of God. It's I who am the victim here – sold to the enemy of my people for the sake of a treaty which no longer holds, sold to a man old enough to be my father, a man who's been as little a husband to me as I've been wife to him.' She looked at Marc, daring him to contradict her, then dropped her voice to appeal directly to him. 'But all that's over now. Loarn will break the treaty, and I'm no more use to you, my Lord King. You've been kind to me, and generous, but I'm not the woman you want me to be.'

Don't do this! Brangianne thought, appalled. *Don't appeal to his better nature. This man has more than one nature.* But Yseult kept on.

'Put me aside, as so many of your Council have called upon you to do. I have no value now, either as a wife or a hostage. I'll never give you a son.' She put her hand on her belly as if to deny the very idea. 'So let me go. I ask nothing from you, no return of my dowry, no lands or titles, no jewels or dresses, not even the name of Queen. I ask only for my freedom. Please – let me go.'

'Let you go to *him?*' Marc's voice fell like a blade in the silence of the hall.

'To go where my heart leads me.'

'Trystan is banished. His escape proves his guilt. I won't allow you to go to him.'

'So you declare me guilty too? You who know better than anyone where the guilt of this matter lies? We're not married. I'd rather be married to the lowest peasant than you!'

Oh, Yseult!

She could have walked away, but her pride had stopped her. Once Trystan was free, her rebellious spirit had surfaced and thrown off the shackles of the long lie, but other shackles would bind her now. Would bind them all.

'You want your freedom from me?' Marc demanded. 'You'd rather be married to the lowest peasant? Very well. If that's what you want.'

'Please, Sire—' Brangianne begged. 'You can't do this! If you do, I'll—'

'Don't threaten me!' He turned on her, his face flushed with anger, and she knew it was no use. Her threat had never been real. If she declared the King guilty of incest, who'd believe her now? The aunt of an adulterous Queen and a foreigner at that?

'For the gods' sake, Marc!' Corwynal began.

'Don't speak to me! You helped him escape.'

'I've been here all the time!'

'Get out of my sight. Get out of Galloway – both of you!'

But Brangianne had no intention of leaving Yseult, and Corwynal didn't move. He was still scanning the room, searching for someone – Aelfric perhaps? Did he have a plan to rescue Yseult from this dreadful situation? But the door was still guarded by

Andrydd's men, and the mood in the hall had changed once more. Brangianne felt it shift and darken as if wolves were circling. She looked for Kaerherdin, hoping he might intervene, but could no longer see him.

'Give her to me!' Andrydd's eyes were hot with desire.

'No, to me,' another of the Councillors called out.

'It's God's will that you give her to me,' Hereydd insisted.

'I'm giving her to none of you!' Marc snarled. 'I said the lowest peasant, and I meant it!'

Yseult's eyes widened as she understood Marc was serious, that by her pride she'd put herself in terrible danger. She'd been a queen, but now she was nothing but a woman, a piece of meat to be fought over and torn apart by men who'd lusted after her from a distance but for whom that distance had now vanished.

'Give her to me, my Lord!' One of the townsmen pushed his way to the front, a tanner, judging by the rank stink of him. Then another, a bargeman perhaps, a dark-skinned man with a leering mouth in which only the stumps of a few teeth could be seen. The townsmen came closer, ignoring the protests of the few women who were there, or even egged on by them. 'Bitch! Whore!' they called out as Yseult's words rebounded on her. *The lowest peasant.*

Marc sat impassively as men crowded about Yseult, snarling at one another like dogs with a bone. Then the nearest of them reached out to touch her dress.

'Enough!' Corwynal strode forward, pushed his way to her, grasped the chair on which Yseult had been sitting, smashed it to the floor and picked up a splintered length of wood. 'The first person to touch her dies!'

A broken piece of wood wasn't much of a weapon, but the crowd backed away, and Brangianne was able push her way to Yseult's side. Still Marc gave no order. What was he waiting for? Did he want to see her torn to pieces before his eyes? Brangianne looked wildly at Corwynal, afraid they too might suffer the same fate, for the shouts had spread out of the hall by then, news running through solid walls and closed doors like the rumour of fire, and there was banging as the crowd outside demanded to be let into the hall.

'Steady.' Corwynal sounded more confident than Brangianne thought he had a right to.

'Where is he?' Yseult was looking around the hall. 'Where *is* he?'

'I don't know. Close. I don't know.'

They mean Trystan. They think he's coming to get her. She realised why Corwynal had been scanning the crowd, and she too began to search for a golden head. But still the cry went up. 'Give her to me! To me, my Lord!' The banging on the hall doors was as loud and rapid as the hammering of Brangianne's heart against her ribs as the crowd lost their fear of a man with a splintered length of wood and two women whose curses they didn't believe, and they surged forward.

Then the banging stopped, and the cries outside turned to screams of terror. A bell was rung slowly but insistently. The doors swung open to let in a cloud of fog that stank of smoke and something much fouler. Out of the fog, a group of figures coalesced, grey-cloaked ragged figures, their clothes in tatters, their torn and stained cloaks marked with a black cross to show they were doomed, men and women who stood on the threshold between this world and the next, half alive, half-dead, creatures of the shadows and nightmares.

Abruptly, Brangianne was back in Dunadd, at Lughnasadh, when men dressed as lepers had tricked their way into the hall. But this was no trick. This was the real thing.

The crowd fell back as they moved into the hall. Some cried out in alarm, but most gave a hissed intake of breath that drew the fog deeper into the hall. Those nearest the main doors slipped out. Others, at the back, made for the other doors and found no resistance, Andrydd's guards having fled. The hall emptied, leaving only a few of Marc's Council with the courage to stay, or those curious to see, from a safe distance, what was going to happen.

The lepers came forward, some limping, one on crutches, his foot badly deformed. Others had missing fingers, and one had no hand at all. They were half-naked and stank of rotting flesh. Their suppurating wounds were bound with rags, and Brangianne was shocked. *They should at least have clean dressings!* But these bandages were old and caked with yellow fluids, fraying tatters that bound limbs and faces. One of the lepers almost certainly had no nose beneath the bandages that covered his face. Another's head was so well-wrapped in the hood of his cloak that Brangianne shuddered, knowing some horror must be concealed, for the rest of his body was marked with oozing wounds, and his clothes were torn and stained black. Yet this was the one who stepped forward.

'Give her to me, my Lord King,' he rasped.

The disease must be in his throat, she realised. He wouldn't have long to live.

'Archers!' Andrydd recovered from his stunned horror and called out to his men. 'Kill them!' But the few who were left eyed one another fearfully and only reluctantly drew their bows.

'No!' It was the Abbott who spoke. 'They're under God's protection. They die at his will, not ours.'

'Leave them.' Marc stared at the lepers in brutal fascination, then let his gaze slide to Yseult. 'God's will,' he repeated as if musing on the idea, then sat back in his chair. 'Take her, then.'

'No!' The protest echoed around the room, but no-one did anything.

'No!' Corwynal whispered, letting the splintered chair leg drop to the floor. 'No!' But he did nothing either, and just stared, his face bloodless, as the leper came forward and held out a diseased hand to Yseult.

'No!' Brangianne's skin crawled. Nevertheless, she stepped in front of Yseult to protect her, but the girl pushed her out of the way.

'This is God's will,' Yseult said clearly to all who were left to listen, then turned to look at Marc. 'Is this your will, my Lord King! Do you give me to this man?'

'If you'd rather take a leper than a King for your husband . . .'

She smiled, as radiant as a bride. 'I would,' she said, and stepped past Brangianne to take the leper's hand. Brangianne felt as if it was her own hand, felt the wounds seep infection into her skin, felt the disease take root and spread. Then the lepers were gone, taking Yseult with them, all of them vanishing into the fog like a dream, like a nightmare. Then she woke up.

'No!' How could she have let it happen? Why hadn't she done something to stop it? Why hadn't anyone? 'I have to go after her.'

A hand caught her arm. 'No,' Corwynal said bleakly. 'It's too late. Let her go.'

'I can't. She needs me and—'

'*I* need you.' He took her by the shoulders. '*I* need you.'

She stared at him. He was trembling, his eyes wide and dark. She'd come out of the nightmare, but he was still in it.

'Arddu warned me,' he muttered. 'He said I'd regret it. Did I save him for *this?*'

'What are you talking about?' Marc had gone, his Council with him, Hereydd and Andrydd and the guards. They were alone. 'We have to go after her.'

'Trystan warned me too,' he went on, still staring at nothing. '*Whatever happens.* That was the message. But I didn't know. I didn't guess! Trystan you *fool!*'

'Trystan? What has this to do with him?'

He came back to himself and took the deep desperate breath of a drowning man.

'Didn't you see? Don't you understand? He was here. That leper was Trystan.'

'You should go,' Corwynal said when the night had dragged itself close to dawn and Trystan and Yseult still hadn't arrived. The fog was thick, dulling sound, but he could still hear the quiet voices of the marsh – the mournful cries of a pair of curlews passing overhead, the trickle of water close by, and the dry rustle of wind in the rushes. Occasionally, one or other of their horses would stamp or snort, setting their harness jingling. But still no-one came.

Getting away had been easier than Corwynal had expected. Trystan's appearance and disappearance had caused sufficient confusion for Corwynal and Brangianne to escape the Mote without detection. It wouldn't be long, however, before someone began to wonder why Yseult had gone off so happily with a leper, where exactly Trystan had escaped to, and where their servants had vanished to along with Trystan's brother, Yseult's aunt and all their horses. The plan had been for Trystan and Yseult to meet them at the ruined hut in the marsh, upriver from the Mote, then head for the coast at Rascarrel Bay where Corwynal had arranged for Maredydd to take them to Rheged. But much of the cold Midwinter night had passed and still Trystan and Yseult hadn't turned up.

'They'll come,' Aelfric said. 'Be patient.'

'You should go.' It was a conclusion Corwynal been trying to avoid. 'Don't you understand what Trystan's done?'

'Stupid bugger,' Aelfric agreed without heat.

He doesn't understand. He didn't see what I did. The terror of it still ran through him, turning his nerves to smoke. He'd seen, in a horrible foreshadowing, Trystan's face disfigured, his eyes desperate, and Arddu's warning had rung through him like the tolling of a death bell. *One day you will wish he had not lived.* He'd seen into the abyss in the hall of the Mote, and he was still shaking with the horror of it.

'Everyone should go.' he insisted. 'Trystan's a danger to everyone around him.'

Aelfric laughed. 'Nothing new there!'

'Brangianne, tell him.' She was a healer. She'd understand.

'Tell him what?' she asked tartly. 'That you're going to sacrifice yourself? Well, I can't speak for Aelfric and Oonagh, but I'm staying, whether you like it or not.'

'But he touched those creatures, and Yseult touched him.'

'They're not creatures. They're people. Yes, they're people with a terrible disease, but as for touching them, I've known priests who've cared for lepers for many years without contracting the disease.'

'Years? But his hands—'

'You thought that was leprosy? That it strikes that quickly? No, his hands were blistered from the fire. What he did was stupid beyond belief, but it's not a death sentence, and, even if it was, do you think I'd let you face it alone? So stop being so stupid and selfish. We're together now, and if we're to stay together we need to find somewhere we'll be safe. Start thinking about that, and leave me to worry about whatever else might happen.'

'—you stupid bugger,' Aelfric added for good measure. Oonagh snorted in agreement.

Years, she'd said. Maybe never. His fears dissolved into the fog, and even as they did so, the little wind shaking the rushes increased in strength, and the Midwinter dark eased as the fog tore apart into pale streamers lit by a waxing half moon that sailed across a sky studded faintly with stars. Shapes emerged from the darkness – the ruined hut, the hobbled horses, the bleak expanse of marsh, the mudflats and river beyond, Aelfric a bulwark against the night, one hand on his axe, the other around Oonagh's shoulders. And Brangianne, who stepped towards him and into his arms.

'I love you,' he whispered into her hair.

'Then don't leave me,' she whispered back before pulling away. 'Listen . . .'

'Horses!' Aelfric had heard it too and, crouching, ran a little way towards the main track. He returned a few moments later. 'Torches,' he said. 'Coming our way.'

'We'll have to split up,' Corwynal said. 'Aelfric, you draw them off. Brangianne and Oonagh, head north. I'll wait for Trystan.'

'No need,' said a voice from the marsh, and two figures emerged from the last streamers of fog.

'Trys?' Corwynal was torn between relief and a profound desire to strangle him.

'Who else? Did you think we weren't coming? Why can't you trust me for once?'

It was too much. Corwynal had been frightened, but now he was furious.

'Do you know what you've done? What you've risked? Don't you know what might happen to both of you? To the rest of us?'

'It won't,' Trystan said shortly, going over to the horses and boosting Yseult into the saddle of her bay mare.

'What did you do with the leper's cloak, Trys?' Brangianne asked.

'Got rid of it,' he said. 'Got rid of everything I had on and made Yseult change as well.' He was wearing a ragged tunic and leggings, Yseult a brown dress tied with rope. 'Had to steal it. That's what delayed us. Now, if Corwynal's finished complaining, can I suggest we get out of Galloway before they catch up with us?'

'How?' Corwynal asked, vaulting into Janthe's saddle. The torches were nearer now, a ribbon of fire in the night. The breeze carried the smell of horses and smoke as the riders trotted along the track by the river. To the south, on the headland beyond the Mote, a flame bloomed. Moments later it was answered on the far side of the river, then again, on the high land behind Rascarrel Bay.

'Shit,' Trystan said as they watched the beacons spread west and east, summoning riders and ships to pursue the faithless Queen and her trickster lover who'd made a fool of the King and his Court. From the Mote, easing their way into the ebbing tide, the dark shapes of warships could be seen on the silver of the estuary. 'Shit, *shit!*' Trystan exclaimed. 'So much for making for Rheged.'

'Where then?' Corwynal asked.

'North? Up the river valley then cut across west? That's the quickest way to Strathclyde.'

'And the most obvious. Look.' Corwynal pointed down the valley. The group following them had split up, some heading west and north, taking the old trackway that led to Trystan's proposed escape route. The bulk of their pursuers carried on, heading straight towards them. Leading them was a tall man on the moorland pony he favoured, the best tracker Corwynal had ever known.

'Kaerherdin,' Trystan muttered. 'I should have known. Where then?'

Find us somewhere safe, Brangianne had told him. They'd have to outrun the Selgovian or, failing that, outsmart him, and that meant making for the one place Kaerherdin wouldn't expect them to go.

'North,' he said. 'Then east.'

'To Lothian? Gododdin?' Trystan asked.

'Neither. To Selgovia. We're going to demand sanctuary from the one woman on earth least likely to give it. We're going to your wife.'

'They're still after us,' Aelfric announced.

Brangianne turned in the saddle to look back down the valley but couldn't see anything. Corwynal could, however, for he nodded and exchanged a glance with Trystan.

'Kaerherdin guessed then. Pity.'

Pity? A Galloway warband was only a few miles behind them, despite all the doubling back they'd done, all the riding through rivers and over cloud-wreathed moorland. And all to make for a country unlikely to welcome them. How could Corwynal remain so calm? Indeed, he was more than calm. He was alive. All of them were. Trystan's eyes glittered with excitement. Yseult, riding beside him, was so filled with the fire that was her true nature Brangianne thought she could warm her cold hands at her. Aelfric was smiling and even Oonagh seemed ready for anything. *I'm not made for this.* It was a conclusion she'd come to not long after they'd escaped from the Mote, two days before and God knows how many miles in the saddle. She shifted her weight to ease the ache in her back and thighs and tried to ignore the grumbling of her stomach and the worrying absence of feeling in her toes. She was cold, hungry and very, very frightened.

'Beacons.' Trystan nodded nonchalantly at the head of the valley. 'They've seen us then.'

'Good,' Corwynal said.

Good? What about any of this was good? She gripped her reins tightly and tried not to look to her right where the slopes fell dizzyingly away down to the valley floor. The track slanted across the western side of a great bowl in the hills, narrowing as it climbed until there was only enough space for a single rider and, once they reached the snow-line, the rutted track was slicked with ice. One false step and . . .

'Let's get moving.' Trystan kicked his horse into a canter. A canter! He was leading the party, closely followed by Yseult, who clicked her tongue at her mount and sped after him. Corwynal, behind Yseult, looked back at Brangianne.

'All right?' he asked.

No.

'Yes.'

'We'll be fine. Kaerherdin won't lead a Galloway warband into Selgovia, and we're almost there now. The Selgovian warband were Trystan's men once. They'll let us in.'

'But will his wife?'

'Essylt? I can handle Essylt,' he said. Then his calm assurance faltered. 'I hope. Come on. Follow me . . .'

She gritted her teeth, gripped the reins and kicked her horse forward, following her man. They were together now, and they were going to stay together. Once they reached the top of the pass they'd be safe.

But they weren't.

'Damn him! *Damn* him!' Trystan reined in his grey stallion as the gradient eased and the track broadened at the head of the pass. A line of horsemen was waiting for them by a tall stone that stood to one side of the track. On the other side was a carved wooden pole on which was mounted a bleached skull that rocked in the wind, twisting on the pole and seeming to watch them. But, gruesome though this was, Brangianne was more alarmed by the horseman who pushed his way through the others, a tall man on a lathered pony, a man she'd assumed was behind them.

'How did he get ahead of us?' Trystan wanted to know.

'Kaerherdin knows these hills,' Corwynal said and smiled wryly. 'You'll have to do some talking to get yourself out of this one, Trys.'

Trystan glanced back down the track. The Galloway men had reached the head of the pass. The Selgovian warband had advanced to form a line behind Kaerherdin. Brangianne threw an anguished glance at Corwynal, but he shook his head bleakly. If either of the horsemen stepped over the line formed by the stone and the skull-topped post there would be a fight, and not only would they be caught in the middle, they'd be the cause.

'I'm not going to talk,' Trystan said grimly. 'I'll fight. The Selgovian warband are mine, and I'll fight Kaerherdin if I have to.'

'It's not your death he wants,' Corwynal said. 'It's mine.'

'Stop!' Brangianne burst out. 'Why do men always have to fight? Once you've spilled blood, no matter whose it is, there will be no going back. So stop it, both of you.'

Corwynal blinked, not used to being talked to as if he was a naughty child, but he nodded. 'She's right, Trys. Ignore Kaerherdin. Appeal directly to your men. He can't have had time to tell them much, and they may not believe him. Remind them what you've been through together. I'll talk to Andrydd. Brangianne, you come with me, and, if we fail, you'll have to persuade Kaerherdin to back down.'

Brangianne's heart sank; she didn't want to face Kaerherdin's justified resentment, but speaking to Andrydd had been her idea, so she followed Corwynal back the way they'd come to meet him at the head of the pass.

'It's not you I've come for,' the Lord of the Fleet said shortly. 'Just the girl. I'm here to take her back to Galloway.'

'To Marc?' Corwynal asked. 'He gave her away. You heard him in the hall. He gave her to a leper.'

'And we all know who the leper was, don't we? We were tricked.'

'That doesn't matter,' Brangianne cut in. 'Marc didn't know that at the time. None of you did. And yet you didn't try to stop it. Worse, you asked for her yourself.'

Andrydd reddened at that. 'That's beside the point. Marc's come to his senses now.'

'Then he'll have the sense not to risk war with Selgovia,' Corwynal said. 'It will gain him nothing but a girl who doesn't want him and lose him his best fighting men, you among them. You know that as well as I, so back off.'

'You're still in Galloway,' Andrydd glanced significantly at the marker stone and the line of horsemen behind it. 'And it doesn't look as if the Selgovians want to let you in.'

'They will,' Corwynal said shortly, wheeled his horse and trotted back. Brangianne followed him but, looking back, saw Andrydd smile, for it was clear Trystan had failed.

'Your turn,' Corwynal said when she caught up with him. This was what it meant, being together with this man. He was a fighter. So she'd have to be one too. He'd fight to protect her. Now it was her turn to protect him, to protect all of them, even though she had no weapon.

'Kaerherdin – please listen to me—' she began.

'You're offering yourself to me? Is that the deal?' His eyes were like flints. She glanced back, but Corwynal, as she'd insisted, was out of earshot.

'Do you imagine I think so little of you?'

There was a momentary slackening of his rigid expression before it hardened once more.

'Did he send you to plead with me?'

'No,' she lied. 'I came on Yseult's behalf.'

'You made a fool of me. She made a fool of my sister.'

'I made a mistake. We were friends. We should never have tried to be more. I cared for you, Kaer. I still do. But I forgot I only had half a heart to give and you deserved more than half. I fooled myself, not you. We don't choose who we love. If you could have chosen, you wouldn't have picked me. Love isn't convenient. Yseult didn't want to love Trystan, nor he her. They tried very hard to hate one another. Are they to be punished for failing? I'm sure your sister didn't mean to love Trystan but, since she does, she'll surely help him now.'

'But not his lover.'

'No, perhaps not. That's for you to do. You saw what happened at the Mote. You saw how Marc gave away his own wife to a man he believed to be a leper. He gave her to a lingering horrible death, and no-one, including you, tried to stop him.'

Like Andrydd, he reddened, and she pressed home her advantage. 'No matter what you think of her, no-one deserves that. If you don't give her sanctuary, she'll be forced to return to a man who would have killed her in such a way. Can you live with that?' He flicked a glance at Yseult, and Brangianne, seeing his resolution falter, knew she'd won. 'We only want shelter for a night or two. We don't want to stay – only to be allowed to travel on to Iuddeu. Your sister need never know.'

The line of riders had lengthened as more rode out of the woods in answer to the call of the beacon, and one of the new arrivals had pushed forward and overheard them.

'Too late. She already does.'

'Essylt?!' Kaerherdin whirled his horse to stare at his sister, Trystan's wife.

She's only a girl! Brangianne thought. Essylt, Queen of Selgovia, was a small slight creature with the body of a child, but there was nothing childlike about her bearing, or the expression in her pale blue eyes that were regarding Brangianne with cool appraisal.

'So, you're the one,' she said simply. 'I've heard much about you.'

From whom? Brangianne wondered. *From Corwynal?* He'd recognised Essylt too, but his face was closed and wary, and the

Queen's expression, glancing briefly at him, was unreadable. There was history there, Brangianne realised, and wondered what lay between them.

'Ninian spoke of you,' Essylt said. 'As did my men, those who returned from the war in Dalriada. And my husband whom you healed. I believed he was going to Dalriada for your sake. Corwynal convinced me I was wrong, but I wasn't, not entirely, was I?'

'Trystan never cared for me in that way. You've no reason to hate me.'

'No,' the Queen agreed. 'Indeed, I'm in your debt for your care of my men. So, I'm willing to give you sanctuary in Selgovia.'

'Thank you! And . . . and . . . ?'

'—and Corwynal, who was my Steward once. And Aelfric, whom I remember.' She smiled at the Angle before turning her speculative gaze to Oonagh.

'Oonagh's his . . . his wife,' Brangianne said.

Essylt nodded, and only then did she look at Trystan and Yseult. She hadn't done so until now, not because she didn't want to, but because she was afraid. But a Queen can't afford to be afraid, and now, with a visible squaring of her shoulders, she forced herself to look at her husband and his lover, and Brangianne heard her give a low moan that was half desire, half hatred.

Trystan slid from the saddle of his big stallion and knelt at his wife's feet.

'My Queen,' he murmured.

'And this is . . .?' Essylt looked down at her rival, antipathy in every line of her body. Yseult had dismounted too. Standing there, wearing an ugly brown dress, muddy and dishevelled from the journey, her nose red with the cold, her hair tangled, Yseult was beautiful, and Essylt hated her.

'This is Yseult, Princess of Dalriada and the former Queen of Galloway,' Trystan said.

'She's Marc's wife.' Andrydd had ridden to the marker stone, but was careful to keep his mount on the Galloway side of the border. 'I've come to take her back.'

Essylt ignored him. 'The *former* Queen?'

'He gave me away,' Yseult said. 'To a leper. I think that makes me the former Queen.'

'You were set aside then?'

'Yes.'

'Marc wants her back,' Andrydd insisted.

'And you are . . . ?'

Andrydd's mouth thinned at Essylt's cool enquiry, and he looked to Trystan and Yseult, but neither offered to introduce him.

'I'm Andrydd, Lord of Loch Ryan and Master of the Galloway Fleet.'

'You're a long way from the sea, Master of the Fleet,' Essylt observed. 'You may have Marc's authority on his seas, but I wonder if you have it in these hills. You come here making demands, but how do I know you speak for your King? If he wants this . . . this woman returned to him, he must write to me in his own hand under his own seal.' She smiled faintly. 'I give you my word that I'll give the matter my full consideration, but I warn you that I'll act in the interests of Selgovia, not Galloway.'

Andrydd opened his mouth to protest then closed it again, realising, for the moment, that he was beaten.

'You're willing, then, to give his wife sanctuary in Selgovia?'

'No. I give his former Queen sanctuary,' she said. 'And do you know why?' She swept her gaze to include Trystan and Yseult, their companions, Kaerherdin and the Selgovian warband, Andrydd and his men, and raised her voice. 'Shall I tell you all why? I give this woman sanctuary because no queen should ever be put aside. Do you hear me? Never. A queen is a queen until she dies.'

And a husband is a husband. A consort is a consort. Brangianne glanced at Trystan. He'd dropped his eyes, understanding only too well the price of their sanctuary. And Brangianne understood that they weren't safe after all. Not here. Not in Selgovia.

PART II

SELGOVIA, IUDDEU, RAINEACH AND ATHOLL,

WINTER AND SPRING 487-488 AD

WEAKNESSES AND STRENGTHS

Six of them were after him, big men on big horses. Ferdiad was on foot, running blindly through a blizzard, stumbling through thigh-deep heather, patches of scree, and drifts of soft wet snow. It had become his speciality, running away, but a glance behind him showed the riders were gaining on him, so he dived into a dip that concealed a half-frozen stream and slid down its steep bank, hoping to all the gods that this was the right stream.

Is it? he demanded of Arddu, but the God just laughed.

He looked back once more. The riders had slowed a little, fearful for their horses' legs on the rocky slope that dipped down to the river, but they were still close enough for Ferdiad to smell them. There were slashes of red across their faces and one of them carried a red pennant.

I just need to make it to the river . . . He slithered and stumbled down the stream until it plunged over the edge of a low cliff to the river below. Ice-slicked boulders pocked the surface of the fast-flowing water. *Shit!* Running away ceased to be an option. He'd have to stand and fight, and fighting, unlike running, wasn't his speciality. But he swung his shield from his shoulder, fumbled it onto his arm with frozen fingers, drew his sword, backed to the edge and glanced down at the river. Was he man enough to make the jump down onto those jagged ice-skimmed rocks? *No*, he concluded, *I'm not.*

The leader of the six riders laughed at his predicament, muttered something that made the others snigger, tossed his reins to one of his companions and leapt to the ground, drawing his own sword in one swift professional movement, then, for good measure, an axe.

Great! Ferdiad braced himself, but even as he did so, chaos erupted as an animal the size of a hind burst out of a small stand of scrub willow, a little man clinging to its back, two others howling alongside him. The Rider's stallions went mad as the deer – or rather the pony, a mare in season – shot past them. The leader's horse took off after the mare, closely followed by two others. One of the remaining horses bucked its rider and the others circled fruitlessly as their riders tried to restrain their mounts.

Ferdiad smiled at the leader. 'It's just you and me now.' He lifted his sword, but the man didn't raise his shield. He wasn't even looking at him. His whole attention was on something happening behind Ferdiad, something that made him throw his weapons down in disgust.

'Bugger!' he said feelingly. 'You underhand bastards!'

'I think we can take it from here.' Marius, Ferdiad's unit leader, pushed past him as he and the rest of his unit emerged from their hiding place below the lip of the cliff and took control of the red unit's mounts and men. 'Good plan though,' he added. 'Oi! You lot!' he yelled at the three little hunters who were dancing between the hooves of the Riders' frustrated stallions, still howling. 'Tell them to leave off. We can go back to camp now.'

'Tell them yourself,' Ferdiad muttered, sheathed his sword, unstrapped his shield and swung it back onto his shoulder.

'What's up with you?' Marius asked. 'We won, didn't we?' He nodded at the red pennant, now in his men's possession, together with their own black one, and the rest they'd captured. 'We're the champions! Who'd have thought it?'

Not you. Ferdiad remembered Marius' fury when he learned that his unit had been landed not only with the useless Dalriad they'd taken prisoner at the border, but three of the little Forest People.

'A poet and three savages?' he'd asked in astonishment. 'What use are they?'

The savages hadn't understood his words, but his tone had been clear enough and they'd bared their teeth at him, as displeased to be under his command as he was to have them. They might have murdered the Riders and Ferdiad in the night if Azarion, whom they worshipped as a god, hadn't told them not to. It hadn't been a good start, and Ferdiad still shuddered at the memory of his first night sharing quarters with these men. He'd lain awake all night imagining a hand on his thigh, a voice in his ear, but all they'd done was snore very loudly. The following night he'd been too exhausted to stay awake.

If he'd thought his training sessions at Dun Sgiath had been hard, he now knew that Azarion had been kind to him. Mornings in the camp of the Dragon-riders were for training, with sword and shield, with spear and axe and knife. He excelled at none of them, and these men weren't kind. Afternoons were for mock battles between units. Sometimes they went on into the long winter night, in snow and rain, in mud and bog, in forest and loch. Ferdiad forgot what it was like to feel warm and dry. Worst of all was that they never, ever won.

'It's you bastards,' Marius complained, lumping Ferdiad in with the Forest People. 'Dead-weights.'

He had a point. He was a man with one hand, whose fighting abilities were limited, and whose ideas had no value. In Marius' opinion, he was just someone to be protected and whose sole purpose was to communicate with the savages he had no use for. That had to change, Ferdiad decided, and he was the one who had to change it.

He began to tell stories. They'd huddle around a meagre fire wherever they'd camped and he'd tell them tales of battles, of courage and trickery. His tales were from Eriu to begin with, but all peoples have their stories, and gradually the Riders began to tell theirs. Ferdiad would embellish them and translate them into the tongue of the little hunters which, as Azarion had promised, was similar enough to the Attecott tongue for him to talk to them. The Forest People, in their turn would tell stories of their own that Ferdiad would translate for the Riders. He built a bridge of words, fragile perhaps and inclined to sway in the wind, but with time the two peoples came to understand one another. The Riders helped Ferdiad improve his skills, and the Forest People showed him how to read the land. Marius began to use his disparate unit in new ways and, when they worked, Ferdiad was careful to let him think they were the Unit Leader's own ideas. Once they started to win, Marius began to ask Ferdiad for his advice and sometimes even took it. They became a unit with strengths and skills none of the other units had, and now they'd proved it by beating all the others.

'So, are we done now?' Ferdiad asked Azarion when they got back to camp and the winning unit were invited to share The Dragon's fire. The other units had been sent hunting and had come back with two hinds and a boar, so they ate well for once, and the feeling returned to Ferdiad's fingers and toes as his sodden filthy clothes steamed in the heat of the fire. It even stopped snowing, and the sky cleared to let a waning sliver of a moon soar over the mountains, rimming them in silver and bleaching the plain by the river to a pallid frozen grey. He shivered, knowing it would turn colder as the long winter night deepened. There would be frost on his blanket come the morning, for the ground beneath him was like iron. The shallows of the river would be frozen, and the loch, black beneath the moon, would have a skim of ice across its surface by dawn. And he'd be no closer to his goal of being good enough to face Corwynal of Lothian in single combat.

'Do I detect a trace of bitterness?' The Dragon leant forward to poke at the fire. The other men in Ferdiad's unit were sprawled on the far side, some talking quietly, others already asleep, rolled in their cloaks and furs, too tired to notice the cold. Ferdiad was exhausted too, but his anger kept him warm and awake.

'You promised me—'

'I promised nothing. I gave you an opportunity and a task. And you succeeded.'

'In your aims, not mine.'

Azarion shrugged. 'You came to learn and you did.'

'I came to learn how to defeat one man. You said I'd learn how to defeat six.'

'And you did. Your unit won, against all the odds.'

'You know that's not what I meant. My unit might have won, but I didn't. Not alone.'

'Is being alone so important?'

'Yes.'

Azarion smiled ruefully. 'Gave you a hard time, did they? I was afraid they might. But you survived it. You've learned to be part of a unit, to fight back-to-back, to trust your comrades. More importantly, you've discovered your own strengths.'

'My strengths turn out to be telling a good story and running away.'

'Marius told me you excel at tactical thinking. He thinks very highly of you.'

Ferdiad snorted. 'That's not the impression he gave me.'

'Men are complicated creatures. He might not have told you, but I believe him. So stay. Help me. Don't you see what I'm building here? An army of units that can act alone. Not an army of champions, but of units of men, comrades who fight together, who use the various strengths of their men, whether they're fighters or thinkers, scouts or swordsmen.'

'I can see what you're trying to do, but I don't see why. Who are you going to lead this army against?'

'Me? I'll lead them against no-one. I'm too old to be The Dragon, and I know in my heart I'll be the last of them. The world's changing,

Ferdiad, and this army is part of that change. That's why I want you to stay.'

'I didn't come here to help you. I have a purpose. One you and Ciaran between you, have been deliberately keeping me from. Did you think I'd give up? Forget who stole my hand and ... so much more? Well, enough is enough. I'm leaving. I'm going to find Corwynal of Lothian, and then I'll destroy him. I should have left months ago.'

'I can't stop you. But it's a dream, the dream of a boy, not a man.'

'It's all I have, all I want,' he said, clinging desperately to the boy's dream. 'If I survive it—'

'You won't.'

'You think he'll kill me?'

'Is that the only possibility?'

I could kill him. But that wasn't what Azarion meant. A shudder passed through him, and Arddu's voice hissed through the crackle of the fire. *He could laugh at you, as he did once before.*

'It must be my death or his.'

Azarion clicked his tongue in irritation. 'Why throw your life away? Ciaran saved your life for a purpose, as he saved mine. Be part of that purpose, Ferdiad.'

'I'm not turning aside from *my* purpose for the sake of the mad dreams of two old men, whatever they might be. Ciaran sent me to you so you could teach me how to fight, but even now your men defeat me with humiliating ease. I've learned nothing.'

Azarion frowned as if Ferdiad was a pupil who'd failed to grasp some fundamental principle. 'You've learned a great deal, though mostly about yourself. But if you want to fight Corwynal, you'll have to know him too. A man has to know his opponent, as I keep telling you. So, ask yourself what makes him the man he is? What shaped him? What does he love, hate, fear? What makes him strong? What makes him weak? Do you know, for example, that he's two men who fight one another, and that when one of them dies the one who's left will be stronger? You're more alike than you think, for you're two men too – the one who walks his own path, and the one who listens to that trickster God of yours.'

Don't listen to him! Don't trust him!

Azarion's voice cut through the hiss of Arddu's warnings. 'If you survive your encounter with Corwynal, be very sure that the part of you that survives is a man you can live with. But you won't survive that encounter as things stand. You'll need to weaken him first. You need to find out where he's weak.'

He touched Ferdiad lightly on the shoulder and got to his feet, pulled his cloak about him and vanished into the dark. The men who'd been talking on the other side of the fire had fallen silent and were snoring quietly. Ferdiad was tired, but he didn't join them. Instead, he sat by the fire for the whole of that winter's night, watching the moon sink behind the mountains, the stars brighten then fade. He thought about death and life and choices, of weaknesses and strengths. The Dragon was right. He'd be a fool to face Corwynal before he'd discovered his weaknesses. He needed first to find out why he was two men, and how to defeat both of them. And so, when morning came, creeping reluctantly over the mountains, he saddled his horse and headed south to find the one man who could tell him.

A wolf was fighting a snake at the edge of a cliff. At first the snake appeared to be winning, for it twined itself about the wolf's legs, but the wolf stabbed down with a spear, impaling the creature which, in its death throes, wound itself about the spear, breaking it and leaving the wolf without a weapon. But he still had a shield and the snake was still alive, despite being nothing more than a painted symbol on the shield, the serpent and broken spear. The wolf bent down to pick up something in his jaws – a human hand made of silver – but as soon as he touched the hand it melted, flowing like mercury and glowing like forged steel, until it was no longer a hand

but a sword, a lost and ancient sword. The wolf was no longer on the edge of a cliff but on the ridge of a great mountain range, looking south into a landscape consisting of a grid of squares, and the wolf shrank until he was a design carved on one side of a gaming piece. On the other was the serpent and broken spear . . .

Blaize woke with a crick in his neck, no feeling in his feet, and a burning sensation that spread from his belly to his back.

'Curse you, Ciaran,' he muttered, struggling to his feet and, since his feet were numb, falling heavily to his knees in front of the trunk that stood in the corner of his little room in Iuddeu's citadel. He threw back the lid and rummaged inside, tossing out the skull of a cat, a jar of dried-up salve, a belt with the buckle missing, a torn shirt, a dented silver cup and several water-stained manuscripts. Eventually, he found what he was looking for, right at the bottom beneath a mouldy piece of fur that might once have belonged to an otter; a carved wooden box. But when he opened it, he discovered, to his disgust, if not his surprise, that it was empty.

I should have got more from Brangianne when I was in Galloway. But he hadn't needed her special powder while he'd been there and hadn't had time to go searching for her. Now he wished he had, and he cursed Ciaran once more, though it wasn't entirely his fault. Other people were to blame for the state of his stomach – Trystan for beginning that disastrous affair with Yseult, Corwynal for not stopping it, Feargus for getting himself so inconveniently killed, and Ferdiad for not being dead after all.

'Ferdiad's changed,' Ciaran said after telling Blaize the story of the lost hand.

'But it won't be for the better,' Blaize objected. 'And if I know Ferdiad he'll be blaming Corwynal for everything and planning his revenge.'

'No doubt. Which is why I encouraged him to go on a journey,' Ciaran said. 'He wants to kill Corwynal in a fair fight, so I sent him to Azarion so he could learn how to do that.'

'What?!!'

Ciaran was old. He must be well into his seventies. Few men reached that age at all, far less with all of their faculties. The gods knew that even Blaize, a mere youngster in his fifties, had noticed some of his own deserting him. Had the old Abbot gone senile? But Ciaran's eyes were as sharp as ever, as were his powers of observation.

'You think I'm mad?' he asked with a faint mocking smile.

'I've come a long way to discuss Feargus' death with you,' Blaize said stiffly. 'And I find you're playing games with my nephew of whom, despite everything, I'm fond.'

He'd been on his way back to Iuddeu from Galloway when he'd heard about Feargus, for he'd gone via Strathclyde. It was the longer route, but easier in the winter, and while he was in Alcluid a ship from Dalriada had arrived with the news. So Blaize had abandoned his plan of resting for a couple of days, requisitioned a fast horse and thundered the length of the wall in record time – not bad for a man in his fifties – to let Arthyr know. A few days later a messenger arrived from Galloway, sent by Corwynal, confirming Feargus' death.

'Who killed him?' Arthyr asked.

'Creonn, apparently.'

'But actually . . . ?'

'I don't know, but I expect it was Loarn.'

'Find out for certain.'

So Blaize had ridden west once more, a gale of wind and rain behind him, had paid an inordinate amount of silver to the master of a fishing boat to take him to Dalriada and, having arrived, half-drowned and with a cold coming on, had gone to St Martin's to find out what he could. There, in a less than reassuring discussion with Ciaran, he'd learned things he'd rather not have known. Then he'd returned to Iuddeu, having been on the road for what felt like an eternity, in winter, in snow and mud, in a storm of winds, and a tempest of political troubles. Small wonder his stomach was bothering him. He was cold and tired and hungry and suspected he smelled, since washing hadn't been a priority. Now all he wanted to do was sleep, and not dream – especially that particular dream which, however one interpreted it, was not an encouraging one.

'Everything's changed,' Ciaran had told him. 'Everything will have to be rethought.'

'You saw this coming?'

'Not Feargus dying like that. But the troubles in Galloway? I should think anyone could have predicted those.'

Maybe instead of going back to Iuddeu, Blaize should have headed for Galloway once more, but it was too late now. He'd arrived in Iuddeu in a blizzard. He'd seen the snow coming, sweeping out of the hills to the south, hills already white down to the tree-line and beyond. The passes would be blocked and ships stormbound by the southerly gale that was bringing the snow. But there was little point in any case, for Corwynal would have got out of Galloway as soon as he heard the news about Feargus. He'd have made for Rheged or Gwynedd, as Blaize had advised him, to wait for the political storm to blow over. If it ever did.

Blaize looked dolefully at the empty wood box, wondered what he'd done in a previous life to have deserved this one, and wished he'd never pledged himself to Ciaran's vision. 'Damn you,' he muttered, then, in a fit of temper that sent a spurt of pure fire through his belly, threw the box across the room. It clattered into the corner, knocking over a Raven Dance board and scattering the pieces to the floor. 'Typical!' he thought irritably, thinking back to the board set out in Ciaran's room and the way the Abbot had looked at it. 'Everything will have to be reconsidered,' he'd said. 'Including Ferdiad's position.'

'He has no position! He's not – as I keep telling you – to be trusted.'

'I think he can be trusted to act according to his nature.'

'Which is that of a snake.'

'In part,' Ciaran agreed. 'So bear that in mind when – if – he comes to you. We must all be part of his journey, a journey that, if it does nothing else, will keep him away from your nephew until such time as his goal changes.'

'And if it doesn't?'

'Then one or other of them will die. Probably Ferdiad.'

Was that what the dream meant? The snake broken by the wolf? If Ferdiad was mad enough to challenge Corwynal, then that would be the outcome.

Thinking about Ferdiad had given him a headache to add to his other pains, but he was going to have to pull himself together and report to Arthyr. *I'm getting too old for this.* He dragged a hand down his face and felt several days of itchy stubble on his cheeks and jaw. Perhaps he'd better shave, wash at least and change out of his wet clothes – his boots were sodden. He ought to get something to eat; bread and milk might help his stomach. But he didn't have the energy for any of these things and just sat there on his pallet, staring at the chaos in his room.

'Gods, it stinks in here!' A tall figure flung the door open, marched in, kicked an empty flagon out of the way, stepped carefully through the mess on the floor and threw back the shutters of the small window that looked out onto Iuddeu's inner courtyard, letting in a rush of freezing air and rather too much light for a man with a headache.

'You!' Blaize exclaimed, without any real surprise.

'Me,' Ferdiad agreed.

'So, are the rumours about Gwenhwyvar and Bedwyr true?'

Blaize glanced around to see who was listening, but he and Ferdiad were alone in their corner of the hall. Nevertheless, he lowered his voice to answer.

'It's true there are rumours,' he confirmed. 'As to their veracity, I couldn't possibly say. Not that it's any business of mine or yours, so please concentrate on the game.'

'I don't need to.' Ferdiad swept a lazy glance across the board that lay between them. 'I'm winning, in case you hadn't already noticed.'

Actually, Blaize had. Ferdiad was beating him, and not for the first time. Hitherto, there had been few who could beat Blaize at Fidchell; Ciaran, and Rifallyn, more often than not. Corwynal when he put his mind to it, and both Lot and Arthyr were dangerous opponents. But Ferdiad appeared able to win without trying, and Blaize wouldn't be playing at all if there had been anything else to do. But the snow that had driven him to Iuddeu a month before had set in with a vengeance, and travelling any distance was virtually impossible, which also meant no news had reached Iuddeu since Midwinter. To be cooped up in Iuddeu with no news was bad enough, but with Ferdiad . . . ?

'I don't know why I play with you,' he muttered as Ferdiad moved a spearman to spring a trap Blaize hadn't seen coming.

'You play with me because we're stuck in Iuddeu together and, apart from Arthyr, I'm the only person with whom you can have an intelligent conversation. So, Blaize, do you want to converse, or have your revenge in another game?'

Blaize shook his head and shivered. The fires in the hall were dying down, it being the night of Imbolc, and wouldn't be lit until the morning.

'It's too dark to play.' The torches, like the fire, had been allowed to burn out, and the only illumination came from the little Imbolc lamps that flickered on each table, each beam, and at each door and shuttered window, and filled the hall with acrid tallow smoke. There had been the usual celebration down on the water-meadows below the fort, but the freezing temperatures had driven most of the men back to the hall, and now they sat with cloaks and furs about their shoulders and hot wine in their stomachs.

The women had disappeared. They had their own ways of celebrating Imbolc, for this was the night of Briga, Saint Brigid as they'd begun to call the Goddess of hearth and home. To men, however, it was still the Night of Thresholds, a night when Blaize would have to make a decision, one way or the other.

He glanced across the board at Ferdiad, whose green eyes flickered like those of a cat in the faint light from the little lamps. *Is Ciaran right? Has he changed?* Ferdiad was certainly different from the man who'd come to Iuddeu a year before in search of an ally against The Dragon. Now he was here, in part, on The Dragon's behalf. But that wasn't the only difference.

'I'm Ferdiad Silverhand now,' he'd announced when he'd arrived in Iuddeu five or six days before. Blaize had been fascinated by the artifice of the hand, but Ferdiad seemed to regard it as a minor nuisance, and if he was angry at the loss of his hand, or hated the man who'd struck it off, he concealed it well. But he'd always been good at that, so no change there. Yet in other ways he was different. He was certainly stronger physically, and was wearing a sword that, by all accounts, he knew what to do with. Perhaps that was the reason he was more at ease with himself. Quixotic unreliable Ferdiad had become stronger and harder and considerably more dangerous.

Yet, despite these changes, Blaize still sensed something broken inside the man, something that would give way if anyone made the mistake of relying on him. He suspected the real Ferdiad, the one behind all those shields and mirrors, was very different from the man who sat opposite him, smiling faintly, a challenge in his unsettling green eyes. Only once had Blaize seen beneath Ferdiad's armour, on the night he'd arrived in Iuddeu and Blaize had told him Feargus was dead. There had been no simulation in either his shock or grief.

'I didn't know you cared for him,' Blaize said when Ferdiad had mastered himself.

'Neither did I.'

And a man who didn't know himself was dangerous indeed.

So why had he come to Iuddeu? Why, night after night, did he seek out Blaize's company? Why, night after night, did he talk about everything and anything, amusingly, engagingly, informatively, and only lightly touch on Corwynal, Trystan or Yseult as if they were nothing more than half-forgotten acquaintances. Had the changed Ferdiad come to his senses and accepted that Corwynal, in striking off his hand, had saved his sanity and possibly his life, and that vengeance was not only ridiculous – for how could anyone hope to face Corwynal in single combat and survive? – but unnecessary? He hadn't even asked where Corwynal was.

Too many questions. Why? What if? Whether? But on the Night of Thresholds, the night balanced between winter and spring, doubt seemed an appropriate state of mind. To trust, or not to trust? To tell, or not to tell? Blaize knew Ciaran wanted to bind Ferdiad to his purpose, and he could see why. The Brotherhood needed new blood. They were all getting old, and Ferdiad was young, intelligent, knowledgeable, flexible . . .

Blaize picked up one of the gaming pieces, a polished disc of holly, the fine-grained wood carved with the likeness of a sword on one side and a staff on the other. Those who followed Chrystos said it was an Abbot's staff. Others believed it belonged to a druid, but both understood that the staff represented knowledge, as the sword symbolised strength. On impulse, thinking of his dream of the gaming piece with the wolf and serpent carved on opposite sides, he tossed the piece onto the board where it spun on its edge. The light of the flickering Imbolc lamps picked out the carvings and, as it spun, sword became staff became sword, over and over, until they were one and the same. Eventually, the piece slowed and fell, settling onto the empty board between them, the staff symbol uppermost, for knowledge.

Blaize made his decision then – because of the dream, because of Ciaran's need, because of his own doubts, and because the little Imbolc lamps were burning their way through this long winter night. And as soon as he made it, he knew a threshold had been crossed, and that his own death would result from it, that Ferdiad would be part of it, and that other deaths and other griefs would come of it also.

He was wrong about so many things, but he was right too. The decision had been made, and though the threshold lay before him, uncrossed as yet, he wouldn't step back. For if he did, the lamps that burned this night would go out, one by one, and the morning would bring no dawn.

'I've changed my mind,' he said. 'Let's play again, but not this game. There's another one I want to show you . . .'

THE GAME

'**L**isten!'

Brangianne woke to Corwynal's voice in her ear, his breath on her cheek, and she was back in the barn in Carnadail, in the sultry heat of summer, listening to Trystan plucking a harp. She'd been happy then.

'Listen,' he repeated. She opened her eyes to find herself in a dark little guest hut in Meldon, the main settlement of Selgovia, at the end of winter. There were skulls hanging from the rafters. She'd got used to those, but not to the incessant wind that blew through the cracks in the wall. The place was freezing, but she was happy here too.

'Listen to what?' She snuggled beneath the blankets and furs and pressed the whole of her body against the warmth of his. He put his arms around her and laughed softly.

'Have you gone deaf, woman? Listen!'

All she could hear was the sounds of the settlement – the voices of men and women, horses whinnying and stamping in the horse-lines, a flock of chickens squabbling, a pig snuffling outside the door, and water dripping. There was nothing unusual about any of that.

'The snow's melting,' he said. 'The thaw's come at last so we'll be able to leave, thank the gods!'

There was relief and excitement in his voice, but Brangianne's heart sank. She'd come to like living in Meldon, despite the cold. She liked these odd taciturn people. She'd even grown fond of Essylt, their Queen, and had spent time discussing healing with her. But she'd known their stay in Selgovia couldn't last for ever. Sooner or later they'd have to leave, and that would be for the best. Nevertheless, she was happy. She and Corwynal were together, and there was no hiding anymore. She was able to spend much of her days and all of her nights with the man she loved, and finally – *finally* – they'd been able to talk, to tell one another their hopes and fears for the future, and confess secrets neither had told anyone else. Not all of them of course. For her part, Brangianne hadn't told him about the child she'd lost – his child. And he'd been reticent about his childhood. There was something dark there, some shadow her love couldn't banish. But he'd tell her one day. She could wait; the rest of their lives lay before them. All they needed was somewhere to build a life together, and, until that morning, when the thaw had reached the snow-girt uplands of Selgovia, she'd hoped it might be in Meldon. But that was just a dream. There were too many tensions in the land-locked pagan land, too many embittered hearts.

Facing Kaerherdin had been difficult at first. His antagonism had been bad enough, but the pain he tried and failed to hide had been worse. She was a healer; she was supposed to heal pain, not cause it. So she'd been relieved when he left Meldon not long after they'd arrived, after a furious argument with his sister, and had gone back to the border fort where they'd spent the first night in Selgovia. The argument would have been about Trystan and Yseult, Brangianne assumed. Kaerherdin must have told his sister everything that had happened in Galloway – the rumours, the trial, what everyone believed to be the truth. But Essylt had refused to believe him, and had sent him away.

Poor child! Essylt was like Marc, suspecting the worst but refusing to face up to it, though she was far from being a fool. She might be young, might look like a child, but there was steel behind those pale blue eyes, and she ruled Selgovia with a firm hand. Brangianne knew Corwynal liked her; he'd been her Steward once, and at one time was supposed to have married her. 'Should I be jealous?' she'd asked, teasing him. 'Did you love her? 'I think there's enough jealousy in Selgovia without you adding to it,' he'd replied wryly.

Yseult and Essylt hated one another, as might have been expected, and Trystan, trying to please them both, was looking harassed. One of them, sooner or later, was going to shatter the pretence that Trystan was Essylt's husband and Yseult nothing more than the unjustly wronged wife of his uncle.

'Why can't he just tell her?' Yseult paced to and fro in the guest hut she'd been given. Her servants, who were probably Essylt's spies, were absent for once, and Yseult was giving full rein to her famous temper. 'Why can't he simply ask for his freedom? No, *demand* it! She's nothing to him, and if she hasn't worked that out by now, I feel sorry for her! Well, I've had enough. If he won't tell her, I will!'

'Don't! Please, Yseult. We're here on sufferance already. I know it's been too long, but there's not much we can do about the weather. As soon as it improves, we'll leave, and you can forget all about her.'

But Brangianne knew Yseult brooded on the woman Trystan had married, and had begun to doubt Trystan's love. The happiness that had burned through her like a fire when they'd escaped from Galloway, laughing at the world, had died back to ashes, and despite the fact that she was beautiful and Essylt wasn't, she was jealous of the little Queen. 'He never comes to me,' she complained.

'How can he when your servants are with you all the time?'

'He goes to *her!*'

Brangianne didn't think he did, but Yseult refused to listen and carried on complaining.

'It's the child,' Oonagh said later. 'She'll get over it.'

'I don't notice you turning into a shrew.'

'No, but then I'm not unhappy, am I?' She placed a complacent hand on her swelling stomach. Yseult was about a month behind her, and, though her initial sickness had gone, there was, thank goodness, no visible sign of her pregnancy as yet, not in the clothes she was wearing. Feeling the cold, she kept herself bundled up in her fur cloak and warmest clothes, even in Meldon's hall, which Essylt took as an insult to her hospitality.

'Are you cold, my lady? I'm afraid we're a hardy people and tend to forget about the softness of you lowland folk,' she said waspishly. 'No doubt you'll be glad to return to the luxuries of Galloway when the snows clear – if your husband will have you back, that is.' She placed a possessive hand on Trystan's arm.

Yseult looked to Trystan to defend her, but he just closed his eyes as if he was weary of it all.

'He doesn't love me!' Yseult wailed later. 'I left Marc for a man who doesn't love me!'

Yes, Brangianne thought, *it's past time we left Selgovia*. Now the thaw had arrived, bringing the world with it.

'Brangianne?' Oonagh was outside, hammering at the door. 'Corwynal? You'd better come . . .'

They looked at one another in alarm, jumped up, scrambled into their clothes and went outside.

'A messenger's arrived,' Oonagh told them. 'From Galloway.'

When they reached the hall there was no-one with Essylt but Kaerherdin. Presumably he'd accompanied the Galloway messenger who'd brought the letter Essylt was reading. She didn't look up when they came in, not even when Aelfric and Trystan arrived, nor, a few moments later, when Yseult came into the hall, having received the same warning.

'Where's the messenger?' Corwynal asked Aelfric quietly.

'At the gatehouse. He's to take an answer straight back.'

Corwynal nodded. 'Get the horses.' Aelfric and Oonagh left the hall, but Essylt still didn't look up, and Brangianne had to suffer

Kaerherdin's reproachful gaze as he took in her dishevelled appearance, and his look of hatred at Corwynal. But she bore it calmly. *I'm not ashamed. Why should I be?*

She was so taken up with staring Kaerherdin down she didn't notice Essylt had gone white until the parchment slipped from her fingers and fell to the floor. It rolled towards Corwynal who stooped to pick it up. Kaerherdin stepped forward to retrieve it, but Essylt lifted a hand. 'Let him read it,' she said in a flat voice. 'Let him read it out loud.'

'It's Marc's own hand,' Corwynal said. 'And his seal.'

Brangianne, remembering the Marc they'd left at the Mote, expected a letter full of vitriol and demands, but this was from a King who'd recovered his senses. He stated, quite simply, that accusations had been made against his wife, Yseult, alleging adultery with his nephew, Trystan of Lothian. A trial had been held, but both of the accused had escaped before it had finished. The trial, however, had continued in their absence, and both had been found guilty.

'Guilty,' Essylt said in a hollow tone. 'Of adultery.'

'I *told* you!' Kaerherdin said triumphantly. 'But you wouldn't listen.'

'Be silent!' she snapped. 'You were in Galloway. Why didn't you stop this happening?'

Kaerherdin opened his mouth then closed it with an audible click of his teeth. Essylt wasn't a woman who could be reasoned with at this moment, because she was close to breaking. Like Marc, she was facing the one thing she'd always dreaded, the thing she'd closed her mind to.

'Read out the sentence,' she ordered Corwynal.

'Banishment for Trystan,' he announced, without surprise but, reading on, his eyes widened as at something unexpected. 'And for Yseult – forgiveness. Her position's to be restored. She's to continue as his wife and Queen of Galloway.'

Yseult laughed at that. 'I don't want his forgiveness. I don't want to be his wife or his Queen. I'm not going back.'

'Yes, you are.' Essylt glared at her. 'Read to the end,' she told Corwynal.

He read on, looking troubled as he did so, and looked up. 'He demands Yseult's return to Galloway. If she's here in Selgovia, she must be sent back. Failure to do so will have regrettable consequences, he says. He means war.'

'She's not going back,' Trystan said flatly.

'You think I'd go to war with Galloway for *her?*' Essylt snarled.

'You needn't,' Corwynal said quickly. 'We'll leave Selgovia. You can tell Marc's messenger you're sorry, but he's too late, because we've already left. Tell him we've gone to Iuddeu to put Yseult's case to Arthyr.'

'No,' she said stubbornly. 'She's going back to her husband. And my husband is staying here, with his wife.'

She was a Queen. She thought that gave her the power to force the world into the shape she wanted, a world where people loved where they ought to, not where they did. *Poor child*, Brangianne thought once more. She'd never give up. She'd always cling to Trystan, the shining knight of her dreams. She'd cling to the vision and not the man. Even now, she imagined she could turn the man into the vision. His silence should have told her otherwise, and the fact that he left it to Corwynal to speak.

'Essylt, please . . . We all make mistakes. Trystan's at fault here, in so many ways, but you aren't without fault too, and nor am I. This marriage was over long ago. We both know that.'

She flushed a little as if remembering something she'd put to the back of her mind. Brangianne shot a look at Corwynal who was giving the distinct impression of a man trying not to say too much. *Should I be jealous?* she'd asked him. She'd been jesting. Now she wondered if she'd been right to do so. There was a threat in his voice. *Don't make me tell everyone.*

'Let Trystan go,' he went on. 'Give him his freedom, not for his sake but for yours. There are many men who'd be proud to be chosen by you, men who'd give you children.'

What? Brangianne stared at the man she thought she knew, but clearly didn't. He was holding Essylt's gaze, like a man facing an opponent.

'No,' she said stubbornly, and Brangianne heard him sigh.

'Essylt—' he began.

'Leave it,' Trystan cut in. 'It doesn't matter. None of this matters. I want my freedom, but I'm not going to beg or threaten. I'm just going to take it.' He put an arm around Yseult's shoulders. 'In truth I've taken it already. Yseult's my wife in everything that matters. She's the other half of my soul, and soon to be mother of my son.'

Essylt's high colour vanished, and she turned as pale as freshly-skimmed milk. Her face crumpled first, then her body, and she slumped in the chair, bending over as if her spine had broken. Her face dropped into her hands, and a strange sound came from her, a low moan of distress that by degrees rose to a wail of grief and became a shriek of anger. It was a sound that came from the ground beneath them, a wind that swirled into the hall, shaking the walls and the rafters. The hangings billowed outwards like an army going into the attack, and the skulls hanging from the roof danced, their jawbones clacking with the laughter of the insane. It was a sound that rooted everyone to the spot with horror as Essylt slid from the chair to the floor, and crouched over, one arm clutching her body as if to hold herself together, the other beating the ground with her fist.

Brangianne was the first to move. She went over and crouched beside her then put an arm around her shuddering shoulders. 'My Lady . . . Essylt . . .'

'You don't understand,' she whispered.

'I do,' she said quietly. 'I know what it is to want a child and believe another woman has stolen it.'

The wailing stopped abruptly and Essylt's sobs eased. She looked up, her red-rimmed eyes staring into Brangianne's. 'He won't give you a child, you know,' she hissed, glaring at Corwynal before throwing off Brangianne's arm. She rose unsteadily to her feet, then took her seat once more, arranging her skirts around her for all the world as if the last few moments hadn't happened.

'Get out,' she said calmly. 'All of you, get out. Leave my lands and never come back.' Her eyes were still rimmed with red, but they were as hard and lifeless as a dried-out river pebble as she turned to Trystan. 'You're no longer my Consort. You no longer command my warband. My brother holds that position now.' Kaerherdin smiled at that. 'You'll never again call on me or my men, and if you ever go to war you can expect to find Selgovia among your enemies. Well . . . ?' she snapped. 'What are you waiting for? You wanted your freedom? Then take it. You want to live the rest of your life with that slut? Then take her.'

Kaerherdin drew his sword. 'You heard my sister. Get out before I kill you.' He looked from Trystan to Corwynal. 'Both of you.'

He wasn't a match for either of them, far less both, but it didn't matter. Trystan and Yseult turned towards the door, but Corwynal, ever the peacemaker, ignored Kaerherdin's threat and stood his ground.

'Essylt, please, not like this . . .'

'I curse you,' Essylt said, no longer a poor child but a woman with revenge in her soul. She pointed her finger at Trystan. 'You think to live for love? You will die for it! And I'll be there to see you die.' She swept her finger about the room, pointing to each of them in turn. 'All of you will be there, watching him *die!*'

It had been entertaining at first, but now Ferdiad was weary of the battle with Blaize – the feint and counter feint, the thrust and parry, the ground gained and given. After several days of being trapped by the weather in Iuddeu with Blaize he was only a little closer to finding out what he'd come for.

Corwynal hadn't been in Iuddeu, to his relief, for he knew he wasn't ready to meet him, though Corwynal's presence in Iuddeu had only been a remote possibility. He was probably still in Galloway, for he wouldn't leave Trystan, and Trystan was unlikely to leave Yseult, no matter who she was married to. But maybe they'd left. If so, where might they have gone? Rheged seemed the most likely place, not only because it was the sensible option, but because Blaize had carefully not mentioned it.

But that wasn't what he was here to find out, and Ferdiad was getting tired of questions, no matter how subtle. Maybe he should just come out with it.

Tell me your nephew's secrets so I can kill him.

Tell me why you want to kill him.

He couldn't do that, so he'd turned to other sources of information. Arthyr had pulled back the troops from the outposts before the snows arrived, so the fort was full of bored men with little to do but gamble and gossip, men who'd served all over the Kingdoms of the North, and some of them remembered Corwynal of Lothian. By carefully sifting snippets of information, Ferdiad was able to piece together his enemy's history and discover a gap, a time when it wasn't clear where he'd been or what he'd been doing, the time after he'd left The Island but before he'd returned to Lothian, the time he'd been in Atholl.

But Blaize headed him off whenever the question of Atholl came up. 'I've no idea,' Blaize had claimed. 'I was banned from Atholl many years ago and haven't been back.'

Interesting! Ferdiad had thought, but hadn't pressed him further. He'd learn no secrets in Iuddeu. He'd have to go to Atholl itself, a place that didn't welcome strangers.

He yawned and stretched. It was late, and the hall had turned cold, but he'd grown so used to the freezing conditions in Raineach that it felt luxurious, and he was reluctant to get back on the road once more. Anyway, Blaize had promised him another game, a different game . . .

At first sight, the board, set out on a chest in Blaize's cramped and smelly chamber, looked like any other Fidchell board. It was laid out in squares, ready for the carved wooden pieces, but when Blaize moved one of the little Imbolc lamps closer, Ferdiad saw an irregular pattern of colour beneath the grid. It looked more like a map than a game – because that was what it was. Before him, in miniature, lay the Kingdoms of the North, from the Wall to the Orc Islands, from the lands of Gododdin to those of the Smertan. The pieces were different too, being carved with the signs of the Kingdoms and others he didn't recognise. This game – if it was a game – was much more complicated than Fidchell.

'This is our world,' Ferdiad concluded, looking across the board at Blaize, who was watching him narrowly as he picked up one piece after another. 'This is Arthyr.' He fingered a counter with a carving of a bear on one side, then picked up another that had been set to one side, and saw, with a sorrow that still surprised him, that it bore Feargus' sign of the swan. Its place on the board had been taken by a piece bearing Loarn's symbol of the gull. This, he understood, was their own times. This was the battle, and here, within the gridded board, might lie the answers he was looking for, though, as ever, there were more questions than answers. 'What's this?' He picked up a piece carved with an oak-leaf, the same symbol as the one on the medallion hanging about his own neck.

'You'll find out,' Blaize said. 'If you want to play, that is.'

'You'll have to tell me the rules.'

'There are none.'

They played for the whole of that night. The little Imbolc lamps sank lower and lower, their flickering light washing the board with sudden piercing illumination, as if through clouds drifting over a sunlit upland. It seemed to Ferdiad that they played with the world itself, like gods, that on their board men died and were reborn, triumphed or were defeated, and kingdoms waxed and waned like the tides. He hadn't expected to be any good at a game he'd never played, especially one with no rules, but it came easily to him, and though Blaize won at first, Ferdiad beat him the next time. Even when they changed sides, they were evenly matched, first one winning then the other. Finally, however, as light seeped through the cracks in the shutters and the lamps guttered out to coils of acrid smoke, they played a game neither could win.

'You see?' Blaize asked quietly. This, then, was where Blaize had been leading him, this point of balance, this threshold on the Night of Thresholds. 'Nine times out of ten, one side or other will win, and the board – our world - will be washed in blood. If Arthyr can hold the Kingdoms between the Walls together, he'll win. If Drest Gurthinmoch can hold the Caledonian Confederacy together, he'll win. It doesn't matter. Either way we lose.'

'We?'

Blaize shrugged. 'People. Our descendants – not that either of us is likely to have any. What do you think will happen to the monasteries if the Caledonians win? Or to the druid schools if Arthyr wins? Either way, knowledge will be lost and, once lost, it's gone forever, and whoever wins will rule a diminished people all the more easily crushed by the forces of chaos.'

'A bleak view, Blaize.'

'But not without hope. There's one other outcome.' He gestured to the board between them, the pieces set out in a stalemate. 'This one. So, do you understand now?'

Ferdiad looked down at the board, at the pieces, their positions, and remembered how, in this last game, they'd moved. He picked up one of the counters carved with the oak-leaf and turned it over to find the symbol of the wolf, of Lothian. One after another, he turned over the oak-leaf counters to discover other symbols carved there, some of which he recognised and some he didn't. He set them back once more and looked at Blaize. 'What do you call yourselves?' he asked and had the satisfaction of seeing that Blaize hadn't expected him to understand so quickly.

'The Brotherhood. Although we aren't brothers, nor even all men.'

Scathach, Ferdiad thought. *Azarion too. That's what his army is for – to hold the balance. And there will be others.*

'So, I'm to be a piece in this game of yours, am I?' He tugged at the medallion about his neck, breaking the thong, and laid the piece down on the board. 'Ciaran gave me this.'

'That doesn't mean you're a piece. It means Ciaran believes you could become a player,' Blaize said evenly. 'That's what we are. By playing the game, we try to bring about this outcome, this balance, for only in balance will everything of value survive. If it doesn't, the dark will come and there will be no dawn. But even if that happens, we still have a role – to be the last lamp, to be a memory and a story, to be the last song sung.' He reached out to snuff out the remaining Imbolc lamp that still bore a flame, but when he'd done so a spark still remained in the wick and it flared back into life once more, a flame that burned briefly before guttering away to nothing. Ferdiad imagined he heard the note of a harp, the last note of a song, humming its way to silence.

'So what you're offering is a long fight against the odds, then a life on the run? At best?'

Blaize didn't even smile. 'Yes.'

'And the price?'

'You know what the price is. This is no time for mindless vengeance.'

'Then why—' He leant across the board towards Blaize, '—is no one other than you trying to stop me? Why am I still alive?'

'Because Ciaran believes in you.'

Ferdiad leant back. 'And what do you believe?'

'That he's wrong. That you're a wild piece, a force for the very chaos we fight to conquer. I believe you're wedded to a dark god who'll never let you go. That you're a snake who sheds its skin, a snake who consumes himself. That you should never – ever – be trusted.'

Blaize's voice was hard and very, very certain.

'Plain speaking for once,' Ferdiad said with a smile to conceal his disquiet at the other man's words. 'So why are you telling me all this?'

'Because Ciaran asked me to, and I trust *him*. Because I hoped there was a chance, even if it was a faint one, that he was right about you. But he isn't, is he?'

Ferdiad shook his head. 'I intend to kill Corwynal of Lothian. And it isn't mindless.'

Blaize shrugged. 'You can try. But I warn you – you won't succeed. You won't be *allowed* to succeed.'

'Why? Is he one of you?'

Blaize laughed sourly. 'No.'

'But he's important?'

'Everyone's important,' Blaize replied a little too quickly.

Ferdiad looked down at the board once more. Corwynal might be the son of a king, but he was unacknowledged. Trystan was the one who mattered for Lothian, so it must be Trystan who was Lothian's wolf piece. Yet there were two wolves on the board since it was Atholl's symbol also. Corwynal of Lothian was also Talorc of Atholl. *He's two men*, Azarion had told him. *One of them has to die.* Which one though? He looked across at Blaize, but Blaize' attention was on the piece Ferdiad had slammed down on the board, his own. He'd turned it over to look at the symbol carved on the back – the snake crossed with the broken spear – and seemed surprised by what he saw, for his eyes flew – for a moment – to Atholl.

'It's just a game,' Blaize said with a shrug, tossing the piece back to Ferdiad. 'It's all nonsense.' He swept the board free of the counters, scooped them into a bag and folded up the board. 'But it's passed the night and look – it's morning.' He threw back the shutters to let the dawn air flood in, but it wasn't as cold as it had been. During the night of Imbolc, while the little lamps had burned to mark the turning of winter into spring, the weather had changed. The wind had swung to the south, and the air was milder, the fort loud with the sound of water dripping from the blankets of snow on the thatched roofs.

'Weather's turned,' Blaize observed. 'The roads will be open now, so I guess you'll be on your way. Where were you thinking of heading?' It was as if the night hadn't happened, the games hadn't been played, the offer made or refused, the secret concealed. It was as if they were friends, brothers even.

Ferdiad considered saying nothing and letting Blaize sweat, but in the end he relented. 'Dalriada. To kill Loarn.'

'Why?'

'Oh, just mindless vengeance. As you pointed out, it's a failing of mine. But then, all men have their weaknesses.'

Blaize nodded, but said nothing more, not even goodbye.

Ferdiad left by the west gate and travelled some way on the road that led to Loch Laoimin, but before he'd reached the final fort in Arthyr's line of glen-blocking fortifications, he'd deciding it was time to lose the tail Blaize had sent after him. It was easy. He hadn't spent time with the Dragon-riders without learning how to lose a tail, and by the end of the day he was heading across country for Atholl and for answers.

The medallion was back around his neck, the oak leaf on one side, the snake on the other, the symbol he didn't understand. But Blaize had recognised it and been so surprised that his guard had dropped. In a fold of Ferdiad's tunic was another piece, one he'd snatched while Blaize had bent down to recover a couple of counters that had fallen to the floor. This was the wolf piece of Atholl and, carved on the reverse, was the same symbol. Which had to mean something. Something significant. Because Corwynal of Lothian might not be important, but Talorc of Atholl was. The world would be a different place once he'd killed him.

Destroyed him, Arddu reminded him, speaking for the first time since he'd left Raineach. *And once you've destroyed him, you'll destroy Ciaran of Dalriada and his Brotherhood. The gods are not mocked. No mere man can control the fates of men. No man may play the game of Kingdoms and expect to win. No man can make himself a god. No man can hold back the dark.*

'Of course not.' But even as Ferdiad pledged his allegiance to Arddu, he hid in the deepest chamber of the ruin that was his soul the memory of a flame in the last Imbolc lamp, and the sound of a harp humming into silence.

'Blaize?! Where the Five Hells have you been?'

Arthyr stormed into the hall and marched over to Blaize, who looked up in surprise. He'd been in the hall for the past few hours as Arthyr might have discovered if he'd bothered to ask.

Blaize had been celebrating with a quiet-eyed man of medium height and unremarkable features, a man no-one noticed, someone so anonymous even Blaize had trouble calling him to mind, despite the man being his most reliable agent.

'He headed west. I followed him as far as Malling before I lost him, but it looked as if he was making for Dalriada,' he told Blaize.

As Blaize had hoped. He'd been afraid he might still be going after Corwynal, and though neither of them had mentioned Rheged, that was probably where Corwynal was. There or Galloway. But it looked as if Ferdiad had other matters to attend to first. *I'm going to kill Loarn.* Blaize didn't doubt he intended to and wondered if he ought to warn Ciaran. On the other hand, the world would be a better place without Loarn, and had the added benefit of being a distraction from Ferdiad's avowed intention of getting revenge on Corwynal. So Blaize's nephew would be safe, at least for the moment.

Ferdiad needs time, Ciaran had told him. *This conviction that he needs to kill Corwynal, whatever the reason, must be allowed to die like a fever. They mustn't meet until Ferdiad's ready to see what he risks. So persuade him. Tell him who we are and what we do. Intrigue him. Challenge him. Turn his mind in another direction.*

So Blaize had done as Ciaran asked and told him about the Brotherhood. *So you think to offer me a long fight against the odds then a life on the run?* Well put. Ferdiad had seen right to the heart of it, which was why Ciaran wanted him to join them. But why give Ferdiad a medallion with that particular symbol on the reverse?

It didn't really matter, however, given that Ferdiad had refused – at least for the moment. But, whatever he decided in the end, Blaize had done his best, and that contributed as much as anything to his good mood – a mood that darkened now at the sight of Arthyr's face. The War-leader was holding, crushed in one visibly shaking hand, a roll of parchment. Whatever it contained must be serious indeed to have this effect on a man not given to displays of public emotion.

'Read it!' He tossed it to Blaize, then loomed over him while he read the contents.

'Oh,' he said weakly once he finished, and his good mood trickled away like wine from a spilled cup.

'I thought you'd dealt with all that.'

All that. Even now Arthyr would not put a name to it, for 'all that' was the rumours about Trystan and Yseult that had reached Iuddeu at the beginning of winter, rumours that Blaize, on returning from his trip to Galloway, had dismissed as no more than gossip, not because they were false – they weren't – but because that was what Arthyr wanted to hear. Because if the whispers in Galloway were true, the whispers in Iuddeu might be true also. And Arthyr didn't want to believe them, which accounted for his anger.

'I believed they'd gone to Rheged,' Blaize said, cursing Corwynal. Had he no control over the boy at all?

'Well, they haven't. If they had, Marc wouldn't be demanding – *demanding!* – his wife's return. Which means they're still in the Lands between the Walls.' He scowled at the crumpled parchment. 'He'll have sent this to everyone, you know. God knows when. The weather's held up messages all over the country. But it can't be a co-incidence that I just received a message from Lothian—'

'Trystan's in Lothian?' Blaize asked hopefully, but Arthyr's scowl deepened.

'Lothian is one place he isn't, because Rifallyn's written to me enquiring about the current location of his son and heir. Worse, he's on his way to Iuddeu to 'discuss the matter'. The letter precedes him, so he could arrive at any time.'

Which was a distinctly unpleasant prospect. Blaize might expect Corwynal to control Trystan, but Rifallyn expected Blaize to control Corwynal. And while Blaize might have an acerbic tongue when it came to the failings of his minions, his half-brother's sarcasm could eat through metal.

So, where *were* Trystan and Corwynal? If they hadn't gone to Rheged, Dalriada would have been the next most obvious destination – until Feargus had got himself killed so inconveniently. Strathclyde then? Dumnagual would be delighted to embarrass Marc, but wouldn't risk war with Galloway. The same went for South Manau and Gododdin. So, if they were still north of the Wall and weren't in Lothian, that just left Selgovia. But surely Trystan wouldn't take another woman, especially the Queen of a neighbouring kingdom, to his own wife?

'Where are they?' he muttered. It was a rhetorical question, but Arthyr leant both fists on the table in front of Blaize and growled at him.

'They're here, in Iuddeu. They just arrived. Trystan and Marc's wife, Corwynal and some woman claiming to be the girl's aunt, that Angle, and a red-headed woman with a tongue in her head and no fear of using it. They demand sanctuary,' Arthyr went on. 'Marc demands his wife back. Rifallyn demands to know where his sons are. And, to complete this charming state of affairs, I've also received a letter from Loarn – appalling Latin, the man's a barbarian – notifying me of his accession to the throne of Dalriada, pointing out that all treaties will have to be renegotiated and informing me that since his son was betrothed to Yseult prior to her marriage to Marc her marriage is therefore invalid and so he demands – *demands!* – that I return her to him.'

Blaize doubted if Yseult had ever been betrothed to Domangart, but the truth didn't matter.

'This is . . . not good,' he said.

'A masterly piece of understatement! Well, Blaize, you're my advisor. So, advise me.'

Blaize took a deep breath and tried to calm the thudding of his increasingly unreliable heart. Bemoaning the situation and trying to apportion blame wasn't going to help. It was the consequences that needed to be dealt with.

'First – you reply to Loarn,' he said with decision. 'You congratulate him on his accession to the throne, look forward to good relations and meeting him in person, blah, blah, blah. You make no reference to this supposed betrothal and mention in passing that you understand Yseult has left Galloway but you're unaware of her present location. He won't have his own spies in Iuddeu, not yet. As for Rifallyn, if Trystan's here you'll have no difficulty in answering that particular demand. Assuming they're still here when he arrives, you can leave Corwynal to deal with his father.' *Rather him than me*, he thought thankfully. 'With regard to your 'guests', I suggest you arrest them, pending further enquiries.'

Arthyr had already done so. The women had been consigned to Gwenhwyvar's care – which might distract her from Bedwyr for a time. Trystan, Corwynal and Aelfric had been disarmed and taken to Arthyr's private chamber.

'This is outrageous!' Trystan complained as soon as Arthyr entered the room, Blaize behind him. A couple of Arthyr's men were guarding the door, spears in hand, but Arthyr gestured for them to leave. Then, without speaking, he took his chair, the only one in the room, and stared coldly at his guests. Blaize shot a glance at Corwynal in which reproach was mixed with exasperation, but Corwynal spread his hands as if there had been nothing he could have done.

'Is it true?' Arthyr demanded.

'Is what true?' Trys asked.

'You know perfectly well! Don't waste my time.'

'It's true,' Corwynal admitted.

'And now you demand sanctuary for yourself and your brother's lover?'

'Ask,' Corwynal said quickly before Trystan could speak.

'Ask. Demand. It makes no difference. Do you realise the position you've put me in by coming here?'

'Where else were we to go?' Trystan asked.

'Rheged?' Arthyr replied dryly. 'Eriu?' He glanced at Aelfric. 'The lands of the Angles? Anywhere outside my jurisdiction.'

'We'd intended to go to Rheged, but Marc made that impossible,' Corwynal said.

Arthyr's lips thinned. 'Marc's written to me. Do you know what he demands?'

Corwynal and Trystan exchanged a glance. 'I can guess,' Trystan replied. 'Marc sent Essylt a message demanding Yseult's return.'

'So, you were in Selgovia,' Arthyr concluded grimly. 'That must have been . . . uncomfortable.'

'Somewhat,' Trystan replied with an irrepressible grin. 'But we always intended coming to Iuddeu, for justice.'

Arthyr's eyebrows shot up. 'You steal the wife of the King of Galloway – your own uncle – and you come here demanding *justice?!*'

'He gave her away!' Trystan said hotly. 'To a leper. Please, Arthyr, let me explain—'

'Not you. We'll be here all day.' Arthyr jerked his chin at Corwynal. 'You tell me.'

By the time Corwynal had finished his unadorned account of events, Blaize felt a certain sympathy for his nephews. Marc had always been unstable. Now, quite possibly, he was mad, which was yet another problem that would have to be dealt with. But not now.

'You can't send Yseult back to Marc,' Trystan said when Corwynal had finished.

'I could send her to Loarn,' Arthyr offered. 'He seems to think she belongs to him. The girl must be a beauty!'

'She stays with me.'

'She's not staying here.'

'You refuse, then?'

'What did you expect? Did you imagine I'd give you back command of that fort? Well, I'm not. It's Gaheris' now.'

'He wouldn't mind,' Trystan said blithely.

'No, but Lot would.' Arthyr leant forward, his grey eyes boring into Trystan's. 'I can't afford trouble between any of the Kingdoms. The Caledonians are mustering. We'll be at war with them later this year, but I can't go to war with trouble at my back, or one king or another refusing to send me his troops. So, let me make myself clear. You're under arrest. So are your womenfolk. I'll let it be known I'm sending Yseult back to Marc, or Loarn, once she's recovered from her journey. At some point in the next few days, you'll break free from your imprisonment – I gather you have a talent for that – and rescue Yseult from her somewhat lax incarceration. You'll flee Iuddeu, and I'll send men after you but they'll lose your trail. I'll have to punish them, and your jailers, for their incompetence, but that will be on your conscience, not mine. You'll go into hiding. I don't care where, and I don't want to know, but if I'm forced to discover you've taken refuge in any of the British Kingdoms north of the Wall, I'll personally drag you from your lair and hand you over to Marc. Is that clear?'

Blaize looked at Corwynal but he'd closed his eyes. *The man looks tired. He's too old for a life on the run.* But Trystan's eyes were sparkling. 'Perfectly clear,' he said. 'Thank you.'

'You won't thank me if I'm forced to support Marc against you,' Arthyr growled. 'And what's more—'

They never discovered what else Arthyr had to say, for his words were drowned out by the sound of a horn from the lookout tower, blaring out a warning of armed men approaching the citadel.

'Marc . . . ?' Corwynal's eyes widened in alarm.

But Blaize, forewarned, knew who this had be.

'Worse,' he said feelingly. 'It's your father.'

MANY MEETINGS

The bull's blood was still dripping from Domech's hands when the acolyte from Dun Caled arrived at the Nemeton. The boy, waiting nervously outside the sacred enclosure, paled dramatically at the sight of the blood splashed across Domech's face and chest, running down his arms and dripping from his fingers. But he recovered quickly and dropped to his knees at Domech's feet, bending to touch his head to the ground. A couple of Domech's attendants hurried over, one with a bronze basin of water, the other with his robe.

'The sacrifice went well, my Lord?' one asked as Domech washed the blood from his hands.

Domech nodded as he shrugged himself into the robe. 'Much is now clear to me,' he said solemnly.

It wasn't exactly a lie, because what was now abundantly clear to him was that he knew nothing. As for the sacrifice, it could have gone better, and he wished someone else could have performed it. But it was his responsibility, as Archdruid, to dispatch the sacrifice in the sacred enclosure into which only he was permitted to go. At least that had the merit of enabling him to keep his secret, which was that he had no problem with the concept of violence and death but didn't enjoy it in such a . . . personal capacity. He hated the smell of blood, the stench of the beast's ordure, and the accusing look in its eyes. So he'd hesitated when he should have struck cleanly, and, instead of falling neatly at Domech's feet, the beast had staggered, bellowing, and the blood spurting from the severed artery had spattered Domech's face and chest.

Nevertheless, he'd collected the bull's blood in a stone basin and poured it on the altar stones: the white stone of Ludus, the red of Vitiris, the black of Ase, and the stones of all their attendant gods. But then there was nothing, no sound, no tremor in the earth, no vision, no sudden understanding, not a single portent, just a movement of air that might have been a sigh of disappointment. What had he done wrong? Was the bull the wrong colour? The day not as auspicious as he'd believed? There had been clouds in the south the previous night, blanketing the stars, a skein of geese heading north as dawn broke. Unwisely, perhaps, he'd ignored them.

'Have the bull flayed,' Domech said curtly. It was a desperate measure, for one didn't lightly undertake the bull dreaming, but, given the absence of signs, he'd be forced to spend the night alone in the sacred enclosure, wrapped in the stinking skin of the animal, its blood congealing and freezing, for it promised to be cold. He probably wouldn't even sleep, far less dream the answers to the questions that plagued him.

Where is Corwynal of Lothian and how do I get him here?

He wasn't entirely relying on signs or dreams, however. There were more reliable ways to get answers, but the heavy snow further south, followed by flooding, meant the few traders who normally came to Dun Caled in the spring hadn't yet arrived. Even his best, if most expensive, spy hadn't come, the one who could be relied on to get news to Domech before anyone else. This year in particular was no time to be blind and deaf to the world outside Atholl, not with the High Druid breathing down his neck . . .

He'd forgotten the boy at his feet, and almost tripped over him, which would have been undignified. His hand twitched for the sacrificial knife at his waist, but, with an effort, he controlled himself. His attendants, druids of the first class, mustn't know the sacrifice had been a failure, mustn't wonder why he was in such a bad mood. The High Druid's spies would be among them, so he had to be careful.

'What do you want?'

'Someone's come to Dun Caled,' the boy muttered, his head still on the ground. 'A man.'

'Someone?' Was it his spy? Had Maredydd arrived at last?

Domech jerked the boy to his feet, took him by the throat with a hand that still stank of blood and looked into the boy's eyes. Few could withstand Domech's stare, and he used it mercilessly. 'What sort of man?'

'A . . . a foreigner, my . . . my Lord,' the boy squawked.

'A trader?'

'No. Not a trader.'

Domech's hand tightened and the boy's eyes bulged. He had to force himself to let go. 'What is he then?' The boy fell back to the ground and scrabbled out of Domech's reach.

'Don't know, my Lord.'

'You *don't know?* Domech's voice dripped ice.

'He's wearing a sword, but he's not a warrior. He's not a druid either, and—' The boy swallowed audibly. '—he has a silver hand.'

'A silver hand?'

'Like in the story, my Lord.'

'You listen to stories?' Domech turned on his attendants. 'Is that what they teach them in the Druid College these days? Stories?'

'No, my Lord,' they replied in unison, visibly shocked – or pretending to be.

'What do we do with story tellers who come to Atholl?' He turned back to the boy, his voice patient now, a teacher's voice. 'The same as we do to the priests of Chrystos. And what is that?'

'We kill them, my Lord,' the boy whispered.

Domech hated story tellers as much as he hated the priests. Sometimes they were one and the same thing. Story tellers brought the world to Atholl, dreams and ideas that sullied the pure well of their own traditions. Atholl was the oldest of the Caledonian kingdoms, the wellspring of what it meant to be Caledonian, the place of the Ancestor. Its culture was not to be despoiled by foreigners with their foreign ideas. Traders were carefully watched and not permitted to pass beyond Dun Caled. All others were disposed of, the Christian, Ninian, being one notable exception – another source of irritation on an extremely irritating day.

'Then why is this man not dead?' he asked, not unreasonably.

'Because he said he brings greetings from Ma . . . Maredydd.' The boy stumbled over the unfamiliar name. 'He wishes to speak to you, my Lord, about . . . about The Exile.'

His two attendants and the boy gazed at him in astonishment as his face twitched and shuddered, and the dried blood cracked and flaked. The sacrifice hadn't failed after all.

'Forget the bull,' he said curtly, controlling himself. 'And you—' He gestured to the boy, still sprawled on the ground. 'Go back to Dun Caled and bring this man to me.'

He turned his back on everyone, strode back into the sacred enclosure and shut the gates behind him. The blood now, a vast pool spreading out between the stone altars, was congealing, but Domech stepped deliberately into the pool and fell to his knees. Then he let the smile come, the one he'd struggled to hide, a smile that split his face like an axe. 'Thank you,' he muttered. 'Thank you!'

There was no reply. He didn't expect one. Distantly, however, half-imagined, he heard the sound of laughter . . .

By the time the stranger arrived at the Nemeton, Domech had washed the stink of blood off his hands and face and was wearing his best robes, the ones embroidered with the symbols of sun and stars. A golden sun hung about his neck and his hair was bound back in a silver ring. It emphasised his nose which, like his smile, had been likened to an axe, but he wasn't displeased by the comparison. An axe was a fearful weapon, and fear was a useful tool for a man not permitted to bear arms, which was why he'd decided to meet the man in the Oak Grove, the place he thought of as the heart of Atholl. The common people might venerate The Mountain, but to Domech and his colleagues this circle of trees was infinitely more powerful, a place of ancient sacrifice, not only of bulls and other animals. Men had once been sacrificed here.

They didn't do that anymore and Domech was both relieved and disappointed the tradition had been allowed to lapse. Relieved that he didn't have to perform such a sacrifice himself, but disappointed because such a death might have its uses. In the old days, the gods would gather like rooks in the leafless branches of the canopy and might do so once more if this stranger was sacrificed. He could, at the very least, threaten to do so. The man must be made to understand the power of the gods of Atholl and, more importantly, the power of Atholl's Archdruid. Truths would spill from him like the blood that had once fed the roots of these ancient oaks.

They brought him in to the sound of drums. Domech heard them from some way off, the slow *doom, doom* of the deepest drums, their rhythm increasing as they approached the Grove. By the time the stranger was thrust into the centre of the trees they were beating at the speed of a frightened man's heart. Prisoners had been known to soil themselves before now. But this man, even on his knees, wasn't as cowed as he should have been, and he lifted his head to look curiously about the Grove. Domech's own gaze was locked not on the stranger's face, but on the hand he'd flung out when he'd been pushed to his knees, a hand made of silver.

Only when Domech had torn his eyes from that strange and fascinating appendage did he look at the man's features. They too were silver; his hair a gleaming fall of it, and his eyes, a cold green, as icy as Domech's own, glittered like moonlight falling on ice. The man continued to look about the Grove, more curious than afraid, taking in the trees and, standing between them, silent and unmoving, like black sentinels, some of the Domech's attendants. Only once he'd done so did he turn that curiously analytical gaze on Domech himself.

Domech knew how he looked. He was taller than most, his dark robes, richly embroidered, emphasising his height, the staff his authority. Men usually bowed without hesitation.

This one laughed.

'I know you, don't I? I've seen you before! No-one could mistake that—' His lips twitched. '—that countenance.' He got to his feet, dusted himself off fastidiously and proved to be as tall as Domech, lean rather than thin, his clothes travel-stained but worn with a strange elegance. His movements had the controlled grace of a warrior though he bore no weapon; those would have been taken from him at Dun Caled.

'It was on The Island, wasn't it?' the man went on, his Caledonian perfect if archaic, with the vowel sounds of the west. Had this stranger been trained on The Island of Eagles? If so, he must have been one of the last of them, being at least ten years younger than Domech. 'You were always with two others,' the man went on musingly, then his eyes widened. 'By all the gods, one of them was Blaize, wasn't it?' He laughed again, an echo of the laughter Domech had heard in the sacred enclosure.

Domech snapped his fingers at his attendants. 'Leave us.' He had the distinct impression this man wasn't going to spill truths like blood after all, and that any truths he offered might be truths Domech didn't want known. Certain mysteries had to be preserved, including any hint that Domech might once have been young.

'Your name?' he demanded once they'd gone.

'Ferdiad of . . . let's see . . . lately of Dalriada.' the man said with a smile.

'There weren't any Dalriads on The Island that I recall.'

'I wasn't a Dalriad then. And don't try to remember me. You won't. No-one does. But I remember you and Blaize. I've just spent a less than illuminating few days in his company. He sends his love, by the way.'

'I doubt that,' Domech said dryly. Blaize had been more rival than friend. 'And I doubt he encouraged you to come to Atholl.'

'He didn't,' Ferdiad, said breezily. 'He doesn't know I'm here.' He smiled once more. For a weaponless man in an oak grove in Atholl he smiled a great deal too often.

'You spoke of a man called Maredydd.'

'Friend of yours, is he? He's everyone's friend, everyone's spy. They all pay for the same information, and think they're getting it first. Poor man; he has a very sore throat and can't speak. It's possible he may never speak again.' He touched the silver hand, moving the fingers to turn the fist into a claw, and Domech had a vivid image of those silver fingers around a man's throat. 'But he told me everything first,' Ferdiad added. 'So I can tell you. And, what's more, I can interpret it for you. There are matters I know about that Maredydd doesn't understand. I'm like Maredydd, you see, but better.'

'A spy?'

'A collector of information. I'm a curious man, in both senses of the word. But, unlike Maredydd, I don't sell my information. I trade it.'

Domech drew himself up to his full height. 'You think to bargain with an Archdruid of Atholl? Don't you know where you are? Don't you know that no foreigner is permitted beyond Dun Caled?' He expected to see the fading away of that infuriating smile. 'Do you know what happens to those who've seen what you've seen?'

'Something painful or humiliating, I expect.' The man appeared unmoved. 'Atholl isn't known for its hospitality to wanderers such as I. Do you imagine me ignorant? I'm not, which should tell you how much I have to offer you. You asked Maredydd to find out about the man you know as The Exile. I have that information, and more. So, yes, I expect to bargain.'

'Any information you have will be taken from you,' Domech said coldly.

'You intend to torture me?' The man's eyebrows shot up. 'I wouldn't bother if I were you. I've been tortured before and those who did so are all dead. None died well, and the last things they saw in life were my eyes.' Domech shivered. The man wasn't smiling now and he moved closer, dropping his voice. 'The last one was a druid. I cut out his heart and offered it to Arddu.'

'You killed a druid?' Domech whispered, wishing he hadn't sent his attendants away. That hand . . . Those eyes . . .

'I sacrificed him. So don't – ever – threaten me.'

Domech had given the gods blood and they'd given him nothing in return, or so he'd thought. But his offering hadn't been in vain after all. He might not like the messenger, but the gods had listened to him for once.

'What do you want?' He expected the man to smile in triumph, but he didn't.

'I want what you want. I want Corwynal of Lothian whom you know as Talorc of Atholl. I want to know his secrets and how to destroy him. But first I'll keep my side of the bargain.' He strolled over to one of the oaks, sat down among those blood-drinking roots, crossed his legs and smiled broadly. 'I'm going to tell you a story . . .'

'Do you remember the last time we met?'

The candles on the altar flickered in the draught and the narrow windows high in the walls were darkening as the late afternoon light was swallowed by rainclouds sweeping in from the west. The outriders of the storm had already reached Iuddeu to fling a handful of raindrops against the door of the chapel. Corwynal shivered; the place was cold, half in shadow, and, as ever, the shadows were deepest about his father. All he could make out was the gleam of eyes as his father turned to watch him come in.

'Of course I remember.' Corwynal went to sit beside him on a bench close to the altar. He would have preferred to meet anywhere but here – the place he'd married Ealhith, named his son, and made promises he'd broken.

'You look tired.' His father turned to look at him, critical and disapproving. 'You should get some rest. You're not as young as you once were.'

'None of us are,' Corwynal replied, though his father didn't seem to age at all.

'I gather Trystan's grown up – and into folly. Can you explain how this lamentable situation came about?'

'It's a long story.' Corwynal was as tired as he looked. They'd been riding for days, for the ground was still frozen, and the meltwater from the heavy snow fall had flooded the lower lands, forcing them to make long detours around farmland that had turned into marshy loch. All he wanted to do now was sleep, rather than explain anything to this most difficult of men.

'I'm sure it is. We haven't seen one another for over a year. But you owe me an explanation, so I suggest you begin.'

Corwynal kept his account brief and to the point. His father would guess at much he hadn't said. He gave him facts, not opinions, explanations rather than excuses, and evasions instead of lies, since the old man would see through those.

'You have a talent, Corwynal, for turning a tale of high romance into something utterly banal,' his father observed when he'd finished. 'Which is strange given that Trystan can do the opposite. But the facts are clear. Trystan has stolen the wife of Marc of Galloway and abandoned his own. Well, I suppose I should have expected it. He has an excellent example in you.'

'I don't excuse him or me,' Corwynal said stiffly.

'You're in love,' Rifallyn said with a curl of his lips as if the word tasted bitter. 'In you it's excusable, since you're of no consequence, but Trystan can't afford it. Love and politics don't mix.'

'I know.' Corwynal wondered if his father had ever loved his mother. Or Gwenllian. He'd certainly never loved him.

'This woman – I forget her name– is she beautiful?'

'Yseult? Exceedingly.'

'No, her aunt. Your – how shall I put it? – companion.'

'Her name's Brangianne. And no, most men wouldn't consider her a beauty.'

'But you're not most men, and you're no longer young and foolish – or so I'd hoped, given that you're a father now, even though you've forgotten it. Caradawc's three now. He can walk and talk, but still has to learn the word 'father'. You haven't seen him in over a year, haven't seen the other one at all, haven't even named him.'

'Ealhith can give him whatever name she chooses.'

'A son should be named by his father. He looks like you, you know. He reminds me of you when you were born.'

'Then perhaps he's better off without a father.'

It wasn't often Corwynal could penetrate his father's armour of cold disinterest, but perhaps he'd succeeded for once, for his father didn't immediately reply, and when he did his voice was softer. 'I suppose I deserved that. But I didn't come to talk of the past, which can't be changed, but of the future which must be managed. So, tell me, what will you do now?'

'I don't know. We came to Iuddeu for sanctuary. Arthyr has refused it and I don't blame him. I assume Marc wrote to you?'

His father nodded. 'His Latin's improved. That surprised me, but nothing else did. The man was always unstable.'

'Trys won't send Yseult back to him.'

'No, I can see that now. None of the others will give you sanctuary you know.'

'We haven't entirely run out of options, though I know we'll have to leave the Lands between the Walls.'

His father frowned. 'Are you sure you've fully explored the options within Arthyr's jurisdiction?'

'I've considered them all. Dumnagual might take us, then sell Yseult to Marc when it suited him. The same goes for Lot and Caw.'

'You've forgotten someone.'

'Essylt? She threw us out of Selgovia.'

'I meant me,' his father said dryly. 'I meant Lothian. Trystan is Lothian's heir. Do you think I'd refuse him sanctuary? And you're my son.'

'I...'

'Yes, yes,' his father said testily. 'You swore you'd never return to Lothian until I begged you. I'm not begging you – let me make that clear – but I wouldn't object to your return, if only for the sake of your sons.'

'There would be conditions, I assume?' His father never did a thing for only one reason. 'You'd expect me to give Brangianne up.'

'I'd leave that to your conscience ....'

We were meant to be together. Would that be one more promise he'd have to break?

'You'd accept Yseult as Trystan's wife? And he'd still be heir to Lothian, his son after him?'

'If that's what he wants. But I suspect what he actually wants is leadership of Lothian's warband, so I'll give him that too. We'll need him – and you too, I suppose – when we go to war.'

'War? With whom?'

'With Galloway of course,' his father said in a matter-of-fact tone. He turned and looked at Corwynal with a twist to his lips that might have been amusement. 'Did you think it could be avoided?' He shook his head. 'There's always been bad blood between Marc and I. A marriage averted it once. It's ironic, therefore, that another marriage will be the cause of it.'

'No,' Corwynal said flatly. 'Marc's army's too big and Arthyr will have to support him. Lothian will be crushed.'

His father shrugged. 'It's Trystan's role in life – to go to war in a hopeless cause and die gloriously in battle. You taught him to live by the sword, so let him die by it. Or at least let him make the choice for himself.'

'No. You said you won't beg me to return to Lothian. But I will beg you – don't make Trystan this offer. There are other options.'

'Which are ...?'

'Which are none of your business.'

His father was silent for a moment. Most of the candles had blown out, leaving a lingering smell of incense and smoke, and shadows were gathering with the night. 'I suppose I deserved that too. Very well. I'll leave before Trystan thinks to look for me. Pity. I would like to have met her.'

'Yseult?'

'No, Brangianne. I'm curious to meet the woman who's won your fickle heart. Ah well, maybe one day . . .' He rose to his feet, a tall man, unstooped with age. 'Do you have a message for Ealhith?'

'Only that I'm sorry.'

Rifallyn waited. They both knew it wasn't enough. 'The boy,' Corwynal went on reluctantly. The boy who looked like him, but who must inherit nothing from him but his looks. 'Name him Taliesin.'

'A dreamer's name? What if he dreams of you?'

'He won't,' Corwynal said. 'You won't let him.'

They'd probably have made him row if he'd had two hands, so there were, Ferdiad supposed, surprising advantages to having only one. The way people looked at him was another, their eyes going on first acquaintance to an arm that ended in nothing, or a silver fist, which allowed him time to observe their reaction. That gave him an edge, and in Atholl, one needed every edge one could find.

It had been touch and go with the Archdruid, and there had been moments when Ferdiad had wondered if he'd leave the Oak Grove alive. So falling in with Maredydd had been a stroke of luck. The information the Rheged trader was bringing north was worth silver to him, but Ferdiad knew how to turn it into gold. Ironically, the events Maredydd came to whisper about had been due to Ferdiad in the first place, though even in his wildest dreams he hadn't expected his simple act of malice to have led to such a political storm. He'd taken Yseult to Carnadail to break a boy's heart, and in doing so might have begun a war.

Maredydd was to have helped Trystan, Yseult and the others escape by ship to Rheged, but no-one had turned up, so he'd made up the fee for their passage in other ways, having been paid in advance for news of a certain half-Caledonian. He'd headed north by sea, reaching Alcluid long before news of events in Galloway had arrived by land. In Maredydd's place, Ferdiad would have gone first to Iuddeu, but the trader had always been greedy. News that comes second is worthless, so once the snow had melted, he'd headed straight for Atholl. Unfortunately for him, he'd met Ferdiad on the road, not far from Dun Caled. Maredydd hadn't wanted to tell him anything at first, but Ferdiad had been... persuasive. He'd never liked the man, a greedy opportunist who'd sell his own mother for a profit, but he'd let him live in the end, though he'd never whisper another secret. His silver hand had seen to that.

Ferdiad had taken the news to Atholl himself, knowing what Maredydd wouldn't know – that Trystan would be on the run, Corwynal with him, and they'd find sanctuary in none of the British lands. Which meant they'd be forced north. To Atholl. Where else could Talorc of Atholl go to be safe from Marc?

He was glad, however, he hadn't been fool enough to have voiced this conclusion to Domech, for it had turned out Atholl was the last place on earth Corwynal would ever seek sanctuary.

'Curse you, Blaize!' he muttered as the boat swept up the loch, knowing now how many of Corwynal's secrets Blaize had kept. Had he played him? Had the game Ferdiad had found so intriguing been nothing but a lie within a lie within a lie – a distraction, a temptation, a trick? Yet it still troubled his dreams, that game of kingdoms, that promise. *You too could be a player.* He was determined he would be, but not in the way everyone expected. He had no allegiances anymore and was a snake who could shed its skin. Blaize might be playing the game with Ciaran standing behind him, but no-one was going to stand behind Ferdiad telling him what to do. Yet the game was for two people, so who was Ciaran playing against? Was it the gods themselves, the forces, as Blaize had put it, of chaos? If so, it was breath-taking in its ambition, so breath-taking Ferdiad was tempted to throw in his lot with the old Abbott, if only to be gloriously on the losing side. But no, that was exactly the sort of distraction he had to avoid. He'd come to Atholl for a purpose, to learn what he could about Corwynal of Lothian. And now he knew.

They called him The Exile here. His name was not to be spoken. They'd buried it beneath a stone, which meant something to these people. He'd killed an Archdruid, a kinsman. He'd only been fifteen. There had been a certain pleasing symmetry in that. Ferdiad had also killed a druid when he'd been fifteen, though not an Archdruid. And, in Corwynal's case, a child had been involved. Corwynal had fled Atholl – Blaize, curse him, had helped him escape – and now Atholl wanted him back.

Domech hadn't told him everything of course. Ferdiad was slightly aggrieved about that since he'd been uncharacteristically generous with his own information. It had been a risk, for he might have rendered himself of no further value. But the Archdruid wasn't a fool. Atholl might like to think it could keep out the world, but it couldn't, not anymore, and Domech needed someone like Ferdiad.

'I'm like Maredydd, but better,' he'd claimed and set about proving it.

Why do you want him back? he'd asked. For justice, for punishment, long overdue. Which made *why now?* the more interesting question. But he hadn't pressed it. He had a good idea in any case. *If Drest Gurthinmoch can hold the Confederacy together he'll win* . . . Domech might have power in Atholl, but he'd have a superior in the High King's court, someone who required him to do something impossible – get back to Atholl a man who'd every reason not to come. Yes, Domech needed Ferdiad.

'I'll help you,' he'd promised.

'How?'

Ferdiad had no idea at all, so had just smiled. 'Trust me,' he'd said.

He'd been allowed to leave the Oak Grove with his life and his remaining limbs intact, but that didn't mean he was trusted. He was listened to, his information weighed and judged. He wasn't exactly a prisoner but wasn't free either. He could go where he wanted, but never alone. Had he tried to leave Atholl, he would have been stopped. It didn't matter though, not yet. There were still things he had to find out and things he needed to learn. He requested and was given a sparring partner and access to a weapons-smith. He needed to improve and change his technique. He still had a man to kill, but was beginning to understand that, in Atholl, he had rivals in that ambition. *Is Corwynal important?* he'd asked Blaize. Surely it wasn't just because he'd killed an Archdruid? Was it because war was coming? If the Confederacy was to win, the gods might require a sacrifice in the old way. A man, rather than an animal. It was permissible, he understood, to sacrifice a criminal. Was that why?

But if anyone was going to sacrifice Corwynal of Lothian, it would be Ferdiad of wherever he was from, not some axe-faced druid. That didn't, however, address the problem of getting the cursed man into Atholl in the first place, and the additional difficulties Domech had made him aware of. There were other powers in Atholl, apparently, a King of sorts and a Royal Lady who'd have to be persuaded Talorc of Atholl should be brought back for justice – a task Ferdiad had offered to undertake.

'How?' Domech had wanted to know.

'Trust me,' he'd repeated.

Which was why he was being rowed down an outrageously long loch into a headwind so cold it threatened to strip flesh from bones. Mountains rose all around the loch, lifting from the black depths of the water to thrust their heads into the sky – a hard white edge against a blue so pure it thrilled Ferdiad's heart. There were settlements on the banks, crannogs standing in the shallows, clusters of houses on the shore, strips of fields, fishing boats in the water, and the smell of spring in the air. He'd seen horsemen descending a valley that ran into the hills, light glinting from their spears. There had been deer on the crest of a hill, a lone wolf stalking them. Any land at the tail-end of winter was a hard land, but Ferdiad had the impression there would be little softening here, even in summer, and that this land of high mountains and deep lochs bred hard men. It was a land that had shaped, to some extent, the man he'd come to destroy.

He wondered if the women were hard too. Men he could manipulate, but women were trickier, being unpredictable and surprising. He could tell this Royal Lady, Seirian – wasn't that a Briton name? – disturbed Domech in some way, and when Ferdiad had said 'trust me', the man had agreed, not because he did, but because he wanted to. She had power, then, in this hard land, so he was surprised her dwelling place was a crannog no bigger than any of the others they'd passed. Dun Caled had a faded glory about it, the Nemeton at the foot of a loch an ancient dignity, but this place was just a home. Washing flapped from a line strung between two trees. Fish were drying on a frame. A couple of children were playing with a hound puppy, others fishing from a spit of rock. Two women were quarrelling, a man feeding a pig in a sty, muck being spread on a field, and the wind was ripe with dung. A long jetty ran out into the loch from the Crannog, but his boat rowed into a small dock near the shore. A serving woman, sitting at the entranceway darning a cloak, looked up when they arrived and glanced suspiciously at the token Domech had given Ferdiad to present. She looked him up and down, seemed unimpressed, snorted at his druid minder then jerked her head at the Crannog to indicate that he could go in.

Having seen the settlement, he wasn't surprised to find that the place reflected its messy domesticity. A fire crackled and smoked in a central hearth, and the walls were covered with brightly woven hangings to keep out the draughts. Bunches of herbs hung from the rafters and the place smelled sweetly pungent. A loom stood to one side, a half-finished strip of cloth on the frame, baskets spilling hanks of wool onto the floor. A chair had been placed close to the hearth, but it was empty, and the only occupants of the residence of the Royal Lady of Atholl were a young girl and a man, both so engrossed in the game they were playing they didn't notice Ferdiad coming in.

'I'd move this one if I were you.' Ferdiad crouched beside the girl and touched a finger to one of the counters. Despite a spirited defence, she was losing.

'I was about to.' She looked up at him, and it was as if he'd been punched in the stomach. She had Corwynal of Lothian's eyes. Was the girl, somehow, his daughter? But no, that was impossible. Some kin then? He'd have kinsmen in Atholl, other than the one he'd killed. So Ferdiad shouldn't have been surprised. Yet this wasn't the only surprise to be had.

'Ferdiad?'

The man was staring at him. Men did that, especially now, but this was different. This man knew him, a man with a pleasant face, unruly brown hair, grey eyes, a man who'd once been a boy.

'Ninian?' Surely it couldn't be? Not in Atholl. Not a foreigner and a follower of Chrystos, for the man – boy – was wearing a small wooden cross openly about his neck. '*Ninian?*' he repeated incredulously. The man grinned, and he was a boy once more.

'Ninian! Do you know how long I looked for you? Why aren't you dead?' All those graves he'd dug up! And here he was, calmly playing Fidchell with a child.

'God protected me,' Ninian said simply. 'Why were you looking for me?'

'Feargus sent me to find you.' Then it occurred to him there was something Ninian couldn't have known. 'He's dead now.' He hadn't intended it to sound so flat. He saw shock, then sorrow, and felt it himself once more.

'He was a great king,' Ninian said.

'The world's certainly less interesting without him.'

'What happened?'

'A long story.' Ninian caught sight of his hand and his eyes widened. His sorrow was harder to take this time, for Ninian would know what music had meant to him. 'A very long story,' he said dryly. 'No doubt you've one of your own.'

Ninian didn't answer at first. He looked down at the board then reached out to move a counter. His hand was scarred and stiff, both hands actually. Ferdiad had known Ninian had been crucified but until this moment hadn't appreciated just what that meant.

'I was supposed to die,' Ninian said gently. 'But I lived, and that put the man who did this to me under certain obligations.'

'Domech?' Ferdiad guessed, and Ninian nodded.

'I'm permitted to live in Atholl, even to practice my faith. I came to bring those I can to God. But mainly I came to forgive the man who did this to me.' He lifted his scarred hands.

Ferdiad stared at him. *Forgive him?* How could he even think of it? As well to ask Ferdiad to forgive Corwynal of Lothian for the loss of his own hand – and other things.

'Does it still hurt?'

He'd forgotten the girl. He looked down to see that she'd slipped her hand into his silver fist as if he might close her fingers on hers.

'Yes,' he said, surprising himself.

'Poor man.' She stroked the back of his silver hand, then caught sight of his medallion, which had fallen free when he'd bent down. 'My father has one of those!'

'Your father?' So there was one of Ciaran's Brotherhood in Atholl. That could be useful – or dangerous. 'Where's your father?'

'On The Mountain.'

'Which mountain?'

'She means he's dead.' The voice came from the doorway, where a woman was silhouetted against the light beyond. Ferdiad had the strangest feeling she'd come in some time before, and had been standing there, watching and listening.

Now, having spoken, she moved into the room, into the firelight. She was tall for a woman, slim, his own age, dark hair touched with silver, her carriage erect, proud even, her gaze direct. Once more there was a blow to his stomach. She too had eyes the colour of a summer storm and features he knew and hated. Finally, he understood who she was and what, and he knew the answer to *why?* and *why now?* He knew the biggest secret of the man he'd come to destroy. He heard the sound of a counter, carved with a wolf, sliding into its place on the board, and knew how it was supposed to be played. He should have guessed! All the clues had been there on the board, in the game of kingdoms. *You won't be allowed to succeed,* Blaize had told him. Now he understood why not.

But, being who and what he was, he began, irresistibly, to laugh.

YOU WILL KNOW HIM

They left Iuddeu after being there for only a few days, which
Oonagh thought was a shame. She'd rather liked the place,
a stronghold built on a rock with a settlement that
sprawled between the rock and a winding river, a bustling place of
markets and barracks. It reminded her of Dunadd, and though the
people spoke foreign, as they had at The Mote, they seemed friendly
enough.

They'd been prisoners, however, the women separated from the
men as soon as they'd arrived. But it had been a comfortable prison,
and they hadn't exactly been confined, though they'd been guarded
by the Queen's household. The Queen herself, however, was reason
enough for them to leave Iuddeu, for Gwenhwyvar had hated Yseult
on sight. Until Yseult arrived, the Queen of Western Manau had
been known for her beauty, but, to Oonagh's critical eyes, she was
no more than pretty. Her reputation was due more to a certain
animation, the flash of her eyes, the quickness of her smile, whereas
Yseult's beauty was bone deep, and Gwenhwyvar didn't relish the
contrast.

We won't be here long, Oonagh had predicted, and she'd been
right. They were to move on to a distant fort that lay somewhere to
the northeast, four days' ride away. There was good land there,
Aelfric had told her, without promising anything, but Oonagh had

hoped she might make a life for herself in that far-off fort, a life with the child to come and its father.

That hope had been dashed.

'Bastard!' Aelfric jerked his chin at the man leading the small party of competent-looking horsemen escorting them not northeast, but northwest. The man was called Arthyr. He wasn't a king, but that hadn't stopped him from banishing them from the lands he governed. 'After all the fighting we did for him!'

A letter had come, apparently, a letter much like the one sent to that child Trystan had married, the little Queen of Selgovia. Threats had been made that couldn't be ignored.

'I *liked* that fort,' Aelfric complained. 'And if we couldn't go there, we could have gone to Lothian,' he added, scowling at Corwynal who was riding ahead, talking to Arthyr. 'He's a stiff-necked bugger, and so's his father.'

Oonagh hadn't met the father, the king who'd come to Iuddeu not long after they'd arrived but who'd left almost immediately. There was bad blood between him and his two sons. *Fathers and sons*, she thought. *Fathers and daughters . . .*

'I *wanted* to go to Lothian,' Aelfric muttered. Oonagh said nothing. She knew he had a sister there, Corwynal's wife. Oonagh was curious about her too, but not enough to make her want to go to Lothian. So she didn't point out that there was nothing stopping Aelfric from going wherever he wanted. Nothing but loyalty, shared experience and friendship.

'They need us,' she reminded him, jerking her head at Trystan and Yseult, Corwynal and Brangianne. 'Poor creatures. How would they manage without you and me?'

It was no less than the truth. Dreamers, the lot of them. Songs did that to you – they addled the brain with all that talk of love and honour, and the gods knew what else. If Trystan and Yseult hadn't listened to songs, they might have had more than a particle of sense between them, but as it was . . . Oonagh sighed. As well ask for the moon. The world was as it was, the people in it the way they were, and no amount of wishing was going to change that. So best get on and do what you could, even if it took you to some difficult places.

'We need you,' Corwynal had told her the night before they'd left Iuddeu when she, for one, hadn't known where they were going. 'We can't stay in the lands of the Britons,' he explained. 'And now Loarn is King, we can't risk going back to Dalriada. Anywhere in Caledonia is out of the question. Which only leaves one place we can go, one man we can appeal to. One man *you* can appeal to.'

Who was the last man on earth she wanted to ask a favour from, a man who lived in the last place on earth she wanted to return to.

After finding her father, she'd lost him once more because he'd been right. The father she remembered was dead, and Azarion, the man with his face and memories, was The Dragon now – King to two peoples she had nothing in common with and who lived in a land that had been grim enough in summer and would be grimmer still the rest of the year.

'I warned you,' her father had said when after a month of trying to fit in with the life of the Dragon-riders, she'd accepted she never would. To be fair, he had indeed warned her, and had tried to dissuade her from accompanying him when he'd returned to Raineach, but she'd insisted on going with him. 'You won't like it,' he'd told her. Annoyingly, he'd been right. And so, when word came, by those strange little forest hunters, that the Princess of Dalriada was to marry the man who'd defeated The Dragon – Eoghan, Steward of Dalriada – and her father had decided to journey to Dunadd to contest this assertion, she'd been glad to leave Raineach behind and go with him.

'I can't afford to care for you,' he'd told her on that journey.

'You care for your people.'

'They need me. You don't.'

She'd never forgive him for that.

'I'm not going on my knees to that man!' she told Corwynal when she understood what he expected her to do.

'No-one's asking you to. But your child needs a safe place to be born, as does Yseult's. All children deserve that, don't they? And Yseult will need you when her time comes.'

Oonagh glanced sharply at him. He knew then. Oonagh had given birth to five children, and all those births had been easy. But Yseult, with her slim hips, would have a harder time of it.

'She needs you,' Corwynal told her. 'But it won't be for long. Only until her child's born. It'll be summer by then, and we'll be able to make our way to the west coast and find a ship to take us south to Rheged or Gwynedd. But that's for the future. It's now that matters.'

'I've never liked you,' she muttered.

'You don't have to.'

'I won't beg,' she insisted.

'No.' A smile flickered at the corners of his lips. 'I don't expect you will.'

'And I won't forgive him,' she added. 'Or you.'

'Naturally. So – you'll do it?'

Bastard! she thought as they rode north along good roads. You had to say that for the Britons; their roads were decent enough, even in winter. The curved surface allowed the water to run off, and there were ditches on either side to take it away. Romans, a tribe of Britons she assumed, had built them, she was told. They'd built the forts too, and the lookout posts, ruins most of them, though Arthyr and his men had put them into some sort of order, rebuilding the walls and roofing the barracks and stables, so they had shelter on the way to Loch Laoimin.

Once beyond the last fort, however, the road ended, and they had to pick their way along a track that wound its way up the narrow rocky shore on the eastern side of the loch. To begin with, where the loch was wide and islanded, Oonagh could make out settlements on the far shore and fishing boats out by the islands. The folks there paid tribute to Dunadd, she was told, which was why they were travelling the more difficult but uninhabited eastern shore. Further north, the loch narrowed, the going got harder, and the weather turned wet. The slopes were riven by streams in spate and were thick with thorn and bracken. The track rose and fell in a vain attempt to follow level ground, and they had to lead the horses more often than not and take shelter in stands of pine that creaked warningly in the rising wind. There were places people weren't meant to live, Oonagh thought. This was one of them, and they were travelling towards another.

Eventually, they reached the head of the loch and followed a river that ran swiftly through wet meadows of rough grass. They climbed steadily, and it wasn't long before they were picking their way between patches of melting snow. She saw herds of deer grazing on the heights, horses little bigger than sheep, but no people. Nevertheless, Oonagh was aware of eyes watching them as they moved up the valley, following the river to its source, passing old clearings, strange mounds and traces of fields. She smelled fox and badly-tanned skins but saw no-one until they crossed a watershed and descended into the wider valley of yet another river.

He was waiting for them there. Even at a distance she recognised him, a tall man on a black horse – that Devil from Carnadail. He was wearing neither the golden helmet, nor any armour, yet there was armour in the way he held himself. Beside him were six Dragon-riders and, on foot, a couple of the forest hunters – the reason he'd known they were coming.

I won't beg, she reminded herself. *Nor will I forgive.*

'You shouldn't be here,' he said when they reached the line of horsemen.

'I don't *want* to be here,' she said, though he'd been speaking to Corwynal.

'We had no choice,' the Caledonian said, but her father just raised an eyebrow.

'All men have choices, women too.' He turned his gaze to Yseult, and Oonagh saw a softening that belied his words. 'I knew you'd be trouble, girl, when I first set eyes on you.' Then he looked at the men. 'You, I've no quarrel with. Indeed, I could use you, but

Raineach's no place for women, especially one who's being hunted.'
His seamed face cracked in a sort of smile at their surprise. 'Yes,
even here we get news of the outer world, though we don't welcome
it. So, knowing what I now know, I regret I can't risk helping you.'
He pulled on the Devil's reins to turn away.

'You owe me,' Oonagh said.

He turned back, reluctantly.

'I repaid you.' He jerked his head at Trystan. 'And I gave you the
opportunity of making your life here, though you chose not to –
wisely, in my view. But coming back wasn't wise.'

'I don't ask for myself.'

'You ask for them?' He indicated the others with a jerk of his head.

'I ask for your grandchild.' She placed a hand on her belly. 'The
child I carry. My son. A child of your blood.'

His eyes widened at that, and the Devil sidled beneath him. Even
the Riders regarded her with renewed respect. Blood mattered to
these people.

'You left me,' she reminded him. 'Do you know how long I looked
for you? When my mother died, I looked for you when they burned
her body. When I married, I looked for you to be glad for me. When
my children were born, I looked for you to rock the cradle. When I
lost everything, I looked for you to help me grieve. But you never
came. You owe me for the years of silence.'

She hadn't known she was going to say such things. Everyone
around her moved uneasily. She wanted to weep but knew she
mustn't, so she held his eyes with hers. 'You *owe* me!' she hissed.

'Then you have my protection, you and your child,' he said. 'But
your companions do not.'

Oonagh could sense Aelfric swelling with indignation but knew
he'd let her go if it came to it. Yseult knew it too and put a hand on
hers. 'It's all right, Oonagh. It's as I expected. Go with your father.
Be safe.'

'It's not all right.' She turned to Azarion. 'Don't you understand?
My family are dead, my mother, my husband, my children, my son.

You forced me to find another family, and this—' She gestured to her five companions, the men and women she'd ridden with, fought beside, laughed and cried with. '—this is my family now. You accept all of us or none.'

A king has to make a judgement. A leader has to be more than a man, more than a father.

'Very well.' He reined the Devil back to make a gap in the line of horsemen, a doorway to sanctuary, and gestured for them all to pass through. 'Welcome home,' he said dryly.

Beyond him, down in the valley, Oonagh saw the camp she remembered, the walled palisade, huts within, smoke pluming from roofs. Beyond the walls were paddocks and horses, a few ploughed fields. Snow lay in the hollows and ditches and the grass was sere and brown. There was mud everywhere. She'd been right. It was grimmer in the winter. *Home? Is that what it is?* And because she was tired, and only because of that – let there be no doubt – Oonagh began, uncontrollably, to weep.

You will know him, her mother had told her. *But you may not love him, nor he you.*

She was ready for that. She was no longer a girl with a girl's dreams.

She didn't expect that he might hate her or laugh at her. She was the Royal Lady of Atholl. She wasn't used to being laughed at.

She'd seen the boat coming down the loch, fighting the headwind, a tall man in the bow. At first, she'd assumed it was Domech, but when the boat drew closer she saw she was mistaken. Not enough gold. She'd had business in the settlement, and when she'd returned the boat had docked and the rowers were resting in the boathouse. A druid was standing on the walkway to the Crannog, his face pinched with disapproval, but he wasn't the tall man she'd seen. From inside the Crannog, she heard Ninian's lilting voice, then another, a little deeper, with the same inflexion, though both were speaking Caledonian. She could move softly when she chose, and at first neither man noticed her standing by the door. Then the stranger looked up and she saw someone who was beyond strange.

He had silver hair but a young face, and his voice was silver too. So was one of his hands. There had been rumours of a stranger – a foreigner – at the Nemeton, a man with a silver hand, but she'd discounted them. In Atholl, stories formed and grew, and ran from settlement to settlement, changing as they did so, like the wind on the loch. The druids liked to play with words, to explore the world through metaphor, and sometimes they confused their explanations for the truth. But Seirian knew what was true. Wasn't she the memory of the tribe? This rumour was nothing more than a throw-back to some old tale. Or so she'd thought.

Kirah had slipped her hand into that silver one, though it wasn't real, wasn't alive. Nevertheless, Seirian wanted to snatch her daughter away, though she sensed it was too late for that, that it was too late for a great many things.

'Where's your father?' the stranger had asked Kirah.

'On The Mountain,' she'd replied.

'Which mountain?'

'She means he's dead.' Seirian moved into the room, into the light, allowing him to see her. The meeting of their eyes felt like a blow, and she saw it was the same for him. His eyes widened. They were an astonishing colour – the cold green of the loch in winter. He wasn't handsome, but his face was an arresting one, narrow and clever, shadowed by something painful. She watched his eyes darken, and there was a flash of something hurtful in his face that left behind a backwash of hatred. Then he laughed.

'Ferdiad!' Ninian hissed at him. 'Don't you know who this is?'

'I do now!' Incredulity had joined the hatred. 'You were the child, weren't you? The one he tried to kill.'

Which meant he wasn't here for her. He was here for *him*.

'His name isn't—'

'Yes, yes,' he interrupted testily. *His name is not to be spoken,* he intoned. 'But that's going to be somewhat of an inconvenience so, if you'll forgive me, I'll name him – Talorc of Atholl, Corwynal of Lothian. I've come to Atholl to kill him.'

She laughed. She owed him that at least. She laughed as she might at a child. 'You men,' she said indulgently, though she'd never felt less indulgent. 'You think to solve everything by killing one another.'

He looked taken aback by that. It was a momentary triumph, for she had the distinct impression he was rarely at a loss. 'Don't you want him dead?'

'I want him as he is – as he should be – forgotten.'

'But you haven't forgotten him, have you? You can't, any more than I can.'

'That's your problem, not mine,' she said. 'But whatever your ambitions with regard to . . . that man, you've come to the wrong place. He isn't in Atholl and never will be. He was exiled for crimes against me and my kinsman and will remain exiled. Domech may bend to the exigencies of the time, but I won't.' She glanced at the doorway to the Crannog, behind which the druid would be memorising this conversation. 'I assume you've been sent to persuade me, but I can't be persuaded. She stepped to the doorway and gestured to the waiting druid. 'Take this man back to the Nemeton.'

'No,' Kirah objected. 'I want him to stay.'

'What you want has no bearing on the matter,' she snapped. 'Ninian, a word. Kirah, you come with me.'

'But—'

'No arguments.' She marched to the end of the pier and stood there, looking out at the loch, at the waters, dark with wind that carried the heady resinous scent of the deep forests that cloaked the lower slopes of the mountains. Why hadn't she seen this? She heard Ninian's footfall behind her, and Kirah's lighter steps, but carried on looking at the water. 'Who is he?' she asked.

'His name's Ferdiad,' Ninian said. 'He was Fili to Feargus of Dalriada who is – was – my King. He's a poet and a singer, a satirist. He knows the histories of Dalriada. I suppose he's like you in a way – the memory of the tribe.'

Which, in the circumstances, was the last thing she wanted to hear. 'And what sort of a man is he?'

It took Ninian some time to gather his thoughts. 'A complicated one,' he admitted. 'Impossible to like, or dislike. He can be charming, or cruel, and can't be trusted. They called him The Snake, and he was proud of the name. In the Triads, he was known as the first of the three devious men of Dalriada. Yet when he sang, and played the harp, there was no deception there. He was loyal to Feargus and The Morholt, who's Dalriada's champion and—' he broke off, glanced at Kirah and shifted awkwardly. '—his friend,' he finished lamely.

Lover, she thought, knowing what that look, that evasion, meant, and might have laughed at herself if she hadn't been so sure and so wrong. He didn't just hate her. He didn't like any women. It wasn't uncommon; there were men of his persuasion among the druids, even among the warriors. Masculine societies bred that sort of closeness. It had never concerned her; men and women took their pleasures where they wanted, and why shouldn't they? But she'd never expected it to touch her own life.

'Why does he hate . . . that man so much?'

'I don't know. You'll have to ask him yourself. But you won't, will you? You and I have talked of many things, but whenever I begin to speak of Corwynal, you change the subject.'

'Because I know you want me to forgive him, as you forgave Domech. But that's impossible.'

'Not impossible. Necessary.'

'Ninian . . . she sighed. 'Not this again . . .'

'Mother . . .' Kirah was tugging at her dress.

'Not now, Kirah,' she said curtly. 'I know you mean well, Ninian, but—'

The tugging was more insistent. 'Mother, the man—'

'The man's gone,' Seirian said shortly.

'No, he hasn't,' said another voice, the one that had laughed at her. She whirled around to find the stranger standing behind her.

'How dare you! What are you doing here!' He was standing on her jetty, the place of sacrifice, the place of the Goddess – *her* place, to which no man might come without invitation. Even Domech's druid hadn't dared, and he stood, irresolute, at the far end.

'I'm apologising.' The man went down on one knee before her, a graceful gesture which, nevertheless, held a hint of mockery. 'To the Goddess of the Waters, to you, to everyone. We began badly and I'm sorry. But you look so like him . . .'

She flinched at that. 'Get up. Go,' she said curtly.

'No.' It was Kirah again. 'I don't want him to go. I *like* him.'

The man looked startled but smiled a peculiarly charming smile. 'There's a first,' he said dryly.

'You don't like children,' Seirian concluded.

He tilted his head to one side to consider the question. 'I've not had much contact with them. I was one myself once, but not for long. I envy them, I suppose, for an innocence I don't remember.' He looked down at Kirah. 'But this one isn't entirely a child.'

Too perceptive. She turned to her daughter. 'Kirah, I've a task for you. I want you to entertain that druid.' She nodded at the man waiting at the end of the jetty. Kirah's eyes lit up with mischief, and she went running off to engage him in some deep conversation.

'Poor man,' the stranger murmured, making Ninian laugh, but Seirian wasn't ready to be charmed.

'Tell me why you're here and what you want, and say it as briefly as possible.'

'Briefly? You wound me. I used to be a poet, you know. We aren't, as a group, inclined to brevity, but I'll do my best. Briefly then, I had a friend once. He was the Champion of Dalriada and—'

'Was?' Ninian interrupted.

'Was. He was killed in a challenge, by Trystan of Lothian.'

'By Trystan? But why?'

'Ninian, if you keep interrupting, I won't be able to obey the Lady's command and be brief. Why doesn't matter. He killed him and he had help – from his half-brother, the man who's not to be named in Atholl.'

'Half-brother?' Seirian exclaimed.

'Surely Ninian told you about him? No? Well, that doesn't matter either. It's sufficient that my friend died at the hands of Trystan and Corwynal of Lothian. Then there's this.' He held up his silver hand. 'I used to make music, the one thing that gave meaning to my life, and Corwynal of Lothian took that from me.'

'Corwynal cut off your hand?' Ninian exclaimed in horror. 'Why?'

'That doesn't matter either. He did it, and I've been hunting him ever since.' He turned to Seirian. 'Was that brief enough for you? I've reason to hate him. So have you. We should be at one in this.'

'Ferdiad, please, think what you're saying . . .' Ninian began.

'Oh don't go all Christian on me, for the gods' sake! I had enough of that from Ciaran. I want Corwynal of Lothian dead, unpleasantly, and by my hand.' He turned to Seirian. 'And I want you to help me. Domech needs him back for reasons we both understand, but I want him back because Atholl's the last place he'd want to go, the place he *has* to go, the place where I can destroy him.'

Destroy, Seirian thought, shivering. Not just killed, *destroyed,* wiped from the world as his name had been. Was that possible? Was that what she wanted? Ninian had spoken of forgiveness, promising it would bring her peace, but she hadn't believed him. Perhaps destruction would give her that peace.

'Don't listen to him, Serian,' Ninian begged her, but she ignored him and looked up at the man with the cold eyes.

'He's exiled. You know why. He should have been punished, but he fled, so why should he come back, no matter what Domech promises him?'

'He'll come back if he has no choice. He's on the run, banished from the Lands between the Walls. Oh, not for anything he's done. It's because of a girl.' He glanced at Ninian. 'Her name's Yseult.'

'Yseult?' Ninian's voice was strangled.

'Part of the long story,' the man went on. 'But, for the Lady, I'll be brief. She was married to the King of Galloway, but not happily. She fled, with Trystan of Lothian, and therefore with Corwynal of Lothian, who'd do anything for his brother.'

'Trystan?' Ninian's voice was faint, his colour worse. 'Yseult and Trystan?' He swayed a little and Seirian reached out to steady him. Then he smiled a fractured difficult smile. 'But why not, after all . . .' He turned and stumbled away, like an old man.

'Oh dear,' the stranger said. 'Still carrying a torch for Yseult, I see.'

For a girl he'd never even mentioned. Seirian had thought Ninian wedded to his god, that if he didn't see her, it was for this reason alone. Clearly, she was wrong.

The man was watching her watch Ninian and drawing his own conclusions. *I hate you. You think to use me as you use Domech, for your own purposes.*

'I never want to see that man again as long as I live. So why should I help you?'

'Because you want justice and punishment as I do, and I can be your instrument. Because I know what makes him weak, and I want to make him weaker. And because I now know his place in the game of kingdoms, a place I intend to take from him. Then there's this. . .'

He moved closer. She had her back to the loch and there was nowhere for her to go. She felt his breath on her cheek as he bent towards her, and her heart fluttered. *You will know him and he you.* Hatred wasn't as much of a barrier as she'd expected. His hand cupped the side of her face, his fingers on her skin, the tips calloused. He'd been a harper, she remembered. His fingers moved down her neck to her throat and she stopped breathing, though her heart was hammering. Then he took hold of the chain that hung about her neck and pulled it free. The medallion had hung between her breasts since Maelcon had died, a secret even from Kirah.

'And this . . .' The man raised his silver hand to tug aside the laces at the neck of his tunic and let a medallion of his own fall free, a carved wooden medallion the same as the one she wore. *Someone will need your help one day,* Maelcon had whispered, pressing his medallion into her hand, the air rasping in his failing lungs. *You will know them by this.*

But that wasn't what made her heart stop entirely. It was the sign on the reverse, the sign she hadn't expected to see ever again. The serpent, crossed by the broken spear, the royal symbol of Atholl.

'He's to be punished.'

Domech regarded the Dalriad suspiciously. 'But she'll let him back?'

He'd expected the man to fail. Domech had failed, so how could a stranger succeed when he hadn't? Perhaps he'd wanted him to fail, wanted that self-confidence to be dented. Yet here he was to confound Domech's expectations, even if he regarded his success as being of little moment. 'With that condition.'

'Punished, how?'

'Painfully, I expect. Fatally, even. We didn't discuss the method. But it doesn't matter. Once he's in Atholl he'll be under your authority, not hers. She doesn't want to speak to him, or even see him.'

'But she'll permit him to come back. How did you persuade her?'

He ought to know how. He'd sent Belig with him and told him to listen to everything that was said and report back. But the Dalriad had had the temerity to go out to the place of sacrifice, unasked. Seirian hadn't looked pleased but hadn't sent him away. Worse, she'd sent that child of hers to distract Belig, and even the Christian priest had left, so Seirian and the Dalriad had spoken alone.

'Charm,' the man replied, with a glinting smile. 'You should try it.'

Domech felt the by now familiar spurt of annoyance that turned his stomach to acid and made him wish he'd had the man killed in the Oak Grove. He still could – once he'd outlived his usefulness. For the moment, however, he needed the Dalriad with the silver hand, needed to know what he was saying and to whom.

They were alone in Domech's own hut at the Nemeton. It wasn't luxurious – he wasn't a King – but it was comfortable enough, with furs on the sleeping pallet, hangings on the walls and, in the centre of the room, a fire in which burned the five sacred woods permitted an Archdruid, together with herbs that sweetened the air. Close to the fire stood two chairs, one – the larger – his, the other for any guest he might care to invite. There was no wine; Domech didn't approve of wine and had banned its import into Atholl. Nor was there ale, for he needed to keep his head clear, and spring-water was good enough for him, if not for the foreigner who took one sip, made a face and laid his cup down, then sprawled back in his chair, smiling mockingly. Domech had come to hate that smile.

Charm, indeed! An Archdruid didn't need charm; he had fear. Yet this man had persuaded Seirian when he hadn't. *How* had he charmed her? He wasn't, in Domech's opinion, an especially good-looking man. His face was too thin, those eyes too . . . disturbing. And it wasn't as if the man even *liked* women. Wanting to test him, Domech had sent him one of the younger druids, the pretty blonde one. He'd been rejected, he was informed, but with regret and a caress explicit enough to confirm in the young druid's mind the man's inclinations. Had this not been the case, Domech wouldn't have sent him to Seirian. Ferdiad of Dalriad was a foreigner, and she might, out of pure spite, have chosen him as Consort. In the circumstances, however, that wasn't a danger.

'It was good to see Ninian again,' the man said idly, but a glint in those disturbing eyes told Domech he knew *everything.* Once more, there was the familiar burning in his guts that came at even the mention of the Christian, Ninian. 'Which surprised me,' the Dalriad went on. 'Oh, not to see him – I had a feeling he wasn't dead – but that I was glad.' He frowned as he pursued this thought. 'I never had much to do with him in Dunadd. He was only a boy, but now he's a man with a purpose. *You* did that, and I rather think you'll live to regret it, but, for the moment, he's useful, or he will be . . .'

He swung his legs to the floor and leant forward, firelight leaping on his face. 'Did you send someone west, as I suggested?'

Domech shifted irritably but nodded. 'Yes. He should be back any day now.'

'Good. Can you deal with Ciniod? He'll be suspicious – and rightly. I can talk to him if you like—'

'No!' The last thing Domech wanted was this man being charming to Ciniod. The King-regent was considerably more malleable than Seirian. 'I'll deal with him.'

'Good. Then all we need do is wait.'

And so they waited, and while they did so the man made himself at home in the Nemeton. He asked for a sparring partner and Domech, unwilling to let the Dalriad out of his sight, sent to Dun Caled for one of Ciniod's warband. And so, as Imbolc eased its way towards Beltein, bringing the usual changeable weather of crisp sunshine interspersed with sharp showers, mornings at the Nemeton were enlivened by the sight of the two men sparring. Initially Domech had expected the lack of a hand to be a disadvantage, but it appeared to have the opposite effect, unsettling his opponent. And sometimes the Dalriad laid aside the silver hand and fitted his left arm with a viciously sharp hook, as much of a weapon as the sword in his other hand.

His greatest weapon, however, was his tongue, for the Dalriad could talk a bear down out of a tree. He liked the sound of his own voice and talked for the sake of talking. He was popular with the other druids, and spent most evenings in their hall, debating this question or that. He was knowledgeable and well-travelled, with a fund of stories and poems which he translated into passable Caledonian. *Is there no end to the man's talents?* Domech wondered resentfully. Only one thing had the power to silence him: the sound of a harp. His face would go still, as if a shield had been flung up, and he'd make some excuse to leave. A weakness then, in a man who appeared to have no other, in a man who was complex and difficult, irritating and amusing, whose memory was astonishing and who used his intelligence like a sword. He was half warrior, half druid, an uneasy and dangerous combination, a man who needed to be watched, to be kept close.

And so he was with Domech when the messenger came, the one who'd been sent west, ostensibly to trade for stallions. He hadn't succeeded – the Dragon-riders were notoriously grudging with their breeding-stock – but on this occasion it didn't matter.

'He's there, my Lord.'

Domech caught the Dalriad's expression, but, as ever, it was too complex for easy interpretation. Triumph, naturally, and the satisfaction of being right, but there was something else that might be fear or, equally, might be longing.

'Alone?' the Dalriad asked the messenger.

'No. Others were with him. Two men and three women.'

'Good.'

'Who are they?' Domech asked, irritated the Dalriad was the one asking the questions.

'A big one, hair the colour of straw?' the Dalriad asked, and the messenger nodded. 'That will be Aelfric, of the Angle nation. A warrior, one to be feared, but so too is the younger, who's more golden, more . . .' He stopped as if afraid to say something he might regret. 'That will be Trystan of Lothian, Champion of Galloway. No-one has beaten him. As for the women, there will be two with red hair, one with dark. The darker red-head is Oonagh. She pretends to be a servant but she's very far from that. The other with the auburn hair is Yseult. She's known as the Flame of Dalriada, and she's the reason they're in the North at all. The dark-haired one is

Brangianne, her aunt, a healer, sister to Feargus, who used to be King of Dalriada. All of them must come to Atholl.'

Domech waved a hand at the messenger, dismissing him. 'Why? What use are they? We want only one man.'

'Because you – we – want that one man weak, and these people are his weakness. So, we need them here too, making him weak.'

'Seirian will never agree—'

'She will, and it will be because a few years ago in Selgovia, you failed to kill a Christian. Your gods didn't save him for nothing. He'll persuade her, and I'll persuade him to do so. As for you—' He clapped Domech familiarly on the shoulder. 'This is what you're going to do, and how you're going to do it . . .'

PART III

RAINEACH AND ATHOLL,

SPRING 488 AD

THE SACRIFICE

'**D**o you understand now?'

Azarion swept his hand to encompass the long valley of Raineach, the horse-paddocks and hayfields, greening now in a reluctant spring that had come late to the land. On both sides of the river, mountains pressed in, their summits lost in the clouds. For once it wasn't raining, and Corwynal and Azarion were making the most of the break in the weather to exercise their horses. It was good to get away from the Dragon-riders' camp with its mud and the all-pervading stench of horse-dung and mould.

Raineach wasn't a land. You couldn't call a single river valley a land. It was a place no-one wanted, guarded to the south by the narrow route from the deserted end of Llyn Llumonwy, to the west and east by mountains, and to the north by the Wolf Moor, a vast expanse of upland, still pocked with icy lochans. The Moor was passable in high summer when it was dry, or in deep winter when it was frozen, but for the rest of the year it was a treacherous bog, frequented by deer and wolves, and men who wanted to test themselves against both. A no-man's land, en route to nowhere. But without a land, how could a people be a people? The Dragons-riders weren't a people; they were an army. In the summer they ranged far into the lands to the north, heavy cavalry for hire. In the winter they returned to their spartan quarters, and only then was it possible to see how few of them there were. But no-one saw that, for strangers weren't welcome. Those who came through curiosity or ambition either stayed, if they were army material, or died. There were few women and no children. It was a hard uncompromising place, so, yes, Corwynal did indeed understand.

They'd been an Ala once, Azarion had told him, a troop of five hundred auxiliary cavalry, Sarmatian in origin, though later recruits had been from other nations. They spoke camp Latin, worshipped the sword and their horses, and carried the dragon banner. No-one except for Azarion knew why anymore. There were less than a hundred left, so you couldn't even call them an army.

'We deal in fear and reputation, not numbers. If anyone chose to attack us in strength, we'd lose. We wouldn't die easily, but die we would. The only reason we're still here is that we've never had anything anyone wanted. Until now.'

There was a warning there – as if he'd needed one.

Corwynal had been uneasy from the start. They were in Raineach under sufferance, and only because of Oonagh rather than any obligation Azarion might have felt towards him. There were secrets too, conversations begun then cut off after a frown from Azarion. The name Silverhand had been mentioned then denied. Who or what that was, Corwynal hadn't been able to find out. Perhaps it was nothing, perhaps everything. Either way, he didn't want to be in Raineach any longer than necessary.

'We'll leave as soon as Yseult's child's born. The end of May, Brangianne thinks.'

'And go where?'

'West, to the coast. We'll find a boat and head south.'

'That's Creonn country. They don't love you or Trystan. Or indeed my Riders. Not after we helped you, which might have been a mistake on my part.'

'Why did you?'

Azarion shrugged. 'To make a point, I suppose. That we had

standards. An army our size has, above everything, to believe in itself. I needed them to believe I could change them. That change has begun, but I need time to complete it. If I'm granted time, we'll move out of this valley and into the world. We're going to become something.'

'What?' *And for whom?*

Azarion smiled. 'That remains to be seen.'

'Arthyr's afraid you'll side with the Caledonians.'

'Arthyr's right to be afraid. But I could side with him, which might worry Drest Gurthinmoch. This summer or the next there will be war and my Riders need to fight on the winning side. Then this valley can go back to the Children of the Forest.'

Corwynal had seen few of the little hunters since they'd been in Raineach. They hibernated, he was told, like bears, dreaming the winter away, their flocks and herds hidden in secret places. No-one would see them until the end of spring, and even then it would be difficult to see them at all.

'It's all I can do for them,' Azarion said sadly. 'Some of them will come with me, those willing to forget their past. I've begun to make my two peoples into one, but not all have been persuaded. Those who remain will inherit a land no-one wants. Some of them will survive, but most will vanish, taking what they know with them. All I can do is give them a chance. I need time for that too, but time is something I no longer have.'

They'd ridden for half the morning, from the main camp that guarded two high passes. One of those passes headed west then south, through Creonn country, to bring a rider out at the head of the loch that speared into Dalriada's heartland. The other led north towards the Moor. To the south, by the shores of another loch, lay a camp used for training exercises, but Azarion and Corwynal were heading for the southern outpost of Raineach, the palisaded camp they'd seen when they'd arrived a month before. To the southwest, the land rose to a watershed between two mountain massifs. Here, by the camp, the river that had carved out the narrow paddocks and fields of Raineach took an abrupt turn south then east – towards Atholl.

Corwynal shivered. Until arriving in Raineach, he hadn't appreciated how close Atholl was.

'They leave us alone on the whole,' Azarion told him as they drew closer to the southern camp. Corwynal had seen no-one else all day, but now he could make out a group of riders returning from a patrol. They were heading for the camp which was built on a slight rise overlooking a ford across a river and the trackway that led east to Atholl. Beyond the ford another patrol was also returning to the camp. 'But, from time to time, we're plagued with small parties of warriors with something to prove, intending to steal rather than buy our horses,' Azarion went on. 'We send them back on foot without their weapons. Humiliation rather than death. We have to be careful. We can defend Raineach against horse thieves, but a full warband would be beyond us. A lot of the Atholl warriors would die, of course, and die badly. But fortunately, they don't want our horses – or indeed anything – enough to risk it. Until now, that is.'

The little shiver of disquiet solidified to a cold lump of fear. Had Marc's hand stretched as far as Raineach, as far as Atholl? Had he made not only threats but promises? Was there a reward for Yseult's return, a reward big enough to tempt The Dragon? He reined Janthe in, reached for the Devil's reins and pulled him to a halt too.

'You've sold Yseult?'

Azarion jerked the Devil's reins away. 'You think I'd sell a woman and her unborn child?'

The Riders approaching the camp from the south were behind them now, the others to the east almost at the ford. And Corwynal could see they weren't Dragon-riders after all.

'It's not Yseult they want,' Azarion said softly. 'It's you.'

Corwynal looked behind him, but it was too late. The Dragon-riders had spread out, filling the space between camp and river. He could try to break through them, but, even if he succeeded, where would he go? South, he decided, past the camp and down to Llyn Llumonwy. But even as he made this decision, another group of Riders emerged from the camp, and he was surrounded.

'You *traitor!*' He whirled Janthe, determined not to be taken without a fight.

'It's not as bad as you think.'

Not bad?! The riders from Atholl had reached the ford by then. They were druids rather than warriors, dark-cloaked and weaponless, but still powerful. Leading them, bearing a skull-topped staff, a gold sun about his neck, was Domech, the man who'd crucified Ninian, the man Corwynal had sworn to kill.

'He just wants to talk,' Azarion insisted.

'What is there to talk about?'

But Corwynal knew what they wanted. He'd killed an Archdruid and a child and, with Blaize's help, escaped retribution. *Not bad?* How could things be worse? Those deaths couldn't be compensated with a fine. Only another death could make recompense. His. And it wouldn't be a clean one.

'I haven't sold you,' Azarion insisted. 'My Riders won't let them take you; it's you who'll do that.' He nodded at Domech, who murmured something to one of his companions then, alone, trotted his horse across the ford and into Raineach. 'Come.' Azarion swung down from the Devil. Janthe danced beneath Corwynal, picking up his fear and readying herself for action, but there was nowhere to go and nothing he could do, so he too swung to the ground as Domech did likewise.

'Dragon,' The man greeted Azarion with a nod.

'Archdruid,' The Dragon replied.

'So they made you Archdruid,' Corwynal concluded. 'Despite your failure. The boy lived. Did you know? You tried to bind me with his death, but he lived.'

'I know,' Domech replied evenly. 'But I told you at the time you'd come back.'

'I'm not back. If you want me, you'll have to send warriors, not druids. Your threats are empty.'

So was his bravado, and everyone knew it.

'I don't believe I've made any threats,' Domech replied. 'I'm here to make you an offer.'

'An offer? What do you have I might want?'

'To belong to Atholl once more. Your blood's Caledonian.'

'And Briton.'

'In the North, it's the mother's blood that matters.'

'Among my people it's the father's.'

'Your people have banished you.' The druid raised an eyebrow. 'Do you think we don't hear of these things? Do you think we haven't watched you and waited? We can be patient when it suits us. And here you are.' He waved a hand at the Riders and the druids, at the mountains and the river. 'Trapped like the wolf you are.'

'So, kill me. I'm unarmed.'

'But still dangerous. Don't take me for a fool. I'm Archdruid of Atholl, and that still counts for something, even in these difficult times. But difficult times require difficult solutions. In a perfect world, I'd have you dragged back to face the retribution you deserve. In a perfect world, you'd face the three-fold death.' Corwynal's guts shrivelled inside him, but he managed to hold Domech's cold grey eyes as the Archdruid continued. 'But the world's far from perfect. It may be that other forms of punishment will suffice.'

'Good of you,' Corwynal muttered. 'I'm not tempted, however.'

The Archdruid's eyes flashed and he visibly controlled an angry retort. 'There are those among us who want you back.'

'Why?'

'You know why.'

'So you're prepared to bend the law in the hope that I might prove . . . useful to some among you. But there will be others who don't want me back, and I doubt you can protect me from them. So, no, I don't accept this generous offer, and you didn't expect me to.'

'No. I didn't. Nevertheless, the offer had to be made.'

'So now we come to the threats?'

Domech gave a small rancid smile. 'Indeed. Ciniod doesn't know you're here because I haven't told him. Once I do, I won't be able to stop him from leading the warband into Raineach. It will be a foolish thing to do, but Ciniod's a foolish man, as you'll remember. Half his warband will perish, but there will also be deaths among the Dragon-riders who can ill afford it.' Domech glanced swiftly at Azarion. 'Yes, we know this too.' Then he turned back to Corwynal. 'You're not alone. You're with people you care about, people who will, I regret to say, be targets of Atholl aggression.'

So, the bluffing was over, the threat made clear. Azarion had known or suspected this, hence all those cut-off conversations, that denied name. Who was Silverhand?

'Shall we return to the offer?' Domech smiled at Corwynal's silence. 'Which is this. If you willingly give yourself up to the judgement of the Druid College, your companions will be offered sanctuary in Atholl, safe-guarded by whatever oaths you require. Atholl will be more comfortable than Raineach, especially for your women. One of them, I understand, is being searched for, but she'll be safe in Atholl.'

I won't be, Corwynal thought, then turned to Azarion. 'You've agreed to this?'

'I had no choice.'

'What of Oonagh?'

The older man's face twisted. 'Oonagh must make her own choice. She won't like this and will blame me, but if she goes to Atholl she'll be safe too – because you'll guarantee it.'

'So, I'm to be sacrificed,' he concluded. 'And Yseult and the others are to be hostages.' The presence of the women closed down his options. Alone, with Aelfric and Trystan, he would have risked fleeing west through Creonn country, but not with the women, two of whom were big with child. He'd said they'd be together, that they'd be a family, and sacrifices have to be made for your family, your son, your unborn grandson, the woman you loved. Which meant he had no choice, but that didn't mean he wouldn't fight to survive whatever Domech had in mind for him.

'I require your oath that my companions will be safe, sworn on whatever you hold most dear.'

The Archdruid nodded without hesitation. 'Then I swear on Atholl itself. And because I care for Atholl above all things, I also swear I'll do my best for you in the matter of your crimes, despite my own opinions, though I can't promise things won't be... difficult. There are powers in Atholl other than mine, as you'll remember.'

'I remember. So, I have one further condition...'

The man's face fell when he made it. 'I don't think—' Domech began.

'That's my condition,' Corwynal insisted.

Domech opened his mouth then closed it once more with an audible click of teeth. 'I'll see what I can do. I'll have an answer in a few days. Be ready to leave when I return.' He pulled himself into his mount's saddle and trotted back over the stream.

'And I've a condition for you.' Corwynal turned to Azarion once the Archdruid and his party were on their way back to Atholl.

'Which is?'

'Tell the others nothing.'

A month before, Brangianne had never wanted to ride anywhere ever again. Now she was glad to be on the move once more.

Raineach had been disappointing – a cold barren place in winter with little improvement when the spring finally arrived. The people were just as cold, and so much stranger even than the Britons. She'd seen few women, and not a single child. Oonagh told her the men had 'summer-wives', women of the surrounding tribes, and there would be children too, but they didn't come to Raineach until they were old enough to fight, by which time they were no longer children.

Raineach didn't strike her as a good place to bring a child into the world. It was too cold, too wet, too spartan, and Brangianne didn't feel welcome there. She'd made an effort, offered Azarion her healing expertise, but had been turned down. The Riders had their own healers, she was told.

The only consolation was that they were all together. They might be uncomfortable, but at least they were safe, though safety soon lost its charm. Trystan and Aelfric in particular were bored. They sparred with some of the Riders and played dice with them, but even Trystan failed to charm them into anything approaching friendship. It was as if they'd been warned not to get too close, not to tell them anything. Oonagh was worse than bored. They were her people, yet she didn't seem to like them. She wanted to change things, but wasn't allowed to, and this was a source of friction between her and her father. It was as if he wanted to prove to Oonagh how wrong she'd been to come to Raineach.

Brangianne was inclined to think he was right. *Only until the children are born,* she kept telling herself. It wouldn't be long now. Two months for Oonagh, three for Yseult. Both were visibly pregnant, both tired now, both beginning, as women did, to turn in on themselves. Oonagh was blooming, but Yseult's pregnancy wasn't going well. She was listless, often sick, and complained of pains in her back. The damp affected her more than the others, and she developed a racking cough she couldn't throw off.

Which was why, when the offer came of sanctuary in a land further east, lower and therefore warmer, drier too, Brangianne was enthusiastic. But Corwynal, who'd grown increasingly distant while they'd stayed in Raineach, had closed himself off completely in that infuriating way he had.

'East? But isn't that Atholl?' Trystan asked. 'I thought you couldn't go back there, that it wasn't safe for you.'

'I was wrong. And I have assurances. Oaths have been sworn, and if there's one thing you can trust about Atholl, it's that an oath matters. You'll be safe.'

You, Brangianne noted. Not *we*. When she questioned him further, he brushed away her concerns, but his expression was guarded. If she could have spoken to him alone, she might have got through to him, but that wasn't possible. For warmth, they all slept in the one room of the barracks, together with their horses, a smelly insanitary arrangement she disapproved of. There was no privacy by night, and during the day he made excuses to avoid being alone with her – until the night before they were to leave when he took her by the hand and led her outside. It was raining heavily, as usual, but there was a little shelter to be had under the eaves of the barrack block.

'Are you going to tell me what's going on?' she asked.

'No,' he said, and took her face between her hands.

'But—'

'No.' He silenced her protests with his mouth, his hands, his body, and kissed her with a desperation that frightened her.

'I don't want to go to Atholl,' she said when he let her go.

'Neither do I, but we have no choice.'

So here she was, riding east into danger, despite all his assurances. They'd been met where the river turned east by three dark-clad riders. They hadn't been armed, which had relieved her, but her relief was short-lived.

'Are they druids?' Trystan asked curiously.

Corwynal nodded, and Brangianne, looking more closely, saw their foreheads had the same tattooed pattern of a coiled snake as Blaize.

'I thought they'd be marked with the wolf,' Trystan said.

'The warriors are, but there are none here. They'll be at Dun Caled, the Royal Residence, which lies in the east of Atholl, close to the border with Arthyr's domain. But we're not going that far.'

They had an escort by then. The three druids who'd met them rode in front. Three more had fallen in behind, but she'd seen others, dark-clad men who stood by the side of the track running close to the river as it squeezed itself between yet more mountains. Eventually, the high ground drew back a little and the river wound its way through meadows and fields, and Brangianne saw the first signs of habitation. They were only summer shelters to begin with, but further down the valley roundhouses appeared, smoke pluming from their thatched roofs. That was when the drums began. One of the druids standing beside the track slowly beat a bodhran. It sounded like the beat of a dying heart. *Doom, doom.* Was it a threat? It was hardly a welcome. Brangianne glanced at Corwynal. He looked pale, and his jaw was clenched. The sound fell away behind them, but further down the valley there was another, deeper, its beat faster. From high on the hillside came the sound of a horn, echoing from slope to slope. There were more fields by then, a few cattle, horses and goats grazing, with sheep on the higher ground, and there were people too, normal people – farmers and their families, men, women and children, all of them standing to watch them go by. No-one waved and no-one spoke. They just watched, expressionless, as their party rode by.

'There are a few things you need to know about Atholl,' Corwynal said abruptly. The track was wide enough now for three to ride abreast and she, Corwynal and Trystan were riding together.

'Only a few?' Trystan asked, irrepressible as ever.

'Listen. I've come to an arrangement with the Archdruid. That's why there are no warriors here to meet us. There are three powers in Atholl, and the Archdruid, as head of the College of Druids, is one of them. The second is Ciniod who leads the warband and is effectively King. Then there's the Royal Lady, mother to the next King and the next Royal Lady, priestess of Latis, Goddess of the Waters. The three of them never agree on anything, which is Atholl's weakness and its strength, for it means no one person can become too powerful. The Archdruid wants me back for reasons I'm not entirely clear about. Ciniod, who's a sort of cousin of mine, doesn't. The Royal Lady holds the balance. That's why I've asked her to guarantee your safety, not Ciniod who hates me, or Domech whom I don't trust.'

'You trust this Royal Lady?'

'I've never met her. I don't know who she is, but she owes her position to me.'

'Why does the Archdruid want you back?' Trystan asked. 'And why you?'

Corwynal shrugged. 'I was trained on The Island of Eagles. Atholl sent me there, so they think they own me.'

It wasn't an answer. There was something he wasn't telling them, and Trystan knew it as well as Brangianne. 'But if the King hates you . . . And wasn't that Caledonian who offered for Essylt his son? Broichan or something like that. He called you a kinslayer, and that's true, isn't it? You told me so yourself. So why—'

'I've dealt with all that,' Corwynal cut in. 'Can't you trust me for once without arguing? Look, we're about to reach the loch . . .'

The hills had closed in once more, and the river was running more swiftly, falling noisily down a series of falls. The track ran close to the river, through woods of oak and ash. The short spring day was drawing to a close as the sun set behind them, but there was light ahead. The woods opened up, and a vast expanse of water lay before them, catching the last of the light and throwing it into the air – a loch lying between mountains that swept steeply down to its shore. There was a larger settlement here, more roundhouses, a granary, stables, more people watching, more druids, more drums, a circle of stones, some of them carved and painted with designs she'd seen on Corwynal's body. Out in the loch, looking as if they were floating, were crannogs like those in Dalriada.

'Look, Yseult!'

Yseult looked up and smiled for the first time in days, for they'd often stayed in a crannog near Dunadd to escape the summer stench of the fort. So when Brangianne learned they were to spend the night in one, she began to think more kindly of Atholl, despite the drums and the druids, the silent people, and Corwynal's distance. But she was too tired to question him and, in the morning, they set off once more, riding down the loch with their druid escort. The day was fair, the loch sparkling, and there were fishing boats out on the loch, and more crannogs on the far side. Her disquiet began to ease. In contrast to Raineach, Atholl looked prosperous.

'This is the heart of Atholl,' Corwynal told her, indicating the loch, which slid through the mountains like a snake, its eastern end hidden behind a fold in the hills.

A good place, she thought. *Better than Raineach.* But the druids, with their drums and horns, still disturbed her; one of them had crucified Ninian.

They travelled through steep woods and eventually reached a settlement built about a large crannog that stood with its feet in the loch, a long jetty curving out into the water. A small harbour on the other side sheltered a number of small boats. A river ran out of the hills, its outflow close to the crannog, and there were fields, roundhouses of various sizes, barns and stables – and a building Brangianne hadn't expected to find in Atholl.

'A church!' she exclaimed.

'Nonsense!' Corwynal said until he too saw the little bee-skep shaped building with a crude cross lashed above the open doorway. 'What's that doing here?'

It was a mystery she forgot as soon as they rounded one of the huts and saw yet another group of druids waiting for them on the far side of the stream. The ones who'd escorted them from Raineach had been simply dressed in black, but this group wore tunics in every colour imaginable – red and blue, green and yellow. All wore gold about their necks, torcs and chains, discs and symbols, and the hems and sleeves of their tunics were richly embroidered. Their faces – a mixture of middle-aged and old – were tattooed with the same snake symbol but they bore others on face and arms, a double-disc symbol prominent among them. Most had a staff of some kind, decorated with feathers or strips of leather, but one was topped with the skull of a small animal – a cat? – its eyes set with jewels. The man who bore this staff wore a large gold disc around his neck, its edges rippling in the sun. But it was the man's face that drew the eye. a hard face with deep-set stone-coloured eyes above a long narrow nose. This, Brangianne decided, must be the Archdruid.

They all reined in at the sight of the group and she glanced at Corwynal, who'd gone very still.

'The entire Druid College,' he murmured. 'I *am* honoured.'

A crowd had gathered by then, curious but silent. Then a girl ran out, a child of about seven. She ran straight to Corwynal and said something. He looked down at her, laughing, then froze. A woman in the crowd called out to the girl and she ran back. Abruptly, the drums, which had been beating all the way to this settlement, fell silent. Everything stopped. Everyone waited. In the silence, Corwynal dismounted, splashed across the stream and knelt in front of the Archdruid.

'Lord!' he said clearly, then spoke a few words in Caledonian, to which the druid nodded.

'Wait!' Trystan dropped to the ground and strode across the stream. 'I know you, don't I?' he said to the druid.

'Trystan!' Corwynal got to his feet, his brows snapping together, but the druid just raised a hand.

'We met in Selgovia, Prince Trystan,' he said in passable Briton. 'But it's to Atholl I bid you welcome.' He shifted his cold gaze to Brangianne and the others, lingering on each in turn. She shivered as his gaze fell on her. 'I bid you all welcome.'

'You crucified Ninian!' Trystan burst out.

'Trystan, I warned you—' Corwynal began.

'Bastard!' Aelfric dropped to the ground too and strode forward to join Trystan, his fists balling. Neither had their weapons – they'd been warned to keep them out of sight – but both looked dangerous, and some of their druid escort moved to protect the Archdruid, staffs at the ready. Once more, however, the Archdruid raised his hand.

'You're correct,' he said calmly, waving the guard away. 'But he survived, as will become apparent . . .'

There was a scream from behind Brangianne. Yseult had dropped awkwardly from her horse and was stumbling towards someone who'd emerged from the crowd, a dark-haired man dressed in the habit of a priest of Chrystos. 'Ninian!' She threw herself at him, almost knocking them both off their feet. 'Is it really you?!'

Ninian? Surely it couldn't be Ninian! He'd been a boy. This was a man, as slight perhaps, with the same brown curly hair, but so much older than the Ninian Brangianne remembered.

'Ninian!' Trystan and Aelfric had also turned at Yseult's scream and, setting aside for the moment their quarrel with the Archdruid, went over to greet him. 'What are you doing here?' Trystan wanted to know.

'It's a long story,' Ninian said, then grinned. 'I live here.' He gestured to the settlement, the little church, the Crannog. 'I'm the guest of the Royal Lady of Atholl, and now you are too.'

Brangianne's fears vanished. This land no longer felt so strange. She looked about, searching for this Royal Lady so she could thank her for looking after Ninian, then noticed that while they'd all been crowding around Ninian the fleet of small boats, which had been in the little harbour when they arrived, were being rowed swiftly down the loch. The Druid College had left, taking Corwynal with them.

'No!' She ran across the stream and down to the water's edge, Trystan beside her.

'Corwynal!' Trystan yelled.

'Look after the women!' he called back. 'You and Aelfric – I charge you with this!'

Then he was gone, as the boats disappeared down the loch.

'He knew!' Trystan kicked a stone in anger. 'He lied to us! Now he's the druids' prisoner, so I suppose we're prisoners too.'

'Not prisoners.' A woman wearing a hooded cloak was standing behind them. A child – the one who'd run out – was holding her hand and looking up at them with interest. 'You're guests,' the woman went on, speaking the Briton tongue in an unfamiliar accent. 'My guests. I'm the Royal Lady of Atholl.'

The child looked up at Trystan with a strange intensity. Her eyes, Brangianne noticed uneasily, were the colour of storm clouds. Perhaps they were common in Atholl, or maybe the girl was some relation of Corwynal's, the woman also. Perhaps that was why she'd made them her guests.

'My name,' the woman added, 'is Seirian.' She waited, as if for a reaction, as if they should have known her name, then threw back the hood of her cloak.

Brangianne found herself staring at Corwynal as he must have looked ten years before, as he would have looked if he'd been born a woman. They could have been twins, but for the age difference, but even so, she must – surely – be—

'You're his sister!' Trystan had reached the same conclusion. He laughed, a laugh in which amusement was mixed with anger and exasperation. 'That's why they want him! That's why we're here!'

Brangianne stared at Trystan, not understanding. 'Don't you see?' he asked. 'Didn't he tell you how they do things here? Descent is reckoned through the mother. This lady is the Royal Lady, and her mother would have been the Royal Lady before that – and Corwynal's mother. That makes him King, Brangianne. Corwynal's the King of Atholl!'

Domech had asked Ferdiad if he'd like to go with the party of druids to meet Corwynal at the border with Raineach. It was a measure of how things had changed that he'd asked. Domech didn't trust him – he wasn't a man much given to trust – but he'd come to listen to him, and that was what mattered. It had taken time to win the man's confidence, but eventually Domech came to share certain observations with Ferdiad, ones he wouldn't have made to an underling, for an underling could turn out to be a rival or a spy. The

High Druid in Dun Tarvos had put Domech in an difficult position, but Ferdiad had been able to offer a possible solution. Domech hadn't agreed, but it would form part of his thinking, part of what Ferdiad was shaping here in Atholl, the game he was playing. It wasn't quite the game Blaize had proposed, though there were certain similarities.

He'd refused Domech's offer. 'He'd recognise me, even at a distance. I'd like the fact of my continued existence to come as a surprise. It won't be a pleasant one. He thinks Seirian's dead also, and that must continue too, until the right moment. But leave Seirian to me.'

Domech hadn't liked that. Ferdiad suspected he had more than a political interest in the Royal Lady of Atholl. Another interesting fact to be used at a further date.

'Ciniod could be a problem,' Domech had mused.

'Not if he's kept in ignorance.'

Domech had laughed. Some of the druids on the other side of the meeting hall at the Nemeton had looked up, startled. Domech wasn't given to laughter. 'Keeping Ciniod in ignorance has never been a difficulty. It's the reverse that's challenging.'

Ferdiad had decided to rise to the challenge. Not saying where he was going – he was no longer being tailed – he'd ridden to Dun Caled to relieve Ciniod of his ignorance of certain matters. It had been difficult to stop him from setting off to complain to Domech, but, by a mixture of charm and threats, Ferdiad had managed it. 'Wait,' he'd advised a man not given to patience. 'If you want to remain King, wait until I say so.'

Ciniod was a stupid, stubborn man, but Ferdiad found an ally in his son. 'I think you should listen to him, Father.' Broichan was not only more intelligent than his sire, he was young and good-looking in that dark Caledonian way Ferdiad found so disturbing. It was a distraction he didn't need, so he tried to ignore it, and instead told Ciniod how long he was to wait, where he was to go, and what to do when he got there.

'What about Seirian?' Ciniod wanted to know.

'You can leave Seirian to me,' he promised Ciniod as he'd promised Domech, but that was easier said than done. Seirian, with something suspiciously like panic, had refused to meet Corwynal. She'd taken some persuading to allow him return to Atholl at all. The medallion had done its work, though she hated him for using it against her. But since she hated him already, that was no loss. Odd, that hatred. Was his ability to charm women beginning to wane? Perhaps if she hadn't looked so much like Corwynal, he might have made a better job of it. Not that it mattered, because she'd done what he wanted, whether because of the medallion or, more likely, Ninian. As soon as the boy understood that Yseult was at the heart of this affair and might be in trouble, he'd bent his own persuasive talents to the woman who, in Ferdiad's estimation, would have given Ninian anything, including herself. Which was amusing when you thought about it.

'I've never asked you for anything before,' Ninian had said after Seirian's flat refusal to allow 'that man' and anyone to do with him to enter her beloved Atholl. 'I know you hate Talorc, and I understand why, but the others have committed no crime. Don't punish them for being his friend, as you didn't punish me. Grant them sanctuary as he asks. You don't have to see him if you don't want to . . .'

But she did, for, with unconscious but delicious irony, Corwynal, not knowing the child he thought he'd killed had survived to become the Royal Lady of Atholl, a woman who hated him, had made as a condition of his return that the Royal Lady rather than Domech offer sanctuary to his companions. In other circumstances, that might have been a clever move, and Ferdiad could imagine Domech's displeasure at that condition. Not that it mattered, for the Council had Corwynal in its power, and it wouldn't be long before Ferdiad's revenge began to take its shape.

Soon . . . Arddu murmured.

So why didn't it feel like triumph?

He'd heard the drums first, booming along the loch. They'd been beating out all the way from the border. The man returning was a king as well as a criminal. There had been druids lining the way, the people told to watch but stay silent. Ferdiad imagined how unsettling that would be, how alien.

Beside him, at the back of the crowd that had gathered at the Crannog, Ninian shaded his eyes against the too-bright sunshine. Ferdiad would have preferred to be alone, but hadn't been able to shake his countryman off. He'd spent too much time with Ninian recently, listening to his story. He still couldn't understand how Ninian could bring himself to forgive the man who'd crucified him, but Ninian placed great store on forgiveness and had urged Ferdiad to search for it in his own heart. *I'd have trouble finding a heart at all, far less anything resembling forgiveness,* he'd told him. Ninian had offered to pray for his soul. *Oh, I sold that to the forces of darkness years ago!* he'd replied, which had the merit not only of being true but shocking Ninian into silence, though not for long.

'There they are! Look! There's Trystan!'

Ferdiad didn't look. He'd been waiting half the day, but still wasn't ready for that. He'd thought he was until Ninian's exclamation sent his heart thumping, the heart he'd found all too easily as he remembered the last time he and Trystan had met, and his humiliating declaration of a love that could never be returned.

'Don't you hate him?' he asked Ninian, still avoiding that flash of golden hair to search for the girl with auburn locks, someone Ninian was avoiding as fervently as Ferdiad was avoiding Trystan.

'Why should I? He deserves her. I don't.'

'Must you be so nauseatingly humble?'

Ninian flushed and Ferdiad regretted saying something so unnecessarily cruel. But he was having difficulty here, for there was one other person in that group of riders he couldn't bring himself to look at – the man who'd struck off his hand, the man he'd brought to this place so he could destroy him – so he was relieved when the riders disappeared behind the roundhouses at the edge of the settlement. Nevertheless, his missing hand throbbed with the old familiar pain, until a little hand slipped into his silver fist.

'Don't do that,' he said irritably, feeling his missing fingers close over the child's, which was ridiculous since he didn't like children. But this one, as he'd pointed out to her mother, was very far from being a child so he talked to her as if she was an adult. Few adults, however, said what they were thinking, himself least of all, but this girl was alarmingly honest, knowing and yet innocent. She was everything a child of her age ought to be, everything he hadn't been allowed to be.

'Leave him alone.' He'd smelled Seirian's perfume before she spoke so had known she was there.

'I thought you were going to hide in the Crannog.'

'I'm not that much of a coward,' she said curtly. 'If that man's come to Atholl I must see him sooner or later.'

She was wearing a cloak, and, like his, the hood was drawn up to shadow her face.

'See, but not be seen?'

'For the moment,' she said coolly.

Another drum had started up. Impressive though they were, they were giving Ferdiad a headache; the beat was unsettlingly close to the rhythm of his own racing heart.

Any moment now! The crowd craned forward and the druid escort emerged from behind the distant roundhouses, their 'guests' close behind them. It wouldn't be long before he'd see him again, the man he'd come to Atholl to destroy. He'd feel the hatred he wanted to feel, *needed* to feel. But that wasn't what happened.

It was Trystan he saw, Trystan his eyes went to, Trystan who made his heart race, Trystan who filled the organ he denied having. His body weakened, his knees went slack, and something like joy expanded inside him. Despite *everything!* Why wasn't this dead? Had this been inside him all the time, waiting to ambush him, despite Ciaran's assurance that his love was no more than a longing to be like him? He had to tear his eyes away, but it was a struggle, and by the time he did so, it was too late. Ninian was staring at Yseult with his soul in his eyes, but he'd missed Seirian's reaction to Corwynal. He'd wanted to witness her hatred, to share it, to let it feed his own, but if it was there, he couldn't touch it and had only his own to rely on.

But when he allowed his gaze to slide to the dark-haired man leading the group of strangers, it wasn't hatred he felt. Nor was it triumph. It was—

Before he could give it a name, Kirah slipped her hand from his silver one, pushed her way through the crowd and ran across to the dark-haired man who, though he didn't know it, was her uncle.

Seirian gave a gasp of alarm and took a step forward, but Ferdiad pulled her back. 'Do you *want* him to see you?'

'But—'

'He won't harm her,' Ninian said quietly.

Corwynal reined in, having seen Kirah come flying towards him. He was smiling – she was probably the first person in Atholl who'd welcomed his return – but Ferdiad saw the smile falter when he looked down at the girl. *Those eyes!* Ferdiad thought. *He'll know! She could ruin everything!* She was speaking to him now. Corwynal didn't reply and just stared after her as she ran back into the watching crowd, wriggling her way back to her mother.

'What did you say?' he demanded.

'I told him who I was,' she said, and he groaned.

'What *exactly* did you say?' Seirian demanded.

'I said I was Kirah. That's all.'

'That wasn't all though, was it?' Seirian asked sharply.

Kirah looked mulish. 'I told him it was going to be all right.'

It's going to be all right? What in the Five Hells did that mean?

'But it isn't,' Seirian said coldly. 'Not for him. Not if I have anything to do with it.'

Nor me. Ferdiad looked at Corwynal and tried to feel *something*. But it was as if he was playing a game he no longer cared about, as if Corwynal was a piece that could be discarded or not, a piece who was moving, willingly or otherwise, into the clutches of the Druid College who were waiting for him on the other side of the stream.

Corwynal didn't seem to care either, despite knowing what was at stake, for he dismounted without fuss, walked across the stream and knelt at Domech's feet. And still Ferdiad felt nothing.

'Oh dear!' Ninian said. 'I think there's going to be trouble . . .'

Ferdiad tore his gaze from the kneeling man to see that Trystan had leapt down from his grey stallion and splashed across the stream to join his brother and shout at Domech.

Oh, shit! Ferdiad had forgotten that Trystan would recognise the druid from Selgovia, and so would Aelfric. The Angle had followed Trystan, his fists balled. There would be bloodshed if he didn't do something fast.

'Ninian! Show yourself!' he snapped.

'But—' Ninian's gaze flicked to Yseult, and his face paled.

'Don't be so bloody pathetic!' Ferdiad gave him a push, and only just in time. Yseult caught sight of him as he emerged reluctantly from the crowd, gave a scream of delight and dropped from her horse.

Trystan, hearing her scream, whirled about and stared at Ninian in disbelief. Then the joy came. Ferdiad saw his eyes sparkle, his lips curve in a smile, watched him stride over to Ninian, affection springing into his face.

Oh, gods! he thought weakly, but Arddu was no help here. Seirian was watching him closely, seeing too much, understanding too much.

He pulled his gaze from Trystan. Yseult was embracing Ninian like a long-lost brother; he supposed that's what he was to her. *Poor Ninian.* Then he noticed how awkwardly she was standing, how she held a hand to her unnaturally swollen stomach – except there was nothing unnatural about it. *She's carrying Trystan's child,* he realised with a kind of wondrous awe. That was why she'd run from Galloway. That was why she was here, why they were all here. For an unborn child.

He was so busy sliding this piece into place, too busy watching everyone greet Ninian with unconcealed joy, too busy trying not to feel envious – though why should he feel envious? – that he didn't notice Corwynal had taken the opportunity to disappear. Without saying goodbye to anyone, he'd gone with the Druid College to the boats. They were rowing down the loch with the south-westerly breeze behind them and were well off the shore before anyone noticed. Trystan and Brangianne ran to the edge of the loch, Trystan shouting after him. Corwynal shouted something back, but Ferdiad couldn't make out what he said.

'So, he's gone,' Seirian said, half to herself, her voice toneless. 'They have him now.'

'It's what you wanted.' It was what he wanted too wasn't it? She looked at him but didn't reply then shook her shoulders back in a gesture he recognised from her brother – that of someone taking up a burden.

'I appear to have some guests,' she murmured. 'I suppose I must greet them. Will you—' She hesitated. 'Will you come with me?'

For what? Moral support? He shook his head. 'Not yet.'

She nodded, once more understanding too much, and went down to join Trystan and Brangianne, who were still staring at the boat taking Corwynal away. She said something to them and threw back her hood. Remembering his own, he could imagine their surprise. He saw Trystan understand and heard him laugh. They'd know now why they were there, though they wouldn't understand what was going to happen. There had to be triumph in that. Surely?

But as he stepped away from the crowd, needing to be alone to savour his triumph, it wasn't triumph he felt. Or hatred. It was nothing. Nothing at all.

16

THE OAK GROVE

K irah would have to be beaten, Seirian decided. This defiance was unacceptable. Not only had she run off to speak to ... that man, but, after being expressly told not to go anywhere near the strangers, she'd escaped to the roundhouse that had been given to Seirian's 'guests'. It was enough to exasperate the most placid of mothers, and Seirian had never been that. Indeed, she was shaking with so much fury she frightened herself.

It will be simple, Ferdiad had said. *You offer these people sanctuary, and Domech will take your ... that man away. You needn't speak to him or see him, and, as for your guests, you've servants don't you? So you don't have concern yourself with them either.*

She'd known it couldn't be that simple, but she'd wanted to believe him. She thought he could make her believe anything if he chose. But it hadn't been simple; nor was it likely to be.

She could hear her daughter's voice inside the guests' roundhouse, the big one down by the loch. Ferdiad had told her of the magnificence of Dunadd, and Seirian was determined Atholl wouldn't be outdone. The bed-places had been piled with furs, fleeces and brightly woven blankets, and the walls were hung with woven panels telling the story of Atholl's past and pride, richly illustrated with the symbols of their tribe. She'd also given them Ninian, so what more could they want? Not the company of a seven-year-old child.

'Kirah! Come out immediately!'

She could have sent a servant to fetch her. It might have been more seemly, but she knew her daughter wouldn't tamely submit to a servant's command. She'd have to go in herself. She'd have to speak to them. She'd have to think about why they were there, and who they'd come with.

She hadn't meant to watch his arrival. Ferdiad had been right; she'd intended hiding in the Crannog until he'd gone. But pride and anger had forced her out. Hooded and invisible, she'd felt safe in the crowd, and had drawn strength from Ninian's quiet core of calm, and from Ferdiad too, which was strange, for she didn't think he was a man one could lean on. Oddly, however, it had helped to know someone else was having as much difficulty with all this as her.

Why does he hate him so much? It wasn't just the hand, she'd decided. It was something deeper, something older.

But it turned out it was love rather than hate he was struggling with. *Why did he have to be the one?* she'd wondered when she'd seen his reaction to the golden-haired young man. *How am I supposed to fight this?* She'd turned to Ninian, but his calm had fled, stolen by the auburn-headed girl who rode beside the young man. She was beautiful. They both were. *I should hate them.* But for some reason she couldn't. All her hatred was consumed by one person, the man who'd robbed her of a childhood, the dark-haired man who led the group of strangers.

But even from the safety of the crowd, she'd been afraid to look at him. *I'll fall,* she thought wildly, feeling dizzy as she remembered the night on The Mountain, the rocks rushing up to meet her. *I can't look at him,* the coward whispered. *Not ever?* the braver part of her asked. *Not yet,* came the reply.

Instead, she stared at the young man who was his half-brother. *And mine.* That was a difficult-enough thought to deal with. Then she turned to the auburn-haired girl, daughter of a king, wife of another. She was clearly a heart-breaker, and Ninian's wouldn't be the only one. A red-haired woman rode behind her, visibly pregnant, her face fierce, her gaze disapproving and suspicious. A big – very big – man with hair the colour of straw rode beside her. Finally, Seirian turned her attention to the dark-haired woman who rode at the rear, the one Ferdiad had told her about. She was aunt to the auburn-haired girl, sister to the king he'd served, and lover of the man they both hated. Seirian had expected to hate her too, had imagined her to be proud and beautiful. But she was neither. *How can you love him?* she'd wanted to ask.

'Kirah!' she called one more time, but the only reply she got was a squeal of laughter, so she took a deep breath and pushed the leather door-hanging aside.

Kirah was whirling through the air, her hands in those of the young man. He was swinging her around so fast her feet had left the floor, and they were both laughing. But when the man caught sight of her, he slowed, lowered Kirah to the floor and steadied her.

'I apologise, my Lady. I was making the acquaintance of my niece.'

His niece! How dare he! Kirah's face fell at the sight of her mother's expression, and she stepped away from the young man and smoothed down her hair. 'I'm sorry, but I can't play with you anymore,' she said regretfully. 'I'm to be the Royal Lady of Atholl one day.'

'I'm to be the King of Lothian one day,' the young man replied, making a face, which made Kirah giggle. 'I think we should play while we still can.'

'Kirah!' Seirian held out a hand and Kirah came reluctantly to heel. She turned, dragging Kirah behind her, to make her escape.

'My Lady! Please wait!' The dark-haired woman had followed her out of the roundhouse. Seirian tried to get away, but Kirah, dragging her heels, slowed her down, and the woman caught up with her. 'I wanted to thank you.'

'That's unnecessary,' Seirian replied coldly, speaking in the Briton tongue, but it was clipped and lacked the lilt of the other woman's. 'You're a guest of Atholl. Few strangers come here, but those who do have guest rights. We aren't barbarians.'

'That isn't what I meant. We're grateful for your hospitality, of course, but I particularly wanted to thank you for looking after Ninian. We're all fond of him and were worried about him, so it's a relief to find him alive and well. He was my apprentice, in Dalriada. Perhaps he told you. I'm a healer . . .'

Seirian looked curiously at the woman. She was certainly no beauty. Her hair, an indeterminate shade of brown, had escaped the ribbon with which she'd tied it back, and it was tangled about her rather long face. Her eyes, however, a greenish brown, were large and expressive, and she was smiling warmly, despite Seirian's antagonism, and regarding her with the same curiosity.

'I'm sorry. I'm staring at you. But you look so like him . . .'

Seirian stiffened. He'd stolen her childhood. Now it seemed he'd also stolen her face.

'He never mentioned he had a sister.' The woman looked down at Kirah and smiled. 'Or a niece.'

'I'm dead to him. And he to me.'

'But why? He's your *brother!*'

'Why? Because my brother tried to kill me. Because he almost succeeded. Because he doesn't know he failed.'

The woman's eyes widened with shock, and, in the stunned silence, Seirian turned and walked away.

Ferdiad was waiting a little way east of the settlement with two horses.

'Come on,' he said. 'There isn't much time.'

Seirian didn't like horses. When she had to travel, she did so by boat. Only on the rare occasions that she went to Dun Caled did she ride. She was used to being helped into the saddle and looked pointedly at Ferdiad, but he looked pointedly at his missing hand and shook his head. She kept forgetting about the hand.

'You didn't tell me anything about them, these 'guests' of mine,' she complained, as they picked their way along the track that led through woods along the edge of the loch.

'I told you the facts. That was all you wanted to hear. So, now you're curious?'

'I'm more curious about why we're riding.'

'Because there's someone in your household who reports to Domech. If we'd left by boat it would have been too public. Domech won't want you at the Nemeton, but we'll be there before he realises we've left the Crannog. I know who the spy is, by the way.'

So did she, as it happened.

'I let him think you were meeting me,' he went on. 'The man will probably report to Domech that we're lovers. Ridiculous of course, but I'm sure you'll enjoy denying it.'

It was dark enough under the trees to conceal the heat that rose into her face.

'Quite ridiculous,' she agreed, her voice over-shrill. 'Given that you're in love with that young man.'

He didn't reply. It was a hit then, right through his armour.

'Does he know?'

'Unfortunately, yes,' he replied curtly. 'Can't you go any faster?'

She kicked her horse, pushed the animal past Ferdiad and cantered on along the track, giving herself up to speed, the smell of spring in the air, the rush of wind on her face, and didn't slow down until they'd reached the end of the loch.

'Tell me then, about my guests,' she asked, having allowed him to catch up with her.

He did so, telling her of their histories and characters, but there was an absence in everything he said, and she knew there was a man in those gaps, a man shaped of nothing, as he'd been all her life. She was riding to fill that space with a death, or worse than a death.

Twenty warriors were waiting for them where a track descended steeply from the hills to the south.

'Ciniod.' She inclined her head to one side; it was more than he deserved.

'We had an agreement,' he growled. 'You were to refuse.'

'I was persuaded of a better way to handle matters.' She threw Ferdiad a look of dislike. He'd used the medallion, her last gift from Maelcon. *Help whoever bears this*, he'd said but had died before he could tell her why. Ferdiad had told her, but she wasn't sure she believed him. He was using her, as he was using all of them, to get what he wanted, whatever that was. This meeting with Ciniod must have been arranged when it was known Talorc would be returning. *Talorc.* She surprised herself with the use of his name. The man shaped of nothing had a name once more, as well as a place in Atholl. Well, she'd see about that.

'He's here then?' Ciniod asked Ferdiad.

'On his way to the Nemeton. The Druid College won't waste time. They'll try him today, I reckon.'

'Domech will let him off.'

'Not necessarily. But, either way, you both have to be there. You have rights, and Domech needs to be reminded of that.'

Ferdiad, Seirian thought, was weaving them all into a knot of such complexity only a sword would be able to cut through it.

'I want that man dead,' Ciniod stated, uncompromisingly. He'd never been a subtle man.

'You'll get what you want,' Ferdiad said soothingly. 'If you do exactly what I tell you . . .'

'Guilty.'

A thrush was singing in the canopy of one of the oaks, its song achingly sweet. Corwynal looked up, searching for the bird among the leafless branches, but couldn't see it.

'Guilty,' another one of the Druid College confirmed.

The Sacred Grove was a clearing in a hollow in the wood that lay between the Nemeton and the river. Venerable old oaks ringed the clearing, but the trees beyond them, on the slope, were younger. The hollow formed an amphitheatre and had a natural acoustic, and people would once have stood on the slopes to watch what took place in the clearing. But there was more undergrowth now, and even the trees were taller and broader than Corwynal remembered, for twenty-five years had passed since he'd last stood there, when he'd been brought to the Grove by his grandfather, Urguist, Archdruid at the time, to be told what would happen on The Mountain on the night of Midsummer. He'd been sixteen. Two days later the old man was dead by Corwynal's hand, having fallen from the cliffs to his death among the rocks.

Twenty-five years before, he'd been standing; now he was kneeling, his hands tied in front of him, facing judgement for that crime and the other – the child, his own sister, cast into the abyss. She'd been seven. He'd hated her, but she hadn't deserved that.

'Guilty,' said the next.

The older ones among the Druid College, including Domech, would have been there that night. They'd seen what they'd seen, so their verdict was inevitable. He hadn't tried to defend himself, because it didn't matter. Nothing mattered except for the sound of singing, but it was no longer the thrush. This was something else, something made up of the hush of the breeze in empty branches, music that rose from the ground beneath his knees, from the roots of the trees, the rocks of the earth. This was the song of Atholl. As soon as he'd crossed the river from Raineach, he'd heard it, and as he'd journeyed east it had grown stronger. There had been drums and horns all along the loch, but even they hadn't drowned out the song, the humming note of . . . what? Recognition? Welcome? He'd never thought of Atholl as his home. Lothian was. Yet Atholl knew he was there. It was . . . unexpected, since what he'd braced himself for was something older and darker, the voices of the greater gods, Ase and Vitiris, Taranis and Ludus. And Arddu. They were all there, of course, waiting like an army behind a ridge, ready to attack. But this song belonged to the lesser gods of stream and pool, of spring and rock. The little gods were welcoming him back.

It will be all right. What had the girl meant? Did she mean for him? For the others? Neither? Both? Her eyes had been the same colour as his own, the same as those of the child he'd killed.

'Not proven.'

That was the last of them, the words unexpected enough to jolt Corwynal from his introspection. It was one of the younger druids from the College.

'Explain yourself!' Domech looked incensed.

'I wasn't there, but from what some of you have said the Archdruid, the child and the . . . accused . . . were alone. Everyone saw the result, but no-one saw the cause. Perhaps the Archdruid stumbled.'

'The accused has had the opportunity to explain what happened and has chosen not to.' Domech glared at Corwynal who just shrugged.

'There's no point. You've all decided I'm guilty. Nothing I can say will change that. I'm not being judged for a kinslaying. I'm being judged for the choice I made.'

'A choice you continue to make.'

He smiled ruefully. He was on his knees, hands tied, in an oak grove in Atholl. 'There comes a time in a man's life when he no longer has a choice.'

'No,' Domech agreed with a thin smile. 'It's we who have the choice here. You're deemed guilty of the crimes of which you're accused. That judgement was never in doubt.' He glared at the young druid. 'What we now have to consider is your punishment.'

Corwynal's knees were aching, his thighs trembling with the effort of holding his position. *Oh, just get on with it!* But Domech was determined to savour his triumph.

'Death is an option, naturally,' Domech mused, glancing around the Grove at the Druid College sitting beneath the circle of trees, and at the prisoner in the centre.

In times of trouble, men had died in the Grove, most of them badly. Usually they were criminals, though in the oldest of days it was a king who was killed, sacrificing himself willingly for the sake of the tribe. Corwynal was both criminal and king, but far from willing; he didn't want to die for Atholl.

But he didn't think death was what Domech had in mind, even if some of the College were nodding to themselves. He wouldn't have come to Atholl if he'd believed that. He was here to be *used*, a piece in a bigger game Domech was playing. Politics must have shifted in Atholl or beyond. Domech had said as much in Raineach and had even given him his word he'd do what he could for him. That might mean nothing, but no druid, especially an Archdruid, is permitted to lie, so Domech was on his side, at least for the moment. The College might condemn him, but Domech would either overrule them or persuade them to a more lenient punishment, expecting Corwynal to be suitably grateful. He was to become a weapon to defeat Domech's enemies. That probably meant Ciniod, Ciniod the fool, Ciniod the King-regent. He was only King as long as Corwynal stayed away, or some child grew up to take his place. It was strange he wasn't here, calling for his death.

And what of the Royal Lady, the woman he'd expected to meet at the Crannog? The Lady's role, as his mother's had been, was to hold the balance between the ambitions of King and Archdruid, to act in Atholl's interests, to remember the past and plan for the future. Whose side was she on? Ciniod's? Domech's? His? Could he trust a woman he'd never met? He smiled at that particular thought. He could trust no-one.

'Talorc!'

Domech's voice drew him back to the Grove. The Archdruid was glaring at him. 'Since we're debating the possibility of your death, you might do us the courtesy of listening!'

'I'm sorry my Lords.' They were all frowning at him, even the younger one. 'I was listening to my God, to Arddu.'

It wasn't true – he wouldn't listen to Arddu ever again – but it startled them. Hadn't they known which god had chosen him? Perhaps it made a difference, perhaps not, but when the College came to give their opinions, only half of them called for his death.

'Then it's for me to decide,' Domech said, a hint of satisfaction in his voice. He'd expected this.

Here it comes, Corwynal thought – the speech that would be entirely for his benefit. The reminder of what he'd done, who he'd become. A reminder too of Urguist. There might be tears in Domech's eyes. They might even be real. Domech had revered the man. Corwynal had too, until the end, until that last impossible demand . . . He was drifting away again when he should be listening. This was Domech's moment – justice tempered with mercy.

'Death! That's what he deserves! Death!'

Corwynal looked up, startled. Domech was on his feet, glaring at a man who'd come into the Grove, a big man of Corwynal's age, bearing the marks of good living. His face was red, his eyes veined, and his hair, once bright, was dull with grey. *He's put on weight,* Corwynal thought. Behind Ciniod, beyond the margins of the Grove, were ranged about ten warriors.

'How *dare* you!' Domech snarled. 'This is the Sacred Grove of Atholl!'

'How dare *you!*' the man retorted. 'How dare you bring this man here! *I* am the King. This should not have been concealed from me!'

'This judgement is our business, not yours,' Domech said in a clipped voice. 'And you're King-regent, not King.'

Ciniod shifted the grip on his sword and pointed it at Domech. 'So, you plot against me? You think to replace me with *this?*' He glanced at his warriors, and Corwynal recognised Broichan among them. 'Come on lads, let's take him.' He stepped towards Corwynal, still waving his sword, but the warriors eyed one another uneasily, reluctant to enter the Grove without permission.

'No blade may be borne here,' Domech declared. 'No blood spilled, but at our command.'

'Then command me, and I'll carve him into pieces.'

'Put your sword up or face the wrath of the gods.'

The blade in Ciniod's hand wavered. He scowled at Corwynal, at Domech, at the entire Druid College, but slammed it back into its scabbard. 'I'm the King. He's a kinslayer and a traitor. He fought against us two years ago.'

'I fought the Dalriads,' Corwynal pointed out. 'They were your allies until Caledonia betrayed them, making them your enemies. And when I fought Caledonians, last winter, they were from Circind, which has always been Atholl's enemy. So when was I a traitor?'

'In Selgovia!' Broichan shouted. 'You fought us there.'

'You were trying to kill me!'

'You're a criminal. I was entitled to kill you!'

'Enough!' Domech cut in. 'It's unseemly to wrangle in this most sacred of places. We're here to judge this man. He's been judged and found guilty of the crime of kinslaying, for which he must atone. Now, *step out of the Grove!*'

Ciniod glowered at Domech but didn't move. He'd always been stubborn as well as stupid, but his son was of purer metal.

'Come, father. Let's hear the decision of the Druid College. It may be what we both want.'

Ciniod scowled but moved back to the edge of the Grove to join the waiting warriors. The Druid College took their seats once more, but Domech remained standing. Corwynal was left in the centre of the Grove. The thrush had stopped singing, but he could still hear the hush of the wind, the distant bark of a fox, and the humming of the little gods. *I haven't betrayed you*, he promised them.

It was said the little gods had made the Grove, that they'd planted the acorns and watered the trees with dew. It was said they were the first of the gods, that the greater gods came later and, seeing the Grove, decided to make something of their own to show how powerful they were. So they made a mountain. You had to respect gods who could do that, and it was to those gods Domech spoke, not the others. It was with their voice.

'Who is this man?' he asked abruptly, pointing at Corwynal and regarding each of the College in turn, then Ciniod and his warriors. 'Who is Talorc of Atholl, who calls himself Corwynal of Lothian? Is he Briton or Caledonian? King or criminal? Exile or tribesman? We, all of us, have an opinion on the matter. We have searched our souls, our memories, our knowledge of the law. Some of us, perhaps, have asked ourselves what we feel about this man.' He smiled faintly. Domech wouldn't be one to consult his feelings. 'But none of us *knows*,' he went on. 'Only the gods truly know the shape of a man's heart, the disposition of his loyalties. Only the gods, great and small. This man has done terrible things in our eyes. He defiled the Sacred Mountain with death. But who can say what prompted his actions? He will not tell us. Did he perhaps, see the future? He has not said so. Was it the gods themselves who made him do what he did? Did they use him to shape the future that Midsummer night? Who can say? Only the gods themselves. This man had passed all the warrior tests and had answered all the questions of the wise. There was one final test, however. Did he fail? We don't know. The Archdruid who asked him that question is dead, killed by this man's hand. If he'd gone on to face the night of trial alone on The Mountain and give himself up to the judgement of the gods, what would have happened? We don't know. He might have returned as our King. He might not have returned at all. *We don't know!* But we must find out. This is my judgement. He must spend a night of trial on The Mountain. The gods will judge him. Let them punish him if he deserves punishment.'

Corwynal could have stopped it there. He could have told them what Urguist's test had been and how he'd failed it. But this was a chance. Midsummer, the time of testing, was some months off. Anything could happen between now and then.

'No!' Ciniod, predictably, objected. 'He should not have this opportunity!'

'You've had it,' Domech said. 'You've ruled as a King, yet every year at Midsummer you've chosen not to take the one test that might confirm your kingship.'

'No-one asked me to!' he complained. Domech didn't reply, but the curl of his lip made clear his thoughts. *A true king wouldn't wait to be asked.*

'This then is my judgement,' Domech concluded. 'That Talorc, son of Gaelen, Royal Lady of Atholl, should face the trial of the gods on The Mountain. If he returns, he's free to challenge Ciniod for the position to which he was born. If not, it will be the gods who've punished him. Are you in agreement?'

He looked around the College. Some nodded. Others looked uncertain, but no-one spoke up.

'Good. Then he'll be taken to the Mountain two days from now at the Spring Solstice.'

Two days?! A ripple of shock ran about the Grove. *Two days?!* Corwynal's bowels clenched. No-one went to The Mountain except at Midsummer when the dark powers of the gods were held in check by the strength of the sun. He stared at Domech. If he'd wanted him dead, why go through all this? Why bring him here at all? Panic made his thoughts swirl, but eventually he groped towards an answer. It was a question of balance. If he survived, his own rights couldn't be questioned, rights he'd owe to Domech. If he didn't, Domech's decision would be seen to be the right one. Either way, Domech won. But that meant it must be possible to survive, because Domech needed him alive.

'Do you accept this judgement?' Domech asked.

There comes a time in a man's life when he no longer has a choice. That was what he'd said.

'Willingly,' he said now. *The sacrifice goes consenting.* 'I'm ready to go to The Mountain.'

And I will be waiting for you there, Arddu murmured in his blood, his bones, the chambers of his heart, in the dark recesses of his soul. *I will be waiting.*

'Curse the man!' Ferdiad muttered when Ciniod went storming into the Grove 'I told him to wait!'

It was his own fault; he should never have let Ciniod out of his sight. But too much hung on what was happening in the Grove and he'd wanted to see, so he'd moved down the slope to where a clump of holly concealed him from any watching eyes. Seirian had gone with him and was beside him now, her face pale, her body racked with shudders.

'I hope you're not changing your mind.'.

She shook her head, but he wasn't convinced. 'If Domech does as I expect, it will be no punishment. You'll have to change that.'

If only Domech did as Ferdiad wanted . . . If only Seirian did as they'd agreed . . . If only Ciniod didn't ruin everything . . . If only . . . If only . . . There were too many people involved, too many minds that weren't his own.

But as he watched and listened, Ciniod's demands were ignored and Domech raised his voice to make his judgement. Ferdiad sighed with relief; Domech had listened to him after all. Corwynal was to be sent to The Mountain in two days.

Tell me about The Mountain, he'd asked Seirian.

Once she'd done so, he knew he'd won. He knew how to destroy Corwynal of Lothian, how to make him weak, how to make him beg for death – a death on Ferdiad's terms. Seirian would help him do that, thinking she was giving him to the gods. In a way she would be, but Ferdiad would be the gods' weapon.

Now all she had to do was intervene, but she hesitated, and he knew why. She didn't want to face the man who'd tried to kill her. She'd only been seven. He could imagine the fear she must have carried inside her for the whole of her life, how afraid she was, not of the man kneeling with his hands bound, but of that fear.

He took her hand in his good one, and her fingers quivered in his, like a fawn shivering in the undergrowth. He ought to say something reassuring. *I'm here to help you*, he could say. But he didn't because he wasn't. 'I know,' he said in the end. 'I do know.'

She gripped his fingers painfully and got to her feet. A threshold had been crossed, and her body was quiet now, her shoulders thrown back as she entered the Grove.

'No,' she said clearly. 'It isn't enough.'

There was silence for a moment, and Ferdiad thought he heard murmuring from the trees, from the earth. Then it was drowned out as the Druid College muttered their objections. Unnoticed, Ferdiad slipped closer to conceal himself behind one of the sentinel oaks.

'Lady . . .' Domech cleared his throat. 'You shouldn't be here.' Ferdiad could imagine the Archdruid's regret that he hadn't posted guards in the woods around the Grove. But why should he? The sanctity of the place should have been protection enough. Ferdiad, for one, had been relying on it.

'I'm not here as the Royal Lady of Atholl,' she declared. 'I'm here as a victim, come to demand redress.'

Corwynal was staring at her, his eyes wide with disbelief. He was seeing a woman who should have been dead, a woman he'd killed when she'd been a child. He'd be struggling to think, to rearrange the world in his head. *Good. It will be decided before he realises what's happening.*

'Redress, my Lady?' Domech asked. 'He's been judged by the Druid College and found guilty of his crimes against you and others. Punishment has been determined, and it's not trivial.'

'It's not *enough!*'

'We're giving him to the gods on the Mountain. You think this insufficient?'

'His crimes were against my family – and his. His crime was to kill his own ancestor.' She paused and Ferdiad held his breath. 'I invoke the trial of the Ancestor in the old way,' Seirian stated, and Ferdiad sagged with relief. Until this moment, he hadn't been sure she'd go through with it.

'Such a trial hasn't been used in generations,' Domech said weakly, his voice almost drowned out by the speculative murmur from the Druid College, some of whom were nodding. The warriors just looked puzzled.

'Perhaps Atholl had diminished as a result,' Seirian replied. 'No man should rule Atholl unless he's spent a night alone on the Mountain.' She cast a look at Ciniod, full of disdain. 'But a King must rule not only because the gods decree it but because he's born to it, in blood and bone, in the lineage of his ancestors. A King should be born on the Mountain, but first he has to die. He must go into the tomb!'

'No!' Corwynal's voice cracked, his panic evident even from that single syllable. 'Please, Seirian, no!'

She stiffened and the muscles of Ferdiad's neck spasmed in sympathy as she turned to look at the man who'd tried to kill her all those years before. He could tell she'd stopped breathing and wondered if her heart had stopped too when she looked, for the first time in twenty-five years, at the man who thought her dead. At her brother, the man she'd just consigned to a lingering death.

'Yes,' she said.

'No. Listen. Let me explain—'

'There's nothing to explain. You did what you did.'

'I thought I'd killed you! I've lived with that!'

'And, now that you face punishment, you regret it?'

'No – yes – no. Listen.' He glanced about the Grove at the avidly listening druids and warriors. 'Not here. Let me speak to you alone.'

She laughed incredulously. 'Alone? You failed once. You think to try again?'

He lifted his hands, showing that they were tied. 'Hardly. Let me explain. This concerns no-one but you and I.'

'It concerns all of Atholl,' Domech cut in, trying to take control once more. 'You had a chance to explain to the College but refused to do so.'

'It didn't matter then. Now it does. Seirian, *please*. For the sake of our mother—'

She struck him hard across the face. His head jerked to one side and he rocked but didn't fall. A trickle of blood ran down his jaw from the corner of his mouth.

'I'll kill him for you!' Ciniod strode into the Grove, unsheathed his sword, gripped Corwynal by the arm and hauled him to his feet. 'Forget all this talk of gods and Ancestors. I'll kill him now.'

'Have you no pride?' Seirian whirled on him. 'No respect for tradition? He's not yours to kill. He's the gods'. Do you hear me? *The gods*!'

He stepped back, cowed by her ferocity, his sword falling to his side, and Seirian turned to Corwynal once more. 'Come then,' she said simply and moved towards the edge of the Grove.

'Are you mad?' Ciniod demanded. 'The man's *dangerous!*'

'I'm not afraid of him,' she said coolly and kept on walking, Corwynal following. No-one tried to stop them. They were walking, Ferdiad realised, with not a little consternation, straight towards him.

This is your sister,' his mother informed him about six months after they'd left Lothian. She was looking down at a small squalling bundle with the private smile that had always been his alone. 'Her father's far away, so you'll have to protect her.'

But he'd resented the child. He was full of resentment in those days – for the father who'd sent him away, for his mother's brother, King Bruide, who despised him for the Briton blood of which he was so proud. Now this creature, stealing his mother's love away. He ran away, intending to make his way back to Lothian, but was caught and beaten. After he'd been brought back for the third time, they'd sent him to The Island from which there was no escape, and he'd returned only infrequently to Atholl, hoping each time to be greeted with the news that, in the way of small children, his sister had succumbed to a fever. Then, when he was fourteen and she was five, she did. She could have died, they'd told him, expecting him to be glad she hadn't. 'So at least you'll have each other . . .'

It was his grandfather, Urguist, Archdruid of Atholl, who broke it to him that his mother had caught the same fever after insisting on nursing her daughter herself. But, unlike his sister, she'd hadn't survived it and had died, leaving so many things unspoken. If he'd been there, he could have stopped it, he told himself. He would have fought death itself. In his grief, resentment had turned to hatred. Yes, he'd wished his sister dead, but he'd never considered killing her himself. What had happened two years later had been an accident. Except she wasn't dead after all.

'Well?' she asked, once they'd left the circle of oaks. 'What do you want to explain?'

She refused to look at him, but he couldn't take his eyes off her. It was like looking into a mirror, or into the past. He recognised his mother in the fall of her hair and the shape of her unsmiling mouth. But that straight nose was his father's, as was the tilt of her cheekbones. The only feature they didn't share was a dented scar in her forehead that ran into her hairline, the sort of scar that might have been made by falling onto rocks.

'Why aren't you dead?' he asked, stupidly.

'My grandfather's body broke my fall,' she said coldly. 'I was knocked unconscious and they couldn't find me. But what do you care? You hated everyone in Atholl.'

It wasn't true. He'd been fond of his grandfather, the only person who'd cared about him when his mother died. Urguist had been patient with his grief and fury. He'd been the one to explain what that death meant; because he was his mother's only son, the King's only royal nephew, he was destined to be the next king of Atholl.

It was Urguist who persuaded him to carry on with his training on The Island. Privately, Corwynal still intended returning to Lothian, for Atholl held nothing for him anymore. Then, after defeating The Dragon, he'd been trapped there – until his uncle, King

*Bruide, had died in a hunting accident and Corwynal was brought
back to Atholl.*

*There would be tests, Urguist explained, to determine if he was
worthy of being the next King. He could have refused, but pride got
in the way. I'll show them, he'd thought. I'll show them Corwynal of
Lothian is good enough to be their king. Then I'll leave and never
come back. He'd no doubt he could pass the tests of skill at arms,
for The Dragon was already teaching him in secret. The tests of
knowledge would also be easy, for they were training him on The
Island to become a druid and he had a good memory. But the final
test would be hard, his grandfather warned him. It was a test of his
obedience to the gods, something difficult, something he might not
want to do. The test would be made by Urguist, as Archdruid, but
he wouldn't tell him what it would be. 'You'll succeed,' he'd told him.
'Then you'll spend a night alone on the Mountain to be tested by the
gods themselves. But you'll succeed in that too, because you're your
mother's son.'*

'I didn't hate my grandfather.'

'Only me, then,' his sister – *his sister!* – said bitterly.

'My mother died because of you.'

She gasped. 'You blamed *me?*'

'I had to blame someone, and I'd always been jealous of you. I
was fourteen when she died, Seirian. Life was black and white for
me then. I hated you as a child hates, but I never wanted you dead.'

'So why did you try to kill me? Why did you kill my grandfather.'

'Because of the test. Didn't you hear what it was? No, he spoke
in Briton. I'd forgotten that. So you wouldn't have understood. *I*
didn't understand. I didn't believe him, not at first, but when I did,
I still didn't understand.'

'What are you talking about?'

'He asked me to kill you.'

She laughed. 'Are you mad? He loved me. And I was to be the
next Royal Lady. That makes no sense.'

'It was a test,' he insisted. 'It wasn't supposed to make sense. It was to be a test of my obedience. I didn't understand until later that he expected me to refuse, *wanted* me to refuse. *That* was the test. I had to show I could make the choice a King has to make, even if it meant going against everything I'd been taught. But I didn't understand that, so I suppose I failed. I was so angry he could think me capable of killing a seven-year-old child, my own sister, even one I thought I hated, I raised a hand. I don't know why. I didn't intend to strike him, but perhaps he thought I did. He stepped back, stumbled. His staff caught in the cleft between two rocks and he lost his balance. You were holding on to him, but when I reached out you wouldn't take my hand. Then you were both gone . . .'

He still felt the horror, the disbelief, the longing to turn back time. He still heard the silence that fell before the screaming began, still heard the voice, close by, speaking a single word in the Briton tongue. 'Run!' Without thinking, he had. It was night, but there was still light in the sky, so he kept low. 'Down here!' That same voice, urging him to hide among the rocks. He heard them searching for him, fail to find him, and return to look for the bodies of his grandfather and sister. They didn't find them either, and in the end everyone left, women keening, children crying, warriors and druids cursing. Only then did he wonder who'd saved him – a druid who looked vaguely familiar, his dark hair tied back into a silver ring. 'I'm your uncle,' he'd said dryly. 'Your other uncle. Your father's brother.'

'It was an accident,' he insisted, twenty-five years later.

'I don't believe you.'

He hadn't expected her to.

'Please, Seirian, don't send me into the tomb.'

Panic surged and his vision blurred at the edges. He had to lean against a tree to steady himself. 'Anything but that.'

She shook her head. 'If you're as innocent as you say, the gods will spare you.'

'My life perhaps, but not my sanity. If I'm trapped underground, I'll go mad, and I'd rather end my own life than lose my mind.'

She looked at him for a long moment, her face expressionless. 'If our Ancestor favours you, you'll find the means to end it in the tomb.'

His heart was racing, his breathing shallow and rapid. 'If I go into that tomb, I won't come out sane. I can't go in there—'

'You can if you care about the people who came to Atholl with you.'

'What do you mean?'

'If you want my guests to remain my guests and not my prisoners, you'll go, willingly, into the earth.'

'But you promised they'd be safe with you!'

'Safe, yes. But nothing more.'

Deep inside himself, deeper than the nerves where Arddu lurked, he knew he was beaten. Everything he'd done – *everything* – had been to protect those he loved. If he was to go on protecting them, he had to make this sacrifice.

He bent his head and stared down at his bound hands.

'But I'll make one concession,' she said.

He looked up, but there was no softening of her expression.

'You'll go willingly into the tomb. There you may kill yourself or not. I don't care. But if you survive it, someone will be waiting for you. If you're mad, he'll kill you, as one would kill a mad dog. If you're sane . . . ? What happens then will be as the gods decree. Do you accept these terms?'

He closed his eyes and nodded. When he opened them again, she'd gone back to the Grove, and some of Ciniod's men were coming to get him. *I could run,* he thought for one insane moment. He wouldn't get far, but he could fight, even with his hands bound. Or he could let Ciniod kill him after all. But even as he considered the possibility, he knew he couldn't do it, and anyway, his retreat was cut off. A figure was standing between him and the woods beyond the Grove, a figure crowned like a stag. *Arddu?* he murmured. But when the God stepped towards him his face shifted and the God was gone, leaving behind a man who, like Seirian, ought to be dead, a man with a silver hand that swung up and hit him hard on the jaw and brought the darkness down.

'I'll be waiting for you there,' the man said, and his voice was silver too as all light vanished. 'On the Mountain. I'll be waiting.'

'You don't approve.' Seirian turned to face Domech, the only one of the Druid College left in the Grove. The others had gone, some of them taking the unconscious prisoner with them. She refused to give him a name. Even Ferdiad, flushed with triumph, had vanished.

'I . . . I'm not sure yet.'

It wasn't like Domech to be so uncertain. The world had indeed changed.

'What you've done here was . . .' He searched for the word. 'Disproportionate.'

She smiled at that. 'He won't come back, you know. The gods will judge him. The Ancestor will judge him.'

'The Ancestor is nothing more than bones in a tomb. What will happen up there will be the will of men, not gods.'

'And women.'

Domech smiled without humour, already planning to subvert her, to subvert the will of the gods. He probably intended getting that man out of the tomb, to make him grateful and forge an alliance that would ensure his own power. He wouldn't know that Ferdiad would be there to stop him, that Ferdiad didn't have gratitude in mind. Quite the reverse.

Should she have agreed to that? Should she put Ferdiad at risk? Her role was one of balance, but was this balanced?

She was tired all of a sudden and had an intense desire to fold herself into dreamless sleep. She longed for the sound of the loch, of shore birds, of wind in the aspens along the water's edge.

'When we meet again, Seirian, Atholl will be a different place,' Domech said as she walked away. She looked back as she crested the rise beyond the hollow of the Grove. The Archdruid was still there, unmoving, like a standing stone, ancient and watchful.

It was nightfall by the time she reached the Crannog. It had begun to rain and the wind had picked up, driving waves across the loch. She was soaked and shivering. Seirian's woman built up the fire, found her a blanket and brought her some warm milk. Kirah was asleep, so she gathered her in her blankets and handed her to the woman to take to her own dwelling on the shore.

Alone at last, she sat by the fire, listening to the lapping of water, the cries of night birds, and the wind in the thatch, but the calm she searched for eluded her. She began, to her own surprise, to weep, quietly to begin with, but her weeping quickly turned to sobs and she had to clamp her hands over her mouth to stop herself from screaming.

I won't think of the past! She'd sleep, she decided, and when she woke the world would be different. But sleep refused to come, and she lay awake all night, tossing from side to side, first shivering then sweating as if she was in a fever. In the end, she got up, pulled a cloak about her shoulders and went to the end of the pier. The water was black under a moonless sky, but as she stood there it slowly turned to grey. The sun was rising behind the hills, striking fire from the mountains to the north. They still held snow on their summits, she noticed. The Sacred Mountain would be equally snow-bound, and it would be bitterly cold on the night of the Spring Solstice. A man could die of that alone.

Eventually she went back to the Crannog and barred the door. Her women came for orders, but she sent them away. Later Kirah came, but she sent her away too. 'Go to the strangers,' she said.

'But you said—'

'I was wrong. They're our guests. Entertain them for me. I have other matters to attend to.'

But she did nothing. She sat in her carved wooden chair, her chin propped on one hand, and watched the dappled light travel across the room, watched it grow then fade once more. She thought about the past and the future, about lies and truth, about what had happened and what had not and why, about fires in the night and falling, of her name being called out, of a man with her face, her blood. The day passed slowly and, when night came, she gave herself up to the dreams, knowing they'd be bad, but that they must be borne for the sake of the answers that would lie within them.

In the morning, she knew what to do. She unbarred her door, gestured to one of the women waiting by the shore, gave her instructions, and returned to the Crannog to dress herself with care. She was the Royal Lady of Atholl after all. Then she waited for her guests to come.

'So,' she said to the first of them, making the demand she'd make of them all. 'Tell me about my brother.'

17

THE TOMB

It wasn't easy, climbing the Mountain. Seirian had told him how to find the way up the cliff and had looked briefly at his silver hand but said nothing, for which he'd been grateful. He'd left the hand behind reluctantly, for it was part of who he was now, of who he'd been *made*, but the hook had proved more useful among the rocks and had saved him more than once already. It would be ironic if the Mountain killed him before he'd got his revenge on the man he'd come for.

Once he reached the summit, however, it wasn't the Mountain that was trying to kill him but the weather. He hadn't expected it to be quite this cold, or for there to be so much snow. His thick woollen cloak, which had been perfectly satisfactory down in the valley, was woefully inadequate in his hiding place behind some rocks close to the edge of the plateau.

The druids who'd come ahead of the others to open the tomb had brought wood and lit a small fire, but Ferdiad could only look longingly at that bright spark of flame and wonder if, like his nemesis, he'd survive until the morning. He almost envied him, trapped in the tomb; at least he'd be out of the wind.

They'd brought Corwynal to the summit before sunset, for the druids would want to be well down the Mountain before darkness fell. There were gods up here, apparently.

I will protect you, Arddu murmured, but Ferdiad wasn't reassured. No god could protect him from the cold.

He was too far away from the tomb to see what was happening but he could make out Domech whose profile was unmistakable. The man, dressed like a king in a fur-lined cloak, must be Corwynal. Ferdiad looked enviously at cloak, but they took it away before putting him in the tomb. He didn't struggle, and Ferdiad wondered if he'd been drugged. Then they sealed the entrance and left, hurrying away across the snow-streaked scree, making for the top of the sacred way that would take them back to the foot of the Mountain.

Just you and me now. And the gods. And the ghosts. And whatever dwelled in the Tomb.

Domech and the others would come for him in the morning, but that was many hours away. Until then, Corwynal was to be tested. Domech had been close-lipped about the details, but Ferdiad gathered that a degree of courage was required, a certain ingenuity, an ability to withstand his ghosts – and what man doesn't have ghosts? Many of those tested in this way had failed. Some had lost all reason by the morning. Others had died. *What of?* he'd asked, but Domech just smiled.

Ferdiad had returned the smile, knowing, as Domech didn't, of Corwynal's fear of being underground. He wanted him terrified. He wanted him weak. *You need to learn everything that makes him weak*, Azarion had told him. Some of those weaknesses had driven him to Atholl. Now another would crush him. Ferdiad understood fear. He'd been frightened once, had turned to the one person who could help him, only to be rejected. Now it was that man's turn to be frightened.

Yessss, Arddu whispered. *Humble him. Rob him of his self-respect. Drive him to his knees. Make him beg.*

'For what?'

His life. His sanity. His soul.

It was death Ferdiad had in mind, but only at the end, when he'd made him understand that by what he'd done – and not done – he'd created the monster who'd come to destroy him.

If the cold doesn't get the monster first, Ferdiad thought, shivering in his inadequate cloak.

The sun set in a blare of red, and the temperature fell even lower. The stars were chips of ice in a black sky, but they dimmed when the moon rose, transforming the Mountain into a rocky field of snow. The tomb was a shallow cairn of stones piled over the chamber that had been built into the Mountain centuries before to house the bones of a nameless hero. Other bones lay about on the summit plateau, those of kings, warriors and druids, but these were invisible beneath the snow, though Ferdiad could hear their ghosts, a thin wailing in the wind that hated life. The ghosts didn't bother him; perhaps they recognised the death in his heart and approved. Maybe that was why the gods left him alone also, though he felt them draw near to watch him, with neither approval nor censure. The moon was close, the sky and the stars pressing down, sucking warmth from the world, and he felt exposed, his thoughts and intentions splayed out for the gods to pick over.

There was only one way into the tomb but there were two ways out. That was the secret. A cool-headed man with a certain way of thinking could get himself out unaided. Corwynal would not be coolheaded though, not once Arddu had finished with him, not once he'd fought the ghosts of his own past. Then it would be Ferdiad's turn.

It took him some time to find the other entrance, for it lay under the snow, and he had to do so silently for he didn't want the man in the tomb to hear him and think he was being rescued. Hope was the last thing Ferdiad wanted Corwynal to have. Not yet, not until he was in a position to betray that hope as he'd betrayed Ferdiad's.

The entrance lay beneath a thin slab of rock carved with Caledonian symbols Ferdiad didn't recognise. From above, it could be moved easily by someone with two hands, but it was harder for

Ferdiad, and it took him some time to pull it away. The tomb beneath him exhaled a foul odour of long-dead bones and mouldering stone, but he ignored the smell and lay down, his head close to the entrance, and threw his cloak over both his head and the entrance way to prevent any light reaching the tomb and revealing the way out. It was colder now, the rocks beneath him icy, the warmth of his body melting the snow and soaking his leggings and shirt, but hatred and anticipation kept him warm as he waited for the man in the tomb to find the courage to face his deepest fear – only to understand he still had to face his ghosts: the men he'd killed, the women he'd betrayed, the lies he'd told, the secrets he'd kept. And among the ghosts would be the first of his victims – the boy from The Island, the boy who lived in a tomb in Ferdiad's mind, behind a barred door, the boy who whispered in the dark, a stunted inarticulate monster.

Corwynal didn't know where he was at first. Ideas and images came at him through a fog, appearing then vanishing once more before he could catch hold of them. *I won't go mad.* That was one thought, but he didn't know what it meant. Why should he go mad?

It was completely dark and bitterly cold. There was stone and dust beneath him, and a sour taste at the back of his throat that made him want to throw up. He was desperately thirsty. *Will I last until morning?* Why should he wonder that? What's going to happen then? His heart was beating slowly, like a drum. There had been drums, hadn't there? *I won't go mad,* he reminded himself. *I'll survive this.* He wasn't sure what 'this' was or why or when or what or . . . He sank beneath the surface of his mind, like a fish submerging in deep water.

When he woke once more the drug had worn off, and he knew the answers to all the questions. His heart was hammering now. *I won't go mad!* He clutched at this determination as a drowning man might grasp a spar. *I won't open my eyes.* Unconsciousness lay beneath him like a black pool. He wanted to dive in and drown himself in its darkness. *I won't wake up. I won't cry out. I won't* ... Determination can only take you so far, he discovered. He woke, opened his eyes, saw nothing, understood where he was, and screamed.

He was in a tomb, stone beneath him, stone – horrifyingly – above him, a hand's-breadth from his face. He stretched out his right hand and his trembling fingers brushed stone. So too with his left hand. There was rock beneath his feet. He was breathless, wondering how much air was in the place and how long ... *I won't scream!* But he did, deafening himself. *I won't beg.* But he did, over and over. *Please ... Please!* No-one heard him or, hearing, did anything. He wasn't sure which was worse. But why should anyone help him? He was here for a reason. He'd *agreed* to this. He was here to be tested, and already he'd failed. Panic rose like a tide, squeezing his heart, his lungs, closing his throat, filling his mouth, swirling dizzily. *I'm going to faint,* he thought, welcoming the spiral into unconsciousness. But even that betrayed him, and he remained horrifyingly aware of where he was.

I'll survive this. I won't go mad. Think! He forced himself to inhale slowly and deeply. Panic receded a little, and reason returned, together with memory – the journey to the Mountain, the night in the Inn at its foot, stars in the sky, a setting moon, the black shape of the Mountain lying in the west, in his future, snow-crowned. It had been raining the following day, but during the long trudge to the summit the rain had turned to snow. Despite the fur-lined cloak, he'd been shuddering, though not entirely with the cold. There had been fire, though, a pulse of red in an expanse of white, smoke in an impossibly blue sky, the sun dropping behind the Mountain, great sheets of flame in the west. There had been ale, warmed and flavoured with bilberries. He hadn't noticed the bitterness until it was too late. Things had been strange after that, blurred, time blurring too. They'd taken his cloak away, had lowered him to the ground when his legs, unaccountably, gave way. The sky above him was red as they slid him head-first into the tomb. Then darkness. Then a deeper darkness. *I'm not here to die*, he reminded himself firmly. He was here to be tested, though he didn't know what was supposed to happen. He remembered the tales, but not the details. Some failed. Some succeeded. Some went mad. Some died. He wasn't sure he wanted to know how. But all he had to do was survive one single night without going mad. Domech had told him he'd come for him at daybreak, and druids didn't lie, but time in the tomb moved differently from the world outside, and morning seemed a long way off. Would he last that long, with the rock so close to his face he was convinced he was suffocating? *I have to get out!* he thought, panicking, then wondered if that was the test. The getting out.

Shudders were running through him continually by then. He wished they'd left him the cloak or that he was wearing his own clothes, rather than the ones they'd insisted he wear – soft deerskin leggings and a shirt belted with the woven hides of all the sacred animals of Caledonia – symbolic perhaps, but they failed to keep out the cold. His boots were wet, and his feet were numb. A man could die from a night in such cold.

Think! Remember! They'd put him in head-first and sealed the passage behind him, so that must be the way out. He wriggled in that direction and used his feet to push against the boulders that blocked the entrance, but there was no movement, not even when he kicked out in frustration, bruising his heels. He tried to turn so he could probe the passage with his fingers and perhaps pull some of the boulders away, but the space was too narrow to allow him to turn. All he could do was to slide onto his stomach. He laid his head down and sobbed.

Don't cry! Think!

He wiped his face and licked the tears from his hand. It didn't do much for his thirst, but it was something. *I'll survive this.* There was rock below and above him, rock on either side, a blocked passage at his feet, but one direction remained. He reached forward, his fingers shaking. They met nothing. The passageway in which he lay carried on, sloping downwards, narrowing until it was little more than the width of his shoulders.

No! Panic surged once more. *I can't!*

But he was here to be tested, so this must be the test. This had to be the way out. The passage must lead somewhere.

It took him a long time to find the courage to begin, to quell the hammering of his heart, to slow his breathing. *Think!* But not of the passage, not of the rock trying to crush him. He thought instead of everyone he loved, and who loved him. There were, to his surprise, more than he'd expected – Trystan, Brangianne, Ealhith, Blaize, Ninian, even Aelfric. He remembered each of them in turn as he groped his way down the passage, letting love take him down into the dark, into the earth, away from any possibility of moonlight.

There was a bad – a very bad – moment when his shoulders jammed. The rock ahead offered no purchase for his fingers, but he pushed with his feet and forced himself through.

Don't think! But he couldn't stop himself. *I can't go back now!* If he came to a narrower place he'd be trapped. He was whimpering by then, scrabbling at the rock, tearing his nails. His hands were bleeding, his mouth so dry he couldn't swallow. Panic surged once more and . . .

. . . and he was out. One last narrowing. One terrifying moment when the rocks squeezed him, tore through his shirt, gouged his skin. He fought this constriction of rock in a birthing passage of darkness, but at last he was through, slipping blood-smeared and wailing like a new-born child. He'd come here to die and be reborn. He'd hoped it would be into the light, but it wasn't. He'd hoped this would be a way out, but it wasn't. It was a way in – to the place where he was truly to be tested. What he'd been through was nothing, he understood, compared to what lay ahead in this chamber in the Mountain where ghosts dwelled. And where they would drive him mad.

His breath was ragged, his heart drumming, his fingers trembling on stone – dressed stone that fitted smoothly together. He fumbled his way along the wall, searching for another way out, but the wall was smooth, and it wasn't long before he was back where he'd started. There was dust beneath his feet and something that cracked when he put his weight on it. He bent down and groped along the floor, his fingers shaping skulls and rib-bone, finger bones and the round discs of a spine. They were grouped in little huddles with nothing to say who these men were, for there was no armour, no weapons, no jewellery, no trace of clothing. But he knew who they were for all that. They were the failures.

Frantically now, he searched around the margin of the chamber once more, but, apart from where he'd emerged, the walls were smooth, curving upwards to a ceiling that was out of reach. Only when he'd done so twice did he grope his way to the centre and find a low rocky plinth covered with more bones. But where the others were huddled together, this skeleton lay extended – a man who hadn't died in this place but who'd been placed there. Because this was his tomb. The Ancestor's. These pathetic piles of bones were his descendants. As was he.

I'm not here to die! he told himself firmly, but he'd begun to believe that was a lie, that no-one would be coming for him in the morning, that he wasn't there to be tested but—

You are here to be sacrificed.

The voice was soft and sinuous, a snake crawling inside his head.

'Arddu?'

Who else would be here at the end? I have come to claim your soul, Talorc of Atholl. I'm the reason you are here – to be punished. You turned from me. But it is not too late. Give me what I want, and I will show you the way out . . .

Corwynal scrambled backwards, for he could see eyes now, gleaming in the dark – a snake's eyes, then a wolf's, then a stag's. A shape formed on the plinth, a figure coalescing from shadows, lit by a light that had no source, no colour, a light that wasn't of the world as he knew it, light that gleamed on a spread of antlers, on the massive gold torc, on the scales of the ram-headed serpent that coiled across his shoulders. Designs on the figure's naked body mirrored those on his own. Arddu stroked the serpent reflectively and beneath his hand it became at first a hare, then – stupidly – a salmon, then an eagle that perched on his forearm. Beside him were crouched other animals, the bull, the horse, the wolf, the boar – eyes, gleaming, watching him as predators study their prey. They shifted and changed as he watched, heart stopped, breath caught. The bones on the plinth glimmered through the coruscating shiftings of this impossible light.

'You're not here,' he said desperately.

Of course I am not here! the God said testily. *I am nowhere and everywhere. I am inside you as I have always been since you killed a kinsman on this mountain. You have been mine since then, and you are mine now. When you rejected me, you were still mine. And now I have come to claim you.*

'What do you *want* from me?!'

What does any god want? Your soul. Worship – yours and your people's. Sacrifice – yours and your people's. Blood on altars. Hearts open to the sky. Promise me that, and I will help you. Take the power you were born to take. I will show you the way, and all I want in return is your allegiance, body and soul.

It was too heavy a price. Arddu had taken so much from him already, but he couldn't give him his soul, couldn't give up the one thing that would take him beyond the veil when he died. His soul was his passage to the afterlife and all the lives he might live. Without his soul, he'd be lost forever, and everyone he loved would be lost to him too.

'I'd rather die!'

You are no use to me dead. You think I would let you kill yourself? You think you can escape what waits for you here? You think this madness? It is not. Not yet. You have not even begun to suffer. You will offer me your soul willingly before the end.

Then he vanished and Corwynal was in darkness once more, but he wasn't alone. The ghosts had been gathering, only held in check by the god who'd abandoned him.

'Don't . . .' he begged Arddu. 'Don't leave me . . .'

But he couldn't make the promises Arddu wanted, not if the price was his soul. Yet if the price of his soul was his sanity, what then? His legs crumpled and he slid down the wall to rest on his heels, his head in his hands, tears trickling between his fingers.

Don't cry, said a different voice. Fingers smoothed the hair back from his forehead. It had been a long time since anyone had done that.

'Mother?'

Her arms went around him, and the scent of her hair enfolded him. He gripped her closely with a sob of relief. 'Are you really here?'

This is the tomb of the Ancestor. Where else would I be?

'Can you help me?'

Of course I can help you, Corwynal, she said reassuringly, then pushed him roughly away and struck him hard across the face, sending him spinning across the chamber. *But why should I? I asked only one thing of you – that you protect your sister. And you failed me.*

'But—'

Too late. She was gone, but someone else was there, another woman, a different scent.

You said we'd be together, Brangianne reminded him. *You promised, but you always break your promises. You lied to me!* And she struck him too.

'Please, Brangianne, just listen—'

But she was gone too, and another woman took her place, a girl.

You took me when you were drunk and didn't even remember! *Did I mean nothing to you?*

She didn't strike him, but her accusations were like a blow. She'd given him two sons, and he hadn't even seen one of them.

'Ealhith, I'm sorry . . .

You only care about one of your sons, she said bitterly. *You only care about Trystan.*

She disappeared, and Trystan was there instead.

'Trys . . . help me . . . keep me sane. You know what madness is. Save me from it. Please, Trys, I'll do anything.'

Anything? Like telling me the truth? Why can't you tell me? Are you ashamed?

'I'm afraid. But I'll tell you anything you want.'

Too late, Corwynal, Trystan said, his voice fading.

'Trys, please . . .'

Oh, don't be so pathetic! Did I save you on this mountain for nothing? Blaize complained.

And, of course, his sister was there too in the dark.

You were supposed to love me! Seirian snarled. It was his sister who'd put him in this place. How had she known of his fear of enclosed places? Someone must have told her. Trystan? No, that wasn't possible. Blaize then? But she'd never met Blaize, or Rifallyn, who was her father too.

And, naturally, the wolf of Lothian was one of his ghosts, as cold and critical as ever. *You betrayed me,* his father reminded him. *I suppose you're giving up,* he added sourly. *You always gave up too easily.*

'Please . . . father.'

You never called me father, Rifallyn complained. *I never called my own father that either. It made it easier to kill him.*

'I won't kill you,' he said tiredly. Even here, even now, at the end, the old obsession.

You will. You won't be able to help yourself. And then you'll take Lothian . . .

Then he was gone too, but he still wasn't alone for, one after another, they came at him out of the dark. His grandfather – his father's father – the man who'd kicked him and called him a half-breed. There would be no help from him. Nor from his other grandfather, the one he'd killed on this very mountain. He'd disappointed all of them, had been weak and cowardly, proud and thoughtless. He wasn't worth saving, even by the men and women he didn't know, for others came too, druids and Royal Women, warriors and chieftains, a proud lineage that had ended in him. Not one of them would help him.

I will.

It was the voice of the Ancestor himself. The Swordsman, they'd called him, the one who'd bound the tribes to his will and fought the Romans until they'd left, never to return. They said he'd borne a cursed sword, sky-metal forged, ancient and powerful, a king sword. The man's name had been forgotten, but the name of his sword was remembered. Caledan – the hard one.

'You? You'll help me?'

Why not? I was a man like you. I was brave at times, a coward at others. I was proud and thoughtless. I did what no-one else could do, but I failed in the end. I was no father's son, or mother's son. I was a bad husband and a worse father. I was as flawed as any man, and if I had a name, no-one remembers it now. Why shouldn't I help you? Come closer...

Corwynal crawled towards the plinth and touched bones, rib bones, finger bones, the solid discs of a spine, metal—

Metal?

Cold beneath his fingers, half-buried in the dust among the bones, was a long shaft of metal, smooth, ridged, its edges sharp. A sword, the blade flared like a flame, the hilt cast in flowing curves, a faceted jewel set in the pommel. Its grip fitted his hand like a glove, as if it had been made for him.

It was. It was made for anyone with the courage to claim it. They call it Caledan...

The sword dropped from his suddenly nerveless fingers as he remembered Seirian's words. *If our Ancestor favours you, you'll find the means to end it in the tomb.*

I said there was a way out... The serpent had returned and was hissing in his ear. The wolf's hot breath was on the back of his neck and he knew there was no Ancestor, that the voice had been a trick. It had been the God's, for Arddu had brought him here not only to be punished but tempted.

Are you ready to take your own life? You won't be the first. What do you think the other men died of? But it is not yet your time to die. There are ghosts still to come for you – the men you killed, the women you took without kindness, the boy you betrayed. So, shall we begin with the boy?

Corwynal groped for the sword among the bones and dust but couldn't find it. Had it ever existed? Was that a trick too?

The boy knows how you feel, Corwynal of Lothian. Alone in the dark with no one to help you. The voice fell down to him, as if from a great height. *You don't remember, don't you? The boy who begged for your help? The boy you turned your back on?*

A drop of water splashed onto his face. Then another. He groped for the sword once more, and this time he found it.

All of Atholl is waiting, Domech thought as he paced the courtyard of the Inn at the foot of the Mountain, wrapped in a heavy fur cloak to keep out the cold, for the rain of the day before had eased and the temperature had dropped. *Or is it just me?*

He looked at the Mountain, a black shape rimmed with white against a moon-washed sky, and wondered what was happening up there. *Bring him back,* the High Druid had ordered him. *Allow him to be King, but make sure he knows who to thank.* The rite of the tomb was surely the best way, but, as the night dragged by and sleep eluded him, Domech began to wonder if he'd done the right thing.

It's the will of the gods now, he'd told his assistants after they'd sealed the entrance. They were in the place of the gods after all. The others looked about fearfully, for the Mountain at the Spring Solstice was a very different place from the one they went to in celebration at Midsummer. Snow lay on the ground, the wind was cold enough to strip skin, and the sky was bleeding in the west. Later, once they'd reached the safety of the foot of the Mountain, the setting moon had emerged from the clouds, and Domech was glad he was no longer still on the Mountain, for the place would be stranger still by moonlight. Even from the Inn, he could make out the glow of the moon on snow – or ghosts.

Domech didn't believe in ghosts. Or gods. He was Archdruid, servant of gods he didn't believe in because, like all archdruids before him, and all true kings, he'd spent a night on the Sacred Mountain, waiting in terror for the judgement of the gods he worshipped. But what had happened had been much more terrifying. What had happened was nothing. No voice. No visions. No presence. All certainty gone from the world. He'd gone there to be tested, but the only test was the one he'd forced himself to succeed at every single day since that night – that of keeping this revelation to himself.

The tomb, however, was a different matter. That was a test of a man's courage, his ingenuity, his ability to free himself. Talorc had been provided with the means, though he didn't know it. It was unlikely he'd be able to free himself, however, so Domech, personally, would rescue him at daybreak. For which he'd be overwhelmingly grateful. But what if he was too late? Some men lost their reason before the night ended. Others killed themselves. And what if the worst happened and he succeeded without Domech's help? So many questions. So many doubts. What happened was out of his hands now, he thought as he stared at the Mountain and waited for the night to pass. It was in the hands of the gods. Who didn't exist . . .

Seirian wasn't waiting. She was hurrying. Haste was needed for it had taken all day. There were as many facets to a man as the people

who knew him. Some had little to say, some too much. Some were
guarded, some too open. The boy, her half-brother, talked the most,
laughing, rueful, exasperated. Honest? She wasn't sure about him
or any of the others. They had their reasons for what they said and
what they concealed. They had concerns, and with good reason, for
the druids had taken the man these strangers cared about to the
Mountain. She wondered how deep the snow would be and thought
about another man with a long climb ahead of him at the end of the
day. There were many ways for a man to die on a mountain,
especially in winter. She'd sent one man to his death, possibly two.
One was her brother. The other . . . she wasn't sure what he was or
could be. He wore a medallion about his neck that was a copy of her
own, the same symbol that had been pricked out on her brother's
arm. It symbolised balance in an unbalanced world. Dark and light.
Life and death. She had to be certain, but she might be too late.

'Hurry!' she said once they reached the far side of the loch where
horses were waiting. She thought about distances and the difficulty
of the road by night, of opposition perhaps. She was afraid they
wouldn't be in time, but they had to try. Seirian, unlike Domech,
believed in the gods and the Goddess who'd graced her own life, but
didn't believe they were on the Mountain. Nor did she think they
acted alone. They used men - and women– to make a difference to
the world. And there were more than two men on the Mountain in
actual fact.

'Hurry!' she said.

They came at him from all directions, batwings sweeping his face,
though they weren't bats, and it wasn't his face they touched but
his mind, and they screamed at him with mouths of teeth and
blood. He didn't know half of them. He'd never seen faces in the
sweet music of sword and death but he saw them now –young and
old, frightened, defiant, furious. His dead. And not just the dead.
There were others, men he'd maimed, humiliated, beaten,

despised. There were women too. He didn't know them either, hadn't been interested in their faces. They'd only been bodies bought with silver, whores and slaves, Even his first war-trophy was there, snarling at him, the girl he'd abandoned for Gwenllian. And she was there too, a ruined beauty, a red wound in a black and white room, screaming his name. *Corwynal! Corwynal!* He crouched on the plinth, his arms over his head, but still his ghosts came, clawing at his sanity.

I have to get out!

Another drop fell, icily cold, and trickled down his face like a tear. That was when the boy came.

He'd forgotten the boy on The Island, but now he was back, lifting his eyes from the ground as he'd never done in life, looking at Corwynal with empty sockets for eyes. But why? *You did the worst thing you could have done. You gave him hope when he had none.*

A fourth drop fell, striking him like a pellet of ice, as if falling from a great height. Abruptly, the voices vanished. *A great height?* He looked up but couldn't see anything. Why was water dripping? There was snow on the Mountain and it was freezing. There was no reason for snow to melt.

He'd saved the boy from four older boys who'd been beating him. He would have done the same thing, more readily, for a dog. They'd been older and bigger, but Corwynal, having just learned he was to be removed from the warrior school, had been furious and wanted to fight someone. He hadn't exactly won, but he hadn't lost either, and eventually, threatening retribution, they'd slunk off. He'd held out a hand to the boy, but he'd stared at the hand as if he'd never seen one before. He wasn't weeping, though he was as bloody from his beating as Corwynal was from the fight. He hadn't even raised his eyes. He'd gathered himself together as if he was a broken puzzle that had been badly put together, then scrabbled into a nearby storehouse. Corwynal had gone after him but the boy had vanished. Then he'd forgotten all about him, but now he wondered what hope he'd given him. Had it been as fragile as Corwynal's was now, shivering and dying as he reached up and felt nothing?

He climbed onto the plinth, scattering bones, and tried again. Still nothing, though the air was colder higher up, less foul, and moved ever so slightly. One last attempt. He jumped down, retrieved the sword, climbed back onto the plinth and probed with the tip. It touched stone, more stone and . . . nothing. There was a jagged gap in the roof, the width of his shoulders, and nothing that he could reach beyond it. Had the ceiling fallen in at some point in the past? But there were no stones lying in the chamber and the bones, directly below the gap, were still intact. It must be another way in – or out. He laid down the sword and leapt for the edge of the gap. He didn't reach it. He tried again and again. Once, his fingers touched stone but could find nothing to grip.

How does it feel? the boy whispered. *To be given hope and have it taken from you?*

He got down from the plinth and sank down onto his heels. There was a way out but he couldn't take it, not without a rope. The sword was his only way out now.

You were the boy's way out, but you left him behind to become what he became.

The boy on The Island had been, what? – seven? – maybe more, a scrawny little creature, ragged and filthy. His hair, under the grime, had been fair, unusual enough to make Corwynal notice him. He was a slave with Attecott blood, which probably accounted for his filthy appearance. The slaves on The Island were treated well on the whole, but the Caledonians of the West, the Carnonacs, hated the Attecotts of the outer islands. They believed them to be half-animal, cannibals who coupled with their mothers, who worshipped cruel and faceless gods, creatures of the night and of nightmares. But Corwynal, who'd heard such things said of Caledonians by Britons, didn't believe any of that. *Poor child*, he'd thought, and promptly forgot him.

He hadn't seen the boy again, but hadn't looked for him either. He'd been too absorbed in his secret training with The Dragon, and the lessons he was forced to learn in the druid school, both of which left him with little leisure to think, though he was aware, sometimes, that he was being watched. It wasn't until after he'd defeated The Dragon and been forced to become the weapons-master in his turn, that he'd seen the boy once more. He'd just learned that his uncle, the King of Atholl, had died, and he was to go back to Atholl to take up the position he didn't want.

Take me with you, the boy had begged in his thick accent. *Teach me to be like you.* He'd laughed. But not at the boy. He'd laughed because why would anyone want to be like him? Trapped on The Island in a role he didn't want, forced to return to Atholl to become someone he had no desire to be, cut off from the only place he could call home. But he was already planning his escape. It would be difficult and dangerous, and, if it succeeded, he'd have to find his way through miles of hostile territory while being hunted by the best hunters in Caledonia. It wasn't a journey he could take a child on.

I'll do anything, the boy had insisted. *I'll let you do anything. It wouldn't matter if it was you . . .* Then he'd told Corwynal, his eyes down, his voice devoid of expression, what that meant, what had been done to him, and what, exactly, he was offering. Corwynal had been no innocent, but these things went far beyond his experience, even his imagination. He'd been appalled, disgusted and angry.

You forced him to offer himself to you. All he had was himself. You gave him hope, then took it away again. You couldn't even turn him down. You couldn't even say no. You walked away without saying anything!

He'd said nothing and turned his back on the boy because he'd known what this would mean. He'd gone to the Head Druid and told him what the boy had said and named the druid who'd mistreated the child. The Head Druid had seemed unsurprised but assured him the matter would be dealt with. All of this, however, had taken time, thus destroying any possibility of escaping the warriors who'd come to take him back to Atholl. And so, furious with himself – and the boy – for ruining his one chance of freedom, he'd left The Island behind and with it all memories of the boy. He'd done his best for him then consigned him to the past.

You left him behind to become what he became, instead of . . . But why should you care about a child's dreams? Why should you care why he chose his name and who he thought you were – the hero out of a story.

Corwynal buried his face in his hands. He was no hero. He was as frightened now as the boy must have been, and he didn't know how much longer he could take being this afraid. *I have to get out. If only I had a rope . . .*

His stomach lurched. He did have a rope, or something like it. He had the belt, woven from strips of the hides of all the sacred animals. Feverishly, he unwound the belt and twisted it into a rope. It wasn't long but might be long enough. He tied it into a loop, got onto the plinth, scattering bones, and threw it upwards. It fell back but he tried again, and again, and again. At last, it caught on a projection. He tugged it gently, then more firmly, and it held, even when he put his whole weight on it. There was strength in the hides of bull and boar, of stag and horse, and perhaps there was magic too. He dragged off his shirt, folded it into a makeshift scabbard for the sword, and tied it behind his back. Then he took hold of the rope and hauled himself up until he was able to grasp a shelf of rock. Shoulders cracking, he pulled himself higher until he found a toehold. Then he was in the shaft and climbing. And all the time the boy's voice was reaching down to him.

If you'd helped him, he could have been anything. But do you know what he turned into instead . . . ?

A druid may not lie, so when the Head Druid had told Corwynal he'd deal with the matter he'd believed the boy would be safe. But he must have dealt with the matter by killing the boy, thus turning him into one of Corwynal's ghosts.

So why should I help you now? the boy's ghost asked as Corwynal groped his way upwards, finding hand and footholds in the dark. The ghost was no longer talking about the boy. The ghost *was* the boy, but it was a boy's voice no longer. It belonged to a man, a man who lay between him and freedom.

You left me alone. Now you're alone and no-one is coming to get you. No-one! You're not here to be tested. You're here to be sacrificed. But I can help you, even though you didn't help me, though you'll have to beg, as I begged. So beg, Corwynal of Lothian. BEG!

The voice had changed once more. This was a god's voice, Arddu's voice, a god determined to bring him to his knees, using the boy who'd become a man to do so. He wanted Corwynal to beg, to promise him anything, as he'd done before. *Anything!* He'd given his life, and his heart, but he wasn't going to give him his soul, wasn't going to give Arddu what every god wanted. Unconditional worship.

It was still dark above him, but Corwynal could smell snow and wind, and no-one, ghost, god or man, was going to keep him from that. He pulled the sword from its makeshift scabbard and stabbed upwards. He heard fabric tearing, then a cry of pain, and he was blinded by daylight. He scrambled the rest of the way up and over the lip of the shaft until he was out, in the open, under a vast sky, dimly lit by a false dawn, on a field of snow and rocks in a bitingly cold wind.

He threw back his head and laughed with relief and triumph. There were no gods here, or ghosts, but there was a man. Blood trickled from a cut across his cheek and he was wrestling one-handed – since he only had one hand – with a sword that had jammed in its scabbard.

He should have been a ghost, the last of his dead as the boy had been the first. But Ferdiad was no ghost, because he wasn't dead. Ferdiad – horrifyingly – had been the slave on The Island. And Ferdiad had come to kill him.

18

THE FIGHT ON THE MOUNTAIN

'You're alive!' That was all Corwynal said. He was standing there, bare-chested, a sword – a sword? – held loosely between his fingers.

This isn't how it was supposed to be! Ferdiad thought wildly. *He wasn't supposed to get out without my help. He was supposed to be on his knees, weaponless, weak with terror and guilt. He was supposed to beg.* Instead, blood was seeping from a cut across Ferdiad's cheekbone that had only just missed his eye, and he was trying to wrestle his sword from its frozen scabbard. He wasn't supposed to have a sword, and now he has one and I don't.

'No,' Corwynal said, which was no answer to anything.

'No, what?' Ferdiad finally managed to free his sword from the frozen sheepskin that lined the scabbard – a mistake a more experienced man wouldn't have made. It wasn't a good start. None of this was. He should have been in control, but he'd never felt less in control of anything.

'I'm not going to kill you.' To Ferdiad's astonishment, Corwynal tossed the sword to the ground. 'Not with this.'

'Aren't you afraid?'

'Afraid?' Corwynal was shivering with the cold, even after he'd pulled on his shirt. It was snowing again, lightly as yet but, from the look of the sky, more snow was on its way. 'Of course I'm afraid! I was very, very, frightened down there.' He nodded at the entrance to the chamber, a black hole in the rocky expanse of the Mountain. 'But I guess that's what you wanted?'

'Only part of it.'

'What more do you want? An explanation? I can give you one. An apology? You can have it. I shouldn't have left you on The Island. I shouldn't have forgotten you. But I thought I'd done the right thing.'

'The right thing?! Do you know what happened after you left? They asked Uuran to leave, but he took me with him, to Eriu, and there was no escape. Can you imagine what my life was like after that? To punish me, he turned me into what he was. For years I was his creature, until I killed him. It was a bad death, so he succeeded. I killed the boys too, the ones who tortured me.'

Corwynal turned pale but didn't look away. 'So you came to Atholl to kill me? Why not years ago? You've had plenty of opportunities.'

Ferdiad opened his mouth and closed it once more. He'd never had an answer to that.

'I'll tell you why – because Arddu stopped you,' Corwynal went on.

Don't listen to him, the God hissed in his nerves.

'Arddu stopped you because he needs me to be his. It wasn't that druid who made you his creature; it was Arddu. He's used you to bring me to Atholl. You think you're here to kill me, but you're not. If you were, I'd be dead now – down there.' He gestured to the tomb entrance and shuddered. 'It's not me who's here to be sacrificed. It's you – with that.' He glanced at the sword lying at his feet. A beautiful thing, a long, flared blade, the hilt set with gold wires, the pommel with a dark jewel. 'Do you know what it's called? Caledan. The hard one. The Swordsman's sword. It has power, Ferdiad, the power to bind men to the one who claims it, but it can only be claimed by death. So I'm not going to claim it. Swords have two edges and this one's no exception. Power and Grief. That's its secret name – Grief-bringer. But I've had enough grief in my life; I don't want more.'

'I don't care!' Ferdiad wanted it to begin. He wanted it to be over. 'I'm not here to die. I'm here to fight you and defeat you, to make you understand I didn't need you, because I've made myself into what I begged you to make me. And when I've defeated you, I'll make you beg for your life. My eyes will be the last thing you see before you die. So pick up that sword!'

Ferdiad stepped towards Corwynal, gripping his own sword tightly, ready for the other man to scoop up the weapon, ready to parry the blow.

'No,' Corwynal stepped back a pace.

'Coward!' Ferdiad wanted to weep with frustration.

'Yes, coward,' Corwynal replied evenly. 'But I'm not afraid of you. It's that sword I fear, because if I claim it, if I kill you, I'll become Arddu's creature as you are, ready and willing to do his bidding. He wants me to take that sword, and Atholl, to war. He wants me to bring back the old worship, to bring back human sacrifice, for you to be the first.'

Liar! He's a liar! Don't listen to him!

Arddu's voice was screaming through him and fire was running through his veins, a burning coruscating pain that threatened to consume him. The only way to stop it was to drive his blade through the heart of the man he hated. All he had to do was lift the blade and thrust. But hands were on his arms, gripping him tightly.

'Don't you see? He needs me alive, because only I can be a king. Only I will have the power to give him what he wants. What use has he for you except as a tool? He made you bring me here, for that.' He gestured at the sword lying at his feet. 'And now your usefulness is over, so don't listen to him. Fight him, not me. I bargained away my life in Lothian to Arddu, then my heart. But I won't give him my soul.'

He turned to Ferdiad, and his face was calm in the growing light. 'Please, Ferdiad. We can fight him together, the two of us.'

The rising sun was throwing long black shadows across the Mountain and scattering the loch in the west with plates of shimmering light. In the east a little light was seeping past the edges of the clouds. Once the sun was fully up, there would be others here on the Mountain.

Make him fight you!

'I need to fight you,' Ferdiad said desperately.

'You only have one hand.'

Ferdiad lashed out. The tip of his hook tore through Corwynal's tunic and sliced across his chest. 'Because you took my hand from me!'

'I saved your life!'

'What life? Fight me!'

'With my bare hands? Like last time?'

Ferdiad flushed at the memory of that humiliation but forced himself to smile. 'Things are different now. I've a sword in my hand, and I know how to use it. The Dragon taught me.'

The surprise in the other man's face was the only satisfying thing that had happened. 'Then there's this.' He lifted the hook. 'It's not without its uses, even for a man with only one hand. And I don't expect you to fight me with your bare hands. There are other weapons here. Look behind you.' He gestured to Corwynal's twinned swords which he'd carried up the Mountain and were now lying beside the tomb. 'You have no excuse.'

Corwynal glanced at his weapons, and the coil of rope lying beside them. 'I see. You intended getting me out but wanted me to beg first. Alright, if that's what you want. Please, Ferdiad, I beg you, don't do this. You may have learned to fight, but it won't have been for long. I may be older than you, and I'll confess to being tired and somewhat emotional after my . . . ordeal . . . but years of experience count. It wouldn't be an equal contest.'

He was right. Everyone had been telling him so, and in his heart Ferdiad knew it. But he couldn't step away from this.

'Let's see, shall we?'

Corwynal looked at him steadily, his face still, his eyes drifting to the sword in Ferdiad's hand, the hook in the other. Then he nodded, went over to pick up his twin swords, unsheathed and hefted them, then sank into a crouch.

'Stop playing with me!'

Ferdiad's blade swung low, forcing Corwynal to step back on ground that was a mixture of snow, ice and the tilting planes of winter-riven rock. He stumbled and fell heavily but managed to roll to one side as the other man's blade crashed down onto the ground beside his shoulder, sending sparks flying.

'I'm not playing!' This was no training match but a fight to a death that, despite his claim, was increasingly likely to be his own.

Ferdiad's blade fell once more, but Corwynal blocked it as it came down, heaved up and threw Ferdiad back. The Fili stumbled in his turn, giving Corwynal enough time to get to his feet and brace himself before the next onslaught.

The man was quicker than he'd expected. The Dragon had trained him well, and that hook, viciously sharp, was a fearsome weapon. Corwynal's shirt was already soaked with blood from the slash across his chest. He now had a similar gash along his thigh and had lost one of his swords to the hook, for when he'd parried one of Ferdiad's thrusts, the hook had slid along his blade, caught the cross-piece and torn the sword from his grasp. It had fallen into a crevice between rocks, so now he had only one with which to defend himself.

Years of experience count, he'd assured Ferdiad confidently. Confidence counted too. But he was far from confident, and the other man had him at a disadvantage. Corwynal was still shaken from his night in the tomb and was fighting badly, defending when he should be attacking.

He switched his blade to the other hand, hoping to surprise the other man, but he was expecting it. The Dragon would have taught

Ferdiad all the tricks he'd taught him. Corwynal feinted low then turned the blow into a backswing, hoping to use his weight to tear Ferdiad's sword from his grip. He'd tried it before and failed, and he failed once more.

'You're not *trying!*' Ferdiad screamed as their blades grated together and locked. Corwynal twisted, broke the lock and thrust Ferdiad back. This time it was the Fili who slipped on the treacherous surface and went sprawling.

Kill him! Arddu screamed inside him, but Corwynal shook his head and stepped back. *Kill him!*

'No!'

He had to hold onto that decision; he'd kill no-one on the Mountain, certainly not at Arddu's bidding. He'd defend himself but not attack, and he wouldn't let the music take hold of him. He could hear it in the distance, and longed for the cold clarity the music would bring, but knew he might not be able to control it, and Arddu would use that lack of control to force him to his will. On the Mountain, he had two enemies to fight.

Give in or give up, Arddu hissed at him, as Ferdiad, with a sob of frustration, rolled to his feet and launched himself at Corwynal once more.

'What do you think I am?! A child to be toyed with? Fight, curse you!'

The hook lashed out, and Corwynal lurched back to avoid losing an eye.

He blocked, parried, and hacked at the other man's sword but not his body, all the while fighting the sense of self-preservation that might drive him into the music and into Arddu's power. And that was tempting for, right then, he needed all the help he could get. He was exhausted, aching, bruised, bleeding and desperately thirsty. His feet were frozen and half-numb, his boots too thin to keep out the cold or the snow, and sweat was running down his spine and turning into ice. The light was bad and getting worse, for a bank of clouds had swallowed up the rising sun. The wind had picked up, sending swirling clouds of spindrift that bit into his skin and stung his eyes.

I just have to survive until morning,' he'd told himself in the tomb. He had survived, and it wouldn't be long before Domech and his minions arrived. A powerful druid could halt two armies in the midst of a battle, but Corwynal wasn't sure Domech could dissuade Ferdiad from killing him. He'd come close several times already.

I have to find something! He needed a way to attack Ferdiad verbally, to use some weakness to get through to him, even though that would mean fighting Arddu on two fronts, for the God would be screaming in Ferdiad's mind too. He could hear a distant echo that wasn't an echo at all. *Kill him! Kill him!* Arddu wanted a death here and, despite what Corwynal had told Ferdiad, it no longer seemed to matter whose it was. All the god needed was for one of them to kill the other, so he could turn the survivor into his creature.

Who is your enemy? The old Abbot's question pealed like a bell at the back of his mind. Here, on Atholl's Sacred Mountain, he knew it was Arddu, the god who'd claimed him when he'd killed his grandfather, the god who'd driven him, step by irrevocable step, back to Atholl to become his slave, the god who'd let Ferdiad kill him if he couldn't bend him to his will. Arddu was Ferdiad's enemy too, but he didn't understand it. Corwynal had to make him see it.

'How did the druid die? The one you killed.' He turned a deep thrust on the left and sprang back.

Ferdiad's eyes flickered in surprise at the question. Then he smiled a thin cruel smile.

'Badly – as you will.' The hook swept towards him, but Corwynal jerked out of reach. 'I cut the heart from his body while he lived and offered it to Arddu.'

Corwynal's bowels loosened at that. Was Ferdiad beyond saving? 'And the others?' he asked. Blades clashed, slid together.

'Equally badly. You really want the details?'

Corwynal thrust him away. 'Did you feel better?'

Ferdiad let his blade drop, but only for a moment.

'I don't want your *understanding!*'

'You didn't kill them for yourself. You killed them at Arddu's bidding.'

'No.' He thrust wildly, but Corwynal had expected it and smashed the blade aside.

'Then why not me?'

'You're here now.' Ferdiad lunged towards him but was unsettled by these questions. His thrust went awry, and Corwynal nearly managed to beat the blade out of his grip. The balance was shifting, and Corwynal could no longer hear that distant beat of music that wasn't his own. It was Ferdiad's, and music would be important to him.

'You're making mistakes,' he said, hammering his sword at Ferdiad's. The Fili's defence faltered for a moment, but he spun away too quickly for Corwynal to take advantage of the hesitation. 'You're not doing this for yourself. It's for Arddu. Kill me and you'll never find music again.'

He wasn't sure if that was true, but Ferdiad wouldn't know that, and he could see the doubt in the other man's face. He drove forward, forcing Ferdiad to retreat, step by step, to the edge of the cliff.

'Satisfied?' he asked. 'Is this playing? Is this not taking you seriously? Go on then – do what you came to do. Kill me. Tell everyone you killed Corwynal of Lothian single-handedly. But you'll know it's not true. Arddu is with you every step of the way, telling you what to do. Kill me and you'll never be alone ever again. And there will be no ending.'

Ferdiad stood in the place his grandfather had stood twenty-five years before. All it had taken was a step back and the old man had fallen to his death on the rocks far below. Corwynal didn't want that to happen again. He gathered himself and lunged at Ferdiad who blocked it easily, but as he did so Corwynal twisted, putting the whole weight of his body behind the movement, his whole reserves of energy, into one desperate stroke. Their blades crashed together, sung together in a peal of metal, and Ferdiad's sword, torn from his grip, went sailing into the dark to clatter on the rocks far below. Behind Corwynal, the rising sun flashed through a gap in the clouds and caught Ferdiad in a wash of golden light. His face was calm now, and remote.

'No ending?' There was a hint of amusement in the Fili's voice. 'But you'll give me one. A story has to end doesn't it? The hero has to defeat the monster so everyone can live happily ever after.'

'I'm no hero,' Corwynal said. 'I never was. And you're no monster.'

With that, he threw his own sword over the cliff to join Ferdiad's on the rocks at the bottom. 'Cuchullain killed Ferdiad in the story, but I'm not going to.'

He was already turning away so didn't see Ferdiad's face change, didn't see his left arm move, his missing hand lash out, but he felt the hook bite deep into his own left hand. His palm tore open as Ferdiad jerked back, pulling Corwynal back towards the edge. For a moment, staring into Ferdiad's furious eyes, he was balanced between past and present, between the old man losing his balance and himself. He reached for the edge as he fell, but his torn hand, slick with blood, lost its grip. The edge slithered away and he landed heavily on an overhanging slab of rock. The momentum of his fall rolled him over the edge, but this time his good hand found something to cling onto, a lip at the edge of the slab. There was nothing below him. The cliff was still in shadow, and he swung free, the muscles of his shoulder screaming as he sought desperately and futilely for a toehold.

'How does it feel having only one hand?' Ferdiad had climbed down the cliff to crouch on the slab from which he was hanging.

'Is this your revenge for that?' His left hand was a throbbing bleeding mess.

'Part of it,' he said evenly. 'This is where you beg.'

Corwynal looked up. *My eyes will be the last thing you see before you die.* Cold green eyes. If the boy on The Island had ever looked up, Corwynal might have recognised him in Ferdiad. Why had the boy never looked up? 'I'm not begging.' His fingers began to slip. 'Not to Arddu. Not to you.'

'Very well – let me give you a hand.' Ferdiad reached down and offered Corwynal the hook, every edge of which was a blade. 'Oh, wait, I forgot. I don't have one. So, this is justice. A hand for a hand. A death for a death. Hope for hope. This is where you killed your grandfather wasn't it? And where you tried to kill your sister. An appropriate place for you to die, don't you think? Unless you *beg!*'

'What's the point if you're going to kill me anyway? I'd just want to know why. You wouldn't look at me on The Island. Not once. So look at me now and tell me why not. Then I'll let go and you'll have what you want.'

'You're not in a position to make demands,' Ferdiad turned away and squinted into the growing sun.

Corwynal's shoulder was a mass of fire now and the muscles in his arm were cramping. 'Tell me! Look at me! You said your eyes would be the last thing I'd see. So *look at me!*'

Ferdiad fought, but no longer with the God. Now it was with himself.

'What is it you're too ashamed to admit? What is it I have to die for? *Look at me!*'

Against his will, fighting all the way, Ferdiad's head turned towards him, his cold green eyes on his.

'All right,' Ferdiad said quietly. 'You win. It's true. I didn't look at you because I was ashamed. Because I was a fool. Because I stole the name of a hero's friend. Because I needed a hero. Then you came and saved me and became my Cuchullain. I worshipped you because of it and because you were an outcast, like me. I worshipped you hopefully, painfully, and you didn't even notice me. Until I . . . I disgusted you, and you laughed at me then betrayed me.

But I didn't blame you, because I loved you and hated myself. That's why. That's why . . . everything.'

Corwynal's fingers slipped over the edge. 'I'm sorry,' he said as he fell.

Pain burst in Ferdiad's head and flared through his blood, his nerves, his bones. Worst of all was the pain in his wrist, the weight trying to tear his hand off.

Let him go! Arddu was screaming, deafening him.

His hand – his good hand – gripped the other man's wrist. He'd almost been too late, had grabbed him as he'd fallen. *I loved you.* What true hate didn't have love at its source? And he'd both loved and hated Corwynal of Lothian with a passion that unnerved him.

So kill him! Arddu raked talons through his mind. *Let him fall!*

For the whole of his life, Ferdiad had been ashamed of that love – as unwanted as he himself had been. Yet, despite everything he'd suffered, a little flame of hope had lingered deep in his damaged soul, something to hold on to in the dark. So perhaps that was why he was holding on now, his shoulder cracking with the strain, his muscles burning. He jammed his hook between two rocks and though the leather straps bit deep into his upper arm he was able to pull Corwynal up far enough that he could crawl onto the slab.

You defy me? Ferdiad wanted to laugh. To have surprised a god!

You defied me! The voice was cold, implacable, enormous. It filled the world, ran shuddering through his body and drove him towards the edge. He'd never be free of that voice, that presence, not until he was dead. So why not—

'No!' A hand jerked him back. 'Don't listen to him! Look at me!'

Slate-blue eyes bored into his, but the bottom of the cliff, in shadow, was calling to him. He'd be able to rest there. There would be no voice, no pain, in that shadow. *Peace, Ferdiad. Freedom . . .*

'Don't listen to him!' The pull on his arm balanced his desire to fall. 'Listen to me! You fought and defeated me. You can fight Arddu. He has nothing more than the power you give him.'

'No-one can fight a *god!*' Pain flared once more, and he folded into it, groaning. *If I tell you to kill yourself, you'll do it. You can't defy me.*

But it seemed he could. Amazingly. 'No!' he croaked, almost blacking out with the pain. 'No! No! *No!*' He screamed like a child. But he wasn't a child anymore. 'No,' the man said, and stepped back from the edge.

Silence fell like a blade. The pain in his head vanished. There was only the sound of the wind and the harsh desperate panting of two men who'd fought a god.

'Has he gone?' he whispered.

'For the moment. If he was ever here.' Corwynal leant back against the cliff and shut his eyes. 'If he really was a god. Maybe the things we call gods are nothing more than parts of ourselves, and Arddu was the worst part – the guilt and fear and shame. Listen, Ferdiad – I laughed, but not at you. I didn't despise you. I was angry, but not at you. I went to the Head Druid on The Island to demand justice. Maybe that was naïve, but I didn't betray you, and if it made things worse, then I'm sorry. I made things worse for myself too, and blamed you for it, but that was wrong. And I was wrong to forget you.'

For twenty-five years, Ferdiad had wanted this: an explanation, an apology. He'd wanted other things too, impossible forbidden things: love, revenge, death. But now it was time to forget them. Now it was time to forget Arddu too. Forgetting was sometimes the best choice.

So this is freedom, he thought, wonderingly. A strange feeling. A sparkling iridescent calm. It didn't last long. Pain returned – but it was the simple, if agonising, pain in his body. Not his mind. And his sense of self returned too, who he was, who he'd made himself.

'An interesting philosophical point,' he observed dryly. 'But we'd be better employed trying to get back up this cliff. We have, after all, two good hands between us.'

Corwynal laughed and, after a moment, so did Ferdiad. It was possible, surprisingly, to laugh.

'Domech isn't going to be pleased,' Corwynal observed.

It was then that Ferdiad remembered something he'd forgotten about. Sometimes, forgetting wasn't the best choice after all. 'It's not only Domech we have to worry about.'

Then he told Corwynal what he'd done.

By the time they'd climbed back to the plateau once more, the warband had appeared out of a snow-shower. They'd reached the boulder-field and were heading for the tomb and the two men.

'Go,' Corwynal said urgently. 'It's me they want.'

'I persuaded Ciniod to kill you if I failed. I'm honour-bound to stay.'

'Honour? So you're the hero now? And neither of us with a weapon between us.'

Ferdiad glanced over the edge of the cliff. Harpstring was down there somewhere, along with one of Corwynal's swords, but there was no time to retrieve them.

'I have this.' He held up his hook. The stump was aching and the straps were loose. 'Then there's that.' He crouched down to retrieve Corwynal's second sword from the crevice into which it had fallen. But the other man shook his head.

'You keep it. I have another.' He went over to the entrance to the tomb and picked up Caledan, the sword he'd refused to use. 'But I'm not going to use it as a weapon.'

'I see,' Ferdiad said, understanding and, as part of that understanding, kicked the unused coil of rope down the shaft into the tomb, then turned to face the approaching men. They were within bowshot now, Ciniod leading them, Broichan by his side. 'How do we do this? Back-to-back like heroes?'

There were thirty of them, which took heroism into the realms of stupidity. Nevertheless, Ferdiad began to hear music in his head, the music he found when he fought. He looked at the sun, rising beyond the clouds, at the blue of the sky in the west, the white

Mountain, the glitter of light on the loch where the sun caught it, the man by his side. All impossibly precious.

'Side by side,' Corwynal said. 'Like friends.'

Ferdiad wanted to weep at that, but forced himself to laugh instead. 'Friends? Isn't it a bit soon for that? I just tried to kill you, in case you'd forgotten.'

'That wasn't you.'

'Listen,' Ferdiad said urgently, for the men were closer now and there wasn't long to say all the things that needed to be said. 'I didn't defeat you, and you know it.'

'I seem to remember hanging by my fingertips.'

'You know what I mean. And what I said . . . I didn't intend to burden you with that.'

'It took courage to say it. I'd like the courage, to tell someone . . . something I'm ashamed of.'

It was a confirmation of something Ferdiad had long suspected. 'You should tell him, you know—'

'Tell who what?' The voice came from behind them, and Corwynal whirled around. Ferdiad, recognising the voice, turned more slowly. Two men clambered over the edge of the cliffs where Ferdiad had climbed to the plateau.

'Trys! What in the Five Hells are you doing here?' Corwynal demanded.

'I heard you were in trouble,' Trystan said lightly, running his eyes over his . . . father? . . . and frowning at his torn hand. 'Where else would I be?' His gaze shifted to Ferdiad who braced himself, remembering the last time they'd met, but all he could see in Trystan's face was the same joyous welcome he'd given Ninian. 'Ferdiad!'

'What's that snake doing here?' Aelfric wanted to know.

'Saving my life,' Corwynal replied.

'What happened to your hand?' Trystan asked, then his gaze shifted and flew to Ferdiad's face. 'What happened to *yours?*'

'Long story.'

'This is no time for stories, long or short.' Aelfric hefted his axe and nodded at the approaching men, all of whom had drawn their weapons and lifted their shields. 'Ten each,' he muttered in satisfaction, as if a lesser number might not be worth bothering with.

'Seven and a half, actually,' Ferdiad said. 'But you can have my half.'

'You can use that thing?' Aelfric glanced at the sword in Ferdiad's hand.

'I think we're about to see.' Trystan moved to the left to protect Corwynal, and Aelfric moved to his right.

It was all impossibly calm. *Is this what it's like? To be with comrades facing your enemies?* Was this what had been missing all his life? The irony of finding this out only now didn't escape him. He glanced at Trystan beside him, bracing himself for the weakness he'd felt at the Crannog, but that had gone, though the joy remained. The Mountain had changed him in more ways than he'd thought possible.

'There will be no fighting,' Corwynal said firmly, and stepped past Trystan, holding Caledan above his head. Everyone in Atholl had been brought up on tales of the Swordsman and his magic sword, so they all recognised the weapon. 'You know what this means?' he called out.

The men halted, uncertain. They wouldn't have wanted to come here, even in the light of day. They believed there were gods on this mountain. And now they faced a man with a mythical sword, and two strangers one of whom, to Ferdiad's eye, had all the golden looks one might expect of Ludus of the sun, and the other, bearded and bearing an axe, must resemble Taranis, god of thunder. *What does that make me?*

'You think you're King now?' Ciniod stepped towards Corwynal, his sword in his hand.

'I know you're not.'

'You've no right to be here. You're not from Atholl!'

'I've more right than you. I went into the tomb to die and was reborn. You've never chosen to be tested in that way, but if you had you wouldn't have succeeded. You're too fat.'

There was a faint snigger from among his men, and Ciniod reacted predictably.

'I'm not too fat to fight you!'

'Why should I do that?' Corwynal said. 'Why should I kill the leader of my warband?'

My warband. Mine, Ferdiad noted with delight.

'What? But—'

'But if you no longer wish to hold the position, I can always give it to your son,' Corwynal added, startling Broichan. 'Except I suppose you want to fight me too,' he went on, turning to the younger man. 'But I'm tired of fighting.'

'I'll fight him for you,' Trystan offered, eyeing Broichan.

'Who in the Five Hells are you?' Ciniod demanded.

'Corwynal's – sorry – Talorc's half-brother. I'm Trystan, heir to Lothian and—' He stopped and grinned ruefully. 'Well, just Lothian now I suppose.'

'And you?' Ciniod asked the big Angle.

'I'm Aelfric of Gyrwum in Bernicia. And once I've pulled your guts through your nostrils, I'll take you all on, every last one of you.'

None of Ciniod's men understood what he was saying, for he was speaking in Gael, but they understood the gist of it. They raised their shields, lifted their swords and edged closer.

'No-one—' declared Domech, shoving his way through the line of warriors, a small pack of druids at his heels. '—is fighting anyone.' He strode towards Corwynal, brushing Ciniod aside, and fell to his knees at his feet. 'My Lord King,' he said loudly and clearly

His druids knelt also. Then Trystan and, more reluctantly, Aelfric. Then Ferdiad. He'd thought Corwynal a hero once, but he wasn't that. He was a king. A man was allowed to love a king, wasn't he? One by one, the warriors also knelt, Broichan last of all, pulling his father to the ground with him.

'Don't imagine *I'm* going to kneel, you stupid, *stupid* man!'

Brangianne burst through the pack of warriors, went straight over to Corwynal then, despite her words, knelt at his feet.

'Please, my heart, don't kneel to me.' He bent down to raise her, but she slapped him away and grasped his injured hand.

'I'm not kneeling,' she said tartly, fishing in a bag that hung from her shoulder. 'I'm trying to see what you've done to your hand. Hold still!'

The other woman came more slowly. The warriors all made way for her.

'My Lord King,' Seirian said stiffly, stopped before him and prepared herself to kneel, but Corwynal stopped her.

'The Royal Lady of Atholl kneels to no man.'

'But she can apologise,' she said quietly, and Ferdiad knew how much that must have cost her.

Corwynal held out his good hand to her. 'We both have apologies to make, in time. And many other things to say to one another.'

'And to me! I *like* stories!'

Seirian stiffened, and she was no longer the remote and untouchable Royal Lady of Atholl but a mother and an exasperated one at that. 'Kirah, I told you to stay . . . Oh, why do I bother!'

Domech cleared his throat, got up from his knees and gestured for his druids to do likewise.

'This is an abomination!' he declared. 'There should be no-one here but the King and myself, and yet I find half of Atholl here. This is not some feast-day market. This is a place of the gods and you—' he pointed his finger one by one at Ciniod, Broichan and all the warriors, '—have by your impiety desecrated the Sacred Mountain. Now go, before I decide to banish you all from the rites.' He snapped his fingers at one of his own men, who came forward with the cloak Corwynal had been wearing the previous day, and Domech laid it tenderly about Corwynal's shoulders. The two men looked at one another in calculation, and Ferdiad had to repress a smile.

'I'm grateful to you, Lord Archdruid,' Corwynal said, and Domech's shoulders sagged with relief. 'I would ask you now to resanctify the Mountain and make the place fit for the gods once more. And lay bare the tomb.'

'But—'

'The bones of the Ancestor should be laid in the light. No man should ever have to go into such darkness to face his destiny. See to it.' He smiled thinly, then allowed his smile to broaden as he looked around at them all. 'Well, I don't know about the rest of you, but I'm hungry . . .'

He headed for the top of the sacred way, and everyone followed, everyone except Domech and Ferdiad.

'There's a rope down there,' Ferdiad said nodding at the shaft that led to the tomb. 'It wasn't used, but maybe it's best no-one finds out about it . . .'

Domech looked at him uneasily. 'What happened here?'

'Long story,' he replied. 'A very, *very* long story.'

PART IV

ATHOLL,

BELTEIN TO LUGHNASADH 488 AD

THE KING OF ATHOLL

We have many things to say to one another. Seirian reminded herself sourly of those words when, a month after the events on the Mountain that had changed so much, she still hadn't really spoken with the man she struggled to think of as a king, far less a brother.

Yet in a few days it would be Beltein, and, in a solemn ceremony at the Nemeton, he'd be invested with the great silver chain of Atholl and formally named King. In truth, however, he was already ruling, and Atholl was beginning to change. Some of those changes weren't surprising; traders, in small selective numbers, had been invited to Dun Caled with their wares, and agreements had been reached with the Dragon-riders of Raineach. Tentative overtures made to Circind had been rejected, however, and though Drest Gurthinmoch had been informed of the return of Atholl's King, he'd yet to reply.

That Seirian knew these things wasn't surprising. She still had her sources, though she hadn't needed them, for there was now a Royal Council to advise the King, its members chosen by him. To her surprise, Seirian had been invited to be part of it, her advice sought, even taken, though not always.

Domech, naturally, was furious. He'd expected to be Talorc's sole advisor, and he disapproved of the Council in general and its members in particular, for it included not only herself, some of the other druids and the older warriors, but Atholl's former King-regent Ciniod, whom everyone had expected to be put to death. Was it weakness that Talorc had chosen not to? Or confidence? Seirian couldn't make up her mind. Indeed, the man she refused to think of as a brother remained a mystery to her, not least because he avoided being alone with her. When they met, he treated her with the respect due to the Royal Lady of Atholl, as if they weren't related, as if neither had almost caused the death of the other.

'He's afraid.' Brangianne was stripping leaves from a bunch of young willow while Seirian spun, the woollen thread thinning and twisting in her fingers.

'Of me?' Seirian, laid down her spindle and looked at her in surprise. Indeed, there was much about the other woman that surprised her. She was Talorc's lover, apparently, but spent little time with him in Dun Caled, preferring, she said, the quiet of the Crannog settlement where her niece and servant, both in the late stages of pregnancy, remained. She didn't seem to be interested in wielding the power she must have, in being a queen, and had laughed at the idea. 'I wouldn't be any good at it, and Corwynal – Talorc – knows it. Anyway—' she added, sobering. '—he has a wife already. And two sons. In Lothian.'

In Lothian, where his – and Seirian's – father ruled, a man she couldn't begin to imagine. Surely that was one of the things they should be talking about?

'He doesn't talk about his father,' Brangianne told her. 'Or his wife and sons. And he'll struggle to talk to you.'

'He speaks to everyone else.' Seirian's sources had told her he listened not only to the advice of his Council but to the opinions of farmers and fishermen, hunters and smiths, basket-makers and leatherworkers.

'But few women,' Brangianne said. 'He isn't comfortable with women.' Brangianne gave a faint, reminiscent smile. 'To your brother, the ruling of Atholl is a small thing compared with dealing with a sister he didn't know he had. Has he been avoiding you? I thought he might. But then you've not tried to get his attention, have you? I don't blame you, though. It's not easy being the sister of a king. But I was one once, so I know he needs you.'

'Needs me? For what?'

'I don't know. I doubt he knows. But you ought to find out. He'll go to the Mountain before they make him King. He'll need to think, and he likes to be up high when he thinks. He'll be alone . . .'

And so Seirian had crossed the loch and made her way to the Inn at the foot of the Mountain to confront the man who, if Brangianne was to be believed, was both afraid of her and needed her.

'What are you doing here?'

He was, as promised, alone, but Seirian could see neither fearn or need, just suspicion and annoyance.

You're alike, Brangianne had told her. *In more ways than you think.*

Seirian hadn't asked what she meant by that but had a good idea. Proud and unyielding, independent and determined to need no-one.

'Why shouldn't I be here? I've as much right as you – no, more – to be here.' She caught herself – this wasn't helping – and attempted a smile. 'I came for the talk you promised me.'

'Not now,' he said curtly. 'Not here.'

He is afraid, she understood. *And so am I.*

'Up there then?' She nodded at the Mountain. 'That's where you're going, isn't it?'

The snow had disappeared from the heights, and the rowans were heavy with blossom, the birches tossing their new leaves in the wind. The day was fine, the sky streaked with high feathers of cloud. Even Atholl's incessant wind had died down, and the mild air smelled of growing things. She looked up at the Mountain sailing against the sky; the ascent would be long but not daunting – not as daunting as the conversation they were going to have. 'We can talk on the way.'

But he set such a fast pace she struggled to keep up and panted with the effort, but anger forced her on. 'How dare he treat me like this!' she muttered to herself, then wondered if she deserved it. She'd had him entombed though he'd begged her not to. She'd sent Ferdiad to fight him if he got out. She'd persuaded Ciniod to kill him if Ferdiad failed.

'Why did you want to come here?' she asked as the gradient eased and she managed to catch up with him.

'Everyone believes there are gods here,' he said as they picked their way across the boulder field. 'You and I – and Domech – know that's not true. But it means no-one comes here, and I wanted to be alone, to think.' He stopped and turned to look into the sun, eyes narrowed. She followed his gaze into the long distances that lay beyond the pale summit of stones, beyond the darker hills that lay between the Mountain and the loch, beyond the foothills of the uplands that separated Atholl from the lands of the Britons. Those lands were hidden by the hills but she could imagine fields and rivers, settlements in broad plains, a land bounded by something they called a sea. But she'd never seen a sea and couldn't imagine a body of water larger than her loch. Was that what he was searching for? The sea?

'I wanted to see Lothian,' he said.

'And can you?' His eyes were screwed up, and a pulse leapt in his throat. His lips were half-parted as if he saw or imagined—

'No.' He turned away and strode across the boulders to the summit rocks, leaving her struggling to follow.

The tomb had gone. The boulders that had formed its walls were piled in an open hollow, the exposed slabs of quartzite blinding in the light, their surface as yet unmarked with the lichen that pocked the rest of the rocks. Some bones lay on one great slab but most had fallen to one side, swept away by rain and wind. She crouched to pick one up, but, brittle with age, it crumbled in her fingers. A winter would see them vanish, and all that would remain would be memory, more resilient than bones.

The summit rocks were the same as they'd always been, but there too memories were more substantial than stone. There was too much past here, hers and his, too much violence on both their parts. *You're alike.* If that was true, he was here for the same reason as her, to resolve the past and decide about the future, so she knew the question he'd come here to ask.

'You're here to decide what sort of king Atholl needs and if you can be that man,' she said. 'Even though you know it would mean saying goodbye to Lothian.'

His eyes widened. 'How did you know?'

'The Goddess speaks to me. She knows the hearts of men.' Then she shook the words away. That was the Royal Lady speaking, not Seirian. 'Shall I tell you what Atholl needs? A strong king. A man who understands the past and has the strength to learn from it. A man who listens and weighs opinions before making a judgement. A man who makes allies out of his enemies when he can but is resolute in the defence of his people and his land when he can't. A man who makes hard choices and bitter sacrifices. A man who, by accepting the responsibilities of power, accepts that, in all the ways that matter, he'll always be alone. A man who—'

She stopped. Her throat had closed, and her eyes prickled with tears. She was describing not a king but a Royal Woman.

'Seirian . . .' He reached out to her, but she stepped back.

'Is that what Atholl's going to get?' she asked. 'Is that you?'

He turned away and folded his arms across his chest. He'd abandoned the bronze armband he'd been wearing when he'd first come to Atholl, and the symbol of Atholl's royal house, of serpent and broken spear, was clear for anyone to see. The skin had been pale at first but was no longer, as if his body had accepted his heritage more easily than his mind.

'I don't know,' he said, half to himself. 'But I can tell you what sort of king I'd like to be. A Steward. I was a Steward in Lothian and . . . other places. I was a man who cared about the harvest and the law, about winter stores and seed crops, who dreaded a long winter or war. I was a man who lay awake in the night, thinking about new types of plough or breeds of sheep. My fingers were always stained with ink.' He unfolded his arms and looked down at his hands, spreading the fingers and turning them over. There was no trace of ink now, just the callouses of a swordsman and a healing scar across his left palm. 'I was despised as a servant,' he went on. 'And I had enemies, for every time I made a decision there were those who lost, and they had longer memories than those who gained. There were times when I felt alone, but I never was, not really, because I had people I cared about. Even when they didn't care for me, they were the people I fought for, the people I made sacrifices for. They were why I came to Atholl.

'It seems to me a king should, above all, be a servant to his people. He should care for them as he cares for his own family, be a peacemaker in a sea of enemies, and let his enemies live because one day he might turn them into allies. Some will see that as weakness, and perhaps they're right. I don't know. I can't see into the future. I can only shape it according to the sort of man I am, with all my manifest flaws. So, in truth, we're not talking about the sort of king I'll become, only of who I am – full of doubt, groping my way in the dark in a desperate attempt to avoid chaos. And there's no clarity to be found, even here.' He swept one arm about the land lying below them. 'Lothian lies behind me now, but I can't see the way ahead. Can you? Am I the sort of king Atholl needs, or deserves? Tell me, Seirian, you who're so sure of everything.'

But she wasn't. She too was groping in the dark. They were alike. Brangianne was right about that, and about something else. He did need her.

'Shall we put it to the test?' she asked. 'Shall we have the conversation we've both been avoiding? Not the one about the past but the future? Shall we talk about enemies and allies, of family and sacrifice? About how to avoid chaos? I know you've been talking to Domech, and he'll have told you I've been . . . Intransigent is the word he favours. He'll have told you about the threats he used and how those threats brought you back. And he'll have told you it's your turn to make threats. You need me to take a Consort, someone to bolster your position – and his. He'll have suggested I be offered as part of your negotiations with Circind, or with Drest. Am I right?'

He smiled. 'Word for word. Is that what you think I'm going to do?'

'No, because you're cleverer than that. You see further. You don't want to be bound to Circind or Drest. You'll look for another solution. But whatever it is, I know I'll be part of it. I tried to have you killed, and I need to make reparation for that, so I'll accept your judgement, your decision, whatever it is.' She smiled at him, at her judge, at the man who'd take her freedom away. 'There – I've made it easy for you.'

'I don't need you to make it easy,' he said. 'A king sacrifices himself, not his family. And you, Seirian, despite everything, are part of my family. I make no demand, no suggestions. You may do what you choose, choose who you want, and I'll support you. I'll even support your refusal to choose. I give you your freedom.'

'My . . . my freedom? But why?'

'Because, long ago, I promised to protect you, and I failed. If there's reparation to be made, it's I who needs to make it. So I'll protect your freedom for as long as I can, though there will be consequences. I can't have Atholl torn apart by factions, so must name an heir. If you choose not to have a son, my heir will be Broichan. With time, I can shape him into a worthy successor.'

'And if I do decide to have a son?'

'Then I'll fight for him as I'd fight for you, though it would be simpler – and safer – for you to choose Broichan to father him. But it's your choice, Seirian. Yours.'

Freedom. Choice. Such gloriously impossible concepts. Family, though. She hadn't expected to be made part of his family, to be the sister of a man who might be too similar to her for comfort but whom she'd come to respect.

He'd come to the Mountain for answers, but they'd been inside him all the time. It was she who'd needed answers, and now she had them. Or some of them at least. She picked her way down the summit rocks, found a flat-topped boulder and sat down. It was warm out of the wind and heat radiated from the sun-bleached stone.

'So,' she said when he sat down beside her. 'Tell me all about my family.'

For so long there had only been her and Kirah. Now there were others – a half-brother and a father, nephews. And an uncle.

'You won't like him,' Talorc warned her, though his smile was affectionate. 'But you can decide for yourself since you'll meet him in a few days. I've invited him to the kingmaking. His name,' he added, 'is Blaize.'

'You think it's a trap?' Arthyr asked Blaize after reading the letter that purported to be from Ferdiad.

'If so, it's not very subtle, which isn't Ferdiad's style.' Blaize read through the letter once more, an invitation to a kingmaking, in Atholl. Ferdiad didn't say who the king was to be. Blaize's presence was requested. *Previous misdemeanours are now seen to be more in the way of misunderstandings and your exile from Atholl is therefore revoked.* Now that *was* Ferdiad's style; the man couldn't use one word where ten would do the job with rather more élan. *And in case of any understandable apprehension, I've included a token that will guarantee safe passage to Dun Caled.* The token was a flat wooden disk with the sign of the wolf carved on one side. *We look forward to seeing you at Beltein.* Who was 'we'? *You'll find some old friends here, including Domech, who sends his love, by the way.*

That last part was certainly a lie.

'You trust Ferdiad?' Arthyr asked. 'If it really is from him.'

'Gods, I've never trusted him! But I think it must be from him. The druids of Atholl are pretty hard-line, and don't approve of writing. I can't say I do either when it brings something quite as irritating and intriguing as this. The Latin's impeccable, as is the handwriting. Yes, it's definitely Ferdiad. What I don't know is what he's up to, but I guess I'll have to go to find out. A new king in Caledonia can't be ignored, especially one in Atholl.'

'Does this mean war?' Arthyr glanced at the map on his desk. 'The Caledonians have been suspiciously quiet of late.'

'I agree. Something's going on north of the frontier, though I doubt we'll see war before the harvest, certainly not until after Lughnasadh, given that the Caledonian harvest's always later than ours. But this—' He tossed the letter back to Arthyr. '—this might be the beginnings of it.'

'We're not ready for a full-blown war this year, not after that Galloway business, though it seems to have blown over. I assume the run-away lovers are still in Raineach?'

'I can't think where else they might be, but I'll try to find out when I'm in Atholl.'

Old friends. What did that mean? Blaize picked up the token and turned it over. On the back was another sign, the serpent and broken spear that symbolised the royal house of Atholl, the sign on the medallion Ciaran had given Ferdiad. And what did *that* mean? He would like to have consulted Ciaran about all this, but there wasn't time. Beltein was only a few days away.

'Be careful, Blaize.'

'Oh, I'll be careful,' he said fervently.

Ferdiad met him at the border by the ferry that crossed the river downstream of Dun Caled on a bright windy day with the promise of summer in the air.

'What's this all about?' Blaize asked as soon as he'd coaxed his reluctant gelding off the raft. He was equally reluctant, for the two warriors who'd been waiting with Ferdiad were eying him disapprovingly. But after a word from Ferdiad they trotted off along the track that led upstream. Behind him, the ferry slipped back across to the other side of the river. For good or ill, he was in Atholl now.

'Nervous, Blaize?' Ferdiad asked sweetly. 'Justifiably, given what happened the last time you were here. But there isn't anything to fear. You got my letter, I assume.'

'A letter which told me nothing.'

'I didn't want to spoil the surprise. Now come along. You're a day later than I expected, and I've been hanging about this ferry since daybreak.' He eyed Blaize critically. 'I do hope you've got something else to wear. You can't be presented to Atholl's new king looking like that. He's very particular, you know.'

It was a game, of course. Ferdiad would drop hints and clues all the way to Dun Caled, and Blaize was expected to put the puzzle together before they got there. Well, he wasn't playing a game in which Ferdiad held all the pieces, so he lapsed into a sullen silence which failed to depress Ferdiad's irritatingly high spirits as he pointed out various features on the way, much as one might to any visitor. Eventually, Blaize could stand it no longer.

'You appear to like Atholl,' he remarked.

'I do. It suits me.'

Blaize glanced at the man riding loosely at his side and wondered what it was about him that was different. He looked taller somehow, his silver hair longer and lifting in the breeze, his shoulders broader, a man comfortable in his own skin for once. He seemed – and this wasn't a word Blaize would ever have associated with Ferdiad – happy. 'You're staying then?'

'Why not? I lost one King, but in Atholl I've found another to equal Feargus. In all the good ways, that is. He's not half as devious.' Ferdiad grinned. 'He has me for that.'

'And your position is . . . ?'

Ferdiad shrugged. 'Advisor, I suppose. Not bard, sadly.' He glanced down at his silver hand. 'But I compose the odd poem, the odder satire and far too many riddles. I have my uses. As you will. It was me who suggested you be invited, you know. Domech didn't want me to, of course. That bit, in my letter, about him sending his love – that wasn't true. He's Archdruid now, and a man at bay, not sure what to make of his new king. He doesn't like change, but changes are being made. That's why you're here. In times of change, the Brotherhood should be represented, don't you think?'

Ferdiad was wearing his medallion openly, Blaize noticed. He'd know what the sign on the reverse meant now, if not how it related to himself, something that had been puzzling Blaize ever since he'd seen it. Maybe when they reached Dun Caled, the mystery would be solved.

'We need to talk about the Brotherhood,' Ferdiad went on, sounding serious for the first time, diffident almost. 'I want to be part of it.'

'Then stop playing games!'

Ferdiad smiled his green glinting smile, and all seriousness was gone. 'But it's all a game, and this particular game's so tempting! You know me, never one to resist temptation. I doubt that will change. Anyway, here we are . . .'

They'd passed some settlements on the banks of the river, and a fort not far from the ferry, but as the river had narrowed the track had risen steadily through woodland until the river lay far below them. Then, suddenly, they were out of the trees and Dun Caled reared above them – walls of fire-fused stone barred with iron-studded oak gates guarded by men wearing the wolf of Atholl. Beyond the outer gates were yet more walls crowned with a wooden rampart. Banners flew from the heights, the wolf once more, together with Atholl's royal symbol, the serpent and broken spear. There were more gates, men who saluted Ferdiad with respect and who glanced curiously but disapprovingly at Blaize until Ferdiad handed over his safe-passage token, whereupon they straightened and saluted him also, and waved them on through the gates. Beyond these lay only one building, the royal residence of Dun Caled, a building so tall it rivalled both Dunpeldyr and Dunadd in splendour, though it was much older, its wood faded to silver. Servants bustled to and fro between hall and various out-buildings that housed kitchen, brewery and storerooms, but the hall itself was empty – a high echoing space that smelled of freshly cut meadowsweet. The upper windows were open, carved columns rose to smoke-stained rafters, and a line of glowing firepits ran down the hall to the raised platform at the far end on which stood three chairs.

'Silverhand!' Something small sped across the hall towards them and grabbed Ferdiad about the knees, almost knocking him over.

'Steady, infant!' He caught up the child – a girl of about seven, and swung her under his arm.

'I'm not an infant!' The girl struggled in Ferdiad's grip, but not very hard. 'Put me down! This is unseemly!'

'As was your greeting.' Ferdiad set the girl back on her feet. 'Blaize, may I present Kirah, the future Royal Lady of Atholl,' he said gravely. 'Kirah, may I present—'

'He smells funny,' the girl announced, wrinkling her nose.

'Granted, but—'

'Kirah!' A woman came towards them from the back of the hall, passing from darkness into a wedge of light thrown from one of the high windows.

'The man's here,' the girl announced, running towards her. 'And he smells funny.'

Blaize stared at the woman. He recognised her features, for they were his nephew's and his own, and his understanding of the world altered, as if he was standing on a shifting field of scree. She'd fallen. Surely she'd fallen!

'I thought you were dead! We – that is—'

'This is—' Ferdiad interrupted.

'I *know* who this is!' Blaize's head was hurting now. 'I have to tell Corwynal! He believes—'

'No, he doesn't. Not anymore.' A man was now sitting in the central chair. The moving field of scree, still carrying Blaize with it, reached the bottom of the mountain and everything slid into place. 'Ferdiad hasn't told you, has he?' Corwynal asked resignedly and frowned at Ferdiad. 'I told you to write.'

'I did write, though I may have left out a few things . . .' Blaize looked from one to the other. *I've found a king to equal Feargus.* Not to obey, however. That wasn't Ferdiad's style. But that meant . . . 'You?' he asked, looking at Corwynal but seeing the board in Ciaran's room, seeing a piece carved with both wolf and serpent slide neatly into place. He was wearing the royal tattoo openly, Blaize noticed. 'You're the King?'

'I will be tomorrow, at Beltein. Which is why you're here. We've a lot to talk about, but first – since effectively I'm King already – there's something I've always wanted to do. Guards!' he called out, and the two men at the door hurried over. 'Arrest this man!'

Blaize looked about in alarm, but everyone was smiling.

'And give him a bath!'

They met later that day on the ramparts that overlooked the river far below. Corwynal had always liked being up high, and Blaize found him leaning on the edge, gazing morosely into the dark waters of the Tava. But he turned and smiled when Blaize appeared, freshly bathed, smelling of some sort of flower, and wearing clothes that weren't his own.

'I'm sorry about the bath, but it was too tempting. There aren't many advantages to being King, so I have to indulge the few I have.'

'Why am I here, Corwynal?'

'To advise me.'

'You seem to have Ferdiad for that, but if you're asking me for advice, it would be this; don't trust him. The last time I last saw him, he was intent on killing you.'

Corwynal shrugged. 'He tried and failed, though my hand will never be the same.' He spread his fingers and winced. A newly healed purple scar ran across the palm of his left hand. 'I suppose, in the circumstances, it was justice,' he said reflectively, then took a deep breath. 'I'd better tell you everything . . .'

It took some time, but by the time he'd finished Blaize understood much that had puzzled him and had a new view of the world. *How much of this does Ciaran know? How much of this did he plan?*

'So—' Corwynal said once he'd reached the end, '—what am I supposed to do?'

'Do? Rule, as you've been doing. Carefully. Keeping Ciniod as warband leader was a clever move, though, as I recall, he was a waste of space.'

'His son Broichan isn't though. If it comes to war, I'll give him the command. And it will, Blaize. It will come to war. So whose side am I on? Oh, I know what you're going to say – that I've already chosen a side. My family's in Atholl now: Brangianne, Trystan, Yseult, Aelfric, Oonagh, even Ferdiad. Then there's Seirian and Kirah. I'm here for all of them. But it doesn't feel right, Blaize. I keep thinking about Lothian, about my father not knowing he has a daughter, about Arthyr and Bedwyr and the lads. I hear Arthyr's strength and influence are growing, but I also hear stories of Drest Gurthinmoch's ambitions. So it *will* come to war between the Britons and the Caledonians, and Atholl will be the key. So, what do I do?'

'I think,' Blaize said slowly, his mind on the game that couldn't be won, 'you're here to keep them apart.'

'How?'

'I don't know, Corwynal. I really don't know.'

The token arrived about midday, carried by one of Corwynal's messengers. *I should call him Talorc now,* Brangianne thought. But even a month after the crowning she still thought of him as

Corwynal, which was strange since she'd known him as Talorc when they'd first met. But that man had lied to her. Corwynal hadn't, though he still had secrets. What had happened on the Mountain, for example.

'Are you leaving today?' Seirian asked. She would have had a good idea of what the messenger carried, the special token that was for Brangianne alone, the serpent and spear on one side, a swan on the other, a token with an unspoken message. *Come. I need you.*

Brangianne smiled and felt the familiar turning over of her insides, half desire, half simple happiness. *We'll be together*, he'd promised. And now they were, for most of the time at least, when she was with him in Dun Caled. The rest of the time she spent at the Crannog settlement with Yseult, Oonagh and Ninian, together with Seirian and Kirah. Kirah was enchanting and exasperating in turn – a typical seven-year-old – but Brangianne still hadn't made up her mind about Seirian. Her looks, so similar to Corwynal's, were unsettling, her position in Atholl society so much like that of a queen. She'd tried to have Corwynal killed, which wasn't easy to forgive, though, to be fair, Corwynal had almost succeeded in killing her when she'd been a child. Atholl was like that – a hard and uncompromising place, but Brangianne felt safe there. And if she was safe, so were the others. Even Corwynal was as safe as any king could be, or make himself, though it wasn't easy, and there were times when he was a man at bay.

'I feel as if I'm walking on eggshells,' he said after one particularly gruelling Council meeting. Then he'd smiled. 'I don't know why I'm complaining. I was Steward of Lothian, and now I'm Steward of Atholl. There's no difference, except in Atholl I don't have a king to deal with.'

Only an Archdruid. Brangianne didn't like Domech for all sorts of reasons. Even if he'd been a more approachable person, she doubted if she could ever accept someone who'd done such terrible things to Ninian. Ninian might have forgiven him, but Brangianne couldn't. Oddly, Domech approved of her, though his reasons made her like him even less.

'As the King's concubine—' he'd informed her, '—you have no status in Atholl, and nor would any children, if you had any, or were likely to.'

She'd hated him for that and had wept for days afterwards because he'd confirmed what she'd begun to believe – that she was barren. It didn't help that she was surrounded by other women's fertility. Oonagh had given birth to a son a week before, and both mother and child were thriving. 'I only breed sons,' Aelfric had announced complacently. He'd named his son Osric but didn't spend much time with him. He had his duties in Dun Caled as part of Corwynal's honour guard, he explained. Trystan was part of the guard too, but it didn't stop him making one excuse after another to visit the Crannog settlement. He spent as much time as he could with Yseult and was determined to be with her for the birth.

Oonagh had snorted at that, and Seirian had shaken her head. Brangianne agreed with them; the birthing chamber was no place for a man. 'It won't be born for a month yet,' she pointed out.

'He,' he corrected her. 'He will be a son.'

In the end Yseult herself sent him away. 'Just let me rest, Trys. Go back to Dun Caled. Brangianne will send for you when it's time.'

After it's over, Brangianne decided. 'She doesn't need you, Trys,' she told him. 'The people she needs right now are me and Oonagh and Seirian. And Ninian.' His expression had darkened at that. 'The person who needs *you* is your brother,' she went on. 'Go back to Dun Caled and guard him for me. You and Aelfric are the only people I trust to shield him from all the people who want to harm him.'

There were too many of those for comfort. Ciniod, the previous king – or something like a king – appeared to have accepted the situation. He was lucky to be alive, and he knew it. But Brangianne was less sure about his son Broichan, an ambitious young man who was biding his time. The Archdruid was on Corwynal's side, but the

Druid College was divided, apparently. Then there were the other Caledonian kingdoms. Corwynal had tried to negotiate with Circind, but a meeting on the border had ended in bloodshed. Corwynal hadn't been hurt, but that was largely due to his bodyguard, the core of which was Trystan, Aelfric and – surprisingly – Ferdiad.

She still didn't know what to make of Ferdiad. In many ways, he was the man she remembered – acid-tongued, amusing, unreliable, irreverent, inclined to do a thing and ask permission afterwards. But the healer in her saw that something that had been broken inside him was beginning to heal. What had happened on the Mountain? Neither man would say, though the evidence of a fight between them had been clear enough. Corwynal's hand had taken a long time to heal. *How did you do that?* she'd asked. *I fell,* he'd replied and changed the subject. He'd certainly fallen – his body had been a mass of bruises with one rib broken – but she'd guessed what had happened to his hand since she'd seen Ferdiad sparring with Trystan, wearing a vicious-looking hook instead of his usual silver hand. Trystan had beaten him, but she still didn't trust the Fili.

Nor did she trust Blaize, Corwynal's uncle. He was still in Atholl whispering in his ear, much to Domech's annoyance. Blaize and Domech were constantly at one another's throats. *Like two wolfhounds squabbling over a bone,* Corwynal had said feelingly. *Thank the gods for Ferdiad. If he wasn't here to mediate, I'd have to do it myself. And I have enough troubles.*

Which was why he needed her, not for advice but just to be there, a calm reflective presence, someone to sink into, to settle his soul inside hers and find himself there. She was his home in a place that didn't feel like home. *What am I doing here?* he'd asked once, half-asleep. But she couldn't tell him. No-one, even his advisors, could tell him that.

The messenger was waiting. All she needed to do was throw on a cloak and step into the boat. The wind was from the southwest so they'd make good time to the foot of the loch where horses would be ready to take them to Dun Caled. She'd be there by nightfall.

'I don't think you should go,' Seirian said.

Brangianne stared at her in surprise. 'Why not?'

'I saw something in the waters. A birth.'

'But it's too soon.'

Seirian shrugged. 'A child comes when it comes.'

Brangianne was a physician and Seirian no more than the occasional midwife for the women in her charge, but Brangianne had come to respect the visions Seirian claimed came from the Goddess of the waters. So she sent the man back to Dun Caled with the token and the message that she'd come when she could. Only when he'd left and the boat had lifted its sail and was making its way down the loch, did she turn back to Seirian.

'What else did you see in those waters of yours?'

'A death,' Seirian said gravely. 'I saw a death.'

'She says she'll come when she can!' Trystan was breathing hard, having run up from Dun Caled's lower gate where he'd been waiting for Brangianne to arrive with news of everyone at the Crannog. 'What does that mean?'

Corwynal was sitting in the great hall by one of the fire-pits, reading a message from The Dragon, but now he laid it aside. 'I imagine she means what she says,' he replied. 'That message was supposed to be private,' he added, a complaint Trystan brushed aside as irrelevant.

'Something's wrong,' he said abruptly.

'Nonsense. There's still a month to go.'

'Something's wrong,' Trystan insisted. 'I *know* it!'

'Nothing's wrong, so you can stop pacing about Dun Caled waiting for news instead of doing your duty.'

Corwynal smiled to take away the sting of his mild reproof. He understood how Trystan was feeling, for he'd felt the same way twenty years before. But he was determined Trystan wouldn't suffer as he had when the time came. He'd keep him away from the screams, the blood, the death, and the knowledge that he'd caused all three. Not that death was inevitable, but the possibility had to be faced. Women died in childbirth.

'I'm going to the Crannog,' Trystan announced.

'No, you're not.'

'What are you going to do? Arrest me?'

'Yes, if your oath of fealty isn't sufficient.' Trystan scowled at that. 'Curse it, Trystan, the one advantage of being King should be that people do what you tell them without arguing. I'd hoped you might keep your word, but it looks as if you can't. The first thing that comes along that you want to do, and all promises are forgotten. You're supposed to be part of my honour guard, but honour doesn't seem to come into it for you.'

'Corwynal, *please!*' Trystan dropped to his knees beside him. 'Something's wrong. If she dies and I'm not there . . .'

'She won't die.' But he'd begun to share Trystan's unease. 'Very well, go then,' he said shortly, wondering if he was making a mistake. 'But I'm coming with you.'

Trystan stared at him. 'Are you *humouring* me?'

'Yes, I'm humouring you, but only because I need to visit the Crannog myself. I've business with my sister.' It wasn't entirely a lie. 'We'll leave in the morning.'

'No, now.'

Corwynal scowled, not relishing the thought of riding through the night, even the short night of late May, but gave in.

By the time they reached the Crannog, the following day, he wished he hadn't.

Trystan, milk pale, winced as yet another scream rose from the Crannog where Yseult was fighting to give birth – a fight begun the previous day, a fight she seemed to be losing.

'I can't bear this!' Trystan whispered.

'You caused it,' Corwynal said brutally, feeling sick and terrified and twenty once more, listening to a woman scream in Dunpeldyr's cold hall. *We should never have come here!*

From time to time, one or other of Seirian's women would leave the Crannog with bundles of blood-stained linen and look disapprovingly at the two men waiting on the shore. As men, they'd been refused entry, and Corwynal had been glad of it, even though it had begun to rain. The sounds were bad enough.

'She's going to die, isn't she?' Trystan said. 'And it will be my fault.'

Corwynal feared it was possible. Was that his fault too? Did a man bequeath his own history to his son? He'd lost the woman he loved and gained a son instead, but he was determined it wouldn't be the same for Trystan. This son wouldn't shape Trystan's life as his had been shaped. He wouldn't imprison him as he'd been imprisoned. This son would have him on his side – a grandfather pretending to be an uncle. Brangianne, so quietly desperate for the child he couldn't seem to give her, would make this child her own. In time, if Seirian couldn't be persuaded to take a Consort or Broichan didn't shape up, Atholl would need an heir. Why not this one?

'What are you two doing here? Apart from getting wet.'

Oonagh was scowling at them from the Crannog's walkway, her own child asleep in a sling across her back. 'If Aelfric had anything to do with you being here, I'll have his guts. Go away!' she said and turned to go into the Crannog.

'What's happening, Oonagh?' Trystan begged.

Another scream rose then faded away. 'A birth,' she said shortly, swept aside the door hanging and disappeared.

And a death. Corwynal remembered how it had snowed on the night of Imbolc when Trystan had been born, how the birthing chamber had been red, how she'd screamed, and how his name had been called out by a dying woman, changing everything.

'My mother died in childbirth,' Trystan said, as if following Corwynal's thoughts.

You should tell him, Ferdiad had said – as if he didn't know that. Maybe this would be the time – when it was over, one way or the other.

'And Yseult's mother,' he added, turning even paler, as if this had only just occurred to him.

They waited, braced for each scream, getting steadily wetter as the rain soaked through their cloaks. Eventually, however, as at Dunpeldyr, silence fell, broken by the sound of a child wailing. Trystan clutched Corwynal's arm, his whole body shaking. 'My son . . . ?'

The door-covering was swept back and Brangianne came out. She walked slowly down the walkway to the shore, like an old woman. Her apron was stained with blood and there was a smear of blood on her forehead, but she'd taken the time to wash her hands. She looked over at Corwynal, a message in her eyes, but Trystan failed to see it and ran over to her. 'Yseult . . . ?'

'I'm sorry, Trys. I did everything I could.' Her eyes were rimmed with red. 'The child came too soon.'

'Can I see her?' Trystan's voice was held together only by the strength of his will.

'I don't think—'

'Trys, please, come away.' Corwynal laid a hand on his arm. He mustn't see it – the red room and the eyes open in death. Green, they'd be, not blue. But Trystan pulled away.

'I have to see her.' He pushed his way past Brangianne and went into the Crannog. Brangianne took Corwynal's hand and gripped it tightly, but didn't say anything and, together, they followed Trystan.

There was too much light, too many people, and the place was so pungent with the smell of childbirth Corwynal wanted to retch. The child wailed and women whispered, shocked at seeing men there. Seirian looked up and snapped a command that sent her women scuttling away, then followed herself. Only Brangianne and Oonagh remained. And Ninian.

'What are you doing here?' Trystan demanded.

'I'm a healer,' Ninian said gently.

'A failed one, it appears,' Trystan said harshly, and Ninian dropped his eyes.

Yseult was very still, very pale. They'd covered her with a blanket and there were no signs of blood. Her eyes, thankfully, were closed. Trystan dropped to his knees beside her.

'Please, Trys, don't.' Brangianne tried to pull him away, but he laid his head on Yseult's chest and wept.

'Trystan.' The voice was faint and exhausted, and the eyes, when they opened, were dull and far-away. A wave of horror gripped Corwynal when he understood. It took a little longer for Trystan to do so and lift his head.

'You're alive? Then . . .'

He stared wildly at her, at Brangianne, and the wailing child in Oonagh's arms, a child already a week old. Then he noticed, pushed against the wall, a little chest, in which something small and very still was swaddled in linen.

'Where's our son?' Yseult asked faintly.

'Yseult, my heart—' Brangianne began.

'Our son's dead,' Trystan said bitterly.

Yseult wailed, the high inhuman wail of something mortally wounded, then turned from Trystan to reach out to Ninian. Trystan got to his feet, stumbling in his haste, shouldered past everyone, and made for the door.

'Trys, wait!' Corwynal followed him. 'Listen to me—'

'There's nothing you can say. *Nothing!* So leave me alone. All of you. *Just leave me alone!*'

20

DUN TARVOS

'What have you decided to do?'

Ferdiad was annoyed he had to ask. He was used to knowing what someone was thinking, but Corwynal, increasingly, eluded him. The problem, of course, was obvious to the meanest intelligence. Atholl was ruled by a King whose loyalty to the Caledonian Confederacy was questionable at best. If it came to war – and it *would* come to war – whose side would he take?

'The trick—' Blaize told him, '—is to avoid war entirely.'

'Quite a trick,' Ferdiad remarked. 'But, assuming the trick doesn't work, what are the alternatives?'

'Keeping out of it.'

'Or, somehow, holding the balance until a truce can be negotiated?' It was a stab in the dark, but he was pleased to see Blaize's eyes fly to his. 'Ambitious, Blaize. But then the Brotherhood *is* ambitious, isn't it?'

He still didn't know much more about the Brotherhood than he'd learned in Iuddeu, but it would be interesting to know what they made of the latest development or, indeed, if they were behind it. A message had just reached Atholl, an invitation to Corwynal, and whoever he wished to bring with him, to visit the High King at Dun Tarvos at Midsummer *to discuss matters of mutual interest*. Ferdiad didn't know if Corwynal was going to accept the invitation or not. 'Obey the summons, you mean,' Corwynal said sourly. 'Curse the man! Why now?' He smashed a fist on the stone rampart in frustration. Ferdiad hadn't been surprised to find him there. The King of Atholl went to the ramparts to think; he'd had been up there a lot recently.

'Why now?' Ferdiad repeated. 'That's obvious. It's a week until Midsummer, which only leaves you enough time to get there if you hurry. That will be deliberate. At Midsummer, because that means you'll miss the Midsummer celebration on the Mountain, which would consolidate your grip on Atholl. At Midsummer, because it's not too late for war, if that's what he wants to discuss. The harvest in the North will be later than in the Lowlands. If I was a War-leader, that's when I'd strike. Clever man. But he wouldn't be High King if he wasn't. So, are you going or not?'

'I can't refuse,' Corwynal ran a hand down his face and made that gesture with his shoulders Ferdiad had come to recognise. He nodded, accepting burdens of his own.

'What do you want me to do?'

Why was he still in Atholl? Why hadn't he left after the events on the Mountain? Why had he dropped to his knees and offered Corwynal of Lothian – now Talorc of Atholl – his sword and his mind, a pledge of fealty no-one believed, including himself? Was it no more than curiosity? Or because he'd begun so much of all this that he ought to stay and see the game played out? He couldn't shake off the suspicion that he wasn't outside the game, looking in, but, on the contrary, had already taken his place on the board. He still had the medallion with the snake and broken spear on the back. He knew now it was the sign of Atholl's royal house, but not what that had to do with him. Ciaran must know, so perhaps he should go back to Dalriada, to St Martins, and pin the old man against the wall with his silver hand until he told him everything. Except he wasn't sure, in his heart, he *wanted* to know everything.

'Who will you take?' he asked, when Corwynal didn't answer his question. 'Me, I hope. I've a mind to see this High King for myself. And you'll take Blaize, I expect,' he added sourly for Blaize was his rival for the ear of Atholl's King. Corwynal would listen to both, silently compare their advice, then make his own decision. Sometimes he agreed with Blaize, sometimes with Ferdiad. Domech was another rival, both his and Blaize's. Ferdiad found it amusing to set Blaize and Domech against one another, drive them to extreme positions then present himself as the voice of reason. No wonder Corwynal looked exhausted, he thought guiltily. 'You'll have to take Domech,' he went on. 'Wild horses wouldn't keep him away. But Trystan can't go.'

Corwynal shook his head. 'No. He's too much of a Briton. He'll be furious, since if I don't take him, he won't have an excuse to avoid Yseult.'

'I know of few men who wouldn't do anything to avoid a woman's tears. He blames himself for dragging her away from Galloway – all those miles, ridden at speed. He blames Yseult too for grieving so . . . extravagantly. But they're both young. Given time, they'll find comfort in one another.'

He didn't believe it, but it was what Corwynal wanted to hear. Ferdiad had become a master of the judicious silence. Corwynal didn't need to know that the dead child lay between Trystan and Yseult like a sword. The promise of the child had held the Galloway party together on their flight north, but, now it had gone, the fault lines were appearing, like the cracks in a frozen river before it breaks up in the spring thaw. Yseult couldn't stop weeping, and Trystan was unable to bear her tears. Oonagh, feeling guilty about bearing a healthy living child, had taken Osric to Raineach. Aelfric, who'd escorted her to the border, had been unnaturally quiet ever since, as if he was thinking, and an Angle, given to thinking, might be a danger to them all. Then there was Brangianne who, before the birth and death of the child, had spent as much time as she could with Corwynal, but now refused to leave the Crannog, claiming Yseult needed her. Corwynal had gone himself to bring her back, but they'd quarrelled and she'd remained there. Seirian, on the other hand, had abandoned the Crannog for Dun Caled and was making Corwynal's life difficult.

'Do you understand women?' Corwynal asked in something like despair.

'Me?' Ferdiad laughed, then saw Corwynal was serious. 'What did you and Brangianne quarrel about?'

'I'm not sure. I said something about how Trystan and Yseult could have another child, and she told me that was exactly the sort of thing a man would say, that when a child's lost it's lost forever and can't be replaced. I was being insensitive, apparently.'

'Maybe you were. The child would have been hers to raise, so she's grieving as much as Yseult. It won't have helped that you have three sons already, and Brangianne's no longer young.'

'I should appoint you my special advisor on women.'

Ferdiad laughed once more, but Corwynal was serious about that too.

'In that capacity, since you're so sensitive, and I'm not, you can do something for me. Go to the Crannog and persuade Brangianne and Yseult to come to Dun Caled. They'll be safer here.'

'You expect trouble?'

'I'd be a fool not to, but it's just a precaution. I'd go myself, but I don't have time if we're to leave for Dun Tarvos.'

'You've heard that Yseult wants to return to Galloway?'

'Yes, but she can't,' Corwynal said shortly. 'So you can talk her out of that too. Once you've been to the Crannog, meet us at the Nemeton. We'll leave for Dun Tarvos from there.'

'*We* being?'

'Me, you, Blaize, Domech, a couple of the Druid College, half my honour guard, including Broichan, but not Trys or Aelfric.'

Ferdiad laughed. 'Trys will love that! He hates Broichan.'

'I can't leave him behind if Trys is to stay. One of these days they'll lock horns, and I want to be there when it happens, not halfway across Caledonia. Anyway, I want Broichan under my eye, and on my

side, but I can't see how to tempt him or threaten him. Can you?'
Despite the warmth of the summer's day, Ferdiad turned cold.
He'd wanted to be trusted, to be tested. He'd hoped Corwynal would
ask him to do something difficult and dangerous. Not this.
'You want me to seduce him?' he asked pointedly.
'Of course not!' But a little colour mounted in Corwynal's face.
'I could, you know,' Ferdiad insisted. 'Man or woman. If I
choose. It's just a game after all. It's when it isn't that I fail.'
Why was he saying this? Because of Trystan? Because Corwynal
had been his enemy and wasn't any more? Because of a word
spoken on a mountain? Because he was confused? Ferdiad didn't
like being confused, and it made him angry. 'What do you want
from me?'
It was a big question, but Corwynal chose to take it at face value.
'For you to discover Broichan's ambitions and weaknesses. For you
to befriend him. That's all.'
'A fine line.'
'I think you're used to treading fine lines. But if you cross it, it
would be your choice, not at my command.'
'Maybe one day you'll give me something really difficult to do.
Then perhaps you'll trust me.' His voice sounded bitter in his own
ears but Corwynal met his eyes without flinching.
'Perhaps I already do.' He pushed himself away from the
rampart against which he'd been leaning. 'But for the moment, the
difficult tasks fall to me. I have to break the news to Trys that he's
not going to Dun Tarvos, and then—' He made a face. 'Then I have
to speak to Seirian.'
Ferdiad's good humour was restored. 'Rather you than me,' he
said. 'On both counts!'

When Ferdiad reached the Crannog settlement later that day, it was
to find Yseult weeping and Brangianne looking harassed.
'Hasn't she stopped since the last time I was here?' he asked.

'Barely. She's sick. Oh, not physically. If she were, I could do something about it. It's her mind that's unwell.'

'Is she still taking about going back to Galloway?'

Brangianne nodded. 'She hates Atholl. She says she's cold all the time. She misses the sea. She's grieving for the child and for Feargus too. She wants her father and, despite the way Marc behaved at the end, all she remembers is that he treated her like a daughter.'

'Going to Galloway isn't going to solve any of her problems. And Corwynal won't let her go.' She looked at him in surprise. 'Come on, woman! Feargus was two men, man and king, and Corwynal's the same. The man might do what's best for Yseult, even if it means letting her go back to Galloway. But the King can't. She's a political prize, and he needs all the advantages he can get.'

He told her about the summons but, typical woman, she only listened to what concerned her personally.

'He's going without saying goodbye?'

'He sent me. I'm sorry; I know I'm a poor substitute. He wants you to go to Dun Caled where you'll be safe.'

'Is there danger?'

'There's always danger.'

Later he went to find Ninian. He was sitting in a patch of sun outside his little hut, looking down at the loch. Ferdiad sat down beside him, leant back against the warm wall of the hut and let the tension ease out of his body. There was something about Ninian, a calm that came off him like a scent. And Ferdiad had come to destroy it.

'Where are all your converts?'

'I don't have any.' Ninian smiled ruefully. 'Even though the Caledonians are a godlier people than Britons or Gaels. Their life moves to the rhythm of their beliefs, and I sometimes wonder if the names we give our deities matter as much as the way we let them rule our lives.'

'You're wasting your life in Atholl, Ninian. It's time you left.'

Abruptly, the calm was gone. 'I . . . can't.'

'Because of Yseult? If you care for her so much, you'll go.'

It was clear to Ferdiad at least that he cared very much. Ninian's youthful ardour hadn't left him. Rather, it had turned into a quiet little lamp that burned steadily and constantly, but was easily eclipsed by Trystan's erratic fire. In her grief, however, a little light was what Yseult needed, and what she'd turned to. Trystan, not understanding, resented her dependence on Ninian, and used it as yet another excuse to stay away.

'You're coming between them,' Ferdiad said bluntly. 'Is that what you want?'

Ninian gazed down at his laced hands. 'Trystan's not the right man for her.'

'Are you? Even if you were, she's married to another man, in the sight of the god you believe in, and to whom she wants to return. Maybe she's fallen out of love with Trystan. Maybe not. Maybe she needs time to find herself once more. Who knows? So, let's find out.'

You too could be a player, Blaize had said.

'Go to Galloway,' Ferdiad suggested. 'Negotiate a return for her, if you think that's the best thing.'

'Does Corwynal know about this?'

'No.'

'Then why suggest it?'

Good question. Why *was* he doing this? For Yseult, of whom he was oddly fond? For Trystan, who'd get over her in time? For Corwynal, who needed to break his ties to the south if he was to be a true king in Caledonia? Or for himself, because he wanted to be a player? Some would lose, of course. Brangianne would have to choose between Yseult and Corwynal – but maybe that was a good thing. Ninian might break his heart, but it was breaking already. Then there was Seirian, who needed to make a decision, and Ninian's presence wasn't helping her with that.

'Because it's for the best – for everyone.'

But a player can make mistakes, especially one who's only just begun to play the game, a player who'd set a little piece free to move on the board. Ferdiad saw it as the solution to several problems, two or more birds with one arrow, a pattern shaped in a world he didn't fully comprehend. It would suck him in, though he didn't know it. It would suck them all in.

Blaize had heard about Dun Tarvos but had never been there. He knew where it was and what – the stronghold of the Vacomag tribe of Badenoch and Mar, whose King, Drest Gurthinmoch, was also High King of the Caledonians. He'd expected to be impressed, therefore, but he hadn't expected to be quite this impressed.

The stronghold itself stood on the highest part of a promontory that overlooked the northern firth. To landward, it was protected by three enormous walls, each pierced by a single gate overlooked by a watchtower. In the bay below the promontory lay the ships that were the fort's strength – the black-hulled Caledonian galleys that were the scourge of the east coast, each of them flying Dun Tarvos' symbol of the bull. It was a fitting symbol for the Vacomag tribe – tenacious, dangerous, easily goaded and ready to wield its killing horns. The sign of the bull was everywhere, on pennants, on carved stone panels in the walls, and on the tunics of the armed guards who flanked the entranceways.

'Are we walking into a trap?' Corwynal asked softly, as they approached the first of the gates.

The timing of the summons had meant they'd had to ride at speed. Fortunately, the weather had remained fair, and the short nights meant they'd been able to travel for most of each day. Blaize was used to it, but the druids had suffered, and Domech looked even more pained than usual. The journey up the Great Glen had been easier, for a horse-transport had been waiting for them, its crew clearly surprised they'd turned up after all.

'We cut across Raineach,' Talorc explained, an apparently idle statement that was duly noted. Atholl was forging alliances with its neighbours and becoming a force to be reckoned with once more. But that didn't mean this wasn't a trap.

'Probably.' Blaize glanced back at the Atholl party who looked, to his eyes, impressive enough. Corwynal had insisted they ride the final miles to the fort rather than take the offered ship. It wouldn't do to have the King of Atholl arrive green with seasickness, for any weakness would be noted. Blaize could sense eyes on them, assessing everyone in their party – Corwynal in his black tunic with the silver wolf of Atholl and the heavy silver chain of kingship around his neck. Domech in his regalia with his two underlings looked equally impressive, as did Corwynal's honour guard. Even Blaize had been forced into something clean and less comfortable than his usual garb. Then there was Ferdiad, with his silver hand and silver hair, looking exotic and dangerous. But the man had his uses, and now, having taken on the role of Herald, he approached the gates and in a ringing voice, from which all trace of his Gael accent had been ruthlessly stripped away, he announced the arrival of Talorc, King of Atholl, and related his ancestry, right back to the Ancestor himself – more ancient than that of Drest Gurthinmoch. That too would be noted. As would the weapon Corwynal was carrying.

'What are you going to do with the sword?' Blaize had asked several times already but hadn't received a satisfactory answer. Nor did he now.

'I don't know. It depends on what happens.'

'You know what's going to happen. You'll be required to state, and possibly prove, your allegiance to the Caledonian Confederacy.'

'Oh, I think I can do that,' Corwynal replied obscurely as he and his entourage were waved through the first of the gates.

Two more gates followed and a great many more bulls. At the last gate, however, Blaize saw other symbols on the pennants fluttering in the wind – the hound of Circind, the boar of the

Taexels, the salmon of the Verturons and all the totems of the tribes
of the North and West – the ram, the owl, the raven and the eagle.
'They're all here,' he said bleakly and glanced up at Atholl's wolf
fluttering over their own party. 'So it means war.'

On the other side of the gate in the final wall lay the original
stronghold of Dun Tarvos, Fort of the Bull. Beyond that was the sea,
cold and clear, the horizon a sword blade notched with the black
sails of Caledonian war and trading galleys. The stronghold itself
sprawled out on the high ground at the end of the promontory, a
cluster of the usual buildings found in any stronghold – granaries,
storerooms, bake and brew-houses, stables and dormitories, all of
them surrounding the biggest roundhouse Ferdiad had ever seen.
Below the settlement on slightly lower ground was a different sort
of sea. A multitude of tents were pitched there, half-market, half-
garrison, for it was Midsummer, and the gathering at Dun Tarvos
was, by all accounts, the greatest of any in the North. The place
smelled of horses and smoke, smelting metal and tanneries, horse
and human dung, and too many men.

Is it a trap? Corwynal had asked Blaize who'd replied
somewhat vaguely. It was both trap and test, a series of tests, and
they'd only passed the first. The final one would be getting out of
Dun Tarvos alive, especially if it came to war, which judging from
the standards flying over the gate, looked likely. It accounted for
Corwynal and Blaize's grim expressions, both in marked contrast
to Broichan's.

'Now we'll see what he's made of!' Broichan whispered,
crowding his mount against Ferdiad's, his eyes glittering with
excitement. Ferdiad smiled but didn't reply. Broichan hadn't been
much of a challenge to befriend. Vain, he was ready to believe any
flattery. Ambitious, it had only taken a few sympathetic words for
him to unburden himself of all his resentments. 'The Britons have

the right of it in one way,' he'd said. 'A son should follow his father in the kingship.'

'Among the Gaels any man of royal blood can succeed if he's chosen,' Ferdiad told him. 'All he needs is the support of the previous king.'

'Broichan wants to be King,' he'd reported to Corwynal as they'd approached Dun Tarvos. 'If you make him enough promises he'll be loyal, but he'll betray you if you can't keep them.'

Corwynal had nodded but made no comment.

A messenger, who'd run off to the roundhouse once they'd passed through the last gate, came back, looking harassed. *As if they didn't actually expect us.* Nevertheless, the King of Atholl, together with any advisors he wished to accompany him, was bidden to the High King's presence. Corwynal told Broichan to see to the Atholl party's accommodation, so only four of them, Corwynal, Blaize, Domech and Ferdiad, entered the great roundhouse where, judging by the smell of freshly-baked bannock, roast meat and ale, the Midsummer feast was still in progress. They were in time then.

Silence fell and spread through the vast space of the hall. Laughter faltered, shouts lost themselves among the high rafters, a song stopped mid-verse, and hands stilled the strings of a harp. The hall was packed, but the crowd parted to let them through. All they could hear was the crackling of a fire in the centre of the hall, and the creak of benches as men shifted their positions to stare at the new arrivals. Then there was a faint susurration, like wind in summer grasses, as the whispers began. Atholl had come after all, its half-Briton King flanked by his Archdruid, another man who looked suspiciously like one of the priests of Chrystos, and an odd-looking man whose left hand was made of silver.

'Welcome.' The voice was deep and uninflected. It belonged to a man seated in a chair on the far side of the fire-pit. He was one of several ringing the fire, but his authority was evident in both his face and bearing. He wasn't a big man and was neither young nor old. His dark hair, woven in warrior braids, was streaked with silver, and his short beard had the badger mark of middle-age. His eyes were dark and deep-set beneath heavy brows that surmounted a sharp nose. This had to be Drest Gurthinmoch, High King of the Caledonian Confederacy.

'Are we?' Corwynal asked mildly.

'If you weren't, you wouldn't have got this far.' Drest smiled, a flash of white teeth in his black beard, and waved a hand at an empty space that had been made on the benches standing around the fire. 'Come, sit. Eat. Drink. Be welcome.' He nodded at the other men sitting around the fire. They wore symbols Ferdiad had seen on the flags outside and must be the Kings of the Caledonian Confederacy. Ferdiad didn't think they looked very friendly, and neither did their advisors, Archdruids and warriors, who sat behind them.

'You know everyone?' Drest asked Corwynal, knowing he didn't. But on the journey to Dun Tarvos, they'd been tutored by Domech so they knew who'd be there and where their allegiances lay.

'By reputation.' Corwynal glanced from one to the next as he took a seat by the fire. Ferdiad, Domech and Blaize found stools close by, and food and ale were brought, but no-one said anything until they'd all eaten and drunk, thus accepting Drest's hospitality and the protection that implied. The silence ended then, but so too did any pretence at politeness.

'You're known also by reputation, Talorc of Atholl,' said a sharp-featured nervous looking man with fair hair and cold grey eyes. He wore the hound of the Veniconn on his tunic and was probably Elpin of Circind. 'As a traitor and a kinslayer.'

'Kinslayer? Yes. I accidentally killed my grandfather. But I've atoned for that crime. As for being a traitor, who am I a traitor to?'

'To the Caledonians. You fought for the Britons in the war three summers ago.'

'Against the Gaels. As Ferdiad—' Corwynal waved his hand at him. '—Ferdiad Silverhand, lately Fili to Feargus of Dalriada, will confirm.'

Ferdiad found the High King's eyes on him – dark and unreadable. 'Do you so confirm?'

'Yes, Sire. My king was defeated by the Britons after being betrayed by those who claimed to be his allies—'

'Old history!' Elpin cut in. 'I speak of more recent treachery. I speak of how this Talorc, who claims to be of Atholl, manned a fort in my lands at the behest of the mercenary from Gwynedd.'

'This I will confess to,' Corwynal said mildly. 'I was given the opportunity of fighting my mother's people but turned it down in favour of a fort further east and the chance to fight Circind. Atholl has always fought Circind. Does that then constitute treachery?'

'Not to my mind,' Drest said. 'The Dog has always been at odds with the Wolf.'

'But need not be,' Corwynal said. 'I sent an embassy to Circind in the hope that we might resolve our differences, but my messenger was returned to me without his head.'

'Indeed?' For the first time Drest showed some emotion, and a faint frown furrowed his forehead, though it wasn't clear with whom he was displeased: Elpin for rejecting the offer out of hand, or Corwynal for making an approach that should have been made by the High King, and his expression didn't lighten as he turned to Corwynal. 'You have an enthusiasm for peace?'

Corwynal shrugged. 'War has its place, but peace is generally better for business.'

'The business of what?'

'Trade. Prosperity. Growth. Expansion. Justice. And—'

'Justice?!' A tall red-headed man leapt up, spots of colour on pale cheekbones, a fish brooch on his shoulder. That would be Deort of Fortru, the one they called the Dispossessed, for his lands were now part of Western Manau. He was the reason they were all there. 'It's easy for Atholl to speak of justice, safe behind its mountains! Where's the justice for Fortru?' Beside him a bull-necked man with the symbol of the boar on his tunic – Gede of Buchan – nodded in agreement.

We could do with a map, Ferdiad thought. A map would explain the leanings of the kings around the fire. With Fortru lost to the Britons, the fleeing people of Fortru, the Veniconn, had been granted lands between Gede's territory and Drest's, both of whom might have had other plans for those lands. With the loss of Fortru, Atholl and Circind were on the frontier with the Britons, with Dalriada to the west. Drest himself held the lands of Mar and Badenoch at the north end of the Great Glen and had subjugated the Decans of Ross. West of the Glen lay the tribes of the western seaboard, the squabbling fluid coalition of the people of the Ram, the Creonn, the Carnonacs, the Caerenn. They weren't true Caledonians, though they were kin to them. In the far north were the lands of the bird tribes, the Smertons, Lugaids and Cornavs. Far to the south, isolated now, was the Caledonian kingdom of Fife, but, looking around, Ferdiad couldn't see anyone from Fife, or indeed from the Orc islands beyond the mainland. Nor were there any Attecotts – but no-one ever invited the Attecotts to anything.

So, who'd be for war? Circind, Fortru and Buchan, obviously. Drest possibly, and if so then the Decans would follow and so too, with one eye on Drest's growing influence, would the bird tribes. The Ram people probably wouldn't be interested. Such a war would be far from their own lands and their ambitions tended in any case to their south, to Dalriada, now in Loarn's hands.

What would Atholl do? That was the question. That was why Ferdiad was here, to find out what Corwynal intended. He knew what Blaize wanted, of course. They both knew there would be war, if not this year, then the next, but Blaize didn't want a victor. He wanted the game to reach stalemate. Atholl's role, in Blaize's opinion, was to stand aside and let the Caledonians and Britons slog it out. Then, when one or other threatened to win, Atholl would throw its forces in support of the loser and impose an uneasy peace – until the next time when some other pretext for war would present itself. It wasn't, and never would be, about justice. It was about ambition, territory and influence, none of the things Corwynal had talked about.

'So you'd go to war with the battle cry of justice on your lips?' Corwynal looked around at the assembled kings. *You*, Ferdiad noted. *Not we*. He wouldn't be the only one to mark that slip. 'Where's the justice in war?' Corwynal went on. 'It lies with the victor. This fight has already been fought and lost. Fortru lost to the Romans. Yet, only a few years later, the people of Fortru were back in their lands as if they'd never left. Now they've been lost once more, to the Britons, so why not do as you did once before, Deort, and simply wait?'

'Wait? While this warlord Arthyr grows strong?'

'While he grows complacent. Until he thinks the North beaten and turns his eyes south once more. Arthyr isn't from the North. He's From Gwynedd, and his enemies aren't the Caledonians but the Saex, who come in increasing numbers to the eastern coasts far to the south. You may not have come across them yet, but you will. They're seamen as you are, fierce warriors as you are. One day you may find yourselves allying with the Britons to fight them.'

'Prophecy?' Drest asked dryly. 'Are you skilled in such matters? I doubt it. So perhaps we should consult the wise men of our various kingdoms. Come, my Lord Archdruids, tell us all what you see in the future.'

'Blood,' said Domech promptly. 'I see blood.' He meant war of course, the war he wanted to seal Atholl's position in the Caledonian Confederacy.

'Blood,' Circind's Archdruid confirmed and was echoed, one by one, some more reluctantly than others, by all the Archdruids.

'Blood, you say?!' A maniacal cackling burst out from someone seated behind the High King. A little man Ferdiad hadn't noticed emerged, an ancient man, not a hair left on his head, and few teeth in his mouth. His body was bent and twisted with the bone disease, and perhaps his mind was bent too for he carried on cackling 'Blood!' as if this was a good joke. Eventually, however, he wiped his streaming eyes and controlled himself while Drest looked down at him with both affection and, to Ferdiad's eyes, anticipation.

'Blood!' the old man scoffed. 'Easy for you to say, young Domech. Easy for you all to say. If tomorrow my Lord King cuts his finger on his eating knife will there not be blood? Won't your prophecy be fulfilled? What future doesn't have blood in it in one form or another? The trick is knowing who's blood it is and why it's there.'

'Do you, my Lord?' Drest asked respectfully.

My Lord? Ferdiad, who'd assumed the old man to be some old and indulged servant of the king, looked again and saw that, while the bones were twisted, the eyes were those of a raptor, cold and hard and far-seeing – eyes that turned not to the High King or the others, not to Domech or Corwynal, but to Blaize.

'Yes,' he said shortly, reaching up to finger something at his neck, something on a thong that swung out and caught the light from the firepit – an oak-leaf medallion.

Blaize gave a swift intake of breath. He hadn't known. He'd probably expected – as Ferdiad had – to meet one of the Brotherhood in Dun Tarvos but hadn't imagined it to be the High Druid himself.

'You see more, my Lord High Druid?' Drest asked.

'I see that we stand on the edge. Of what I cannot yet say.'

'And do we step over?'

'That's for you to decide. All of you,' the old man said irritably as if tiring of these questions. He limped back to his stool and closed his eyes, and his head drooped as if he'd fallen into the swift sleep of the elderly.

Drest nodded. He'd kept his own counsel, and his expression was unaltered. He'd listened as Corwynal had listened, but the person he reminded Ferdiad of in that moment was Arthyr, and he thought of Arthyr's map, a map that existed in this hall too, though it lay in the High King's head, and perhaps in the High Druid's also. The map that was the board and the game, a game about to become more deadly.

'So,' Drest said quietly. 'What do we decide?'

'War,' Deort of Fortru said and was quickly echoed by Elpin of Circind and Gede of Buchan. The kings of the bird tribes hesitated, but they too declared for war. The Ram tribes declined. They had a war of their own in mind, they said. *Against Loarn*, Ferdiad assumed, not knowing if he was pleased about that or not.

'You say nothing,' Drest asked Corwynal.

'I await the High King's view, for it seems that unity is required in such an undertaking.'

'And if I choose war?' Drest asked. Forcus, the King of Ross, a thin-faced dark-haired nervous looking man, hadn't spoken, but his opinion didn't matter since he'd do as Drest told him. He flushed darkly but kept his silence. 'Will Atholl join us? Or would you prefer to join our enemies for whom you've already fought? Will we see the wolf banner arrayed against us?'

'Yes. For the wolf is Lothian's symbol also. But, as for Atholl, I believe there's a third choice. Atholl could remain neutral and fight for neither side.'

Ferdiad glanced at Blaize for this was the stance he'd urged Corwynal to take, but his eyes were still on the High Druid. Beyond Blaize, Domech's eyes blazed with fury at Corwynal's statement, for he'd urged war.

'And so, since I choose war, will that be your position?' Drest asked. The others muttered, Elpin cursed and Deort spat his disgust. But Drest appeared unsurprised and, if anything, mildly disappointed by Corwynal's predictability.

'No,' Corwynal said. 'I too choose war. I would join you.'

'What?' Blaize asked, snapping upright.

What? Ferdiad wondered. *What's he playing at?*

Drest's disappointment vanished, and he looked, for the first time, in less than full control of the situation. 'Why?' he rapped out. The Kings had fallen silent and their silence spread beyond them to their advisors and retainers, so though Corwynal spoke quietly, everyone heard him.

'Because there comes a time in any man's life when he has to make a choice, and for me this is that time. I'm of both Briton and Caledonian blood. I thought I'd made a choice long ago to be a Briton, and I've fought their enemies. But what do I have to show for my loyalty? They call me 'The Caledonian' in the lands of the Britons. My father rules Lothian and has chosen my younger brother as his heir. Arthyr doesn't trust me and gave me no command. The fort you speak of was never mine. I hadn't expected to be welcome in the lands of my mother, for I'd believed myself outcast for the killing of a child. But, though she lived to become the Royal Lady of Atholl, I had another crime to atone for, the death of my grandfather, who was once the Archdruid of Atholl. Yet, when I returned to Atholl, I was judged fairly. I was given a chance to seek the gods' judgement, and they judged me worthy. I was reborn from the tomb as were the Kings of old. Such a thing changes a man and makes him see his life – and loyalties – differently. I've been granted the trust of my people and, through the gods, the right to rule them, and it's them I'd fight for. But if I'm to join you, I have a condition. I must have the trust of the whole Caledonian Confederacy, and to that end I bring you a gift and a demand in one. I must lead the combined armies of the North against the Britons.'

'What?!' Blaize had gone white. Even Domech looked startled. The Kings were stunned into silence by his presumption. Drest continued to stare at Corwynal, but his expression was unreadable.

'Why you?' he rapped out.

'Why him?' The High Druid had woken up, and his eyes were shining with amusement as he looked at Corwynal. 'Tell him, boy.'

'Because I have this,' he said, unsheathing the Ancestor's sword. Drest's men sprang forward to protect their Lord, but Corwynal had shifted the blade to lay it across his palms so everyone could see what he held there. The light rippled across its damascened surface, the jewels in the pommel sprang into vivid light and its whole fractured history glittered for all to see.

'Because,' Corwynal said softly, 'I have the Sword.'

21

LET'S DRINK TO CHAOS

The pain began behind his breastbone and spread around his chest in a tightening band. Sometimes it extended down his left arm. Usually it faded after a while, but not this time.

'Are you all right?' Ferdiad asked.

'I'm fine,' Blaize croaked, though his heart was racing and he was light-headed and breathless, dizzy and sick. His skin was cold, though he was drenched in sweat.

It's just the heat, he told himself, for the weather had turned hot and sultry, with the promise of thunder later that day. But he knew there was more to it than the heat.

'You don't look fine.' Ferdiad reined in his horse.

'My state of health is no concern of yours!' Blaize snapped but didn't object when Ferdiad waved the rest of their party on. They were east of the Great Glen by then, and the worst of the climb up the Spean was behind them. It wouldn't be long before they reached the northern part of Raineach. Apart from summer herdsmen on the high pastures, it was largely uninhabited, so Blaize could afford to rest for a while, and maybe the pain would go away.

'We're still two days from Atholl.' Ferdiad unearthed a beaker from his pack and dropped to the ground to fill it with water from a stream.

Two days from Atholl perhaps, but Blaize would have to go further – to Arthyr, to tell him what had happened and explain why he'd failed. But he still didn't know why, despite asking the man he seemed no longer to know.

'Why?' Corwynal repeated. 'You heard what I said in Drest's hall. Weren't those reasons enough? A man has to choose. You've been telling me that all my life.'

Was it my fault? The question kept Blaize from sleep, and every time he asked it, it brought on the pain in his chest.

'Did you see this coming?' he asked Ferdiad, having dismounted to sit at the edge of the stream. It annoyed him that he had to ask. Blaize had known Corwynal all his life and should have predicted this. But Ferdiad had made a special study of his nephew, so perhaps he'd seen the resentment and ambition Blaize had missed – though there was always another possibility. 'Did you put him up to this?'

Ferdiad laughed. 'Me? I was as surprised as everyone, including Drest, who didn't strike me as a man who enjoys being surprised. What did he say to Corwynal? Did he tell you?'

Blaize scowled. The single most important conversation at Dun Tarvos had taken place in his absence.

Drest had been the first to react to Corwynal's insane demand that he lead the combined armies of the North. He'd risen to his feet and proved to be a big man who towered over the other kings. *We're dead men!* Blaize had thought. But Drest had just jerked his chin at Corwynal. 'A word . . .' He'd left the hall, the silent crowd parting before him, and Corwynal had calmly followed. Blaize had wondered if he'd ever see him again, but it wasn't long before the two kings had returned, and the feast had gone on as if nothing had happened. An accommodation had clearly been reached, but what and why, where and when?

'What did you talk about?' Blaize asked Corwynal as soon as he was able to exchange a private word with his nephew. 'And what in the Five Hells are you playing at?'

'This isn't a game, Blaize. We spoke of strategy, but you'll understand if I'm unwilling to discuss it.'

'Don't you trust me?'

'I can't afford to,' he'd said quietly. 'Not anymore.' Then he'd turned away.

'He didn't tell me.' Blaize fished in his tunic for the pot the High Druid had given him, sprinkled some of the powder into the cup Ferdiad had filled with water, swirled it around and swallowed it, grimacing at the taste. 'Foxglove,' he said in reply to Ferdiad's raised eyebrow.

'I see.'

'What do you know of it?'

'Enough. Does Corwynal know?'

'Talorc; that's what we should be calling him now. And no. Anyway, I'm fine now.' It wasn't entirely true, but his heart was slowing and the pain was easing away. Returning the cup to Ferdiad, he headed for his horse, but the Fili put a hand on his arm to prevent him from mounting.

'You got that from the High Druid, didn't you? What did he say to you?'

It wasn't a conversation Blaize wanted to remember.

'You!' the High Druid had said once Corwynal and Drest had left the hall and the stunned disbelieving outraged silence had started to fill with whispers. 'No, not you!' he said crossly as Domech, evidently expecting a summons, got to his feet. 'You,' he said, pointing at Blaize. 'A word,' he added in deliberate echo of the High King. 'Well?' he asked as Blaize, alarm banishing stunned disbelief, didn't move. 'Come along. I won't eat you.' He leered at him with empty gums. 'Not with these teeth.' He turned and hirpled from the hall with surprising speed, leaving Blaize to follow him out of the great roundhouse and over the courtyard to a low building near the wall. Blaize took it to be a storeroom at first, for it was lined with shelves, each of which was packed with jars and baskets, pots and bowls. A couple of stools stood in the middle of the room, dangerously close to a brazier, and there was a pile of blankets in one corner. This must be where the man lived, Blaize surmised. The High Druid rummaged about the shelves, muttering to himself, then gave a cry of triumph and held out a little pot to Blaize.

'Take this. A couple of pinches in water. Tastes like shit, but it will help with the chest pains. Won't cure you though, and you'll be dead within the year. Not prophecy, in case you're wondering. Experience. What you need to decide is how best to make use of your death.'

Blaize sank down onto one of the stools as the man beamed at him.

'Don't worry! You'll know what to do when the time comes.' He patted Blaize on the shoulder. 'Everything will be fine – except for you, naturally, since you'll be dead. But never mind. Now, off you go, and send me the other one. The one with the silver hand. I've something to explain to him.'

'He didn't tell me anything that made any sense,' he told Ferdiad. 'Why, what did he tell you?'

'Nothing that made any sense either,' Ferdiad said shortly, and Blaize knew he was lying.

They mounted once more and caught up with the rest of the Atholl party – Corwynal riding between Domech and Broichan, the honour guard ahead and behind him.

'Do you think he's mad?' Ferdiad asked abruptly. 'The High Druid. He was the only one who wasn't surprised by what Corwynal did. Or maybe he didn't care. But how could he not care? Unless he's so old he's gone senile. He's even older than Ciaran . . .' His voice tailed off, and he stared, unseeing, into the distance.

Blaize shuddered, for Ferdiad was echoing his own suspicions. He'd always assumed Ciaran was the mind behind the Brotherhood, behind the game. But what if it was this old man, and what if the old man was indeed mad or simply wrong? Or malign? Worse, what if there was nothing, no plan, no controlling mind, no game, no anything?

'It's as if—' Ferdiad continued distantly, '—there were no gods. No meaning to anything. Nothing to believe in. Nothing to trust.'

Trust? A strange word coming from Ferdiad. 'I didn't think you trusted anyone or anything.'

Ferdiad laughed. 'Oh, there are a few things I trust, and I'll tell you one of them. When we get back to Atholl and Trystan finds out what's happened, there will be a confrontation to end all confrontations!'

Blaize's spirits rose. If there was one person who could talk Corwynal out of his insane decision, it was Trystan.

Aelfric didn't like Atholl. He didn't like the mountains or the weather or the people. He didn't like the sound of their language and had made little effort to learn it. If he shouted loud enough in Briton, they understood him – when he had any need to be understood – which he didn't. He sometimes felt as if he was invisible. He, Aelfric of Bernicia, of Gyrwum, invisible! But why else had Corwynal gone north without him? Aelfric was supposed to be part of his honour guard, his shield brother in a fight and as much of a battle companion as Trystan, who'd been left behind too and had been complaining about it ever since. Aelfric didn't blame him; the boy was as bored as he was, and the trip to Dun Tarvos, wherever that was, had sounded entertaining, or at least dangerous, which was much the same thing.

He'd spent the afternoon in the armoury, sharpening his weapons, but it hadn't taken long, and he still had the rest of the day to get through. He could go to the hall; there would be food, drink, dicing, and maybe a serving wench or two. But even the prospect of those attractions failed to raise his spirits. What he really wanted, he realised, was the feel of a ship beneath his feet – a proper ship, not one of those glorified skiffs they used in Atholl. He wanted the wind in his face, the smell of the sea in his lungs. Or, failing that, a fight would do, anything to relieve the boredom of being stuck in Dun Caled trying to avoid Oonagh.

Aelfric missed the old Oonagh, the one who gave as good as she got, who was always up for a fight either with words or . . . the other. There had been times when she'd ridden him the whole night long . . . He smiled reminiscently, stirring at the thought, but it wasn't long before the smile – and the stirring – faded. That woman was gone. Now it was all, *Not tonight, Aelfric, I'm too tired*, or *Don't; you'll wake the child.* Osric. His child. A son. Good pair of lungs, he had. One day he'd be a fine warrior, but for now he was just an inconvenience. 'Bring him to me when he's old enough to carry a sword,' he'd told Oonagh, only half in jest.

'And between now and then you don't want to see him?' she'd snapped. 'My father takes more interest in Osric than you do.'

'Then go back to your father if he's so understanding.'

The argument had been acrimonious but hadn't been followed by the usual making up of their differences. It was all depressingly familiar; this was why he'd left his wife in Bernicia after the second boy was born. That had been a good few years ago, and the boys must be seven or eight by now, so maybe he should go back. Given that no-one needed him in Atholl.

He was surprised how much he minded about being left behind, especially when Corwynal had taken that snake, Ferdiad, and his mad uncle, Blaize, neither of whom Aelfric liked or trusted. He assumed he'd been left to keep an eye on Trystan and the women, but it would have been nice if someone had actually asked him, even though neither of those tasks, in the absence of actual danger, posed much of a challenge.

It's time to leave, he decided. *When Corwynal comes back.* Because he wasn't leaving without telling him to his face what he thought of him and his abandonment of Ealhith, since he obviously had no intention of ever going back to Lothian. And then—

'Aelfric?! You'd better come!' Trystan was ashen and tight-lipped.

'Trouble?' Aelfric asked hopefully.

'Trouble,' Trystan confirmed. 'Corwynal's back.'

'He's all right?'

'No. He's gone mad. Come on!' Trystan hovered impatiently in the doorway to the armoury while Aelfric gathered his weapons, then went racing off towards the hall.

'Mad, how?' Aelfric asked when he caught up with him.

'There's to be war,' Trystan announced. 'It was decided at Dun Tarvos. The Caledonians are going to fight the Britons.'

Aelfric's spirits rose – maybe he'd stay after all – then they faltered. He knew Corwynal. He hated war. He'd keep Atholl out of it. No wonder Trys was angry.

'We have to talk him out of this madness,' Trystan said.

'You won't persuade him to fight Arthyr,' Aelfric pointed out.

Trystan stopped half-way across the courtyard below the hall. 'That's not what we need to do. He's going to war – with the Caledonians. And he intends to lead it!'

Aelfric didn't believe him, but when they reached the hall and he saw the expressions on the faces of those who were there, he knew it must be true.

'You can't do this!' Trystan marched through the whispering crowd of warriors to confront Corwynal, his fists on his hips, his eyes flashing dangerously.

But the Caledonian just sat in his chair, that big silver chain about his neck, his face a mask.

'I can, and I will,' he said. 'Did you think there were no consequences to coming to Atholl? You pledged me your fealty—'

'Not for this!'

'Ah! So your sacred promise had conditions attached to it?'

'Yes, when it comes to fighting my friends – who're your friends too!'

Corwynal's lips tightened and he leant forward, one fist on his knee. 'Don't be such a child! You drove us here. You, Trystan. Not me. You forced me into this. You forced me to make a choice, and perhaps you think that choice was a difficult one to make. But it wasn't. Atholl is my Kingdom. Why should I go back to Arthyr? What waits for me there? What waits for me in Lothian?' I'll tell you what. Responsibility but no power. Nothing of honour. Yet, despite that, Trystan, I would have served you as its king – if you'd ever shown the slightest interest in being Lothian's king. But no, you had other ambitions. You wanted to be someone greater than any king. For a while, I believed in those ambitions, but you squandered them for the sake of a girl who was never yours and who's grown tired of you now.'

What are you doing, man? Aelfric wondered, for Trystan was white-faced and trembling with rage. *This is no way to handle him!*

'But now you've a chance to redeem yourself,' Corwynal continued.

'To be a traitor like you?!'

A hiss ran around the room. It was packed, Aelfric noticed, with the younger members of Atholl's warband, that bastard Broichan's cronies. And that druid was there – whatshisname – Domech, fair bursting with amusement, not only at Trystan's humiliation but at Blaize who was slumped in a chair, his head in his hands, while Ferdiad stood in the shadows, the firelight gleaming on his silver hand and silver hair and those cursed cold eyes.

'You call *me* a traitor?' Corwynal asked softly. 'Your own brother?'

'You're no brother of mine!' Trystan retorted shrilly.

'No – he's your *King!*' Broichan stepped forward. 'You'll address him with respect!'

Trystan whirled, his eyes blazing, his hand dropping to the weapon that had been taken from him – as Aelfric's had been – when they'd entered the hall.

'I'll show my so-called brother as much respect as I have for you, you Caledonian shit!'

Broichan launched himself at him.

'Aelfric!' Corwynal called out. 'Separate them!'

'Separate them yourself. You caused it.'

Corwynal folded his arms across his chest, and two of the warband sprang forward to do Corwynal's bidding. 'So, you defy me too?' he asked him.

'You're behaving like an arse,' Aelfric retorted. 'So, yes, I'm defying you. I've had it with Atholl, and with you, you stupid bastard.'

Time to go, he decided. If Caledonia was going to fight the Britons, the south would be vulnerable, and the Angles would be on the move – into Gododdin at least, maybe further. He had to get back to Lothian and persuade Ealhith to leave. It must be clear to her by now that her husband didn't care about her. Oonagh? He felt regret and guilt, but Oonagh would manage without him. She was the managing sort.

'Come on, Trys,' he said, taking the boy's arm. 'Let's get out of here. It's a long way to Iuddeu.'

Blaize got to his feet. 'I'm coming with you.'

Corwynal laughed. 'You don't imagine I'm going to let any of you go? Broichan . . .'

And it had to have been pre-arranged, for Broichan snapped his fingers and half the warband fell on them. Blaize struggled ineffectually, but Trystan fought like a wolf. Aelfric fought too, but there were simply too many of them. Then something crashed onto the back of his head and darkness swept in from the edges of his vision. The last thing he saw was Corwynal's face. His lips were smiling, but his eyes weren't. Then everything went black.

'. . . and the troops from Badenoch will have to come this way . . .'

The warriors had left, and the servants had been sent away by the time Ferdiad returned to the hall, having completed the tasks Corwynal had given him. Only Broichan and Domech remained with Corwynal, and all three were looking at the floor. The rushes and strewing herbs had been swept aside, and Corwynal, his knife scoring the beaten earth beneath, was explaining the plans for the coming campaign. Ferdiad, who liked maps and, even more, explanations, moved quietly to join them, but didn't go unobserved. Corwynal looked up, a question in his eyes, to which Ferdiad replied with a brief nod. Domech narrowed his eyes suspiciously. That man would suspect his own mother.

'The traders,' Corwynal explained. 'I sent Ferdiad to deal with them. I don't want rumours reaching Iuddeu . . .'

'Good thinking!' Broichan said with a grin which faded as he wondered whether he should have suggested it himself. Corwynal was riding him hard, and the boy was as tense as a strung bow. *There's steel in him*, Corwynal had said. *But it needs to be tempered.*

'Here,' Corwynal used the tip of his dagger to indicate a place east of Dun Caled, to the north of the river, before it bent south towards the lands of the Britons. 'This will be the gathering place.'

'The fort the Romans left?' Domech pursed his lips in disapproval. 'An ill-omened place, full of spirits.'

'Then drive them out,' Corwynal said. 'You and however many of the Druid College it takes. It's too good a site to avoid because of ancient history.'

Ferdiad agreed, for he'd been to the place, and it was vast, as you might expect of a legionary camp. The combined Caledonian force could camp there with ease. The interior buildings had long since crumbled away, but the ramparts still stood though they protected nothing now but sheep.

'I'm giving you command of the camp, Broichan. And of the Atholl warband.'

'Me?' Broichan's eyes widened. 'But my father leads the warband.'

'In peacetime, perhaps. But war requires someone with more . . . decision.'

'A heavy responsibility for a young man,' Domech remarked.

'Is it? Trystan's younger, and he wouldn't hesitate.'

'I'm not hesitating!' Broichan said hotly. 'I can do it.'

Broichan glanced at Ferdiad who nodded encouragingly. 'Of course you can.' He'd spent the journey to Dun Tarvos persuading Broichan of his rights and abilities. It hadn't been difficult.

'You'll have Domech to advise you,' Corwynal assured him. 'And me when I can. Then if I fall in battle . . .'

He left that thought unspoken, but everyone knew what he meant. Command of the warband was tantamount to declaring Broichan his heir. Not that it was up to Corwynal, for the Druid College and the Royal Lady would have their say, but the opinion of the warband would count for a great deal, and Broichan, knowing this, turned first white then red.

'But you won't fall,' Broichan said with something like regret. 'You can't. You have the Sword.' His eyes dropped to the jewelled hilt of the weapon hanging at Corwynal's left side, the sword about which so many tales were told, including that it made its bearer invulnerable. Ferdiad watched Broichan's expression change, the pride in this unspoken acclamation darkening to something more like desire. The Sword seemed to have that effect on men, Ferdiad had noticed, though he didn't feel it himself. But Corwynal, seeing Broichan's expression, touched the hilt of the weapon that had never left his side since he'd found it. *Does he sleep with it?* Ferdiad wondered and decided to ask Brangianne.

The opportunity to do so presented itself sooner than he'd expected for, just then, the side door of the hall slammed open and Brangianne herself marched up to Corwynal.

'Tell me it's not true! Tell me you're not doing this!' She caught sight of the map scratched on the floor. 'You are, aren't you?!' She stepped forward, but Ferdiad, seeing her raised arm, caught her wrist. 'Let go of me you . . . you *snake!* Was this your idea?' She glared at him before shifting her attention to Domech. 'Or yours?' Then she noticed who was absent. 'Where's Trystan? Aelfric? Blaize, even?'

'In prison,' Corwynal said laconically. She stared at him in disbelief then sagged into herself.

'I thought I knew you,' she said dully, but after a moment she rallied. 'Are you going to put me in prison too?'

'No. You're coming with me.'

'To war?! How *dare* you!'

'I dare because men will die, and others will be wounded, and you're a healer. You may think you don't know me, but I know you. You'll go whether I order you to or not.'

'I hate you,' she hissed, tore herself from Ferdiad's grasp and marched off, slamming the door behind her.

Corwynal looked down at the map, carefully brushed the lines away and kicked the rushes back. 'Leave me,' he said quietly. 'All of you.' He went over to his chair, sat down, leant back and closed his eyes. He didn't open them when the door closed behind Domech and Broichan or when Ferdiad, picking up a flagon of wine and two cups, poured wine into them and pressed one into his hand.

'Drink,' he said, sitting down on the dais, stretching out his legs and taking a mouthful of wine. It was thin and acid but alcoholic enough for warmth to spread pleasantly through him.

'What part of *leave me, all of you* did you fail to comprehend?' Corwynal hadn't tasted the wine but his voice was slurred.

'I didn't fail to comprehend. I failed to obey. So are you going to remind me of my oath and have me imprisoned? Or would you prefer a report? Drink the wine – there will be precious little in Atholl from now on.'

'The traders?'

'One got away.'

'You think he'll go to Arthyr?'

'Oh, I should think so, but he'll say what he's been told to say.'

I'm enjoying this! Ferdiad thought. Being a warrior was all very well, but this was who he really was – a snake who, once more, had shed his skin to emerge anew, glittering and deadly.

'And Trystan? Did you see him? Did he understand?'

Ferdiad shook his head. 'Not yet. But he'll have time to think about it. They all will. It won't do them any harm and, in Blaize's case, it may do him some good – he's not well. But you probably knew that.'

Aelfric had only just been coming around when, overseen by Ferdiad, the prisoners had been manhandled into the boat that was to take them downriver to the fort overlooking the ferry crossing.

'Sorry about all this, Blaize,' he'd said as the boatmen took their positions at the oars.

'So, you decided to be a snake after all,' Blaize concluded sourly.

'Shall I silence them, Lord?' one of the boatmen asked.

'Let them talk. It can do no harm.'

'How can you be part of this?!' Trystan demanded as he struggled fruitlessly with his bonds.

'Because I swore an oath, Trys, as you did. It may surprise you – it certainly surprises me – but I'm going to hold to it. But maybe we'll meet again quite soon in happier circumstances, so don't do anything foolish.' That last was spoken in Gael, though it made no difference for all the response he got. 'Take them away,' he'd told the boatmen and watched them disappear downriver into the glitter of sun sparkling on the water before returning to Dun Caled.

Corwynal took a deep swallow of his wine. 'In a single day I've alienated everyone I care about.'

'It was necessary.'

'They called Feargus the Fox. What will they call me? Talorc the Traitor? Corwynal the Coward?'

'One or the other. If you survive. Which is unlikely.'

Corwynal smiled. 'Why do you serve me, Ferdiad?'

'Because . . .' Because of an oath? No, neither of them believed that. Because he'd loved him once and perhaps still did? No – that would begin too difficult a conversation. 'Because, to my surprise, I have to serve someone. And, though this whole business is undoubtedly madness, I find I'm enjoying it.'

'It's not a game, you know.'

'Yes, it is. Life's a game. So's death.'

Corwynal shook his head and leant back against his chair. 'Broichan didn't ask how the army was going to cross the river. Did you notice? I have to confess to a certain . . . disappointment in him.'

Corwynal shifted like a man who's been wounded in the belly and is trying, vainly, to hold himself together. First Trystan, then Brangianne . . .

'I'll have to speak to Seirian . . .' he went on. 'But I can't.'

And service sometimes meant taking up burdens you didn't want to.

'Then I will,' Ferdiad poured more wine into Corwynal's cup. 'Drink that, then get some sleep,' he advised. 'Or you'll be no use to anyone. There's a lot to do between now and Lughnasadh.'

'Chaos,' Corwynal murmured, staring into his wine. 'That's what we face.'

Ferdiad raised his own cup. 'Then, for the gods' sake, let's drink to chaos.'

Seirian cast the last of the dawn offerings onto the surface of the loch and watched them drift away, blown by a little wind that had sprung up along the shore, rustling the rushes and driving back the insects pluming from the dew-soaked vegetation. Out on the loch, at the end of the pier, the breeze had blown the insects clear, and she was free to stare down into the water that lay, dark and mysterious, beneath her feet. The loch was a calm unassailable presence, and she breathed it in like the scent of summer roses, allowing it to slow her pulse. Then, when she was as calm as the waters, she closed her eyes and opened herself to vision.

Blood. Screaming. Horses and men. The wail of a carnyx. Two wolves, snarling at one another. A broken silver chain lying in the mud . . .

Her eyes flew open. The serenity that came with the offering had vanished. Her heart was hammering, her mouth dry, as fury erupted from the place in which she'd tried to confine it. But it was too vast to be contained. *How dare he!* Her fists balled at her sides as she remembered how passionately Talorc had spoken of peace. *How dare he not consult me!* He hadn't even sent anyone to tell her he'd returned from Dun Tarvos to bring Atholl to war. And that he was going to lead it.

How could she have misjudged him so badly? She'd watched him closely since that surprising conversation on the Mountain, had listened to him as he spoke to others, watched how he persuaded men to his will even when it went against theirs. Ciniod had been placated, Domech listened to, Broichan moulded. She'd believed he'd been crafting something that might last, but all he'd been shaping was a route to his own ambitions. She blamed the Sword. That lump of metal and jewels had no more magic than any other sword, but men believed in it; that was its power. But she hadn't expected Talorc to fall under its spell, despite it never leaving his side. No, there was some other force behind this change, not an object but a mind more devious than her brother's. And she knew whose it had to be.

A blackbird gave a warning call from the woods on the far side of the stream, as clear as a trumpet in the still dawn air, so she was prepared for the jingle of harness and the soft clop of hooves. Too late, someone had come to tell her. Was it Talorc himself? She unclenched her hands and forced the anger back into its prison, because if he'd come himself she didn't know what she'd do or say, though it would surely be violent. But no, he wouldn't dare. He'd send Trystan to charm her and laugh away her apprehensions. Or Blaize who'd tell her truths she didn't want to hear – but at least they'd be truths. She waited, heard the creak of the Crannog walkway, then nothing, and knew it was neither of them and she'd be given neither charm nor truth. She knew those footsteps from the way they vibrated in wood and water rather than air, the step of a lynx, the faintest slither of scales. He'd sent Ferdiad.

She kept her back to him until his shadow fell on her before turning to face him. The sun, lifting above the hills, blinded her briefly and cast an aureole of silver about his head. He must have seen the fury in her face, for he took a step back as if to ward off an attack, his left arm rising, the silver hand catching the sunlight.

'If you've come to tell me Atholl's at war, you needn't have bothered. I know.'

'Of course you know!' he replied scornfully. 'But you don't know why. He had no choice.'

'There's always a choice.'

'Some choices are unacceptable. You think Atholl should have stayed neutral? How long do you think Atholl could survive on its own? The first thing that would happen would be that the victor – whoever won – would make Atholl suffer for not joining them. Is that what you want?'

'He told me he'd do everything to prevent a war.'

'He did.'

'Then why is he *leading* it?!'

'He's *controlling* it. Come on, woman! You've watched him work.'

'I've watched you too,' she said incautiously. 'I've seen you whisper in his ear. You speak of control when it's you who's behind every one of his decisions!'

He laughed in genuine amusement. 'You flatter me if you think I've that much influence.'

'I *believed* in him!' she burst out.

'Then believe in him still. I do.'

'Why?'

For the first time, he didn't have a ready answer, and ran his fingers through his hair, then smiled with something of Trystan's unconscious charm. 'You like to ask difficult questions, don't you? He asked me – before I came here – why I served him, and I didn't have an answer. I still don't. All I know is that when I hated him and tried to kill him, I was wrong. As you were wrong to help me. And you're wrong now. I might ask you to trust me in this, but you won't, and I don't blame you. But trust yourself. Trust that belief. Because I am right and you are wrong.'

She was standing with her arms crossed protectively across her chest to hide how much her hands were shaking. But he stood loosely, relaxed. She'd noticed that in him since he'd come back from the Mountain, and while she'd gone to Dun Caled to watch her brother, that was only part of it. She'd gone to watch Ferdiad too, to try to understand why she was drawn to him despite everything she knew about the man. She'd noticed how, since the Mountain, he was more at ease with himself, more inclined to laugh with amusement rather than malice. And he wasn't as frivolous as he sometimes pretended. His contributions at the Council meetings were incisive and well-judged. And yet . . . And yet . . .

'Why didn't Talorc come himself? Why send you?'

'He didn't send me. I offered to come. I didn't think the inevitable criticism you'd subject him to would do him any good. He asked me to apologise. I gather that has something to do with a conversation you had with him – a promise he's had to go back on.'

'He promised me my freedom,' she said bitterly.

He raised an eyebrow. 'You're no more free than he is. No-one's free.'

'You are.'

'Am I?' He tilted his head to one side and considered the matter. 'Well, maybe. But if I am, it's because no-one depends on me, or cares very much whether I live or die. Is that the sort of freedom you want?'

'He promised me—'

'Did he? Think what he said.'

What had he said? *I'll protect your freedom – for as long as I can. A King sacrifices himself, not his family.*

She felt the blow of it somewhere below her heart. 'He doesn't expect to come back, does he?'

He regarded her with a respect that had been missing until now, as if she'd understood something he hadn't expected her to.

'He doesn't expect to survive, no.' He raised an eyebrow. 'Did you think that Drest, if he wins, would let him live? Or Arthyr? What matters to Talorc – if not me – and what should matter to you, is what comes after. You believed in him when you should have believed in Atholl, in what he's shown you it can become.'

'In his hands. But he won't just be sacrificing himself. War isn't about one man. How many men will have to die for Atholl's future? What future will it have? But why should you care? All that matters to *you* is one man, the man you tried to kill once and failed. You hope to see him die at someone else's hands.'

He stared at her. 'You think this is about revenge? That I'm supporting this war to kill one man? That I might be capable of that? That it might even be true?' He was more shaken than she'd expected.

'No – yes – I don't know. I don't know what to think.'

'Then don't think,' he said harshly. 'Don't imagine. Rely on the evidence. He asked me to give you something.' A bag, holding something heavy, was slung from one shoulder. He opened it and brought out the thing she'd seen in her vision, broken and lying in the mud, the silver chain of Atholl. He held it out to her with both hands, silver on silver and flesh, before laying it at her feet. 'He gives it into your keeping. To do with as you see fit. I rather think he expects you to give it to Broichan when the time comes.'

As he'd warned her. Broichan, whom he'd been shaping for kingship. Broichan who was easily influenced, whom she'd seen laughing with Ferdiad, a hand on his shoulder.

'Broichan, who is your lover,' she said coldly.

'Broichan who is *not* my lover. But I'll make him so if I have to. He needs to be . . . guided.'

If I have to. Not from love then, but duty – a duty that was properly hers, who was of Atholl, as he was not. 'Is there no other choice?'

'For you or me, Seirian? I don't see one.'

'For both of us. I could do as everyone has been demanding, and choose a Consort, but not Broichan. I could choose someone who's not of Atholl but who's bound to it by oath and . . . and affection. A man of intelligence and subtlety.'

'You have someone in mind?' he asked dryly, apparently unable to think of such a person.

'You,' she said with a lightness she didn't feel, and saw his swift intake of breath, the way he held it, sensed the mind working furiously behind eyes that bored into hers.

'You're joking, I assume.' His voice was ice-cold. It was, she supposed, the rejection she'd expected, even deserved.

'Of course,' she said quickly, knowing she had to make a jest of it, and not only for her own pride. 'I was making a point about choices. Or perhaps I was offering to save you from Broichan who would bore you rather quickly I think.' She saw him breathe out. 'I thought it might amuse Kirah.'

He laughed, though it sounded forced. 'Good reasons, but not good enough, even in jest. So, what do I tell Talorc?'

She crouched to pick up the chain. It was heavier than she expected and she could imagine the weight of it about her neck, the burden of kingship. 'That I . . . understand.'

He nodded. 'It's more than he'd hoped for.'

Then he was gone, turning his back on her and striding down the pier to the Crannog, across the walkway to the shore where he leapt onto his grazing horse, gathered the reins and set off for the loch trackway. She heard him urge his mount into a gallop along the dangerously narrow path. He'd ridden through the night and now he was riding back, as if he was escaping.

'Was that Silverhand?' Kirah came out of the Crannog, rubbing sleep from her eyes. The settlement was waking up, yawning in the morning light. 'Why didn't he stay?'

'I don't know.' Seirian crouched down and pulled her daughter into her arms. 'Do you?'

'He was afraid,' Kirah said.

'Of me?'

'Of himself.'

22

THE FERRY CROSSING

'**O**h, stop pacing, Trys, and sit down, for the gods' sake!' Trystan ignored Blaize and carried on striding from one side of their prison to the other and back again. 'I can't bear this!' he complained.

'Yes, you can. You've borne it for half a moon already. What *I* can't stand is your constant going on about it.'

'You expect me to take this lying down?'

'Why not? Aelfric is.'

Aelfric was snoring gently on the pile of straw that served them as somewhere to sleep, his hands clasped over his well-fed belly. The food was good and plentiful, the place dry enough, and they hadn't been ill-treated, but they were closely guarded. Their prison was a cave at the base of a cliff, with no opening apart from the metal grill that formed the door. Aelfric had tested the door when they'd arrived and declared the place impregnable. 'We won't get out without help,' he'd said. Help, Blaize thought, was unlikely to be forthcoming.

'You'd do better devoting your energy to charming the guards,' Blaize told Trystan. 'Try to find out what's happening.'

Blaize hated not knowing what was going on. It was almost as painful as recognising how badly he'd handled things. If he'd been thinking straight on the return from Dun Tarvos, he might have anticipated all this and headed straight for Iuddeu before anyone knew he'd gone, rather than relying on Trystan to persuade Corwynal to change his mind. He hadn't, and maybe – just maybe – Corwynal was right. Blaize no longer knew what to think. All his certainty had deserted him, and he felt its loss as keenly as his loss of freedom.

Trystan, on the other hand, was furious with everyone, including himself. The things Corwynal had said to him so publicly had been brutal, but Trystan had come to understand they might have been deserved. 'It's all my fault,' he'd said at one point.

'Nonsense!' Blaize had retorted. 'It's not *all* your fault. Just mostly.' But it wasn't long before Trystan resumed railing against fate, his brother – and Ferdiad.

'I can't believe he just stood by and let it happen,' Trystan complained, but Blaize didn't think the Fili had been as passive as that. 'I'm going to kill him when I get out of here,' Trystan declared.

'Not if I get to him first.'

'Oh, Ferdiad's all right.' Aelfric woke up and yawned expansively. Blaize and Trystan looked at him in astonishment, for Aelfric had never trusted the Dalriad. 'He's just cleverer than both of you, and *that's* what you can't stand.'

The guard was changed regularly, which wouldn't be on the orders of Broichan, who was in charge of the fort where they were held. It would be at Corwynal's or Ferdiad's insistence, both being aware of Trystan's ability to charm. As soon as Trystan got on good terms with one guard, the man was replaced and he had to start all over again, which meant they'd learned little.

The cave in which they were incarcerated had been an armoury at one point, but it had been emptied of weapons, leaving behind the smell of lanolin and iron that affected Trystan like a war-horse hearing battle trumpets. To be in prison when he might be at war was tearing him apart and making him forget everything and everyone – the woman he loved, the brother he resented, the friend he blamed. All he wanted was to be part of the fight, and that fight would be soon. A chance remark made by one of the guards before he'd been replaced had told them it would begin at the full moon before Lughnasadh, only a few days away. They also knew who'd be leading the Atholl warband. Not Ciniod – a fool, according to Trys – but Broichan. This they'd learned from Broichan himself when he'd come to boast and taunt Trystan. To have appointed Broichan as warband leader was the worst thing Corwynal could have done, for Trystan already resented the boy because of the attention Corwynal had given him. 'At least Arthyr needn't worry about the Atholl warband,' Trystan declared. 'Not if it's led by that blustering idiot.'

But Blaize wasn't so sanguine about Broichan's lack of abilities, and the planned date of the attack was worrying, for Arthyr had expected it to be later. If only he'd managed to get away to warn Arthyr! But he hadn't, so it wasn't Trystan's fault. It was his - and Ferdiad's, of course.

'That snake!' he muttered. 'That devious bastard! That traitor!'

The guard – he'd been changed again, Blaize noticed – moved closer to the door. It was raining steadily outside, and the man, heavily cloaked, had sought the shelter of the cliff that overhung the cave. Blaize had been muttering in the Gael tongue so the man wouldn't have understood him, though it wouldn't have mattered if he had. The whole world was welcome to his opinion of that Dalriad serpent. 'When I get my hands on Ferdiad, I'll shove his grinning face so far up his arse he'll be shitting teeth for years.'

'I doubt that's physically possible,' the guard remarked in the musical accent of the Royal courts of Dalriada. Trystan looked up. 'Ferdiad!' Aelfric opened his eyes. 'About time,' he muttered. 'Did you bring our weapons?'

'Naturally.' Ferdiad lifted the beam that barred the door. 'What?' He looked from Trystan to Blaize, his lips twitching at their expressions. 'I said I'd come, didn't I?'

'When?'

'At the dock. I said I'd see you again in happier circumstances and advised you not to do anything foolish. Didn't you understand? Aelfric did.'

Blaize turned on the Angle. 'You bloody, *bloody* man!' Aelfric grinned as the door swung open and Ferdiad came in. He dropped a heavy bundle that clanked reassuringly.

'You'll notice I've not only brought your weapons, but arranged for it to be raining, which is both good and bad. Good because no-one's likely to notice us as we make a run for the ferry. Corwynal and the women are already there, with the horses. But bad because the river's running fast, and it'll be hard to get across, with no possibility of swimming our mounts if we're cut off. So, let's get going.' He tossed them a cloak each. 'Well? What are you waiting for? There's going to be a war. Do you want to be part of it or not?'

'On whose side?' Trystan asked.

'Whose side do you want to be on?' Ferdiad was standing in front of the door, a sword in one hand, that wickedly sharp hook strapped to his other arm.

'Corwynal's,' Trystan said, without hesitation.

'Right answer,' Ferdiad replied.

'What do you mean 'you don't know'?' Domech demanded of a defiant Broichan.

'I can't be expected to know everything!'

'You can – and are – expected to know everything. That's what being in command means. So, once again, how many men did you leave to guard the bridge of rafts?'

'I didn't leave any,' Broichan admitted sullenly. 'Talorc said he'd take care of the rafts, so I assumed—'

'You *assumed?* It was a word Domech was hearing all too frequently, usually coupled with the assertion that 'Talorc was taking care of that'.

'Does it matter?'

'*Does it matter?!* Of course it matters! Did you imagine the Britons wouldn't notice the sudden presence of a bridge? Or might not attack it?' And listen—' The rain, thundering down with the violence of a summer storm, was battering on the roof of the command tent at the Roman camp so loudly they had to shout. 'Even in the unlikely absence of spies, the river will be trying to tear the rafts from their moorings. At the very least, you should have left men to check the hawsers were holding. So, see to it. Right now.'

'But Talorc—' Broichan protested, but Domech quelled him with a look, and the boy went off, leaving the Archdruid to wonder what he was doing there and whether the spirits of the long-gone Roman invaders had returned, bringing the rain to destroy all their plans. Yet the rain was the least of Atholl's problems. The biggest was Broichan himself. Talorc had misjudged him, Domech thought, but so had he. The boy had more steel than his father, but lacked experience – which could be remedied – and imagination – which couldn't. Talorc should have taken charge himself. Domech might not have approved of everything the new King of Atholl did, but he couldn't fault him on his attention to detail, and his reasons for giving command to Broichan had been compelling.

'The boy needs experience,' Talorc had said. 'This is the only way he'll get it. If he's to succeed me, he needs to prove himself capable of command.'

'Surely he'll not succeed you for many years?'

Talorc had shrugged. 'Hopefully not, but war is unpredictable. If we lose, I'm not likely to survive. If we win then . . . well, let's just say that Atholl has supplied many High Kings in the past and I see no reason why it shouldn't do so once more – with or without Drest's approval. And if I'm in Dun Tarvos, Atholl will need a king of its own. Broichan is the only possible choice.'

'So Seirian . . . ?' Domech asked tentatively; Talorc was touchy about his sister.

'Seirian has, for the moment, chosen not to be part of Atholl's future. But she may change her mind. I gave her a taste of power while we were away in Dun Tarvos, and you and I both know how difficult that is to give up. Once the war's over, and she sees

Broichan ruling in Dun Caled, she'll know what she has to do to wield that power once more. Broichan will always need to be . . . guided. I hope Seirian will be the one to do so, because you'll be in Dun Tarvos, with me.'

The High Druidship! A thrill of triumph swept through him; he'd been right to bring Talorc back to Atholl. It was all working out like a dream. Except now, in the rain and mud and chaos of the old Roman camp, he was beginning to wonder if his dream might not be a nightmare in disguise.

'Talorc said he'd be here by now.' Broichan had returned, shaking rain from his cloak. Now he looked up at the sound of horses outside, men calling out greetings. 'That will be him.'

But it was some of Broichan's own men. 'What are you doing here? You're supposed to be guarding the ferry.'

'Silverhand came to say we were relieved, that everyone should be in the camp ready for the assault.'

'And you were replaced by . . . ?' Domech asked.

'Men from Dun Caled.'

'You saw them?'

'Well, no,' the leader said. 'But I assumed—'

'Is Silverhand with you?'

'He said he'd wait for the King then ride for the camp, but I expect the rain's delayed them.'

Domech had a bad feeling about all this. About Silverhand. About Talorc. About the prisoners in Broichan's fort who, very likely, were prisoners no longer. About Talorc's women, especially the one who'd said, 'I thought I knew you'. Maybe she really did know him. Then he thought of Broichan and his inexperience and the consequent need for Domech personally to deal with all the details Broichan hadn't considered. About the constant questions and complaints – the Badenoch men too close to the tents of their old enemies, the men of Ross, the lack of spears, of fodder. About conflicting orders, those from Broichan countermanded by Talorc who Domech had naively assumed had been trying to moderate the boy's misguided zeal. Even Ciniod had turned up, demanding to know who was in charge. Wasn't Talorc supposed to have dealt with him? Domech was convinced the gods were laughing at him, and the rain they'd sent, turning the camp into a stinking sea of mud, felt like a symbol of the morass of deceit into which he'd been sucked. *Ferdiad!* he thought bitterly. *Blaize!*

'Get back to the fort!' he yelled at the men who'd just arrived. 'Now, curse you!' A druid's curse wasn't taken lightly, and they leapt for their mounts. 'And someone find me a horse!'

'But Talorc—' Broichan began yet again.

'Talorc, you fool, is escaping! And he's taking the Sword with him.'

'Get on the ferry!'

'Not unless you come with me!'

Brangianne's hood had blown back, and her rain-soaked hair trailed like weed across her pale face. She was shivering, but her lips were tight and determined – a look Corwynal knew all too well.

'I'll be right behind you,' he lied. 'Trust me.'

'Trust you? You didn't trust me.'

'I explained all that. Now, get on that cursed ferry!'

'I know you. You'll send me across then stay here.'

'For the gods' sake woman, I have to wait for the others!'

'Then I'll wait too!'

Oonagh and Yseult, together with their horses, had already crossed to the other side of the swollen river. In calm weather three horsemen could cross at once, but, with the river bucking and heaving as it swept down between the island that sheltered the ferry and the shore, it was barely safe for two. Or, in the whiningly repetitive complaint of the ferryman, better for none to cross at all.

Where are they? Corwynal wished he hadn't allowed Ferdiad to go to the fort rather than him. *You're too important,* Ferdiad had informed him, though he wasn't. It was what he carried that mattered. Caledan hung by his side as usual, but he'd no intention of using it to take a life, of giving it the power of its secret name – *Grief-bringer*. If he had to fight, he had his twin swords in their shoulder harness. But if everything went to plan, he wouldn't need to fight at all. All they had to do was get across the river then cut the ropes on which the ferry ran. Ferdiad and the others would have dealt with the bridge of rafts that was to have carried the Caledonian forces over the river. The rafts would be scattered all down the river, some sunk, most mired in the marsh where the Tava met the Isla.

They should have been here by now. He wiped the rain out of his eyes and peered eastwards. The sky was still a dark mass of low clouds, the river only slightly paler than the surrounding water-logged land. All he could hear was the roar of water sweeping by on either side of the island, drowning out the hiss of rain. A tree trunk swirled in the flood, its branches snagging briefly on the ferry ropes before being swept on down the river. The body of some animal, a dog perhaps, shot by. The horses were growing increasingly restive, Janthe jibbing and whinnying, when he saw them. Three – no, four – horsemen rode towards them, one trailing the others. They were riding hard, in poor visibility, on bad terrain, which meant they were being followed. Moments later he saw their pursuers; at least twenty horsemen were riding after them.

'Come on!' he urged Brangianne and turned to the ferryman. But the man, taking advantage of his inattention, had vanished. Cursing, Corwynal grabbed the bridles of the two horses and dragged the reluctant animals onto the ferry. By the time he'd tethered them, Aelfric had thundered down the slope, pulled up at the edge of the river, slid off his mount and hauled it onto the ferry.

'Can you work this thing?' Corwynal yelled over the roar of water. The ferry ran on two huge hawsers that stretched across the river. A third rope pulled it from one side to the other. Aelfric gave it a look and shrugged.

'It's a boat, isn't it?' Then he did what Corwynal should have done, grabbed Brangianne about the waist and deposited her on the craft. 'Can you hold them off till I get back?'

'Corwynal, no!' Brangianne called out, but it was too late. Aelfric had cast off the rope tethering the ferry to the shore and was hauling it out into the river. Heart in his mouth, Corwynal watched the frail craft tilt and buck in the current, making the horses rear. It could overturn. One of the horses could kick Brangianne over the side. She could drown. But none of these things happened, and, in any case, it wasn't long before he had other matters to deal with.

'Corwynal, you *bastard!* I'm going to *kill* you!'

Trystan reined Rhydian down to his haunches, slid from his back and drew his sword in one fluid movement, but he was grinning as he did so, as alive and burning as a lamp.

'The rafts?'

'Gone.' Trystan laughed. 'Took some doing though, and, as you'll have gathered, they're after us.'

Corwynal glanced back across the river. The ferry had reached the other side, slightly downstream, and Brangianne was leading the horses ashore. *She's safe.* Aelfric had shifted to the other end of the ferry and, muscles cording, was pulling it into the current, back to the other side. He wouldn't reach them before the riders, but that no longer mattered. All the women were safe. Now to make sure everyone else was safe too. The gut-wrenching terror that had dried up his mouth and soured his belly began to ease, making space for a little flicker of joy to burst into life.

'We're about to have a fight on our hands.' He returned Trystan's grin, drew his twin swords and raced to the top of the incline that led from the main river-track to the ferry dock. Then the joy faltered; Blaize, still riding awkwardly was only just ahead of the pursuing men. Ferdiad, who'd almost reached the ferry, glanced back, reared his horse to a stop, turned it with a savage jerk of the reins, and rode back.

'He can't—' Trystan reached for Rhydian to go after him.

'He can. We have to hold the crossing until Aelfric gets back. I can't do it alone.'

It wasn't true. Where the river curved around the island, the overhanging riverbank was steep and fringed with a scrub of alder, blackthorn and gorse. The only way to the ferry was down the incline that had been cut into the bank. A single man could hold it, but two would be better. He glanced back at the river. Aelfric was half-way across now. They only had to hold the approach to the ferry until he made it back.

Further down the track, Ferdiad crashed into the leading rider of their pursuers. The man's horse went down in a squealing thrash of hooves, forcing the riders behind to swerve to avoid it. Blaize cantered past Ferdiad, his mount leaping forward with a scream as Ferdiad, pulling his own horse about, struck it hard across the rump with the flat of his sword, and, together, Ferdiad and Blaize galloped for the ferry. Trystan leapt for Blaize's horse and dragged it to a halt, allowing Blaize, who looked dazed, to slide awkwardly from the saddle.

'Get on the ferry, Blaize!' Ferdiad dropped from his own mount, jerked on its reins to turn it, and struck the animal making it canter into the path of the oncoming riders. 'Forget the horses! There's no time—'

Nor was there. The riders were on them in a thunder of hooves and mud, spears flying, swords stabbing. Corwynal ducked a spear and struck out, and his blade caught on leather and flesh. The rider cried out and his horse squealed as both rider and saddle fell heavily to the ground. On Corwynal's left, Ferdiad slashed low with that vicious hook, and blood sprayed across Corwynal's face as he turned to block the thrust of a spear.

'Stop them!' The voice rang out over the cries and curses of the swirling riders. A deep voice, used to being obeyed, a voice trained from infancy. 'Get the Sword!' Domech screamed.

Ferdiad ducked a spear-thrust that would have taken him in the throat. '*Look out!*' he yelled, but Corwynal was already moving, left then right, thrusting up, swinging back, muscles burning, nerves protesting, rain dripping from his hair, joy surging as, side by side, the three of them held off the Atholl troop. Trystan was screaming out a battle cry that was half words, half music, as the Atholl men, dismounted now, came in for the kill. But it was they who died. Trystan's sword swept past Corwynal to take a man in the throat. Ferdiad's hook slashed across another man's eyes. Corwynal's own blades arced high, then low, to fell another. If any man screamed, he didn't hear it, for all sound was drowned out by the drums and horns and the high unearthly harp-song of his own soul, a battle song that merged with the music of the men fighting at his side, silver and gold on a darkening day.

'I want them alive!' Domech thundered out. The Atholl men didn't fall back, but there was a lessening of the pressure of the attack – until someone pushed forward.

'Out of my way!' A single warrior shouldered his way past the spearmen, a swordsman, tall, broad-shouldered and young.

'Broichan!' Trystan snarled and hefted his sword.

'No!' Corwynal caught at his arm in panic and glanced at Ferdiad. *This isn't part of the plan!* But Ferdiad just shrugged.

'Back off, Broichan,' Corwynal called out. 'There are three of us.'

'I don't care how many there are of you!' Broichan glanced at Trystan and Ferdiad, but his whole will was concentrated on Corwynal. His eyes were feverish, his lips half-parted, for the two things he wanted most in the world would be won or lost here – Corwynal's death and thereby his own succession, and the sword all men desired. 'I'm going to kill you, Talorc the Traitor!'

'You'll have to kill me first!' Trystan tore himself from Corwynal's grasp and threw himself at Broichan in a clash of iron. Both disengaged then swung together once more – two stags at the rut, both powerful, both trained from infancy, a lifetime of fighting behind them. Steel blurred and crashed, slid and thrust, but neither was touched by the other's blade. Neither could break through the other's guard.

'What are you doing?!' Domech shouted, not at the combatants but at the men who'd fallen back to watch the fight everyone had been anticipating for months. 'Get them!' He pointed at Corwynal and Ferdiad, but no-one did anything, and the fight went on.

We're going to get out of here! It was the first time Corwynal had allowed himself to think beyond the next few moments. All they'd needed was time, and Trystan was giving them that. Behind them, Aelfric had reached the bank and the gangway slammed down onto the slipway. 'Come on! Corwynal, Trys – *come on!*'

Aelfric's cry broke Trystan's concentration. Only briefly, but it was enough. He parried awkwardly, and Broichan's right blade scraped the length of his to smash against the hilt and tear it from his grasp. Broichan grinned, stepped back, his left-hand blade sweeping in a crashing blow that would have taken Trystan at the knees. Impossibly, he dived below it, then rolled, coming up behind Corwynal to snatch Caledan from its sheath.

'No!' But it was too late. Trystan surged to his feet, the blade in his hand rising with him to take Broichan in the belly and up behind the breastbone.

'*No!*' Corwynal breathed into the sudden stillness.

'Run!' Ferdiad hissed, clutching his arm.

'RUN!' Aelfric yelled from the ferry. '*RUN!*'

They tore down the incline and leapt onto the ferry. Aelfric had already dragged the protesting Rhydian on board. Now he thrust the animal's reins at Trystan and hacked through one of the hawsers holding the ferry to the shore. The remaining hawser creaked as it took the whole weight of the craft. 'Quickly!' Ferdiad shouted as the Atholl men began pounding down towards them, Domech shouldering his way through the mob.

'Where's Blaize?' Corwynal demanded.

'He was right behind me—'

Aelfric slammed his axe down. The hawser parted and the ferry swung out into the current, tethered to the far shore by the hauling rope.

'There!' Ferdiad shouted, pointing at the shore. Blaize was crouched beneath a tree, a fist pressed to his chest. Had he been wounded?

'Jump, Blaize!' Trystan yelled, for an eddy of the current had swung the ferry back towards the bank, and it was only a leap away. 'He can't,' Ferdiad said, swearing.

Corwynal took a step back, readying himself to make the leap ashore but was slammed backwards and stumbled into Trystan and they both sprawled beneath Rhydian's feet as Ferdiad made the leap Corwynal had intended. He landed badly but made it to Blaize's side, hauled him to his feet and dragged him down to the edge of the water. The ferry bucked as the back-eddy fought with the current and drifted a little closer.

'Jump!' Corwynal yelled, but just then an uprooted tree slammed into the side of the ferry, forcing the tilting craft out into the main current. The bank swept away and the two men were engulfed by a mass of Atholl warriors. But before they went down Ferdiad held up his left hand with its vicious steel hook and called out something defiant that made Corwynal catch his breath on a sob. Then Ferdiad and Blaize vanished, and the ferry was trying to buck Corwynal and Trystan into the river.

He hadn't planned for this. He hadn't planned for any of this. They were supposed to have got away without detection. Blaize was to have gone with him to Arthyr. Ferdiad was to have stayed with Broichan. Broichan was supposed to be the next King of Atholl. He wasn't supposed to be dead.

'Did you have to kill him?' he demanded of Trystan. 'And with that sword?'

'It was him or you.' Trystan shrugged. 'Does it matter?'

Corwynal shook his head, but not because it didn't. He'd made an error of judgement. If he'd trusted Trystan with the truth, none of this would have happened. 'He was supposed to be King.'

'They'll find someone else. But why should you care? You've made your choice.'

'Have I? Give me back Caledan, Trys.'

He saw in Trystan's eyes the same hunger he'd seen in Broichan's.

'It's mine. Give it to me,' he repeated. There was a battle of wills in the look they exchanged, accusation and blame, but eventually, if reluctantly, Trystan handed it over.

Corwynal thought about throwing it into the river. He hadn't claimed it for himself, but now it had taken a life. *Grief-bringer.* Whose grief though? His or Trystan's? Both? The river, roiling and swirling beneath the bucking ferry, seemed to want him to throw the Sword into its depths. But the moment passed, and he slammed it back into its sheath as the ferry grounded on a bank of shingle down river from the crossing place. They waded ashore, Trystan dragging Rhydian, and made it back to the women. Brangianne threw herself at him, weeping with relief and terror and fury. 'You . . . you . . .'

'Traitor!' The word tore through the roar and hiss of the river. 'I curse you and your line. I curse you to death and beyond. I curse you to grief beyond all imagining. I curse you in the name of the gods of Atholl and the land you abandoned. Your name will be buried and you will die forgotten, an old and broken man . . .' The rest of Domech's words were whipped away by the wind.

'He's not pleased, is he?' Trystan said lightly, then sobered. 'What will he do to Ferdiad and Blaize?'

Corwynal forced himself to shrug. 'Blaize is a druid so they can't touch him. And Ferdiad can talk himself out of anything.'

Neither believed it.

'What did Ferdiad shout?' Trys asked. 'Something about difficult and dangerous, I thought. Then a name. It sounded like 'Cuchullain', but that doesn't make any sense.'

Corwynal said nothing and looked across the river, at the man still mouthing curses, at the place where he'd failed to protect all his family. 'Let's go,' he said, turning his back on Atholl. 'Arthyr will be waiting.'

Even after all these years, Arthyr still found the waiting intolerable. Better the swift unthinking response to an unexpected attack than knowing it was coming when he wasn't even remotely ready.

The moon before Lughnasadh. He hadn't believed the warning at first. Then he had. The frontier had been too quiet, which spoke of men gathering for a purpose other than the usual opportunistic summer raiding of the young bucks of the tribes. There was a mind behind this, a knowledge of where and when they'd be weak. And he knew who that mind belonged to – Corwynal of Lothian, now Talorc of Atholl, a man who, to Arthyr's chagrin, he'd sent north himself.

But he'd done what he could in the short time he'd been afforded, had manned the signal stations, reinforced the glen forts and summoned the levies. Most of the kingdoms had sent their warbands with promises of more men on the way. They'd probably arrive too late.

Five thousand. That's what the trader had told him. So now he knew when and how many, if not where. But he had a good idea. There had always been one weakness along the frontier, an over-reliance on the swift-flowing Tava river that separated Caledonia from the lands further south. There was a signal station, isolated in marshy land close to the confluence with the Isla, but the nearest fort was back at Bertha, where it guarded the only decent ford across the Tava.

They said the river had taken a different course in the days of the legions, that a great fortress had been cut off by that change of course and now lay abandoned on the northern bank. There had been a bridge once, but it had been swept away generations before. Arthyr had sent men to scout the riverbank and they'd reported the building of rafts, said they were being lashed one to the other to make a bridge of rafts big enough to take an army of five thousand. He'd sent men, under cover of a storm that had swollen the river to flooding point, to cut the rafts loose, but they'd just returned, wet, exhausted and frustrated; they'd found no bridge. Had they got lost, Arthyr wondered, or had the bridge – if bridge it was – been nothing more than a feint? Were the Caledonians intending to strike further east out of the lightly guarded valleys of Strathmore while he waited miles away? Because it was the morning after the full moon now, and nothing had happened except—

'Riders!'

Arthyr squinted north, as the sun, emerging from a break in the clouds sweeping towards the sea, trailing showers in their wake, threw a glitter of light from the sodden marshy land. 'How many?' Five thousand, he'd been told. A dark tide of Caledonian warriors who'd sweep them all away.

'Six, Sire!'

'Six? My horse – quickly!'

Six men, coming from Atholl, riding loosely, one of them – a big man – bearing a branch of willow, the sign of parley. He was fair-haired, unusual among the tribes, as was one of the other riders. Then Arthyr saw that there weren't six men after all, for three of the riders were women, and he recognised all of them. 'Stay here,' he told his bodyguard, kicked his horse into a trot and rode to meet them.

Trystan recognised the horse, a deep-chested roan with a white blaze on its forehead, before he saw who rode it. 'It's Arthyr!' he declared.

'Take the women to the camp, both of you,' Corwynal said. Aelfric eyed him sharply, as did Brangianne, but neither protested, and they all trotted off. Only Trystan hung back and would have spoken, but Corwynal shook his head. Caledan – Trystan's taking of it and what he'd done with it – lay between them.

'Go, Trystan,' he said tiredly. 'Arthyr and I have business to discuss.'

'The war?'

Corwynal nodded, and Trystan gave him a grin that stabbed him in the heart. 'Talorc the Traitor' they'd name him in the North. What would they call him in the south by the time he'd finished? Trystan wheeled his horse and rode after Aelfric and the women, raising a hand to Arthyr as they passed, and it wasn't long before they'd disappeared into the low hills where the Britons were camped. A cluster of standards fluttered from the skyline, but the army itself was out of sight to conceal their numbers – or lack of them. They were all there, Arthyr's bear, Galloway's raven, Strathclyde's salmon, Goddodin's boar and Selgovia's tree. And Lothian's wolf. *Is the old wolf there?* Corwynal didn't relish the meeting and could imagine his father's dry disappointment. *So you thought you could be a king, did you? Thought you could lead them all to war? Now here you are, alone, a traitor to everyone you care about. And what have you done with Blaize . . . ?*

'So?' Arthyr's voice broke through his introspection as he reined in his mount beside Janthe and leant on the saddle horn.

'So it's over, for the moment at least. The bridge has gone, the ferry also, and the Tava is flooded all along its length, though I can't take credit for that. Atholl has no leader and neither does the army.'

'A respectable achievement,' Arthyr said dryly. 'If only temporary, for all these things can be mended.'

'I'm aware of that. I bring you nothing but an opportunity to talk.'

'You're their spokesman?'

In other circumstances, Corwynal might have laughed at that. 'Hardly, given what I've done. I'm just the translator. It's not me you'll be talking to but someone who can deliver on whatever you agree between you. But there will be conditions. My conditions.'

'You're in a position to make conditions?'

'Yes.'

'You're on their side?'

'No, nor yours either. Or perhaps I'm on both your sides, though I doubt if anyone will see it that way.'

'And this person with whom I'm to negotiate?'

Corwynal turned in the saddle and looked back, something he hadn't allowed himself to do until now, afraid there would be nothing to see. But there was. A single rider on a black horse. They'd managed to repair the ferry then, as he'd expected. He closed his eyes in relief; until this moment he hadn't known if this would happen, or if he'd imagined a certain private conversation in Dun Tarvos. Now, as promised, he'd come, alone – and Corwynal was going to betray him.

'Sire.' He turned to Arthyr as the man rode up. 'I have the honour to present Drest Gurthinmoch, King of Badenoch and Mar, High King of the Caledonian Confederacy.' Then he turned to the man who held Caledonia in the palm of his hand. 'My Lord King, may I present Arthyr of Gwynedd, King Consort of Northern Manau, and War-leader of the Lands between the Walls.'

The two men assessed one another. Both were big men, one dark, one fair, both silvering into grey, both on the wrong side of middle-age, both fighters by necessity and politicians by desire, men who could see beyond the here and now, men who could compromise.

'We have five thousand men,' Drest stated. 'You've barely a third of that number.' He glanced at the hill. 'Despite that brave show of standards. If we cross the Tava, you'll be slaughtered.'

'Indeed,' Arthyr agreed. 'But I notice your men are still on the other side of the river.'

'The bridge will be rebuilt.'

'By which time my reinforcements will have arrived.'

Drest threw back his head and laughed. 'Honour is served. We've both made our empty threats. But neither of us is here for that.' He leant towards Arthyr, eyes glittering with amusement and anticipation. 'What then are your demands?'

The two men argued, Corwynal translating. Drest wanted the old Fortru lands back. Arthyr wasn't prepared to yield them, but other concessions could be made. The map could be redrawn. Strathmore – difficult to defend – could be returned to Circind if, in return, the Caledonian fleet was withdrawn to the north. The glen-blocking forts would be abandoned and the new frontier would be the Tava, but Fife would become subject to the Britons' control. Arthyr and Drest argued back and forward, made threats and promises, but in the end an agreement was reached.

'What's to stop either of us from going back on this . . . arrangement?' Drest looked to Corwynal for the first time.

'This is.' Corwynal drew the sword of The Ancestor from its sheath. 'Its name is Caledan.'

Arthyr's eyes opened wide, softening as he looked at the sword glittering in the wan sunlight, desiring it as so many other men had desired it. 'I thought Caledon was a story out of the old days.'

'It is a story. That's its power, it's magic. But, like all magic, it has a dark side, for they also call this sword Grief-bringer. Grief is the price of power for the one who wields it and I, for one, want neither power nor grief. Nevertheless, I'll unsheathe Caledan if either of you go back on the agreement.'

I'm not ready for war, Drest had said in Dun Tarvos. *Now you, a Briton, have forced me to it – yet you want it no more than I do. What is this then? A challenge for the High Kingship?'*

I want neither war nor the High Kingship. Yet both will be forced on me unless . . .

Unless . . . ?

He'd told Drest what he proposed. He'd suggested a strategy, a date, a place, told him what might come of it and how it could be guaranteed. Now Arthyr understood it too.

'You'd fight against whoever breaks the treaty? And because of the Sword, men will flock to your side?' He eyed Corwynal narrowly, and Drest's smile deepened for this was what had been agreed. A promise. A threat. A lie.

'No,' Corwynal said, the first of his many betrayals.

'What?' Drest demanded. 'You swore!'

'I lied. So did you.' He turned to Arthyr. 'And you're lying too. How long before one of you provokes the other and forces me to join you? That's not what I want.'

'What *do* you want,' Arthyr asked irritably.

Right then what he wanted was to slide out of the saddle, lie down on the ground, pull the earth over himself and dream of a world in which everyone didn't hate him.

'I want my sons to grow up without having to fight. I want my niece to become Lady of Atholl and nothing more. I want Oonagh's child to be able to decide where he belongs. I want a generation of peace in the lands of the North. And that's why I'm giving Caledan to you, Arthyr, if you're willing to accept it.'

'What?' Arthyr asked in surprise.

'*What?!*' Drest was more furious than surprised.

'But there are conditions,' Corwynal went on. 'My conditions. The Sword won't be unsheathed against the Caledonians. Instead, you'll use it against your true enemy, the Saex.' *And the Angles. I'm sorry, Aelfric.* Second of his betrayals. 'But if the Lands between the Walls are attacked by the Caledonian Confederacy, you'll ride north to defend us. This you'll swear. And one day, when you're dead, the sword will return to its rightful place in Atholl.' He turned to Drest. 'One day the old lands of Fortru will be held by Caledonians once more, either by war, or treaty. But it won't be in your lifetime, my Lord King, or mine. Do you agree? Do you both agree?'

Drest narrowed his eyes at him. 'No more conditions?'

'I want Blaize back, and Ferdiad. Domech has them.'

Drest pursed his lips. 'I have no authority over a land with no king. Perhaps if you'd given me the Sword . . .' He shrugged. 'This I can't agree to, but to everything else, yes.'

It was the answer he'd expected, but he'd had to try. Blaize would understand. So too would Ferdiad. He'd sacrificed them as he'd sacrifice everyone else. Two more betrayals.

'And me?' Arthyr asked. 'You have conditions for me also?'

He told him then. None of them were impossible. All of them were in Arthyr's interests, and he nodded, distractedly, his mind already racing into the future, into the great dream he now had a chance of achieving. 'I agree,' he said.

Corwynal handed him Caledan, Grief-bringer, thus burdening him with a name that would live forever and a doom that would turn his tale into tragedy. Something tore away inside him, a future, fame, everything he'd ever wanted until he'd discovered he wanted so much more. His fear of the Sword hadn't left him, however. He still felt sick from the taint of Trystan taking Broichan's life, and sensed the price of that death shivering into their futures, a doom that couldn't be avoided any more than Arthyr could avoid his.

Drest watched the exchange, his face sour. 'One day, Talorc of wherever you belong, I'll tear your guts out through your throat.' He clicked his tongue, wheeled his horse and trotted off, heading for the ferry and the Caledonian lands on the other side of the newly agreed border. Corwynal didn't bother translating those last words.

It was over. War had been avoided. Men who might otherwise have died would live to farm their lands, to bring up their children. There was hope for the future, for a little while at least. A generation? He doubted it, but it was better than nothing, though there were still sacrifices to be made. That was what a king did. He made sacrifices, not only of himself but of everyone he cared about. Blaize and Ferdiad, trapped in Atholl, Seirian whom he'd promised to protect, Aelfric turned into an enemy, Oonagh forced to make an impossible choice, Trystan and Yseult whose long dream was over. And Brangianne who'd never, ever forgive him.

23

BETRAYAL AND SACRIFICE

It had been raining when they'd left Iuddeu all those months ago, but Brangianne hadn't minded the weather. She'd been happy because Corwynal had promised they'd be together and, despite the dangers and discomfort of the journey, that was all that mattered. Now, returning to Iuddeu once more, the sun was shining in a clear rain-washed sky the colour of harebells, and that promise had been broken.

I thought I knew you! she'd yelled at him in Dun Caled.

You do, he'd said quietly. There had been a message in that, but she hadn't understood it. Now she did.

I should be furious, she thought dully. What she felt, however, was nothing – no anger, no tears, nothing to burn away this cold feeling of impending loss as she watched the man she loved sever his ties with everyone he cared for.

'No war?' Trystan had been incredulous at first when Corwynal had joined him and Aelfric in the camp of the Britons. 'Why not?'

'Because neither side can afford it,' Corwynal had replied, once he'd dismounted from Janthe and given her into the care of a groom. 'Arthyr hasn't enough men, and Drest has other problems to deal with.'

'This is your doing.' Trystan was tight-lipped with fury.

'I can hardly be blamed for those two realities.'

'But you were *there!*' Trystan glanced back north to where the three men had met not far from the river. All around them, the camp on the south side of a low hill was breaking up. Arthyr's men would remain to ensure the Caledonians didn't cross the river after all, but there was no sign of them, and the smoke, which for days had plumed from the many campfires in the old Roman fort on the north bank of the river, had vanished. They were leaving, as were the Britons, and there would be no war. Not that day, not that season. 'So, tell me the deal,' Trystan insisted.

Corwynal hesitated. Arthyr had announced that an agreement had been reached and had given a number of orders relating to the camp, before withdrawing to his command tent, together with the leaders of the various warbands. Neither Corwynal nor Trystan had been invited. Nor had Aelfric, though there was no reason for Arthyr to consult an Angle. Nevertheless, it was to Aelfric that Corwynal looked. *What has he done?* Brangianne watched him carefully from the doorway of the tent she, Yseult and Oonagh had been given, and saw grief and guilt in a face that had grown steadily more difficult to read since they'd arrived in Atholl.

'Arthyr's given up Strathmore,' he said.

'What? All the forts? Everything we fought for?'

'It can't be held. Not without a standing army. It makes sense. In return, the Caledonian fleet will withdraw from the east coast. The frontier will be the Tava. We get Fife.'

'*We?* This seems like a very good deal for the Caledonians,' Trystan said bitterly.

'I'm not on one side or the other. I just want peace.'

'At any price?'

'Personally, yes.'

It was then that Trystan noticed. The weapon, that had hung from Corwynal's side ever since he'd returned from the Mountain, the blade that had been part of him, was gone.

'Caledan—?'

'I gave it to Arthyr.'

'To *Arthyr?*'

'It's a sword for war. Not for me.'

'But you said there wasn't going to be a war.'

'There isn't. Not here.'

'You could have given it to me.'

'And what would you have done with it? Used it to kill someone else you didn't care for?'

Trystan stiffened at that. 'I saved your life,' he said quietly, turned on his heel and walked away.

Brangianne glanced at Aelfric who could usually talk Trystan out of a sulk, if sulk it was, but Aelfric was staring at Corwynal, his normally ruddy face ashen.

'What's Arthyr going to do with it?'

'I don't know.'

'You *do* fucking know! You *traitor!*'

Aelfric had called him that before, but this time he meant it, and he balled his fists and strode off, muttering.

She looked at Corwynal as he watched Aelfric go. His eyes were unfocussed, and he was unaware of her until she went over to put a hand on his arm.

'Don't.' He pulled away.

'There's more, isn't there?' He closed his eyes, took a single breath, let it out and dropped his face into his hands. 'What is it?'

'*Don't!*' he muttered. 'I don't deserve your comfort.'

'Why? What have you done?'

He raised his head. His eyes were dry, bleak hollows in a haggard face, and she stepped back from what she saw there – not what he'd done, but what he was going to do.

He walked away without replying, leaving her prey to a hollow sickness sourced in apprehension and the foreknowledge of loss. He had no destination at first, just away. She saw him pause and make the gesture that turned her heart over – that of a man shouldering a burden. He went to one of the cluster of tents above which a standard flew. A wolf – the wolf of Atholl. She didn't

understand why it was there among the Britons, until she
remembered. Not Atholl. Lothian. He'd gone – reluctant and
afraid – to see his father.

It wasn't until they'd been in Iuddeu for a few days that Brangianne
learned what Corwynal had done and what had been exacted for the
gift of that cursed sword. Peace had come at a price, but wasn't
there always a price?

No sooner had Arthyr spoken in Iuddeu's hall than the whole
fort was buzzing with the news.

'He's leaving! Arthyr's leaving!'

'Not yet,' some objected. 'Not until the spring.'

Who'd protect them then? Who'd be War-leader when he was
gone? That the Lands between the Walls had managed without a
War-leader for years was forgotten. That there was no war to fight
was also forgotten. Names were suggested, but one name emerged
from all the others – Trystan of Lothian. And Selgovia. Don't forget
Selgovia. And Galloway? No, best not mention Galloway.

For this was the price Trystan was being asked to pay for the
War-leadership.

'You're going back to him?' he demanded of Yseult, having
stormed into Yseult's guest chamber in the fort. 'Back to Marc?
After everything?'

Yseult had been expecting this confrontation and had begged
Brangianne not to leave her. Now she reached for Brangianne's
hand and clung to it for courage.

'It's for the best, Trys.'

'The best for who? Us?'

'There's no 'us' anymore. No-one will let us be 'us'. That's why I'm
going back to Marc. He wants me.'

'And you want him?'

'He cares for me.'

'*I* care for you.'

'I can't be what you need. I'm not strong, not anymore, and I'm tired, Trys. I just want to sleep.'

'With Marc?'

She shook her head, flushing. 'He won't... He's agreed. Ninian—'

'Ninian!' he exploded. 'I might have known he'd be behind this!'

Brangianne said nothing. Let him blame Ninian if he liked, Ninian who felt so strongly about the sanctity of marriage in the sight of God. But the idea of going to Marc to negotiate Yseult's return wouldn't have been his. It would have been Ferdiad's idea, which meant Corwynal had, at the very least, known of it. Better to blame Ninian than Corwynal who had so much else to answer for. But Yseult wasn't prepared to stand by and let Ninian be blamed either.

'How dare you!' she snapped, with something of her old fire. 'Don't tell me you've been offered the War-leadership for nothing! You're going back to *her*, aren't you? To Essylt. Your wife.'

'It's been suggested,' he said stiffly. 'But I won't, if you'll stay with me.'

'Oh, grow up, Trys!'

'Don't you love me anymore?' With those words he turned into a lost little boy, and even though Brangianne suspected he wasn't as lost as he pretended, her heart went out to him. Yseult softened too. In a moment she'd open her arms and he'd fall into them and Brangianne would have to beat a hasty retreat.

'Trys ...' she said warningly. 'Yseult ...'

Did it make a difference that she spoke? Did either of them actually hear her? A threshold loomed and passed by as Yseult stepped back.

'No, Trys,' she said gently. 'I don't think I do.'

Yseult waited until he'd walked stiffly out of the little chamber, until they heard the sound of his footsteps quickening as he broke into a run. Only then did she fall to her knees, her hands clamped across her mouth to keep the wail inside her. 'I lied!' she whimpered, over and over. 'I lied.'

'You said the right thing,' Brangianne insisted, though she wasn't sure she had. Yseult seemed not to hear her and crawled into bed, pulled the blankets over her head and wept and wept. Brangianne left her to it and escaped to the terrace – only to find yet another weeping woman.

'Treacherous pig!' Oonagh scrubbed tears from her face as she glared down at the lower courtyard where a party of horsemen wearing the wolf symbol of Lothian were riding out through Iuddeu's gate in a sudden summer shower. Among them was a big man on a bigger horse, his axe by his side, a sword on his back, his possessions in bulging saddlebags. Aelfric, it seemed, was leaving too.

'Going back to his people,' Oonagh said resentfully. 'He means his wife. He and Corwynal had a huge argument. I thought they'd kill one another, but it never came to blows. Better if it had . . .'

'What will you and Osric do now?' The child, oblivious to his mother's anger and his father's imminent disappearance, was, despite the rain, sleeping soundly in a basket at Oonagh's feet. 'Go to your father?'

Oonagh shook her head. 'Not yet. Raineach's no place for an infant. Maybe when he's older . . . No, I was planning on going to Galloway with you and Yseult. The gods know how you'd manage without me—'

She stopped, her face falling. 'Oh, shit!'

Me and Yseult?

'He hasn't told you, has he?'

Brangianne understood it then. Trystan and Aelfric were going back to their wives. So was Corwynal. That's why he and Aelfric hadn't come to blows.

'Where did he go?' she asked urgently, but Oonagh just shrugged. 'Away. He'll not be back until he's summoned up the courage to face you.' She smiled thinly. 'Could take some time.'

Brangianne ran down to the stables, stumbling in her haste, yelled at one of the stable boys and, a few moments later, was riding out of the gate.

'If Oonagh's sent you to reason with me, you're wasting your time,' Aelfric declared when she'd caught up with the Lothian party. 'And you won't get Corwynal to change his mind. Anyway, he isn't here.'

'I'm not here to see you, or him.' She kicked her mount forward, her heart in her mouth, for she'd come to see – as reluctantly and fearfully as had Corwynal – Rifallyn, King of Lothian. His father.

She hadn't spoken to him until today, had only been aware of him as a dark presence in the distance. He was a big man, stooped a little with age, but still rode a big chestnut as if he'd been born in the saddle.

'Let her through,' he said when his bodyguard would have kept her away. His voice was deeper than she expected, and softer. He regarded her without expression, amber eyes in a dark face. 'I know who you are.' He reined in his mount, pulled it away from the party and trotted towards a small copse, leaving her to follow.

'He doesn't look like you,' she observed once they reached the shelter of the trees.

'He looks like his mother. As, I believe, does his sister.'

'He told you then.'

'Twenty years too late. A long time to keep such a secret.'

'That's unfair. He thought she was dead.'

'That he'd killed her,' he corrected her. 'He has a talent for kinslaying, my son. He left Blaize – my half-brother – in the hands of his enemies.'

'Blaize was dying.' She was still annoyed with herself that she hadn't understood what was wrong with him. 'But Corwynal tried to save him.'

'He could have traded that sword I've been hearing so much about for his uncle's life. But he chose not to. Instead, he bargained it away for something he wanted more.'

'For peace. Is that so terrible?'

'For peace? You think that was his motivation? You think he just wants everyone to be friends and stop killing one another? No. There's only one thing he truly cares about, and that's Lothian.'

'He cares for Atholl too.'

'Poor Atholl,' he said dryly. 'A man has to choose where his loyalties lie as he has to choose between two women.'

'So you've forced him to choose Ealhith?'

'The mother of his children.' The pain of that was like the lash of a whip. 'No. That was his idea. I've never forced him to do anything.'

He tilted his head to one side and regarded her narrowly. 'You're not as I expected,' he said. 'My wife – Trystan's mother – was very beautiful.'

'And I'm not. I know it. I suppose Ealhith is?'

He shook his head. 'Ealhith is . . . homely. But she has great sweetness of temperament.'

'And I have not,' she said, tartly, making him smile – a smile that transformed his face in the way the same smile transformed his son's.

'You look at me and think we're not alike, Corwynal and I,' he said. 'But we are. We both care rather more for a land than a woman. Much safer, you see. We both understand the balance between winning and losing. And we both understand punishment. I sent his mother back to Atholl to punish myself. Now he sends you to . . . wherever it is you'll go. Galloway, I expect.'

She understood then that this was fruitless, that she'd lost. 'While he goes back to Lothian, to his wife,' she concluded bitterly.

'Oh, he's not going to Lothian!' Rifallyn raised an eyebrow at her surprise. 'He swore an oath – didn't he tell you? And I intend to hold him to it. He won't come back until I beg him, and I'm not ready to do that. I'd like to live a little longer, to see my grandsons grow into boys, if not men.'

'I . . . I don't understand.'

'I told you. He's a kinslayer. And one day he'll kill me.'

'I don't believe you.'

He shook his head sadly. 'But he does. He does.'

'How do you think they'll kill us?' Ferdiad tried to sound as if he didn't care one way or the other.

'Oh, I expect it'll be swift, whatever it is,' Blaize replied idly, and Ferdiad knew he was lying.

They'd been judged in the Oak Grove of the Nemeton in front of the full Druid College presided over by an incandescently embittered Domech. The decision had never been in doubt. They were deemed to be spies for the Britons – a crime against Atholl and the gods. The sentence had never been in much doubt either.

'Death!' Domech snarled. 'On the night of the Horned Moon.'

That being half a moon away, they'd been imprisoned somewhere near the Nemeton in a foul-smelling chamber dug into the ground. The sides curved upwards to a shaft covered by a boulder except when food and water were lowered down to them or the bucket they'd been provided with hauled up. Their prison was half a man's height with only enough floor space for two men to lie down, though not comfortably for it had been raining ever since Lughnasadh, and the boulder failed to stop water from trickling down the shaft and turning their prison into a nightmare of mud.

'I wish they'd get on with it,' Ferdiad complained. 'The prospect of more than a few days of your company in this far from salubrious residence is enough to drive a man insane.'

'Insanity would be one way to escape,' Blaize mused. 'Were you thinking of taking it?'

Ferdiad shuddered as panic surged. It was as if he stood on the edge of a cliff with an overwhelming desire to jump. Yes, he was tempted. Sometimes he dreamed he was back in that underground passage on The Island, waiting for his enemies to come and get him. When he woke, reality wasn't much different from his nightmare. The only consolation was that he wasn't alone, and that, in a man who'd always craved solitude, was the most disturbing thing of all. There were times when only the sound of Blaize's prosaic voice and his own vestiges of pride kept him from screaming.

'It's your own fault you know,' Blaize went on. 'If you hadn't jumped off the ferry, I'd have the place to myself.'

'I thought I was saving your life, you ungrateful sod.'

'I didn't know you cared.'

'I don't, but if I hadn't jumped, Corwynal would have done so. Unlike him, I was dispensable, so here I am, about to be dispensed. Anyway, I thought I could do it. If that cursed tree hadn't come down the river at that moment, I would have got you back on the ferry.'

'Cuchullain. That's what you shouted. What did it mean?'

'Nothing. It's just a story . . .'

Blaize was silent for a long time, the only sound in their stony prison their own breathing – Ferdiad's slow, fighting panic, Blaize's lighter and faster, the breath of an ill man. That had been another temptation. They'd been searched for weapons before being forced into their prison, but Blaize's little twist of foxglove powder had been overlooked or dismissed. Was there enough to poison a man? If Ferdiad took it from Blaize, how long would he last without it? Not long, Ferdiad reckoned. Which meant he had the power to render them both corpses long before the new moon. So why not? Why cling to life? Why hope when there was no reason to do so?

'Speaking of stories, would you like me to tell you one?' Blaize asked. His breathing had changed, as if he'd made a decision.

'Does it have a happy ending?'

'It doesn't have an ending at all. Not one I can make. It's the game – all of it. As much as I know. It's what I've done, or tried to do, and why. It's what I would have done if... if it had been possible. It's my successes, my failures and my hopes. A little self-indulgent, I admit, but perhaps you'll indulge me.'

'Why now?' Ferdiad asked. 'Because it's too late for me to interfere in this grand plan?'

'Because – finally – you care about something other than yourself. Because – finally – without intending it, you've become part of it all. Because when I'm dead, someone has to carry on. And because Ciaran was right about you all along.'

Ferdiad laughed, but hysteria caught hold of his voice, so he reached for anger instead.

'Too cursed late, Blaize, in the circumstances!'

'Who knows? I still have hope – for you, if not for myself. And anyway, we've a lot of silence to fill, so unless you want to tell me your life-story...'

'Talk then,' Ferdiad said curtly. 'I'm listening.'

He didn't, not to begin with, but gradually, unwillingly, he was drawn in as Blaize spoke of peoples and kingdoms, of treaties and alliances, of strengths tempered, weaknesses rooted out, of spies and informants, of traders and fishermen, of messages written in Latin by priests, or signs carved on wood by druids, of meeting places and times. He spoke of individuals with dreams or abilities, and of those who had neither. He spoke of the Brotherhood who knew of these things, and whose one aim was to tend the flame of knowledge wherever they might find it, in monasteries protected or threatened by kings, in druid schools and warrior training camps. Because the darkness was coming, long foretold, long foreseen.

'Chaos,' Blaize said. 'That's the enemy. No matter what form it takes, no matter whose face it wears. Ambition without vision. Power without responsibility. Justice without mercy. War.'

'But that's what we have. How did you intend to stop it?'

'Corwynal was supposed to stop it, to keep out of it, not choose Atholl. Nor side with Arthyr. Not take sides at all. He was supposed to pick up the pieces.'

'Perhaps he didn't want there to be pieces to pick up.'

'He should have trusted me in Atholl,' Blaize complained. 'But he trusted you instead.'

'He needed to deceive Domech, and deceit is my speciality. He needed Domech to believe him if he was ever to get away. Imprisoning you and the others was just to prove where his loyalties lay. Broichan wasn't supposed to die, though. If Trys hadn't killed him, we could have talked our way out of this.'

'Domech . . .' Blaize muttered. 'It was always going to come to this.'

His voice was hoarse. How long had he been talking for? Hours? Days? Ferdiad felt a touch on his arm, a hand gripping his wrist. 'Will you promise me something? If there's a chance for you to escape, will you take it, no matter what it is?'

'Are you joking? Of course I will! If I thought it would save me, I'd get down on my knees before Domech and suck—'

'Don't jest!'

'I wasn't.'

'Promise me!'

It was an easy promise to make, but there was more. 'And don't look back. I'm going to die in any case. Don't jump off the ferry this time. Don't . . . interfere.'

'Interfere with what?'

Blaize's grip tightened, but he didn't reply. The stone had been moved aside but not, this time, to lower food and water or to haul up the noisome bucket. This time a looped rope dropped down. How many days had passed? All of them. The sky above was bright with fading sunlight, clouds the colour of steel-streaked blood-red with sunset. It was the night of the horned moon, the night they were to die.

'Were you intending to avoid me until it was too late?'

Corwynal turned slowly at the sound of that all too familiar voice, and his heart sank like a stone in a well for, coward that he was, he'd intended exactly that. Now she'd found him in Iuddeu's lower town, in a dusty granary filled with sweetly-smelling piles of drying grain, for the harvest had been a good one. Peace and a good harvest. What more could a man want? More, it seemed. A great deal more.

'I thought it was for the best.' He half-turned towards her. She was standing in the doorway, her back to the light that turned her into a silhouette rimmed with gold as the dust from the grain swirled in the treacherously bright sunlight.

'Best for who? You? Me? Didn't you think I deserved an explanation?'

'You didn't need an explanation. No-one else knows me like you do.'

The silhouette folded in on itself as she stepped into the granary. 'I've always been afraid I'd lose you to Trystan. I knew, if you had to choose, you'd choose him, and there was a time when I hated you for that. Then I realised that if Trystan was my son, I'd choose him over you, so I forgave you. But I never expected to lose you to a land, even though you warned me.'

'Warned you?'

'In Carnadail. You spoke of the land you wanted to live in, of hills and fields and people, of harvests and stock, of fletchers and fishermen, a land that, without war, could grow. I think I began to love you then, because, even if it was no more than a dream, it was a good dream. I came to believe we could build that dream in Carnadail. But your dream was bigger, and your love was older. Lothian was your first love, wasn't it? You left it for love, and ever since then it's been at the back of your mind. If Trystan wasn't so bound up in your plans for Lothian, I believe you'd sacrifice him too.'

'That's not true—'

'You've sacrificed me. Why not him?'

'I've sacrificed myself.'

'As your father sacrificed himself by sending you and your mother away?'

He turned his back on her, unable to bear the expression in her face.

'Since you were avoiding me, I went to speak to your father,' she went on. 'I wanted to understand. But in the end, I learned more than I wanted to know.'

'That's always a risk with my father.'

'I don't think I truly knew you until I met him,' she said reflectively. 'You're alike in ways you'd both deny – cold ways, calculating ways. You're both prepared to balance one passion against another, to step back from humanity and take refuge in abstractions, because it's so much safer. You're a coward, Corwynal of Lothian, in all the ways that matter. You can't even *look* at me!'

Her hand gripped his shoulder and turned him to face her. She was no longer a silhouette but a woman he loved, a woman weeping because of him.

'My poor love!' She slid a hand to his face. 'You can't solve the world's problems, but you wouldn't be the man I love if you didn't try. Yes, I do still love you, despite you being such a coward. And I know you love me. That's why we're here, isn't it, saying goodbye? So many people have suffered for that great dream of yours – Blaize and Ferdiad lost, Aelfric embittered, Trystan and Yseult separated – that you have to share their suffering by not allowing us to be together. I understand. And I forgive you.'

'I don't deserve your forgiveness.'

'I know – but you have it.' She wiped away her tears with the back of her hand and ran a thumb below his eyes to wipe away his. 'It will be all right, you know,' she said. 'Shall I tell you what will happen? I'll go to Galloway with Yseult. I have a half-finished infirmary there, and it will absorb my energies for a while. In time

Yseult will have a child by Marc, and she'll love it as she would have loved Trystan's child. She'll grow fat and lazy and lose her beauty, but Marc will still care for her. I'll turn thin and sarcastic and we'll all be content. Trystan will give Essylt a child which will free him for the grand adventure of being War-leader. In time, your father will die, and Trys will become King of Lothian with you at his side, and your wife at your side. You'll raise your sons together, and you'll be content too.' Her voice was breaking, but she held it together. 'We won't be happy without each other, but we'll be content.'

Forgiveness, understanding and hope – none of which he deserved, for he hadn't given her the one thing she wanted above even himself.

'I would have given you a child if I could,' he blurted out. She stiffened and drew back, letting her hand fall. His skin cooled in its absence. 'I dreamed you with a child in your arms, and it was a true dreaming,' he insisted, though it hadn't been his dream but Ciaran's prophecy.

'You didn't dream who its father would be?'

He shook his head. 'Not me, for in my dream I wept. But we were together. This isn't the end—'

'It is. It has to be. You dreamed of another life, a path untaken. There's always such a path, Corwynal, always a different world. In that world we might never have met, never loved, never lived. But we have to walk the path that lies before us, and mine takes me to Galloway.' She raised a hand to his face once more, then the other, held him between her palms and kissed him without passion, but with friendship, regret and farewell. Then then she let him go and went out into the gentle sunlight of the peace and good harvest for which he'd paid this terrible, terrible price.

They were to be killed when the moon set behind the hills, in a circle of stones not far from the Grove that was the heart of the Nemeton.

The sky was darkening as the sun set, but clear of cloud, the rain of the past weeks having edged away to the south. The circle was lit by torches that burned before each of the stones, and the Druid College were waiting, standing between the uprights, Domech smiling from his place between the two largest stones. Others crowded in behind, acolytes and the younger druids, all straining to see, but all Ferdiad could look at was the central recumbent stone slab, on which stood a block of oak and a broad-bladed axe. His bowels turned to water at the sight.

'You have a choice.' Domech came to stand over him and Blaize as they knelt in the centre of the circle, their hands – or in Ferdiad's case, hand – tied behind their backs. 'To you, Ferdiad of Dalriada, the one they call the Serpent, I've decided to be merciful.' Ferdiad looked up quickly, the hope he'd thought crushed into submission flaring into life. But when he saw Domech's expression, he knew there was no hope. The block and axe took on a darker meaning. Standing to one side of the stone, eyes blank, was one of Domech's henchmen.

'You can die, here in this Grove. Or you can be exiled. But first, since you've stolen Atholl's honour, you'll suffer the penalty of a thief, to lose a hand. And since you've only one . . .'

Panic surged once more and Ferdiad forced himself to concentrate on anything that might stop him losing consciousness: the smell of the damp earth beneath him, the distant shimmer of the careless stars, the bark of a fox in the woods above the Nemeton, the taste of the wind on his parched tongue, and the warmth of Blaize's shoulder as it came to rest against his, steadying him.

'When did you become such a sadist, Domech?' Blaize asked. 'Was it when you tortured Ninian?'

'Be silent!' Domech struck him across the face, sending him sprawling onto his side, before rounding on Ferdiad.

'Choose! Death or life?'

A life with no hands? A life of being dependent on someone to care for him? But who would care? He'd rather die – which was the other option.

'This is an abomination!'

Seirian's voice was cold and clear as she strode into the stone circle. If she'd been there all the time, Ferdiad hadn't seen her. Had she come to see justice done as she had when she'd condemned her own brother?

'You're here to observe, Seirian,' Domech said. 'Not to interfere or comment.'

'You're about to kill my uncle, and you expect me to stand meekly by and let you do it?'

'I'm about to have your uncle killed,' he corrected her. 'He's been judged. The judgement was unanimous, the sentence inevitable. This is within the law, so there's nothing you can do.'

'This means war between us,' she hissed. 'War!' she repeated, raising her voice, and swept her gaze about the circle to look at each of the College in turn. Some of them moved uneasily.

'Please, Seirian,' Blaize said. 'You can't save us both.'

Save us both? What did that mean?

'Blaize—'

She stopped, bit her lip, tears welling.

'Don't. There's no need. We don't know one another well, but I can tell you your father would be proud of you.'

Whatever that meant, it strengthened some resolve in her, for she blinked back her tears and turned, dry-eyed, to Ferdiad. There was no hint of sympathy or regret in her expression, though there was no reason why she should feel either of these things.

'Which do you choose? Death or mutilation?' she asked crisply. 'Would you like me to choose your fate for you?'

Unbidden, a bubble of laughter welled up inside him. *This is ridiculous!* Yet the temptation was irresistible, one last throw of the dice in a game he'd never play again.

'I'd be honoured, Lady, if you'd make the choice on my behalf,' he said formally since it no longer mattered; he was going to die, one way or the other. Either here, swiftly, in public, or later, after considerable pain, in privacy, in his own way. It was, if you thought about it, quite funny. Blaize clearly thought so, for he was laughing softly. But Domech wasn't. He was looking at Seirian in sudden consternation as she laid a hand on Ferdiad's shoulder.

'You heard him, my Lord Druids,' she called out. 'This man, Ferdiad of Dalriada, has given his fate into my hands, and I accept it. And him. I choose him as my Consort.'

What?!

'Shut up, you fool!' Blaize hissed as Ferdiad opened his mouth to protest.

'You can't do that!' Domech screamed. 'He's a criminal. He's condemned to death.'

'And now I condemn him to life! It's my right – isn't it, my Lords? Is this against any of the Laws? Isn't this what you've been urging me to do for years? Which of you can say I can't do this?'

No-one spoke.

'Untie him,' Seirian snapped at Domech's swordsman who did so without looking at Domech, but when he moved to untie Blaize also, the Archdruid gestured him away.

'Not him,' he snarled. 'A choice has been made, but it wasn't him. He's going to die and you—' His glare raked Seirian and Ferdiad, '—you'll both watch!' He turned to his man. 'Kill him – as slowly and painfully as possible.'

'Wait!'

Ferdiad hadn't heard Blaize use his druid voice before, but now it rang out in all its authority, and the man who was reaching for his knife stepped back.

'Kill me as you will – as painfully and slowly as you wish. I've been judged, and I accept both judgement and punishment.' He swept his gaze around the Druid College. 'I'll go willingly to the gods you think I betrayed, and they'll judge me. You believe I've harmed Atholl, and perhaps I have. So let me make recompense. Let me offer myself as a sacrifice in the old way.'

The old way? Ferdiad glanced at Seirian. Her hands had flown to her mouth and her eyes were wide with horror. 'What?' he asked

Blaize, half stepping towards him before being stopped by the look he threw him and the mouthed reminder. *You promised!*

'No,' Domech said flatly.

'Am I not acceptable to the College? Am I not one of you? How many years – no, *generations* –has it been since one of you has gone willingly in the old way?' Then he turned to Domech and lowered his voice. 'Haven't you the stomach for it?'

'What's happening?' Ferdiad hissed at Seirian.

'He's offering his soul as a gift to the gods. It's a very great sacrifice, for the soul never returns and only a willing sacrifice, one who understands what's at stake, may undertake it. An Archdruid must carry out the killing, once the sacrifice has been—' She swallowed painfully. '—marked.'

Ferdiad still didn't understand. Despite all his threats, Domech's reluctance was evident. It was as if he was being judged, and he paled visibly when one of the College, after conferring with the others, stepped forward.

'The sacrifice is acceptable.'

A drum began to beat, a soft irregular rhythm which came from the ground itself. Perhaps it was Blaize's heart. Perhaps it was Ferdiad's own.

'Prepare him,' Domech said heavily, stripping off his embroidered overtunic so he was naked from the waist up, his skin ashen in the torchlight, the druid patterns black. *There will be blood then. A lot of it.* Domech gestured his man away and two druids came forward to untie Blaize's bonds.

Run, Blaize! But Blaize just stood there, smiling faintly, as the rhythm of the drums changed. The two druids stripped away his clothes to leave him naked and vulnerable. But still he smiled, even as the first druid unsheathed his curved knife, touched it to his chest, and cut into the skin. Blaize's smile faltered, and he gasped but didn't cry out as the knife cut through old tattoos, curving up and down and around, carving out the design of the wolf of Atholl. For a moment the design was sharp before it blurred in blood. The druid spoke a few words then stepped back, sheathing his knife. *Is that it?* Then another of the College came forward to make his own mark on Blaize's body, this one on his back. One after the other, they laid open his skin on chest and back, flank and thigh, on arm and shoulder, until he was inscribed with the symbols of the gods and sheeted in blood that pooled around his bare feet and ran in little channels around the altar stone.

Beside him, Seirian had her hands over her mouth as she gagged. Ferdiad's own gorge rose and fell and rose once more. Miraculously, Blaize was still on his feet, though he was shuddering now, his jaw rigid, his eyes squeezed shut. But he opened them as Domech came forward. There was no skin left to cut open but Ferdiad understood the Archdruid's task was to send Blaize to the gods, his soul carried in the arms of the horned moon. A knife was in Domech's hand, but it was shaking. He touched it to the ruin of Blaize's chest, below the breastbone, angled upwards to strike into the heart.

Do it! End this! But Domech hesitated. Blaize's whispered something. A plea? An accusation? A cry rang around the circle, but it wasn't Blaize. The knife dropped, unused. Domech turned and fled into the dark as Blaize slumped heavily against the stone.

Ferdiad ran to his side. 'You did it, Blaize! You won! They'll have to set you free now! Blaize?'

Blaize was looking beyond him, his face the blue grey Ferdiad had seen before, his lips white. His sightless eyes were on the cleft of the hills into which the crescent moon had dipped unnoticed, a vessel holding a given soul on its journey beyond this world and the next. The drumbeat was gone, and Ferdiad knew it has been Blaize's heart he'd heard earlier. And now it had stopped.

There were times to weep, and this ought to be one of them. A man Seirian had barely known, but whose blood she shared, had given his life – and his soul – to the gods. Other women might have wept, but she couldn't allow herself to be other women. Not yet.

'Lift him onto the altar,' she told two of the druids, and when they'd done so she covered what was left of Blaize with her own cloak. 'Let him lie here until sunrise, then take him to the Mountain. I'll come at sunset to conduct the rites.'

No-one demurred. No-one mentioned Domech.

She turned to the man whose freedom she'd bought at the cost of her own. 'Come,' she said shortly. 'We need to talk. But not here.'

Ferdiad looked at her without understanding, not seeing her. He was elsewhere, following a soul as it began its journey into oblivion, and didn't reply. Nor did he speak as they walked from the Nemeton to the river, not even when they were rowed to the loch then down its black waters to the Crannog. She didn't speak herself until she'd watched the boat head back north. Apart from a single torch, the Crannog was in darkness. She'd sent Kirah and her women ashore. It was the middle of the night, well past moonset.

'You stink,' she told him. 'There's a gravel pool at the stream's outfall. Use it.'

He went meekly to do her bidding. It wouldn't last long, that meekness, but it had its uses. She had her own bathing place closer to the Crannog in the roots of the alders. She stripped off her clothes and gave herself to the water to let it wash away the smell of blood, then wrapped herself in a cloak and went to find him.

He was still in the pool, lying on his back, his eyes on the sky, his body a colourless blur below the surface of the water, the light of the torch outside the Crannog turning his silver hair to gold. She picked up his clothes and threw them away. He became aware of her and stood up without self-consciousness, though he kept his mutilated arm behind his back. *He's well made*, she decided, noting the broad shoulders, the narrow hips, the muscled thighs, the pale unscarred skin. But she felt no desire for him and nor, evidently, did he for her.

'My clothes—' he began. The meekness was gone.

'—are only fit for burning.'

'Then you'll have to find me some new ones. I need to be on my way, and I'd like to be beyond the frontier by dawn.'

'Not yet. There's something you have to do first.'

'You're not going to hold me to it? I'm terribly grateful to still be alive and reasonably intact, but I don't think—' He backed away when she stepped into the water.

'Not that. It's something else you have to do. To weep. To allow yourself to weep. For your friend.'

She watched his control shatter. It hadn't been meekness after all. His face crumpled and his body folded in on itself. She reached him as he fell to his knees, and staggered as his arms clutched her. The weight of his body fell on hers, pulling her cloak away, but he didn't notice she was naked beneath it, didn't notice she was a woman. He was weeping like a child, and she was soothing him like a mother, holding him and rocking him and murmuring nothings. He was clinging to her, his cheek against her cheek, his mouth reaching blindly for hers. He tasted of salt and peat as the river poured over them, dragging them into the pool. The waters of the loch pulled them from the shallows into its depths. Her hair flowed around them both like weed as his hand moved over her, from neck to shoulder to breast. And still he was oblivious to her, as if she was nothing more than shelter, a cave in which he could hide himself, a panicked flight that beat into her and through her, the wings of a trapped falcon, a moth striving for the moon.

'I'm sorry,' he said later when they lay, spent, like beached fish on the shore. 'That wasn't supposed to happen.'

Wasn't it? But she said nothing. He sat up, retrieved her cloak from the pool and laid it about her shoulders. It was sodden, heavy and cold, but served to cover the marks of his fingers, his mouth, a faint constellation of bruises beneath a sky of stars. They walked back in silence to the Crannog, and she blew up the fire and found two blankets. Still she didn't speak, and allowed the sound of the

Crannog to fill the silence – the crackle of the fire, the hush of the wind, the creak of wood and rope, the slow lap of water and, from further away, the call of a curlew. She watched Ferdiad's breathing ease, his gaze fall into the fire and go far beyond it.

'He wasn't my friend,' he said. 'Except perhaps at the end. I lack the capacity for friendship. This hand—' He held up the stump of his left arm that he'd tried to hide and regarded it curiously as if it belonged to someone else. '—this *absence* of a hand tells you everything you need to know about me. That I can't be what you want or need.'

'What do you imagine I want you to be? A lover? A husband? A servant? A spy? An assassin?'

'I think you need all of these things.'

'I'm not so foolish as to expect to find them all in one man,' she said tartly. 'I would . . .' She hesitated, choosing her words with care. '. . . allow you to find your own role. I demand nothing, exclude nothing.'

'And hope for everything? I don't deal in hope.'

'Then shall we speak of life instead? I didn't save your life because I felt sorry for you; it was so you could save mine.'

'I doubt you're in that much danger.'

'No? What do you think will happen in Atholl now? Its king has turned traitor, and I'm his sister. Until last night, I'd refused to take a Consort. I've declared war on Domech and, by extension, the entire Druid College. Ciniod will demand to be King, and I can't think of anyone likely to oppose him. Once I held the balance in Atholl between Domech and Ciniod, but Domech has been weakened by his failure last night, and Ciniod will be stronger because of what Talorc has done. So how can I hold the balance now? How can I survive? You say you're not capable of friendship, but that doesn't matter, because I don't need a friend. I need an ally.'

'You need a son.'

'You may have given me one.'

His eyes widened. 'No! I . . . No, you can't know that.'

'Why are you so afraid of the possibility?'

She didn't expect him to answer, for that question had gone deep.

'I was a child once,' he said in the end.

'And were unhappy?'

'Unhappy would be one word for it,' he said dryly.

'So surely you'd protect your own child from such unhappiness?'

'—and live with the terror of failure?'

She laughed at that. 'You think I don't feel that terror? That I don't wake up every morning with that fear, or dream of failing every single night? That's what it means to have a child. It's not something you can choose or not choose.'

'I can't live like that.'

'Other men do. Talorc does.' She raised an eyebrow at his surprise. 'You thought I didn't know? That I don't have a brother and half-brother, but a brother and a nephew?'

'I can't be like him. It makes him vulnerable, tortured, conflicted, doubtful, guilt-ridden.'

'It makes him human. I think . . .' Again, she chose her words carefully. '. . . that love is difficult for you. You believe it doesn't matter, but search for it anyway, and when you come close it turns into something else. So you think it betrays you. You say you don't deal in hope, but I believe it's hope that drives you, the quest for a harbour for your soul. I said something in the stone circle I didn't understand at the time, but now I do. I said I condemned you to life. That's what I would do, Ferdiad, condemn you to the terror and fear of loving a child. I need a son. And a son needs a father.'

'I survived without a father,' he said stubbornly.

'And look how you turned out!' she retorted.

'Look, Seirian, I'm grateful to you, but you'd do better choosing one of the warriors or the younger druids and letting me go.'

'I'm not holding you here. I'm merely offering you a choice.'

'I'm tired of choices.' He drew his hand down his face. 'I'm tired of everything. I need to sleep.' He looked at her. 'Alone.'

'Of course.'

'And I'll leave in the morning.'

'If you wish.'

She remained by the fire after he'd stumbled to one of the sleeping alcoves and waited until he was asleep before quietly dressing herself. Once she'd done so, she roused Kirah and one of her servants and gave them precise instructions, before returning to the Crannog. Ferdiad was deeply asleep by then, lying on his back, as vulnerable as he'd feared he'd become.

I hope this is worth it, she thought crossly. Then she went back to the fire, stared into its faintly glowing depths, and remembered all the things she'd said about love, of which she knew so little. She thought of Maelcon, more friend than lover, of lovers who'd meant nothing to her, of a brother she'd hated before coming to respect, of the way he'd spoken of Lothian and how it had resonated within her. There were so many sorts of love it was strange there was only one word for them all. There should be different names for the love of a man, a friend, a father, brother, mother, child, country. And once she'd thought of these things, she went to one of her chests, brought out the royal chain of Atholl and held it in her hands. *Do with it as you see fit*, had been her instructions.

By dawn the boat with her servant was coming back, and Ferdiad was stirring.

'I found you some clothes.' She nodded at a pile she'd placed beside him, then went outside to allow him to dress. He joined her at the end of the pier not long afterwards.

'Thank you and . . . I'm sorry. For everything.'

'Where will you go?'

'Iuddeu to begin with. Then wherever Corwynal is. I'll have to tell him about Blaize. After that . . . ? I don't know. I swore an oath to Atholl's king, but I'm not sure what that means now. And there's an old man I'll have to tell about Blaize. I wonder what happened to—'

'Here.' Blaize's medallion lay in her palm, flaked with dried blood. He looked down at it for a long time, but didn't pick it up.

'This is the other path, isn't it?' he asked heavily. 'To take that and carry on. To be part of it.' He lifted his clenched fist and shook it at the sky. 'Curse you, Blaize!' Then he looked at her accusingly. 'You know what the medallion means?'

'Only in part.' She wished Maelcon had told her more.

'And this?' He pulled out his own medallion, the one with the royal sign of Atholl.

'Oh, yes. I know what it means – that you're bound to Atholl's Royal House. I've always known that, but not how.'

He picked up Blaize's medallion and brushed away the worst of the dried blood. 'The High Druid told me about that, but I chose not to understand him. Now I do, but I still don't like it, so I'm not promising anything,' he warned her. 'Not faith or fidelity or trust or anything like that.'

'No,' she agreed, taking Blaize's medallion from him and tying it around his neck to join his own.

'An ally, you said. No more.'

'My enemies to be your enemies.'

He fingered the medallion, his lips pursed, his eyes sharpening. 'There's one way—' She forestalled him by unclasping her cloak. Beneath it, she was wearing the silver chain of Atholl. It was heavier than it looked and cut into her shoulders. She'd need help to bear its weight. 'You'd already thought of it,' he said accusingly, reaching out to touch the silver links.

'You swore an oath to a king. Can you swear one to a queen? Can you make me a queen, Ferdiad? It will be difficult and dangerous, but—'

'Silverhand!'

Kirah's voice rang like a bell over the still waters of the loch. She was standing in the prow of the boat Seirian had sent in the night to the Nemeton, waving something that glinted silver in the dawn light. As soon as the boat touched the dock, she leapt ashore and ran down the pier towards them. 'Silverhand,' she declared triumphantly, holding the hand out to him, its straps dangling.

'The druids gave it to you willingly?' Seirian asked.

'Not willingly. But I made them.' She helped Ferdiad strap the thing on his arm and, to Seirian's surprise, he let her do so. 'You've got Blaize's medallion,' Kirah observed. 'He's dead, you know. I saw the moon. I watched it carry him across the sky.'

'You were outside last night, to see the moon?' Seirian asked, without surprise.

'Of course.'

'Last night?' Ferdiad asked. 'You were outside last night? You watched?'

She nodded. 'Have you made me a brother?'

'You're a monster,' he said with conviction.

'I'm the future Royal Lady of Atholl,' she corrected him.

'The two aren't mutually exclusive,' he said dryly as he tightened the final strap.

Kirah pondered this for a moment before sliding a hand into his silver one. 'Come along. There's lots to do if you're staying. You *are* staying, aren't you?'

'Yes, Kirah,' he said meekly. 'I'm staying.'

PART V

THE LANDS BETWEEN THE WALLS,

AUTUMN 488 AD

24

AFTERMATHS

'Ninian! By all the gods, it's good to see you! I was beginning to worry . . .' Corwynal flung an arm about Ninian's shoulders, drew him into Meldon's hall and sent a servant running for food and drink. 'So – tell me everything.'

Ninian laughed weakly. 'Let me catch my breath first!'

He was pale beneath the dust of his journey and thinner than Corwynal remembered. The journey to Galloway wasn't a long one, so he should have been back in Selgovia weeks before. Had something happened in Galloway? Was—?

'Brangianne's fine,' Ninian said quickly.

Something that had been wound tightly inside him began to loosen; if she was alright, nothing else mattered. 'You should rest. You look done in.'

'Don't fuss. I just want to sit for a while on something that doesn't move beneath me.' Ninian glanced at the roof of the hall where the skulls hung like grinning moons. 'Maybe outside in the sun. Is Trystan here?'

'No. He's off hunting somewhere. Why? Is Yseult—?'

'She's fine too. I was just wondering because—' He broke off as a servant arrived with ale and a platter of bread and mutton, but he waved it away. 'Not ale. Can you bring me some spring water? And I don't eat meat now, but if there's any cheese . . . ?'

They went outside and found a bench in the sun. In the clear afternoon light, Ninian was even more ethereal than he'd seemed in the hall, and Corwynal knew he was responsible for that since he'd asked Ninian to go to Galloway on his behalf. 'Essylt's missed you.'

'Oh dear!' Ninian said ruefully. 'I expect she wants to unburden herself, so you'd better tell me what to expect.'

'Oh, nothing new. She and Trystan aren't getting on any better. I don't know the details, because he doesn't tell me anything. He does his duty as a husband, but without any joy, it seems to me. He's fulfilled his bargain with Arthyr, and now he's just waiting – for Arthyr to leave, for my father to die, for Marc to die. He's being patient, but patience and Trystan have never been easy bedfellows. Essylt got what she wanted, only to discover she doesn't want it anymore, but she's too proud to tell him.'

'Poor Essylt. All she wants is for someone to love her, but everyone she turns to lets her down.'

Corwynal shifted uneasily since he'd been one of them, and was relieved when Ninian changed the subject.

'The rest of the harvest went well?'

'Well enough.' It was well into September by then, and the last of the grain was in the granaries. Selgovia had little land for cereals, but the weather had been good for the whole of the summer, and the crops had yielded more than usual. The same was true of most of the Lands between the Walls. The situation further north was otherwise. The rain that had fallen in Atholl before Lughnasadh had barely let up for the whole of the following month and had ruined the Caledonian harvest. That, as much as the agreement Corwynal had brokered between Arthyr and Drest, would ensure peace for the coming season at least. An omen, it was said. A warning from the gods. There would likely be starvation north of the Tava, come the spring. But these were rumours only, and no real news had come south of the river.

'You've not heard anything then?' Ninian asked.

Corwynal shook his head. For weeks after they'd escaped from Atholl, leaving Blaize and Ferdiad behind, he'd expected one or the other to come riding into Iuddeu complaining that they'd been abandoned. But neither had come, and his hopes of either of them still being alive were fading.

'I'll find out,' Ninian said. 'I'll go to Atholl and send word to you. One way or the other.'

'It's too dangerous.'

'No more than before. But first, let me tell you about Galloway . . .'

Shortly after Lughnasadh, Ninian had travelled to Galloway with Yseult and Brangianne, much to Trystan's displeasure; he hadn't forgiven Ninian for negotiating Yseult's return to Marc. Trystan himself, together with Corwynal, had gone to Selgovia – back to Essylt – as he'd promised. Perhaps he'd hoped things would go badly in Galloway and Yseult would return to him once more, but a few weeks later Ninian arrived in Meldon to report that she'd been received with rejoicing by a contrite Marc. Every honour had been heaped on her and Brangianne, and no-one in Galloway, on pain of death, was to mention the trial or the cause of it. As far as Marc was concerned – and Galloway had been instructed to believe – Yseult had spent the past seven months in Iuddeu at Gwenhwyvar's invitation. Marc intended to wipe out the past. *A new beginning*, he'd declared. But Corwynal knew Marc of old. New beginnings had all too often fizzled out, so he'd asked Ninian to return to Galloway once more and report back to him. But everything seemed to be as well as could be expected.

'Yseult's better,' Ninian told him. 'Less gloomy. More . . . alive.'

'A child?' Corwynal asked hopefully. A child by Marc would replace the one she'd lost. More importantly, it might convince Trystan his relationship with Yseult really was over. But Ninian shook his head.

'Not that I know of. But she seemed happy enough.'

'And Brangianne?'

'Busy with the infirmary, as you might expect.'

'And does she . . . ? Is she . . . ?'

Ninian smiled. 'Alone? Yes. Kaerherdin isn't in Galloway.'

The relief made him dizzy. When he and Trystan had arrived in Meldon, Kaerherdin had had a furious argument with Essylt and demanded she choose between him and Trystan. Predictably, she'd chosen Trystan, and Kaerherdin had stormed out of Selgovia, muttering threats of vengeance. Corwynal was relieved at first, but began to worry Kaerherdin had gone to Galloway. Yet why shouldn't he? Brangianne deserved someone who could give her his whole heart, someone to help her forget him. But Corwynal didn't want to be forgotten. Like Trystan, he was waiting for something to happen – a death perhaps. His father's. Marc's. Or perhaps he was waiting for a woman to ride north to tell him that, since he hadn't gone back to his wife after all, here she was. If she came, he didn't think he'd be able to send her away again.

'I went to Lothian,' Ninian said, cutting into his thoughts. 'That's why I'm late. I went to Dunpeldyr.'

Corwynal's dream of a woman riding north had, regretfully, to be put to one side. 'You saw Ealhith?'

'Yes, though it wasn't easy. She was being guarded.'

'By my father?'

'By her brother. Aelfric's in Dunpeldyr, trying to persuade her to forget about you, given that you broke your promise.'

'How does he imagine I can keep my promise when my father refuses to have me in Lothian?'

'He thinks you should defy your father, storm into Dunpeldyr and take her by force. That's what he'd do.'

Corwynal grunted. He could imagine Aelfric doing exactly that. 'I can't. I swore I wouldn't go back until my father begged me, and that's a promise I won't break.'

'So, it's pride then? On both your parts?'

'Pride? It must seem so but, no, on his part it's fear. He believes I'll kill him one day. I've no desire to, but maybe I'm afraid he's correct. Even so, he has no right to keep Ealhith in Lothian. If she wanted to be with me, she could come to Meldon.'

'He's not stopping her leaving. Only your sons. I rather fear he loves them.'

Corwynal dropped his face into his hands. Had it all been for nothing? His self-punishment? His sacrifices, not only of himself?

'What do I do then?' he asked Ninian. 'Give up? Ask Brangianne to come back? Forget the woman I married in the sight of your god? The children I fathered on her? I haven't even seen the youngest one. Should I forget Lothian, live out my life as Steward of Selgovia, and watch Trystan fall into bitterness as he waits for my father to die and the woman he loves to forget him?'

'I think you should resist despair,' Ninian said gently, patting his shoulder. 'Because I did achieve something in Dunpeldyr. Ealhith has agreed to meet you at Trimontium, two weeks from now.'

'With my sons?'

'Probably not.'

Corwynal didn't see what could be achieved by such a meeting but didn't say so to Ninian.

'No matter. It will be good to see Ealhith. Thank you, Ninian. One day they'll make you a saint!'

'Unlikely!' Ninian smiled, but after a moment his smile faded. 'I heard something else in Dunpeldyr – that Trystan's been in Lothian. Not in Dunpeldyr itself, but on the border. Did you know?'

Corwynal frowned because he didn't, though that wasn't surprising. Trystan didn't tell him anything these days. But, when challenged, he didn't deny it.

'Why shouldn't I go to Lothian? I didn't swear some stupid oath. Lothian will be mine one day; don't forget that. I was out hunting and ran into some of the lads. We got talking about old times, that's all. Lothian's warband remembers me fondly, which is more than can be said of Selgovia's.'

'Give them time, Trys.' Corwynal didn't need to remind him of the reasons for the warband's coolness – the slaughter in Dalriada,

Trystan's betrayal of Essylt, Kaerherdin's departure. There were many reasons for Selgovia's warband to have fallen out of love with their young commander. But Trystan was used to being loved.

'Time,' he muttered. 'It's slipping away, day by day, month by month. And nothing ever happens.'

'I'm going to Trimontium in a couple of weeks,' Corwynal ventured. 'I've . . . some business there. Do you want to come with me? Remember the last time we were there? The Mansio . . . ?' He hoped Trystan would laugh at the memory of the fight with the miller and how they'd set the place on fire. But Trystan didn't laugh. It had been three years before, and Trystan wasn't the same man anymore. Neither was he.

'No,' Trystan said shortly and walked away.

Ninian headed north a week later, and a few days after that Corwynal left too, taking the river track that would lead to Trimontium. Trystan had left Meldon also, saying he was going hunting once more. Corwynal suspected he was going to meet up with the Lothian warband, but didn't object. It was better Trystan was away hunting than moping about Meldon or, worse, heading for Galloway.

The last of the harvest was in by then, and there was little for a Steward to do before the cattle slaughter at Samhain. Even so, Essylt complained about him leaving. 'You're not coming back, are you? I'm going to be left here to rot. First Ninian, then Trystan, now you.'

Poor Essylt. She'd shone so brightly once. Now she loved and hated in equal measure. And so he was glad to go, even though the journey was likely to be a wasted one. It was good to be alone for once, to travel mindlessly through Selgovia's warm golden woods, with the river rushing along beside him, foxes yowling in the darkness beyond his fire and the smell of autumn in the chill of the night air. In some strange way, it was a time between times.

Trimontium, when he reached it, was as busy as ever. The Mansio by the gate was packed and the innkeeper sufficiently harassed to have forgotten the Caledonian from Lothian who, together with his companions, had caused so much trouble three years before.

He was a day early so bought a place in the dormitory and went to the common room to nurse a jug of ale and listen to the rumours. As ever, they were half nonsense, half-truth.

Arthyr's leaving, they say. In the spring. Lot can't wait to see the back of him. Lot? Didn't he bring him here in the first place? More fool him! Nah – Lot's no fool. He'll make himself High King now, for who's to stop him? And if Lot's High King, that'll be good for Gododdin, good for business.

None of this surprised Corwynal. Things would be interesting, come the spring. If Lot became High King and Trystan didn't do anything stupid before then, Lot would make him War-leader, the position Arthyr had promised him. Inevitably, Lot would call on Corwynal to serve him in some capacity or other, and he might not be averse to doing so. Perhaps this was what both he and Trystan were waiting for, and—

'Corwynal? Is it really you?' A youngish sandy-haired man slid into the booth opposite him and, for a moment, Corwynal didn't recognise him.

'Gaheris?' He looked older. He *was* older.

'What are you doing here?' Gaheris wanted to know.

'I'm here to meet someone.'

'Not Trystan? No, you can't be. He's— That is, I don't know where he is. Haven't seen him in a couple of moons.' Gaheris flushed – always a weakness. 'Right,' he said. 'Got to go. Good to see you . . .' Then he was gone, shouldering his way through the crowd.

Moons? Surely Gaheris hadn't seen Trystan in years? And he hadn't asked where he was or how he was - which meant he knew, that he was probably going to meet him.

'He went north,' the gate-warden said, when he followed Gaheris, only to see him riding away from Trimontium with some others. 'Him and ten men.'

Hardly a hunting trip then. Corwynal considered going back to the Mansio, saddling Janthe and riding after him, but decided against it. Whatever Trystan was up to, he'd hardly welcome Corwynal's interference, and, anyway, that wasn't the reason he'd come.

It was late the following morning before Ealhith finally arrived, by which time he'd grown steadily more nervous. So when she stepped into the Mansio's common room, deserted at that time of the day, he couldn't think of anything to say at first.

'You're alone?' he asked in the end, stupidly.

'My . . . escort's outside.'

'No, I meant—'

'Your sons? They're in Dunpeldyr.'

'They're well?'

She nodded. 'Caradawc's quite a little man now, and Tal's cutting his second tooth.'

'Tal?'

'Taliesin,' she said curtly. 'The only thing I've had from you in all these years. A name. But you're not interested in teeth or childhood illnesses or . . . or anything at all.'

'That's not true! I'm here, amn't I?'

She looked at him, her light blue eyes clear and cold. 'You're thinner,' she said. 'Older. I've not seen you for a year and nine months.

A year and nine months in which he'd grown older, and she'd . . . grown into herself. He'd seen the beginnings of it in Iuddeu when they'd married. Now she was a poised and confident young woman, one who made the most of her looks. Her straw-coloured hair was smooth and glossy and plaited in an elaborate style that made her neck look longer but exposed the scar on the left side of her face. She'd hidden it once but did so no longer. *This is who I am*, she was saying. He supposed she was the nearest thing Lothian had to a queen. And he was nothing more than the reluctant Steward of Selgovia. Did she still love him? Oddly, it mattered.

'I'm sorry,' he said. 'Things have been . . . complicated. I would have come to Lothian for you if I could.'

'Ah! That stupid oath which, conveniently, you refuse to break.'

'My father doesn't want me in Lothian.'

'You don't *understand* your father.'

That at least was true. 'Then will you come to Meldon? Or Iuddeu? Or Trimontium?'

'Aelfric wants me to go back to Bernicia with him.'

It was like a blow in the chest, for he hadn't thought of this possibility. 'Will you go?'

'Without my children? I'll go nowhere without them. Can't you understand that? I love them, and so does your father. He's their grandfather, but he's been more of a father to them than you. If you want to see them, you must come to Dunpeldyr. You have to resolve this thing with your father. Not with me. Just . . . talk to him.'

'I've tried.'

'Then you haven't tried hard enough or said the right thing. One day you'll have to find the words. One day you'll be forced to choose between your father and Trystan – and it may be sooner than you think.' She looked up as the door to the common room opened and got to her feet. 'Goodbye, Corwynal.'

'Wait—' Then he saw who'd come in. 'What are you doing here?'

'Did you imagine I'd let my sister ride half-way across Lothian on her own?' Aelfric glowered at Ealhith. 'Did you tell him?'

'That I'm going to Bernicia? No. I told him – as I told you – that I'm going nowhere without my children.'

'Not *that!* Gods, woman! Tell him.'

'Tell me what?'

Aelfric and Ealhith shared a glance, but it was Ealhith who spoke.

'It's Trystan,' she said. 'The warband have declared him King of Lothian, and they're heading for Galloway to take Yseult back from her husband.'

'No women,' Marc insisted when the messenger – his spy – had arrived from Lothian with word of Trystan's lunacy. 'Just the warband, travelling light, no camp-followers. I'll meet him in the field. I'm not cowering in the Mote waiting for him to come to Galloway. What does he take me for? No, my love, I'm not risking you,' he informed Yseult when she asked if she could go with him. 'God knows what treachery he's planning.'

Yseult glanced at Brangianne, with something of her old fire in her eyes, but when she turned to Marc her expression was all sweetness and light. 'But he'll think you don't trust me. Take me, my Lord. It will prove to him I've made my choice; that I'm your wife and can never be his. If he sees me with you, your Queen, your loving wife, perhaps he'll realise this war is hopeless. I don't want anyone to die because of me.'

Poor Marc, Brangianne thought. *Besotted enough to believe her.*

'I have to go,' Yseult said later once she and Brangianne were alone. 'I need to see Trystan again. And perhaps, somehow . . .'

Somehow, they could be together once more. Poor Yseult, living this impossible dream. For living she was. The deathlike exhaustion that had plagued her since the death of her child had lifted at last, and she was alive once more. But with the return of life had come pain and hope in equal measure. So when Ninian told Yseult he was going back to Selgovia, she hadn't tried to keep him in Galloway. 'Give Trystan a message. Tell him I still love him, despite everything I said . . .'

'Tell him she's happy,' Brangianne told Ninian privately.

'But she isn't.'

'No, but tell him she is. And, in time, she will be. If she and Marc could just . . .' She sighed. In every respect Yseult was the perfect wife, or at least playing the role so perfectly everyone was fooled. But she and Marc still slept apart, though Brangianne didn't know whether this was at Yseult's insistence or Marc's fear of failure. Whatever the reason, it meant there would be no child, and a child was what Yseult needed. A child would prove to Trystan it was over, but it would take time – time that, thanks to Trystan, they no longer had.

'Trystan will have some plan, won't he?' Yseult asked. 'We'll get away, just the two of us. We'll find a valley no-one knows about. He can hunt, and I can . . . do whatever peasant women do. And we'll be happy . . .'

This hopeless impossible dream was all she lived for.

'I'll make Marc take me,' she said fiercely. Brangianne was sure he wouldn't let her go, but to her surprise, the next day, when the warband were about to set off, he relented. Not only could Yseult go but, if they wanted, Brangianne could accompany her, together with that servant of theirs.

'Of course I'm going!' Oonagh informed them. 'Someone has to keep an eye on you. Anyway—' She flushed and scowled. '—if there's a fight brewing, that fool of an Angle's bound to be there . . .'

And wherever Trystan was, Corwynal would be there too . . .

So the three women set out – or rather three women and a child since Oonagh wouldn't leave Osric behind – all three of them nursing the foolish hope that they'd see the men they loved before they all got themselves killed.

'How did you persuade him?' Brangianne asked Yseult as they rode north through Galloway's autumn-russet woods. Marc rode ahead of them but he kept turning back and smiling at Yseult in a rather disturbing way. 'What did you say?'

'I didn't *say* anything,' Yseult said. 'I had to get him to trust me, and there was only one way to do that. It was disgusting, but it didn't last long. Now he's even more in love with me than ever. Poor Marc. I only did it so I could go to Trystan . . .'

Poor Marc indeed, but if this insane war could be averted, it might lead to better things.

'You could have a child,' Brangianne suggested hopefully.

'Not by Marc,' Essylt said flatly. 'Never by him.'

'So, Blaize is dead,' Arthyr said gravely. 'I'd suspected as much when the reports stopped arriving.'

Ferdiad had found the War-leader in Iuddeu's Council room, poring over a map he hadn't seen before, one that showed the lands to the south of the great wall, lands Ferdiad had never visited and – given the distances involved – had no desire to.

He knew what Arthyr's plans were; he'd made it his business to find out. Information was power, and, for Atholl's sake, he needed that power. So as soon as the immediate consequences of Seirian's claim to the throne had been dealt with – some of it violent, some of it at his hands, or hand – he'd sought out the informants and spies Blaize had told him about. He'd been Ferdiad the Serpent once, but now he was Ferdiad the Spider, someone who gathered rumours and whispers, who tugged a strand here and there and made things happen. He'd become a player in the game of kingdoms and kings – and queens – and felt oddly and terrifyingly alive.

There was to be a child, Seirian told him. It would be a boy. He didn't know how she could know that but didn't doubt her. His first reaction has been terror, his second . . . less easy to define.

'So you can go now,' she informed him.

He'd argued about that. They argued about everything. 'I suppose I'm dispensable now, so you're sending me away – despite everything I've done for you.' He'd done a great deal, as it happened.

'After everything you've done for *us*,' she corrected him. 'We're allies, remember – though I hadn't expected having an ally would be such a *fight*.' She smiled. She enjoyed the fight as much as he did.

'Go. I set you free. You've been useful to me, to Atholl. But Atholl doesn't stand alone. We need to know what's happening beyond its borders, and my brother should be told about Blaize. Go to Lothian, Ferdiad. Serve me by being my eyes and ears on a world I've never seen. Come back and tell Kirah and I all about our Briton kin – and about the sea.'

He'd left Atholl in an autumn gale but had first gone to Raineach to see Azarion. Only after he'd done so did he head for Iuddeu. It had rained most of the way. His bones ached and his muscles were stiff, but he still had a long way to go, to Lothian to find Corwynal.

'He's not there,' Arthyr told him. 'Some disagreement with his father apparently, which I can well believe. He went to Selgovia. He's Steward there, though I've a mind to bring him back to Iuddeu when I leave.'

Arthyr intended going south in the spring, leaving a settled North behind him. The Caledonians had been quiet, so he'd begun to dismantle the glen-forts of the Strath and transfer the men to new fortifications in Fife. An old Roman fort by a crossing of the Tava was being rebuilt. Lot, a king of Gododdin whom Ferdiad didn't know, was likely to name himself High King, and Arthyr would support him in that before he left. If Trystan behaved himself, Lot would make him War-leader in Arthyr's place. The boy had steadied, Arthyr said, had gone back to his wife in Selgovia. Yseult had returned to her husband, Marc, King of Galloway, and been received with joy and honour. So that whole sorry business was over.

'I only have a few problems to sort out here,' Arthyr finished, glancing briefly across the room where Bedwyr was dicing with a couple of Arthyr's other captains. *He means Gwenhwyvar and his best friend,* Ferdiad thought. 'And I could always do with more men,' Arthyr went on quickly. 'I don't want to deplete the garrisons I'm leaving behind.'

But here, to Arthyr's astonishment, Ferdiad had some good news for him.

'Dragon-riders? They'd fight for me?'

Ferdiad nodded at the sword Arthyr bore on his left side, the sword that had scarred Ferdiad's cheek and come close to losing him an eye. Caledan. 'They'll fight for that. Azarion's decided it's time they left the shadows. They were Romans once, and you're the last of the Romans, so they'll fight under your banner when you go south. They're a day's ride behind me. I came ahead to warn you – a troop of Dragon-riders is a terrifying sight if you're not expecting them.'

Arthyr's half smile of disbelief flared into a grin that took years from him, and Ferdiad understood why men followed this man. 'Now that's worth celebrating! Bedwyr! Culhwch! Did you hear? You there—' he snapped his fingers at a servant. 'Bring wine – the best. Jump to it man!' Then he turned back to Ferdiad and flung an arm around his shoulders.

'Blaize never trusted you,' he said with disarming frankness. 'So I didn't. But it's good to be wrong.' He caught sight of Blaize's medallion; Ferdiad was still wearing it about his neck. 'I don't suppose—?'

Ferdiad shook his head and slipped from Arthyr's embrace. 'No,' he said with some regret, for this was a man worth following. He might not be a king but he had a king's heart. 'I'm not Blaize's replacement.'

'You could come south with me. I need men with your talents.'

'I have . . . responsibilities in Atholl.' It wasn't a word that came easily to his lips. 'You'll find other men like me.'

'Maybe.' Arthyr looked up. A servant – a different one from before – had come in, laid down a tray with a pottery flagon and silver cups and was standing waiting for instructions, but his eyes were on Ferdiad rather than Arthyr, and he made a sign he'd come to recognise.

'You can go. We'll pour our own,' Arthyr said impatiently.

'Wait. He's one of Blaize's men. Let him speak.'

Moments later he wished he hadn't, that he'd remained in ignorance, that he hadn't been present to see the shattering of Arthyr's shining plans, to see a man, famously even-tempered, quiet and reliable, whether it be on the battlefield or in the Council chamber, lose his temper quite so spectacularly.

He picked up the flagon and flung it across the hall, narrowly missing one of his men. It crashed against the wall in a shower of wine and shards of pottery.

'No! No! *No!*' Arthyr leant on the table, hunched over his shaking fists, took a deep breath, then another, and looked up at the messenger.

'Say it again,' he said in a tone of dangerous calm.

'Trystan of . . . of Lothian—' The man cleared his throat and his voice dropped a register, '—has raised Lothian's warband, and they're heading for Galloway.'

'Does Marc know of this?'

'He will by now, my Lord. One of Marc's spies left Dunpeldyr and headed south after the rumours started to go about. I remained to get more information, then came north as quickly as I could. The Lothian warband was to gather at this ruined fort.' The man pointed to a position in the hills south of Dunpeldyr. 'The night before the Solstice.'

'Christ's Blood – that was last night!' But that wasn't all.

'They expected to meet men from Gododdin,' the man added.

'Gododdin? Lot? That's all I need!' Arthyr stared down at the map, judging distance and terrain.'

'Here.' He stabbed his finger down at the map, on the line of an old Roman road that ran from Caer Lual to Dun Eidyn. 'Trystan will have to take this route south. Marc, if he's fool enough to leave Galloway – and Marc always was a fool – will take this road north. I need to get between them . . .'

He rapped out a series of commands that sent Bedwyr and his other captains running off to deal with horses and men, weapons and supplies. They could raise fifty by nightfall. If they force-marched through the night, they'd reach the road by dawn. There was a good road down to the northern wall then they'd follow the Cluta upstream. If the rain held off, there would be a moon. The

Dragon-riders can follow. It sounds as if I'll need them.' He glanced at Harpstring at Ferdiad's side. 'You can use that? You'll come? I'll need every man I can get if I'm to stop a war – because that's what this is likely to turn into. A war.'

'I'll come,' Ferdiad said. 'Though I can't promise I'll fight or, if I do, who I'll fight for. I'll come because I need to see Corwynal, and wherever Trystan is Corwynal will be there, because he'll be trying to stop this too. But you'll need to find me a horse. My own's spent.'

In the end it was two horses he needed.

'Ninian? Ninian!'

Ferdiad was surprisingly glad to see him, and even more surprisingly touched by Ninian's own delight. 'You're alive! Blaize—?'

'—isn't.' Ferdiad hadn't told Arthyr the details and had no intention of telling Ninian. 'His heart gave out.' It was as good a description as any. 'What are you doing here?'

'I was heading to Atholl to find out what happened to you and Blaize.' He frowned at Ferdiad. 'You could have sent word.'

Ferdiad supposed he could but hadn't considered the manner of Blaize's death to be something to put in a message.

'Not about Blaize,' Ninian said. 'About you, being alive. Did you think no-one cared?'

'Why should they?'

Ninian shook his head in exasperation. 'I guess you're on your way to see Corwynal? Well, you'll have a long journey.'

Because it turned out that Corwynal had left Selgovia, but not with Trystan. Worse, he didn't know what Trystan had done, and neither did Ninian. So Ferdiad told him. 'I need to find a horse,' he finished.

'Find two. I'm coming with you.' The boy looked exhausted but determined. 'Trystan's in trouble,' he said simply. 'And that means Yseult's in trouble too.'

'We've been here before,' Aelfric reined in his labouring gelding on the last rise of the moors and stretched to ease the ache in his hips. A valley lay below them, and, in the growing light, he could make out the silver coil of a river and the pale thread of a road running alongside it. To the south of them, on the far side of the valley, a hill, crowned with a signal beacon, rose abruptly out of the lower-lying land.

The journey should have taken two days, but he and Corwynal had done it in a single night, and both horses were spent. Aelfric's big grey was lathered and heaving, and Corwynal's chestnut mare was drooping. The Caledonian reached forward to clap her shoulder, and she lifted her head gamely and whickered softly. 'Not far, girl,' he whispered to her. 'Not far.'

'Are you listening to me?' Aelfric asked. 'We've been here before.'

I shouldn't have come. I should have taken Ealhith back to Dunpeldyr. But when Corwynal had announced that he was going to stop Trystan, Aelfric had decided to go too. 'The lads will see Ealhith safely home.' He'd jerked his head at three men who'd joined them in the Mansio's common room, older men of the Dunpeldyr guard.

'I don't need you.'

'I'm not going for *you*.'

That was all that had been said about anything other than the matter in hand – of getting to Trystan before he and his men met Marc's. *Up that way . . . Across that hill . . . If we cut down there . . .* They'd gone right across country, over the moors on a cold night lit by the seed moon, waning from the full, which turned the streams cutting the heather-dark slopes to silver. Thank Odin for the moon, but it had still been a nightmare of a journey – like the last time they'd ridden this way in an attempt to stop the Dalriads from joining the war with the Caledonians. They hadn't succeeded then and were unlikely to succeed now. Aelfric had expected Corwynal to be furious with Trystan, but he just looked frightened, and that made Aelfric more than a little uneasy.

'We've been here,' he insisted. 'Three years ago.'

Corwynal nodded. 'You're a better horseman now than you were then.'

Aelfric snorted. 'But you're as much of a fool. You got yourself captured then.'

'And you, unless you've forgotten, were a slave.'

Oddly, he'd forgotten that – until now. 'Don't think I've forgiven you for that – or for anything else.'

'So why are you here?'

Aelfric didn't know. He owed this man nothing, not even a promised death, for he'd given up on that oath a long time before. *I'm just here for the fight,* he told himself, except he wasn't. He was here to stop a fight – and that was a first. *I must be getting old.* Then he understood he wanted to stop the fight because he didn't know whose side he was on. Was it Trystan's – who seemed to have lost his mind once more? Or Corwynal's – who by that deal with Arthyr had put Aelfric in a very difficult position? Now he was in another difficult position, because he'd have to make a choice, and Aelfric didn't like choices. He liked things to be clear and straightforward, but life wasn't that simple. *I really* am *getting old,* he thought irritably, stretching his back, which clicked alarmingly. The sun was rising behind them now, and something flashed on the slopes to the north of that solitary hill. Aelfric screwed up his eyes until he saw them; horsemen approaching from the northwest. Which meant it wasn't Trystan. Or Marc.

'Arthyr?' Corwynal sagged with relief.

Arthyr! Aelfric scowled. He might not know who he was going to fight for, but it certainly wouldn't be Arthyr.

'He'll stop this,' Corwynal declared. 'If anyone can.'

But if Arthyr succeeded, he'd be free to head south, taking war to the Saex and Angles. So maybe Aelfric should be helping someone start a war here. Not stop it.

'Why are you here?' Corwynal asked one more time.

'Fuck knows,' Aelfric said miserably, because he didn't.

By the time Corwynal and Aelfric reached the floor of the valley, Arthyr had already set up camp in a bend of the river below the signal hill.

'You're not with Trystan then,' Arthyr concluded when Corwynal found him in a makeshift shelter beneath a stand of alders.

'I didn't know.' It sounded pathetic even in his own ears.

'Can you talk him out of this?'

It was the question Corwynal had been asking himself all the way from Trimontium, but he still didn't know the answer. Trystan had gone too far this time. It was as if Corwynal had forged a sword, bright and strong, only to have it turn in his hand and cut him to the bone. This was no adventure on Trystan's part, no mad escapade, no high spirits, no laughing in the face of death. He'd involved Lothian this time, had allowed himself to be named King and risked a war that couldn't be won. And all for the sake of a woman who, if Ninian was to be believed, was living happily, or happily enough, with her husband. Something had gone wrong inside Trystan. Maybe it was the lingering effects of The Dragon's poison, or Trystan's thwarted obsessive love for Yseult. *Or maybe it's my fault, my doom, my blood in his.* Whatever the reason, it was Corwynal's responsibility to stop him.

'He's an hour away,' Arthyr said after exchanging a few words with a scout. 'There's no sign of Marc yet. Maybe he won't come.' He didn't believe it any more than Corwynal. If Marc was sensible, he'd wait for Trystan in Galloway. But Marc had never been sensible. 'I've fifty men,' Arthyr went on. 'Trystan has around a hundred. Marc will have more. I've more men coming, but they won't arrive before tomorrow. Trystan also has men from Gododdin, apparently. I hope to God it's not Lot.'

'It'll be Gaheris,' Corwynal said tiredly. 'He'd do anything for Trystan, but he's not got a brain in his head.'

Arthyr nodded distractedly then moved away to deal with some question, and Corwynal became aware of someone watching him. He felt the cold brush of antagonism and turned to see Kaerherdin leaning on the saddle-horns of a rangy roan gelding.

'So, your precious Trystan's turned feral. I suppose it was only a matter of time, but I wonder if you'll be able to control him this time.'

'Why are you here?'

'I'm one of Arthyr's men now.'

'Arthyr doesn't need men like you.'

Kaerherdin scowled at him. 'He needs every man he can get, because it's going to come to a fight, and I thank the gods for it; I've wanted to fight you and that treacherous brother of yours for a very long time.' He smiled once more, kicked his horse, and cantered off in the direction of the horse lines.

'Old friends make bad enemies,' said a voice from behind him. 'Old enemies, on the other hand, are another matter.'

Ferdiad was leaning against one of the alders, his arms crossed, amusement in his green eyes. 'No – I'm not the ghost you clearly believe me to be.' And to prove it, he stepped forward and gripped Corwynal by the arm.

'I thought you were dead!' he said stupidly, staring at the man who'd been Ferdiad the Serpent before transforming himself into Ferdiad Silverhand. Now he'd changed his skin once more. The calm that had followed the storm in Atholl was gone now, and Corwynal understood how unnatural that calm had been, as if it was the still surface of water untouched by wind or life. Now Ferdiad glittered, his eyes dancing, his expression flaring from amusement to irony to empathy.

'Do you know how many people have said that – *I thought you were dead* – in just that way? As if they were disappointed I'm not?' Then the self-mocking smile faded. 'Blaize, however *is* dead. I'm sorrier than I expected to be. I should have sent word, but I wanted to tell you in person. So—' He spread his hands, one flesh, one silver. 'Here I am.'

'You know what Trystan's done?'

'Young fool,' Ferdiad said without heat. 'I heard in Iuddeu. But you'll stop him.'

'How?'

'You'll think of something.'

But Trystan was only an hour away, so there wasn't much time to think of anything. He glanced at the signal hill that rose above the camp and Ferdiad, following the direction of his gaze, groaned.

'This predilection of yours for high places is very wearing,' he complained as they walked to the foot of the hill and found a little track that climbed through heather up an increasingly stony hillside and led to a shoulder of the hill and thence to a flat little peak that was lower than and separate from the true summit. Looking towards Lothian, through the rain sweeping down the valley, blurring the slopes and woods, Corwynal caught a flash of light from the distant shoulder of a hill, then another. If that was Trystan, his troop wasn't moving fast, so must be unaware of Arthyr's men blocking their way. The scout was right. They were at least an hour away.

'Tell me then,' Corwynal said to distract himself from his inability to think of anything he could do. 'About Blaize.'

It wasn't an easy telling, nor an easy listening, and Corwynal felt sick by the end. 'A bad death,' he said, thinking of the man he'd known, his flesh carved to ribbons, dying on a stone slab in Atholl.

'No. It was a good death. He died for a reason, for something he believed in, by his own will. He helped keep Atholl safe, Seirian safe, me safe.'

'I hope you killed Domech.' Corwynal wished he could have killed him himself but, to his surprise, Ferdiad shook his head.

'I was too late. The morning after Blaize's death, Domech woke up, weakened and unable to speak. It's not uncommon in men of his age and temper. But for a man like Domech to be unable to speak is a living death, so I let him live.'

'But Seirian's safe, you said? I suppose she had to take Ciniod as Consort.' Corwynal sighed. He'd promised her freedom, but it had only been the freedom to have no choice at all. 'I was afraid she'd have to.'

'Ciniod's dead,' Ferdiad said dismissively. 'A show of ruthlessness was required, and he was a victim of that necessity. But it wasn't dishonourable. He was offered the chance to fight and took it. I pretended it was more difficult than it was.'

'You killed him? Then Seirian—?'

'—chose me as Consort. That's why – how – she saved me from Domech.'

'She chose you? I didn't think you were . . .' Words failed him.

'What? Attracted to women after all? I'm not. I'm certainly not attracted to Seirian who's infuriating and stubborn and . . .' Ferdiad gave a self-mocking laugh once more. '. . . much like yourself. So, it's not a love match, if your romantic heart was looking for one. We're not even friends. We are – as she keeps reminding me – allies, which means she's recognised I'd make a bad enemy. She's Queen now, or rather Queen-regent, since I gather there's to be a child – a son apparently.'

'Yours?'

'So she tells me,' Ferdiad said distantly and turned to watch the approaching party of horsemen. They were nearer now and Corwynal could see, or imagine he saw, a fair head among the leaders. 'Is it worth it?' Ferdiad asked, all hint of self-mockery gone from his voice. 'The grief? The terror? The . . . impotence?'

Corwynal, who, right then, felt all of these things, shook his head. 'I don't know. It's not easy. I don't think it's supposed to be easy.'

Ferdiad, lost in his own tortured fears, continued to watch the Lothian riders, 'You have a father, don't you? Yes, of course you do. He's Seirian's father also. I keep forgetting that. Do you . . . care for him?'

'I'm not sure. Being a son isn't easy either.'

'I never knew my father,' Ferdiad said. 'Whoever he was, he

raped my mother. I think of him sometimes, wonder if he's still alive and what I'd say to him before I killed him as painfully as I could devise.' His voice was relentless, but he shook off the chill of revenge, and when he spoke once more he sounded reflective. 'Maybe sons are put on earth to destroy their fathers. When you think of it, it makes sense – the old wolf killing the young and taking his place. We're, all of us, nothing more than animals at heart.'

Corwynal shuddered at this echo of his father's dream, and Ferdiad, seeing it, laughed shortly. 'I'm sorry. Not a very tactful metaphor in the circumstances.' He glanced at the approaching riders 'We should get back. Arthyr will want to ride out to meet them and I expect you'll want to go with him.'

'What am I to say to him? How am I to stop this?'

Ferdiad regarded him thoughtfully. 'Tell him you're his father?'

Corwynal shook his head. How could he persuade Trystan of anything after telling him he'd lied to him for the whole of his life?'

25

THE CHALLENGE

'**I**'m not losing men because of an internal squabble.' Arthyr glanced around at his captains and the other interested parties, which included Ferdiad, Aelfric and, to Corwynal's surprise, Ninian.

'It's more than a squabble,' Corwynal objected. 'And you're War-leader.'

Arthyr dropped his hand to Caledan's hilt. Like Corwynal before him, he kept it by his side at all times. 'Very well. Since there are bigger issues at stake.' He frowned at Aelfric who was standing behind Corwynal. 'I brought my men so I could argue from a position of strength, but since you're here – since you've failed to prevent Trystan from acting like an idiot – you can do the arguing.'

'Listen, Arthyr. There's a solution . . .' It was the only way out he could see. 'Trys needs a challenge. Being Selgovia's Consort isn't enough. Nor is the prospect of succeeding you. Yseult will always be in Galloway, always within reach. He needs to be sent away from the North. Offer him a position as one of your captains. You know what he can do, what he's done in the past. Use him in the south to fight the Saex.'

He'd been conscious of Aelfric's eyes boring into the back of his head. Now he felt his breath on his neck.

'You treacherous bastard!' he hissed.

'No,' Arthyr said flatly. 'Why should I reward him? Why should I trust him? He showed promise once, but this obsession with another man's wife has ruined him.'

There was a small careful silence in which no-one looked at Bedwyr. But if Arthyr was aware of it, or intended saying any more on the subject, they didn't find out, for just then one of his scouts galloped up from the south, dismounted and muttered something that made Arthyr's eyes sharpen.

'Marc's on his way,' he announced. 'Right – let's go and talk to Trystan. I want Bedwyr, Culhwch, Kaerherdin, Corwynal and . . .' He hesitated. 'Ferdiad.'

'I'm coming too,' Aelfric declared. 'I've a stake in this!'

Arthyr regarded him narrowly, judging whether it was worth the fight if he was to refuse, then, concluding it wasn't, nodded his assent.

'And me,' Ninian said. 'Trystan's a Christian. As a priest, maybe I can remind him of what that means.'

Arthyr was clearly sceptical of any priest influencing Trystan but agreed that too.

The eight of them rode out in a smirr of rain to meet the Lothian men and waited by the bend in the river where the track ran close to a wooded hillside. In the distance, but close enough to be counted, were Trystan's troops, a hundred and twenty or so strong. Lothian's wolf flew above them, as did Gododdin's boar.

'Young fool!' Arthyr muttered. 'I wouldn't care to be in Gaheris' boots when Lot finds out.'

This didn't seem to have occurred to Gaheris, however, for he showed no signs of anxiety when he, Trystan and Madawg, who, as Lothian's warband leader, bore the wolf standard, rode ahead to meet them.

'This is none of your business,' Trystan told Arthyr.

'I disagree,' Arthyr said mildly. 'What you do after I leave isn't my concern. But, as you'll have noticed, I haven't left yet. Go back to Lothian, Trys.'

'Not without Yseult. She's mine.'

'Don't be a fool, Trys!' Corwynal cut in.

Trystan ignored him. 'If Marc gives me Yseult,' he went on, 'I'll disband my men and leave, renouncing all claims – to Lothian, to Selgovia, to anything in the North. None of you will see me again.'

Madawg frowned at Trystan; clearly this hadn't been the arrangement. Gaheris looked puzzled, but was happy to go along with anything Trystan decided, as he always did.

'Do you seriously imagine Marc will just give her up to you?' Arthyr asked.

'Yseult doesn't want to be with him.'

'She went willingly enough. No-one forced her.'

'She's happy,' Corwynal insisted.

'Yseult's *pretending* to be happy,' Trystan retorted. 'But she isn't.'

'We aren't here to debate a woman's happiness or lack of it,' Arthyr said. 'What man ever truly knows a woman's heart?' He glanced at Bedwyr as he said this, and Bedwyr looked away. 'We're here to debate the position we find ourselves in. It won't have escaped your notice that I've camped between your warband and Marc's. If you want to fight him, you'll have to fight me first. The reverse is also the case, as I'll be explaining to Marc. But you put me in a difficult position, Trys. You're in the wrong here. I ought to support Marc and may decide to do so. Alternatively, I may choose to stand aside and let the two of you slog it out between you. The world would be a simpler place without either of you. So now might be the time to consider who's on your side and who isn't.'

Trystan lifted his chin and regarded each of them in turn – Arthyr whom he respected and admired to the point of worship but whom he'd disappointed, Bedwyr and Culhwch, fighting and drinking companions who'd be so no longer, and Kaerherdin, once a friend, but whose sister he'd betrayed and was betraying even now. Then there was Ferdiad whose love Trystan had rejected, and as for Aelfric . . .

'Whose side are you on?' he asked the Angle who'd been his shield brother in so many fights.

'Not his.' Aelfric jerked his head at Arthyr. 'But that doesn't mean I'm on your side, you fucking idiot!'

'I'm on your side,' Ninian said quietly, to everyone's surprise, including Trystan's, for his jealousy of Ninian in Atholl had been bitter, vocal and unfair, but Ninian kicked his horse forward and rode to join him.

'And your god?' Trystan smiled wryly at him. 'Is he on my side?'

'He's your god too, Trys, so of course he's on your side. He's on everyone's side.'

Trystan had won one priest and not a single warrior, but still had someone to ask. His eyes slid slowly to Corwynal's, who braced himself to meet them.

'And you – brother? Whose side are you on?'

Corwynal didn't – couldn't – reply.

'Come,' Arthyr said to the others. 'Let's leave the brothers of Lothian to find a solution to this impasse.' He hauled on the reins to turn his mount, kicked him into a canter and headed back to the camp. Bedwyr, Culhwch and Kaerherdin followed him, and, after a backwards glance – full of resentment on Aelfric's part and empathy on Ferdiad's – they followed the others, leaving Corwynal alone with Trystan, the smell of woodsmoke and rain-washed heather all around them.

'I'm not on anyone's side,' he said.

'You have to choose.' Trystan jerked his chin at Gaheris who wheeled his mount and rode back to re-join Trystan's troop. 'You too, Madawg,' he added. 'But leave me the standard to remind my brother why we're here.' Madawg tossed him the staff with the wolf banner, but Trystan fumbled the catch. The staff slipped between his fingers and fell to the ground, and the banner ended up in a muddy puddle pocked with the rain that was falling heavily now. Madawg moved to dismount but Trystan made an angry gesture. 'Leave it. Go back,' he said harshly, staring down at the banner, a white look about his lips. Then he looked up and gave a thin-lipped smile.

'Do you reckon that was symbolic? Maybe it was. Well? What do you have to say? But I warn you, if it's a lecture you have in mind, you can save your breath.'

'I think you're beyond being lectured to, beyond anything I can say. But I still have to say it. Don't do this, Trys.'

Trystan waited for more, then gave a short laugh. 'That's it? That's the extent of your argument?'

'It's the heart of it. Don't do this. Just walk away – leave Lothian, leave Yseult. Leave everything and . . . walk away.'

'Leaving her behind? I can't.' He made an impatient gesture with one hand. 'I know what you're going to say – that I can. I've tried. You may not believe me, but I *have* tried. God knows I've tried, but it's like having my soul torn in two, and I can't bear it anymore. I can't live like this any longer.'

'You'd give up everything for Yseult? For a *woman?*'

'Yes – but surely you understand that?'

'I gave up Brangianne.'

'You gave her up for *Lothian*. That's why you're here – because I might take away the one thing you care about more than anything, the place you'd give everything up for, the place you love more than Brangianne or . . . or me.'

'That's not true.'

'It is! Everything you do is for Lothian. You raised me to be Lothian's King, not caring if that was what I wanted. You even left Lothian for its sake, not mine. Everything you've done, or not done, and everything you've persuaded me to do, or not do, has been with one thought in your head – how will this affect Lothian? You might have stayed in Atholl, thinking you could control the Caledonians and thus keep Lothian safe, but when you couldn't, when it came to war, you betrayed Atholl and Caledonia for the sake of Lothian. You made that peace for *Lothian!* You sold me to Arthyr and Selgovia. You sold Yseult to Marc. And all the time I believed you were right because I believed you cared about me. But you don't.'

'I *do* care about you!'

'Then why are you fighting against me?'

'I'm not fighting against you.'

'But you're not with me either. You've broken all your promises. Do you remember in Galloway, when you came to talk me out of fighting The Morholt, you told me I'd fall in love with some beautiful woman one day, and you wouldn't try to stop me?'

'Those were simpler times, Trys. That was before Yseult. I wish I'd never said what I said. I wish you'd never met her.'

'And lived my life as half a person? She completes me,' Trystan said simply. 'All I want to do is spend the rest of my days with her, away from everyone, not hurting anyone, just her and me. Alone. Is that so much to ask?' He held out a hand in appeal, then let it fall.

'Apparently it is. But I'll prevail, you'll see. All you have to do is watch. I'll either win and leave the North, or I'll lose. Either way you win. Either way you get Lothian. It will be my gift to you.'

'Lothian isn't mine to take or yours to give.'

'It is now. Rifallyn's deposed. It wasn't my idea, but when it was forced on me I knew it was right. It's not his anymore, and Lothian needs a king, so you'll take it, protesting all the way, no doubt, but you *will* take it.'

'You're wrong, Trys. And you can't win. Marc will have more men than you, and Arthyr, for all his talk of standing between you, will have to side with him. You'll lose. Yseult will lose. A lot of men with no reason to die will do so, though they don't deserve it. And then what? Their sons, their cousins, their friends, will want revenge, and Lothian will find itself at war with Galloway. Lot will be forced to support Lothian and fight Marc, and Strathclyde will get involved. Selgovia, whose warband hates you and so hates Lothian, won't keep out of it. Where will all this end? Where? Don't do this!'

Trystan looked at him steadily, unmoved, still waiting, but Corwynal could think of nothing more to say. 'Must I beg? Must I get down on my knees before you and beg? Because I will. Trystan – I beg you not to do this.'

But Trystan's expression, instead of softening, just hardened. 'Is that the best you can do? If it is, we've nothing more to say to one another – brother. But you can give Arthyr a message from me. He wants a solution to the impasse. So this is my proposal. No-one need die. I'll fight anyone Marc or Arthyr chooses in single combat. If I win, I get Yseult. If I lose, I'll leave the North and never come back.'

And, leaving Lothian's wolf standard lying in the mud, he jerked Rhydian's reins, wheeled him tightly and galloped back to his men.

'The boy's a fool,' Arthyr declared when Corwynal took Trystan's proposal back to him.

'He isn't, actually.'

Corwynal looked around the rough shelter that served as Arthyr's command tent, expecting to see the dirty irascible figure of his uncle standing at Arthyr's shoulder telling him something he didn't want to hear. But it was Ferdiad, doing much the same thing.

'He's not,' Corwynal said. 'If Marc agrees to this, he'll be the fool, because if Trys wins – and he fully expects to – you'll have to back him when Marc reneges on the agreement – which he will.'

Arthyr swore quietly under his breath. 'Marc *will* agree,' he said. 'He's nothing to lose, and if he has reinforcements coming up the road he'll be glad of any delay.'

Another of Arthyr's scouts had reported Marc's forces to be in the hills to the south, almost the same number as Trystan had. Marc's own scouts must have seen Arthyr's camp in the valley, for the Galloway men stopped and made camp some distance away on the slopes of a hill.

'But Trystan will win.' Corwynal was feeling a little less sick about the whole business.

'I can't afford for Trystan to win,' Arthyr said. 'If he loses, the Lothian men will lose heart and it will be over. But if he wins, there will be a fight I'll have to take part in. Trystan *has* to lose, so—' He looked from one man to the next, '—who's going to fight him?'

'I will,' Culhwch said. One by one, Arthyr's men put themselves forward, but Arthyr smiled and shook his head at each of them.

'I will. It's my right to fight him.' Arthyr's smile faded for it was Kaerherdin who'd spoken.

'It's no-one's right,' Arthyr said curtly. 'I don't want Selgovia brought into this mess – and I doubt you could beat him anyway.'

Kaerherdin flushed and didn't reply; Arthyr was right. Bedwyr hadn't put himself forward, but he didn't need to. Everyone knew Arthyr would choose him if Marc had no candidate. Arthyr's men were murmuring among themselves. It would be a good fight, they were saying, well worth coming all this way for. Good old Trystan for suggesting it. Some of them wandered off, already taking bets on who'd win.

'Right,' Arthyr said, a grim expression on his face 'Bedwyr, Culhwch, Kaerherdin – you come with me. Let's see what Marc has to say for himself . . .'

Yseult demanded the right to go and meet the men riding towards them from the camp further up the river.

'After all, this is about me,' she said, with some justice, and Marc relented, even allowing Brangianne to attend her, though he surrounded them both with more warriors than Brangianne thought necessary, given that only four men rode to meet them.

Yseult's colour was high, her eyes glittering, her lips bitten to crimson and parted with excitement, and raindrops sparkled on her hair. She expected Trystan to be one of the riders, but Brangianne knew he wouldn't be such a fool as to face Marc with only three other men. One of them might be Corwynal, however, and her heart was thudding painfully as the men approached. But as they drew closer she saw, with a dull thud of disappointment, that he wasn't one of them, though there was a man who made her heart thump in a different way – Kaerherdin. With him was Arthyr, Bedwyr at his side, and a third man Brangianne didn't know.

'What are you doing here?' Marc asked Arthyr.

'Trying to stop this foolishness,' Arthyr said evenly. 'So, I have a proposal. Galloway's Champion to meet Lothian's Champion in single combat to settle this stupid business.'

Single combat? Brangianne wondered what madness this was, for surely Lothian's Champion would be Trystan himself, and surely – *surely* – he'd win. Marc must have thought so too, for he glanced sharply at Arthyr. 'Galloway's Champion to fight Trystan, you mean.'

'Indeed. Does Galloway have a Champion who'd be willing to meet him?'

'I would have met him myself if I'd been a few years younger,' Marc declared.

A few decades, Brangianne thought waspishly.

'I hope, my Lord, you're not thinking of it.' Yseult leant over to put a hand on Marc's arm.

'You think your old husband couldn't do it?' he asked coyly, taking her hand in his and smiling fondly.

'Of course you could, but I should still fear for the safety of my husband, who isn't as old as he pretends!' she said, matching his loving smile with her own.

Brangianne, knowing what Yseult had done to get herself there, turned away, sickened.

'This is a ridiculous proposal,' Marc stated. 'Trystan knows Galloway doesn't have a Champion since he held that position himself before he betrayed us.'

'Then allow me to offer Galloway one of my own men to stand as your Champion.' Arthyr inclined his head to the three men who were with him.

Marc's eyes narrowed in speculation and he looked from one to the next, his gaze alighting first on Kaerherdin, whom he knew. 'Well, boy? You must want to fight Trystan after everything he's done. You'd be welcome in my camp, you and any men you care to bring with you.'

Kaerherdin opened his mouth to speak, but Marc's attention had already passed on. 'Culhwch, isn't it?' he said to the man Brangianne didn't know. 'A fine fighter. But not a patch on Bedwyr, eh?' His eyes slid to Bedwyr, who blushed rosily. 'Your reputation goes before you.'

Brangianne looked at Bedwyr with growing alarm, for if that reputation was correct, he might beat Trystan. Bedwyr was a big man, softly spoken, Arthyr's shadow and, if the rumours were to be believed, Gwenhwyvar's shadow also.

Marc looked at Bedwyr, then Arthyr, then Bedwyr again, and smiled.

'You choose, Arthyr,' he said magnanimously. 'Anyone you choose. Let the fight settle it.'

'Perhaps we should ask Queen Yseult's opinion,' Arthyr said, turning to her. 'Do you understand what's at stake here, my lady?'

'I do.' She drew herself up in the saddle, not so much Galloway's Queen as Feargus of Dalriada's daughter. '*I* am at stake. If your Champion wins, Trystan will give up his claim to me. If he wins, I'll go to him. So why ask my opinion? I'm nothing more than a prize to be won. But if by being won or lost a war is avoided, then I'm content.'

'Very well.' Arthyr's distaste for the whole business was evident. 'The fight will begin at dawn tomorrow and I'll support whoever wins.'

'But I've one small condition,' Marc said as Arthyr turned away. He was still smiling, but it was the smile of a weasel. 'I want Trystan of Lothian dead – one way or the other. The fight must be to the death.'

'You can't agree to this, Arthyr!' Corwynal insisted when the War-leader returned from meeting Marc. 'Not a fight to the death!'

'Why not?' Arthyr shook rain from his cloak. 'One man dead instead of hundreds?'

But which man?

'You there—' Arthyr called to one of his men. 'Call the Captains.'

Word of Marc's demand had flown about the camp, and quite a few Arthyr hadn't summoned turned up as well, but one was missing.

'Where's Kaerherdin?' Arthyr asked and was told he'd left the camp. 'God's Blood! I should have known . . . He's gone to Marc, curse them both. Still, one man won't make a difference.'

'He hasn't gone to Marc.' Corwynal was chillingly certain. 'He's gone to Meldon, and he'll come back with the Selgovian warband to fight for anyone willing to fight Trystan.'

Arthyr dropped his face into his hands, his fingers kneading his temples as if to force his brain to think, and when he looked up, his face was haggard.

'Right. This is what will happen. The fight will be at dawn, and it *will* be to the death. But it has to be Trystan's death. That's the only thing that will stop all this from turning into a war.'

'No!' Corwynal burst out. 'He won't agree. I won't let him! I'll go to him and—'

'You'll stay here,' Arthyr said harshly, with a glance at a few of his men who edged warily towards Corwynal, their hands fingering their weapons. 'You think I'm going to let you fight against me? No, you'll stay here. You failed to persuade him once, and you'll fail again.'

Corwynal glanced around, seeking a way out. He had to get to Trystan, to warn him and make another attempt to get him to back down. Aelfric was at the back of the crowd, head and shoulders hunched to avoid being noticed. If the Angle could just make some sort of diversion . . . But Aelfric folded his arms across his chest and shook his head. Ferdiad, on the other side, also shook his head and made a sign urging Corwynal to wait. *Wait for what?*

'Listen, Corwynal,' Arthyr said tiredly. 'Marc may be a treacherous bastard, but it was Trystan who started this. He stole another man's wife, and there has to be consequences for that. If he doesn't want to risk being defeated, he can walk away, but if he does, his reputation will be in ruins, and he knows it. So he'll fight. And that means I need someone who can defeat him.' He looked around at his men. 'But it won't be Bedwyr.'

'But Arthyr—' Bedwyr began.

'No. I saw what Marc was thinking – that I might have reason to risk your life. But he's wrong. I need you alive.' He grasped the other man by the shoulder and shook him. 'I *need* you.' The two men looked at one another, and Gwenhwyvar no longer lay between them.

'Who then?' Bedwyr asked.

'I'll do it myself,' Arthyr said, his voice stern but weary.

The protests came from all around him, Bedwyr foremost among them.

'You can't,' he said simply. 'Because I need *you* alive. Anyway—' A slow smile lit his face. '—you aren't good enough.'

Arthyr returned the smile. 'Then I need to find someone who is.' He looked to his men, judging and assessing each of them, waiting for someone to step forward. But no-one did so, and not because they weren't prepared to die for Arthyr – they'd risked their lives for him often enough in the past – but they weren't willing to fail him. The foul taste of fear in Corwynal's throat began to diminish. If Arthyr couldn't find anyone, then Marc's gamble would have failed and Trystan would win by default. There would still be a war and, since Corwynal couldn't think how to stop it, he'd have to fight in that war, at Trystan's side, where he should have been all along.

'I could beat him.'

Heads swivelled and the fear in Corwynal's throat almost choked him, for Aelfric had shouldered his way through Arthyr's men to stand before the War-leader. 'I could have beat him in Lothian—' He threw Corwynal a resentful look. '— if he hadn't had help.'

'You can't!' Corwynal said desperately. 'You wouldn't. He's your friend.'

'You were my friend too. But friendship doesn't seem to count for much.'

'You'd do this?' Arthyr asked, his relief palpable.

Aelfric nodded. 'For a price.' The two men looked at one another. Aelfric didn't need to say what the price was, and Corwynal held his breath as he watched Arthyr struggle with the implications.

'I'm not backing out of fighting the Saex. Or their allies,' he said eventually, and Corwynal was able to breathe once more.

Aelfric shrugged. 'Then we've reached a – what was that word you used? – an impasse.'

'I'll find someone,' Arthyr insisted without conviction. 'And then—'

A cry of challenge rang out, followed by the whinny of horses and the shouting of men, and one of Arthyr's men came running.

'It's Lothian!' he gasped. 'They're here!'

Swords slid from scabbards, spears were hefted and shields raised, but only a handful of men stepped into the firelight from the shadows beyond. While they'd talked and argued, night had fallen on Arthyr's camp. The new arrivals wore the wolf of Lothian, but they hadn't come to fight, for they weren't Trystan's men. Corwynal recognised three of them. As did Aelfric.

'What are you lot doing here? I told you to— Odin's Balls!' Accompanying the Lothian guardsmen was the slight, exhausted, but determined figure of a woman. 'Ealhith! You shouldn't be here!'

'I tend to agree,' said a voice from the darkness, and a figure moved into the light. Firelight glittered faintly on the wolf embroidered on his black tunic, and over his shoulders he wore a rain-speckled wolf-skin cloak as dense as the shadows from which he'd coalesced.

'I believe you're discussing the death of my heir,' Rifallyn of Lothian said, his amber wolf-eyes on Arthyr. 'You didn't think I might have an opinion on such a matter?'

Arthyr was rarely at a loss, but he was now. 'Sire, I apologise. It's a . . . a difficult situation.'

'Indeed! That's why I'm here,' Rifallyn said mildly, removing his riding gloves one finger at a time. 'They tell me I'm no longer King of Lothian.' He smiled his humourless wolf-smile. 'But I beg to differ. So, shall we set about solving this dilemma of yours?'

He swept his cold golden gaze around the assembled men, looking at each in turn and appearing to find them wanting. He noted Aelfric's presence with a nod, and Ferdiad's with a raised eyebrow as if he'd heard of him. He left Corwynal to last, and he braced himself for his father's usual disappointment. But there was nothing in his expression, nothing at all.

'Come, Corwynal,' his father said softly, before walking back into the night.

'I have to warn him!'

'Ssshh.' Brangianne held Yseult hard against her and let the girl break her heart in her arms. Her sobs, muffled against her shoulder, were all the fiercer for having been held in until they were alone.

A fight to the death?! Brangianne hadn't been able to believe her ears when she'd heard Marc's condition. *To the death?!* Yseult had dropped her eyes to conceal her terror, a pulse beating wildly in her throat. Brangianne had seen the faint tremble of a body about to break, and she'd pushed her horse between Yseult's and Marc's to draw his attention away from his wife.

'How can you suggest such a thing?!' Trystan's your only—'

'My only nephew,' Marc cut in with a hard blue glare. That night, that claim, was to be forgotten. Trystan was no longer his son; he was a rival. '—and a treacherous one at that. I should have had him put to death when I had the chance. Now let Arthyr do it.' He'd jerked his chin at the four men riding back to their camp. 'Because he will,' he snarled.

'I feel sick.' Yseult put a hand to her mouth. 'Excuse me . . .' She slid from her horse, stumbled to the shelter of some bushes and Brangianne heard the sound of retching.

'You're a monster!' she told Marc, pulling her horse away to follow Yseult, but he caught her wrist and pulled her back.

'What ails her?'

Fear? Grief? Disgust? You choose.

'Is she breeding?'

Feeling sick herself, she tore her arm away. If she'd had the power, her look would have turned him into a worm crawling in the mud beneath her feet. But all she could do was bend towards him and hiss her hatred in his face. 'If Trystan dies, I'll destroy you!' She dropped to the ground, followed Yseult, held her as she retched, then coaxed her back to the camp and into the small tent they shared with Oonagh.

'The man's a fool!' Oonagh declared when she heard about Marc's condition. 'He's condemned another man to die, because who could possibly beat Trystan?'

Yseult looked up hopefully and sniffed back her tears, but Brangianne had seen one man who could – Bedwyr, Arthyr's friend. Then she remembered another: Aelfric, who'd left Iuddeu in a temper. The possibility must also have crossed Oonagh's mind for she paled dramatically.

'Men!' she muttered. 'Why do they have to be so *stupid?!* And what's Corwynal doing? He stopped a war between the Britons and Caledonians. Why can't he stop *this?*'

Brangianne had been asking herself that question all the way from Galloway. Because he didn't know? Because he couldn't? Because – something cold and heavy settled on her stomach at the thought – because Trystan had gone too far this time and struck at the heart of everything Corwynal cared about. But surely even he—

'I have to speak to him,' she said.

'Yes!' Yseult looked up, thinking she was speaking of Trystan, and scrubbed away her tears. 'They won't let me leave, but you could go. Tell him he mustn't agree to this. Tell him to forget about this war and be patient. Tell him – remind him – about the valley. He'll know what I mean. Tell him I'll wait for him there. He has to live. Nothing else matters. Tell him I never stopped loving him. Make him see that's all that matters.'

Brangianne wasn't sure any of that would help, but she agreed and didn't say it was Corwynal she wanted – needed – to see.

Marc's men were more concerned with keeping men away from the camp than preventing one woman from leaving – as long as it wasn't Yseult. Brangianne told them she had a lover in Arthyr's camp – which she did – and they let her go. Arthyr's men were more efficient, and marched her, none too gently, to one of the biggest campfires in the camp that spanned the valley where Arthyr himself was sitting with some of his men. Corwynal wasn't among them.

'He left the camp,' Arthyr said shortly, looking like a man who couldn't see a way out of the position he'd been put in.

'Let me go to Trystan,' she urged, for Corwynal – surely – must have gone to talk him out of whatever he was planning. 'Let me take him Yseult's words. Perhaps they'll persuade him to go back to Lothian.'

'Yseult's the reason all this is happening,' Arthyr complained.

'Let me try, my Lord.'

'Very well,' he said gravely. 'Tell him about Marc's demand, and say I've accepted it.'

The stone settled on her stomach once more. 'Who's going to fight him?'

'He'll discover that in the morning.' Arthyr got to his feet. 'I'll find someone to take you to his camp.' He looked about, then gestured to someone she hadn't expected to see again, or be glad to see.

'Ferdiad! You're alive!'

Ferdiad uncoiled himself from a place by the fire and sighed. 'So they tell me,' he said dryly. 'Well, come along, if you insist on going on this fool's errand.'

They left Arthyr's camp and walked north along a track to a flicker of fires within a patch of woodland. It had stopped raining and the sky had cleared to reveal the first of the stars. The temperature was dropping, as were her spirits.

'You won't achieve anything,' Ferdiad warned her. 'Corwynal didn't.'

'Is he with Trystan?'

'No – he's with his father. The former King of Lothian as opposed to the current one. He's chosen sides, Brangianne.'

'I don't believe that. Trystan's his *brother!*'

'We both know that isn't true.'

She wasn't surprised he knew, only that he'd kept it secret until now. Had he guessed, or had Corwynal told him? Not that it mattered. 'What's going to happen?'

'Someone's going to die. Corwynal just has to decide who it is.'

'But—'

A shout rang out, and they were surrounded with men who bore the symbol of a snarling wolf on their tunics and steel in their fists, but when one brought a torch they lowered their weapons, taken aback by the sight of a woman and a man with a silver hand.

'We're friends,' Ferdiad said. 'This is the Lady Brangianne who saved Trystan's life in Dalriada, and I'm Ferdiad of . . . of Atholl. We've come to speak to Trystan.'

'He's with his priest.'

'Brangianne brings a message from the Lady Yseult. He'll want to hear it, priest or no priest.'

They found Trystan in a clearing in the woods where a small fire burned. He was sitting on the trunk of a fallen tree, crouched over the fire. The priest, his hood drawn up against the chill of the night was sitting beside him, a hand on his arm, but when he saw them approach, he murmured something and moved into the shadows, leaving Trystan alone in the little grove, staring into the fire, his face haggard in the firelight. *He's afraid!* Brangianne had never seen him afraid before. *He knows about Marc's demand, and now he's afraid.*

'Trystan . . .' He looked up at the sound of her voice and his face stiffened. His eyes slid past her, past Ferdiad, into the darkness beyond them. But once he understood that the man he'd half-expected wasn't with them, his face relaxed.

'I thought you were dead,' he told Ferdiad, who sighed.

'I'm hard to kill.'

Then Trystan turned his gaze on her. 'Whatever you have to say, you can save your breath.'

She'd expected no less. 'It's my breath to waste, so let me speak. Marc's lost his mind. He's insisting you fight to the death.'

His eyes widened at that. So he *hadn't* known! Then why—?

'Good old Marc!' Trystan threw back his head and laughed. 'Predictable to the end!' Then he sobered. 'Is he kind to her?'

She nodded. 'Yseult's convinced him she loves him, and, fool that he is, he believes her. But he's wrong. It's always been you—'

'I know. She lied to me to set me free, but I don't want to be free. Not of her.' He stared down into the fire for a long time. 'You'll stay with her, after . . . after tomorrow? Whatever happens?'

'Of course. But why must you fight? That's what she sent me to tell you. She doesn't want you to fight for her but to be patient. She asked me to remind you about the valley and say she'll wait for you there, no matter how long it takes. Marc's an old man, Trys. He won't make old bones, not the way he lives. He'll die one day, sooner than you imagine perhaps.'

'That one day will be far too late. It's already too late. What will happen, will happen now. I couldn't stop this even if I wanted to – and I don't want to.'

'Trystan—' She moved towards him but he jumped up and backed away.

'No! Go back. Tell Arthyr I accept – as if he had any doubt I would. Who's it to be?' He glanced at Ferdiad. 'Not you?'

'I'm too fond of my own skin to risk fighting you, Trys. I don't know who'll be chosen. It hasn't been decided.'

Trystan nodded. 'It'll be Bedwyr I expect. Good. Now go back, Brangianne. Tell Yseult I never doubted her, but it's I who must wait for her.'

'Please, Trys—' She stepped towards him, intending to shake some understanding into him, but once more he backed off.

'It's no use, Brangianne. It's too late.'

'It can't be.'

'It is.' The priest, advancing from the darkness, threw back his hood to reveal a man younger than she'd imagined him to be. And not actually a priest.

'Ninian?! What are you doing here?'

'Hearing Trystan's confession – for which we require privacy. Go back to Yseult, Brangianne. And Ferdiad – go back to Corwynal.'

He'd been weeping and was trying to hide it.

'What's wrong?'

'Ninian brought me unhappy news,' Trystan said before Ninian could speak. 'Blaize is dead – as we all suspected.'

Blaize? Brangianne felt a sharper grief than she'd expected for Corwynal's irascible old uncle. She'd rarely seen Blaize and Trystan together but knew Trystan's affection ran deep. Yet that didn't account for his fear. And Ninian hadn't really known him. So, why—?

'How did you escape?' Trystan asked Ferdiad, who was staring at Ninian with the same bafflement.

'Oh, it's a long story. I'll tell you one day.'

Trystan's face twisted into something like regret, but he forced himself to smile. 'I'd like that. Now go. Take Brangianne back to Yseult.'

'Won't you come, Ninian?' Brangianne asked. 'Yseult would so like to see you.'

Ninian glanced at Trystan with the same regret.

'You won't leave me, will you, Ninian?' Trystan asked, with something close to desperation.

'I won't leave you.' Ninian put a hand on his shoulder. 'Now then, there's that matter of a confession . . .' Trystan allowed himself to be led away but turned to Ferdiad as he left the circle of firelight.

'Tell Corwynal I've always—'

'You can tell him yourself, Trys,' Ferdiad cut in gently. 'Tomorrow, after your fight.' He reached out a hand to clasp Trystan's but he leapt back.

'Don't touch me!'

Ferdiad let his hand drop. 'Trys, I was just—'

'Go,' Trystan said harshly. '*Go!*' He pushed Ninian aside and ran off into the night. Ninian exchanged a moment's silent regard with Ferdiad before going after Trystan.

'Something's wrong,' Brangianne said as they walked back down the road. 'I've never seen him like this.'

Ferdiad didn't say anything. He wasn't a man to show his emotions, but Brangianne could tell Trystan's rejection had hurt him badly. 'I think—' he said eventually, '—that Trystan, at the grand old age of – what is he? Twenty? – has just realised he's not immortal.'

They passed through the Lothian guard without incident, but when they reached Arthyr's camp Brangianne found trouble waiting.

'Where the fuck have you been?' Aelfric demanded. 'And why in the name of all the gods did you let Oonagh come with you, with the *child!* Don't you know there's going to be a war?'

'I don't remember Oonagh ever did what *you* told her to do!' Brangianne replied tartly.

'Well, you can take her back, right now! She came looking for you.'

Brangianne doubted that. Oonagh would have been looking for Aelfric – and she'd found him.

'Where is she?'

'With my—'

'Aelfric!' Ferdiad cut in.

'What?' Aelfric turned red but remained pugnacious. 'Bloody women, always poking their noses into men's business!' He took Brangianne by the arm and marched her to a small fire where she found Oonagh talking animatedly to another woman. The woman had Osric on her knee, but when she saw Aelfric approaching, she handed the child back to Oonagh and got to her feet. Brangianne found herself looking at a slight young woman with long fair hair woven into a plait, a livid scar across one cheek and rain-coloured eyes that bore a striking resemblance to Aelfric's own.

'This is my sister, Ealhith,' he said half-proudly, half-defiantly. 'Corwynal's wife.'

26

A TERRIBLE SYMMETRY

'Well? What do you have to say for yourself?'

Corwynal closed his eyes. He was seven once more and had been caught in the armoury, fighting his own shadow with a broken knife he was pretending was a sword when he should have been practicing his letters with Dunpeldyr's ancient priest. He'd learned then it was better to make no defence, to confess his crimes quickly and accept his punishment.

'I've failed. In everything that matters, I've failed.'

'Quite,' his father said dryly. 'If somewhat sweeping.'

They were alone. His father's men had made camp at the foot of the hill Corwynal had climbed with Ferdiad earlier that day. There were two folding chairs on either side of a fire. His father lowered himself into one and gestured for him to sit in the other.

'Perhaps you could be more specific about these . . . failures?'

This, he understood, was to be his punishment.

'I thought I could make Trystan into a king everyone could be proud of, but I failed. I tried to keep Lothian from war and believed I'd done it, but I've failed there too. I betrayed Atholl, my friends, Trystan's future, and my own heart, for the sake of peace, yet tomorrow a war will begin, unless Trystan dies in this foolish, *foolish* contest, Trystan whom I've fought all my life to keep from harm. Instead, I allowed him to fall into this madness, and it will suck everyone in. He doesn't listen to me anymore and accuses me of caring more for Lothian than him, of abandoning him – because if I'm still on his side, why am I here?' He discovered, to his horror, that he was weeping, and dashed the tears away. 'And I allowed Blaize to die a terrible death.'

His father looked at him impassively, giving no hint of his thoughts. 'Begin with that, then. Tell me how Blaize died.'

It was the last thing he wanted to talk about, but he knew it had to be done, so he told his father as tonelessly as Ferdiad had told him, staring into the fire as he did so, unwilling to see his father's grief, for, in their way, the two men had been close.

'Blaize was always a fool!' His father's voice was angry, his eyes dry.

Corwynal looked up. 'A brave fool. He died for something he believed in – to save Atholl from chaos – and to save your daughter.'

'To save your mother's daughter,' Rifallyn corrected him, then raised an eyebrow at Corwynal's surprise. 'Didn't you know? She was the only real woman in his life, though she was never more than kind to him. Why do you think he rescued you from Atholl when you failed so spectacularly to stay there? For you? No, it was because you were her son. Why do you think he tried, all your life, to get you to go back? Because that was the birthright she'd given you. And that, in part, was why I sent you away. Lothian had nothing to offer you.'

'It was my home. It didn't have to offer me anything.'

'You were seven,' Rifallyn said disparagingly. 'A boy with a boy's dreams. You were clever, but wanted to be a warrior. You were ambitious, yet could see no further than serving in the warband. But they would never have accepted you.'

'Because I was a half-breed,' he said bitterly, remembering.

'The other boys called you that, didn't they? Children can be cruel. But you forget what it was like in those days – constant raids by Caledonians from Circind and Fife, civil war between the Walls, rebellion and anarchy. War can bring out the best in some men, but in most it brings out the beast, and I should know. It was in those wars that I killed my father.'

Corwynal had wondered when they'd get around to that.

'I didn't want to,' his father went on. 'But it had to be done, even though I knew my actions would have consequences. I was acclaimed King by the landholders who'd suffered under my father's rule, but the priests and the warband thought I should do penance for my crime, and I agreed with them. But you know all that.'

Not from you, Corwynal thought, for he'd learned these things from Lot. 'So you sent my mother away, and me with her,' he said, trying to keep the hurt from his voice. 'I thought it was *my* penance. That I'd done something wrong.'

His father shook his head. 'If anyone did anything wrong, it was your mother for not telling me who and what she was. I like to think she was afraid I'd send her back, that she'd wanted to stay. It was Blaize who told me, Blaize who insisted I had no right to keep your mother in Lothian with no honour, no future. He was right, of course, and it was him I listened to, though he was barely more than a boy then. But Blaize was . . .' he shrugged. 'Blaize was Blaize. He made me understand what my punishment had to be. I was to send you both away and allow your mother to believe I'd made a choice between her and Lothian. Letting her believe that was *my* penance. She had another life to live, and I wanted her to live it without regret. You too.'

'But why—?'

'Listen, and don't interrupt! Your mother must have hated me very much when she left. She didn't even tell me she was carrying my child, and she cursed me as she left. She told me that one day my son would kill me. And, knowing what she was, how could I doubt her? Don't you see, Corwynal? That became my real punishment – a life of waiting for someone to come and take Lothian from me as I'd taken it from my father. But I was determined no-one would do so. I'd given up your mother and you, but I was going to keep Lothian. I fought for Lothian, bled for Lothian, and lost everything I cared about for Lothian, because it was all I had. And tomorrow – no, today, I won't let Lothian start a war it can't win. I'll do everything I can to prevent it. Do you understand me?'

His father was close now, leaning forward, his wolf-eyes boring into Corwynal's own. The fire had died down to a glow in woody ash, and the cold of the starlit night had seeped like a mist through the camp. The fire glow threw strange red lights into a face that was suddenly unfamiliar. He still didn't understand what his father was trying to tell him, but it didn't matter. Only one thing did. He hadn't done anything wrong. Not when he'd been seven. His father had sent him and his mother away because he'd cared for them both.

'Why did you try to make me hate you?'

His father grunted and leant back into the shadows. 'You really don't understand, do you? And I thought you were clever! Isn't it obvious? I knew what my doom was. When you came back to Lothian, I knew it was yours too. It's no small thing to kill your own father. It . . . mars a man's life. It robs him of respect and honour, and it's always there, at the back of your mind, a wound that never heals, a guilt that wakes you in the middle of the night, a regret for the things said and not said. If it was my doom, I'd accept it when the time came. But if it was yours, I wanted you to do it lightly, believing it to be right. I had to give you a reason, Corwynal. I *needed* you to hate me.'

'I don't. And I'm not going to kill you.'

His father sighed. 'You can't see the future.'

'I can! I did! I dreamed Trystan's death and it happened exactly as I'd seen it, but he didn't die. I *changed* the future. You *can* fight your own fate. Blaize taught me that.'

'You think I haven't fought? What do you think that shameful alliance with Galloway was all about, Corwynal? I didn't want to marry again, but I knew if I did, I could have another son, and perhaps that one would be my doom, a son I could make hate me, since I seem to have failed with you. Then Trystan was born.'

Corwynal turned cold and was aware of the world hanging on his next words. He saw his father's eyes on his, old and wise and . . . knowing.

'Trystan's not your son. He's mine.'

He braced himself for fury, accusation, a bone-deep disappointment, disgust, betrayal, all the things he'd feared for over twenty years. But his father just nodded.

'Good,' he said, then raised an eyebrow at Corwynal's surprise. 'You must have known I suspected. I knew he wasn't mine, so I feared he might be Marc's son. There were things she said, you see . . . I thought you must know about Gwenllian and Marc, and had brought me this faithless enchanting woman as revenge for sending you away.' He smiled wryly, as if at an old and painful memory. 'Yes, in spite of myself, I was enchanted. I thought, fool that I was, that with her by my side I might fight myself free of the shadow that had hung over me for so long – until I saw that you and she . . . Did you imagine I didn't notice?

'She had to make men love her, didn't she? I saw you were under the same enchantment, and for a time I hated you. That's why I made you choose Trystan over the life you wanted. Gradually, however, I came to think he must be your son. Not mine. Not Marc's. Which meant the doom remained for both of us, but I couldn't send you away once more. I needed an heir – that much had always been true. I knew you couldn't be that, not with your Caledonian blood. So I made you stay to turn him into someone to succeed me. I let you love him but couldn't love him myself – he was *her* son. I watched you turn him into the man you wanted to be, a great shining hope for the future, for Lothian. I watched you love him, and Lothian, and tried to use both those loves to make you hate me.

'So when Lot brought war, I saw an opportunity to bring the matter to a head and force you to choose between staying in Lothian and leaving with Trystan. You chose Trystan, chose to put yourself in danger, to risk your life for him. I didn't understand that in choosing Trystan you *had* chosen Lothian, that in your mind the two were inextricably linked. Even then, I tried to keep you with me, to keep you safe, but in the end I had to let you go. I was tired, Corwynal, tired of the hate, the fear. I decided to send you away once more, hoping that this time you might not come back, that you'd make a life for yourself away from me, from Lothian, and somehow the fate I believed in could be avoided. I made you swear that foolish oath, knowing you'd hold to it. I knew I mustn't weaken and beg you to return. I hoped you'd forget Lothian, but you can't, and Trystan's right. You care for Lothian as I care. And you won't let Lothian go to war tomorrow any more than I will. Oh, do stop weeping, Corwynal! There's nothing to weep about.'

'All these years . . . ! Could you not have told me *anything* of this?'

'You know now why I couldn't.'

'So why are you telling me now?'

'Because I can see a way to avoid the doom that binds us together.'

'There is no doom! Because I won't kill you! I won't take Lothian from you!'

'You will. I've seen it, dreamed it. I've seen the knife in your hand.'

'This one?' Corwynal pulled his knife from its scabbard and thrust it at the other man's throat, his hand trembling. 'See – I have a knife in my hand. Now watch—' He tossed it into the fire. 'It's just a dream, nothing more than . . . I don't know, guilt, remorse. You give it a name.'

'I dreamt your mother's death,' his father said. 'One night my heart stopped, and I knew. I saw her lying on a raft, flowers about her feet, on the waters of a loch lying between mountains. Was that not the way of it?'

'I don't know. I wasn't there,' Corwynal said stubbornly, though he knew it was likely.

'And I dreamed you lying in a tomb on a mountain.'

'Then you were wrong! I did lie in a tomb, but I wasn't dead.'

'I know that,' his father said gently. 'Because, in that dream, my heart kept on beating.'

'You didn't dream of Seirian,' Corwynal insisted. 'She looks like my mother. When you see her—'

'I won't,' Rifallyn said harshly. 'Not in this life.' He stared into the fire, at the knife slowly turning red. Then he shook himself free of whatever thoughts had gripped him. 'Now, enough of this. I've indulged myself – and you – with these justifications long enough, and the night wears on. I'm tired, Corwynal, and I'm old. I didn't think you'd make me wait so long. I didn't think to find, so late in life, things that were worth living for and fighting for. I couldn't love Trystan, but I've come to love your other sons. I've tried to be a father to them but they're . . . exhausting. They've reached the age when they need a father, not a grandfather. When we last met, I should have told you so, but I was weak and selfish and . . . afraid. So, Corwynal, I beg you – *beg you* – to go back to Lothian for them. Be Lothian's King after me. Trystan doesn't want it, but you do. Not everyone will like it, and there are those who'll remember who your mother was, but you'll fight, as I did. Let Trystan turn himself into a song. It's time for you to stop protecting him. You have other sons to protect.'

He got to his feet, a big man moving slowly, not because it was menacing but because his bones ached. 'So let us go to Arthyr. There's a way out of this, a future in which Trystan doesn't die and Lothian doesn't go to war with Galloway. A solution to so many problems. Blaize was right. Sometimes you have to fight your own fate. So, if Arthyr agrees, will you support me?'

'Of course! But what—?'

'Swear, Corwynal. Swear you'll support me, as your father and your King.'

Corwynal wanted to laugh and weep all at the same time because he was seven once more and he'd fallen down that old well. He was in the dark and the cold and the earth was pressing in on him. He was sick and terrified, and the only thing that kept him from losing his mind was the thought of his father. *He'll come. He'll save me. I just have to be brave. He'll know what to do.* And he had. He'd been beaten for it, but he hadn't minded that, or the lecture that had followed. *Swear you'll never go near that place again!* He'd sworn, not because he was afraid, but because he'd been asked to by his father, the man who'd rescued him then and would rescue him once more, and, though he felt a tremor of unease, the brush of a black moth's wings, he ignored it.

'I swear,' he said.

Arthyr wasn't asleep when Corwynal and his father went to see him, and it was clear he'd failed to find anyone to fight Trystan, for he and Bedwyr were arguing about it beside Arthyr's fire.

'I won't let you,' Arthyr was saying.

'You have no choice, my heart,' Bedwyr said, but Arthyr took his face between his hands and pulled him close.

'I won't let you. I'd rather let Trystan win by default, then fight Galloway with not enough men, than let you risk yourself. It's not your affair, Bedwyr.'

'Quite!' Rifallyn stepped into the firelight, Corwynal at his shoulder, and Arthyr and Bedwyr sprang apart. 'It is, however, *my* affair. Not yours. Not Galloway's. Not Selgovia's. *Mine*. Trystan of Lothian – my son – has declared himself King of Lothian, yet appears to have overlooked one inconvenient fact. I'm still alive and consider myself to be Lothian's King, something I'll do until I die. I dispute his declaration and demand the right to contest it. It's your duty, as War-leader of The Lands between the Walls, to uphold my right.'

'Yes, but I don't see how—'

'If you could just listen,' Rifallyn said testily. 'You young men! I'm offering you a way out of this debacle, and you don't even have the courtesy to listen! Trystan, the young idiot, has offered single combat to anyone of your choice. Marc, fool that he is, has insisted it be to the death. But you haven't found anyone with sufficient of a death wish to fight someone with Trystan's reputation. Very well – here I am. I will fight him.'

Corwynal stared at his father. So did Arthyr and Bedwyr. The old man was sixty years of age, but no-one laughed.

'You can't.' Corwynal found his voice, even though the black moth's wings were beating furiously at him as he understood what his conversation with his father had really been about.

'I can. I'm not incapable, Corwynal. I can still wield a sword. I won't disgrace myself, if that's what you're worrying about.'

It wasn't. 'Trystan won't do it. He'll withdraw.'

'Then a solution will have been reached. But I don't think he will. He won't like it, but not because he loves me, for Trystan and I have never been friends. He'll fight me and kill me and tell himself he's doing it for you.'

'No! Marc won't agree. It would be too . . . easy.'

Rifallyn smiled his humourless wolf-smile. 'It won't be that easy, but you're wrong. Marc will agree because he's no intention of abiding by his bargain, and he's always hated me. Trystan will win and get the woman he loves, but he won't be able to take her to Lothian because he won't be King of Lothian anymore. The warband follow Trystan because he's lucky, but a man who kills his own father loses all his luck, as I've cause to know. They'll return to Lothian, but not with Trystan. They'll return with Corwynal.'

That was when he saw the true horror of what his father planned. There was only one thing he could say.

'Trystan's not your—'

His father was still strong, his hand about his throat choking the words down. 'Would you shame me?' he hissed. 'Would you shame Trystan? Do you imagine anyone would believe you? In the circumstances?'

'I'll tell him, warn him—'

'It would make no difference. Surely you see that?' His father let him go and turned to Arthyr. 'It's the perfect solution. Trystan and Yseult will live out their lives with some degree of honour, far from The Lands between the Walls. He'll console himself with the knowledge that his brother rules Lothian, which he never wanted, and he'll be free to do what he wants. No doubt he'll get himself into trouble of some kind or another and may even get himself killed. But the important thing – the outcome we all want – is that war will be averted. With Trystan gone, Marc will have no reason to invade Lothian. He'll be too busy chasing the fugitives. So you may go south as you planned, Arthyr, to your long fight, with the sword my son gave you to take your wars away, knowing the North will stand firm behind you. So, do you agree?'

'Arthyr, you can't agree!' Corwynal protested.

'Corwynal, please be quiet. I'm an old man, and Trystan's young. I'm tired – of so many things. We've spoken of just a few of them. It's a sacrifice, and there will be some things I'll regret, but I make this sacrifice willingly because it's for Lothian. There will be few to mourn me.'

'Ealhith would. And my sons. And I'd mourn you.'

'I would rather you said that you *will* mourn me. You swore, Corwynal.'

'A foolish oath. Oaths can be broken.'

'Not by you. Arthyr?' He turned to the War-leader, who looked stricken. Eventually, however, he nodded.

'I don't like it, but, yes, it's your right. I too will mourn you.'

Rifallyn smiled his wolf-smile once more. 'I doubt that, but I thank you for saying so. Now I'd like to spend what's left of the night in prayer. Alone. And I'd be grateful if someone could make sure Ealhith doesn't learn of this until it's too late for her to interfere.'

'I will.' Ferdiad stepped from the shadows. How long had he been standing there listening? Long enough, Corwynal realised, from the look in his eyes as Rifallyn walked slowly into the night.

'Let him go,' Ferdiad said. 'There are times when a man should be with his gods and no one else.'

'He's doing this for me,' he said through a throat that was closing up. 'I can't let him. I can't stand by and watch my son kill my father.'

'You must. He's given you a task. Would you fail him?'

Arthyr and Bedwyr had gone and they were alone beneath an uncaring sky of stars. Corwynal was shaking, but when Ferdiad's arms went around him he welcomed their warmth, their strength, though he didn't welcome what he had to say. 'Listen to me; Seirian sent me south in part to find out what sort of man her father was. I haven't met him or spoken with him, but I don't need to. He's like you. You're like him. You would have made exactly the same sacrifice. So let him do this and mourn for him when it's over. But weep for him now. There are times when a man has to weep. I discovered that somewhat to my cost.'

'I can't.'

'You must.' Ferdiad let him go with evident reluctance. 'Wait here. I must go and keep Ealhith away. Will you wait?'

Corwynal nodded and Ferdiad disappeared. He couldn't speak, couldn't move, and didn't want to move, for if he did so, the night itself would move forward into this terrible symmetry. Ferdiad was right. He *was* like his father and he would have made the same sacrifice for the son he loved. How many sacrifices had he already made for Trystan? What did one more matter? Except this time, he was sacrificing his father, a father who, to his surprise and grief, appeared to love him. And that was all he'd ever wanted – not Lothian, not to be a King, not even to be a warrior. To make his father proud, for him to love him. But death, it seemed, was the price of love.

Brangianne was furious with Aelfric. How dare he make her meet this . . . this woman! What had she done to deserve this humiliation? It wasn't as if she could have stopped Oonagh from coming, and Aelfric knew it. And how dare Oonagh be so friendly with Ealhith, even if she was her lover's sister! The worst thing was how they both sat there, talking about the one thing Brangianne didn't share – children. And that hurt.

But when Aelfric's sister stood up, there was no triumph in her eyes. *So you're the one he loves?* Brangianne could see that thought as clearly as the other woman must see her own. *So you're the mother of his sons?*

'Er . . .' Aelfric belatedly realised the awkwardness of the situation, a realisation reinforced by Oonagh kicking him hard in the shins. 'Aargh!'

'We'd better get back,' Oonagh said through gritted teeth. 'Come along, my lady.'

Oonagh hardly ever called her 'my lady', so she must be feeling guilty about talking so freely to Ealhith. 'And as for you—' She poked Aelfric in the chest. 'You stay alive, you big ox, or I'll personally tear your balls off.'

'I won't need them if I'm dead,' he pointed out.

'Gods! Men!' Oonagh muttered, hefted Osric onto her hip and began to walk away, but Aelfric caught her shoulder and pulled her back.

'Stay here,' he said. 'It's going to come to a fight tomorrow, so stay with Ealhith. Rifallyn's men will keep you safe. You too, Brangianne,' he added in a misplaced attempt to make up for his thoughtlessness.

'No. Yseult needs me. I have to get back to the Galloway camp. Are you coming, Oonagh?'

Oonagh was looking at Aelfric, her chin raised in challenge.

'You're fighting for Lothian then?'

He scratched at his beard, irresolute. 'Possibly.'

'And if you survive, you're staying in Lothian?'

'Maybe.'

'With me and Osric?'

Aelfric shrugged.

'Is that an offer?'

'Perhaps,' he admitted.

She sniffed. 'I'll think about it,' she said coolly. 'Come along, Brangianne.'

'Not yet.'

Ferdiad appeared, as Ferdiad frequently did, out of nowhere. One of Arthyr's men was with him. 'Cynog here will see Oonagh safely back to the Galloway camp. Aelfric – you stay with your sister. Rifallyn is praying and doesn't want to be disturbed. Brangianne, come with me. There's someone who needs your help.'

'I don't have anything with me.' Normally, she carried her satchel of medical supplies but hadn't brought it with her.

'You won't need that. Now. Quickly.'

'When did you start to think you could order people about?' Aelfric asked.

'When I got to be Atholl's Queen-Consort.' Aelfric's jaw dropped, effectively silencing him, and Brangianne was sufficiently stunned that she allowed herself to be led away without protest.

'You? You and *Seirian?*' she exclaimed when she recovered the use of her tongue.

'Quite. Your incredulity says it all,' he said wryly. 'Long story, but not tonight. Now, listen to me; it's Corwynal—'

'He's hurt?'

'In a way. He mustn't be left alone tonight. Mustn't be allowed to think. So do anything, say anything, to stop him from thinking about tomorrow. Because tomorrow something terrible is going to happen, and he can't allow himself to be part of it.'

She was frightened now, because she could see Ferdiad was.

'Don't fail me, Brangianne. Don't fail *him.*'

Corwynal was standing by the remains of a fire, staring into the dying flames. There was something desperate about his expression and, though he looked up as she approached, his face didn't change. He gave that little twist of his shoulders she'd come to know, but it was no longer the gesture of a man shouldering a burden. It was someone shattering beneath its weight.

'What's wrong?' She turned to Ferdiad, but he'd gone, leaving behind an echo of his desperate plea. *Don't fail him.*

She went up to Corwynal, laid her head on his shoulder, put her arms about him and felt his heart beat fast and erratic against her own. He neither pushed her away nor welcomed her, and if it hadn't been for that fluttering heart, she might have thought she was embracing a corpse.

'Ferdiad said I should weep, but I can't,' he said blankly.

'What's wrong?'

He gave a short humourless laugh. 'The world's wrong. Tomorrow my son will kill my father. And I'm supposed to stand there and let him do it. How can that be right?'

Something terrible is going to happen. She wanted to protest, to deny the truth of what he was saying, but knew it was too late for that. 'Ferdiad's right. You should weep.'

His arms came about her then and the weight he couldn't bear settled on her own heart, but she bore it gladly. *Don't fail him.* She knew what he needed from her, and so she allowed that unbearable weight to drive her to tears, to give him the permission he needed to weep himself, soundlessly, without words, a shuddering rejection of what tomorrow would bring. *My son will kill my father.* And the most terrible thing of all. *And I must stand by and let him do it.* Could weeping help anyone bear that? Yet he wept, and she held him, thinking as she did so that Ealhith would envy her this, that he should find shelter in her and not his wife. But he needed more than shelter. *Don't fail him. Don't let him think.* She couldn't stop him thinking, so she had to make him think of something else.

'I met your wife tonight,' she said as his weeping eased. 'Ealhith. She seemed . . . nice.'

He drew apart a little and wiped his face on his sleeve. 'I'm sorry—'

'Don't be! It's not your fault I met her, and anyway I was curious. She's . . . fond of you.'

He nodded distractedly, already drifting away into his own thoughts.

'I envied her,' she said desperately and managed to catch his attention.

'Ealhith? Why?'

'She has your— *don't say sons!*—your children. I wanted so much to bear you a child.'

'I know. But I failed you in that.'

'No! It was I who failed you!' She took him by the shoulders and made him look at her. 'Do you remember, in Carnadail, when we said goodbye for the first time? We'd made a child then.' She had him now. 'A son. You didn't fail me. I failed you – and him. He died in my womb, and I birthed him in pain and blood, thinking I hated you because you'd betrayed me. It was only when I lost the child, I knew I could never hate you. I cried out to you so loudly that night you must have heard it. It was Samhain – the night of endings, and just one ending of so many.'

He nodded slowly. 'By Midwinter I'd married Ealhith for the sake of a child who wasn't yours. If I could go back—'

'There's no going back. Only forward. Into the future. *Our* future. You told me of a dream in which I had a child,' she reminded him.

'A dream in which I was weeping but didn't know why.'

'The reasons don't matter. The child does. I want a child, Corwynal. Your child. Our child. A daughter who'll look like you and remind me of you when you've gone – because we're going to say goodbye again, aren't we? Like we did in Carnadail. But none of our goodbyes has been forever, and this one won't be either because of that dream. One day I'll come to Lothian to show her to you, and you'll weep with joy because she's beautiful.'

She took his hand and pulled him, unresisting, into the night. *Don't let him think about tomorrow.* 'I'm here, my love. I'm now.

I'm the future. Hold me. Touch me. Let me be a harbour for you, a place to rest, and one day we'll set sail together. It's only a dream at the moment, but make it real for us both. Give me a child . . .'

Above them, the sky was clear, but the stars faded one by one as the moon rose above the hill that reared over them like a wave. Brangianne was in the wave, in the surge of it; then she was the wave itself, washing him away, washing away tomorrow. Eventually, the moon disappeared behind a bank of mist and he rolled away from her and pulled on his clothes. He crouched down to her, cupping her cheek, and smiled.

'Perhaps I'm weeping in the dream because you're there with our child, but I'm not. Because I'm a ghost.'

He walked away, giving that little twist of his shoulder that was of a man taking up a burden, and this time he didn't break but staggered a little as he bore its weight. She hugged her cloak about her, against the cold, against the dream that was nothing more than a dream, and the knowledge that she'd failed.

Something terrible is going to happen tomorrow. And now tomorrow was today.

Ferdiad hadn't slept, and, since he'd ridden through the previous night without rest, he was dizzy and dissociated from everything – which might be for the best, given what the day would bring.

It wasn't long after dawn, but the mist had cleared and light sprang swiftly into the sky, driving the night back into the woods and slopes of the eastern side of the valley, where the dark pines held on to the shadows, and the birches, golden with autumn, flared like torches as the light caught them. To the west, the hill he'd climbed with Corwynal the previous day was blinding in the sunlight, the fans of scree and boulders catching the sun and throwing it back in a frenzy of reflection. The day was transcendent and treacherous in its beauty, entirely at odds with Ferdiad's mood.

The contest – he forced himself to think of it as a contest and not a slaughter – was to be held down by the river where a stream joined it from the west. Between the river and the stream lay a broad expanse of gravel scattered with tufts of grasses turning sere with autumn. Arthyr's men had cleared it of the larger stones and used them to lay out a perimeter beyond which those who wanted to watch must stand. And everyone wanted to watch.

The Lothian men arrived first and took up position on the far side of the stream. They were joking among themselves with the nervous laughter that comes with the anticipation of violence, though they didn't know who Trystan was to fight. Whoever it was, they expected Trystan to win, but had no illusions about Marc keeping to his bargain. Arthyr's men were nearest to where the contest was to take place, strategically placed to keep Lothian and Galloway apart. But there were too few of them to do that for long, and Arthyr, looking grim, was scanning the margins of the valley – east to where Kaerherdin might bring the Selgovians, south to where Marc's reinforcements could appear at any moment, and west, where the Dragon-riders would come. Neither Lothian nor Galloway had seen the Riders before, and Arthyr was relying on them being sufficiently overawed for the battle to stop before it began. But there was no sign of the Riders as yet, and the morning was wearing on.

Trystan was the first to take position. From a distance he looked relaxed and cheerful as he checked the grip of his shield and flexed his sword hand, but Ferdiad saw signs of strain and could tell he hadn't slept either. His smile was forced, his skin ashen yet slicked with sweat. *Something's wrong,* Brangianne had said, and Ferdiad agreed. Ninian must know what that was, but he couldn't see his fellow countryman among the Lothian men, so turned his attention to the Galloway troop. They'd marched up from their camp further down the valley and had taken up position on the slopes of a low hill – more of a mound really – that overlooked the gravel bank between river and stream. One of Marc's men set two folding chairs on top of the mound and Marc sat down, his arms crossed, but Yseult remained standing, her eyes on Trystan, her soul in her eyes. Brangianne stood at Yseult's shoulder, her cloak wrapped tightly around her against the chill of the wind, which had picked up shortly after dawn and was blowing strongly now.

Had Brangianne succeeded? Had Ferdiad done the right thing in sending her to Corwynal? There had been a long moment when he'd held Corwynal and believed he could be everything he needed – a mind, a body, a distraction from thought, from decision. But he'd let him go and spent the night torn by doubt and desire. It wasn't Samhain, but today, no matter what happened, that at least had to end.

Corwynal was standing quietly beside his father. He wasn't armed, Ferdiad saw with gut-loosening relief. Rifallyn had shed his wolf-skin cloak and without it, in the flat light – for the sun had disappeared behind a bank of cloud – Ferdiad could see how similar the two men were. Rifallyn was older and taller and would once have been broader across the shoulders than Corwynal. But even now he looked formidable in his stillness, in the wolf-gleam of his eyes – eyes that fell coldly on Trystan who turned very still too, like a hare caught in the gaze of an ermine. He must have seen Corwynal beside Rifallyn but gave no sign of it, and shook off his immobility and looked about, searching for Bedwyr whom he expected to fight. But it was Arthyr who stepped forward.

'My Lords, men of Lothian, Galloway, Gododdin and Gwynedd, we're here to see justice carried out . . .'

He spoke well, his voice deep and solemn, a voice that carried without effort even to the men standing at the back, a voice Ferdiad imagined might echo in this valley, these hills and woods, long after this day was over. He spoke of the reasons he'd come north to The Lands between the Walls, of the battle fought against the Caledonians and Dalriads, the peace forged, lands regained. He didn't name names, but everyone knew how much was owed to Trystan. He spoke then of the south, of his plans to take war to the

Saex and Angles. Ferdiad glanced across at Aelfric, standing with some Lothian men – but not Trystan's – Ealhith and Oonagh beside him. His arms were crossed, his brow furrowed in a scowl, but he didn't interrupt as Arthyr went on to talk of battles still to be fought, of glory to be won. He was tempting them, Ferdiad understood. The warbands had been robbed of a fight when Arthyr, Corwynal and Drest had made peace in the summer, but there were fights to come that need not be today. He was taking a risk, of course, hoping the Dragon-riders would arrive before the Selgovians and the Galloway reinforcements. But he couldn't talk forever, and as time went on and still no-one came, the Lothian and Galloway men grew restive and began to stamp their feet, beating out a rhythm into which the Lothian men wove a chant. *Trystan! Trystan! Trystan!*

'Enough!' Arthyr raised his arms for silence. 'We're here to see justice done, under the gaze of the gods, mine and yours. Trystan of Lothian has offered to fight anyone I choose, to prove the right to his two claims. Firstly, he claims Yseult, Queen of Galloway, as his. Marc of Galloway disputes that claim but has agreed that the matter be settled by this contest, Yseult to be given to whichever man lives at the end. Furthermore—' He had to raise his voice over the shouts of the Galloway troops. 'Furthermore, Trystan also claims the kingship of Lothian, a claim that is disputed by Rifallyn, King of Lothian, who has also agreed that the matter be settled by this contest. However, he doesn't agree that I may choose the man who'll meet Trystan in this fight. He demands the right to fight for his own honour himself. And I've agreed.'

The shouting stopped. The muttering stopped. The stamping and chanting stopped, and silence fell. Marc rose to his feet then sank back into his chair once more. Yseult's hands flew to her mouth to stifle a cry of horror. Ealhith cried out and tried to run forward but Aelfric caught and held her back. And for a long moment there was no sound but the moan of the rising wind and the snap of banners, raven, wolf and bear.

Trystan had gone white.

'Do you accept?' Arthyr asked quietly. 'It's no small thing to kill your own father. You understand what it would mean?'

Trystan glanced at the Lothian warband who'd emerged from their stunned incredulity and begun to mutter among themselves.

'Yes,' he said. It was only a breath of sound but everyone heard him.

'It's not too late, Trys,' Arthyr said softly. 'Walk away from this. It's over.'

'No, it's not.'

'So, you'll fight?' Arthyr asked. 'Against your own father?'

'Yes.'

What else could he say? If he walked away, he wouldn't be Trystan of Lothian anymore, not the song he'd turned himself into. He stood there, golden and young and doomed, like the hero of a winter's tale, but it wasn't Trystan Ferdiad was looking at now. His heart was fluttering, waiting for something terrible to happen, the thing he'd tried to prevent, the decision he'd failed to stop being made.

Corwynal stepped past his father.

'No,' he said.

FIGHT TO THE DEATH

Two years before, on the stony beach of a rocky island in the middle of the sea, Corwynal had asked himself a question. *Can a man watch his son die?*

Now, on a gravel bank surrounded by hills, he was asking himself another. *Can a man watch his son kill his own father?*

The answer was simple. The answer was the same. He can't.

'No,' he said.

Protests erupted all around – Brangianne shrill with panic, Ferdiad in desperate denial. Between them, they'd tried to stop him making this decision. Did neither of them know him? Didn't they realise he'd already made it? All he'd needed was time to accept what it meant.

Above the moan of the rising wind, he heard Ninian's voice from among the Lothian men. Ealhith cried out in horror, and, with an oath, Aelfric shouldered his way through the crowd towards him. But none of these protests mattered. Only one did.

'What foolishness is this?' his father demanded, as if Corwynal had committed some childish act of defiance. But the anger in his father's voice was at odds with his stricken expression. 'You swore—'

'I swore to something I didn't understand.'

'Don't you see? This is the only way—'

'There's another way. My way.'

'Corwynal, I beg you—'

'I allowed this to happen. Now I have to stop it. It's not your affair. It's mine.'

He turned to Arthyr, Arthyr who hadn't protested. 'You asked the brothers of Lothian to find a way past this impasse. This is it. We'll fight one another – to the death. Do you accept?'

Arthyr didn't like it; he liked none of this. He glanced around, judging the mood of the warbands. A fight between Trystan and Rifallyn would be no sport at all. This, however . . . He lifted his eyes to look beyond the crowd, judging how long it might be before the men he expected arrived. Eventually, he nodded. 'If both brothers agree.'

Corwynal hadn't looked at Trystan, not after he'd stepped forward, afraid of what he might see – disbelief, derision, betrayal. Yes, there would be betrayal, but not fear, never fear. Reluctance, though? Corwynal wanted so much to see reluctance he dared not look. Perhaps Trystan would decide it was possible to fight an old man he hated, but not his own brother, his guardian, tutor and friend. Perhaps he'd just . . . walk away. But when Corwynal forced himself to meet Trystan's eyes, he saw nothing he expected or hoped for. Trystan was looking at him steadily and calmly, and the only expression he could put a name to was relief.

'I agree,' Trystan said quietly. 'But I won't fight an unarmed man.'

Like everyone other than the participants, Corwynal had come to the place of the contests without his weapons. Now, he moved to go back for his twin swords, but Arthyr stopped him.

'Wait. This was yours before it was mine. Take it now.' He handed him Caledan, and a hiss ran through the crowd, for the meaning of his gesture was clear. Arthyr wanted him to win.

The hilt sang into his palm as it had done in the tomb. It felt right. *Grief-bringer.* Yes, there would be grief that day, though all swords had that power. He hefted it, watched light ripple along the blade, and heard its song.

'You fight with two swords, don't you?' His father pressed the hilt of his own sword into his left hand. Corwynal turned to see tears in the old man's eyes. 'Fight well, my son.' He gripped the hand with the sword painfully in both of his before stepping back. Everyone stepped back.

'So,' Corwynal said. 'Shall we begin?'

Ferdiad had accepted, with both irritation and relief, that he'd never be more than competent as a swordsman, and now he understood that if Corwynal had really been trying to kill him on the Mountain, he wouldn't have lasted very long.

I couldn't do this, he thought, watching the two men circle and come together, listening to the clash of steel, the grunts of effort. The watching crowd was silent but for intaken breaths, and someone nearby was weeping, but he didn't know who it was and didn't care. At some point, he'd heard horses approaching, and there was a surge in the crowd as others joined the press, their whispered questions hissed to silence, but he wasn't interested in who'd come. All he cared about were the two men in the broad expanse of gravel between river and stream – one old, one young, one fair, one dark, both loved. One of them was going to die. But not yet.

How long had it lasted already? Ferdiad didn't know. He couldn't count back his heartbeats, and could only measure time by the circling and clash of the two men and the rhythm they made – the stamp and advance, the flurry of blows blocked and turned, the ring of steel, the whistle as blades swept through the wind, the high impossible keening he'd once heard for himself. Now he was hearing that same song, transmuted and deepened, each note of music layered one upon the next in a flare of chords. He heard the drone of horns and a low throbbing as if drums were beating deep within the earth. Was that the gods? That wild triumphant chanting? Were they here, looking down, scenting death, drawn not so much by the prospect of a life taken, but given?

Trystan struck low, a vicious slice to the shins, but Caledan was already there, blocking the blow, light flashing from the damascened ripplings of the blade. Then Rifallyn's sword in Corwynal's left hand was swinging upwards to catch Trystan's shield and beat it back. Trystan gave way, stepping aside and pivoting, using the momentum of Corwynal's swing to bring his own weapon in a slashing backhand that would have cut Corwynal in two if he hadn't seen it coming and stepped away in time. Even so, the tip of Trystan's blade sliced through his tunic, drawing blood. Both men were bleeding by then, Corwynal from a wound in the thigh, Trystan from a slash in his shoulder. Neither was serious. Neither gave the other an advantage. Neither could find a way through the other's wall of steel to make the killing thrust. Corwynal blocked each of Trystan's blows as if the pattern of the fight lay before him, ready for him to step into. Nothing he tried, however, could penetrate either Trystan's shield or the dancing barrier of his sword. But why should anyone be surprised by that? There was nothing Trystan knew that Corwynal hadn't taught him, nothing Corwynal had held back in that teaching. It was like watching one man fight his own shadow.

'He's not trying.'

Ferdiad didn't take his eyes from the fight, but knew Aelfric was standing behind him, just as he knew Brangianne and Ninian had also made their way to his side. Aelfric didn't say which of them he meant but he was wrong. Each was trying, quite desperately, not to kill the other. Ferdiad, had watched both men fight. He'd seen Trystan defeat The Morholt and The Dragon and had faced Corwynal himself. He'd fought beside both at the ferry between Atholl and the lands of the Britons and he could see that each thrust, each blow, each slash, was a fraction of a heartbeat too late, each backhand carving through the air a hairsbreadth too far away to do any damage. But both men were tiring. Both were human, and one of them, sooner rather than later, was going to make a mistake.

'What will happen?' Brangianne's breath was sour with terror. Ferdiad could taste the same bitterness in his own throat.

'One of them's going to die,' he said harshly, for he could see what she was hoping for – that one of them, somehow, would disarm the other, then throw his arms about his brother and declare the fight over. If only life was that simple.

'Which one?' she asked.

'The one with the most reasons to die,' Ninian said.

Ferdiad glanced at him and knew it had been Ninian he'd heard weeping, but he seemed beyond that now. *Something's wrong,* Brangianne had said.

'What do you know?' he hissed, taking Ninian by the throat with his silver hand – an action that inclined most men to the truth, and Ninian was no exception. Moments later, Ferdiad wished he hadn't asked.

He let Ninian go as all the strength left his body. If Aelfric hadn't gripped his elbow, he would have fallen. Brangianne swayed against him and gasped as if a blade had gone in under her ribs. *Trystan, you fool!*

'Does he know?' Ferdiad asked Ninian.

'He does now.'

'Not Trystan! *Corwynal!*' Ninian shook his head. 'Then he must be told—'

'No!' He'd never heard Brangianne sound so fierce. 'What do you think he'd do if he knew? Not this.' She waved her hand at the fight. Both men were exhausted now. Both had fallen back, breathing heavily. And Ferdiad, his gorge rising, understood.

'Trystan wants this,' Ninian said. 'It's not about Yseult; she's just the pretext. He wants an ending with some degree of honour. He needs Corwynal to give him that ending.'

'But he won't,' Ferdiad said bleakly. He understood now what it would mean to be a father, to ask the question that only had one answer. *How can a man kill his own son?* 'He can't.'

He hadn't expected to find joy, not here, not given what he's here to do. Nevertheless, it's there. He hadn't expected to hear music, for he'd always believed it to be the gift of the god he'd rejected. But he finds that too. He hears the horns and drums of The Island of Eagles. Rain is falling and he knows it's falling in his past.

He's fighting for his life, for sanity. He's fighting memory, and he's in a wood in Lothian with a thrush singing, and a boy with a blade in his hand is laughing down at him. Then they're fighting in that green wood, teacher and pupil, guardian and boy. And Corwynal almost kills him.

But that won't happen today, not in the present he's trying so desperately to forget, and it's not his mind that's fighting on that gravel bank between river and stream. His body is fighting, and all that matters of himself is far away and separate, like a hawk lifting on a thermal of air, gazing down incuriously at the two men at the joining of waters, one old, one young, one dark, one fair, each trying not to kill the other.

He's bleeding now, his thigh sliced open by the edge of Trystan's shield, his chest bruised from the hammer of the shield boss, his tunic torn open, a cut along one rib. His shoulder aches, the one The Dragon dislocated, and his hand, the one Ferdiad's hook tore open, cramps as he grips his father's sword. But none of these wounds will kill him and are little more than a distraction from the place he wants to be – the past. He feels his body move to the rhythm of the drums and find its place inside the network of steel. He feels the air of a blade as it whistles past his face and his own blades thrust and block, feint and parry. He's twisting and reaching, falling back, and down, always in balance, dancing the dance. His body seems to be managing quite well on its own, so he gives himself up to the past, because, right now, that's all he has, all he'll ever have.

Keep up your guard. Again. Better. Now, again. Loosen your grip. Slide, don't jerk. Watch me. Try again. He remembers laughter that wasn't his own. He remembers Trystan going with the warband for the first time, and how, when he'd returned safe and whole, he'd retched with relief and was cold and distant to conceal how afraid he'd been. He remembers promises made and broken, harsh words spoken, apologies made and accepted. He remembers the fights they'd had, shoulder to shoulder, back-to-back, but never – after that wood in Lothian – against one another. Until now. No – that's in the present, and he needs to stay in the past.

He sees a sail with the symbol of a black ship, and knows it comes from a dream. He sees that ship once more, drenched with blood, in a fight that's not his own. He's standing on a shore asking himself a question. What was the answer again? A dog barks and a sword falls, then a man, but not the one he'd feared would fall, though the fear remains and the possibility of death, the taste of it, the smell.

He remembers another ship, being sick, drowning, coming back to life, a woman. Love in the wrong place at the wrong time. The right woman recognised too late. He's always been too late. He understands now that life mirrors itself on the past, that mistakes flow in the blood from generation to generation. There's a madness in that, and the fear of madness, and he wonders, even now, if that was the beginning. He remembers a flight that became a return, a tomb and a sword, a hand held out to stop him from falling. He feels the weight of a chain about his neck and the heavier love of a land denied him. He remembers men and women he's loved, and men and women who've hated him. He's found family where he least expects it, love he doesn't deserve, and knows that love has brought him here and love will take him away. As love should. Because he remembers the question now. *Can a man kill his own son?* And the answer. *He can't.*

'You're not trying!'

He's back. The hawk slides away, and his mind has returned to his body, to the present. Trystan is hissing in his face. Their swords are locked together. Both strain against the other, both in balance. Both give way together, both spring back. Both crouch, breathing hard. But the respite is only for a moment, then they're feinting, parrying, thrusting, blocking. Both know exactly what the other will do and when and how. Corwynal *is* trying. He's trying to die. But he's failing.

'You're not trying either,' he says when he can, his breath ragged, his voice rasping. He's desperately thirsty now. 'It isn't a game, Trys! It's never a game!'

Trystan laughs. 'It's the only game worth playing. Come on! What are you waiting for?'

For the right moment. All your life, I've been waiting for the right moment.

'Don't you have the stomach for it, old man? Why else are you here, if not to take Lothian back?'

Trystan feints left. Corwynal blocks without thought and thrusts forward with his father's sword. Trystan dances away, pivots on his heel and sweeps his own sword in a backhand that would have sliced through Corwynal's stomach if he hadn't been expecting it. But he steps back just in time, and half of him wants to applaud Trystan, because it's not the easiest of moves, and half of him wants to scream because it wasn't good enough, and he knows why. Trystan has no intention of killing him. He falls back, gasping for air. Trystan isn't as winded as he is but pretends to be, and he too falls back.

It's time. This is the moment. There have been too many missed opportunities on both sides. Corwynal has left himself dangerously open on more than one occasion, and Trystan has fumbled too many parries, as if the grip of his sword is loose. But one of them is going to make a mistake, and Corwynal's determined it won't be him. He needs Trystan to be the one to make the mistake, needs to goad him to anger and knows of only one way to do it.

'You're right. It's Lothian I want, Lothian I've always wanted. It should never have been yours. You've no right to it. You're not even a king's son. You're the son of a bastard, a half-breed, a servant. You're the son of everything you've ever despised, the son of a man who's lied to you for the whole of your life. You're *my* son, Trystan.'

Trystan allows his shield to drop. His eyes are the harebell blue of a spring day, but his expression is unreadable.

'Say that again.'

'I'm your father.'

'Again. Louder. Say it so everyone hears it.'

Would you shame me? Would you shame him? But shame no longer matters, and it has to be said. It's the reason he's here. 'I'm his father!' he shouts loud enough for everyone to hear, especially the Lothian warband, who're the ones who matter. Then he lowers his voice. 'I can't kill you, Trystan. A father can't kill his own son.'

But Trystan just smiles and launches himself forward, sword in hand, and Corwynal, not expecting it, loses his balance for the first time and goes down, falling heavily. His left arm slams into the gravel and his father's sword flies out of his grip. His right arm is caught against his ribs, Caledan jammed beneath Trystan's weight. Trystan's sword falls, and steel slides into flesh, past bone and tendon, into muscle. It catches briefly, tugged by the beating of a heart, then slides on into lung. Blood wells, hot and metallic, frothing with breath. Darkness pulses in from the edges of his vision.

'I know,' Trystan whispers. 'I've always known. All I wanted was for you to tell me.'

Someone's screaming. Is it himself? No, it sounds like a woman. The crowd surges and begins to roar like a wave, one that's going to drown him. Then the sounds recede, as if the wave has hissed back out to sea, and all he can hear is a single fading voice.

'Keep her away,' Trystan whispers. 'Keep everyone away.'

In the distance, someone is yelling. 'Keep away! Leave them

alone!'

'Trystan—'

'Don't talk. Listen. I've been so proud to be your son. All I wanted was to make you proud. You gave me a great gift. You gave me life. And now you've given me another gift.'

How can a man kill his own son? He can't. He hadn't. Caledan's hilt is still in his hand, the blade, on which Trystan had thrown himself, deep in Trystan's body. It's still now, no pulse of heartbeat, no breath, just the slow trickle of blood seeping from one body to cover another. Corwynal wants to make a sheet of that blood and pull it over them, to fold them both in its embrace and sleep, holding his son in his arms, as he'd held him once before to break a fever.

'Corwynal.'

He doesn't open his eyes. *Leave me alone.*

'He's dead, Corwynal.'

No. It's me. It was meant to be me.

A shadow falls over him and it begins to rain, fat drops of water that fall on his face and run over his parched lips, tasting of salt. He must be in the sea, in the wave, the one that drowned him. He's drowned before, so he knows what it's like. Some woman – he forgets her name – brought him back to life, but she won't this time. He won't let her. It would have been better if she'd never done so.

'Let him go, Corwynal.' The rain's still falling, and the shadow's still blocking out the light, yet why should there be light? 'Let him go.'

The weight of a loved body lifts from him. He resists briefly before the fight drains out of him. He just wants to sleep.

'Get up. You're not hurt.'

Not *hurt?!* Incredulity at such a statement makes him open his eyes, makes him realise that he is, after all, alive, and that his father is standing over him, holding Trystan's body in his arms. He's weeping, his tears falling on Corwynal's face.

His father lays Trystan down gently, as he never did in life, finds his sword, lays it on the ruin of his chest, closes his hands over it and sets the shield at his feet. Then he crouches down beside Corwynal and takes him in his arms. He's never done that before either. He's holding him with the same anguish with which Corwynal had held Trystan – with a father's desperate fear and equally desperate love.

'It's over, Corwynal,' his father whispers. 'It's all over.'

EPILOGUE

Lothian,

Shortly after Beltein, 489 AD and Spring 491 AD

THE GIFT AND THE STORY

How do you find a place in a dream if the dream isn't your own?

Brangianne looked about the little grove in the wood not far from Dunpeldyr and wondered if this was the place and, if it wasn't, whether things would work out differently. All she could do was wait and see. She'd been alarmingly fatalistic since that dreadful day over nine months before. She still had nightmares in which Trystan ran at Corwynal, and both went down. She shuddered at the memory of the terrible stillness that had fallen, and the knowledge that one of them was dead. Ferdiad had screamed for everyone to leave them alone, and Yseult had struggled in Brangianne's grasp, screaming too – that she had to go to Trystan, that she loved him, that she always had and always would.

Marc's face had turned to stone that day and hadn't changed since. Everyone had stood there, unable to believe it was over, until the old man with the wolf-skin cloak, Corwynal's father, had stumbled towards the two fallen men, and bent to lift Trystan's lifeless body from Corwynal's living one.

Yseult had fainted then, and she wasn't the only one. Essylt of Selgovia had collapsed into Kaerherdin's arms, for the Selgovians had come, unnoticed, halfway through the fight, as had Marc's reinforcements. The Dragon-riders, led by Azarion, had also arrived, and, at Arthyr's command, they'd surrounded the gravel bank to prevent anyone disturbing the two men, father and son, in their grief.

They'd burned Trystan where he lay at nightfall, between river and stream. Ninian had insisted on it, though there was some disquiet among the Christians. Everyone left the next morning. The Selgovians, with a distraught Essylt, had vanished during the night. The Lothian warband left at dawn, accompanied by Corwynal and his father. They rode together, the older man unwilling, it seemed, to let his son out of his sight. Aelfric had gone with them, Ealhith by his side, as were Oonagh and Osric. To Brangianne's surprise, Ealhith had looked back and lifted a hand in farewell before riding off with the Lothian party. The Galloway troops left shortly afterwards, Marc still stony-faced, Yseult wooden and withdrawn, her face and hair grey with the ash from Trystan's pyre, ash she'd refused to wash away for weeks. It was her last act of defiance, and thereafter she did what she was told blankly, a shell of a girl in which no heart beat.

Arthyr's men, Brangianne assumed, had returned to Iuddeu where, shortly afterwards, a King of Gododdin, called Lot, had been named as High King of The Lands between the Walls. Marc refused to go to the celebration, and word sifted only slowly to Galloway. One of the High King's sons, someone called Gawain, became War-leader when Arthyr left for the south. But Brangianne hadn't been interested in any of that; she'd had troubles of her own to deal with in Galloway. But those troubles were behind her, and now, on a sparkling spring day, she was in Lothian following a dream.

Dunpeldyr wasn't far away, according to the keeper of the Inn where she'd spent the night. He'd agreed to send one of his lads with a token for Lothian's Steward. Yes, he'd be in Dunpeldyr, he said. He rarely left the place these days.

How is he? she wanted to ask. *Is he happy? Unhappy?* But the man wouldn't understand the questions or know the answers.

'You making for Dunpeldyr yourself then?' he wanted to know. She shook her head. 'Where then?'

'I don't know,' she said, because she didn't. She could go anywhere. She was free, or soon would be. She could return to Dalriada, for Domangart, Loarn's son, ruled there now, Loarn having suffered an unfortunate and fatal accident. She could visit Ciaran at St Martins.

'He's aged,' Ninian told her. He'd taken the old Abbot news of Blaize's death. 'He took it hard. I doubt he'll last out the year.' Yes, she decided, she'd go to St Martins then travel on to Atholl to see Seirian and the child. A son, apparently. 'They called him Drustan,' Ninian told her. 'And he'll be High King of Caledonia one day or Ferdiad will want to know the reason why. But maybe it would be best not to mention the name to Corwynal when you see him.'

If she saw him. If he came. If he still believed in dreams.

Ninian wasn't with her now, though she'd had his company on the road north and had been glad of it, for she didn't think she could have faced the place by the river and the stream on her own. But when they reached it, there was nothing to be seen, no blood on the stones, no ash on the gravel, only a carpet of little yellow flowers. The hill was still there, of course, as was the place where the Galloway troops had camped, and the copse where the Lothian men had been. But the campfires had vanished and the place was deserted, but for a hawk circling lazily in the spring sunshine. There was little to remind her of that terrible day the previous autumn. Nothing but her own memories.

She and Ninian hadn't stayed long; they'd left their offering among the little yellow flowers and Ninian had prayed. Brangianne had only pretended to pray. Then they'd headed north, and Ninian left her where the road divided and carried on for Iuddeu. From there he'd go on to Atholl, back to his little church and his convert. He had one now. 'It's a start,' he said wryly.

She'd taken the other fork, towards a sea she'd never seen and a hill that, by all accounts, was shaped like a sleeping wolf. But she didn't intend going that far, only to a little grove near an Inn, half a day's ride from the fort. She'd left the girl at the Inn, the one who'd moaned all the way from Galloway. She'd be free of her soon. She'd be free herself, though she didn't want to be.

She dismounted awkwardly and set her horse loose to graze in the lush spring grass. Had there been a horse in the dream? He hadn't said. She settled down in a patch of sunshine and listened to the birds singing and the beat of her own heart until that beat was echoed by the drumming of a single horse on a track. He'd come after all. He'd grown a beard, black shot through with silver. It made him look older and sterner, but kingly.

She got up carefully, for the gift she'd brought him was precious. He reined in on the edge of the grove, his horse rearing at the curb, a grey stallion Brangianne recognised. It was Rhydian, Trystan's horse.

'Where's Janthe?' she asked stupidly.

'In foal.' He swung his leg over the stallion's neck and leapt to the ground, his eyes not on her but on what she was carrying – a sleeping child.

'Mine?'

'Yes.'

He reached out to touch the infant's rosy cheek with the back of his fingers.

'Take her.' She handed him the child, and he took her carefully, a man used to holding children, but the child woke up, opened her eyes and looked up at him. She heard his intake of breath and knew love had entered his heart in the same moment that grief had entered hers. She crossed her arms over her chest to still the pain. The air was cold against her chest where the damp little body had lain.

'Ours,' he said, certain now, for the child had dark brown hair like hers and eyes the slate blue of storm clouds. *Something to remind me of you,* she'd told him. *A daughter.*

She could keep her secret. She'd become good at keeping secrets. She could take the child back from him and walk away. But that wasn't why she was here.

'No – not ours. She's not your daughter. She's your grand-daughter – Trystan and Yseult's – though everyone believes she's mine and yours.'

She told him everything. Yseult had never been strong since she'd lost her child in Atholl, and Trystan's death broke what was left of her spirit. She hadn't told Brangianne she was with child, hadn't had the chance to tell Trystan, and hadn't told Marc. It was only the knowledge that she was carrying Trystan's child that had enabled her to lie with Marc that one time. She never did so again. Marc stopped believing Yseult loved him, or ever could, on the day Trystan died. He wanted nothing to do with her anymore, or Brangianne. So, it was easy . . .

'I did a terrible thing,' Brangianne confessed. 'I'd sworn that if Trystan died, I'd destroy Marc. And that's what I did. A child would have saved him from what he's become. But I told him Yseult had leprosy. I said I'd take her away and care for her until she died, and he let me. He never saw her again. I've allowed him to bear the guilt of that because he deserves it; he would have given her to a leper that day in the Mote. I took her away to a place I'd found – a valley with an abandoned hut. It was primitive and cold in the winter, but Yseult was happy. She believed it was the valley she and Trystan had talked about, that he'd come for her when the child was born. And maybe he did . . .'

It had been easy to pretend it was she who was with child, rather than Yseult. The few people who came to the valley to leave supplies saw her only at a distance and didn't see Yseult at all. Brangianne padded her clothes towards the end and let it be known Corwynal was the father. No-one was surprised at that, including Marc.

Unlike Yseult's first birth, this one had been easy, and there was no reason for her to have died. But she just faded away, talking to Trystan as if he was there.

'Maybe he was. She asked me to care for the child. So, here I am, giving her to you. The world – and Marc – believes her to be yours. Marc must never learn that she's Yseult's, for then he might believe she's his and claim her for his own. But I know she'll be safe with you. I can think of no other man who . . .'

She couldn't go on. She was weeping by then. But something more had to be said. 'Tell Ealhith the truth.'

'What will you do?'

She scrubbed her tears away and tried out a smile.

'I'll travel. I'll go to all the places I've wanted to see. South maybe, to Gwynedd. Maybe even to Rome. No—' She touched his lips with her fingers to still his protest. 'I have to go. Do you think I could stay in Lothian somewhere, waiting for you to visit me in secret? Or watch her growing up at a distance, and not be part of her life? I couldn't bear that. No, I'll go, but not to Rome to begin with. I have to go to St Martin's to make a confession. Then to Atholl to see Seirian and her child. You'd heard?'

He nodded. 'They called him Drustan.' He smiled, somewhat wryly. 'Everyone has tried very hard not to let me find that out, but it's a good name. I wonder how Ferdiad's coping. Badly, I expect.'

'Ninian says not. He was in Atholl not so long ago – he never stops travelling. He was with Yseult and I at the end, and we came north together. We burned her in the hut in the valley and took her ashes to lie with Trystan's.'

'Was she . . . ? Did she . . . ?'

'Have leprosy? No.' She knew why he was asking. 'It's not that infectious. There are priests who care for sufferers for years without catching the disease.'

'But Trystan had caught it?'

'He was . . . unlucky.'

'And it was certain?'

'He had all the signs – the lesions on his arms, the numbness in his hands and feet.' She wasn't entirely convinced, but it was important for Corwynal to believe it. 'His death would have been prolonged, painful and unpleasant.'

'Why didn't he tell me? Why didn't anyone tell me?'

'You know why. You would have taken him away and cared for him until he died, and everyone would have called him Trystan the Leper and forgotten he was ever Trystan the Dragon-slayer. They would have forgotten he'd had the voice of an angel, that he was the hero he'd always wanted to be – the hero he'd been for you, for his father. Eventually, you would have caught the disease too and would have died, equally painfully and unpleasantly, though not alone because I would have been with you. Then I too—'

'Enough!' he said harshly.

'The way he chose was better. He chose *you* to give him the death he wanted.'

'And consigned me to life without him.'

'A life serving people who need you – and now there's another.'

He was still holding the child and Brangianne was glad of it. If he'd opened his arms to her, she would have stepped into them. She would have held him, and been held, and never been able to let him go. But the child was between then, so Brangianne was able to walk away, able to leave him in the grove, tears streaming down his face as they had in the dream.

But dreams are strange and unchancy. Dreams make you do things because you think you've seen the future, because you think you've seen the truth. Sometimes you have, but it's not always the right truth.

She paid the girl she'd brought from Galloway more than she deserved. Corwynal or Ealhith would find another wetnurse for Yseult's child. Brangianne wept a little when the girl was gone, but not for long. She had a long journey ahead of her, and was as free as she ever would be. More than a summer of freedom lay ahead of her – a life of freedom she no longer wanted.

'My Lady!' She looked up without thought at the Innkeeper's voice, though she'd allowed him to think her no more than a wandering healer with a bastard child. But the man wasn't speaking to her. He was bowing and sweeping dust from a bench and sending a servant running for wine. 'The best, mind!'

Ealhith had the look of a woman who'd grown into her own skin and found it comfortable. This slightly-built former slave, with a scar down one side of her face, had turned into Lothian's Queen.

'He told me everything,' she said with a gesture that sent the Innkeeper away.

'You'll care for the child? You'll pretend?'

'She looks like him,' Ealhith said. 'And you.'

It was as Brangianne had feared. Ealhith believed the child to be hers and Corwynal's.

'She looks like her grandparents. Yseult's mother was dark, a beauty. I believe Yseult's daughter will grow up to look just like her. She's not mine, Ealhith. Or Corwynal's.'

Ealhith laid a hand on her arm. 'I didn't think she was. I'm a mother. If she was yours, you couldn't have given her up. So, yes, I'll care for her, and pretend she's my husband's daughter by the healer I hope will come to live with us in Dunpeldyr.'

Brangianne stared at her. 'But—'

'He's given me two children, and I love them more than life itself, more than him, if I'm honest. I'd do anything for them, give them anything. And what I want to give them – what they need – is a father who can laugh more than he does. I think you can help him laugh. So stay, Brangianne. Help me heal him. He needs you.'

And so I stayed in Lothian, and the years passed swiftly as they do. We were, I think, happy, and I grew to love Corwynal's sons by Ealhith, especially the younger quiet one who was so like him. We named Yseult's daughter Ethlin, after her grandmother whom she did indeed grow to resemble. They were good years, golden years of good harvests and peace between the walls, on the whole.

Marc took to drink, which surprised no one, and choked on his own vomit. Andrydd, after killing all his rivals, succeeded him, and now rules Galloway with an iron grip. Dalriada continues to be ruled by Domangart, though there's a new abbot at St Martin's now for, true to Ninian's prediction, Ciaran died the year I moved to Lothian, not long after I visited him. Atholl continues at peace, though they say there are wars further north in the Caledonian Confederacy.

Ninian is, as ever, the best source of news, and he never rests as he journeys from one land to the next telling his stories of angels and trumpets. He still isn't ordained, but I believe they'll make him a Saint one day: Saint Ninian, the man who converted the Caledonians. There are more of them now, and his little church in Atholl had to be rebuilt to house them all. It's presided over by the first of his converts, Domech. He's still unable to speak, but Ninian taught him to write and so communicate. It's strange to think of the Archdruid as a Christian.

Seirian and Ferdiad's child, Drustan, thrives, as does Essylt's daughter. Yes, she had a child in the end. No-one knows who the father is, but I think she looks a little like Ninian. The child turned Essylt into a softer kinder person, though that troubles me, for I know if I'd allowed Marc to believe Yseult's child was his, he too might have been softer and kinder and wouldn't have killed himself with drink. So I had my revenge for a murdered husband and a dead child in Carnadail all those years ago. But despite Ciaran's absolution, it doesn't sit easily on my conscience.

We hear of Arthyr's wars in the south where he's turning himself and his Dragon-riders into a legend. Aelfric went back to Bernicia and carved himself a kingdom on the Gododdin border that troubles the High King and Arthyr alike. He's grown fat over the years and blames it on his wife's cooking. Oonagh was always a good cook. Yes, he took her as his wife. His first wife, it turned out, had been dead for some years. But his sons survived, both of them – as did Oonagh's child – all of them the image of their father, the image of all the little Aelfrics scattered across the kingdoms of the North.

Of Ferdiad there's little news, at least not directly. Seirian told me he's changed and is a calmer man than he used to be. She spoke of a Brotherhood, and I believe he has something to do with it, whatever it is, whatever it does.

Seirian came to Lothian when I sent word her father was failing. I'd grown fond of the old man and had come to see how similar he and Corwynal were. The two men, father and son, were together often, talking quietly of the past, though talking became difficult when Rifallyn suffered the disease of old men and woke one day with a weakness down his left side and a slur in his speech. That was when I sent for Seirian that she might see him, and he her. They both wept, and afterwards she was ready to let him go.

Corwynal killed him in the end, as his father had foretold, and I helped him. Rifallyn woke up one day unable to move or speak, a useless body holding the fleeting remnants of a will. They sent for me, though I could do nothing – except for one thing.

'Shall I send for Corwynal?' I didn't know if he could hear me, but he blinked his assent.

So I told him what had to be done and persuaded him it was both right and necessary.

'How can a man kill both his son and his father?'

'With love,' I said. 'It's the last gift you can give him.'

His father kept his eyes on his son's as he drove the knife through the wall of his chest and into his heart and kept them there until there was no light left.

So, tomorrow, the man I've loved and hated and loved once more will burn his father. Tomorrow he'll set fire to his pyre and send the smoke of his burning far into the sky. Then the Council will make this kinslayer a king, not because they have no choice but because he's the best choice.

'It's cold.' Ealhith shivered as she looked up at the ramparts, a black line against a sky red with sunset, and at the man silhouetted against the fires in the sky, a man wearing a wolf-skin cloak, a man thinking of the future and what the day would bring. And of the past. Of Trystan of Lothian and his place in his story.

Ealhith put a hand through my arm and called to the children – Caradawc, Taliesen and little Ethlin. 'Let's go and bring your father down.'

I watch them go up to the rampart, the two women, the three children – his women, his children. The sun has slipped below the horizon, and the banners of sunset have faded to a faint pink glow in the west. I can't make out his features, but I know he wants to be alone with his memories, as I want to be alone with mine. That's why I ease back into the shadows as they pass by, and only the boy, the youngest one, notices me. I press a silver finger to my lips and he nods gravely, as if he knows me. He has his father's eyes. They all do, but this one has his soul, a soul that calls to mine.

I watch them return to Dunpeldyr's hall, to warmth and light and the company of other people. I think about joining them but choose not to. Instead, I climb up to the rampart myself. It's the middle of the night, moonless but clear, and the stars have turned the sky a dusty grey. To the south, mountains bulk black against the horizon. To the north, the sea gleams faintly. I place my hand where his hand had lain and give myself up to the same memories, to the same story – the tale of Trystan of Lothian and his doomed love for Yseult of Dalriada. They would never have met if it hadn't been for me, and the world would be a different place. So, like the man before me, I pace the rampart and wonder how different Trystan's story would be had I not done what I did, or been who I was.

Dawn is edging the sky before I leave. The constellation of the Rider has set in the west, and the stars in the east have faded. A mist, flowing along the river towards Dunpeldyr from the firth, cloaks the rising sun.

I've finished now. I've reminded myself of everything that happened, as did the man before me, but I've gone further and turned truth into tale. It's no longer his story, not as I've shaped it. It's Trystan's, the tale he would have wanted told, the one I promised him, a shining thing of gold and copper and silver, a tribute paid to a man I loved as hopelessly as I now love another.

It's strange to think that, despite my struggles to become something I dreamed of, and who I've actually become, I remain at heart a nameless teller of tales. Perhaps being nameless is my punishment for stealing a hero's name, and now no-one will ever know who shaped Trystan's tale into legend.

But that doesn't concern me. I've shaped this story not for myself but for my audience, and I know them better than they think. They want something they can remember, something to retell and change as it suits them. And so the truth of kings and kingdoms, of queens and dynasties, of shifts of power and peoples, has been stripped away to leave only this – a golden hero, a beautiful princess, a noble king. No-one wants to know that Trystan was selfish, Yseult impulsive, Marc unstable. Why spoil a good story? And if others are part of it, Corwynal, Brangianne, Kaerherdin, Essylt and The Morholt, they're shadowy figures who come and go, outshone by the gleaming heart of the tale I've made.

Years will pass, and those who remember the truth will die. Wars will be fought and countries rise and fall. People will flee violence or hunger, taking nothing with them but their legends, the last flicker of a waning Imbolc lamp. But my tale will live on as it moves through the world, as it's told in foreign tongues in distant courts, is set to music or laid down in ink, changing as it does so. A man who taught me more than how to fight will become a winged beast, the poison on his blade the fire in the creature's jaws. A glance on a sunlit morning to the echo of a harp will become a love potion. The sign of the black ship will be a ship with black sails, and no-one will remember who wielded the notched sword. The Morholt, whom I loved, will be transformed into a loveless giant. The ending will change, but death will be part of it, as death always is.

The sun is rising now, and the east blazes with light as the rising wind strips the dawn mists away. Today the man who changed my life, the other half of my soul, will burn his father, and Lothian will have another king. But my allegiance, if not my heart, is given to the Queen who's sent me to see the smoke of her father's pyre plume into the sky. She expects me to take my place with the others, as Consort of Atholl, and pretend I've only just arrived. But he will know I haven't and why I've stayed away, and I'm not sure I'm ready for that understanding, as I've not been ready to see him again since the day Trystan died on a gravel field between river and stream.

But our lives will go on, beyond my power to shape. Perhaps the next time we meet, we will be on opposite sides of a battlefield, though we'll both do anything to prevent that, and maybe we'll succeed. I like to think so. Perhaps, when we've passed beyond ambition and duty, passion and shame, we'll be able to sit together in the sunshine, two old men, and tell each other tales of what was and might have been.

But that will be another story . . .

AUTHOR'S NOTE

I very much hope you've enjoyed reading *The Serpent in Spring*.

If you have, I'd love you to **post a review on Amazon**. It needn't be an essay – a couple of lines would be fantastic. Reviews are particularly helpful for authors like me who're just setting out into the stormy waters of self-publishing. It would be great to know you've got my back!

If you've spotted any typos and would like to let me know about them, please contact me through my website or DM me on Instagram. I do really want to know so I can fix them.

If you'd like to find out more about *The Trystan Trilogy* or about what I'll be writing next:

Subscribe to my Newsletter

Not only will you receive exclusive extracts from *The Trystan Trilogy*, but free short stories and a regular newsletter.

Go to **barbaralennox.com/subscribe** or
barbaralennox.wordpress.com/subscribe

or scan the QR code:

HISTORICAL NOTE

The mediaeval romance of Tristan and Isolde was compiled on the continent in the 12th century and later incorporated into Malory's 15th century Arthurian fantasy, *Le Morte D'Arthur*. But it was based on much earlier tales derived from Irish and possibly Pictish sources. These early tales acquired a Welsh flavour, following the resettlement of Britons from Strathclyde in Gwynedd at the end of the 9th century. Subsequently, the same stories were taken to the other Brythonic lands of Cornwall and Brittany where they absorbed local references, and the story is now thought of as being Cornish/Breton. But the original stories were probably set in Scotland/Ireland.

In *The Trystan Trilogy*, the legend has been reworked to include many of the familiar elements of the story, but not necessarily in the same order, and has been set against the 'historical' background of late 5th century 'Scotland'. Historical is a very loose term in this context. Virtually no texts survive from this period and location, so the settings and characters are an amalgam of the little that is known about earlier and later times. Galloway and Strathclyde, for example, are later names, given to the lands of the Novantae and Dumnonni tribes detailed by Ptolemy in his 1st century map of Britain. The Votadini tribe of the east coast gave their name to the later Kingdom of Gododdin. Lothian, a modern term, comes from a reference to Tristan's traditional home being Loonois, which has been equated with Lothian. Dalriada was a real Irish Kingdom, existing both in Ireland and Scotland. It was supposedly founded by Fergus, Loarn and Oenghus, but they are probably mythical. The Caledonian, or Pictish, tribes are also mentioned by Ptolemy, and a list of their kingdoms appears in a 9th century text. The name Atholl probably derives from Alflotha, or new Ireland, a name given to it after the area became part of a Scots-controlled territory.

The character names were taken from the various versions of the Tristan and Isolde legend, and from the oldest Arthurian texts, but have been 'adjusted' to give them more of a 'Welsh' look since the people of the Lands between the Walls (a made-up name) would have spoken Brythonic, a precursor of Welsh. Some names, such as Dumnagual and Ciniod, come from genealogies and king-lists of the period. They may even have been real people, though the historicity of genealogies is very dubious.

All Celtic nations would have celebrated the four fire-festivals of Imbolc, Beltein, Lughnasadh and Samhain, but these are the Gaelic names, since I was unable to find reliable 'British' names for them.

The Trystan Trilogy is a work of fiction, and my intention was to give the reader a flavour of the cultures of the period rather than sticking strictly to the known facts – or lack of them. I've researched as widely as I could on these matters but, inevitably, will have misinterpreted or simply missed available evidence, and for that I apologise.

For further information and a bibliography of sources, refer to the resources/bibliography page of my website.

ABOUT THE AUTHOR

I was born, and still live, in Scotland on the shores of a river, between the mountains and the sea. I'm a retired scientist and science administrator but have always been fascinated by the early history of Scotland, and I love fleshing out that history with the stories of fictional, and not-so-fictional, characters.

Find out more about me and my writing on my websites:

Barbaralennox.com
Barbaralennox.wordpress.com

Connect with me on the following:

Instagram.com/barbaralennoxauthor
Goodreads.com/author/show/19661962.Barbara_Lennox
Pinterest.co.uk/barbaralennox58
Amazon: viewauthor.at/authorprofile

ALSO BY BARBARA LENNOX

The Man who Loved Landscape, a collection of 40 short stories, many of which are set in Scotland, was published in 2020.

getbook.at/Manwholovedlandscape

'Simply the best book of short stories I have read in years.'

The Ghost in the Machine, *poems of love, loss, life and death*, a collection of 69 poems, was published in 2021.

getbook.at/theghostinthemachine

'This is an excellent book, nuanced, accessible, human.'

Related novels:

The Wolf in Winter, first volume of *The Trystan Trilogy*, was published in 2021. getbook.at/Wolfinwinter

The Swan in Summer, second volume of *The Trystan Trilogy*, was published in 2022. Mybook.to/swaninsummer

ACKNOWLEDGEMENTS

I would never have written anything if I hadn't attended the 'Continuing as a Writer' classes, part of the University of Dundee's Continuing Education Programme. These classes were tutored by Esther Read, whose support and encouragement has been unstinting and invaluable. Esther, I can't thank you enough, not only for your help and advice as I mastered the art of short story writing, but for manfully reading through early drafts of *The Wolf in Winter*.

I also want to give a shout-out to all my Instagram pals from whom I learned such an immense amount about the process of self-publishing, and who were always there for inspiration, support and encouragement. Thanks, guys and gals!

At home, my writing buddies, Harry, Rambo and Oscar, the best cats in the world, were with me all the way, usually asleep.

Almost finally, but not least, I'd like to thank my husband, Will, for putting up with all the scribbling and not asking any awkward questions.

My biggest thank you, however, goes to all my readers, especially my ARC team – you know who you are – without whom this book would be nothing more than a footnote in my own imagination.